*To Peter Rowling,*
*in memory of Mr Ridley*
*and to Susan Sladden,*
*who helped Harry out of his cupboard*


献给彼得·罗琳，
为着纪念里德利先生；
献给苏珊·斯莱登，
她帮助哈利从储物间里出来

# HOGSMEADE

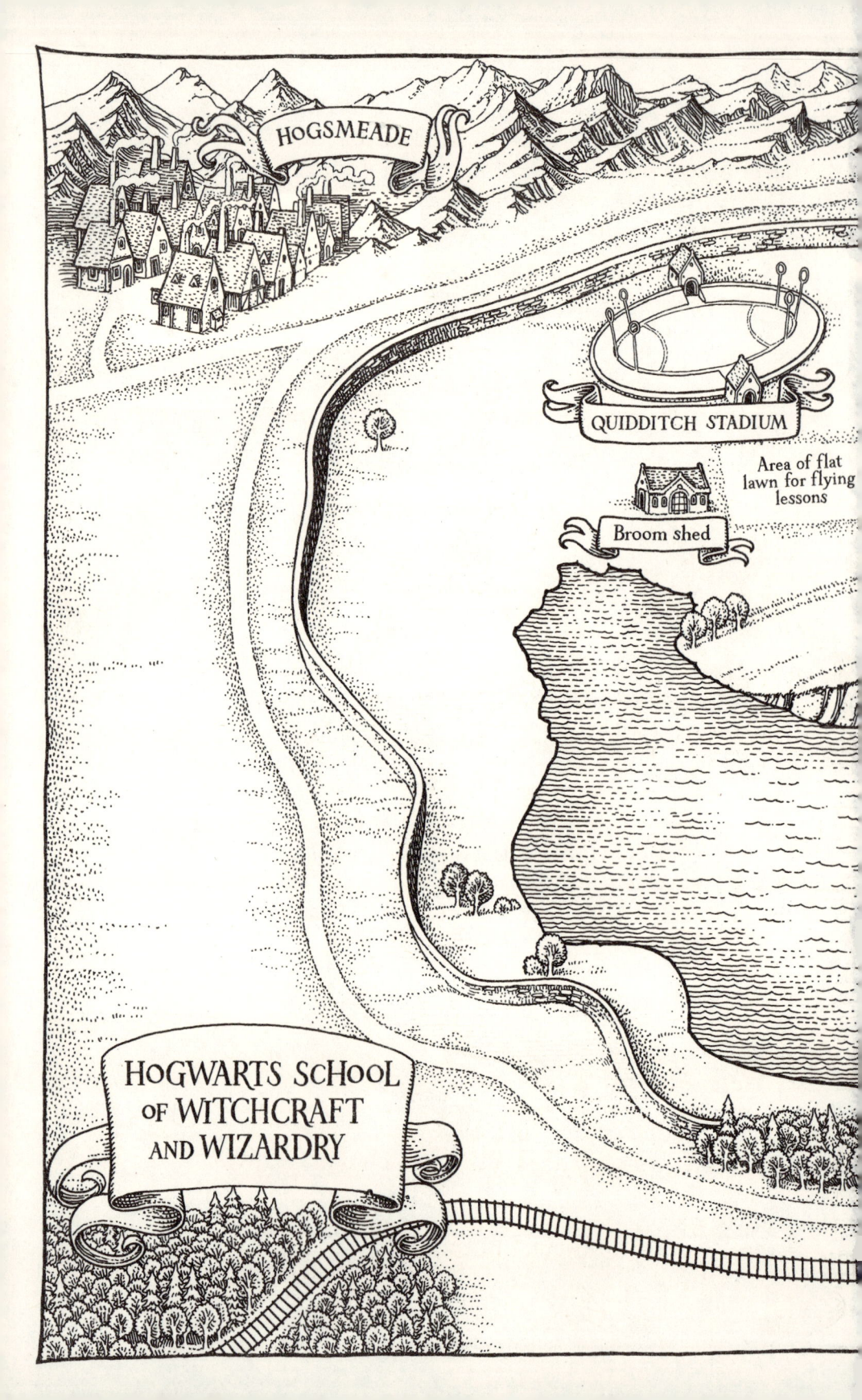

## QUIDDITCH STADIUM

Area of flat lawn for flying lessons

Broom shed

# HOGWARTS SCHOOL OF WITCHCRAFT AND WIZARDRY

# Harry Potter
AND THE GOBLET OF FIRE

# J.K. ROWLING

4

英汉对照版

# Harry Potter

哈利·波特与火焰杯 [上]

〔英〕J.K. 罗琳 / 著

马爱农　马爱新 / 译

WIZARDING WORLD

人民文学出版社
PEOPLE'S LITERATURE PUBLISHING HOUSE

著作权合同登记号　图字　01-2018-5447

Harry Potter and the Goblet of Fire
First published in Great Britain in 2000 by Bloomsbury Publishing Plc.
Text © 2000 by J.K. Rowling
Interior illustrations by Mary GrandPré © 2000 by Warner Bros.
Wizarding World, Publishing and Theatrical Rights © J.K.Rowling
Wizarding World characters, names and related indicia are TM and © Warner Bros. Entertainment Inc.
Wizarding World TM & © Warner Bros. Entertainment Inc.
Cover illustrations by Mary GrandPré © 2000 by Warner Bros.

图书在版编目（CIP）数据

哈利·波特与火焰杯：英汉对照版：上下/（英）J.K.罗琳著；马爱农，马爱新译. —北京：人民文学出版社，2019（2023.9重印）
ISBN 978-7-02-015070-0

Ⅰ.①哈…　Ⅱ.①J…②马…③马…　Ⅲ.①儿童小说—长篇小说—英国—现代—英、汉　Ⅳ.①I561.84

中国版本图书馆CIP数据核字（2019）第040997号

| | |
|---|---|
| 策划编辑 | 王瑞琴 |
| 责任编辑 | 翟　灿 |
| 美术编辑 | 刘　静 |
| 责任印制 | 苏文强 |

| | |
|---|---|
| 出版发行 | 人民文学出版社 |
| 社　　址 | 北京市朝内大街166号 |
| 邮政编码 | 100705 |

| | |
|---|---|
| 印　　刷 | 三河市龙林印务有限公司 |
| 经　　销 | 全国新华书店等 |

| | |
|---|---|
| 字　　数 | 1577千字 |
| 开　　本 | 640毫米×960毫米　1/16 |
| 印　　张 | 66.75　插页6 |
| 印　　数 | 137001—147000 |
| 版　　次 | 2019年7月北京第1版 |
| 印　　次 | 2023年9月第16次印刷 |
| 书　　号 | 978-7-02-015070-0 |
| 定　　价 | 128.00元（上、下册） |

如有印装质量问题，请与本社图书销售中心调换。电话：010-65233595

HAGRID'S HUT

FORBIDDEN FOREST

WHOMPING WILLOW

GREENHOUSES

HOGWARTS CASTLE

HOGSMEADE STATION

# CONTENTS

| | | |
|---|---|---|
| CHAPTER ONE | The Riddle House | 008 |
| CHAPTER TWO | The Scar | 030 |
| CHAPTER THREE | The Invitation | 044 |
| CHAPTER FOUR | Back to the Burrow | 062 |
| CHAPTER FIVE | Weasleys' Wizard Wheezes | 080 |
| CHAPTER SIX | The Portkey | 100 |
| CHAPTER SEVEN | Bagman and Crouch | 114 |
| CHAPTER EIGHT | The Quidditch World Cup | 144 |
| CHAPTER NINE | The Dark Mark | 176 |
| CHAPTER TEN | Mayhem at the Ministry | 216 |
| CHAPTER ELEVEN | Aboard the Hogwarts Express | 234 |
| CHAPTER TWELVE | The Triwizard Tournament | 254 |
| CHAPTER THIRTEEN | Mad-Eye Moody | 286 |
| CHAPTER FOURTEEN | The Unforgivable Curses | 310 |
| CHAPTER FIFTEEN | Beauxbatons and Durmstrang | 338 |
| CHAPTER SIXTEEN | The Goblet of Fire | 368 |
| CHAPTER SEVENTEEN | The Four Champions | 402 |
| CHAPTER EIGHTEEN | The Weighing of the Wands | 426 |
| CHAPTER NINETEEN | The Hungarian Horntail | 464 |
| CHAPTER TWENTY | The First Task | 498 |
| CHAPTER TWENTY-ONE | The House-Elf Liberation Front | 538 |
| CHAPTER TWENTY-TWO | The Unexpected Task | 570 |
| CHAPTER TWENTY-THREE | The Yule Ball | 596 |

# 目 录

| | | |
|---|---|---|
| 第 1 章 | 里德尔府 | 009 |
| 第 2 章 | 伤疤 | 031 |
| 第 3 章 | 邀请 | 045 |
| 第 4 章 | 回到陋居 | 063 |
| 第 5 章 | 韦斯莱魔法把戏坊 | 081 |
| 第 6 章 | 门钥匙 | 101 |
| 第 7 章 | 巴格曼和克劳奇 | 115 |
| 第 8 章 | 魁地奇世界杯赛 | 145 |
| 第 9 章 | 黑魔标记 | 177 |
| 第 10 章 | 魔法部乱成一团 | 217 |
| 第 11 章 | 登上霍格沃茨特快列车 | 235 |
| 第 12 章 | 三强争霸赛 | 255 |
| 第 13 章 | 疯眼汉穆迪 | 287 |
| 第 14 章 | 不可饶恕咒 | 311 |
| 第 15 章 | 布斯巴顿和德姆斯特朗 | 339 |
| 第 16 章 | 火焰杯 | 369 |
| 第 17 章 | 四位勇士 | 403 |
| 第 18 章 | 检测魔杖 | 427 |
| 第 19 章 | 匈牙利树蜂 | 465 |
| 第 20 章 | 第一个项目 | 499 |
| 第 21 章 | 家养小精灵解放阵线 | 539 |
| 第 22 章 | 意外的挑战 | 571 |
| 第 23 章 | 圣诞舞会 | 597 |

| | | |
|---|---|---|
| CHAPTER TWENTY-FOUR | Rita Skeeter's Scoop | 640 |
| CHAPTER TWENTY-FIVE | The Egg and the Eye | 674 |
| CHAPTER TWENTY-SIX | The Second Task | 704 |
| CHAPTER TWENTY-SEVEN | Padfoot Returns | 746 |
| CHAPTER TWENTY-EIGHT | The Madness of Mr Crouch | 784 |
| CHAPTER TWENTY-NINE | The Dream | 826 |
| CHAPTER THIRTY | The Pensieve | 850 |
| CHAPTER THIRTY-ONE | The Third Task | 884 |
| CHAPTER THIRTY-TWO | Flesh, Blood and Bone | 926 |
| CHAPTER THIRTY-THREE | The Death Eaters | 938 |
| CHAPER THIRTY-FOUR | Priori Incantatem | 958 |
| CHAPTER THIRTY-FIVE | Veritaserum | 974 |
| CHAPTER THIRTY-SIX | The Parting of the Ways | 1004 |
| CHAPTER THIRTY-SEVEN | The Beginning | 1038 |

| 第 24 章 | 丽塔·斯基特的独家新闻 | 641 |
| 第 25 章 | 金蛋和魔眼 | 675 |
| 第 26 章 | 第二个项目 | 705 |
| 第 27 章 | 大脚板回来了 | 747 |
| 第 28 章 | 克劳奇先生疯了 | 785 |
| 第 29 章 | 噩梦 | 827 |
| 第 30 章 | 冥想盆 | 851 |
| 第 31 章 | 第三个项目 | 885 |
| 第 32 章 | 血，肉和骨头 | 927 |
| 第 33 章 | 食死徒 | 939 |
| 第 34 章 | 闪回咒 | 959 |
| 第 35 章 | 吐真剂 | 975 |
| 第 36 章 | 分道扬镳 | 1005 |
| 第 37 章 | 开始 | 1039 |

# CHAPTER ONE

# The Riddle House

The villagers of Little Hangleton still called it 'the Riddle House', even though it had been many years since the Riddle family had lived there. It stood on a hill overlooking the village, some of its windows boarded, tiles missing from its roof, and ivy spreading unchecked over its face. Once a fine-looking manor, and easily the largest and grandest building for miles around, the Riddle House was now damp, derelict and unoccupied.

The Little Hangletons all agreed that the old house was 'creepy'. Half a century ago, something strange and horrible had happened there, something that the older inhabitants of the village still liked to discuss when topics for gossip were scarce. The story had been picked over so many times, and had been embroidered in so many places, that nobody was quite sure what the truth was any more. Every version of the tale, however, started in the same place: fifty years before, at daybreak on a fine summer's morning, when the Riddle House had still been well kept and impressive, and a maid had entered the drawing room to find all three Riddles dead.

The maid had run screaming down the hill into the village, and roused as many people as she could.

'Lying there with their eyes wide open! Cold as ice! Still in their dinner things!'

The police were summoned, and the whole of Little Hangleton had seethed with shocked curiosity and ill-disguised excitement. Nobody wasted their breath pretending to feel very sad about the Riddles, for they had been most unpopular. Elderly Mr and Mrs Riddle had been rich, snobbish and rude, and their grown-up son, Tom, had been even more so. All the villagers cared about was the identity of their murderer – plainly, three apparently healthy people did not all drop dead of natural causes on the same night.

# 第 1 章

# 里德尔府

小汉格顿的村民们仍然把这座房子称为"里德尔府",尽管里德尔一家已经多年没有在此居住了。房子坐落在一道山坡上,从这里可以看见整个村子。房子的几扇窗户被封死了,房顶上的瓦残缺不全,爬山虎张牙舞爪地爬满了整座房子。里德尔府原先是一幢很漂亮的大宅子,是方圆几英里之内最宽敞、最气派的建筑,如今却变得潮湿、荒凉,常年无人居住。

小汉格顿的村民们一致认为,这幢老房子"怪吓人的"。半个世纪前,这里发生了一件离奇而可怕的事,直到现在,村里的老辈人没有别的话题时,还喜欢把这件事扯出来谈论一番。这个故事被人们反复地讲,许多地方又被添油加醋,所以真相到底如何,已经没有人说得准了。不过,故事的每一个版本都是以同样的方式开头的:五十年前,里德尔府还是管理有方、气派非凡的时候,在一个晴朗夏日的黎明,一个女仆走进客厅,发现里德尔一家三口都气绝身亡了。

女仆一路尖叫着奔下山坡,跑进村里,尽量把村民们都唤醒。

"都躺着,眼睛睁得大大的!浑身冰凉!还穿着晚餐时的衣服!"

警察被叫来了,整个小汉格顿村都沉浸在惊讶和好奇之中,村民们竭力掩饰内心的兴奋,却没有成功。没有人浪费力气,假装为里德尔一家感到悲伤,因为他们在村子里人缘很坏。老夫妇俩很有钱,但为人势利粗暴,他们那个已经成年的儿子汤姆,说起来你也许不信,竟比父母还要坏上几分。村民们只关心凶手究竟是何许人——显然,三个看上去十分健康的人,是不可能在同一个晚上同时自然死亡的。

## CHAPTER ONE   The Riddle House

The Hanged Man, the village pub, did a roaring trade that night; the whole village had turned out to discuss the murders. They were rewarded for leaving their firesides when the Riddles' cook arrived dramatically in their midst, and announced to the suddenly silent pub that a man called Frank Bryce had just been arrested.

'Frank!' cried several people. 'Never!'

Frank Bryce was the Riddles' gardener. He lived alone in a run-down cottage in the Riddle House grounds. Frank had come back from the war with a very stiff leg and a great dislike of crowds and loud noises, and had been working for the Riddles ever since.

There was a rush to buy the cook drinks, and hear more details.

'Always thought he was odd,' she told the eagerly listening villagers, after her fourth sherry. 'Unfriendly, like. I'm sure if I've offered him a cuppa once, I've offered it a hundred times. Never wanted to mix, he didn't.'

'Ah, now,' said a woman at the bar, 'he had a hard war, Frank, he likes the quiet life. That's no reason to –'

'Who else had a key to the back door, then?' barked the cook. 'There's been a spare key hanging in the gardener's cottage far back as I can remember! Nobody forced the door last night! No broken windows! All Frank had to do was creep up to the big house while we was all sleeping ...'

The villagers exchanged dark looks.

'I always thought he had a nasty look about him, right enough,' grunted a man at the bar.

'War turned him funny, if you ask me,' said the landlord.

'Told you I wouldn't like to get on the wrong side of Frank, didn't I, Dot?' said an excited woman in the corner.

'Horrible temper,' said Dot, nodding fervently, 'I remember, when he was a kid ...'

By the following morning, hardly anyone in Little Hangleton doubted that Frank Bryce had killed the Riddles.

But over in the neighbouring town of Great Hangleton, in the dark and dingy police station, Frank was stubbornly repeating, again and again, that he was innocent, and that the only person he had seen near the house on the day of the Riddles' deaths had been a teenage boy, a stranger, dark-haired and pale. Nobody else in the village had seen any such boy, and the police

# 第1章 里德尔府

那天夜里，村里的吊死鬼酒馆生意格外兴隆，似乎全村的人都跑来谈论这桩谋杀案了。他们舍弃了家中的火炉，并不是一无所获，因为里德尔家的厨娘咋咋呼呼地来到他们中间，并对突然安静下来的酒馆顾客们说，一个名叫弗兰克·布莱斯的男人刚刚被逮捕了。

"弗兰克！"几个人喊了起来，"不可能！"

弗兰克·布莱斯是里德尔家的园丁。他一个人住在里德尔府庭园中一间破破烂烂的小木屋里。当年弗兰克从战场上回来，一条腿僵硬得不听使唤，并且对人群和噪音极端反感，此后就一直为里德尔家干活。

酒馆里的人争先恐后地给厨娘买酒，想听到更多的细节。

"我早就觉得他怪怪的，"厨娘喝下第四杯雪利酒后，告诉那些眼巴巴洗耳恭听的村民们，"冷冰冰的，不爱搭理人。我相信，如果我想请他喝一杯茶，非得请上一百遍他才答应。他从来不喜欢跟人来往。"

"唉，怎么说呢，"吧台旁边的一个女人说，"弗兰克参加过残酷的战争。他喜欢过平静的生活，我们没有理由……"

"那么，还有谁手里有后门的钥匙呢？"厨娘粗声大气地说，"我记得，有一把备用钥匙一直挂在园丁的小木屋里！昨晚，没有人破门而入！窗户也没有被打坏！弗兰克只要趁我们都睡着的时候，偷偷溜进大宅子……"

村民们默默地交换着目光。

"我一直觉得他那样子特别讨厌，真的。"吧台旁边的一个男人嘟哝着说。

"要是让我说呀，是战争把他变得古怪了。"酒馆老板说。

"我早就对你说过，我可不愿意得罪弗兰克，是吧，多特？"角落里一个情绪激动的女人说。

"脾气糟透了。"多特热切地点着头，说道，"我还记得，他小的时候……"

第二天早晨，小汉格顿的人几乎都相信是弗兰克·布莱斯杀死了里德尔全家。

然而在邻近的大汉格顿镇上，在昏暗阴沉的警察局里，弗兰克固执地一遍又一遍重复自己是无辜的。他说，在里德尔一家死去的那天，他在宅子附近只见到一个人，是个他不认识的十多岁男孩，那男孩头发黑黑的，脸色苍白。村里的其他人都没有见过这样一个男孩，警察

## CHAPTER ONE    The Riddle House

were quite sure that Frank had invented him.

Then, just when things were looking very serious for Frank, the report on the Riddles' bodies came back and changed everything.

The police had never read an odder report. A team of doctors had examined the bodies, and had concluded that none of the Riddles had been poisoned, stabbed, shot, strangled, suffocated or (as far as they could tell) harmed at all. In fact, the report continued, in a tone of unmistakeable bewilderment, the Riddles all appeared to be in perfect health – apart from the fact that they were all dead. The doctors did note (as though determined to find something wrong with the bodies) that each of the Riddles had a look of terror upon his or her face – but as the frustrated police said, whoever heard of three people being *frightened* to death?

As there was no proof that the Riddles had been murdered at all, the police were forced to let Frank go. The Riddles were buried in the Little Hangleton churchyard, and their graves remained objects of curiosity for a while. To everyone's surprise, and amidst a cloud of suspicion, Frank Bryce returned to his cottage in the grounds of the Riddle House.

"'S'far as I'm concerned, he killed them, and I don't care what the police say,' said Dot in the Hanged Man. 'And if he had any decency, he'd leave here, knowing as how we knows he did it.'

But Frank did not leave. He stayed to tend the garden for the next family who lived in the Riddle House, and then the next – for neither family stayed long. Perhaps it was partly because of Frank that each new owner said there was a nasty feeling about the place, which, in the absence of inhabitants, started to fall into disrepair.

The wealthy man who owned the Riddle House these days neither lived there nor put it to any use; they said in the village that he kept it for 'tax reasons', though nobody was very clear what these might be. The wealthy owner continued to pay Frank to do the gardening, however. Frank was nearing his seventy-seventh birthday now, very deaf, his bad leg stiffer than ever, but could be seen pottering around the flowerbeds in fine weather, even though the weeds were starting to creep up on him.

Weeds were not the only things Frank had to contend with, either. Boys from the village made a habit of throwing stones through the windows of

# 第1章 里德尔府

们认定这是弗兰克凭空编造的。

就在形势对弗兰克极为严峻的时候,里德尔一家的尸体检验报告回来了,一下子扭转了整个局面。

警察从没见过比这更古怪的报告了。一组医生对尸体做了检查,得出的结论是:里德尔一家谁也没有遭到毒药、利器、手枪的伤害,也不是被闷死或勒死的。实际上,报告以一种明显困惑的口气接着写道,里德尔一家三口看上去都很健康——只除了一点,他们都断了气儿。医生们倒是注意到(似乎他们决意要在尸体上找出一点不对劲儿的地方),里德尔家的每个人脸上都带着一种惊恐的表情——可是正如已经一筹莫展的警察所说,谁听说过三个人同时被吓死的呢?

既然没有证据证明里德尔一家是被谋杀的,警察只好把弗兰克放了出来。里德尔一家就葬在小汉格顿的教堂墓地里,在其后的一段时间,他们的坟墓一直是人们好奇关注的对象。使大家感到惊讶和疑虑丛生的是,弗兰克·布莱斯居然又回到了里德尔府庭园他的小木屋里。

"我个人认为,是弗兰克杀死了他们,我才不管警察怎么说呢。"多特在吊死鬼酒馆里说,"如果他稍微知趣一些,知道我们都清楚他的所作所为,他就会离开这里。"

但是弗兰克没有离开,他留了下来,为接下来住在里德尔府的人家照料园子,然后又为再下面的一家干活——这两家人都没有住很长时间。新主人说,也许一部分是因为弗兰克的缘故吧,他们总觉得这地方有一种阴森吓人的感觉。后来由于无人居住,宅子渐渐失修,变得破败了。

最近拥有里德尔府的那个富人,既不住在这里,也不把宅子派什么用场。村里的人说,他留着它是为了"税务上的原因",但谁也不清楚到底是怎么回事。不过,这位富裕的宅主继续花钱雇弗兰克当园丁。弗兰克如今快要过七十七岁的生日了,耳朵聋得厉害,那条坏腿也比以前更僵硬了。但天气好的时候,人们仍然能看见他在花圃里磨磨蹭蹭地干活,尽管杂草在向他身边悄悄蔓延,他想挡也挡不住。

况且,弗兰克要对付的不仅是杂草。村子里的男孩总喜欢往里德尔府的窗户上扔石头。弗兰克费了很大心血才保持了草地的平整,他们

## CHAPTER ONE   The Riddle House

the Riddle House. They rode their bicycles over the lawns Frank worked so hard to keep smooth. Once or twice, they broke into the old house for a dare. They knew that old Frank was devoted to the house and grounds, and it amused them to see him limping across the garden, brandishing his stick and yelling croakily at them. Frank, on his part, believed the boys tormented him because they, like their parents and grandparents, thought him a murderer. So when Frank awoke one night in August, and saw something very odd up at the old house, he merely assumed that the boys had gone one step further in their attempts to punish him.

It was Frank's bad leg that woke him; it was paining him worse than ever in his old age. He got up and limped downstairs into the kitchen, with the idea of refilling his hot-water bottle to ease the stiffness in his knee. Standing at the sink, filling the kettle, he looked up at the Riddle House and saw lights glimmering in its upper windows. Frank knew at once what was going on. The boys had broken into the house again, and judging by the flickering quality of the light, they had started a fire.

Frank had no telephone, and in any case, he had deeply mistrusted the police ever since they had taken him in for questioning about the Riddles' deaths. He put down the kettle at once, hurried back upstairs as fast as his bad leg would allow, and was soon back in his kitchen, fully dressed and removing a rusty old key from its hook by the door. He picked up his walking stick, which was propped against the wall, and set off into the night.

The front door of the Riddle House bore no sign of being forced, and nor did any of the windows. Frank limped around to the back of the house until he reached a door almost completely hidden by ivy, took out the old key, put it into the lock and opened the door noiselessly.

He had let himself into the cavernous kitchen. Frank had not entered it for many years; nevertheless, although it was very dark, he remembered where the door into the hall was, and he groped his way towards it, his nostrils full of the smell of decay, ears pricked for any sound of footsteps or voices from overhead. He reached the hall, which was a little lighter owing to the large mullioned windows either side of the front door, and started to climb the stairs, blessing the dust which lay thick upon the stone, because it muffled the sound of his feet and stick.

On the landing, Frank turned right, and saw at once where the intruders

却骑着自行车在上面随意碾压。有一两次，男孩们因为互相打赌，还闯进了老宅。他们知道老弗兰克一心一意地护理宅子和庭园，几乎到了一种痴迷的程度，所以愿意看到他一瘸一拐地穿过园子，挥舞着拐杖，用沙哑的嗓子朝他们嚷嚷。每当这时，他们就觉得特别开心。弗兰克呢，他相信这些男孩之所以折磨他，是因为他们和他们的父母、祖父母一样，认为他是一个杀人犯。因此，在那个八月的夜晚，当弗兰克一觉醒来，看见老宅上面有异常的动静时，还以为是那些男孩又想出了新的花招来折磨他了。

弗兰克是被那条坏腿疼醒的，如今他上了年纪，腿疼得越发厉害了。他从床上起来，瘸着腿下楼走进厨房，想把热水袋灌满，暖一暖僵硬的膝盖。他站在水池边，往水壶里灌水，一边抬头朝里德尔府望去，看见楼上的窗户闪着微光。弗兰克立刻就明白了是怎么回事。那些男孩又闯进老宅了，那微光闪闪烁烁，明暗不定，看得出他们还生了火。

弗兰克的屋里没有装电话，而且自从当年为了里德尔一家猝死的事，警方把他带去审问之后，他就对警察有了一种深深的不信任感。他赶紧把水壶放下，拖着那条坏腿，尽快地返回楼上，穿好衣服，旋即又回到厨房。他从门边的钩子上取下那把锈迹斑斑的旧钥匙，拿起靠在墙边的拐杖，走进了夜色中。

里德尔府的前门没有被人强行闯入的迹象，窗户也完好无损。弗兰克一瘸一拐地绕到房子后面，停在一扇几乎完全被爬山虎遮住的门边，掏出那把旧钥匙，插进锁孔，无声地打开了门。

弗兰克走进洞穴般幽暗的大厨房，他已经很多年没有进来过了。四下里漆黑一片，但他仍然记得通往走廊的门在哪里。他摸索着走过去，一股腐烂的气味扑鼻而来。他竖起耳朵，捕捉头顶上的每一丝脚步声或说话声。他来到走廊上，这里因为有前门两边的大直棂窗，多少透进了一点儿光线。他开始上楼，心想多亏了石阶上积着厚厚的灰尘，使他的脚步声和拐杖声发闷，不易被人察觉。

在楼梯平台上，弗兰克向右一转，立刻看到了闯入者在什么地方。就在走廊的尽头，一扇门开着缝，一道闪烁的微光从门缝里射出来，

## CHAPTER ONE  The Riddle House

were: at the very end of the passage a door stood ajar, and a flickering light shone through the gap, casting a long sliver of gold across the black floor. Frank edged closer and closer, grasping his walking stick firmly. Several feet from the entrance, he was able to see a narrow slice of the room beyond.

The fire, he now saw, had been lit in the grate. This surprised him. He stopped moving and listened intently, for a man's voice spoke within the room; it sounded timid and fearful.

'There is a little more in the bottle, my Lord, if you are still hungry.'

'Later,' said a second voice. This, too, belonged to a man – but it was strangely high-pitched, and cold as a sudden blast of icy wind. Something about that voice made the sparse hairs on the back of Frank's neck stand up. 'Move me closer to the fire, Wormtail.'

Frank turned his right ear towards the door, the better to hear. There came the chink of a bottle being put down upon some hard surface, and then the dull scraping noise of a heavy chair being dragged across the floor. Frank caught a glimpse of a small man, his back to the door, pushing the chair into place. He was wearing a long black cloak, and there was a bald patch at the back of his head. Then he disappeared from sight again.

'Where is Nagini?' said the cold voice.

'I – I don't know, my Lord,' said the first voice nervously. 'She set out to explore the house, I think …'

'You will milk her before we retire, Wormtail,' said the second voice. 'I will need feeding in the night. The journey has tired me greatly.'

Brow furrowed, Frank inclined his good ear still closer to the door, listening very hard. There was a pause, and then the man called Wormtail spoke again.

'My Lord, may I ask how long we are going to stay here?'

'A week,' said the cold voice. 'Perhaps longer. The place is moderately comfortable, and the plan cannot proceed yet. It would be foolish to act before the Quidditch World Cup is over.'

Frank inserted a gnarled finger into his ear and rotated it. Owing, no doubt, to a build-up of earwax, he had heard the word 'Quidditch', which was not a word at all.

'The – the Quidditch World Cup, my Lord?' said Wormtail. (Frank dug his finger still more vigorously into his ear.) 'Forgive me, but – I do not

## 第1章 里德尔府

在黑乎乎的地板上投出一道细长的金色光影。弗兰克侧着身子,小心地一点点靠近,手里紧紧攥着拐杖。在离门口几步远的地方,他可以透过窄窄的门缝看见房间里的情景。

他现在看到了,那火是生在壁炉里的。这使他感到很意外。他停住脚步,竖起耳朵,只听见房间里传来一个男人的说话声,那声音显得胆怯、害怕。

"瓶子里还有呢,主人,如果您还饿,就再喝一点儿吧。"

"待会儿再说。"又一个声音说。这也是一个男人——但声音尖得奇怪,而且像寒风一样冰冷刺骨。不知怎的,这声音使弗兰克脖子后面稀少的头发都竖了起来。"把我挪到炉火边去,虫尾巴。"

弗兰克把右耳贴到门上,想听得更清楚些。房间里传来一只瓶子放在某个坚硬的东西上的当啷声,然后是一把重重的椅子在地板上拖过时发出的刺耳的摩擦声。弗兰克瞥见一个小个子男人,背对着门,正在推动一把椅子。他穿着一件长长的黑斗篷,后脑勺上秃了一块。随后,他又不见了。

"纳吉尼在哪儿?"那个冰冷的声音问。

"我——我不知道,主人。"第一个声音紧张地说,"我想,它大概在房子里到处看看……"

"我们睡觉前,你挤些它的毒液,虫尾巴。"第二个声音说,"我夜里还需要补充力量。这一路上可把我累坏了。"

弗兰克皱紧眉头,又把那只好耳朵往门上贴了贴,使劲儿听着。房间里静了片刻,然后那个被称作虫尾巴的人又说话了。

"主人,我能不能问一句,我们要在这里待多久?"

"一个星期,"那个透着寒意的声音说,"也许还要更长。这地方还算舒适,而且那计划暂时还不能实施。在魁地奇世界杯赛结束前就草率行事是不明智的。"

弗兰克把一根粗糙的手指伸进耳朵,转了几下。肯定是耳垢积得太多了,他居然听见了"魁地奇"这样一个怪词,根本就不成话。

"魁——魁地奇世界杯赛,主人?"虫尾巴说,(弗兰克用手指更使劲地掏耳朵。)"请原谅,可是我——我不明白——我们为什么要等

## CHAPTER ONE  The Riddle House

understand – why should we wait until the World Cup is over?'

'Because, fool, at this very moment wizards are pouring into the country from all over the world, and every meddler from the Ministry of Magic will be on duty, on the watch for signs of unusual activity, checking and double-checking identities. They will be obsessed with security, lest the Muggles notice anything. So we wait.'

Frank stopped trying to clear his ear out. He had distinctly heard the words 'Ministry of Magic', 'wizards' and 'Muggles'. Plainly, each of these expressions meant something secret, and Frank could think of only two sorts of people who would speak in code – spies and criminals. Frank tightened his hold on his walking stick once more, and listened more closely still.

'Your Lordship is still determined, then?' Wormtail said quietly.

'Certainly I am determined, Wormtail.' There was a note of menace in the cold voice now.

A slight pause followed – and then Wormtail spoke, the words tumbling from him in a rush, as though he was forcing himself to say this before he lost his nerve.

'It could be done without Harry Potter, my Lord.'

Another pause, more protracted, and then –

'Without Harry Potter?' breathed the second voice softly. 'I see ...'

'My Lord, I do not say this out of concern for the boy!' said Wormtail, his voice rising squeakily. 'The boy is nothing to me, nothing at all! It is merely that if we were to use another witch or wizard – any wizard – the thing could be done so much more quickly! If you allowed me to leave you for a short while – you know that I can disguise myself most effectively – I could be back here in as little as two days with a suitable person –'

'I could use another wizard,' said the second voice softly, 'that is true ...'

'My Lord, it makes sense,' said Wormtail, sounding thoroughly relieved now, 'laying hands on Harry Potter would be so difficult, he is so well protected –'

'And so you volunteer to go and fetch me a substitute? I wonder ... perhaps the task of nursing me has become wearisome for you, Wormtail? Could this suggestion of abandoning the plan be nothing more than an attempt to desert me?'

'My Lord! I – I have no wish to leave you, none at all –'

'Do not lie to me!' hissed the second voice. 'I can always tell, Wormtail!

到世界杯结束呢？"

"傻瓜，因为在这个时候，巫师们从世界各地涌进这个国家，魔法部那些爱管闲事的家伙全部出动了，他们站岗放哨，留意有没有异常的活动，反复盘查每个人的身份。他们一门心思就想着安全、安全，生怕麻瓜们注意到什么。所以我们必须等待。"

弗兰克不再掏耳朵了。他准确无误地听见了"魔法部""巫师"和"麻瓜"这些字眼。显然，这些词都具有神秘的含义，而据弗兰克所知，只有两种人才会说暗语：特务和罪犯。弗兰克更紧地攥住拐杖，更凝神地听着。

"这么说，主人的决心仍然没变？"虫尾巴轻声问。

"当然没变，虫尾巴。"那个冰冷的声音里现在带着威胁的口气了。

之后是片刻的沉默——随即虫尾巴说话了，他的话像湍急的河水一样从嘴里涌出来，似乎他在强迫自己在丧失勇气前把话说完。

"没有哈利·波特也能办成，主人。"

又是沉默，比刚才延续的时间更长，然后——

"没有哈利·波特？"第二个声音轻轻地问，"我明白……"

"主人，我说这话不是因为关心那个男孩！"虫尾巴说，他的声音突然抬高了，变得尖厉刺耳，"我才不在乎那个男孩呢，根本不在乎！我只是想，如果我们使用另外的巫师——不管是男是女——事情就可以速战速决了！如果您允许我离开您一小会儿——您知道我可以自如地伪装自己——我两天之内就回到这里，带回一个合适的人选——"

"我可以使用另外的巫师，"那个冰冷的声音轻轻地说，"这主意不错……"

"主人，这是合乎情理的。"虫尾巴说，口气舒缓多了，"要去加害哈利·波特太困难了，他现在受到了严密的保护——"

"所以你主动提出，要给我找一个替代品来？我想……也许这份伺候我的工作已经使你厌烦了，是吗，虫尾巴？你建议放弃原计划，是不是只想抛弃我呢？"

"主人！我——我没有要离开您的意思，压根儿没有——"

"不要对我撒谎！"第二个声音咝咝地说，"我什么都清楚，虫尾巴！

## CHAPTER ONE   The Riddle House

You are regretting that you ever returned to me. I revolt you. I see you flinch when you look at me, feel you shudder when you touch me …'

'No! My devotion to your Lordship –'

'Your devotion is nothing more than cowardice. You would not be here if you had anywhere else to go. How am I to survive without you, when I need feeding every few hours? Who is to milk Nagini?'

'But you seem so much stronger, my Lord –'

'Liar,' breathed the second voice. 'I am no stronger, and a few days alone would be enough to rob me of the little health I have regained under your clumsy care. *Silence!*'

Wormtail, who had been spluttering incoherently, fell silent at once. For a few seconds, Frank could hear nothing but the fire crackling. Then the second man spoke once more, in a whisper that was almost a hiss.

'I have my reasons for using the boy, as I have already explained to you, and I will use no other. I have waited thirteen years. A few more months will make no difference. As for the protection surrounding the boy, I believe my plan will be effective. All that is needed is a little courage from you, Wormtail – courage you will find, unless you wish to feel the full extent of Lord Voldemort's wrath –'

'My Lord, I must speak!' said Wormtail, panic in his voice now. 'All through our journey I have gone over the plan in my head – my Lord, Bertha Jorkins's disappearance will not go unnoticed for long, and if we proceed, if I curse –'

'If?' whispered the second voice. '*If?* If you follow the plan, Wormtail, the Ministry need never know that anyone else has disappeared. You will do it quietly, and without fuss; I only wish that I could do it myself, but in my present condition … come, Wormtail, one more obstacle removed and our path to Harry Potter is clear. I am not asking you to do it alone. By that time, my *faithful* servant will have rejoined us –'

'*I* am a faithful servant,' said Wormtail, the merest trace of sullenness in his voice.

'Wormtail, I need somebody with brains, somebody whose loyalty has never wavered, and you, unfortunately, fulfil neither requirement.'

'I found you,' said Wormtail, and there was definitely a sulky edge to his voice now. 'I was the one who found you. I brought you Bertha Jorkins.'

'That is true,' said the second man, sounding amused. 'A stroke of

你一直在后悔回到我这里来。我使你感到厌恶。我看得出你一看见我就畏缩，我感觉到你一碰到我就全身发抖……"

"不是这样的！我对主人忠心耿耿——"

"什么忠心耿耿，你只是胆小罢了。如果你有别的地方可去，决不会到这里来的。而我呢，我每隔几小时就需要你喂我，离开你我怎么活得下去？谁给纳吉尼挤毒液呢？"

"可是您看上去强壮多了，主人——"

"说谎，"第二个声音轻轻地说，"我没有强壮起来，几天工夫就会夺走我在你马马虎虎的照料下恢复的一点元气。别出声！"

正在结结巴巴、语无伦次地说着什么的虫尾巴，这时立刻沉默下来。在那几秒钟内，弗兰克只能听见火苗噼噼啪啪燃烧的声音。然后，第二个声音又说话了，声音很低很低，像是从喉咙里发出的咝咝声。

"我用那个男孩自有我的道理，这已经向你解释过了，我不会用其他人的。我已经等了十三年，再多等几个月也无妨。至于那个男孩受到严密保护，我相信我的计划会起作用。现在就需要你有一点勇气，虫尾巴——你得有勇气，除非你希望感受一下伏地魔大发雷霆的——"

"主人，请让我说一句！"虫尾巴说，声音里带着恐慌，"在我们这一路上，我脑子里反复盘算着那个计划——主人，伯莎·乔金斯的失踪很快就会引起人们的注意，如果我们再干下去，如果我杀死了——"

"如果？"第二个声音耳语般地说，"如果？如果你按我的计划行事，虫尾巴，魔法部永远不会知道还有谁死了。你悄悄地去做，不要大惊小怪。我真希望能亲自动手，可是按我目前的状况……过来，虫尾巴，只要再死一个人，我们通往哈利·波特的道路上就没有障碍了。我并没有要求你独自行动。到那时候，我忠实的仆人就会加入我们——"

"我就是一个忠实的仆人。"虫尾巴说，声音里含着一丝淡淡的不快。

"虫尾巴，我需要一个有脑子的人，一个对我绝对忠诚、从不动摇的人，而你呢，很不幸，这两个条件都不符合。"

"是我找到您的，"虫尾巴说，声音里带着明显的恼怒，"是我把您找到的，是我把伯莎·乔金斯给您带来的。"

"那倒不假，"第二个男人用打趣般的口吻说，"真没想到你还能说

## CHAPTER ONE  The Riddle House

brilliance I would not have thought possible from you, Wormtail – though, if truth be told, you were not aware how useful she would be when you caught her, were you?'

'I – I thought she might be useful, my Lord –'

'Liar,' said the second voice again, the cruel amusement more pronounced than ever. 'However, I do not deny that her information was invaluable. Without it, I could never have formed our plan, and for that, you will have your reward, Wormtail. I will allow you to perform an essential task for me, one that many of my followers would give their right hands to perform ...'

'R-really, my Lord? What –?' Wormtail sounded terrified again.

'Ah, Wormtail, you don't want me to spoil the surprise? Your part will come at the very end ... but I promise you, you will have the honour of being just as useful as Bertha Jorkins.'

'You ... you ...' Wormtail's voice sounded suddenly hoarse, as though his mouth had gone very dry. 'You ... are going ... to kill me, too?'

'Wormtail, Wormtail,' said the cold voice silkily, 'why would I kill you? I killed Bertha because I had to. She was fit for nothing after my questioning, quite useless. In any case, awkward questions would have been asked if she had gone back to the Ministry with the news that she had met you on her holidays. Wizards who are supposed to be dead would do well not to run into Ministry of Magic witches at wayside inns ...'

Wormtail muttered something so quietly that Frank could not hear it, but it made the second man laugh – an entirely mirthless laugh, cold as his speech.

'*We could have modified her memory*? But Memory Charms can be broken by a powerful wizard, as I proved when I questioned her. It would be an insult to her *memory* not to use the information I extracted from her, Wormtail.'

Out in the corridor, Frank suddenly became aware that the hand gripping his walking stick was slippery with sweat. The man with the cold voice had killed a woman. He was talking about it without any kind of remorse – with *amusement*. He was dangerous – a madman. And he was planning more murders – this boy, Harry Potter, whoever he was – was in danger –

Frank knew what he must do. Now, if ever, was the time to go to the police. He would creep out of the house and head straight for the telephone box in the village ... but the cold voice was speaking again, and Frank

出这么聪明的话来，虫尾巴——不过，说句实话，你把那女人抓来时，并没有意识到她多么有用，对不对？"

"我——我知道她会有用的，主人——"

"撒谎，"第二个声音又说道，冷冰冰的打趣口吻更明显了，"不过，我不否认她提供的情报很有价值。要不是那个情报，我就不可能想出我们的计划。这个嘛，虫尾巴，你自会得到奖赏。我允许你为我完成一件重要的任务，那是我的许多追随者都争着献上右手去完成的……"

"是——是吗，主人？什么——"虫尾巴的声音又变得恐慌起来。

"啊，虫尾巴，你难道想破坏这份意外之喜吗？最后才轮到你出场呢……不过我向你保证，你将有幸和伯莎·乔金斯一样有用。"

"您……您……"虫尾巴的声音突然沙哑了，他的嘴似乎变得很干，"您……您想……把我也杀死？"

"虫尾巴，虫尾巴，"那个冰冷的声音圆滑地说，"我为什么要杀死你呢？我杀死伯莎·乔金斯是迫不得已。在我审问完之后，她就没有用了，完全没有用了。不管怎样，如果她带着假期里遇见你的消息回到魔法部，人们就会提出许多难以应付的问题。原本应该死了的巫师是不会在路边的小客栈里遇见魔法部的女巫师的……"

虫尾巴又嘟哝了几句什么，声音太低，弗兰克没有听清，但他的话使第二个男人哈哈大笑起来——这是一种十分阴险的笑，跟他说的话一样寒气逼人。

"我们本可以改变她的记忆是不是？可是碰到一个法力强大的巫师，遗忘咒就不起作用了，这一点我在审问她时已经得到证实。不利用一下从她那里得到的情报，这对她的记忆也是一种侮辱啊，虫尾巴。"

在外面的走廊里，弗兰克突然意识到自己攥着拐杖的手已经被汗水湿透了。冰冷声音的男人杀死了一个女人。他谈论这件事的时候，没有一丝一毫的悔意——用的是一种打趣的口吻。这个人很危险——是一个亡命徒。他还在计划杀死更多的人——那个男孩，名叫哈利·波特的，不知道是谁——现在正处在危险中——

弗兰克知道他必须做什么了。这个时候非找警察不可了。他要偷偷溜出老宅，径直奔向村里的电话亭……可是那个冰冷的声音又说话

## CHAPTER ONE   The Riddle House

remained where he was, frozen to the spot, listening with all his might.

'One more curse ... my faithful servant at Hogwarts ... Harry Potter is as good as mine, Wormtail. It is decided. There will be no more argument. But quiet ... I think I hear Nagini ...'

And the second man's voice changed. He started making noises such as Frank had never heard before; he was hissing and spitting without drawing breath. Frank thought he must be having some sort of fit or seizure.

And then Frank heard movement behind him in the dark passageway. He turned to look behind him, and found himself paralysed with fright.

Something was slithering towards him along the dark corridor floor, and as it drew nearer to the sliver of firelight, he realised with a thrill of terror that it was a gigantic snake, at least twelve feet long. Horrified, transfixed, Frank stared at it as its undulating body cut a wide, curving track through the thick dust on the floor, coming closer and closer – what was he to do? The only means of escape was into the room where two men sat plotting murder, yet if he stayed where he was the snake would surely kill him –

But before he had made his decision, the snake was level with him, and then, incredibly, miraculously, it was passing; it was following the spitting, hissing noises made by the cold voice beyond the door, and in seconds, the tip of its diamond-patterned tail had vanished through the gap.

There was sweat on Frank's forehead now, and the hand on the walking stick was trembling. Inside the room, the cold voice was continuing to hiss, and Frank was visited by a strange idea, an impossible idea ... *This man could talk to snakes.*

Frank didn't understand what was going on. He wanted more than anything to be back in his bed with his hot-water bottle. The problem was that his legs didn't seem to want to move. As he stood there shaking, and trying to master himself, the cold voice switched abruptly to English again.

'Nagini has interesting news, Wormtail,' it said.

'In-indeed, my Lord?' said Wormtail.

'Indeed, yes,' said the voice. 'According to Nagini, there is an old Muggle standing right outside this room, listening to every word we say.'

Frank didn't have a chance to hide himself. There were footsteps, and then the door of the room was flung wide open.

A short, balding man with greying hair, a pointed nose and small, watery

了，弗兰克待在原地，像是被冻僵了一样，拼命集中精力听着。

"只要再来一次谋杀……我在霍格沃茨的忠实仆人……哈利·波特注定是我的了，虫尾巴。就这么定了，没什么可说的。慢着，你别作声……我好像听见了纳吉尼的声音……"

第二个男人的声音变了，发出一些弗兰克从未听见过的怪声；他不歇气地发出咝咝声和呼噜呼噜声。弗兰克认为他一定是发病了。

就在这时，弗兰克听见身后漆黑的走廊里传来了动静。他转身一看，顿时吓得呆在那里。

什么东西窸窸窣窣地滑过漆黑的走廊地板朝着他过来了。当那东西渐渐接近门缝里射出的那道壁炉的火光时，弗兰克惊恐万状地发现，那是一条巨蛇，至少有十二英尺长。弗兰克吓得呆若木鸡，站在那里望着它波浪般起伏的身体，在地板上厚厚的灰尘中留下蜿蜒曲折的、宽宽的轨迹，慢慢地越来越近——他怎么办呢？要逃也只能逃进那两个男人正在密谋杀人的房间，可是如果待在原地，这条蛇肯定会把他咬死——

还没等他拿定主意，巨蛇已经横在他面前，然后又神奇地、令人不可思议地滑了过去。它听从门后那个冰冷的咝咝声和呼噜呼噜声的召唤，几秒钟后，它那钻石图案的尾巴就从门缝里消失了。

这时，弗兰克额头上已渗出了汗珠，抓着拐杖的手抖个不停。房间里，那冰冷的声音继续咝咝地响着，弗兰克突然产生了一个奇怪的想法，一个荒唐的想法……这个人能跟蛇说话。

弗兰克不明白这一切到底是怎么回事。现在他最渴望的就是抱着热水袋回到床上。问题是他的双腿似乎不愿挪动。他站在那里，浑身瑟瑟发抖。他努力控制住自己。就在这时，那冰冷的声音猛地又说起了人话。

"纳吉尼带回了一个有趣的消息，虫尾巴。"那声音说。

"是——是吗，主人？"虫尾巴说。

"当然是。"那声音说，"据纳吉尼说，有一个老麻瓜，现在就站在这个房间外面，一字不漏地听着我们说话。"

弗兰克没有机会躲藏了，里面传来脚步声，随即房门一下子被打开了。

弗兰克面前站着一个秃顶的矮个子男人，花白的头发，尖尖的鼻子，

## CHAPTER ONE    The Riddle House

eyes stood before Frank, a mixture of fear and alarm on his face.

'Invite him inside, Wormtail. Where are your manners?'

The cold voice was coming from the ancient armchair before the fire, but Frank couldn't see the speaker. The snake, on the other hand, was curled up on the rotting hearth-rug, like some horrible travesty of a pet dog.

Wormtail beckoned Frank into the room. Though still deeply shaken, Frank took a firmer grip upon his walking stick, and limped over the threshold.

The fire was the only source of light in the room; it was casting long, spidery shadows upon the walls. Frank stared at the back of the armchair; the man inside it seemed to be even smaller than his servant, for Frank couldn't even see the back of his head.

'You heard everything, Muggle?' said the cold voice.

'What's that you're calling me?' said Frank defiantly, for now that he was inside the room, now that the time had come for some sort of action, he felt braver; it had always been so in the war.

'I am calling you a Muggle,' said the voice coolly. 'It means that you are not a wizard.'

'I don't know what you mean by wizard,' said Frank, his voice growing steadier. 'All I know is I've heard enough to interest the police tonight, I have. You've done murder and you're planning more! And I'll tell you this, too,' he added, on a sudden inspiration, 'my wife knows I'm up here, and if I don't come back –'

'You have no wife,' said the cold voice, very quietly. 'Nobody knows you are here. You told nobody that you were coming. Do not lie to Lord Voldemort, Muggle, for he knows … he always knows …'

'Is that right?' said Frank roughly. 'Lord, is it? Well, I don't think much of your manners, *my Lord*. Turn round and face me like a man, why don't you?'

'But I am not a man, Muggle,' said the cold voice, barely audible now over the crackling of the flames. 'I am much, much more than a man. However … why not? I will face you … Wormtail, come turn my chair around.'

The servant gave a whimper.

'You heard me, Wormtail.'

Slowly, with his face screwed up, as though he would rather have done anything than approach his master and the hearth-rug where the snake lay, the

一双小眼睛水汪汪的，脸上带着既恐惧又警惕的表情。

"请他进来，虫尾巴。你怎么不懂礼貌呢？"

那冰冷的声音是从壁炉前那把古老的扶手椅后发出来的，但弗兰克看不见说话的人。而那条蛇已经盘踞在壁炉前破烂的地毯上，如同在模仿一只哈巴狗，样子十分狰狞。

虫尾巴示意弗兰克进屋。弗兰克尽管全身颤抖得厉害，还是攥紧拐杖，一瘸一拐地迈过了门槛。

炉火是房间里唯一的光源，把长长的、蛛网状的影子投到了墙上。弗兰克盯着扶手椅的背后，坐在椅子里的人似乎比他的仆人虫尾巴还要矮小，弗兰克甚至看不见他的后脑勺。

"你什么都听见了，麻瓜？"那冰冷的声音问。

"你叫我什么？"弗兰克强硬地说，既然已经进了房间，既然必须采取行动，他的胆子反倒大了起来。在战场上经常就是这样的情况。

"我叫你麻瓜，"那声音冷冷地说，"就是说，你不是个巫师。"

"我不知道你说的巫师是什么意思。"弗兰克说，声音越来越平稳了，"我只知道，今晚我听到的东西足以引起警察的兴趣。你们杀了人，还在策划着要杀更多的人！我还要告诉你们，"他突然灵机一动，说道，"我老伴知道我上这儿来了，如果我不回去——"

"你没有老伴，"那冰冷的声音慢条斯理地说，"没有人知道你在这儿。你没有对别人说过你上这儿来。麻瓜，不要对伏地魔大人说谎，他什么都知道……什么都知道……"

"你说什么？"弗兰克粗暴地说，"大人，是吗？哼，我认为你的风度可不怎么样，我的大人！你为什么不像个男人一样，把脸转过来看着我呢？"

"因为我不是个人，麻瓜，"那冰冷的声音说，声音很低，几乎被炉火的噼啪声盖住了，"我比人要厉害得多。不过……好吧！我就面对你一下……虫尾巴，过来把我的椅子转一转。"

仆人发出一声呜咽。

"你听见没有，虫尾巴！"

小个子男人愁眉苦脸，仿佛他最不愿做的事就是走近他的主人，走近那条蛇盘踞的地毯；他慢慢地走上前，开始转动扶手椅。椅腿撞

small man walked forwards and began to turn the chair. The snake lifted its ugly triangular head and hissed slightly as the legs of the chair snagged on its rug.

And then the chair was facing Frank, and he saw what was sitting in it. His walking stick fell to the floor with a clatter. He opened his mouth and let out a scream. He was screaming so loudly that he never heard the words the thing in the chair spoke, as it raised a wand. There was a flash of green light, a rushing sound, and Frank Bryce crumpled. He was dead before he hit the floor.

Two hundred miles away, the boy called Harry Potter woke with a start.

## 第1章 里德尔府

在地毯上时,巨蛇昂起丑陋的三角形脑袋,发出轻微的咝咝声。

现在,椅子面对着弗兰克了,他看见了上面坐着的是什么。拐杖啪嗒一声掉在地上。他张开嘴,发出一声凄厉的喊叫。他喊叫的声音太响了,没有听见椅子上那个家伙举起一根棍子时嘴里说了些什么,而且永远也不会听见了。一道绿光闪过,一阵嗖嗖的声音响起,弗兰克·布莱斯瘫倒在地。在倒地之前他就已经死了。

两百英里之外,那个名叫哈利·波特的男孩猛地从梦中惊醒。

## CHAPTER TWO

## The Scar

Harry lay flat on his back, breathing hard as though he had been running. He had awoken from a vivid dream with his hands pressed over his face. The old scar on his forehead, which was shaped like a bolt of lightning, was burning beneath his fingers as though someone had just pressed a white-hot wire to his skin.

He sat up, one hand still on his scar, the other reaching out in the darkness for his glasses, which were on the bedside table. He put them on and his bedroom came into clearer focus, lit by a faint, misty orange light that was filtering through the curtains from the street lamp outside the window.

Harry ran his fingers over the scar again. It was still painful. He turned on the lamp beside him, scrambled out of bed, crossed the room, opened his wardrobe and peered into the mirror on the inside of the door. A skinny boy of fourteen looked back at him, his bright green eyes puzzled under his untidy black hair. He examined the lightning-bolt scar of his reflection more closely. It looked normal, but it was still stinging.

Harry tried to recall what he had been dreaming about before he had awoken. It had seemed so real ... there had been two people he knew, and one he didn't ... he concentrated hard, frowning, trying to remember ...

The dim picture of a darkened room came to him ... there had been a snake on a hearth-rug ... a small man called Peter, nicknamed Wormtail ... and a cold, high voice ... the voice of Lord Voldemort. Harry felt as though an ice cube had slipped down into his stomach at the very thought ...

He closed his eyes tightly and tried to remember what Voldemort had looked like, but it was impossible ... all Harry knew was that at the moment when Voldemort's chair had swung around, and he, Harry, had seen what was sitting in it, he had felt a spasm of horror which had awoken him ... or

# 第 2 章
# 伤　疤

**哈**利直挺挺地躺在床上，呼哧呼哧喘着粗气，好像刚才一直在奔跑似的。他从一个非常逼真的梦中惊醒，双手紧紧捂在脸上。在他的手指下面，那道闪电形的伤疤火辣辣地疼，仿佛有人刚将一根白热的金属丝按压在他的皮肤上。

他坐了起来，一只手捂着伤疤，另一只手在黑暗中摸索着去拿床头柜上的眼镜。他戴上眼镜，卧室里的景物慢慢变得清晰起来，窗外街灯的灯光透过窗帘，给卧室笼罩了一层朦朦胧胧的橙红色柔光。

哈利又用手指抚摸伤疤，仍然疼得厉害。他打开身边的台灯，翻身下床，穿过房间，打开衣柜，朝柜门内侧的镜子望去。镜子里一个瘦瘦的十四岁男孩在看着他，乱蓬蓬的黑头发下面是一对绿莹莹的、充满困惑的眼睛。哈利更仔细地端详镜子里他额头上的伤疤，看不出有什么异常，可是仍然钻心地疼。

哈利竭力回忆刚才梦中的情景。一切都是那么逼真……有两个人他认识，还有一个他不认识……他皱紧眉头，集中思想，拼命回忆着……

他眼前模模糊糊地浮现出一个昏暗的房间……壁炉前的地毯上卧着一条蛇……一个小个子的男人名叫彼得，外号虫尾巴……还有一个冷冰冰的、尖厉的声音……那是伏地魔的声音。哈利一想到这个家伙，就觉得仿佛有一块冰滑进了胃里……

他紧紧闭上眼睛，竭力回忆伏地魔的模样，可是无法做到……哈利只知道，当伏地魔的椅子一转过来，当他——哈利——看出那上面坐的是什么时，他只感到一阵巨大的恐惧，猛地惊醒过来……也许，

## CHAPTER TWO  The Scar

had that been the pain in his scar?

And who had the old man been? For there had definitely been an old man; Harry had watched him fall to the ground. It was all becoming confused; Harry put his face into his hands, blocking out his bedroom, trying to hold on to the picture of that dimly lit room, but it was like trying to keep water in his cupped hands; the details were now trickling away as fast as he tried to hold on to them ... Voldemort and Wormtail had been talking about someone they had killed, though Harry could not remember the name ... and they had been plotting to kill someone else ... *him* ...

Harry took his face out of his hands, opened his eyes and stared around his bedroom as though expecting to see something unusual there. As it happened, there were an extraordinary number of unusual things in this room. A large wooden trunk stood open at the foot of his bed, revealing a cauldron, broomstick, black robes and assorted spellbooks. Rolls of parchment littered that part of his desk that was not taken up by the large, empty cage in which his snowy owl, Hedwig, usually perched. On the floor beside his bed a book lay open; he had been reading it before he fell asleep the previous night. The pictures in this book were all moving. Men in bright orange robes were zooming in and out of sight on broomsticks, throwing a red ball to each other.

Harry walked over to this book, picked it up and watched one of the wizards score a spectacular goal by putting the ball through a fifty-foot-high hoop. Then he snapped the book shut. Even Quidditch – in Harry's opinion, the best sport in the world – couldn't distract him at the moment. He placed *Flying with the Cannons* on his bedside table, crossed to the window and drew back the curtains to survey the street below.

Privet Drive looked exactly as a respectable suburban street would be expected to look in the early hours of Saturday morning. All the curtains were closed. As far as Harry could see through the darkness, there wasn't a living creature in sight, not even a cat.

And yet ... and yet ... Harry went restlessly back to his bed and sat down on it, running a finger over his scar again. It wasn't the pain that bothered him; Harry was no stranger to pain and injury. He had lost all the bones from his right arm once, and had them painfully regrown in a night. The same arm had been pierced by a venomous foot-long fang not long afterwards. Only last year Harry had fallen fifty feet from an airborne broomstick. He

## 第 2 章 伤 疤

那是因为他的伤疤突然剧痛起来？

还有，那个老人是谁呢？当时肯定有一个老人，哈利看见他跌倒在地上。唉，越来越乱了。哈利把脸埋在手里，不让自己看见卧室里的景物，拼命沉浸于那个光线昏暗的房间，然而，这就像试图用双手把水兜住，他越是拼命地想抓住那些细节，它们就越是迅速地从他的指缝里溜走了……伏地魔和虫尾巴刚才谈到他们杀死了一个人，然而哈利记不清那个名字了……他们还在策划杀死另一个人……那就是他……

哈利把脸从手上抬起来，睁开眼睛，使劲儿盯着卧室四周，好像以为会看见什么不寻常的东西。确实，房间里有满满当当一大堆不寻常的东西。在他的床脚旁有一个大木箱，敞开着，露出里面的坩埚、飞天扫帚、黑色长袍和各种各样的咒语书。桌子上放着一只空空的大鸟笼，哈利的白色猫头鹰海德薇平常就在里面栖息。在桌上剩余的地方，胡乱地扔着几卷羊皮纸。床边的地板上有一本打开的书，那是哈利昨晚临睡前看的。这本书上的图画都在动个不停，穿着鲜艳的橙红色袍子的小伙子骑在飞天扫帚上，嗖嗖地飞来飞去，相互掷着一个红色的球。

哈利走过去，把书捡了起来，注视着一个巫师把球投进五十英尺高的圆环，十分漂亮地赢了一球。随即，哈利又猛地把书合上了。魁地奇比赛，在哈利看来，是世界上最精彩的运动，可是此刻也不能吸引他的注意力了。他把那本叫《与火炮队一起飞翔》的书放在床头柜上，走到窗前，拉开窗帘，望着下面的街道。

看上去，女贞路完全符合一条体面的郊区街道在星期六凌晨应该呈现的样子。街道两边的窗帘都拉得严严实实。哈利在黑暗中望过去，看不见一个活物，连一只小猫的影子也没有。

然而……然而……哈利心神不宁地回到床边，坐下来，又伸出一根手指抚摸他的伤疤。令他烦恼的不是伤疤的疼痛，哈利对疼痛和受伤已经习以为常。有一次，他右臂里所有的骨头都没有了，可又在一夜之间全部长好，那真是钻心的疼啊。在这之后不久，还是这条胳膊，又被一根尺把长的毒牙刺伤。就在去年，哈利飞到五十英尺高的空中

## CHAPTER TWO  The Scar

was used to bizarre accidents and injuries; they were unavoidable if you attended Hogwarts School of Witchcraft and Wizardry and had a knack for attracting a lot of trouble.

No, the thing that was bothering Harry was that the last time his scar had hurt him, it had been because Voldemort had been close by ... but Voldemort couldn't be here, now ... the idea of Voldemort lurking in Privet Drive was absurd, impossible ...

Harry listened closely to the silence around him. Was he half expecting to hear the creak of a stair, or the swish of a cloak? And then he jumped slightly as he heard his cousin Dudley give a tremendous grunting snore from the next room.

Harry shook himself mentally; he was being stupid; there was no one in the house with him except Uncle Vernon, Aunt Petunia and Dudley, and they were plainly still asleep, their dreams untroubled and painless.

Asleep was the way Harry liked the Dursleys best; it wasn't as though they were ever any help to him awake. Uncle Vernon, Aunt Petunia and Dudley were Harry's only living relatives. They were Muggles (non-magic people) who hated and despised magic in any form, which meant that Harry was about as welcome in their house as dry rot. They had explained away Harry's long absences at Hogwarts over the last three years by telling everyone that he went to St Brutus's Secure Centre for Incurably Criminal Boys. They knew perfectly well that, as an underage wizard, Harry wasn't allowed to use magic outside Hogwarts, but were still apt to blame him for anything that went wrong about the house. Harry had never been able to confide in them, or tell them anything about his life in the wizarding world. The very idea of going to them when they awoke, and telling them about his scar hurting him, and about his worries about Voldemort, was laughable.

And yet it was because of Voldemort that Harry had come to live with the Dursleys in the first place. If it hadn't been for Voldemort, Harry would not have had the lightning scar on his forehead. If it hadn't been for Voldemort, Harry would still have had parents ...

Harry had been a year old the night that Voldemort – the most powerful Dark wizard for a century, a wizard who had been gaining power steadily for eleven years – arrived at his house and killed his father and mother. Voldemort had then turned his wand on Harry; he had performed the curse that had disposed of many full-grown witches and wizards in his steady rise

## 第2章 伤疤

时，还从飞行着的扫帚上坠落下来。对他来说，稀奇古怪的事故和伤痛已经是家常便饭。既然你进了霍格沃茨魔法学校，并且擅长招惹是非，就绝对无法避免这些事故和伤痛。

上一次伤疤发作是因为伏地魔就在附近，正是这一点使哈利感到不安……此刻伏地魔不可能在这里……伏地魔会潜伏在女贞路？这种想法太荒唐了，绝对不可能……

哈利在一片寂静中凝神倾听。难道他在隐隐期待听见楼梯上传来吱吱呀呀的声音，或者听见斗篷在空中摆动的沙沙声？突然，他微微吃了一惊，他听见表哥达力在隔壁房间发出一声吓人的鼾声。

哈利慢慢鼓起勇气。他真是太傻了。整个房子里，和他住在一起的只有弗农姨父、佩妮姨妈和达力。他们显然都在酣睡，美美地做着梦，没有受到任何干扰。

哈利最喜欢的就是德思礼一家睡着的时候。这并不是说此刻的他们会对醒着的他有什么帮助。弗农姨父、佩妮姨妈和达力是哈利在世上仅有的亲戚。他们都是麻瓜（不会魔法的人），憎恨和蔑视任何形式的魔法，这就意味着哈利在他们家里就像霉菌一样不受欢迎。在过去的三年里，哈利到霍格沃茨上学，长期不在家，他们为了消除别人的疑虑，总是解释说哈利去了圣布鲁斯安全中心少年犯学校。他们明明知道，哈利作为一个未成年巫师，是不允许在霍格沃茨以外的地方使用魔法的，可每当家里出了什么乱子，还是总把责任推在他身上。哈利从来没法对他们说说知心话，也不能告诉他们他在魔法世界里生活的详细情况。想一想，等他们醒了，他去对他们说他的伤疤疼痛发作，并说他担心伏地魔潜伏在附近，这岂不是太可笑了吗！

说到根本，正是由于伏地魔，哈利才到这里跟德思礼一家生活的。如果没有伏地魔，哈利的额头上就不会有闪电形的伤疤。如果没有伏地魔，哈利的爸爸妈妈就会依然活着……

哈利刚刚一岁的时候，有一天夜里，伏地魔——这个一百年来最强大的黑巫师，这个花费了十一年的时间扩展其势力范围的巫师——闯到哈利家里，杀死了哈利的爸爸妈妈。然后，伏地魔又把他的魔杖指向哈利，念了一个咒语——在伏地魔的力量不断发展壮大的过程中，

## CHAPTER TWO  The Scar

to power – and, incredibly, it had not worked. Instead of killing the small boy, the curse had rebounded upon Voldemort. Harry had survived with nothing but a lightning-shaped cut on his forehead, and Voldemort had been reduced to something barely alive. His powers gone, his life almost extinguished, Voldemort had fled; the terror in which the secret community of witches and wizards had lived for so long had lifted, Voldemort's followers had disbanded, and Harry Potter had become famous.

It had been enough of a shock for Harry to discover, on his eleventh birthday, that he was a wizard; it had been even more disconcerting to find out that everyone in the hidden wizarding world knew his name. Harry had arrived at Hogwarts to find that heads turned and whispers followed him wherever he went. But he was used to it now: at the end of this summer, he would be starting his fourth year at Hogwarts; and he was already counting the days until he would be back at the castle again.

But there was still a fortnight to go before he went back to school. He looked hopelessly around his room again, and his eye paused on the birthday cards his two best friends had sent him at the end of July. What would they say if he wrote to them and told them about his scar hurting?

At once, Hermione granger's voice filled his head, shrill and panicky.

*'Your scar hurt? Harry, that's really serious ... Write to Professor Dumbledore! And I'll go and check* Common Magical Ailments and Afflictions *... Maybe there's something in there about curse scars ...'*

Yes, that would be Hermione's advice: go straight to the Headmaster of Hogwarts, and in the meantime, consult a book. Harry stared out of the window at the inky, blue-black sky. He doubted very much whether a book could help him now. As far as he knew, he was the only living person to have survived a curse like Voldemort's; it was highly unlikely, therefore, that he would find his symptoms listed in *Common Magical Ailments and Afflictions*. As for informing the Headmaster, Harry had no idea where Dumbledore went during the summer holidays. He amused himself for a moment, picturing Dumbledore, with his long silver beard, full-length wizard's robes and pointed hat, stretched out on a beach somewhere, rubbing suntan lotion into his long crooked nose. Wherever Dumbledore was, though, Harry was sure that Hedwig would be able to find him; Harry's owl had never yet failed to deliver a letter to anyone, even without an address. But what would he write?

## 第 2 章 伤 疤

这个咒语曾将许多成年巫师置于死地，然而那天夜里，它却莫名其妙地失灵了。咒语并没有结果小男孩的性命，而是反弹到了伏地魔自己身上。哈利安然无恙，只是在额头上留下了一道闪电形的伤疤，而伏地魔却沦为一种半死不活的状态。他的魔法全废，生命奄奄一息。伏地魔逃跑了，长久以来一直笼罩着神秘魔法世界的恐惧消除了，伏地魔的追随者们作鸟兽散，而哈利·波特一夜之间名闻遐迩。

哈利长到十一岁的时候，突然发现自己是个巫师，当时他真是吃惊不小。接着他又发现，在神秘的魔法世界里，人人都知道他的名字，这就更使他感到不知所措了。哈利来到霍格沃茨后，不管走到哪里，都会发现人们转过脸来看他，压低声音议论他。不过，他现在对这一切已经习以为常：过完这个夏天，哈利就在霍格沃茨上四年级了，他已经迫不及待地想回到那座城堡中去。

可是离开学还有整整两个星期呢。他又无奈地望了望自己的卧室，目光落在两张生日卡片上，那是他最要好的两个朋友在七月底寄给他的。如果哈利给他们写信，说他的伤疤疼了起来，他们会怎么说呢？

立刻，他脑子里似乎充满了赫敏·格兰杰的声音：咋咋呼呼，大惊小怪。

"你的伤疤疼？哈利，那可不是一般的事儿……快写信告诉邓布利多！我去查一查《常见魔法病痛》……也许书里会谈到魔咒伤疤……"

没错，赫敏肯定会这样建议：赶紧去找霍格沃茨的校长，同时在一本书里查找答案。哈利凝望着窗外沉沉的深蓝色夜空。现在书本能够给他帮助吗？他感到怀疑。据他所知，经历了伏地魔那样的咒语而活下来的只有他一个人。因此，他不可能看到他的症状列举在《常见魔法病痛》里。那么要不要告诉校长呢？可是哈利压根儿就不知道邓布利多暑假去了哪里。哈利饶有兴趣地幻想着一把银白胡子的邓布利多：穿着长长的巫师袍，戴着尖顶帽，躺在什么地方的海滩上，往自己长长的歪扭的鼻子上抹防晒油。不过哈利知道，邓布利多哪怕走到天涯海角，海德薇也有办法找到他。哈利的这只猫头鹰神通广大，还从来没有它送不到的信，即便没有地址也不要紧。问题是这封信怎么写呢？

## CHAPTER TWO   The Scar

*Dear Professor Dumbledore, Sorry to bother you, but my scar hurt this morning. Yours sincerely, Harry Potter.*

Even inside his head the words sounded stupid.

And so he tried to imagine his other best friend Ron Weasley's reaction, and in a moment, Ron's long-nosed, freckled face seemed to swim before Harry, wearing a bemused expression.

'Your scar hurt? But ... but You-Know-Who can't be near you now, can he? I mean ... you'd know, wouldn't you? He'd be trying to do you in again, wouldn't he? I dunno, Harry, maybe curse scars always twinge a bit ... I'll ask Dad ...'

Mr Weasley was a fully qualified wizard who worked in the Misuse of Muggle Artefacts Office at the Ministry of Magic, but he didn't have any particular expertise in the matter of curses, as far as Harry knew. In any case, Harry didn't like the idea of the whole Weasley family knowing that he, Harry, was getting jumpy about a few moments' pain. Mrs Weasley would fuss worse than Hermione, and Fred and George, Ron's sixteen-year-old twin brothers, might think Harry was losing his nerve. The Weasleys were Harry's favourite family in the world; he was hoping that they might invite him to stay any time now (Ron had mentioned something about the Quidditch World Cup), and he somehow didn't want his visit punctuated with anxious enquiries about his scar.

Harry kneaded his forehead with his knuckles. What he really wanted (and it felt almost shameful to admit it to himself) was someone like – someone like a *parent*: an adult wizard whose advice he could ask without feeling stupid, someone who cared about him, who had had experience of Dark Magic ...

And then the solution came to him. It was so simple, and so obvious, that he couldn't believe it had taken so long – *Sirius*.

Harry leapt up from the bed, hurried across the room and sat down at his desk; he pulled a piece of parchment towards him, loaded his eagle-feather quill with ink, wrote *Dear Sirius*, then paused, wondering how best to phrase his problem, and still marvelling at the fact that he hadn't thought of Sirius straight away. But then, perhaps it wasn't so surprising – after all, he had only found out that Sirius was his godfather two months ago.

There was a simple reason for Sirius' complete absence from Harry's

## 第2章 伤疤

　　亲爱的邓布利多教授，很抱歉打扰你，可是我的伤疤今天早晨疼了起来。
　　　　　　　　　　　　　　　　　你忠实的哈利·波特

　　太荒唐了，这些话别说写下来，就是在脑子里想想都是可笑的。

　　接着哈利又试着想象他另一个最要好的朋友罗恩·韦斯莱的反应。立刻，他眼前浮现出了罗恩的那一头红发，那一张鼻子长长的雀斑脸，脸上带着一种茫然困惑的表情。

　　"你的伤疤疼？可是……可是，神秘人现在不可能接近你啊，是不是？我是说……你知道的，对吗？说不定他又要来害你了，会不会？我不知道，哈利，也许魔咒伤疤总是有点疼的……我去问问我爸……"

　　韦斯莱先生是一位很有资历的巫师，在魔法部禁止滥用麻瓜物品办公室工作，但是就哈利所知，他对咒语的问题并不内行。而且，不管怎么说，哈利可不希望韦斯莱一家都知道他，哈利，为了片刻的疼痛而惊慌失措。韦斯莱夫人比赫敏还要大惊小怪，还有弗雷德和乔治——罗恩那一对十六岁的双胞胎哥哥，他们肯定会认为哈利变成一个胆小鬼。在这个世界上，韦斯莱全家是哈利最喜欢的一家人。他正期待着他们邀请他去住一段时间（罗恩曾经提到魁地奇世界杯赛什么的），他可不愿意自己住在韦斯莱家的时候，大家都紧张兮兮地询问他的伤疤如何如何，那多扫兴啊。

　　哈利用指关节揉了揉伤疤。其实，他真正需要的（要让他自己承认这一点，多少有些丢脸）是一位——是一位像父母那样的人：一位成年巫师，哈利可以坦然地向他请教，而不感到自己显得很傻，那个人应该很关心他，还应该知道怎样对付黑魔法……

　　慢慢地，他的脑子里有了答案。太简单了，太显而易见了，他简直无法相信自己居然想了这么长时间——那个人就是小天狼星！

　　哈利从床上一跃而起，匆匆走过屋子，在桌子旁边坐下。他拉过一张羊皮纸，将鹰毛羽毛笔蘸满墨水，写下亲爱的小天狼星，然后停住了。他不知道用什么词语表达自己面临的问题，同时脑海里还在惊叹，刚才怎么没有一下子就想到小天狼星呢。接着他想通了——毕竟，他两个月前才知道小天狼星是他的教父啊。

　　那么，为什么在那之前小天狼星没有在哈利的生活中出现呢？原

## CHAPTER TWO  The Scar

life until then – Sirius had been in Azkaban, the terrifying wizard gaol guarded by creatures called Dementors, sightless, soul-sucking fiends who had come to search for Sirius at Hogwarts when he had escaped. Yet Sirius had been innocent – the murders for which he had been convicted had been committed by Wormtail, Voldemort's supporter, whom nearly everybody now believed dead. Harry, Ron and Hermione knew otherwise, however; they had come face to face with Wormtail the previous year, though only Professor Dumbledore had believed their story.

For one glorious hour, Harry had believed that he was leaving the Dursleys at last, because Sirius had offered him a home once his name had been cleared. But the chance had been snatched away from him – Wormtail had escaped before they could take him to the Ministry of Magic, and Sirius had had to flee for his life. Harry had helped him escape on the back of a Hippogriff called Buckbeak, and since then, Sirius had been on the run. The home Harry might have had if Wormtail had not escaped had been haunting him all summer. It had been doubly hard to return to the Dursleys knowing that he had so nearly escaped them for ever.

Nevertheless, Sirius had been of some help to Harry, even if he couldn't be with him. It was due to Sirius that Harry now had all his school things in his bedroom with him. The Dursleys had never allowed this before; their general wish of keeping Harry as miserable as possible, coupled with their fear of his powers, had led them to lock his school trunk in the cupboard under the stairs every summer prior to this. But their attitude had changed since they had found out that Harry had a dangerous murderer for a godfather – Harry had conveniently forgotten to tell them that Sirius was innocent.

Harry had received two letters from Sirius since he had been back at Privet Drive. Both had been delivered, not by owls (as was usual with wizards) but by large, brightly coloured, tropical birds. Hedwig had not approved of these flashy intruders; she had been most reluctant to allow them to drink from her water tray before flying off again. Harry, on the other hand, had liked them; they put him in mind of palm trees and white sand, and he hoped that wherever Sirius was (Sirius never said, in case the letters were intercepted) he was enjoying himself. Somehow, Harry found it hard to imagine Dementors surviving for long in bright sunlight; perhaps that was why Sirius had gone south. Sirius' letters, which were now hidden beneath the highly useful loose

## 第2章 伤疤

因很简单——小天狼星被关在阿兹卡班，那座令人恐惧的巫师监狱，看守是一些被称为摄魂怪的家伙。它们没有视力，是专门摄取别人灵魂的魔鬼。小天狼星逃跑后，它们曾到霍格沃茨来搜找过他。其实小天狼星是无辜的——指控他犯的那些谋杀罪行，实际上真正的凶手是伏地魔的追随者虫尾巴，而几乎每个人都以为虫尾巴已经死了。不过，哈利、罗恩和赫敏知道他还活着。就在去年，他们还和虫尾巴面对面地接触过，可是只有邓布利多教授才相信他们的话。

当时，那一个钟头里哈利真是心花怒放，以为自己终于要离开德思礼家了，因为小天狼星承诺在澄清自己的名誉后，就会给哈利一个家。然而，这个机会被剥夺了——没等他们把虫尾巴带到魔法部，就让他逃脱了，小天狼星不得不匆匆逃命。哈利帮助他骑上那头名叫巴克比克的鹰头马身有翼兽逃走了，从那以后，小天狼星就一直逃亡在外。如果虫尾巴没有逃脱，哈利将有一个多么好的家啊。整个夏天，这个念头一直萦绕着他。哈利明知道自己差一点就可以永远摆脱德思礼一家，现在却又不得不回到他们身边，这种滋味真是难受。

不过，小天狼星虽然不可能陪伴哈利，却一直在帮助他。正是因为有了小天狼星，哈利现在才能把学校里用的东西都放在卧室里。以前德思礼一家是绝对不许他这么做的。他们一门心思不让哈利快活，再加上对他的法力十分害怕，所以在此之前的每年夏天，他们都把他上学用的东西锁在楼梯下的储物间里。后来，当他们发现哈利有一个危险的杀人犯当他的教父时，态度立刻就转变了——哈利恰好忘记了告诉他们小天狼星是无辜的。

哈利回到女贞路后，收到过小天狼星的两封信。这两封信不是猫头鹰送来的（用猫头鹰送信是巫师们的惯常做法），而是色彩斑斓的热带大鸟送来的。海德薇对这些花里胡哨的入侵者很不以为然，甚至不愿让它们在它的水盘里喝几口水再动身离开。哈利倒是很喜欢那些热带鸟，它们使他想起了棕榈树和白色的沙滩。他衷心希望，小天狼星不管在哪里，都生活得很愉快。由于担心信件被半道截走，小天狼星从不透露自己的去向。不知怎的，哈利觉得很难想象摄魂怪能在灿烂的阳光下存活很长时间，也许正是考虑到这一点，小天狼星才到南方去了。此刻，小

## CHAPTER TWO   The Scar

floorboard under Harry's bed, sounded cheerful, and in both of them he had reminded Harry to call on him if ever Harry needed to. Well, he needed to now, all right …

Harry's lamp seemed to grow dimmer as the cold grey light that precedes sunrise slowly crept into the room. Finally, when the sun had risen, when his bedroom walls had turned gold and when sounds of movement could be heard from Uncle Vernon and Aunt Petunia's room, Harry cleared his desk of crumpled pieces of parchment, and reread his finished letter.

> Dear Sirius,
>
> Thanks for your last letter, that bird was enormous, it could hardly get through my window.
>
> Things are the same as usual here. Dudley's diet isn't going too well. My aunt found him smuggling doughnuts into his room yesterday. They told him they'd have to cut his pocket money if he keeps doing it, so he got really angry and chucked his PlayStation out of the window. That's a sort of computer thing you can play games on. Bit stupid really, now he hasn't even got Mega-Mutilation Part Three to take his mind off things.
>
> I'm OK, mainly because the Dursleys are terrified you might you might turn up and turn them all into bats if I ask you to.
>
> A weird thing happened this morning, though. My scar hurt again. Last time that happened it was because Voldemort was at Hogwarts. But I don't reckon he can be anywhere near me now, can he? Do you know if curse scars sometimes hurt years afterwards?
>
> I'll send this with Hedwig when she gets back, she's off hunting at the moment. Say hello to Buckbeak for me.
>
> Harry

Yes, thought Harry, that looked all right. There was no point putting in the dream, he didn't want it to look as though he was too worried. He folded the parchment up and laid it aside on his desk, ready for when Hedwig returned. Then he got to his feet, stretched and opened his wardrobe once more. Without glancing at his reflection, he started to get dressed before going down to breakfast.

## 第2章 伤 疤

天狼星的信就藏在哈利床底下那块松动的地板下——这块地板的用处非常大。信上的口气很愉快，两封信都提醒哈利，如果他需要的话，随时可以召唤小天狼星。瞧，哈利现在就有这种需要了，好吧……

黎明前寒冷的、灰白色的天光慢慢地透进房间，哈利的台灯光线似乎变暗了。终于，太阳升起来了，卧室的墙壁被映成了金黄色，弗农姨父和佩妮姨妈的房间里也有了动静。这时，哈利收拾起桌上那些揉皱了的羊皮纸团，又把那封终于写成的信读了一遍。

亲爱的小天狼星：

感谢你给我来信。那只鸟实在太大了，差点进不了我的窗户。

这里的情况没什么变化。达力的节食计划进行得不太成功，昨天我姨妈在他房间里发现了他私藏的甜甜圈。他们警告他，如果他屡教不改，就削减他的零花钱，结果他一气之下，把他的游戏机扔到了窗外。那是一种电脑，可以在上面玩游戏。他这么做真是有点儿傻，现在他心情苦闷的时候，就不能玩《无敌破坏Ⅲ》来消遣了。

我一切都好，主要是因为德思礼一家害怕我一发话，你就会突然出现，把他们全都变成蝙蝠。

不过，今天早晨发生了一件怪事。我的伤疤又疼了。上次疼的时候，是因为伏地魔就在霍格沃茨。我猜想他现在不可能在我附近，对吧？你知道魔咒伤疤会不会在许多年后又疼起来？

海德薇回来后，我就派它把这封信给你送去。它眼下出去捕食了。请代我向巴克比克问好。

哈 利

行，看上去不错，哈利心想。没必要把做梦的事也写进去。他不希望显得自己紧张兮兮的。他卷起羊皮纸，放在桌上，等海德薇回来把它送走。然后，他站起身，伸了个懒腰，又一次打开衣柜。他没有照镜子，就径直穿好衣服，下楼去吃早饭了。

## CHAPTER THREE

## The Invitation

By the time Harry arrived in the kitchen, the three Dursleys were already seated around the table. None of them looked up as he entered or sat down. Uncle Vernon's large red face was hidden behind the morning's *Daily Mail* and Aunt Petunia was cutting a grapefruit into quarters, her lips pursed over her horse-like teeth.

Dudley looked furious and sulky, and somehow seemed to be taking up even more space than usual. This was saying something, as he always took up an entire side of the square table by himself. When Aunt Petunia put a quarter of unsweetened grapefruit onto Dudley's plate with a tremulous 'There you are, Diddy darling', Dudley glowered at her. His life had taken a most unpleasant turn since he had come home for the summer with his end-of-year report.

Uncle Vernon and Aunt Petunia had managed to find excuses for his bad marks as usual; Aunt Petunia always insisted that Dudley was a very gifted boy whose teachers didn't understand him, while Uncle Vernon maintained that 'he didn't want some swotty little nancy boy for a son anyway'. They also skated over the accusations of bullying in the report – 'He's a boisterous little boy, but he wouldn't hurt a fly!' said Aunt Petunia tearfully.

However, at the bottom of the report there were a few well chosen comments from the school nurse which not even Uncle Vernon and Aunt Petunia could explain away. No matter how much Aunt Petunia wailed that Dudley was big-boned, and that his pound-age was really puppy-fat, and that he was a growing boy who needed plenty of food, the fact remained that the school outfitters didn't stock knickerbockers big enough for him any more. The school nurse had seen what Aunt Petunia's eyes – so sharp when it came to spotting fingerprints on her gleaming walls, and in observing the comings

# 第 3 章

# 邀　请

**哈**利来到厨房时，德思礼一家三口已经围坐在餐桌旁了。哈利进门坐下，他们谁也没有抬头看他一眼。弗农姨父那张红红的大脸膛躲在早晨送来的《每日邮报》后面，佩妮姨妈正在把一只葡萄柚切成四份，嘴唇嗫着，包住了她长长的大马牙。

达力阴沉着脸，显得气呼呼的，所占的空间似乎比平常更大。这就很有意思了，因为他平常一个人就能把方桌的一边占得满满当当。佩妮姨妈把四分之一没有加糖的葡萄柚送进达力的盘子，用颤抖的声音说了句："吃吧，小乖乖。"达力怒气冲冲地瞪着她。自从达力暑假回家，带回来期末成绩报告单之后，他的生活便发生了十分痛苦的变化。

对于达力糟糕的学习成绩，弗农姨父和佩妮姨妈像往常一样找到了一些借口：佩妮姨妈总是一再强调，达力是一个很有天赋的孩子，只是老师们都不理解他；弗农姨父则坚持说，他"可不希望自己的儿子变成一个娘娘腔的书呆子"。对于老师批评达力欺负同学的评语，他们也轻飘飘地一带而过——"他虽然是个活泼爱动的孩子，可是连一只苍蝇都不忍心伤害的！"佩妮姨妈噙着泪花说。

不过，在报告单下面，有学校护士小心翼翼写下的几句话，就连弗农姨父和佩妮姨妈都无法找借口遮掩过去。尽管佩妮姨妈哭喊着说达力只是骨头架子大，说他体重过沉只是一种青春期的暂时肥胖，并说他正处在发育成长的阶段，需要丰富的食物和营养，但有一个事实是无法改变的：学校服装库里再也找不到达力能穿得上的裤子了。佩妮姨妈的眼睛，在查看一尘不染的墙壁上的手指印，或观察

## CHAPTER THREE   The Invitation

and goings of the neighbours – simply refused to see: that, far from needing extra nourishment, Dudley had reached roughly the size and weight of a young killer whale.

So – after many tantrums, after arguments that shook Harry's bedroom floor, and many tears from Aunt Petunia – the new regime had begun. The diet sheet that had been sent by the Smeltings school nurse had been taped to the fridge, which had been emptied of all Dudley's favourite things – fizzy drinks and cakes, chocolate bars and burgers – and filled instead with fruit and vegetables and the sorts of things that Uncle Vernon called 'rabbit food'. To make Dudley feel better about it all, Aunt Petunia had insisted that the whole family follow the diet too. She now passed a grapefruit quarter to Harry. He noticed that it was a lot smaller than Dudley's. Aunt Petunia seemed to feel that the best way to keep up Dudley's morale was to make sure that he did, at least, get more to eat than Harry.

But Aunt Petunia didn't know what was hidden under the loose floorboard upstairs. She had no idea that Harry was not following the diet at all. The moment he had got wind of the fact that he was expected to survive the summer on carrot sticks, Harry had sent Hedwig to his friends with pleas for help, and they had risen to the occasion magnificently. Hedwig had returned from Hermione's house with a large box stuffed full of sugar-free snacks (Hermione's parents were dentists). Hagrid, the Hogwarts gamekeeper, had obliged with a sack full of his own home-made rock cakes (Harry hadn't touched these; he had had too much experience of Hagrid's cooking). Mrs Weasley, however, had sent the family owl, Errol, with an enormous fruitcake and assorted pasties. Poor Errol, who was elderly and feeble, had needed a full five days to recover from the journey. And then on Harry's birthday (which the Dursleys had completely ignored) he had received four superb birthday cakes, one each from Ron, Hermione, Hagrid and Sirius. Harry still had two of them left, and so, looking forward to a real breakfast when he got back upstairs, he started eating his grapefruit without complaint.

Uncle Vernon laid aside his paper with a deep sniff of disapproval and looked down at his own grapefruit quarter.

'Is this it?' he said grumpily to Aunt Petunia.

Aunt Petunia gave him a severe look, and then nodded pointedly at Dudley, who had already finished his own grapefruit quarter, and was eyeing

## 第3章 邀 请

邻居们的行踪时总是非常敏锐,却不肯看到学校护士发现的一个事实:达力根本不需要额外补充营养,他的块头和体重已经接近一头幼年的虎鲸了。

因此,在没完没了地发脾气之后,在惊天动地的争吵几乎把哈利卧室的地板掀翻之后,在佩妮姨妈抛洒了无数眼泪之后,新的饮食制度开始实施了。斯梅廷学校护士寄来的减肥食谱被贴在了冰箱上,凡是达力喜欢的食物——汽水饮料、蛋糕、巧克力和汉堡牛排,冰箱中已经一概没有,只有水果、蔬菜,还有一些弗农姨父称之为"兔粮"的食物。为了使达力情绪好一点儿,佩妮姨妈坚持全家人都遵循那个食谱。此刻,她把四分之一的葡萄柚递给了哈利。哈利注意到,他的这份比达力的那份小得多。佩妮姨妈似乎认为,使达力振奋精神的最好办法就是保证他至少比哈利吃的东西多。

然而,佩妮姨妈不知道楼上那块松动的地板下藏着的秘密。她压根儿也想不到哈利根本就没有遵循食谱。当哈利听到风声,得知自己整个夏天可能都要靠胡萝卜过活时,便派海德薇给他的朋友们送信,呼吁援助,他们立刻积极响应。海德薇从赫敏家里带回一个大盒子,里面塞满了无糖的点心(赫敏的父母都是牙科医生)。海格是霍格沃茨的猎场看守,他热情地捎来满满一袋自己做的岩皮饼(哈利连碰都没碰,对于海格的厨艺,他早有领教)。韦斯莱夫人派出他们家的猫头鹰埃罗尔,给哈利送来了一块巨大的水果蛋糕和各种风味的夹肉馅饼。可怜的埃罗尔,上了年纪,体力不支,送完这批货之后,整整休息了五天才缓过劲儿来。后来,哈利在生日那天(德思礼一家连提都没提)一共收到了四份超级大蛋糕,分别是罗恩、赫敏、海格和小天狼星送给他的。到现在还有两个蛋糕没有吃完。哈利期待着回到楼上享用一顿真正的早餐,便毫无怨言地吃着他那份葡萄柚。

弗农姨父气呼呼地从鼻子里哼了一声,放下报纸,低头望着分给他的那份四分之一葡萄柚。

"就这么点儿?"他带着怒气问佩妮姨妈。

佩妮姨妈严厉地瞪了他一眼,然后朝达力的方向点了点头。达力已经吃完他那份葡萄柚,正使劲儿地盯着哈利的那一份,小小的猪眼

## CHAPTER THREE    The Invitation

Harry's with a very sour look in his piggy little eyes.

Uncle Vernon gave a great sigh which ruffled his large, bushy moustache, and picked up his spoon.

The doorbell rang. Uncle Vernon heaved himself out of his chair and set off down the hall. Quick as a flash, while his mother was occupied with the kettle, Dudley stole the rest of Uncle Vernon's grapefruit.

Harry heard talking at the door, and someone laughing, and Uncle Vernon answering curtly. Then the front door closed, and the sound of ripping paper came from the hall.

Aunt Petunia set the teapot down on the table and looked curiously around to see where Uncle Vernon had got to. She didn't have to wait long to find out; after about a minute, he was back. He looked livid.

'You,' he barked at Harry. 'In the living room. Now.'

Bewildered, wondering what on earth he was supposed to have done this time, Harry got up and followed Uncle Vernon out of the kitchen and into the next room. Uncle Vernon closed the door sharply behind both of them.

'So,' he said, marching over to the fireplace and turning to face Harry as though he was about to pronounce him under arrest. '*So*.'

Harry would have dearly loved to have said 'So what?', but he didn't feel that Uncle Vernon's temper should be tested this early in the morning, especially when it was already under severe strain from lack of food. He therefore settled for looking politely puzzled.

'This just arrived,' said Uncle Vernon. He brandished a piece of purple writing paper at Harry. 'A letter. About you.'

Harry's confusion increased. Who would be writing to Uncle Vernon about him? Who did he know who sent letters by the postman?

Uncle Vernon glared at Harry, then looked down at the letter, and began to read aloud:

> *Dear Mr and Mrs Dursley,*
>
> *We have never been introduced, but I am sure you have heard a great deal from Harry about my son Ron.*
>
> *As Harry might have told you, the final of the Quidditch World Cup takes place next Monday night, and my husband, Arthur, has just managed to get prime tickets through his connections at the Department of Magical Games*

## 第3章 邀请

睛里闪动着十分仇恨的光芒。

弗农姨父重重地叹了口气,吹得乱蓬蓬的大胡子都抖动起来,然后他拿起了勺子。

门铃响了。弗农姨父费力地从椅子上站起来,朝门厅走去。达力趁母亲忙着照料水壶,说时迟那时快,把弗农姨父剩下的葡萄柚偷了过去。

哈利听见门口有说话声,什么人在哈哈大笑,弗农姨父简短地回答着什么。随后,前门关上了,门厅里传来了撕纸的声音。

佩妮姨妈把茶壶放在桌上,好奇地环顾四周,不知道弗农姨父去了哪里。她很快就会明白的;一分钟后,弗农姨父回来了,神情大怒。

"你,"他对哈利吼道,"快到客厅里去。马上。"

哈利一头雾水,不知道自己这次又做错了什么。他从桌旁站起,跟着弗农姨父离开厨房,走进隔壁的房间。两人进去后,弗农姨父狠狠地关上了房门。

"好啊,"他说,三步并作两步地走到壁炉跟前,回过身来面对着哈利,就好像要宣布把哈利逮捕法办似的,"好啊。"

哈利真想问一句:"什么'好啊'?"但是他知道,弗农姨父一清早的脾气是惹不起的,而且,他已经因为没吃饱而憋了一肚子火。于是,哈利礼貌地做出一副困惑的表情。

"刚送到的,"弗农姨父说,冲哈利挥舞着一张紫色的书写纸,"一封信。跟你有关。"

哈利更加糊涂了。谁会给弗农姨父写信说他的事呢?在他认识的人中间,有谁会让邮递员送信呢?

弗农姨父恼火地瞪着哈利,然后低头看信,大声念道:

亲爱的德思礼先生和夫人:

我们素不相识,但我相信你们一定从哈利那里听到过许多关于我儿子罗恩的事。

也许哈利已经对你们说过,魁地奇世界杯赛将于星期一夜里举行,我丈夫亚瑟通过他在魔法体育运动司的关系,好不容易弄

## CHAPTER THREE  The Invitation

*and Sports.*

*I do hope you will allow us to take Harry to the match, as this really is a once-in-a-lifetime opportunity; Britain hasn't hosted the Cup for thirty years and tickets are extremely hard to come by. We would of course be glad to have Harry to stay for the remainder of the summer holidays, and to see him safely onto the train back to school.*

*It would be best for Harry to send us your answer as quickly as possible in the normal way, because the Muggle postman has never delivered to our house, and I am not sure he ever knows where it is.*

*Hoping to see Harry soon.*

*Yours sincerely,*

*Molly Weasley*

*P.S. I do hope we've put enough stamps on.*

Uncle Vernon finished reading, put his hand back into his breast pocket, and drew out something else.

'Look at this,' he growled.

He held up the envelope in which Mrs Weasley's letter had come, and Harry had to fight down a laugh. Every bit of it was covered in stamps except for a square inch on the front, into which Mrs Weasley had squeezed the Dursleys' address in minute writing.

'She did put enough stamps on, then,' said Harry, trying to sound as though Mrs Weasley's was a mistake anyone could make. His uncle's eyes flashed.

'The postman noticed,' he said through gritted teeth. 'Very interested to know where this letter came from, he was. That's why he rang the doorbell. Seemed to think it was *funny.*'

Harry didn't say anything. Other people might not understand why Uncle Vernon was making a fuss about too many stamps, but Harry had lived with the Dursleys too long not to know how touchy they were about anything even slightly out of the ordinary. Their worst fear was that anyone would find out that they were connected (however distantly) with people like Mrs Weasley.

Uncle Vernon was still glaring at Harry, who tried to keep his expression neutral. If he didn't do or say anything stupid, he might just be in for the treat of a lifetime. He waited for Uncle Vernon to say something, but he

## 第3章 邀 请

到了几张最好的票。

　　我真希望你们允许哈利去观看比赛，这实在是一次千载难逢的机会；英国已经三十年没有主办比赛了，球票很不容易弄到。当然了，我们很愿意留哈利在这里一直住到暑假结束，并送他平安地乘火车返校。

　　最好让哈利将你们的答复尽快通过正常方式送达我们，因为麻瓜邮差从来没有给我们家送过信，大概根本不知道我们家在什么地方。

　　希望很快见到哈利。

你们忠实的<br>莫丽·韦斯莱

　　又及：但愿我们贴足了邮票。

　　弗农姨父念完了，把手伸进胸前的口袋，抽出一个东西。

　　"看看这个。"他没好气地说。

　　他举起刚才装韦斯莱夫人那封信的信封，哈利拼命憋住才没有笑出声来。信封上到处都贴满了邮票，只在正面留下一小块一寸见方的地方，韦斯莱夫人用极小的字，把德思礼家的地址密密麻麻地填了进去。

　　"她确实贴足了邮票。"哈利说，竭力使语气显得平淡，好像韦斯莱夫人只是犯了一个谁都可能犯的错误。弗农姨父的眼睛里喷出了怒火。

　　"邮差注意到了，"他咬着牙，声音从牙缝里挤出来，"他非常好奇，想知道这封信是从哪儿寄来的，所以摁响了门铃。他大概觉得这件事有些古怪。"

　　哈利什么也没说。换了别人也许不理解，不就是多贴了几张邮票嘛，弗农姨父何至于这样大惊小怪呢。但哈利和德思礼一家共同生活了这么长时间，知道他们对哪怕稍微有点超出常规的事情都特别敏感。他们最担心的，就是有人发现他们跟韦斯莱夫人那样的人有联系（不管这种联系多么疏远）。

　　弗农姨父还在狠狠地瞪着哈利。哈利使劲装出一副傻乎乎的表情。只要他不做蠢事，不说傻话，就有可能去观看一辈子难遇的重大赛事。他等着弗农姨父说点什么，可是弗农姨父只是那样狠狠地瞪着他。哈

## CHAPTER THREE    The Invitation

merely continued to glare. Harry decided to break the silence.

'So – can I go, then?' he asked.

A slight spasm crossed Uncle Vernon's large, purple face. The moustache bristled. Harry thought he knew what was going on behind the moustache: a furious battle as two of Uncle Vernon's most fundamental instincts came into conflict. Allowing Harry to go would make Harry happy, something Uncle Vernon had struggled against for thirteen years. On the other hand, allowing Harry to disappear to the Weasleys' for the rest of the summer would get rid of him two weeks earlier than anyone could have hoped, and Uncle Vernon hated having Harry in the house. To give himself thinking time, it seemed, he looked down at Mrs Weasley's letter again.

'Who is this woman?' he said, staring at the signature with distaste.

'You've seen her,' said Harry. 'She's my friend Ron's mother, she was meeting him off the Hog– off the school train at the end of last term.'

He had almost said 'Hogwarts Express', and that was a sure way to get his uncle's temper up. Nobody ever mentioned the name of Harry's school aloud in the Dursley household.

Uncle Vernon screwed up his enormous face as though trying to remember something very unpleasant.

'Dumpy sort of woman?' he growled finally. 'Load of children with red hair?'

Harry frowned. He thought it was a bit rich of Uncle Vernon to call anyone 'dumpy', when his own son, Dudley, had finally achieved what he'd been threatening to do since the age of three, and become wider than he was tall.

Uncle Vernon was perusing the letter again.

'Quidditch,' he muttered under his breath. '*Quidditch* – what is this rubbish?'

Harry felt a second stab of annoyance.

'It's a sport,' he said shortly. 'Played on broom–'

'All right, all right!' said Uncle Vernon loudly. Harry saw, with some satisfaction, that his uncle looked vaguely panicky. Apparently his nerves wouldn't stand the sound of the word 'broomsticks' in his living room. He took refuge in perusing the letter again. Harry saw his lips form the words 'send us your answer in the normal way'. He scowled.

'What does she mean, *the normal way?*' he spat.

## 第3章 邀请

利决定打破这种沉默。

"那么——我能去吗？"他问。

弗农姨父那张紫红色的大脸微微抽搐了一下，胡子一根根直立起来。哈利觉得仿佛能看到那胡子后面的脑瓜里在想什么：弗农姨父的两个最基本的直觉发生了冲突。让哈利去观看比赛会使哈利高兴，这是十三年来弗农姨父坚决不愿意干的。另一方面，批准哈利到韦斯莱家去过完暑假，就可以比原先盼望的早两个星期摆脱哈利，而弗农姨父是特别讨厌哈利待在他们家里的。弗农姨父大概是为了给自己一些思考的时间吧，又低头去看韦斯莱夫人的信。

"这个女人是谁？"他厌恶地盯着那个签名，问道。

"你见过她的。"哈利说，"她是我朋友罗恩的母亲，上学期结束的时候，她到霍格——她到学校的火车上来接过罗恩。"

他差点儿说出"霍格沃茨特快列车"，如果那样，肯定会使弗农姨父火冒三丈。在德思礼家里，从来没有人大声提到过哈利学校的名字。

弗农姨父肥硕的大脸皱成一团，似乎在拼命回忆一桩很不愉快的事情。

"那个胖墩墩的女人？"最后，他粗声粗气地问，"带着一大堆红头发的孩子？"

哈利皱起了眉头。他觉得，弗农姨父居然说别人"胖墩墩"，真是太滑稽了，要知道他的亲生儿子达力终于完成了他三岁起就显露苗头的生长趋势——变成了一个腰围超过身高的胖墩儿。

弗农姨父又在仔细地看信。

"魁地奇，"他不出声地嘟哝着，"魁地奇——这是个什么破玩意儿？"

哈利又感到一阵烦躁。

"是一种体育运动，"他不愿意多说，"骑在扫帚上玩的——"

"行了，行了！"弗农姨父大声说。哈利有些满意地看到，弗农姨父显得有一点儿紧张。显然，他的神经无法忍受"飞天扫帚"这个词在他的客厅里响起。为了寻求避难，他又低头看信。哈利看到他的口形在念"将你们的答复……通过正常方式送达"。他皱起了眉头。

"通过正常方式，这是什么意思？"他厉声问道。

## CHAPTER THREE  The Invitation

'Normal for us,' said Harry, and before his uncle could stop him, he added, 'you know, owl post. That's what's normal for wizards.'

Uncle Vernon looked as outraged as if Harry had just uttered a disgusting swear word. Shaking with anger, he shot a nervy look through the window, as though expecting to see some of the neighbours with their ears pressed against the glass.

'How many times do I have to tell you not to mention that unnaturalness under my roof?' he hissed, his face now a rich plum colour. 'You stand there, in the clothes Petunia and I have put on your ungrateful back –'

'Only after Dudley finished with them,' said Harry coldly, and indeed, he was dressed in a sweatshirt so large for him that he had had to roll back the sleeves five times so as to be able to use his hands, and which fell past the knees of his extremely baggy jeans.

'I will not be spoken to like that!' said Uncle Vernon, trembling with rage.

But Harry wasn't going to stand for this. Gone were the days when he had been forced to take every single one of the Dursleys' stupid rules. He wasn't following Dudley's diet, and he wasn't going to let Uncle Vernon stop him going to the Quidditch World Cup, not if he could help it.

Harry took a deep, steadying breath and then said, 'OK, I can't see the World Cup. Can I go now, then? Only I've got a letter to Sirius I want to finish. You know – my godfather.'

He had done it. He had said the magic words. Now he watched the purple recede blotchily from Uncle Vernon's face, making it look like badly mixed blackcurrant ice-cream.

'You're – you're writing to him, are you?' said Uncle Vernon, in a would-be calm voice – but Harry had seen the pupils of his tiny eyes contract with sudden fear.

'Well – yeah,' said Harry, casually. 'It's been a while since he heard from me, and, you know, if he doesn't, he might start thinking something's wrong.'

He stopped there to enjoy the effect of these words. He could almost see the cogs working under Uncle Vernon's thick, dark, neatly parted hair. If he tried to stop Harry writing to Sirius, Sirius would think Harry was being mistreated. If he told Harry he couldn't go to the Quidditch World Cup, Harry would write and tell Sirius, who would *know* he was being mistreated. There was only one thing for Uncle Vernon to do. Harry could

## 第3章 邀 请

"我们的那种正常方式,"哈利不等弗农姨父阻止,就接着往下说道,"你知道,就是派猫头鹰送信,巫师们一般都是这么做的。"

弗农姨父显得恼火极了,就好像哈利说了一句大逆不道的骂人话。他气得浑身发抖,紧张地朝窗口扫了一眼,似乎担心邻居会把耳朵贴在玻璃窗上。

"还要我告诉你多少遍,不许在我家里提这些稀奇古怪的事!"他咬牙切齿地说,脸色涨成紫红,活像熟透了的洋李子,"你穿着佩妮和我给你的衣服站在那里,却不知道感恩——"

"那些衣服是达力不穿了才给我的。"哈利冷冷地说。确实,他身上穿的那件无领长袖运动服大得要命,他不得不把袖子卷起五道,才能露出双手,衣服的下摆一直拖到那条无比肥大的牛仔裤的膝盖上……

"不许这样对我说话!"弗农姨父气坏了,浑身直抖。

然而哈利不愿意再忍受。过去他被迫遵守德思礼家的每一条愚蠢的清规戒律,如今那种日子一去不复返了。他没有遵守达力的减肥食谱,也不想让弗农姨父阻止他去观看魁地奇世界杯赛——只要有办法,他就一定争取。

哈利深深吸了一口气,稳定了自己的情绪,然后说道:"好吧,世界杯我看不成了。那么,我现在可以走了吧?我在给小天狼星写信,还没有写完呢。你知道——他是我的教父。"

他成功了。他的话有着神奇的魔力。现在,他注视着弗农姨父脸上的紫色一块一块地褪去,他的脸变得像搅拌不匀的黑加仑冰淇淋。

"你在——你在给他写信?"弗农姨父说,竭力使口气保持平静,但是哈利看到他那双小眼睛的瞳仁突然因为恐惧而缩小了。

"噢——是啊,"哈利漫不经心地说道,"他已经有一段时间没有得到我的消息了,你知道,如果收不到我的信,他会以为我出什么事了。"

他停住话头,欣赏了一下这番话的效果。他简直可以看到弗农姨父梳得一丝不乱的浓密黑发下的思想活动,看到那些齿轮是怎么运转的。如果弗农姨父阻止哈利给小天狼星写信,小天狼星就会认为哈利受到了虐待。如果弗农姨父对哈利说不能去观看魁地奇世界杯赛,哈利就会写信告诉小天狼星,小天狼星就会知道哈利确实受到了虐待。这样

## CHAPTER THREE  The Invitation

see the conclusion forming in his mind as though the great moustached face was transparent. Harry tried not to smile, to keep his own face as blank as possible. And then –

'Well, all right then. You can go to this ruddy … this stupid … this World Cup thing. You write and tell these – these *Weasleys* they're to pick you up, mind. I haven't got time to go dropping you off all over the country. And you can spend the rest of the summer there. And you can tell your – your godfather … tell him … tell him you're going.'

'OK then,' said Harry brightly.

He turned and walked towards the living-room door, fighting the urge to jump into the air and whoop. He was going … he was going to the Weasleys', he was going to watch the Quidditch World Cup!

Outside in the hall he nearly ran into Dudley, who had been lurking behind the door, clearly hoping to overhear Harry being told off. He looked shocked to see the broad grin on Harry's face.

'That was an *excellent* breakfast, wasn't it?' said Harry. 'I feel really full, don't you?'

Laughing at the astonished look on Dudley's face, Harry took the stairs three at a time, and hurled himself back into his bedroom.

The first thing he saw was that Hedwig was back. She was sitting in her cage, staring at Harry with her enormous amber eyes, and clicking her beak in the way that meant she was annoyed about something. Exactly what was annoying her became apparent almost at once.

'OUCH!' said Harry.

What appeared to be a small, grey, feathery tennis ball had just collided with the side of Harry's head. Harry massaged his head furiously, looking up to see what had hit him, and saw a minute owl, small enough to fit into the palm of his hand, whizzing excitedly around the room like a loose firework. Harry then realised that the owl had dropped a letter at his feet. Harry bent down, recognised Ron's handwriting, then tore open the envelope. Inside was a hastily scribbled note.

*Harry – DAD GOT THE TICKETS – Ireland versus Bulgaria, Monday night. Mum's writing to the Muggles to ask you to stay. They might already have the letter, I don't know how fast Muggle post is. Thought I'd send this with Pig anyway.*

## 第3章 邀 请

一来，弗农姨父别无选择，只有一条路可走。哈利可以清楚地看到那个决定渐渐在弗农姨父脑海里形成，就好像那张络腮胡子的大脸是透明的一样。哈利拼命忍住笑，不让自己的脸上露出任何表情。然后——

"那么，好吧。你可以去看这个该死的……这个愚蠢的……这个所谓的破世界杯赛。你写信告诉那个——那个韦斯莱一家，让他们来接你，记住了。我可没有时间把你送来送去。你可以待在那里，过完整个暑假。你不妨告诉你的——你的教父……告诉他……告诉他你要去。"

"好吧。"哈利高兴地说。

他转身朝客厅的门走去，克制住欢呼雀跃的冲动。他要走了……要到韦斯莱家去了，他要去观看魁地奇世界杯赛了！

在外面的门厅里，他差点儿和达力撞了个满怀。达力刚才躲在门后，显然是希望听见哈利被教训一顿。他看到哈利咧着嘴笑得正欢，不由得大为惊愕。

"多么美妙的一顿早餐，是吗？"哈利问，"我吃得真饱啊，你呢？"

哈利嘲笑着达力脸上惊恐的表情，三步并作两步地奔上楼梯，冲进自己的卧室。

他一眼就看见海德薇已经回来了。它蹲在笼子里，用巨大的琥珀色眼睛瞪着哈利，嘴巴碰出咔嗒咔嗒的声音，这通常表示它对什么东西感到恼火。几乎与此同时，令它恼火的东西显形了。

"哎哟！"哈利惊叫。

一个长着羽毛的灰色小网球般的东西猛地撞在他脑袋上。哈利气呼呼地揉着被撞疼的地方，抬头望去，看见了一只很小很小的猫头鹰，小得可以被他握在手掌里。它激动得像一个燃着的烟花，在房间里嗖嗖地飞来蹿去。哈利这才发现，这只猫头鹰刚才在他脚边扔下了一封信。哈利弯下身，认出了罗恩的笔迹，便撕开信封。里面是一封草草写成的短信。

哈利——**爸爸弄到票了**——爱尔兰对保加利亚。星期一晚上的。妈妈正在给那些麻瓜写信，邀请你来我们家住。他们大概已经收到信了，我不知道麻瓜送信的速度有多快。我想不管怎样，我还是派小猪把这封信给你送去。

## CHAPTER THREE   The Invitation

Harry stared at the word 'Pig', then looked up at the tiny owl now zooming around the lampshade on the ceiling. He had never seen anything that looked less like a pig. Maybe he couldn't read Ron's writing. He went back to the letter:

> We're coming for you whether the Muggles like it or not, you can't miss the World Cup, only Mum and Dad reckon it's better if we pretend to ask their permission first. If they say yes, send Pig back with your answer pronto, and we'll come and get you at five o'clock on Sunday. If they say no, send Pig back pronto and we'll come and get you at five o'clock on Sunday anyway.
>
> Hermione's arriving this afternoon. Percy's started work – the Department of International Magical Co-operation. Don't mention anything about Abroad while you're here unless you want the pants bored off you.
>
> See you soon – Ron

'Calm down!' Harry said, as the small owl flew low over his head, twittering madly with what Harry could only assume was pride at having delivered the letter to the right person. 'Come here, I need you to take my answer back!'

The owl fluttered down on top of Hedwig's cage. Hedwig looked coldly up at it, as though daring it to try and come any closer.

Harry seized his eagle-feather quill once more, grabbed a fresh piece of parchment, and wrote:

> Ron, it's all OK, the Muggles say I can come. See you five o'clock tomorrow. Can't wait.
>
> Harry

He folded this note up very small and, with immense difficulty, tied it to the tiny owl's leg as it hopped on the spot with excitement. The moment the note was secure, the owl was off again; it zoomed out of the window and out of sight.

Harry turned to Hedwig.

'Feeling up to a long journey?' he asked her.

## 第3章 邀请

哈利瞪着"小猪"两个字发愣,又抬头看看那只正绕着天花板上的灯罩嗖嗖乱飞的小猫头鹰。他从没见过比它更不像小猪的东西了。大概是罗恩的笔迹太潦草,他没有看清。他接着看信:

不管麻瓜愿意不愿意,我们都要去接你,你绝对不能错过世界杯,不过妈妈和爸爸认为最好还是先假装征求一下他们的意见。如果他们同意,请火速派小猪送来回信,我们于星期天五点钟过去接你。如果他们反对,也请火速派小猪送来回信,我们还是于星期天五点钟过去接你。

赫敏今天下午到。珀西开始上班了——在国际魔法合作司。你在这里的时候,千万不要提跟"国外"沾边的事,除非你想被他烦死。

希望很快见到你。

罗恩

"你安静点儿!"哈利说,小猫头鹰俯冲下来,飞过他的头顶,嘴里叽叽喳喳地叫个不停。哈利只能猜测,它是因为准确无误地把信送到了收件人手里,按捺不住内心的得意。"到这儿来,我要你把我的回信送回去!"

猫头鹰扑扇着翅膀落到海德薇的笼子顶上,海德薇抬起头,冷冷地望着它,似乎是问它敢不敢再走近一步。

哈利又一次拿起羽毛笔,另外抓过一张干净的羊皮纸,写道:

罗恩,一切都没问题,麻瓜说我可以去。明天下午五点钟见。我都等不及了。

哈利

他把信叠得很小很小,那只小猫头鹰兴奋地跳上跳下,哈利费了很大的劲儿才把信拴在它的腿上。信刚一拴好,猫头鹰就出发了。它嗖地从窗口飞了出去,一眨眼就消失了。

哈利转脸望着海德薇。

"你觉得能做一次长途飞行吗?"他问海德薇。

## CHAPTER THREE    The Invitation

Hedwig hooted in a dignified sort of way.

'Can you take this to Sirius for me?' he said, picking up his letter. 'Hang on ... I just want to finish it.'

He unfolded the parchment again and hastily added a postscript.

> If you want to contact me, I'll be at my friend Ron Weasley's for the rest of the summer. His dad's got us tickets for the Quidditch World Cup!

The letter finished, he tied it to Hedwig's leg; she kept unusually still, as though determined to show him how a real post owl should behave.

'I'll be at Ron's when you get back, all right?' Harry told her.

She nipped his finger affectionately, then, with a soft swooshing noise, spread her enormous wings and soared out of the open window.

Harry watched her out of sight, then crawled under his bed, wrenched up the loose floorboard, and pulled out a large chunk of birthday cake. He sat there on the floor eating it, savouring the happiness that was flooding through him. He had cake, and Dudley had nothing but grapefruit; it was a bright summer's day, he would be leaving Privet Drive tomorrow, his scar felt perfectly normal again, and he was going to watch the Quidditch World Cup. It was hard, just now, to feel worried about anything – even Lord Voldemort.

## 第3章 邀 请

海德薇以一种高贵的姿态鸣叫了一声。

"你能替我把这封信送给小天狼星吗?"哈利说,拿起他刚才写的那封信,"等一等……我还没有写完。"

他展开羊皮纸,又匆匆加了几句话。

> 如果你想跟我联系,我将在我朋友罗恩·韦斯莱家过完暑假。他爸爸为我们弄到了魁地奇世界杯赛的票!

信写完了,哈利把它系在海德薇的腿上。海德薇一动不动,出奇地稳重,似乎打定主意要让哈利看看,一只真正的猫头鹰信使是什么风度。

"你回来的时候,我在罗恩家,明白吗?"哈利对它说。

海德薇亲热地轻轻咬了咬他的手指,然后展开巨大的翅膀,发出轻轻的嗖嗖声,轻盈地飞出了敞开的窗口。

哈利望着它消失在空中,回过身来钻到床底下,撬开那块松动的地板,掏出一大块生日蛋糕。他一屁股坐在地板上,大口吃了起来,尽情享受着满心涌动的喜悦。他有蛋糕吃,而达力除了葡萄柚什么都没有;这是一个晴朗明媚的夏日,他明天就要离开女贞路了,头上的伤疤也完全恢复了正常,而且他还要去观看魁地奇世界杯赛。在这样的时刻,是很难为什么事情感到烦恼的——就连伏地魔也不能破坏他的喜悦。

## CHAPTER FOUR

## Back to The Burrow

By twelve o'clock next day, Harry's trunk was packed with his school things, and all his most prized possessions – the Invisibility Cloak he had inherited from his father, the broomstick he had got from Sirius, the enchanted map of Hogwarts he had been given by Fred and George Weasley last year. He had emptied his hiding place under the loose floorboard of all food, double-checked every nook and cranny of his bedroom for forgotten spellbooks or quills, and taken down the chart on the wall counting the days down to September the first, on which he liked to cross off the days remaining until his return to Hogwarts.

The atmosphere inside number four Privet Drive was extremely tense. The imminent arrival at their house of an assortment of wizards was making the Dursleys uptight and irritable. Uncle Vernon had looked downright alarmed when Harry informed him that the Weasleys would be arriving at five o'clock the very next day.

'I hope you told them to dress properly, these people,' he snarled at once. 'I've seen the sort of stuff your lot wear. They'd better have the decency to put on normal clothes, that's all.'

Harry felt a slight sense of foreboding. He had rarely seen Mr or Mrs Weasley wearing anything that the Dursleys would call 'normal'. Their children might don Muggle clothing during the holidays, but Mr and Mrs Weasley usually wore long robes in varying states of shabbiness. Harry wasn't bothered about what the neighbours would think, but he was anxious about how rude the Dursleys might be to the Weasleys if they turned up looking like their worst idea of wizards.

Uncle Vernon had put on his best suit. To some people, this might have looked like a gesture of welcome, but Harry knew it was because Uncle

# 第 4 章

## 回到陋居

第二天中午十二点钟的时候,哈利准备带到学校去的箱子已经收拾好了,里面装满了他上学用的东西和所有他最珍贵的宝贝——从父亲那里继承来的隐形衣、小天狼星送给他的飞天扫帚,还有去年弗雷德和乔治·韦斯莱孪生兄弟送给他的带魔法的霍格沃茨活点地图。他把藏在那块松动的地板下的食物都掏了出来,并把卧室的犄角旮旯搜了又搜,看是否还有遗忘的咒语书和羽毛笔,然后摘下挂在墙上的那张表格,上面标着九月一号以前的所有日子。他每过一天都要在上面的日子上打个叉,只盼着能快点返回霍格沃茨。

在女贞路4号的住宅里,气氛紧张到了极点。很快就要有一群各种各样的巫师来到他们家,这使德思礼一家心情烦躁,神经过敏。当哈利告诉弗农姨父,韦斯莱一家将于第二天下午五点钟赶到这里时,弗农姨父一副大惊失色的样子。

"我希望你告诉过他们穿衣服要得体,那些人真没法说。"弗农姨父立刻就咆哮起来,"我见过你们那类人穿的东西。他们最好穿正常的衣服,那才是得体的。"

哈利微微感到有些恐慌。他很少看到韦斯莱先生或夫人穿着德思礼一家人称之为"正常"的衣服。孩子们也许会在放假时穿几件麻瓜衣服,可是韦斯莱先生和夫人通常都穿着破旧的长袍,只有破旧的程度有所变化。哈利才不在乎邻居会怎么想呢,但他担心,如果韦斯莱一家出现时的样子正是德思礼夫妇脑海中最糟糕的巫师的形象,不知德思礼夫妇将以怎样无礼的态度对待他们。

弗农姨父穿上了他最好的西装。在有些人看来,这大概是表示欢

## CHAPTER FOUR  Back to The Burrow

Vernon wanted to look impressive and intimidating. Dudley, on the other hand, looked somehow diminished. This was not because the diet was at last taking effect, but due to fright. Dudley had emerged from his last encounter with a fully-grown wizard with a curly pig's tail poking out of the seat of his trousers, and Aunt Petunia and Uncle Vernon had had to pay for its removal at a private hospital in London. It wasn't altogether surprising, therefore, that Dudley kept running his hand nervously over his backside, and walking sideways from room to room, so as not to present the same target to the enemy.

Lunch was an almost silent meal. Dudley didn't even protest at the food (cottage cheese and grated celery). Aunt Petunia wasn't eating anything at all. Her arms were folded, her lips were pursed and she seemed to be chewing her tongue, as though biting back the furious diatribe she longed to throw at Harry.

'They'll be driving, of course?' Uncle Vernon barked across the table.

'Er,' said Harry.

He hadn't thought of that. How *were* the Weasleys going to pick him up? They didn't have a car any more; the old Ford Anglia they had once owned was currently running wild in the Forbidden Forest at Hogwarts. But Mr Weasley had borrowed a Ministry of Magic car last year; possibly he would do the same today?

'I think so,' said Harry.

Uncle Vernon snorted into his moustache. Normally, Uncle Vernon would have asked what car Mr Weasley drove; he tended to judge other men on how big and expensive their cars were. But Harry doubted whether Uncle Vernon would have taken to Mr Weasley even if he drove a Ferrari.

Harry spent most of the afternoon in his bedroom; he couldn't stand watching Aunt Petunia peer out through the net curtains every few seconds, as though there had been a warning about an escaped rhinoceros. Finally, at a quarter to five, Harry went back downstairs and into the living room.

Aunt Petunia was compulsively straightening cushions. Uncle Vernon was pretending to read the paper, but his tiny eyes were not moving, and Harry was sure he was really listening with all his might for the sound of an approaching car. Dudley was crammed into an armchair, his porky hands beneath him, clamped firmly around his bottom. Harry couldn't take the

## 第4章 回到陋居

迎的意思,但哈利知道,弗农姨父这么做是为了使自己显得风度不凡,盛气凌人。另一方面,达力看上去倒像是缩小了一些。这倒不是因为减肥食谱终于产生了效果,而是因为达力太害怕了。达力上次与一位成年巫师接触时,裤子后面冒出了一根蜷曲的猪尾巴,佩妮姨妈和弗农姨父只好花钱送他进了伦敦的私人医院,把尾巴割掉。所以,难怪达力现在紧张极了,不停地用手在屁股上摸来摸去,并且躲躲闪闪地从一个房间走到另一个房间,生怕又被敌人当成靶子,重演上次的悲剧。

吃午饭的时候,几乎谁也没有说话。达力甚至没有对食物(农家鲜干酪和芹菜末)提出抗议。佩妮姨妈什么也没吃。她抱着双臂,噘着嘴唇,似乎在咀嚼自己的舌头,就好像在把她希望扔给哈利的愤怒谴责嚼碎了咽下去似的。

"他们肯定是开车来,是吗?"弗农姨父隔着桌子厉声问道。

"哦。"哈利回答。

他倒没想过这个问题。韦斯莱一家准备怎么来接他呢?他们已经没有汽车了。原来倒是有一辆福特安格里亚老爷车的,可是那辆车眼下正在霍格沃茨的禁林里狂奔乱撞呢。韦斯莱先生去年从魔法部借过一辆汽车,也许他今天也会这么做吧?

"大概是吧。"哈利说。

弗农姨父哼了一声,把粗气喷在胡子上。要按惯常的情况,弗农姨父就该追问韦斯莱先生开的是什么车了。他总喜欢根据别的男人开的车有多宽敞、多昂贵来评价他们。但是哈利怀疑,即便韦斯莱先生开着一辆法拉利,弗农姨父恐怕也不会喜欢他。

哈利几乎整个下午都待在自己的卧室里。他无法忍受佩妮姨妈每隔几秒钟就透过网状的窗帘朝外窥视一番的样子,就好像她得到警告,有一只犀牛从动物园里逃出来了似的。最后,到了五点差一刻,哈利才走下楼梯,来到客厅里。

佩妮姨妈正在一个劲儿地把坐垫摆来摆去,就像患了强迫症一样。弗农姨父假装在看报纸,但他的小眼睛一动不动。哈利可以肯定,实际上他正在全神贯注地听着是不是有汽车开来。达力把肥胖的身体挤进了一张扶手椅,肉乎乎的双手压在身下,紧紧地抓住自己的屁股。

## CHAPTER FOUR  Back to The Burrow

tension; he left the room, and went and sat on the stairs in the hall, his eyes on his watch and his heart pumping fast from excitement and nerves.

But five o'clock came and then went. Uncle Vernon, perspiring slightly in his suit, opened the front door, peered up and down the street, then withdrew his head quickly.

'They're late!' he snarled at Harry.

'I know,' said Harry. 'Maybe – er – the traffic's bad, or something.'

Ten past five ... then a quarter past five ... Harry was starting to feel anxious himself now. At half past, he heard Uncle Vernon and Aunt Petunia conversing in terse mutters in the living room.

'No consideration at all.'

'We might've had an engagement.'

'Maybe they think they'll get invited to dinner if they're late.'

'Well, they most certainly won't be,' said Uncle Vernon, and Harry heard him stand up and start pacing the living room. 'They'll take the boy and go, there'll be no hanging around. That's if they're coming at all. Probably mistaken the day. I daresay *their kind* don't set much store by punctuality. Either that or they drive some tinpot car that's broken d– AAAAAAAARRRRRGH!'

Harry jumped up. From the other side of the living-room door came the sounds of the three Dursleys scrambling, panic-stricken, across the room. Next moment Dudley came flying into the hall, looking terrified.

'What happened?' said Harry. 'What's the matter?'

But Dudley didn't seem able to speak. Hands still clamped over his buttocks, he waddled as fast as he could into the kitchen. Harry hurried into the living room.

Loud bangings and scrapings were coming from behind the Dursleys' boarded-up fireplace, which had a fake coal fire plugged in front of it.

'What is it?' gasped Aunt Petunia, who had backed into the wall and was staring, terrified, towards the fire. 'What is it, Vernon?'

But they were left in doubt barely a second longer. Voices could be heard from inside the blocked fireplace.

'Ouch! Fred, no – go back, go back, there's been some kind of mistake – tell George not to – OUCH! George, no, there's no room, go back quickly and tell Ron –'

## 第4章 回到陋居

哈利受不了这种紧张的气氛，就离开客厅，出来坐在门厅的楼梯上，眼睛盯着手表，心脏因为兴奋和紧张而跳得飞快。

然而，五点钟到了又过了，西装革履的弗农姨父已经在微微冒汗。他打开前门，朝马路上左右张望了一下，又立刻缩回脑袋。

"他们迟到了！"他粗声恶气地对哈利说。

"我知道，"哈利说，"大概——嗯——大概交通太拥挤了。"

五点十分……五点一刻……哈利自己也开始沉不住气了。五点半的时候，他听见弗农姨父和佩妮姨妈在客厅里没好气地嘟哝。

"一点儿也不尊重别人！"

"我们或许还有别的约会呢。"

"他们大概以为，如果来晚一点儿，我们就会邀请他们吃晚饭。"

"哼，想都别想，"弗农姨父说，哈利听见他站了起来，在客厅里踱来踱去，"他们带上那男孩就走，不许在这里逗留——那是说他们如果来的话。大概把日子搞错了，我敢说他们那类人根本就没有什么时间观念，要么就是他们开的破车半路抛锚——啊啊啊啊啊呀！"

哈利一跃而起。客厅的门后传来德思礼一家三口惊恐万状地在房间里爬动的声音。接着，达力一头冲进门厅，表情极度恐怖。

"怎么了？"哈利问，"出什么事了？"

达力似乎已经说不出话来了。他用双手紧紧护住屁股，跌跌撞撞地尽快冲进厨房。哈利赶紧走进客厅。

德思礼家的壁炉是被封死的，前面放着一个假炭炉。此刻，从壁炉后面传来重重的敲打声和摩擦声。

"什么东西？"佩妮姨妈已经退到墙边，恐惧地瞪着假炭炉，上气不接下气地问，"什么东西，弗农？"

他们的疑问很快就有了答案。被封死的壁炉后面传来了几个人的说话声。

"哎哟！不对，弗雷德——回去，回去，大概是弄错了——快叫乔治不要——哎哟！不对，乔治，这里挤不下了，快回去告诉罗恩——"

## CHAPTER FOUR  Back to The Burrow

'Maybe Harry can hear us, Dad – maybe he'll be able to let us out –'

There was a loud hammering of fists on the boards behind the electric fire.

'Harry? Harry, can you hear us?'

The Dursleys rounded on Harry like a pair of angry wolverines.

'What is this?' growled Uncle Vernon. 'What's going on?'

'They – they've tried to get here by Floo powder,' said Harry, fighting a mad desire to laugh. 'They can travel by fire – only you've blocked the fireplace – hang on –'

He approached the fireplace and called through the boards.

'Mr Weasley? Can you hear me?'

The hammering stopped. Somebody inside the chimney-piece said, 'Shh!'

'Mr Weasley, it's Harry ... the fireplace has been blocked up. You won't be able to get through there.'

'Damn!' said Mr Weasley's voice. 'What on earth did they want to block up the fireplace for?'

'They've got an electric fire,' Harry explained.

'Really?' said Mr Weasley's voice excitedly. 'Ecklectic, you say? With a *plug*? Gracious, I must see that ... let's think ... ouch, Ron!'

Ron's voice now joined the others'.

'What are we doing here? Has something gone wrong?'

'Oh, no, Ron,' came Fred's voice, very sarcastically. 'No, this is exactly where we wanted to end up.'

'Yeah, we're having the time of our lives here,' said George, whose voice sounded muffled, as though he was squashed against the wall.

'Boys, boys ...' said Mr Weasley vaguely. 'I'm trying to think what to do ... yes ... only way ... stand back, Harry.'

Harry retreated to the sofa. Uncle Vernon, however, moved forwards.

'Wait a moment!' he bellowed at the fire. 'What exactly are you going to –?'

BANG.

The electric fire shot across the room as the boarded-up fireplace burst outwards, expelling Mr Weasley, Fred, George and Ron in a cloud of rubble and loose chippings. Aunt Petunia shrieked and fell backwards over the

## 第4章 回到陋居

"说不定哈利能听见我们呢,爸——说不定他能放我们出去呢——"

于是,好几只拳头重重地砸在电炉后面的壁板上。

"哈利?哈利,你能听见吗?"

德思礼夫妇像两只发怒的狼獾,猛地对哈利发起了攻击。

"怎么回事?"弗农姨父咆哮着问,"他们在干什么?"

"他们——他们想靠飞路粉到这儿来。"哈利说,忍不住想放声大笑,但拼命克制着,"他们可以通过炉火旅行——只是你把壁炉封死了——等一等——"

他走到壁炉跟前,隔着壁板朝里面喊话。

"韦斯莱先生吗?你能听见我说话吗?"

拳头砸墙壁的声音停止了。壁炉台里面有一个人说:"嘘!"

"韦斯莱先生,我是哈利……壁炉被封死了。你们没法从这里出来。"

"该死!"韦斯莱先生的声音说,"他们干吗非要把壁炉封死呢?"

"他们弄了一个电炉。"哈利解释道。

"真的?"韦斯莱先生的声音兴奋起来,"你是说,带电的?有插头吗?太棒了,我一定得见识见识……让我想想……哎哟,罗恩!"

罗恩的声音也加入到他们中间。

"我们在这里干什么?出什么事了吗?"

"噢,没有,罗恩,"弗雷德的声音传了出来,一副讽刺的腔调,"没出事,这正是我们要来的地方。"

"是啊,我们正在享受人生呢。"乔治说,他声音发闷,似乎被挤得贴在了墙上。

"孩子们,孩子们……"韦斯莱先生说道,声音含混,"我在考虑怎么办……好吧……只有这样了……哈利,往后站。"

哈利退到沙发前,弗农姨父反倒向前跨了几步。

"等等!"他冲着壁炉喊道,"你们究竟想干什——"

**梆!**

封死的壁炉猛地炸开了,电炉腾的一下飞到房间那头,韦斯莱先生、弗雷德、乔治和罗恩随着一大堆碎石墙皮被甩了出来。佩妮姨妈尖叫一声,向后倒在咖啡桌上,弗农姨父伸手把她抓住,她才没有摔倒在地。

## CHAPTER FOUR   Back to The Burrow

coffee table; Uncle Vernon caught her before she hit the floor and gaped, speechless, at the Weasleys, all of whom had bright red hair, including Fred and George, who were identical to the last freckle.

'That's better,' panted Mr Weasley, brushing dust from his long green robes and straightening his glasses. 'Ah – you must be Harry's aunt and uncle!'

Tall, thin and balding, he moved towards Uncle Vernon, his hand outstretched, but Uncle Vernon backed away several paces, dragging Aunt Petunia. Words utterly failed Uncle Vernon. His best suit was covered in white dust, which had settled in his hair and moustache and made him look as though he had just aged thirty years.

'Er – yes – sorry about that,' said Mr Weasley, lowering his hand and looking over his shoulder at the blasted fireplace. 'It's all my fault, it just didn't occur to me that we wouldn't be able to get out at the other end. I had your fireplace connected to the Floo Network, you see – just for an afternoon, you know, so we could get Harry. Muggle fireplaces aren't supposed to be connected, strictly speaking – but I've got a useful contact at the Floo Regulation Panel and he fixed it for me. I can put it right in a jiffy, though, don't worry. I'll light a fire to send the boys back, and then I can repair your fireplace before I Disapparate.'

Harry was ready to bet that the Dursleys hadn't understood a single word of this. They were still gaping at Mr Weasley, thunderstruck. Aunt Petunia staggered upright again, and hid behind Uncle Vernon.

'Hello, Harry!' said Mr Weasley brightly. 'Got your trunk ready?'

'It's upstairs,' said Harry, grinning back.

'We'll get it,' said Fred at once. Winking at Harry, he and George left the room. They knew where Harry's bedroom was, having once rescued him from it in the dead of night. Harry suspected that Fred and George were hoping for a glimpse of Dudley; they had heard a lot about him from Harry.

'Well,' said Mr Weasley, swinging his arms slightly, while he tried to find words to break the very nasty silence. 'Very – erm – very nice place you've got here.'

As the usually spotless living room was now covered in dust and bits of brick, this remark didn't go down too well with the Dursleys. Uncle Vernon's

## 第4章 回到陋居

弗农姨父喘着粗气，说不出话来，只是瞪眼瞅着韦斯莱一家。他们都有着一头红通通的头发，还有弗雷德和乔治，这两兄弟完全是一个模子刻出来的，连脸上的雀斑也一模一样。

"这下好多了。"韦斯莱先生喘着气说，掸了掸绿色长袍上的尘土，扶了扶眼镜，"啊——想必你们就是哈利的姨妈和姨父吧！"

韦斯莱先生是个瘦瘦高高的秃顶男人，他伸出一只手，朝弗农姨父走来，可是弗农姨父拉着佩妮姨妈，连连后退了几步。弗农姨父完全说不出话来了，他那套最好的西装上落满白色的灰尘，头发和胡子上也是，弄得他像是一下子老了三十岁。

"哦——是的——对不起。"韦斯莱先生说，垂下那只手，扭头看着炸开的壁炉，"这都怪我，我压根儿没想到我们到了目的地却出不来。您知道吗，我把您的壁炉同飞路网联在了一起——就这一个下午，您知道的，为了来接哈利。严格来说，麻瓜的壁炉是不应该联网的——但是我在飞路网管理小组有一个很管用的熟人，是他帮我办妥的。不用担心，我一会儿就给您弄好。我要点一堆火，把孩子们送回去，然后在我幻影移形离开前，我可以帮您修好壁炉。"

哈利敢说德思礼夫妇对这番话一个字都没听懂。他们都呆若木鸡地瞪着韦斯莱先生。佩妮姨妈站直了身子，摇摇晃晃地躲到了弗农姨父身后。

"你好，哈利！"韦斯莱先生兴高采烈地说，"箱子收拾好了吗？"

"在楼上呢。"哈利朝他笑着，说道。

"我们去搬下来。"弗雷德立刻自告奋勇地说。他和乔治朝哈利眨了眨眼睛，就离开了客厅。他们知道哈利的卧室在哪里，曾有一次在深夜把哈利从卧室里营救了出去。哈利怀疑弗雷德和乔治是想看看达力，他们从哈利嘴里听到过不少关于达力的事。

"好吧。"韦斯莱先生说。他微微摆动着双手，拼命想找到一句合适的话，打破这令人难受的沉默。"你们住的地方非常……嗯……非常漂亮。"

平常一尘不染的客厅，现在到处都是灰尘和碎砖头，因此，这句恭维话在德思礼夫妇听来就不可能受用了。弗农姨父的脸顿时涨得通

## CHAPTER FOUR  Back to The Burrow

face purpled once more, and Aunt Petunia started chewing her tongue again. However, they seemed too scared to actually say anything.

Mr Weasley was looking around. He loved everything to do with Muggles. Harry could see him itching to go and examine the television and the video recorder.

'They run off eckeltricity, do they?' he said knowledgeably. 'Ah yes, I can see the plugs. I collect plugs,' he added to Uncle Vernon. 'And batteries. Got a very large collection of batteries. My wife thinks I'm mad, but there you are.'

Uncle Vernon clearly thought Mr Weasley was mad, too. He moved ever so slightly to the right, screening Aunt Petunia from view, as though he thought Mr Weasley might suddenly run at them and attack.

Dudley suddenly reappeared in the room. Harry could hear the clunk of his trunk on the stairs, and knew that the sounds had scared Dudley out of the kitchen. Dudley edged along the wall, gazing at Mr Weasley with terrified eyes, and attempted to conceal himself behind his mother and father. Unfortunately, Uncle Vernon's bulk, while sufficient to hide bony Aunt Petunia, was nowhere near enough to conceal Dudley.

'Ah, this is your cousin, is it, Harry?' said Mr Weasley, taking another brave stab at making conversation.

'Yep,' said Harry, 'that's Dudley.'

He and Ron exchanged glances and then quickly looked away from each other; the temptation to burst out laughing was almost overwhelming. Dudley was still clutching his bottom as though afraid it might fall off. Mr Weasley, however, seemed genuinely concerned at Dudley's peculiar behaviour. Indeed, from the tone of his voice when he next spoke, Harry was quite sure that Mr Weasley thought Dudley was quite as mad as the Dursleys thought he was, except that Mr Weasley felt sympathy rather than fear.

'Having a good holiday, Dudley?' he said kindly.

Dudley whimpered. Harry saw his hands tighten still harder over his massive backside.

Fred and George came back into the room, carrying Harry's school trunk. They glanced around as they entered and spotted Dudley. Their faces cracked into identical, evil grins.

'Ah, right,' said Mr Weasley. 'Better get cracking, then.'

He pushed up the sleeves of his robes and took out his wand. Harry saw

红,佩妮姨妈又开始咬她的舌头。不过,他们似乎都被吓得不敢再说一个字。

韦斯莱先生在房间里东张西望。凡是与麻瓜有关的事,他都喜欢。哈利看得出来,他特别渴望走过去仔细看看电视机和录像机。

"它们是用电的,是吗?"他很有学问地说,"啊,对,我看见插头了。我收集插头,"他又对弗农姨父说,"还有电池,收集了很多很多电池。我太太以为我疯了,可是你瞧,我说对了吧。"

弗农姨父显然也以为韦斯莱先生疯了。他几乎不为人察觉地向右移动了一点儿,用身体挡住佩妮姨妈,好像他以为韦斯莱先生会突然跳起来,向他们发起进攻似的。

忽然,达力又出现在房间里。哈利可以听见箱子在楼梯上拖动的声音,他知道是这声音把达力吓得从厨房里逃了出来。达力贴着墙根移动,用极度惊恐的眼睛盯着韦斯莱先生,拼命想让自己躲在爸爸妈妈身后。不幸的是,弗农姨父的大块头可以绰绰有余地遮挡瘦巴巴的佩妮姨妈,可要挡住达力,那是根本不可能的。

"啊,这就是你的表哥,是吗,哈利?"韦斯莱先生再次鼓起勇气,尝试着与他们交谈。

"是啊,"哈利说,"他就是达力。"

他和罗恩交换了一个眼色,赶紧又把目光移向别处。他们太想大笑一场了,简直克制不住。达力仍然紧紧捂住屁股,似乎生怕屁股会掉下来。韦斯莱先生倒是真心为达力的古怪行为感到担忧。确实,从韦斯莱先生接下来说话的语气判断,哈利可以肯定他认为达力疯了,就像德思礼夫妇认为韦斯莱先生疯了一样,不过韦斯莱先生感到的是同情而不是恐惧。

"假期过得好吗,达力?"他和蔼地问。

达力呜咽了一声。哈利看到他用双手把肥胖的屁股捂得更紧了。

弗雷德和乔治搬着哈利上学的箱子回到了客厅。他们一进来就东张西望,一见达力,两人脸上同时绽开了一模一样的坏笑。

"啊,好吧,"韦斯莱先生说,"我们最好开始行动吧。"

他捋起长袍的袖子,抽出魔杖。哈利看见德思礼一家三口以同样

## CHAPTER FOUR  Back to The Burrow

the Dursleys draw back against the wall as one.

'*Incendio!*' said Mr Weasley, pointing his wand at the hole in the wall behind him.

Flames rose at once in the fireplace, crackling merrily as though they had been burning for hours. Mr Weasley took a small drawstring bag from his pocket, untied it, took a pinch of the powder inside and threw it onto the flames, which turned emerald green and roared higher than ever.

'Off you go then, Fred,' said Mr Weasley.

'Coming,' said Fred. 'Oh no – hang on –'

A bag of sweets had spilled out of Fred's pocket and the contents were now rolling in every direction – big, fat toffees in brightly coloured wrappers.

Fred scrambled around, cramming them back into his pocket, then gave the Dursleys a cheery wave, stepped forward and walked right into the fire, saying, 'The Burrow!' Aunt Petunia gave a little shuddering gasp. There was a whooshing sound, and Fred vanished.

'Right then, George,' said Mr Weasley, 'you and the trunk.'

Harry helped George carry the trunk forward into the flames, and turn it onto its end so that he could hold it better. Then, with a second whoosh, George had cried, 'The Burrow!' and vanished too.

'Ron, you next,' said Mr Weasley.

'See you,' said Ron brightly to the Dursleys. He grinned broadly at Harry, then stepped into the fire, shouted, 'The Burrow!' and disappeared.

Now Harry and Mr Weasley alone remained.

'Well ... bye then,' Harry said to the Dursleys.

They didn't say anything at all. Harry moved towards the fire, but just as he reached the edge of the hearth, Mr Weasley put out a hand and held him back. He was looking at the Dursleys in amazement.

'Harry said goodbye to you,' he said. 'Didn't you hear him?'

'It doesn't matter,' Harry muttered to Mr Weasley. 'Honestly, I don't care.'

Mr Weasley did not remove his hand from Harry's shoulder.

'You aren't going to see your nephew 'til next summer,' he said to Uncle Vernon in mild indignation. 'Surely you're going to say goodbye?'

Uncle Vernon's face worked furiously. The idea of being taught

## 第4章 回到陋居

的姿势退到了墙边。

"火焰熊熊！"韦斯莱先生用魔杖指着身后墙上的那个洞说道。

壁炉里立刻蹿起火苗，噼噼啪啪地燃得很旺，就好像已经燃了好几个小时。韦斯莱先生从口袋里掏出一个束着拉绳的小袋子，把它打开，从里面捏出一点粉末投进火里，火焰马上变成了碧绿色，火苗蹿得比刚才还高。

"弗雷德，你上路吧。"韦斯莱先生说。

"这就走，"弗雷德说，"哦，糟糕——等一等——"

一袋糖果从弗雷德的口袋里滑落出来，里面的糖滚得到处都是——又大又圆的太妃奶糖，包着花花绿绿的糖纸。

弗雷德伏在地上，手忙脚乱地把糖捡起来，塞回自己的口袋，然后开心地朝德思礼一家挥挥手，向前跨了几步，径直走进火焰中，说了一句："陋居！"佩妮姨妈倒抽一口冷气，打了个寒战。只听嗖的一声，弗雷德不见了。

"好了，乔治，"韦斯莱先生说，"你带着箱子走吧。"

哈利和乔治一起搬着箱子走向火焰，然后把箱子竖了起来，使乔治可以拿得稳当一些。接着，乔治大喊一声："陋居！"又是嗖的一声，他也一下子消失了。

"罗恩，轮到你了。"韦斯莱先生说。

"再见。"罗恩高高兴兴地对德思礼一家说。他朝哈利笑了笑，一步跨进火中，喊道："陋居！"便也不见了。

只有哈利和韦斯莱先生还没有走。

"好吧……那就再见了。"哈利对德思礼一家说。

他们一句话也没有说。哈利朝火焰走去，刚走到壁炉边，韦斯莱先生伸出一只手，把他拉了回来。韦斯莱先生正惊愕地望着德思礼一家。

"哈利对你们说了再见，"他说，"你们没有听见吗？"

"没关系，"哈利小声对韦斯莱先生说，"说实在的，我并不在乎。"

韦斯莱先生没有把手从哈利肩膀上松开。

"你要到明年夏天才能见到你的外甥呢，"他微微有些愤怒地对弗农姨父说，"你总要说一句再见吧？"

弗农姨父气得脸都变了。一个刚刚炸毁他客厅半面墙壁的人居然

## CHAPTER FOUR  Back to The Burrow

consideration by a man who had just blasted away half his living-room wall seemed to be causing him intense suffering.

But Mr Weasley's wand was still in his hand, and Uncle Vernon's tiny eyes darted to it once, before he said, very resentfully, 'goodbye, then.'

'See you,' said Harry, putting one foot forward into the green flames, which felt pleasantly like warm breath. At that moment, however, a horrible gagging sound erupted behind him, and Aunt Petunia started to scream.

Harry wheeled around. Dudley was no longer standing behind his parents. He was kneeling beside the coffee table, and he was gagging and spluttering on a foot-long, purple, slimy thing that was protruding from his mouth. One bewildered second later, Harry realised that the foot-long thing was Dudley's tongue – and that a brightly coloured toffee-wrapper lay on the floor before him.

Aunt Petunia hurled herself onto the ground beside Dudley, seized the end of his swollen tongue and attempted to wrench it out of his mouth; unsurprisingly, Dudley yelled and spluttered worse than ever, trying to fight her off. Uncle Vernon was bellowing and waving his arms around, and Mr Weasley had to shout to make himself heard.

'Not to worry, I can sort him out!' he yelled, advancing on Dudley with his wand outstretched, but Aunt Petunia screamed worse than ever and threw herself on top of Dudley, shielding him from Mr Weasley.

'No, really!' said Mr Weasley desperately. 'It's a simple process – it was the toffee – my son Fred – real practical joker – but it's only an Engorgement Charm – at least, I think it is – please, I can correct it –'

But far from being reassured, the Dursleys became more panic-stricken; Aunt Petunia was sobbing hysterically, tugging Dudley's tongue as though determined to rip it out; Dudley appeared to be suffocating under the combined pressure of his mother and his tongue, and Uncle Vernon, who had lost control completely, seized a china figure from on top of the sideboard, and threw it very hard at Mr Weasley, who ducked, causing the ornament to shatter in the blasted fireplace.

'Now really!' said Mr Weasley, angrily, brandishing his wand. 'I'm trying to *help*!'

Bellowing like a wounded hippo, Uncle Vernon snatched up another ornament.

要来教他学会尊重人,这似乎给他带来了极大的痛苦。

可是韦斯莱先生手里还拿着魔杖呢,弗农姨父的小眼睛扫了一下魔杖,然后非常恼火地说:"好吧,再见。"

"再见。"哈利说完,把一只脚伸进了绿色的火焰,感觉它就像温暖的呼吸。就在这时,他身后突然传来一阵可怕的干呕声,佩妮姨妈失声惊叫起来。

哈利转过身,达力已经不再躲在他父母身后了,而是跪在咖啡桌旁,嘴里冒出一个尺把长的、黏糊糊的紫红色东西,害得他不停地干呕,呜噜呜噜地叫唤。哈利只纳闷了一刹那就明白了,那尺把长的东西是达力的舌头——达力面前的地板上有一张花花绿绿的太妃糖纸。

佩妮姨妈猛地扑向达力,抓住他膨胀的舌尖,拼命想把舌头从他嘴里拔出来。自然喽,达力大声惨叫,呜噜呜噜地叫得比刚才更响了,一边使劲儿想摆脱佩妮姨妈。弗农姨父胡乱挥舞着双手,大发雷霆,韦斯莱先生不得不直着嗓子喊叫,才使他们听见了他说话。

"不用担心,我来解决这个问题!"他喊道,一边举着魔杖,朝达力走去,可是佩妮姨妈叫得更厉害了,并且扑在达力身上,生怕韦斯莱先生伤害他。

"哦,别这样!"韦斯莱先生绝望地说,"办法很简单——都是那颗太妃糖惹的祸——我儿子弗雷德——整天就喜欢搞恶作剧——不过没关系,只是一个膨胀咒——至少我认为是这样——请让开,我可以纠正过来——"

可是德思礼夫妇不仅没有放宽心,反而更紧张了。佩妮姨妈一边歇斯底里地抽泣着,一边使劲拽住达力的舌头,好像下定决心要把它连根拔掉似的。达力在母亲和舌头的双重压力下,似乎要窒息了。弗农姨父已经完全失去了控制,一把抓起餐具柜顶上的一个瓷像,朝韦斯莱先生狠狠地扔过去。韦斯莱先生低头一躲,那个装饰品在被炸毁的壁炉上摔得粉碎。

"好了,别闹了!"韦斯莱先生恼火地说,一边挥舞着他的魔杖,"我是真心想帮助你们!"

弗农姨父像一匹受伤的河马那样咆哮起来,又抓起一个装饰品。

## CHAPTER FOUR  Back to The Burrow

'Harry, go! Just go!' Mr Weasley shouted, his wand on Uncle Vernon. 'I'll sort this out!'

Harry didn't want to miss the fun, but Uncle Vernon's second ornament narrowly missed his left ear, and on balance he thought it best to leave the situation to Mr Weasley. He stepped into the fire, looking over his shoulder as he said, 'The Burrow!'; his last fleeting glimpse of the living room was of Mr Weasley blasting a third ornament out of Uncle Vernon's hand with his wand, Aunt Petunia screaming and lying on top of Dudley, and Dudley's tongue lolling around like a great slimy python. But next moment Harry had begun to spin very fast, and the Dursleys' living room was whipped out of sight in a rush of emerald green flames.

## 第4章 回到陋居

"哈利,快走!快走!"韦斯莱先生用魔杖指着弗农姨父,喊道,"我来解决这件事!"

哈利不想错过这个热闹,可是弗农姨父扔过来的第二个装饰品擦着他的左耳飞了过去。他权衡利弊,觉得最好还是让韦斯莱先生独自对付这个局面。哈利跨进火焰,说了一声:"陋居!"一边还扭头望着。他最后匆匆瞥了一眼客厅,只见韦斯莱先生用魔杖把弗农姨父扔出的第三个装饰品炸成了碎片。佩妮姨妈伏在达力身上尖声大叫,达力的舌头伸在嘴巴外,像一条滑溜溜的大蟒蛇。接着,哈利开始在熊熊的碧绿色火焰中飞速旋转起来,德思礼家的客厅消失了。

## CHAPTER FIVE

# Weasleys' Wizard Wheezes

Harry spun faster and faster, elbows tucked tightly to his sides, blurred fireplaces flashing past him, until he started to feel sick and closed his eyes. Then, when at last he felt himself slowing down, he threw out his hands, and brought himself to a halt in time to prevent himself falling face forwards out of the Weasleys' kitchen fire.

'Did he eat it?' said Fred excitedly, holding out a hand to pull Harry to his feet.

'Yeah,' said Harry, straightening up. 'What *was* it?'

'Ton-Tongue Toffee,' said Fred brightly. 'George and I invented them, we've been looking for someone to test them on all summer ...'

The tiny kitchen exploded with laughter; Harry looked around and saw that Ron and George were sitting at the scrubbed wooden table with two red-haired people Harry had never seen before, though he knew immediately who they must be: Bill and Charlie, the two eldest Weasley brothers.

'How're you doing, Harry?' said the nearer of the two, grinning at him and holding out a large hand, which Harry shook, feeling calluses and blisters under his fingers. This had to be Charlie, who worked with dragons in Romania. Charlie was built like the twins, shorter and stockier than Percy and Ron, who were both long and lanky. He had a broad, good-natured face, which was weather-beaten and so freckly that he looked almost tanned; his arms were muscly, and one of them had a large, shiny burn on it.

Bill got to his feet, smiling, and also shook Harry's hand. Bill came as something of a surprise. Harry knew that he worked for the wizarding bank, Gringotts, that he had been Head Boy of Hogwarts, and had always imagined Bill to be an older version of Percy; fussy about rule-breaking and fond of bossing everyone around. However, Bill was – there was no other word for it – *cool*. He was tall, with long hair that he had tied back in a

# 第 5 章

# 韦斯莱魔法把戏坊

哈利越转越快,胳膊肘紧紧贴在身体两侧,无数个壁炉飞速闪过,快得简直看不清楚。最后他感到有些恶心,便闭上了眼睛。终于,在他觉得速度慢下来的时候,他猛地伸出双手,及时刹住。还好,他差点儿脸朝前摔出韦斯莱家厨房的壁炉。

"他吃了吗?"弗雷德兴奋地问,一边伸过一只手,把哈利拉了起来。

"吃了,"哈利说着,站起身,"那是什么东西?"

"肥舌太妃糖,"弗雷德眉飞色舞地说,"乔治和我发明的。整个夏天,我们一直想找个人试一试……"

小小的厨房里爆发出一阵大笑,哈利环顾四周,看见罗恩和乔治坐在擦得干干净净的木桌旁,旁边还有两个红头发的人,哈利以前没有见过,不过他马上就知道了,他们一定是韦斯莱兄弟中最大的两个:比尔和查理。

"你好吗,哈利?"两兄弟中离哈利最近的那个咧开嘴笑着,伸出一只大手。哈利握了握,感到自己的手指触摸到许多老茧和水泡。这一定是查理,他在罗马尼亚研究火龙。查理的身材和那对双胞胎差不多,比豆芽般的珀西和罗恩要矮、胖、结实一些。他长着一副好好先生似的阔脸,饱经风霜,脸上布满密密麻麻的雀斑,看上去几乎成了棕黑色。他的手臂肌肉结实,一只手臂上有一道被火灼伤的发亮的大伤疤。

比尔站了起来,笑着,也同哈利握了握手。比尔的样子多少令人感到有些意外。哈利知道他在古灵阁,即巫师银行工作,而且上学时还是霍格沃茨的男生学生会主席。哈利一向以为比尔是珀西的翻版,只是年龄大几岁而已,也是那样对违反校规大惊小怪,喜欢对周围的每个人发号施令。今天一看,才知道不是这样,比尔一副很——没有

## CHAPTER FIVE    Weasleys' Wizard Wheezes

ponytail. He was wearing an earring with what looked like a fang dangling from it. His clothes would not have looked out of place at a rock concert, except that Harry recognised his boots to be made, not of leather, but of dragon hide.

Before any of them could say anything else, there was a faint popping noise, and Mr Weasley appeared out of thin air at George's shoulder. He was looking angrier than Harry had ever seen him.

'That *wasn't funny*, Fred!' he shouted. 'What on earth did you give that Muggle boy?'

'I didn't give him anything,' said Fred, with another evil grin. 'I just *dropped* it ... it was his fault he went and ate it, I never told him to.'

'You dropped it on purpose!' roared Mr Weasley. 'You knew he'd eat it, you knew he was on a diet –'

'How big did his tongue get?' George asked eagerly.

'It was four foot long before his parents would let me shrink it!'

Harry and the Weasleys roared with laughter again.

'It *isn't funny*!' Mr Weasley shouted. 'That sort of behaviour seriously undermines wizard–Muggle relations! I spend half my life campaigning against the mistreatment of Muggles, and my own sons –'

'We didn't give it to him because he was a Muggle!' said Fred indignantly.

'No, we gave it to him because he's a great bullying git,' said George.

'Isn't he, Harry?'

'Yeah, he is, Mr Weasley,' said Harry earnestly.

'That's not the point!' raged Mr Weasley. 'You wait until I tell your mother –'

'Tell me what?' said a voice behind them.

Mrs Weasley had just entered the kitchen. She was a short, plump woman with a very kind face, though her eyes were presently narrowed with suspicion.

'Oh, hello, Harry dear,' she said, spotting him and smiling. Then her eyes snapped back to her husband. 'Tell me *what*, Arthur?'

Mr Weasley hesitated. Harry could tell that, however angry he was with Fred and George, he hadn't really intended to tell Mrs Weasley what had

## 第5章 韦斯莱魔法把戏坊

别的词可以形容——"酷"的样子。他个子高高的，长长的头发在脑后扎成一个马尾巴，耳朵上还戴着一只耳环，上面悬着一颗尖牙似的东西。比尔的那身衣服，即使是去参加摇滚音乐会也不会显得不合适。不过哈利看出来了，他的那双靴子不是牛皮而是火龙皮做的。

大家还没来得及说话，就听见一阵轻微的爆裂声，韦斯莱先生在乔治身边突然冒了出来。他气坏了，哈利从没见过他这么生气。

"这不是开玩笑的事情，弗雷德！"他嚷道，"你到底给那个麻瓜男孩吃了什么？"

"我什么也没给他，"弗雷德脸上带着坏笑说，"我只是不小心撒在地上……谁叫他自己捡起来吃的，这可不能怪我。"

"你是故意把它弄撒的！"韦斯莱先生怒吼道，"你知道他肯定会吃，你知道他在减肥——"

"他的舌头肿得多大？"乔治急切地问。

"一直肿到四尺多长，他父母才让我把它缩小了！"

哈利和韦斯莱兄弟又一次哈哈大笑起来。

"这不是开玩笑！"韦斯莱先生大声嚷道，"这种行为严重损害了巫师和麻瓜的关系！我半辈子都在拼死拼活忙着反对虐待麻瓜的工作，结果我自己的儿子——"

"我们不是因为他是麻瓜才给他的！"弗雷德气愤地说。

"是啊，我们捉弄他是因为他专门欺负人。"乔治说，"是不是，哈利？"

"没错，他就是那样的，韦斯莱先生。"哈利很认真地说。

"问题不在这里！"韦斯莱先生气呼呼地说，"你们等着吧，我要告诉你们的妈妈——"

"告诉我什么？"他们身后传来一个声音。

韦斯莱夫人正巧走进厨房。她是一个矮矮胖胖的女人，面容非常慈祥，不过此刻眼睛眯着，露出怀疑的神色。

"你好，哈利，亲爱的。"她看见哈利，微笑着打了个招呼，接着，她又把目光投到丈夫身上，"告诉我，亚瑟，怎么回事？"

韦斯莱先生迟疑着。哈利可以看出，他尽管对弗雷德和乔治很生气，却并不真的打算把事情告诉韦斯莱夫人。韦斯莱先生紧张地望着妻子，

happened. There was a silence, while Mr Weasley eyed his wife nervously. Then two girls appeared in the kitchen doorway behind Mrs Weasley. One, with very bushy brown hair and rather large front teeth, was Harry and Ron's friend, Hermione Granger. The other, who was small and red-haired, was Ron's younger sister, Ginny. Both of them smiled at Harry, who grinned back, which made Ginny go scarlet – she had been very taken with Harry ever since his first visit to The Burrow.

'Tell me *what*, Arthur?' Mrs Weasley repeated, in a dangerous sort of voice.

'It's nothing, Molly,' mumbled Mr Weasley, 'Fred and George just – but I've had words with them –'

'What have they done this time?' said Mrs Weasley. 'If it's got anything to do with *Weasleys' Wizard Wheezes* –'

'Why don't you show Harry where he's sleeping, Ron?' said Hermione from the doorway.

'He knows where he's sleeping,' said Ron. 'In my room, he slept there last –'

'We can all go,' said Hermione, pointedly.

'Oh,' said Ron, cottoning on. 'Right.'

'Yeah, we'll come, too,' said George –

'*You stay where you are*!' snarled Mrs Weasley.

Harry and Ron edged out of the kitchen, and they, Hermione and Ginny set off along the narrow hallway and up the rickety staircase that zigzagged through the house to the upper storeys.

'What are *Weasleys' Wizard Wheezes*?' Harry asked, as they climbed.

Ron and Ginny both laughed, although Hermione didn't.

'Mum found this stack of order forms when she was cleaning Fred and George's room,' said Ron quietly. 'Great long price-lists for stuff they've invented. Joke stuff, you know. Fake wands and trick sweets, loads of stuff. It was brilliant, I never knew they'd been inventing all that ...'

'We've been hearing explosions out of their room for ages, but we never thought they were actually *making* things,' said Ginny, 'we thought they just liked the noise.'

'Only, most of the stuff – well, all of it, really – was a bit dangerous,' said Ron, 'and, you know, they were planning to sell it at Hogwarts to make some money, and Mum went mad at them. Told them they weren't allowed to make any more of it, and burnt all the order forms ... she's furious at them

## 第5章 韦斯莱魔法把戏坊

一时间没有人说话。就在这时,两个女孩子出现在韦斯莱夫人身后的厨房门口。一个长着非常浓密的棕色头发,两个门牙很大,这是哈利和罗恩的好朋友赫敏·格兰杰。另一个身材矮小,一头红发,是罗恩的小妹妹金妮。两个女孩都朝哈利露出了微笑,哈利也对她们笑着,金妮立刻羞红了脸——自从哈利第一次拜访陋居以来,金妮就对他非常迷恋。

"快说,亚瑟,怎么回事?"韦斯莱夫人又问了一句,口气有点儿吓人。

"没什么,莫丽,"韦斯莱先生含糊地说,"弗雷德和乔治刚才——我已经教训过他们了——"

"他们这次又干了什么?"韦斯莱夫人说,"如果又和韦斯莱魔法把戏坊有关——"

"罗恩,你带哈利去看看他睡觉的地方好不好?"赫敏在门口说。

"他知道他睡在哪儿,"罗恩说,"在我的房间,他上次就睡在那儿——"

"我们都去看看。"赫敏严厉地说。

"噢,"罗恩这才心领神会,"好吧。"

"对了,我们也去。"乔治说。

"你们不许动!"韦斯莱夫人大吼一声。

哈利和罗恩小心翼翼地侧身溜出厨房,和赫敏、金妮一起,穿过狭窄的门厅,踏上摇摇晃晃的楼梯。那楼梯曲里拐弯,通向上面的楼层。

"什么是韦斯莱魔法把戏坊?"他们上楼时,哈利问道。

罗恩和金妮都大笑起来,只有赫敏没笑。

"妈妈打扫弗雷德和乔治的房间时,发现了那一沓订货单,"罗恩小声说,"长长的好几页价目表,上面都是他们发明的东西。搞笑的玩意儿,你知道。假魔杖啦,魔法糖啦,一大堆东西。真是太棒了,我从来不知道他们一直在搞发明……"

"好长时间了,我们总是听见他们房间里有爆炸的声音,但从来没想到他们真的在做东西,"金妮说,"还以为他们只是喜欢听响儿呢。"

"不过,那些东西大多数——唉,实际上是全部——都有点儿危险,"罗恩说,"你知道吗,他们计划把这些东西拿到霍格沃茨去卖,大赚一笔呢。妈妈听说以后,简直气疯了,警告他们不许再搞这类玩意儿,还把他们的订货单烧了个精光……她一直在生他们的气,他们拿到的

## CHAPTER FIVE  Weasleys' Wizard Wheezes

anyway. They didn't get as many O.W.L.s as she expected.'

O.W.L.s were Ordinary Wizarding Levels, the examinations Hogwarts students took at the age of fifteen.

'And then there was this big row,' Ginny said, 'because Mum wants them to go into the Ministry of Magic like Dad, and they told her all they want to do is open a joke-shop.'

Just then, a door on the second landing opened, and a face poked out wearing horn-rimmed glasses and a very annoyed expression.

'Hi, Percy,' said Harry.

'Oh, hello, Harry,' said Percy. 'I was wondering who was making all the noise. I'm trying to work in here, you know – I've got a report to finish for the office – and it's rather difficult to concentrate when people keep thundering up and down the stairs.'

'We're not *thundering*,' said Ron irritably. 'We're walking. Sorry if we've disturbed the top-secret workings of the Ministry of Magic.'

'What are you working on?' said Harry.

'A report for the Department of International Magical Co-operation,' said Percy smugly. 'We're trying to standardise cauldron thickness. Some of these foreign imports are just a shade too thin – leakages have been increasing at a rate of almost three per cent a year –'

'That'll change the world, that report will,' said Ron. 'Front page of the *Daily Prophet*, I expect, cauldron leaks.'

Percy went slightly pink.

'You might sneer, Ron,' he said heatedly, 'but unless some sort of international law is imposed we might well find the market flooded with flimsy, shallow-bottomed products which seriously endanger –'

'Yeah, yeah, all right,' said Ron, and he started off upstairs again. Percy slammed his bedroom door shut. As Harry, Hermione and Ginny followed Ron up three more flights of stairs, shouts from the kitchen below echoed up to them. It sounded as though Mr Weasley had told Mrs Weasley about the toffees.

The room at the top of the house where Ron slept looked much as it had done the last time that Harry had come to stay; the same posters of Ron's favourite Quidditch team, the Chudley Cannons, were whirling and waving

O.W.L. 证书数量也让她失望。"

O.W.L. 是普通巫师等级考试，是霍格沃茨的学生十五岁时参加的一种考试。

"那一次吵得可凶了。"金妮说，"妈妈想让他们以后进魔法部工作，像爸爸那样，可他们对她说，他们只想开一家玩笑商店。"

就在这时，二楼平台上的一扇门打开了，从里面伸出一张脸来，戴着牛角边的眼镜，表情很不耐烦。

"你好，珀西。"哈利说。

"噢，你好，哈利。"珀西说，"我不明白是谁弄出这么大的响动。你知道，我正在这里工作呢——为办公室赶写一份报告——可是老有人在楼梯上轰隆隆地乱跑，使我很难集中精力。"

"我们没有轰隆隆地乱跑，"罗恩恼火地说，"我们在走路。如果我们打扰了魔法部的最高机密工作，那么很抱歉。"

"你在忙些什么呢？"哈利问。

"为国际魔法合作司写一份报告。"珀西得意地说，"我们准备按标准检验坩埚的厚度。有些外国进口的坩埚底太薄了——渗漏率几乎以每年百分之三的速度在增长——"

"真了不起，这份报告会改变世界的。"罗恩说，"我想，《预言家日报》会在头版头条登出来：坩埚渗漏。"

珀西的脸涨成了粉红色。

"你尽管挖苦嘲笑吧，罗恩，"他激动地说，"可是必须颁布实施某种国际法，不然我们就会发现市场上充斥着伪劣产品，坩埚底薄，脆弱易碎，严重危害——"

"好了，好了。"罗恩说着，抬脚继续往楼上走。珀西重重地关上了卧室的门。哈利、赫敏和金妮跟着罗恩，又爬了三层楼梯，仍然能听见下面厨房里传来的喊叫声。似乎韦斯莱先生已经把太妃糖的事告诉了韦斯莱夫人。

罗恩睡觉的那个顶楼房间，和哈利上次来住的时候没什么差别：还是到处都贴着罗恩最喜欢的魁地奇球队——查德里火炮队的海报，那些队员们在墙壁和倾斜的天花板上飞来飞去，还不停地挥手致意。窗台上还是

on the walls and sloping ceiling, and the fishtank on the window-sill which had previously held frog-spawn now contained one extremely large frog. Ron's old rat, Scabbers, was here no more, but instead there was the tiny grey owl that had delivered Ron's letter to Harry in Privet Drive. It was hopping up and down in a small cage, and twittering madly.

'Shut *up*, Pig,' said Ron, edging his way between two of the four beds that had been squeezed into the room. 'Fred and George are in here with us, because Bill and Charlie are in their room,' he told Harry. 'Percy gets to keep his room all to himself because he's got to *work*.'

'Er – why are you calling that owl Pig?' Harry asked Ron.

'Because he's being stupid,' said Ginny. 'Its proper name is Pigwidgeon.'

'Yeah, and that's not a stupid name at all,' said Ron sarcastically.

'Ginny named him,' he explained to Harry. 'She reckons it's sweet. And I tried to change it, but it was too late, he won't answer to anything else. So now he's Pig. I've got to keep him up here because he annoys Errol and Hermes. He annoys me, too, come to that.'

Pigwidgeon zoomed happily around his cage, hooting shrilly. Harry knew Ron too well to take him seriously. He had moaned continually about his old rat Scabbers, but had been most upset when Hermione's cat, Crookshanks, appeared to have eaten him.

'Where's Crookshanks?' Harry asked Hermione now.

'Out in the garden, I expect,' she said. 'He likes chasing gnomes, he's never seen any before.'

'Percy's enjoying work, then?' said Harry, sitting down on one of the beds and watching the Chudley Cannons zooming in and out of the posters on the ceiling.

'Enjoying it?' said Ron darkly. 'I don't reckon he'd come home if Dad didn't make him. He's obsessed. Just don't get him onto the subject of his boss. *According to Mr Crouch ... as I was saying to Mr Crouch ... Mr Crouch is of the opinion ... Mr Crouch was telling me ...* They'll be announcing their engagement any day now.'

'Have you had a good summer, Harry?' said Hermione. 'Did you get our food parcels and everything?'

'Yeah, thanks a lot,' said Harry. 'They saved my life, those cakes.'

'And have you heard from –?' Ron began, but at a look from Hermione

放着金鱼缸，里面原先养着蛙卵，现在却是一只大得吓人的青蛙。罗恩的那只老掉牙的老鼠斑斑不见了，取而代之的是那只到女贞路给哈利送信的灰色小猫头鹰。它在一只小笼子里跳上跳下，叽叽喳喳地叫个不停。

"闭嘴，小猪。"罗恩说着，侧身从两张床中间挤了过去，房间里一共放了四张床，挤得满满当当，"弗雷德和乔治也和我们一起住在这里，因为比尔和查理把他们的房间占了。"他对哈利说，"珀西硬要一个人占一个房间，因为他要工作。"

"对了——你为什么管那只猫头鹰叫小猪呢？"哈利问罗恩。

"因为他非要犯傻，"金妮说，"它真正的名字是朱薇琼。"

"是啊，那个名字倒是一点儿也不傻。"罗恩讽刺地说。

"是金妮给它起的，"他对哈利解释道，"金妮觉得这名字特别可爱，我想把它换掉，已经来不及了，猫头鹰只认这个名字，叫它别的，它一概不理。所以现在它就成了小猪。埃罗尔和赫梅斯都讨厌它，我只好把它养在这里。说实在的，我也挺讨厌它的。"

朱薇琼快活地在笼子里蹿来蹿去，发出刺耳的鸣叫。哈利太了解罗恩了，知道对他的话不能当真。原先，他也是整天抱怨他那只老鼠斑斑，可是当他以为赫敏的猫克鲁克山咬死了斑斑时，别提有多难过了。

"克鲁克山呢？"哈利又问赫敏。

"大概在外面的园子里吧。"她说，"它喜欢追赶地精，以前从没见过这玩意儿。"

"看来，珀西挺喜欢工作的，是吗？"哈利在一张床上坐下，看着天花板的海报上那些查德里火炮队队员嗖嗖地飞来飞去。

"喜欢？"罗恩愁闷地说，"如果爸爸不把他硬拉回来，他根本不肯回家。他是个工作狂。你可千万别引他谈起他们老板。克劳奇先生认为……我是这样对克劳奇先生说的……克劳奇先生是这样想的……克劳奇先生告诉我……我看他们现在随时都可能宣布订婚消息。"

"你暑假过得好吗，哈利？"赫敏问，"收到我们寄给你的好吃的和其他东西了吗？"

"收到了，太感谢了。"哈利说，"多亏了那些蛋糕，我才死里逃生。"

"对了，你有没有收到——"罗恩刚说到一半，赫敏瞪了他一眼，

he fell silent. Harry knew Ron had been about to ask about Sirius. Ron and Hermione had been so deeply involved in helping Sirius escape from the Ministry of Magic that they were almost as concerned about Harry's godfather as he was. However, discussing him in front of Ginny was a bad idea. Nobody but themselves and Professor Dumbledore knew about how Sirius had escaped, or believed in his innocence.

'I think they've stopped arguing,' said Hermione, to cover the awkward moment, because Ginny was looking curiously from Ron to Harry. 'Shall we go down and help your mum with dinner?'

'Yeah, all right,' said Ron. The four of them left Ron's room and went back downstairs, to find Mrs Weasley alone in the kitchen, looking extremely bad-tempered.

'We're eating out in the garden,' she said when they came in. 'There's just not room for eleven people in here. Could you take the plates outside, girls? Bill and Charlie are setting up the tables. Knives and forks, please, you two,' she said to Ron and Harry, pointing her wand a little more vigorously than she had intended at a pile of potatoes in the sink, which shot out of their skins so fast that they ricocheted off the walls and ceilings.

'Oh, for heaven's *sake*,' she snapped, now directing her wand at a dustpan, which hopped off the side and started skating across the floor, scooping up the potatoes. 'Those two!' she burst out savagely, now pulling pots and pans out of a cupboard, and Harry knew she meant Fred and George. 'I don't know what's going to happen to them, I really don't. No ambition, unless you count making as much trouble as they possibly can …'

She slammed a large copper saucepan down on the kitchen table and began to wave her wand around inside it. A creamy sauce poured from the wand tip as she stirred.

'It's not as though they haven't got brains,' she continued irritably, taking the saucepan over to the stove and lighting it with a further poke of her wand, 'but they're wasting them, and unless they pull themselves together soon, they'll be in real trouble. I've had more owls from Hogwarts about them than the rest put together. If they carry on the way they're going, they'll end up in front of the Improper Use of Magic Office.'

Mrs Weasley jabbed her wand at the cutlery drawer, which shot open. Harry and Ron both jumped out of the way as several knives soared out of it, flew across the kitchen and began chopping the potatoes, which had just

## 第5章 韦斯莱魔法把戏坊

他便不往下说了。哈利知道罗恩想打听一下小天狼星的情况。罗恩和赫敏都积极参加了帮助小天狼星逃脱魔法部追捕的行动,所以他们像哈利一样关心他教父的安危。可是,当着金妮的面谈论他是不明智的。只有他们和邓布利多教授知道小天狼星是怎样逃跑的,并相信他是无辜的。

"我想他们大概吵完了。"赫敏看到金妮好奇地望望罗恩,又望望哈利。她为了掩饰这片刻的尴尬,说道:"我们下去帮你妈妈准备晚饭,好吗?"

"行,好吧。"罗恩说。四个人离开了罗恩的房间,回到楼下,发现韦斯莱夫人正一个人在厨房里忙碌着,情绪坏到了极点。

"我们在外面的园子里吃饭,"他们进去以后,她说,"这里可容不下十一个人。姑娘们,你们能把这些盘子端出去吗?比尔和查理在摆桌子呢。你们两个,拿上刀叉。"她一边吩咐罗恩和哈利,一边用魔杖点了点水池里的一堆土豆,可没想到用的劲儿大了一点,土豆自动脱皮的速度太快,一个个都蹿到墙上和天花板上去了。

"哎呀,天哪。"她恼火地说,又用魔杖对着一个侧立的簸箕点了一下。簸箕立刻就跳起来,在地板上滑来滑去,把土豆一个个撮了起来。"这两个家伙!"她恶狠狠地说,一边从碗柜里抽出许多大锅小锅,哈利知道她指的是弗雷德和乔治,"真不知道他们会变成什么样儿。没有一点雄心壮志,整天就知道变着法儿闯祸……"

韦斯莱夫人把一口黄铜大炖锅砰地扔在厨房的桌上,将魔杖伸进去呼呼地转着圈儿。随着她的搅拌,一股奶油酱从魔杖头上喷了出来。

"他们不是不聪明,"她把炖锅放在炉子上,又用魔杖捅了一下,把火点着,继续气呼呼地说着,"可那些聪明用得不是地方,除非他们很快振作起来,改邪归正,不然会倒大霉的。从霍格沃茨飞来给他们告状的猫头鹰,比其他所有人的加起来都多。照这个样子下去,他们最后准会被送进禁止滥用魔法办公室。"

韦斯莱夫人又用魔杖捅了一下放刀具的抽屉,抽屉猛地弹开了。哈利和罗恩赶紧跳开,只见抽屉里蹿出好几把刀子,在厨房里飞过,

been tipped back into the sink by the dustpan.

'I don't know where we went wrong with them,' said Mrs Weasley, putting down her wand and starting to pull out still more saucepans. 'It's been the same for years, one thing after another, and they won't listen to – OH, NOT AGAIN!'

She had picked up her wand from the table, and it had emitted a loud squeak and turned into a giant rubber mouse.

'One of their fake wands again!' she shouted. 'How many times have I told those two not to leave them lying around?'

She grabbed her real wand and turned around to find that the sauce on the stove was smoking.

'C'mon,' Ron said hurriedly to Harry, seizing a handful of cutlery from the open drawer, 'let's go and help Bill and Charlie.'

They left Mrs Weasley, and headed out of the back door into the yard.

They had only gone a few paces when Hermione's bandy-legged, ginger cat Crookshanks came pelting out of the garden, bottle-brush tail held high in the air, chasing what looked like a muddy potato on legs. Harry recognised it instantly as a gnome. Barely ten inches high, its horny little feet pattered very fast as it sprinted across the yard and dived headlong into one of the wellington boots that lay scattered around the door. Harry could hear the gnome giggling madly as Crookshanks inserted a paw into the boot, trying to reach it. Meanwhile, a very loud crashing noise was coming from the other side of the house. The source of the commotion was revealed as they entered the garden and saw that Bill and Charlie both had their wands out, and were making two battered old tables fly high above the lawn, smashing into each other, each attempting to knock the other's out of the air. Fred and George were cheering; Ginny was laughing, and Hermione was hovering near the hedge, apparently torn between amusement and anxiety.

Bill's table caught Charlie's with a huge bang, and knocked one of its legs off. There was a clatter from overhead, and they all looked up to see Percy's head poking out of a window on the second floor.

'Will you keep it down?' he bellowed.

'Sorry, Perce,' said Bill, grinning. 'How're the cauldron bottoms coming on?'

'Very badly,' said Percy peevishly, and he slammed the window shut again. Chuckling, Bill and Charlie directed the tables safely onto the grass, end to

## 第5章 韦斯莱魔法把戏坊

开始嚓嚓地切起土豆来。那只簸箕刚才已经把土豆倒进了水池。

"真不明白我们什么地方教育得不对。"韦斯莱夫人说着,放下魔杖,又拽出几口炖锅,"这么多年来一直这样,捅了一个乱子又一个乱子,根本听不进——哦,又不对!"

她从桌上拿起她的魔杖,结果魔杖发出一声刺耳的尖叫,变成了一只巨大的橡皮老鼠。

"又是他们搞的假魔杖!"她嚷嚷道,"我对他们说过多少遍了,不要把这些玩意儿到处乱放!"

她抓起真魔杖,一转身,发现炉子上的奶油酱已经冒烟了。

"走吧,"罗恩从打开的抽屉里抓起一把餐具,急急地对哈利说,"我们去帮帮比尔和查理吧。"

他们撇下韦斯莱夫人,出了后门,进了园子。

刚走几步,他们就看见赫敏那只姜黄色的、罗圈腿的猫克鲁克山,匆匆地在园子里跑来跑去,瓶刷子似的尾巴高高竖着,正在追赶一个东西。那东西沾满泥巴,活像一个长了腿的土豆。哈利一眼就认出那是个地精。它身高不足十英寸,坚硬的小脚啪嗒啪嗒地走得飞快,穿过园子,一头钻进扔在门边的一只惠灵顿皮靴里。克鲁克山把一只爪子伸进靴子,想抓住地精。哈利听见地精在里面疯狂地咯咯大笑。就在这时,房子的另一头传来一声震耳欲聋的撞击声。他们走进园子,才发现这番骚动是怎么引起的。他们看见比尔和查理都拔出了魔杖,正在调动两张破破烂烂的旧桌子在草坪上飞,互相撞击,每张桌子都想把对方从空中打落。弗雷德和乔治在一旁欢呼,金妮哈哈大笑,赫敏在篱笆边徘徊,看样子又觉得好玩,又感到紧张,不知如何是好。

梆的一声,比尔的桌子击中了查理的桌子,把一条桌腿打掉了。这时,头顶上传来一阵清脆的撞击声。他们同时抬起头,看见珀西的脑袋从三楼的窗口探了出来。

"你们能不能小声一点儿?"他吼道。

"对不起,珀西,"比尔笑嘻嘻地说,"坩埚底怎么样啦?"

"糟透了。"珀西没好气地说,砰的一声关上了窗户。比尔和查理轻声笑着,用魔杖指引桌子稳稳地降落到草地上,连着排在一起。然后,

## CHAPTER FIVE   Weasleys' Wizard Wheezes

end, and then, with a flick of his wand, Bill reattached the table leg, and conjured tablecloths from nowhere.

By seven o'clock, the two tables were groaning under dishes and dishes of Mrs Weasley's excellent cooking, and the nine Weasleys, Harry and Hermione were settling themselves down to eat beneath a clear, deep-blue sky. To somebody who had been living on meals of increasingly stale cake all summer, this was paradise, and at first, Harry listened rather than talked, as he helped himself to chicken-and-ham pie, boiled potatoes and salad.

At the far end of the table, Percy was telling his father all about his report on cauldron bottoms.

'I've told Mr Crouch that I'll have it ready by Tuesday,' Percy was saying pompously. 'That's a bit sooner than he expected it, but I like to keep on top of things. I think he'll be grateful I've done it in good time. I mean, it's extremely busy in our department just now, what with all the arrangements for the World Cup. We're just not getting the support we need from the Department of Magical Games and Sports. Ludo Bagman –'

'I like Ludo,' said Mr Weasley mildly. 'He was the one who got us such good tickets for the Cup. I did him a bit of a favour: his brother, Otto, got into a spot of trouble – a lawnmower with unnatural powers – I smoothed the whole thing over.'

'Oh, Bagman's *likeable* enough, of course,' said Percy dismissively, 'but how he ever got to be Head of Department ... when I compare him to Mr Crouch! I can't see Mr Crouch losing a member of our department and not trying to find out what's happened to them. You realise Bertha Jorkins has been missing for over a month now? Went on holiday to Albania and never came back?'

'Yes, I was asking Ludo about that,' said Mr Weasley, frowning. 'He says Bertha's got lost plenty of times before now – though I must say, if it was someone in my department, I'd be worried ...'

'Oh, Bertha's *hopeless*, all right,' said Percy. 'I hear she's been shunted from department to department for years, much more trouble than she's worth ... but all the same, Bagman ought to be trying to find her. Mr Crouch has been taking a personal interest – she worked in our department at one time, you know, and I think Mr Crouch was quite fond of her – but Bagman just keeps laughing and saying she probably misread the map and ended up in

## 第5章　韦斯莱魔法把戏坊

比尔用魔杖轻巧地一点，把那条桌腿重新接上，又凭空变出了桌布。

七点钟的时候，两张桌子在韦斯莱夫人妙手做出的一道道美味佳肴的重压下嘎吱作响。韦斯莱一家九口，还有哈利和赫敏都坐了下来，在明净的深蓝色夜空下用餐。对于整个夏天都吃着越来越不新鲜的蛋糕的人来说，现在就像进了天堂一样。起先，哈利只顾大吃鸡肉火腿馅饼、煮土豆和沙拉，根本顾不上说话。

在桌子的那一头，珀西正在告诉父亲他撰写坩埚底厚度报告的情况。

"我对克劳奇先生说，我星期二就能完成，"珀西挺得意地说，"比他预期的快一些，但我想一切都争取主动。如果我按时完成了，他会感到很满意的，因为目前我们司里的事情特别多，都忙着筹备世界杯呢。我们从魔法体育运动司得不到所需要的支持。卢多·巴格曼——"

"我喜欢卢多这个人，"韦斯莱先生温和地说，"多亏他替我们弄到了这么好的世界杯球赛票。我原先帮过他一个小忙：他弟弟奥多出了点儿麻烦——把一台割草机弄出了许多特异功能——是我把整个事情摆平的。"

"是啊，当然啦，巴格曼是挺可爱的，"珀西不以为然地说，"可是拿他和克劳奇先生一比，我真不明白他是怎么当上司长的！如果克劳奇先生发现我们司里有人失踪，一定会着手调查，而不会听之任之。你知道，伯莎·乔金斯已经失踪一个多月了！到阿尔巴尼亚度假，再也没有回来。"

"是啊，我向卢多询问过这件事。"韦斯莱先生说着，皱起了眉头，"他说在这之前，伯莎就失踪过好多次——不过说句实话，如果是我司里的人，我会感到担心……"

"唉，伯莎这个人确实让人很伤脑筋。"珀西说，"我听说这些年，她从一个部门被赶到另一个部门，惹的麻烦比做的事情还多……但是不管怎么说，巴格曼还是应该想办法找找她。克劳奇先生个人一直很关注这件事，你知道，伯莎以前在我们司工作过一段时间，我认为克劳奇先生还是很喜欢她的——可巴格曼总是哈哈一笑，说伯莎大概是看错了地图，没有到阿尔巴尼亚，而是到了澳大利亚。不过，"珀西派

Australia instead of Albania. However,' Percy heaved an impressive sigh, and took a deep swig of elderflower wine, 'we've got quite enough on our plates at the Department of International Magical Co-operation without trying to find members of other departments too. As you know, we've got another big event to organise right after the World Cup.'

He cleared his throat significantly and looked down towards the end of the table where Harry, Ron and Hermione were sitting. '*You* know the one I'm talking about, father.' He raised his voice slightly. 'The top-secret one.'

Ron rolled his eyes and muttered to Harry and Hermione, 'He's been trying to get us to ask what that event is ever since he started work. Probably an exhibition of thick-bottomed cauldrons.'

In the middle of the table, Mrs Weasley was arguing with Bill about his earring, which seemed to be a recent acquisition.

'... with a horrible great fang on it, really, Bill, what do they say at the bank?'

'Mum, no one at the bank gives a damn how I dress as long as I bring home plenty of treasure,' said Bill patiently.

'And your hair's getting silly, dear,' said Mrs Weasley, fingering her wand lovingly. 'I wish you'd let me give it a trim ...'

'I like it,' said Ginny, who was sitting beside Bill. 'You're so old-fashioned, Mum. Anyway, it's nowhere near as long as Professor Dumbledore's ...'

Next to Mrs Weasley, Fred, George and Charlie were all talking spiritedly about the World Cup.

'It's got to be Ireland,' said Charlie thickly, through a mouthful of potato. 'They flattened Peru in the semi-finals.'

'Bulgaria have got Viktor Krum, though,' said Fred.

'Krum's one decent player, Ireland have got seven,' said Charlie shortly. 'I wish England had got through, though. That was embarrassing, that was.'

'What happened?' said Harry eagerly, regretting more than ever his isolation from the wizarding world when he was stuck in Privet Drive. Harry was passionate about Quidditch. He had played as Seeker on the Gryffindor house Quidditch team ever since his first year at Hogwarts and owned a Firebolt, one of the best racing brooms in the world.

'Went down to Transylvania, three hundred and ninety to ten,' said Charlie gloomily. 'Shocking performance. And Wales lost to Uganda, and

## 第5章 韦斯莱魔法把戏坊

头十足地长叹一声，深深地饮了一口接骨木花酒，"我们国际魔法合作司要做的事情实在太多了，没有闲工夫替别的部门找人。要知道，世界杯之后，我们还要组织一项大型活动呢。"

珀西煞有介事似的清了清喉咙，扭头望着桌子这边哈利和赫敏坐的位置。"你知道我说的是什么活动，爸。"他微微抬高了嗓门，"最高机密的那个。"

罗恩翻了翻眼珠，低声对哈利和赫敏说："自打他开始工作以来，就一直想逗我们问他那是什么活动。大概是一次厚底坩埚展览会吧。"

在桌子中央，韦斯莱夫人正在和比尔争论那只耳环的事，看来这耳环是最近才戴上的。

"……上面还带着一个可怕的大长牙。真的，比尔，银行里的人怎么说？"

"妈，银行里的人根本不关心我穿什么衣服，只要我找回大量财宝就行。"比尔耐心地说。

"你的头发也难看得要命，亲爱的，"韦斯莱夫人说，一边慈爱地摆弄自己的魔杖，"我真希望你能让我修剪一下……"

"我喜欢。"坐在比尔旁边的金妮说道，"妈，你太落伍了。而且，和邓布利多教授的头发比起来，这根本不算长……"

在韦斯莱夫人旁边，弗雷德、乔治和查理正在热烈地讨论世界杯赛。

"肯定是爱尔兰队胜出，"查理嘴里塞满了土豆，嘟嘟哝哝地说，"他们在半决赛时打败了秘鲁队。"

"可是保加利亚队有威克多尔·克鲁姆呢。"弗雷德说。

"克鲁姆是不错，但他只是一个人，爱尔兰队有七位好手呢。"查理不耐烦地说，"不过，我真希望英格兰队能够出线。真是太丢脸了。"

"怎么回事？"哈利急切地问。他暑假里一直守在女贞路，与魔法世界完全隔绝，想起来真是懊恼透顶。哈利对魁地奇充满了热情。他从在霍格沃茨上一年级时起，就进了格兰芬多学院的魁地奇球队，担任找球手。他还拥有世界上最棒的飞天扫帚火弩箭。

"输给了特兰西瓦尼亚队，十比三百九十。"查理愁眉苦脸地说，"表现糟糕透了。威尔士队败给了乌干达，苏格兰队被卢森堡队打得落花

## CHAPTER FIVE   Weasleys' Wizard Wheezes

Scotland were slaughtered by Luxembourg.'

Mr Weasley conjured up candles to light the darkening garden before they had their pudding (home-made strawberry ice-cream), and by the time they had finished, moths were fluttering low over the table and the warm air was perfumed with the smells of grass and honeysuckle. Harry was feeling extremely well fed and at peace with the world as he watched several gnomes sprinting through the rose bushes, laughing madly and closely pursued by Crookshanks.

Ron looked carefully up the table to check that the rest of the family were all busy talking, then he said very quietly to Harry, 'So – have you heard from Sirius lately?'

Hermione looked round, listening closely.

'Yeah,' said Harry softly, 'twice. He sounds OK. I wrote to him the day before yesterday. He might write back while I'm here.'

He suddenly remembered the reason he had written to Sirius and, for a moment, was on the verge of telling Ron and Hermione about his scar hurting again, and about the dream which had awoken him ... but he really didn't want to worry them just now, not when he himself was feeling so happy and peaceful.

'Look at the time,' Mrs Weasley said suddenly, checking her wrist-watch. 'You really should be in bed, the whole lot of you, you'll be up at the crack of dawn to get to the Cup. Harry, if you leave your school list out, I'll get your things for you tomorrow in Diagon Alley. I'm getting everyone else's. There might not be time after the World Cup, the match went on for five days last time.'

'Wow – hope it does this time!' said Harry enthusiastically.

'Well, I certainly don't,' said Percy sanctimoniously. 'I *shudder* to think what the state of my in-tray would be if I was away from work for five days.'

'Yeah, someone might slip dragon dung in it again, eh, Perce?' said Fred.

'That was a sample of fertiliser from Norway!' said Percy, going very red in the face. 'It was nothing *personal*!'

'It was,' Fred whispered to Harry, as they got up from the table. 'We sent it.'

## 第5章　韦斯莱魔法把戏坊

流水。"

韦斯莱先生变出了一些蜡烛,把渐渐暗下来的园子照亮了,然后大家开始享用家里做的草莓冰淇淋。大家都吃完了,飞蛾低低地在桌子上飞舞,温暖的空气中弥漫着青草和金银花的香气。哈利觉得自己吃得很饱。他坐在那里,望着几只地精被克鲁克山紧紧追赶,一边飞快地穿过蔷薇花丛,一边疯狂地大笑。这一刻,哈利真是从心底里感到满足。

罗恩小心地抬头望望桌子周围,看家里人是不是都在忙着聊天,然后用很轻的声音对哈利说:"你说——你最近收到过小天狼星的来信吗?"

赫敏抬头张望了一下,仔细听着。

"收到过,"哈利小声说,"两次。看来他一切都好。我昨天给他写了封信。我住在这里的这段时间,他会给我回信的。"

他突然想起了他给小天狼星写信的原因,真想告诉罗恩和赫敏他伤疤又疼起来的事,告诉他们那个把他惊醒的噩梦……但是又觉得现在这么幸福、满足,他不想让他们担心。

"看看时间吧,"韦斯莱夫人突然说道,一边看了看她的手表,"你们应该上床睡觉了,你们大家——明天一大早要起床去看比赛。哈利,你把学习用品的采购单留下,我明天到对角巷去替你买来。我反正要给其他人买的。等世界杯结束后大概就来不及了,上次的比赛持续了整整五天。"

"哇——真希望这次也这样!"哈利激动地说。

"噢,我可不希望。"珀西假正经地说,"一下子离开五天,那我的文件筐里还不堆满了文件啊,想到这点,真让我不寒而栗。"

"是啊,说不定又有人将火龙粪塞在信封里寄给你呢,珀西。"弗雷德说。

"那是从挪威寄来的肥料样品!"珀西说着,脸涨得通红,"不是给私人的!"

"其实,"大家起身离开桌子时,弗雷德悄悄对哈利说,"那是我们寄给他的。"

## CHAPTER SIX

# The Portkey

Harry felt as though he had barely lain down to sleep in Ron's room when he was being shaken awake by Mrs Weasley.

'Time to go, Harry, dear,' she whispered, moving away to wake Ron.

Harry felt around for his glasses, put them on and sat up. It was still dark outside. Ron muttered indistinctly as his mother roused him. At the foot of Harry's mattress he saw two large, dishevelled shapes emerging from tangles of blankets.

'"S'time already?' said Fred groggily.

They dressed in silence, too sleepy to talk, then, yawning and stretching, the four of them headed downstairs into the kitchen.

Mrs Weasley was stirring the contents of a large pot on the stove, while Mr Weasley was sitting at the table, checking a sheaf of large parchment tickets. He looked up as the boys entered, and spread his arms so that they could see his clothes more clearly. He was wearing what appeared to be a golfing jumper and a very old pair of jeans, slightly too big for him and held up with a thick leather belt.

'What d'you think?' he asked anxiously. 'We're supposed to go incognito – do I look like a Muggle, Harry?'

'Yeah,' said Harry, smiling, 'very good.'

'Where're Bill and Charlie and Per–Per–Percy?' said George, failing to stifle a huge yawn.

'Well, they're Apparating, aren't they?' said Mrs Weasley, heaving the large pot over to the table and starting to ladle porridge into bowls. 'So they can have a bit of a lie-in.'

Harry knew that Apparating was very difficult; it meant disappearing from

# 第6章

# 门 钥 匙

哈利觉得自己刚在罗恩的房间里躺下,还没睡一会儿,就被韦斯莱夫人摇醒了。

"该走了,哈利,亲爱的。"她小声说,一边又走过去唤醒罗恩。

哈利伸手摸到眼镜戴上,坐了起来。外面还是一片漆黑。罗恩被母亲唤醒时,嘴里含混不清地嘟哝着什么。哈利看见床脚处有两个不规则的黑影从乱糟糟的毯子下冒了出来。

"怎么,已经到时间了?"弗雷德睡眼惺忪地问。

大家默默地穿衣服,都困得不愿说话。然后,他们四个下楼走进厨房,一边还在打哈欠,伸懒腰。

韦斯莱夫人正在搅拌炉子上一口大锅里的东西,韦斯莱先生坐在桌旁,核对一扎羊皮纸做成的大张球票。男孩子们走进厨房时,他抬起头,展开双臂,好让他们看清楚他身上的衣服。他穿着一件像是高尔夫球衣的上衣和一条很旧的牛仔裤,裤子穿在他身上有点儿嫌大,用一根宽宽的牛皮带束住了。

"怎么样?"他急切地问,"我们去的时候应该隐瞒身份——我这样子像麻瓜吗,哈利?"

"像,"哈利笑着说,"很不错。"

"怎么不见比尔、查理和珀—珀—珀西?"乔治说,忍不住又打了个大哈欠。

"他们要幻影显形去,不是吗?"韦斯莱夫人说,一边把那口大锅放在桌上,开始把粥舀进一个个碗里,"所以可以睡一会儿懒觉。"

哈利知道,所谓幻影显形,就是从一个地方消失,一眨眼又在另

## CHAPTER SIX  The Portkey

one place and reappearing almost instantly in another.

'So they're still in bed?' said Fred grumpily, pulling his bowl of porridge towards him. 'Why can't we Apparate, too?'

'Because you're not of age and you haven't got your test,' snapped Mrs Weasley. 'And where have those girls got to?'

She bustled out of the kitchen and they heard her climbing the stairs.

'You have to pass a test to Apparate?' Harry asked.

'Oh yes,' said Mr Weasley, tucking the tickets safely into the back pocket of his jeans. 'The Department of Magical Transportation had to fine a couple of people the other day for Apparating without a licence. It's not easy, Apparition, and when it's not done properly it can lead to nasty complications. This pair I'm talking about went and splinched themselves.'

Everyone around the table except Harry winced.

'Er – *splinched*?' said Harry.

'They left half of themselves behind,' said Mr Weasley, now spooning large amounts of treacle onto his porridge. 'So, of course, they were stuck. Couldn't move either way. Had to wait for the Accidental Magic Reversal Squad to sort them out. Meant a fair old bit of paperwork, I can tell you, what with the Muggles who spotted the body parts they'd left behind ...'

Harry had a sudden vision of a pair of legs and an eyeball lying abandoned on the pavement of Privet Drive.

'Were they OK?' he asked, startled.

'Oh yes,' said Mr Weasley matter-of-factly. 'But they got a heavy fine, and I don't think they'll be trying it again in a hurry. You don't mess around with Apparition. There are plenty of adult wizards who don't bother with it. Prefer brooms – slower, but safer.'

'But Bill and Charlie and Percy can all do it?'

'Charlie had to take the test twice,' said Fred, grinning. 'He failed first time, Apparated five miles south of where he meant to, right on top of some poor old dear doing her shopping, remember?'

'Yes, well, he passed second time,' said Mrs Weasley, marching back into the kitchen amid hearty sniggers.

'Percy only passed two weeks ago,' said George. 'He's been Apparating

## 第6章 门钥匙

一个地方重新出现,他心知这一定很难。

"这么说,他们还在呼呼大睡?"弗雷德气恼地问,"为什么我们不能也幻影显形呢?"

"因为你们不到年龄,还没有通过考试。"韦斯莱夫人回敬了他一句,"那两个丫头上哪儿去了?"

她转身冲出厨房,他们听见她上楼的声音。

"幻影显形还要通过考试?"哈利问。

"噢,是的。"韦斯莱先生说着,把球票仔细地塞进牛仔裤后面的口袋里,"前几天,魔法交通司对两个人处以罚款,因为他们没有证书就擅自幻影显形。这可不是一件容易的事,如果做得不对,就会惹出麻烦,后果很严重的。我说的那两个人最后就分体了。"

餐桌上的人除了哈利,都皱起眉头,做出一副苦脸。

"哦——分体?"哈利问。

"他们把自己的半个身子丢下了,"韦斯莱先生说,舀了很多糖浆,拌进他的粥里,"所以,自然啦,他们就被困在了那里,两边都动弹不得。只好等逆转偶发魔法事件小组去处理这件事。告诉你吧,这意味着要准备大量的文件材料,那些麻瓜看见了他们丢下的部分身体……"

哈利突然想到,如果两条大腿和一个眼球被遗弃在女贞路的人行道上,那该是什么情景啊。

"他们没事吧?"他惊恐地问。

"噢,没事,"韦斯莱先生平淡地说,"不过被狠狠罚了一笔。我想他们短时间内大概不会尝试了。你可千万别拿幻影显形当儿戏。许多成年巫师都不愿惹这个麻烦。他们情愿用扫帚——虽然慢些,可是安全。"

"可是比尔、查理和珀西都会,是吗?"

"查理考了两次才通过。"弗雷德嬉笑着说,"他第一次考砸了,在离原定目标以南五英里的地方显形,落到一个正在买东西的可怜的老太太的头顶上,记得吗?"

"是啊,不过他第二次就通过了。"在一片开心的嬉笑声中,韦斯莱夫人大步回到了厨房。

"珀西是两个星期前才通过的。"乔治说,"从那以后,他每天早晨

downstairs every morning since, just to prove he can.'

There were footsteps down the passageway and Hermione and Ginny came into the kitchen, both looking pale and drowsy.

'Why do we have to be up so early?' Ginny said, rubbing her eyes and sitting down at the table.

'We've got a bit of a walk,' said Mr Weasley.

'Walk?' said Harry. 'What, are we walking to the World Cup?'

'No, no, that's miles away,' said Mr Weasley, smiling. 'We only need to walk a short way. It's just that it's very difficult for a large number of wizards to congregate without attracting Muggle attention. We have to be very careful about how we travel at the best of times, and on a huge occasion like the Quidditch World Cup –'

'George!' said Mrs Weasley sharply, and they all jumped.

'What?' said George, in an innocent tone that deceived nobody.

'What is that in your pocket?'

'Nothing!'

'Don't you lie to me!'

Mrs Weasley pointed her wand at George's pocket and said, '*Accio!*'

Several small, brightly coloured objects zoomed out of George's pocket; he made a grab for them but missed, and they sped right into Mrs Weasley's outstretched hand.

'We told you to destroy them!' said Mrs Weasley furiously, holding up what were unmistakeably more Ton-Tongue Toffees. 'We told you to get rid of the lot! Empty your pockets, go on, both of you!'

It was an unpleasant scene; the twins had evidently been trying to smuggle as many toffees out of the house as possible, and it was only by using her Summoning Charm that Mrs Weasley managed to find them all.

'*Accio! Accio! Accio!*' she shouted, and toffees zoomed from all sorts of unlikely places, including the lining of George's jacket and the turn-ups of Fred's jeans.

'We spent six months developing those!' Fred shouted at his mother, as she threw the toffees away.

'Oh, a fine way to spend six months!' she shrieked. 'No wonder you didn't get more O.W.L.s!'

All in all, the atmosphere was not very friendly as they made their

## 第6章 门钥匙

都幻影显形到楼下,就是为了证明他有这个本事。"

过道里传来了脚步声,赫敏和金妮走进厨房,两个人的脸色都显得很苍白,好像没有睡醒。

"我们干吗要这么早起来?"金妮揉着眼睛,在餐桌旁坐下,问道。

"我们要走一段路呢。"韦斯莱先生说。

"走路?"哈利问,"怎么,我们步行去观看世界杯?"

"不,不,那就太远了,"韦斯莱先生笑着说,"只需走一小段路。把大批巫师集合到一起而不引起麻瓜的注意,这是非常困难的。我们不得不非常谨慎,选择最佳时间上路,在魁地奇世界杯赛这样盛大的场合——"

"乔治!"韦斯莱夫人突然厉声喝道,把大家都吓了一跳。

"怎么啦?"乔治说。他假装什么事也没有,可是骗不了人。

"你口袋里是什么?"

"没什么!"

"不许对我说瞎话!"

韦斯莱夫人用魔杖指着乔治的口袋,念道:"飞来!"

一些花花绿绿的小玩意儿从乔治口袋里跳了出来。乔治伸手去抓,没有抓住,它们径直跳进了韦斯莱夫人伸出的手掌中。

"叫你们把这些玩意儿毁掉!"韦斯莱夫人气愤地说,举起手里的东西,那无疑又是肥舌太妃糖,"叫你们扔掉这些劳什子!快把口袋掏空,快点,你们两个!"

这真是令人难受的一幕。双胞胎兄弟显然想把尽可能多的太妃糖从家里走私出去,韦斯莱夫人用上了她的召唤咒,才把那些糖果都找了出来。

"飞来!飞来!飞来!"她连声喊道,太妃糖从各个意想不到的地方嗖嗖地飞出来,包括乔治的夹克内衬里,以及弗雷德牛仔裤的翻边里。

"我们花了整整半年,才研制出这些东西!"弗雷德看到母亲把太妃糖扔到一边,委屈地喊道。

"半年时间花在这个上面,真不错!"韦斯莱夫人尖声说道,"怪不得才拿了那么几个 O.W.L. 证书呢!"

总之,他们离开的时候,气氛不是很友好。韦斯莱夫人亲吻韦斯

## CHAPTER SIX  The Portkey

departure. Mrs Weasley was still glowering as she kissed Mr Weasley on the cheek, though not nearly as much as the twins, who had each hoisted their rucksacks onto their backs and walked out without a word to her.

'Well, have a lovely time,' said Mrs Weasley, 'and *behave yourselves*,' she called after the twins' retreating backs, but they did not look back or answer. 'I'll send Bill, Charlie and Percy along around midday,' Mrs Weasley said to Mr Weasley, as he, Harry, Ron, Hermione and Ginny set off across the dark yard after Fred and George.

It was chilly and the moon was still out. Only a dull, greenish tinge along the horizon to their right showed that daybreak was drawing closer. Harry, having been thinking about thousands of wizards speeding towards the Quidditch World Cup, sped up to walk with Mr Weasley.

'So how *does* everyone get there without all the Muggles noticing?' he asked.

'It's been a massive organisational problem,' sighed Mr Weasley. 'The trouble is, about a hundred thousand wizards turn up to the World Cup, and of course we just haven't got a magical site big enough to accommodate them all. There are places Muggles can't penetrate, but imagine trying to pack a hundred thousand wizards into Diagon Alley or platform nine and three-quarters. So we had to find a nice deserted moor, and set up as many anti-Muggle precautions as possible. The whole Ministry's been working on it for months. Firstly, of course, we have to stagger the arrivals. People with cheaper tickets have to arrive two weeks beforehand. A limited number use Muggle transport, but we can't have too many clogging up their buses and trains – remember, wizards are coming from all over the world. Some Apparate, of course, but we have to set up safe points for them to appear, well away from Muggles. I believe there's a handy wood they're using as the Apparition point. For those who don't want to Apparate, or can't, we use Portkeys. They're objects that are used to transport wizards from one spot to another at a prearranged time. You can do large groups at a time if you need to. There have been two hundred Portkeys placed at strategic points around Britain, and the nearest one to us is up the top of Stoatshead Hill, so that's where we're headed.'

Mr Weasley pointed ahead of them, where a large black mass rose beyond the village of Ottery St Catchpole.

'What sort of objects are Portkeys?' said Harry curiously.

## 第6章 门钥匙

莱先生的面颊时,仍然板着面孔。双胞胎兄弟的态度更坏。他们把帆布背包甩到背上,一句话没对妈妈说就走了出去。

"再见,祝你们玩得痛快,"韦斯莱夫人说,"表现好一点儿。"她冲着双胞胎兄弟离去的背影喊道,可是他们既没有回头,也没有应答。"我中午的时候打发比尔、查理和珀西上路。"韦斯莱夫人对韦斯莱先生说。韦斯莱先生正和哈利、罗恩、赫敏、金妮穿过漆黑的院子,跟在弗雷德和乔治后面出发了。

外面很冷,月亮还高高地挂在天上。只有他们右边的地平线上露出一抹淡淡的灰绿色,显示着黎明正在渐渐到来。哈利一直在琢磨成千上万的巫师赶去观看魁地奇世界杯的事,便快走几步赶上韦斯莱先生。

"您说,大家怎样才能赶到那儿而不引起麻瓜的注意呢?"他问。

"组织工作真是困难重重,"韦斯莱先生叹了口气,"主要的问题是,大约有十万巫师要来观看世界杯,我们当然找不到一个能容纳这么多人的魔法场地。有些地方是麻瓜们进不去的,但是想象一下,怎么可能把十万巫师都塞进对角巷或 $9\frac{3}{4}$ 站台呢?所以我们不得不找一片荒无人烟的沼泽地,并采取一切防备麻瓜的措施。整个部里为这件事忙了好几个月。首先,当然啦,必须把大家到达的时间错开。球票便宜的人只好提前两个星期赶到。一部分人使用麻瓜的交通工具,但人数有限,我们不能让太多的人塞满麻瓜的公共汽车和火车——你别忘了,世界各地都有巫师赶来。当然,还有些人用幻影显形,但必须规定一些安全的地方让他们显形,远离所有的麻瓜。我想附近大概正好有座树林,用作幻影显形的落脚点。对于那些不愿意或不会幻影显形的人,我们就使用门钥匙。这玩意儿的作用是在规定时间内把巫师从一个地方运送到另一个地方。如果需要的话,一次可以运送一大批人。在英国各地投放了两百把门钥匙,离我们最近的一把就在白鼬山的山顶上,我们现在就是去那里。"

韦斯莱先生指着前方,奥特里·圣卡奇波尔村的后面耸立着大片阴影。

"门钥匙是什么样的东西?"哈利好奇地问。

## CHAPTER SIX  The Portkey

'Well, they can be anything,' said Mr Weasley. 'Unobtrusive things, obviously, so Muggles don't go picking them up and playing with them ... stuff they'll just think is litter ...'

They trudged down the dark, dank lane towards the village, the silence broken only by their footsteps. The sky lightened very slowly as they made their way through the village, its inky blackness diluting to deepest blue. Harry's hands and feet were freezing. Mr Weasley kept checking his watch.

They didn't have breath to spare for talking as they began to climb Stoatshead Hill, stumbling occasionally in hidden rabbit holes, slipping on thick black tuffets of grass. Each breath Harry took was sharp in his chest, and his legs were starting to seize up when at last his feet found level ground.

'Whew,' panted Mr Weasley, taking off his glasses and wiping them on his sweater. 'Well, we've made good time – we've got ten minutes ...'

Hermione came over the crest of the hill last, clutching a stitch in her side.

'Now we just need the Portkey,' said Mr Weasley, replacing his glasses and squinting around at the ground. 'It won't be big ... come on ...'

They spread out, searching. They had only been at it for a couple of minutes, however, when a shout rent the still air.

'Over here, Arthur! Over here, son, we've got it!'

Two tall figures were silhouetted against the starry sky on the other side of the hilltop.

'Amos!' said Mr Weasley, smiling as he strode over to the man who had shouted. The rest of them followed.

Mr Weasley was shaking hands with a ruddy-faced wizard with a scrubby brown beard, who was holding a mouldy-looking old boot in his other hand.

'This is Amos Diggory, everyone,' said Mr Weasley. 'Works for the Department for the Regulation and Control of Magical Creatures. And I think you know his son, Cedric?'

Cedric Diggory was an extremely handsome boy of around seventeen. He was captain and Seeker of the Hufflepuff house Quidditch team at Hogwarts.

'Hi,' said Cedric, looking around at them all.

## 第6章 门钥匙

"啊，五花八门，什么样的都有，"韦斯莱先生说，"当然，都是看上去不起眼的东西，这样麻瓜就不会把它们捡起来摆弄……他们会以为这是别人胡乱丢弃的……"

他们步履艰难地顺着黑暗潮湿的小路，朝村庄的方向走去，四下里一片寂静，只听得见自己的脚步声。穿过村庄时，天色慢慢地亮了一些，原先的漆黑一片逐渐变成了深蓝色。哈利的手脚都冻僵了。韦斯莱先生不停地看表。

他们开始爬白鼬山了，脚下不时被隐蔽的兔子洞绊一下，或者踩在黑漆漆、厚墩墩的草团上打滑，根本匀不出气儿来说话。哈利每喘一口气，都觉得胸口一阵刺痛，双腿也渐渐挪不开步子了，就在这时，他发现终于踏在了平地上。

"哟，"韦斯莱先生摘下眼镜，用身上的球衣擦着，气喘吁吁地说，"不错，我们到得很准时——还有十分钟……"

赫敏最后一个登上山顶，她的一只手紧紧揪住衣襟。

"现在我们只需要找到门钥匙，"韦斯莱先生说着，戴上眼镜，眯着眼睛在地上寻视，"不会很大……快找一找……"

大家散开，分头寻找。可是，他们刚找了两三分钟，就有一个喊声划破了宁静的夜空。

"在这儿，亚瑟！过来，儿子，我们找到了！"

在山顶的另一边，星光闪烁的夜空衬托着两个高高的身影。

"阿莫斯！"韦斯莱先生说，笑着大步走向那个喊他的男人。其他人跟了上去。

韦斯莱先生和一个长着棕色短胡子的红脸庞巫师握了握手，那人的另一只手里拿着个东西，像是一只发了霉的旧靴子。

"我给大家介绍一下，这是阿莫斯·迪戈里。"韦斯莱先生说，"他在魔法生物管理控制司工作。这是他的儿子塞德里克，我想你们都认识吧？"

塞德里克·迪戈里大约十七岁，是一个长得特别帅的男孩。在霍格沃茨，他是赫奇帕奇学院魁地奇球队的队长兼找球手。

"嗨，你们好。"塞德里克说，转头望着大家。

## CHAPTER SIX · The Portkey

Everybody said 'Hi' back except Fred and George, who merely nodded. They had never quite forgiven Cedric for beating their team, Gryffindor, in the first Quidditch match of the previous year.

'Long walk, Arthur?' Cedric's father asked.

'Not too bad,' said Mr Weasley. 'We live just on the other side of the village there. You?'

'Had to get up at two, didn't we, Ced? I tell you, I'll be glad when he's got his Apparition test. Still ... not complaining ... Quidditch World Cup, wouldn't miss it for a sackful of Galleons – and the tickets cost about that. Mind you, looks like I got off easy ...' Amos Diggory peered good-naturedly around at the three Weasley boys, Harry, Hermione and Ginny. 'All these yours, Arthur?'

'Oh, no, only the redheads,' said Mr Weasley, pointing out his children. 'This is Hermione, friend of Ron's – and Harry, another friend –'

'Merlin's beard,' said Amos Diggory, his eyes widening. 'Harry? Harry *Potter?*'

'Er – yeah,' said Harry.

Harry was used to people looking curiously at him when they met him, used to the way their eyes moved at once to the lightning scar on his forehead, but it always made him feel uncomfortable.

'Ced's talked about you, of course,' said Amos Diggory. 'Told us all about playing against you last year ... I said to him, I said – Ced, that'll be something to tell your grandchildren, that will ... *you beat Harry Potter!*'

Harry couldn't think of any reply to this, so he remained silent. Fred and George were both scowling again. Cedric looked slightly embarrassed.

'Harry fell off his broom, Dad,' he muttered. 'I told you ... it was an accident ...'

'Yes, but *you* didn't fall off, did you?' roared Amos genially, slapping his son on his back. 'Always modest, our Ced, always the gentleman ... but the best man won, I'm sure Harry'd say the same, wouldn't you, eh? One falls off his broom, one stays on, you don't need to be a genius to tell which one's the better flier!'

'Must be nearly time,' said Mr Weasley quickly, pulling out his watch again. 'Do you know whether we're waiting for any more, Amos?'

## 第6章 门钥匙

每个人都应了声"嗨",但弗雷德和乔治没有吭气,只是点了点头。去年,塞德里克在第一场魁地奇比赛中打败了他们格兰芬多队,这对双胞胎到现在都没有完全原谅他。

"走过来很远吧,亚瑟?"塞德里克的父亲问道。

"还好,"韦斯莱先生说,"我们就住在村庄的那一边。你们呢?"

"两点钟就起床了,是不是,塞德?不瞒你说,我真愿意他早点通过幻影显形考试。不过……没什么可抱怨的……魁地奇世界杯嘛,绝不能错过,哪怕要付出一口袋金加隆——实际上,买票也确实花了那么多钱呢。不过我总算对付下来了,还不算太难……"阿莫斯·迪戈里和蔼地望着周围的韦斯莱家三兄弟、哈利、赫敏和金妮,"亚瑟,这些都是你的孩子?"

"哦,不,红头发的才是。"韦斯莱先生把自己的孩子一一指出,"这是赫敏,罗恩的朋友——这是哈利,也是罗恩的朋友——"

"梅林的胡子啊,"阿莫斯·迪戈里说,眼睛睁得溜圆,"哈利?哈利·波特?"

"嗯——是的。"哈利说。

哈利已经习惯了人们初次和他见面时总是好奇地盯着他,也习惯了他们立刻把目光投向他额头上的伤疤,但这总是让他感到很不自在。

"当然啦,塞德谈到过你。"阿莫斯·迪戈里说,"他告诉了我们去年他和你比赛的事……我对他说,我说——塞德,这件事等你老了可以讲给你的孙子们听,很了不起……你打败了哈利·波特!"

哈利不知道该怎样回答,就什么也没说。弗雷德和乔治又都皱起了眉头。塞德里克显得有点儿尴尬。

"哈利从扫帚上掉下来了,爸爸,"他小声地嘟哝说,"我告诉过你的……是一次意外事故……"

"是啊,可是你没有掉下来,对不对?"阿莫斯亲切地大声说,一边拍了拍儿子的后背,"我们的塞德总是这么谦虚,总是一副绅士风度……但赢的人总是最棒的,我敢肯定哈利也会这么说的,是吗?一个从扫帚上掉了下来,另一个稳稳地待在上面,你不需要具备天才的脑瓜,就能说出谁是更出色的球员!"

"时间差不多快到了,"韦斯莱先生赶紧说道,把怀表又掏出来看了看,"你知道我们还要等什么人吗,阿莫斯?"

## CHAPTER SIX  The Portkey

'No, the Lovegoods have been there for a week already and the Fawcetts couldn't get tickets,' said Mr Diggory. 'There aren't any more of us in this area, are there?'

'Not that I know of,' said Mr Weasley. 'Yes, it's a minute off … we'd better get ready …'

He looked around at Harry and Hermione. 'You just need to touch the Portkey, that's all, a finger will do –'

With difficulty, owing to the bulky backpacks, the nine of them crowded around the old boot held out by Amos Diggory.

They all stood there, in a tight circle, as a chill breeze swept over the hilltop. Nobody spoke. It suddenly occurred to Harry how odd this would look if a Muggle were to walk up here now … nine people, two grown men, clutching this manky old boot in the semi-darkness, waiting …

'Three …' muttered Mr Weasley, one eye still on his watch, 'two … one …'

It happened immediately: Harry felt as though a hook just behind his navel had been suddenly jerked irresistibly forwards. His feet had left the ground; he could feel Ron and Hermione on either side of him, their shoulders banging into his; they were all speeding forwards in a howl of wind and swirling colour; his forefinger was stuck to the boot as though it was pulling him magnetically onwards and then –

His feet slammed into the ground; Ron staggered into him and he fell over; the Portkey hit the ground near his head with a heavy thud.

Harry looked up. Mr Weasley, Mr Diggory and Cedric were still standing, though looking very windswept; everybody else was on the ground.

'Seven past five from Stoatshead Hill,' said a voice.

## 第6章 门钥匙

"不用了,洛夫古德一家一星期前就到了那里,福西特一家没有弄到票。"迪戈里先生说,"这片地区没有别人了,是吧?"

"据我所知是没有了。"韦斯莱先生说,"好了,还有一分钟……我们应该各就各位了……"

他转脸看着哈利和赫敏。"你们只要碰到门钥匙,就这样,伸出一根手指就行……"

由于大家都背着鼓鼓囊囊的大背包,九个人好不容易才围拢在阿莫斯·迪戈里拿着的那只旧靴子周围。

他们站在那里,紧紧地围成一圈,一阵清冷的微风吹过山顶,没有人说话。哈利突然想到,如果这时恰巧有个麻瓜从这里走过,这情景该是多么怪异……九个人,其中两个还是大人,在昏暗的光线中抓着这只破破烂烂的旧靴子,静静地等待着……

"三……"韦斯莱先生一只眼睛盯着怀表,低声念道,"二……一……"

说时迟那时快,哈利觉得,似乎有一个钩子在他肚脐眼后面以无法抵挡的势头猛地向前一钩,他便双脚离地,飞起来了。他可以感觉到罗恩和赫敏在他两边,肩膀与他的撞到一起。他们一阵风似的向前疾飞,眼前什么也看不清。哈利的食指紧紧粘在靴子上,好像那靴子具有一股磁力似的,把他拉过去,拉过去,然后——

他的双脚重重地落到地上,罗恩踉踉跄跄地撞在他身上,他摔倒了。啪的一声,门钥匙落到他脑袋边的地上。

哈利抬起头来,只有韦斯莱先生、迪戈里先生和塞德里克还站着,但也是一副被风吹得披头散发、歪歪斜斜的样子,其他人都跌在了地上。

"五点零七分,来自白鼬山。"只听一个声音说道。

## CHAPTER SEVEN

# Bagman and Crouch

Harry disentangled himself from Ron and got to his feet. They had arrived on what appeared to be a deserted stretch of misty moor. In front of them was a pair of tired and grumpy-looking wizards, one of whom was holding a large gold watch, the other a thick roll of parchment and a quill. Both were dressed as Muggles, though very inexpertly; the man with the watch wore a tweed suit with thigh-length galoshes; his colleague, a kilt and a poncho.

'Morning, Basil,' said Mr Weasley, picking up the boot and handing it to the kilted wizard, who threw it into a large box of used Portkeys beside him; Harry could see an old newspaper, an empty drinks can and a punctured football.

'Hello there, Arthur,' said Basil wearily. 'Not on duty, eh? It's all right for some … we've been here all night … you'd better get out of the way, we've got a big party coming in from the Black Forest at five fifteen. Hang on, I'll find your campsite … Weasley … Weasley …' He consulted his parchment list. 'About a quarter of a mile's walk over there, first field you come to. Site manager's called Mr Roberts. Diggory … second field … ask for Mr Payne.'

'Thanks, Basil,' said Mr Weasley, and he beckoned everyone to follow him.

They set off across the deserted moor, unable to make out much through the mist. After about twenty minutes, a small stone cottage next to a gate swam into view. Beyond it, Harry could just make out the ghostly shapes of hundreds and hundreds of tents, rising up the gentle slope of a large field towards a dark wood on the horizon. They said goodbye to the Diggorys, and approached the cottage door.

## 第7章

## 巴格曼和克劳奇

哈利挣扎着摆脱罗恩的纠缠，站了起来。他们来到的这个地方很像一大片荒凉的、雾气弥蒙的沼泽地。在他们前面，站着两个疲惫不堪、阴沉着脸的巫师，其中一个拿着一块大金表，另一个拿着一卷厚厚的羊皮纸和一支羽毛笔。两人都打扮成了麻瓜的样子，可是太不在行了：拿金表的男人上身是一件粗花呢西服，下面却穿着一双长及大腿的长筒橡皮套鞋；他的同事穿着苏格兰高地男人穿的那种褶裥短裙和一件南美披风。

"早上好，巴兹尔。"韦斯莱说道，捡起那只靴子，递给穿褶裥短裙的巫师。那人把它扔进身边的一只大箱子，里面都是用过的门钥匙。哈利可以看见一张旧报纸、一个空易拉罐和一只千疮百孔的足球。

"你好，亚瑟，"巴兹尔疲倦地说，"没有当班，嗯？有些人运气真好……我们整晚上都守在这里……你们最好让开，五点一刻有一大群人要从黑森林来。等一下，我找一找你们的营地在哪儿……韦斯莱……韦斯莱……"他在羊皮纸名单上寻找着，"走过去大约四分之一英里，前面第一片场地就是。营地管理员是罗伯茨先生。迪戈里……你们在第二片场地……找佩恩先生。"

"谢谢，巴兹尔。"韦斯莱先生说，他招呼大家跟着他走。

他们穿过荒无人烟的沼泽地，浓雾中几乎什么也看不见。走了大约二十分钟，渐渐地眼前出现了一扇门，然后是一座小石屋。哈利勉强可以分辨出石屋后面有成百上千顶奇形怪状的帐篷，它们顺着大片场地的缓坡往上，场地一直伸向地平线上一片黑乎乎的树林。他们告别了迪戈里父子，朝石屋的门走去。

## CHAPTER SEVEN  Bagman and Crouch

A man was standing in the doorway, looking out at the tents. Harry knew at a glance that this was the only real Muggle for several acres. When he heard their footsteps, he turned his head to look at them.

'Morning!' said Mr Weasley brightly.

'Morning,' said the Muggle.

'Would you be Mr Roberts?'

'Aye, I would,' said Mr Roberts. 'And who're you?'

'Weasley – two tents, booked a couple of days ago?'

'Aye,' said Mr Roberts, consulting a list tacked to the door. 'You've got a space up by the wood there. Just the one night?'

'That's it,' said Mr Weasley.

'You'll be paying now, then?' said Mr Roberts.

'Ah – right – certainly –' said Mr Weasley. He retreated a short distance from the cottage and beckoned Harry towards him. 'Help me, Harry,' he muttered, pulling a roll of Muggle money from his pocket and starting to peel the notes apart. 'This one's a – a – a ten? Ah yes, I see the little number on it now … so this is a five?'

'A twenty,' Harry corrected him in an undertone, uncomfortably aware of Mr Roberts trying to catch every word.

'Ah yes, so it is … I don't know, these little bits of paper …'

'You foreign?' said Mr Roberts, as Mr Weasley returned with the correct notes.

'Foreign?' repeated Mr Weasley, puzzled.

'You're not the first one who's had trouble with money,' said Mr Roberts, scrutinising Mr Weasley closely. 'I had two try and pay me with great gold coins the size of hubcaps ten minutes ago.'

'Did you really?' said Mr Weasley nervously.

Mr Roberts rummaged around in a tin for some change.

'Never been this crowded,' he said suddenly, looking out over the misty field again. 'Hundreds of pre-bookings. People usually just turn up …'

'Is that right?' said Mr Weasley, his hand held out for his change, but Mr Roberts didn't give it to him.

'Aye,' he said thoughtfully. 'People from all over. Loads of foreigners. And

## 第7章 巴格曼和克劳奇

门口站着一个男人,正在眺望那些帐篷。哈利一眼就看出他是这一大片地方唯一一个真正的麻瓜。那人一听见他们的脚步声,就转过头来看着他们。

"早上好!"韦斯莱先生精神饱满地说。

"早上好!"麻瓜说。

"你就是罗伯茨先生吗?"

"啊,正是。"罗伯茨先生说,"你是谁?"

"韦斯莱——两顶帐篷,是两天前预订的,有吗?"

"有,"罗伯茨先生说,看了看钉在门上的一张表,"你们在那儿的树林边有一块地方。只住一个晚上吗?"

"是的。"韦斯莱先生说。

"那么,现在就付钱,可以吗?"罗伯茨先生说。

"啊——好的——没问题——"韦斯莱先生说。他退后几步,离开小石屋,示意哈利到他跟前去。"帮帮我,哈利。"他低声说,从口袋里抽出一卷麻瓜钞票,把它们一张张分开,"这张是——嗯——嗯——十镑?啊,对了,我看见了上面印的小数字……那么这张是五镑?"

"是二十镑。"哈利压低声音纠正他,同时不安地意识到罗伯茨先生正在努力地想听清他们说的每一个字。

"啊,原来是这样……我不知道,这些小纸片……"

"你是外国人?"当韦斯莱先生拿着几张正确的钞票回去时,罗伯茨先生问道。

"外国人?"韦斯莱先生不解地重复了一句。

"弄不清钱数的可不止你一个人,"罗伯茨先生说,仔细地打量着韦斯莱先生,"就在十分钟前,有两个人要付给我毂盖那么大的金币呢。"

"真的吗?"韦斯莱先生不安地说。

罗伯茨先生在一个铁罐里摸索着零钱。

"从来没有这么多人,"他突然说道,目光又一次眺望着雾气弥漫的场地,"几百个人预订了帐篷。人们通常是直接上门的……"

"是这样的吗?"韦斯莱先生问,伸手去接零钱,可是罗伯茨先生没有给他。

"是啊,"罗伯茨先生若有所思地说,"什么地方来的人都有。数不

not just foreigners. Weirdos, you know? There's a bloke walking round in a kilt and a poncho.'

'Shouldn't he?' said Mr Weasley anxiously.

'It's like some sort of ... I dunno ... like some sort of rally,' said Mr Roberts. 'They all seem to know each other. Like a big party.'

At that moment, a wizard in plus-fours appeared out of thin air next to Mr Roberts's front door.

'*Obliviate!*' he said sharply, pointing his wand at Mr Roberts.

Instantly, Mr Roberts's eyes slid out of focus, his brows unknitted and a look of dreamy unconcern fell over his face. Harry recognised the symptoms of one who had just had his memory modified.

'A map of the campsite for you,' Mr Roberts said placidly to Mr Weasley. 'And your change.'

'Thanks very much,' said Mr Weasley.

The wizard in plus-fours accompanied them towards the gate to the campsite. He looked exhausted; his chin was blue with stubble and there were deep purple shadows under his eyes. Once out of earshot of Mr Roberts, he muttered to Mr Weasley, 'Been having a lot of trouble with him. Needs a Memory Charm ten times a day to keep him happy. And Ludo Bagman's not helping. Trotting around talking about Bludgers and Quaffles at the top of his voice, not a worry about anti-Muggle security. Blimey, I'll be glad when this is over. See you later, Arthur.'

He Disapparated.

'I thought Mr Bagman was Head of Magical games and Sports?' said Ginny, looking surprised. 'He should know better than to talk about Bludgers near Muggles, shouldn't he?'

'He should,' said Mr Weasley, smiling, and leading them through the gates into the campsite, 'but Ludo's always been a bit ... well ... *lax* about security. You couldn't wish for a more enthusiastic Head of the Sports Department, though. He played Quidditch for England himself, you know. And he was the best Beater the Wimbourne Wasps ever had.'

They trudged up the misty field between long rows of tents. Most looked almost ordinary; their owners had clearly tried to make them as Muggle-like as possible, but had slipped up by adding chimneys, or bell-pulls, or weather-

清的外国人。不仅仅是外国人，还有许多怪人，你知道吗？有个家伙还穿着一条苏格兰短裙和一件南美披风走来走去的。"

"不可以吗？"韦斯莱先生急切地问。

"那就像是……我也不知道……就像是某种交际活动。"罗伯茨先生说，"他们好像互相都认识。就像一个大聚会。"

就在这时，一个穿灯笼裤的巫师突然凭空出现在罗伯茨先生的石屋门边。

"一忘皆空！"他用魔杖指着罗伯茨先生，厉声说道。

顿时，罗伯茨先生的眼神就散了，眉头也松开了，脸上显出一副恍恍惚惚、对什么都漠不关心的神情。哈利看出，这正是一个人的记忆被改变时的模样。

"给你一张营地的平面图。"罗伯茨先生心平气和地对韦斯莱先生说，"还有找给你的零钱。"

"非常感谢。"韦斯莱先生说。

穿灯笼裤的巫师陪着他们一起朝营地的大门走去。他显得十分疲劳：下巴上胡子没刮，铁青一片，眼睛下面也有青紫色的阴影。当罗伯茨先生听不见他们说话时，那巫师小声对韦斯莱先生嘟哝道："他给我添了不少麻烦。为了让他保持心情愉快，每天要念十几遍遗忘咒。卢多·巴格曼只会帮倒忙。到处走来走去，大着嗓门谈论游走球和鬼飞球，完全不顾要提防麻瓜，确保安全。天哪，我真巴不得这一切早点结束。待会儿见，亚瑟。"

他说完便幻影移形了。

"我原本以为，巴格曼先生是魔法体育运动司的司长，"金妮似乎有些吃惊，说道，"应该知道不能在麻瓜周围谈论游走球的，是吗？"

"是的，"韦斯莱先生笑着说，领着他们穿过大门，走进营地，"卢多一向对安全的问题……嗯……有些马虎。但是，你找不出一个比他更富有激情的人来担任体育运动司的领导了。你知道，他原来代表英格兰打过魁地奇球。他是温布恩黄蜂队有史以来最优秀的击球手。"

他们费力地走在薄雾笼罩的场地上，从两排长长的帐篷间穿过。大多数帐篷看上去没什么特殊，显然，它们的主人费了心思，尽可能把

## CHAPTER SEVEN  Bagman and Crouch

vanes. However, here and there was a tent so obviously magical that Harry could hardly be surprised that Mr Roberts was getting suspicious. Halfway up the field stood an extravagant confection of striped silk like a miniature palace, with several live peacocks tethered at the entrance. A little further on they passed a tent that had three floors and several turrets; and a short way beyond that was a tent which had a front garden attached, complete with birdbath, sundial and fountain.

'Always the same,' said Mr Weasley, smiling, 'we can't resist showing off when we get together. Ah, here we are, look, this is us.'

They had reached the very edge of the wood at the top of the field, and here was an empty space, with a small sign hammered into the ground that read *Weezly*.

'Couldn't have a better spot!' said Mr Weasley happily. 'The pitch is just on the other side of the wood there, we're as close as we could be.' He hoisted his backpack from his shoulders. 'Right,' he said excitedly, 'no magic allowed, strictly speaking, not when we're out in these numbers on Muggle land. We'll be putting these tents up by hand! Shouldn't be too difficult … Muggles do it all the time … here, Harry, where do you reckon we should start?'

Harry had never been camping in his life; the Dursleys had never taken him on any kind of holiday, preferring to leave him with Mrs Figg, an old neighbour. However, he and Hermione worked out where most of the poles and pegs should go, and though Mr Weasley was more of a hindrance than a help, because he got thoroughly overexcited when it came to using the mallet, they finally managed to erect a pair of shabby two-man tents.

All of them stood back to admire their handiwork. Nobody looking at these tents would guess they belonged to wizards, Harry thought, but the trouble was that once Bill, Charlie and Percy arrived, they would be a party of ten. Hermione seemed to have spotted this problem, too; she gave Harry a quizzical look as Mr Weasley dropped to his hands and knees and entered the first tent.

'We'll be a bit cramped,' he called, 'but I think we'll all squeeze in. Come and have a look.'

Harry bent down, ducked under the tent flap, and felt his jaw drop. He had walked into what looked like an old-fashioned, three-roomed flat, complete with bathroom and kitchen. Oddly enough, it was furnished in

## 第7章 巴格曼和克劳奇

它们弄得和麻瓜的帐篷一样，可是都一不小心做过了头，画蛇添足地加上了烟囱、拉铃绳或风向标，弄得不伦不类。不过，偶尔也有那么几顶帐篷，一看就知道施了魔法，哈利心想，怪不得罗伯茨先生会怀疑呢。在场地中央，有一顶帐篷特别显眼。它十分铺张地用了大量的条纹绸，简直像座小小的宫殿，入口处还拴着几只活孔雀。再前面一点，又看见一顶帐篷搭成三层高楼的形状，旁边还有几个角楼。再往那边，还有一顶帐篷的门前带有一个花园，里面鸟澡盆、日晷、喷泉等样样俱全。

"总是这样，"韦斯莱先生笑着说，"大家聚到一起时，就忍不住想炫耀一番。啊，到了，看，这就是我们的。"

他们来到了场地尽头的树林边，这里有一片空地，地上插着一个小小的牌子，上面写着：韦兹利。

"这地方再好不过了！"韦斯莱先生高兴地说，"球场就在树林的那一边，近得没法再近了。"他把背包从肩头褪了下来，"好啦，"他兴奋地说，"严格地说，不许使用魔法，因为我们这么多人来到了麻瓜的地盘上。我们要用自己的手把帐篷搭起来！应该不会太难……麻瓜们都是这样做的……对了，哈利，你认为我们应该从哪儿开始呢？"

哈利以前没有野营过。节假日的时候，德思礼一家从来不带他出去，他们情愿把他留给邻居老太太费格太太。不过，他和赫敏还是基本上弄清了那些支杆和螺钉应该在什么位置，而韦斯莱先生在旁边总是帮倒忙，因为每当要用到大头锤时，他都激动得要命。最后，他们总算支起了两顶歪歪斜斜的双人帐篷。

他们都退后几步，欣赏自己亲手劳动的成果。哈利心想，谁看了这些帐篷都不会猜到它们是巫师搭成的，然而问题是，一旦比尔、查理和珀西也来了，就有十个人呢。赫敏似乎也发现了这个问题，用疑惑的目光看了看哈利。这时，韦斯莱先生四肢着地，钻进了第一顶帐篷。

"可能有点儿挤，"他喊道，"但我想大家都能挤进来。快来看看吧。"

哈利弯下腰，从帐篷门帘下钻了进去，顿时惊讶得下巴都要掉了。他走进了一套老式的三居室，还有浴室和厨房。真奇怪，房间里的布置和费格太太家的风格完全一样：不般配的椅子上铺着钩针编织的罩

## CHAPTER SEVEN  Bagman and Crouch

exactly the same sort of style as Mrs Figg's; there were crocheted covers on the mismatched chairs, and a strong smell of cats.

'Well, it's not for long,' said Mr Weasley, mopping his bald patch with a handkerchief and peering in at the four bunk beds that stood in the bedroom. 'I borrowed this from Perkins at the office. Doesn't camp much any more, poor fellow, he's got lumbago.'

He picked up the dusty kettle and peered inside it. 'We'll need water …'

'There's a tap marked on this map the Muggle gave us,' said Ron, who had followed Harry inside the tent, and seemed completely unimpressed by its extraordinary inner proportions. 'It's on the other side of the field.'

'Well, why don't you, Harry and Hermione go and get us some water, then –' Mr Weasley handed over the kettle and a couple of saucepans, '– and the rest of us will get some wood for a fire.'

'But we've got an oven,' said Ron, 'why can't we just –?'

'Ron, anti-Muggle security!' said Mr Weasley, his face shining with anticipation. 'When real Muggles camp, they cook on fires outdoors, I've seen them at it!'

After a quick tour of the girls' tent, which was slightly smaller than the boys', though without the smell of cats, Harry, Ron and Hermione set off across the campsite with the kettle and saucepans.

Now, with the sun newly risen and the mist lifting, they could see the city of tents that stretched in every direction. They made their way slowly through the rows, staring eagerly around. It was only just dawning on Harry how many witches and wizards there must be in the world; he had never really thought much about those in other countries.

Their fellow campers were starting to wake up. First to stir were the families with small children; Harry had never seen witches and wizards this young before. A tiny boy no older than two was crouched outside a large pyramid-shaped tent, holding a wand and poking happily at a slug in the grass, which was swelling slowly to the size of a salami. As they drew level with him, his mother came hurrying out of the tent.

'*How* many times, Kevin? You don't – touch – Daddy's – *wand* – yeuch!'

She had trodden on the giant slug, which burst. Her scolding carried after them on the still air, mingling with the little boy's yells – 'You bust slug! You bust slug!'

## 第7章 巴格曼和克劳奇

子,空气里有一股刺鼻的猫味儿。

"噢,这只是暂时的。"韦斯莱先生用手帕擦着他的秃顶,探头望着卧室里的四张双层床,"我这是从办公室的珀金斯那里借来的。可怜的家伙,他患了腰痛病,再也不能野营了。"

韦斯莱先生拿起沾满灰尘的水壶,朝里面望了一下:"我们需要一些水……"

"在那个麻瓜给我们的地图上,标着一个水龙头,"罗恩说,他也跟在哈利后面钻进了帐篷,似乎对帐篷内部不寻常的空间熟视无睹,"在场地的另一边。"

"好吧,那么你就和哈利、赫敏去给我们打点水来,然后——"韦斯莱先生递过他们带来的那个水壶和两口炖锅,"——我们剩下来的人去捡点柴火,准备生火,好吗?"

"可是我们有炉子啊,"罗恩说,"为什么不能就——"

"罗恩,别忘了防备麻瓜的安全条例!"韦斯莱先生说,因为跃跃欲试而满脸兴奋,"真正麻瓜野营的时候,都是在户外生火的。我见过。"

他们很快地参观了一下姑娘们的帐篷,发现只比男孩的略小一点,不过没有猫味儿。然后,哈利、罗恩和赫敏就提着水壶和炖锅,出发穿过营地。

这时,太阳刚刚升起,薄雾渐渐散去,四面八方都是帐篷,一眼望不到头。他们慢慢地在帐篷间穿行,兴趣盎然地东张西望。哈利这才明白,原来世界上有这么多巫师,他以前从没认真想过其他国家的巫师。

场地上的野营者们逐渐醒过来了。最先起床的是那些有小孩的家庭。哈利还没见过这么小的巫师呢。只见一个两岁左右的小男孩蹲在一顶金字塔形的大帐篷外面,手里拿着魔杖,开心地捅着草地上的一条鼻涕虫,鼻涕虫慢慢地胀成了一根香肠那么大。他们走到男孩面前时,男孩的母亲匆匆地从帐篷里出来了。

"对你说过多少次了,凯文?你不许——再碰——你爸的——魔杖——哎哟!"

她一脚踩中了那条肥大的鼻涕虫,鼻涕虫啪的一声爆炸了。他们走了很远,还听见寂静的空气中传来她的叫嚷声,其中还夹杂着小男孩的哭喊——"你把虫虫踩爆了!你把虫虫踩爆了!"

## CHAPTER SEVEN  Bagman and Crouch

A short way further on, they saw two little witches, barely older than Kevin, who were riding toy broomsticks which rose only high enough for the girls' toes to skim the dewy grass. A Ministry wizard had already spotted them; as he hurried past Harry, Ron and Hermione, he muttered distractedly, 'In broad daylight! Parents having a lie-in, I suppose –'

Here and there adult wizards and witches were emerging from their tents and starting to cook breakfast. Some, with furtive looks around them, conjured fires with their wands; others were striking matches with dubious looks on their faces, as though sure this couldn't work. Three African wizards sat in serious conversation, all of them wearing long white robes and roasting what looked like a rabbit on a bright purple fire, while a group of middle-aged American witches sat gossiping happily beneath a spangled banner stretched between their tents which read: *The Salem Witches' Institute.* Harry caught snatches of conversation in strange languages from the inside of tents they passed, and though he couldn't understand a single word, the tone of every single voice was excited.

'Er – is it my eyes, or has everything gone green?' said Ron.

It wasn't just Ron's eyes. They had walked into a patch of tents that were all covered with a thick growth of shamrocks, so that it looked as though small, oddly shaped hillocks had sprouted out of the earth. Grinning faces could be seen under those which had their flaps open. Then, from behind them, they heard their names.

'Harry! Ron! Hermione!'

It was Seamus Finnigan, their fellow Gryffindor fourth-year. He was sitting in front of his own shamrock-covered tent, with a sandy-haired woman who had to be his mother, and his best friend, Dean Thomas, also of Gryffindor.

'Like the decorations?' said Seamus, grinning, when Harry, Ron and Hermione had gone over to say hello. 'The Ministry's not too happy.'

'Ah, why shouldn't we show our colours?' said Mrs Finnigan. 'You should see what the Bulgarians have got dangling all over *their* tents. You'll be supporting Ireland, of course?' she added, eyeing Harry, Ron and Hermione beadily.

When they had assured her that they were indeed supporting Ireland, they set off again, though, as Ron said, 'Like we'd say anything else surrounded by that lot.'

## 第7章 巴格曼和克劳奇

又走了一段路,他们看见两个小女巫师,年纪和凯文差不多大,骑在两把玩具飞天扫帚上,低低地飞着,脚轻轻掠过沾着露水的青草。一个在部里工作的巫师已经看见她们了,他匆匆走过哈利、罗恩和赫敏身旁,一边心烦地嘀咕着:"居然在大白天!父母大概睡懒觉呢……"

时不时地可以看见成年巫师从他们的帐篷里钻出来,开始做早饭。有的鬼鬼祟祟地张望一下,用魔杖把火点着;有的在擦火柴,脸上带着怀疑的表情,似乎认为这肯定不管用。三个非洲男巫师坐在那里严肃地谈论着什么,他们都穿着长长的白袍,在一堆紫色的旺火上烤着一只野兔似的东西。另外一群中年美国女巫师坐在那里谈笑风生,她们的帐篷之间高高挂着一条星条旗图案的横幅:塞勒姆女巫协会。哈利听见了经过的帐篷里传来只言片语的谈话声,说的都是奇怪的语言,他一个字也听不懂,但每个人说话的声音都很兴奋。

"呵——难道我的眼睛出了毛病,怎么一切都成了绿的?"罗恩说。

罗恩的眼睛没出毛病。他们刚刚走进的这片地方,所有的帐篷上都覆盖着厚厚的一层三叶草,看上去就像从地里冒出无数个奇形怪状的绿色小山丘。在门帘掀开的帐篷里,可以看见嬉笑的面孔。这时,他们听见身后有人喊他们的名字。

"哈利!罗恩!赫敏!"

原来是西莫·斐尼甘,他们在格兰芬多学院四年级的同学。他坐在自家三叶草覆盖的帐篷前,旁边有一个淡黄色头发的女人,肯定是他的母亲,还有他最好的朋友迪安·托马斯,也是格兰芬多学院的学生。

"喜欢这些装饰吗?"西莫笑嘻嘻地问,"部里可不太高兴。"

"咳,为什么就不能展示一下我们的颜色?"斐尼甘夫人说,"你们应该去看看,保加利亚人在他们的帐篷上都挂了什么。你们当然是支持爱尔兰队的,是吗?"她问,眼睛亮晶晶地盯着哈利、罗恩和赫敏。

他们向她保证确实支持爱尔兰队,然后他们又出发了。罗恩嘀咕道:"在那群人中间,我们还能说别的吗?"

## CHAPTER SEVEN  Bagman and Crouch

'I wonder what the Bulgarians have got dangling all over their tents?' said Hermione.

'Let's go and have a look,' said Harry, pointing to a large patch of tents upfield, where the Bulgarian flag, red, green and white, was fluttering in the breeze.

The tents here had not been bedecked with plant life, but each and every one of them had the same poster attached to it, a poster of a very surly face with heavy black eyebrows. The picture was of course moving, but all it did was blink and scowl.

'Krum,' said Ron quietly.

'What?' said Hermione.

'Krum!' said Ron. 'Viktor Krum, the Bulgarian Seeker!'

'He looks really grumpy,' said Hermione, looking around at the many Krums blinking and scowling at them.

'"*Really grumpy*"?' Ron raised his eyes to the heavens. 'Who cares what he looks like? He's unbelievable. He's really young, too. Only just eighteen or something. He's a *genius*, you wait until tonight, you'll see.'

There was already a small queue for the tap in the corner of the field. Harry, Ron and Hermione joined it, right behind a pair of men who were having a heated argument. One of them was a very old wizard who was wearing a long flowery nightgown. The other was clearly a Ministry wizard; he was holding out a pair of pinstriped trousers and almost crying with exasperation.

'Just put them on, Archie, there's a good chap, you can't walk around like that, the Muggle on the gate's already getting suspicious –'

'I bought this in a Muggle shop,' said the old wizard stubbornly. 'Muggles wear them.'

'Muggle *women* wear them, Archie, not the men, they wear *these*,' said the Ministry wizard, and he brandished the pinstriped trousers.

'I'm not putting them on,' said old Archie in indignation. 'I like a healthy breeze round my privates, thanks.'

Hermione was overcome with such a strong fit of the giggles at this point that she had to duck out of the queue, and only returned when Archie had collected his water and moved away again.

Walking more slowly now, because of the weight of the water, they made their way back through the campsite. Here and there they saw more

## 第7章 巴格曼和克劳奇

"我真想知道保加利亚人在他们的帐篷上挂满了什么？"赫敏说。

"我们过去看看吧，"哈利说，他指着前面的一大片帐篷，那里有保加利亚的旗子——白、绿、红相间——在微风中飘扬。

这里的帐篷没有覆盖什么植物，但每顶帐篷上都贴着相同的招贴画，上面是一张非常阴沉的脸，眉毛粗黑浓密。当然啦，图画是活动的，但那张脸除了眨眼就是皱眉。

"克鲁姆。"罗恩小声说。

"什么？"赫敏问。

"克鲁姆！"罗恩说，"威克多尔·克鲁姆，保加利亚的找球手！"

"他的样子太阴沉了。"赫敏说，看着周围无数个克鲁姆朝他们眨眼、皱眉。

"'太阴沉了'？"罗恩把眼睛往上一翻，"谁在乎他的模样？他厉害极了！而且还特别年轻，只有十八岁左右。他是个天才，今晚你就会看到的。"

在场地一角的水龙头旁，已经排起了一个小队。哈利、罗恩和赫敏也排了进去，站在他们前面的两个男人正在激烈地争论着什么。其中一个年纪已经很老了，穿着一件长长的印花睡袍。另一个显然是在部里工作的巫师，手里举着一条细条纹裤子，气恼得简直要哭了。

"你就行行好，把它穿上吧，阿尔奇。你不能穿着这样的衣服走来走去，大门口的那个麻瓜已经开始怀疑了——"

"我这条裤子是在一家麻瓜商店里买的，"老巫师固执地说，"麻瓜们也穿的。"

"麻瓜女人才穿它，阿尔奇，男人不穿，男人穿这个。"在部里工作的巫师说，一边挥舞着那条细条纹裤子。

"我才不穿呢，"老阿尔奇气愤地说，"我愿意让有益健康的微风吹吹我的屁股，谢谢你。"

赫敏听了这话，真想咯咯大笑。她实在忍不住了，一弯腰从队伍里跑开了，一直等阿尔奇接满水离开之后，她才回来。

他们穿过营地返回，因为提着水，走得慢多了。所到之处，总能看见一些熟悉的面孔：霍格沃茨的同学及他们的家人。奥利弗·伍德

## CHAPTER SEVEN   Bagman and Crouch

familiar faces: other Hogwarts students with their families. Oliver Wood, the old captain of Harry's house Quidditch team, who had just left Hogwarts, dragged Harry over to his parents' tent to introduce him, and told him excitedly that he had just been signed to the Puddlemere United reserve team. Next they were hailed by Ernie Macmillan, a Hufflepuff fourth-year, and a little further on they saw Cho Chang, a very pretty girl who played Seeker on the Ravenclaw team. She waved and smiled at Harry, who slopped quite a lot of water down his front as he waved back. More to stop Ron smirking than anything, Harry hurriedly pointed out a large group of teenagers whom he had never seen before.

'Who d'you reckon they are?' he said. 'They don't go to Hogwarts, do they?'

''Spect they go to some foreign school,' said Ron. 'I know there are others, never met anyone who went to one though. Bill had a pen-friend at a school in Brazil ... this was years and years ago ... and he wanted to go on an exchange trip but Mum and Dad couldn't afford it. His pen-friend got all offended when he said he wasn't going and sent him a cursed hat. It made his ears shrivel up.'

Harry laughed, but didn't voice the amazement he felt at hearing about other wizarding schools. He supposed, now he saw representatives of so many nationalities in the campsite, that he had been stupid never to realise that Hogwarts couldn't be the only one. He glanced at Hermione, who looked utterly unsurprised by the information. No doubt she had run across the news about other wizarding schools in some book or other.

'You've been ages,' said George, when they finally got back to the Weasleys' tents.

'Met a few people,' said Ron, setting the water down. 'You not got that fire started yet?'

'Dad's having fun with the matches,' said Fred.

Mr Weasley was having no success at all in lighting the fire, but it wasn't for lack of trying. Splintered matches littered the ground around him, but he looked as though he was having the time of his life.

'Oops!' he said, as he managed to light a match, and promptly dropped it in surprise.

'Come here, Mr Weasley,' said Hermione kindly, taking the box from him, and starting to show him how to do it properly.

## 第7章 巴格曼和克劳奇

是哈利所在的学院魁地奇队的前任队长,刚刚从霍格沃茨毕业。他把哈利拉到他父母的帐篷里,向他们作了介绍,并且兴奋地告诉哈利,他刚刚签约进入普德米尔联队的预备队。接着,是赫奇帕奇的四年级同学厄尼·麦克米兰向他们打招呼。又走了几步,他们看见了秋·张,一个非常漂亮的姑娘,在拉文克劳学院队当找球手。她朝哈利挥手微笑,哈利也忙不迭地向她挥手,慌乱中把许多水泼在了前襟上。哈利为了不让罗恩嘲笑自己,赶紧指着一大群他以前从没见过的十多岁的少年。

"你说他们是谁?"哈利问,"他们上的不是霍格沃茨学校,对吗?"

"大概上的是哪所外国学校吧。"罗恩说,"我知道还有别的学校。不过不认识那些学校的人。比尔以前有个笔友,在巴西的一所学校上学……那是很多很多年前的事了……比尔还想来个交换旅游,可是爸爸妈妈付不起那么多钱。他说他不能去,那个笔友气坏了,给他寄来一顶念过咒语的帽子,弄得他两只耳朵都皱了起来。"

哈利笑了起来,但他没有说他得知还有其他魔法学校时感到多么惊讶。他现在看到营地里有这么多民族的巫师代表,心想自己以前真傻,居然从来没有意识到霍格沃茨并不是唯一的魔法学校。他扫了一眼赫敏,发现她听了这个消息后无动于衷,她无疑早已从书本上或别的什么地方了解到了其他魔法学校的情况。

"你们怎么去了这么久。"他们终于回到韦斯莱家的帐篷时,乔治埋怨道。

"碰到了几个熟人。"罗恩说着,把水放下,"你们还没有把火生起来?"

"爸爸在玩火柴呢。"弗雷德说。

韦斯莱先生的生火工作一点也没有起色,这并不是因为他缺乏尝试。他周围的地上散落着许多折断的火柴,看他的样子,好像非常享受其中。

"哎哟!"他终于划着了一根火柴,惊叫一声,赶紧又扔掉了。

"是这样,韦斯莱先生。"赫敏温和地说,从他手里拿过火柴盒,向他示范应该怎样做。

## CHAPTER SEVEN  Bagman and Crouch

At last, they got the fire lit, though it was at least another hour before it was hot enough to cook anything. There was plenty to watch while they waited, however. Their tent seemed to be pitched right alongside a kind of thoroughfare to the pitch, and Ministry members kept hurrying up and down it, greeting Mr Weasley cordially as they passed. Mr Weasley kept up a running commentary, mainly for Harry and Hermione's benefit; his own children knew too much about the Ministry to be greatly interested.

'That was Cuthbert Mockridge, Head of the Goblin Liaison Office ... here comes Gilbert Wimple, he's with the Committee on Experimental Charms, he's had those horns for a while now ... Hello, Arnie ... Arnold Peasegood, he's an Obliviator – member of the Accidental Magic Reversal Squad, you know ... and that's Bode and Croaker ... they're Unspeakables ...'

'They're what?'

'From the Department of Mysteries, top-secret, no idea what they get up to ...'

At last, the fire was ready, and they had just started cooking eggs and sausages when Bill, Charlie and Percy came strolling out of the woods towards them.

'Just Apparated, Dad,' said Percy loudly. 'Ah, excellent, lunch!'

They were halfway through their plates of sausages and eggs when Mr Weasley jumped to his feet, waving and grinning at a man who was striding towards them. 'Aha!' he said. 'The man of the moment! Ludo!'

Ludo Bagman was easily the most noticeable person Harry had seen so far, even including old Archie in his flowered nightdress. He was wearing long Quidditch robes in thick horizontal strips of bright yellow and black. An enormous picture of a wasp was splashed across his chest. He had the look of a powerfully built man gone slightly to seed; the robes were stretched tightly across a large belly he surely had not had in the days when he had played Quidditch for England. His nose was squashed (probably broken by a stray Bludger, Harry thought), but his round blue eyes, short blond hair and rosy complexion made him look like a very overgrown schoolboy.

'Ahoy there!' Bagman called happily. He was walking as though he had springs attached to the balls of his feet, and was plainly in a state of wild excitement.

## 第7章　巴格曼和克劳奇

他们终于把火生起来了，可是至少又过了一小时，火才旺起来，可以煮饭。不过等待的时候并不枯燥，有许多东西可看呢。他们的帐篷似乎就在通向球场的一条大路旁，部里的官员们在路上来来往往地奔走，每次经过时都向韦斯莱先生热情地打招呼。韦斯莱先生不停地作着介绍，这主要是为了哈利和赫敏，他自己的孩子对部里的人太熟悉了，引不起丝毫的兴趣。

"那是卡思伯特·莫克里奇，妖精联络处的主任……过来的这位是吉尔伯特·温普尔，在实验咒语委员会工作，他头上的那些角已经生了有一段时间了……你好，阿尼……阿诺德·皮斯古德，是个记忆注销员——逆转偶发魔法事件小组的成员……那是博德和克罗克……他们是缄默人……"

"他们做什么？"

"是神秘事务司的人，绝密，不知道他们在做什么……"

终于，火烧旺了，他们刚开始煎鸡蛋、煮香肠，比尔、查理和珀西便从树林里大步向他们走来。

"刚刚幻影显形过来，爸爸。"珀西大声说道，"啊，太棒了，有好吃的！"

他们美美地吃着鸡蛋和香肠，刚吃了一半，韦斯莱先生突然跳了起来，笑着向一个大步走过来的男人挥手致意。"哈哈！"他说，"当前最重要的人物！卢多！"

卢多·巴格曼显然是哈利见过的最引人注目的人，就连穿着印花睡袍的老阿尔奇也比不上他。卢多穿着长长的魁地奇球袍，上面是黄黑相间的宽宽的横道，胸前泼墨般地印着一只巨大的黄蜂。看样子，他原先体格强健，但现在开始走下坡路了。长袍紧紧地绷在大肚子上，试想他当年代表英格兰打魁地奇比赛时，肚子肯定没有发福。他的鼻子扁塌塌的（哈利猜想大概是被一只游走球撞断了鼻梁），但那双圆溜溜的蓝眼睛、短短的金黄色头发，还有那红扑扑的脸色，都使他看上去很像一个块头过大的男学生。

"啊嗬！"巴格曼开心地喊道。他走路一蹦一跳，仿佛脚底下装了弹簧。他显然正处于极度兴奋的状态。

## CHAPTER SEVEN   Bagman and Crouch

'Arthur, old man,' he puffed, as he reached the campfire, 'what a day, eh? What a day! Could we have asked for more perfect weather? A cloudless night coming ... and hardly a hiccough in the arrangements ... not much for me to do!'

Behind him, a group of haggard-looking Ministry wizards rushed past, pointing at the distant evidence of some sort of a magical fire which was sending violet sparks twenty feet into the air.

Percy hurried forwards with his hand outstretched. Apparently his disapproval of the way Ludo Bagman ran his department did not prevent him wanting to make a good impression.

'Ah – yes,' said Mr Weasley, grinning, 'this is my son, Percy, he's just started at the Ministry – and this is Fred – no, George, sorry – *that's* Fred – Bill, Charlie, Ron – my daughter, Ginny – and Ron's friends, Hermione Granger and Harry Potter.'

Bagman did the smallest of double-takes when he heard Harry's name, and his eyes performed the familiar flick upwards to the scar on Harry's forehead.

'Everyone,' Mr Weasley continued, 'this is Ludo Bagman, you know who he is, it's thanks to him we've got such good tickets –'

Bagman beamed and waved his hand as if to say it had been nothing.

'Fancy a flutter on the match, Arthur?' he said eagerly, jingling what seemed to be a large amount of gold in the pockets of his yellow and black robes. 'I've already got Roddy Pontner betting me Bulgaria will score first – I offered him nice odds, considering Ireland's front three are the strongest I've seen in years – and little Agatha Timms has put up half shares in her eel farm on a week-long match.'

'Oh ... go on, then,' said Mr Weasley. 'Let's see ... a Galleon on Ireland to win?'

'A Galleon?' Ludo Bagman looked slightly disappointed, but recovered himself. 'Very well, very well ... any other takers?'

'They're a bit young to be gambling,' said Mr Weasley. 'Molly wouldn't like –'

'We'll bet thirty-seven Galleons, fifteen Sickles, three Knuts,' said Fred, as he and George quickly pooled all their money, 'that Ireland win – but Viktor Krum gets the Snitch. Oh, and we'll throw in a fake wand.'

## 第7章 巴格曼和克劳奇

"亚瑟,老伙计,"他来到篝火边,气喘吁吁地说,"天气多好啊,是不是?天气太棒了!这样的天气,哪儿找去!晚上肯定没有云……整个筹备工作井井有条……我没什么事情可做!"

在他身后,一群面容憔悴的魔法部官员匆匆跑过,远处有迹象表明有人在玩魔火,紫色的火花蹿起二十多英尺高。

珀西急忙上前一步,伸出手去。很明显,他虽然对卢多·巴格曼管理他那个部门的方式不以为然,但并不妨碍他想给别人留下一个好印象。

"啊——对了,"韦斯莱先生笑着说,"这是我儿子珀西。刚刚到魔法部工作——这是弗雷德——不对,是乔治,对不起——那个才是弗雷德——比尔、查理、罗恩——我的女儿金妮——这是罗恩的朋友,赫敏·格兰杰和哈利·波特。"

听到哈利的名字,巴格曼微微愣了一下便恍然大悟,他的眼睛立刻扫向哈利额头上的伤疤,哈利对此已是司空见惯。

"我来给大家介绍一下,"韦斯莱先生继续说道,"这位是卢多·巴格曼,你们知道他是谁,我们多亏他,才弄到了这么好的票——"

巴格曼满脸堆笑,挥了挥手,好像是说这不算什么。

"想对比赛下个赌注吗,亚瑟?"他急切地问,把黄黑长袍的口袋弄得叮当直响,看来里面装了不少金币,"我已经说服罗迪·庞特内和我打赌,他说保加利亚会进第一个球——我给他定了很高的赔率,因为我考虑到爱尔兰前场的三个人是我这些年来见过的最棒的——小阿加莎·蒂姆斯把她的鳗鱼农庄的一半股份都押上了,打赌说比赛要持续一个星期。"

"哦……那好吧,"韦斯莱先生说,"让我想想……我出一个加隆赌爱尔兰赢,行吗?"

"一个加隆?"卢多·巴格曼显得有些失望,但很快就恢复了兴致,"很好,很好……还有别人想赌吗?"

"他们还太小,不能赌博。"韦斯莱先生说,"莫丽不会愿意——"

"我们压上三十七个加隆,十五个西可,三个纳特,"弗雷德说,他和乔治迅速掏出他们的钱,"赌爱尔兰赢——但威克多尔·克鲁姆会抓到金色飞贼。哦,对了,我们还要加上一根假魔杖。"

## CHAPTER SEVEN    Bagman and Crouch

'You don't want to go showing Mr Bagman rubbish like that –' Percy hissed, but Bagman didn't seem to think the wand was rubbish at all; on the contrary, his boyish face shone with excitement as he took it from Fred, and when the wand gave a loud squawk and turned into a rubber chicken, Bagman roared with laughter.

'Excellent! I haven't seen one that convincing in years! I'd pay five Galleons for that!'

Percy froze in an attitude of stunned disapproval.

'Boys,' said Mr Weasley under his breath, 'I don't want you betting … that's all your savings … your mother –'

'Don't be a spoilsport, Arthur!' boomed Ludo Bagman, rattling his pockets excitedly. 'They're old enough to know what they want! You reckon Ireland will win but Krum'll get the Snitch? Not a chance, boys, not a chance … I'll give you excellent odds on that one … we'll add five Galleons for the funny wand, then, shall we …'

Mr Weasley looked on helplessly as Ludo Bagman whipped out a notebook and quill and began jotting down the twins' names.

'Cheers,' said George, taking the slip of parchment Bagman handed him and tucking it away carefully.

Bagman turned most cheerfully back to Mr Weasley. 'Couldn't do me a brew, I suppose? I'm keeping an eye out for Barty Crouch. My Bulgarian opposite number's making difficulties, and I can't understand a word he's saying. Barty'll be able to sort it out. He speaks about a hundred and fifty languages.'

'Mr Crouch?' said Percy, suddenly abandoning his look of poker-stiff disapproval and positively writhing with excitement. 'He speaks over two hundred! Mermish and Gobbledegook and Troll …'

'Anyone can speak Troll,' said Fred dismissively, 'all you have to do is point and grunt.'

Percy threw Fred an extremely nasty look, and stoked the fire vigorously to bring the kettle back to the boil.

'Any news of Bertha Jorkins yet, Ludo?' Mr Weasley asked, as Bagman settled himself down on the grass beside them all.

## 第7章 巴格曼和克劳奇

"难道你们想把那些破玩意儿拿给巴格曼先生看——"珀西压低声音说。可是巴格曼先生似乎根本不认为假魔杖是破玩意儿,他从弗雷德手里接过魔杖,魔杖呱呱大叫一声,变成了一只橡皮小鸡,巴格曼先生哈哈大笑,孩子般的脸上满是兴奋。

"太棒了!我许多年没有见过这么逼真的东西了!我出五个加隆把它买下!"

珀西既惊讶又不满,一时呆在了那里。

"孩子们,"韦斯莱先生压低声音说,"我不希望你们赌博……这是你们所有的积蓄……你母亲——"

"不要扫兴嘛,亚瑟!"卢多·巴格曼粗声大气地说,一边兴奋地把口袋里的钱弄得叮当乱响,"他们已经大了,知道自己想要什么!你们认为爱尔兰会赢,但克鲁姆能抓住金色飞贼?不可能,孩子们,不可能……我给你们很高的赔率……还要加上那根滑稽的魔杖换得的五个加隆,那么,我们是不是……"

卢多·巴格曼飞快地抽出笔记本和羽毛笔,潦草地写下双胞胎兄弟的名字,韦斯莱先生在一旁无奈地看着。

"谢了。"乔治接过巴格曼递给他的一小条羊皮纸,小心翼翼地塞进长袍的前襟里。

巴格曼眉飞色舞地又转向韦斯莱先生。"你能不能帮我一个忙?我一直在找巴蒂·克劳奇。保加利亚那个跟我同级的官员在提意见刁难我们,可他说的话我一个字儿也听不懂。巴蒂会解决这个问题。他会讲大约一百五十种语言呢。"

"克劳奇先生?"珀西说,他刚才因为对巴格曼不满而僵在那里,像一根电线杆子,此刻突然兴奋得浑身躁动不安,"他能讲两百种语言呢!美人鱼的、妖精的,还有巨怪……"

"巨怪的语言谁都会讲,"弗雷德不以为然地说,"你只要指着它,发出呼噜呼噜的声音就行了。"

珀西恶狠狠地白了弗雷德一眼,使劲地拨弄篝火,让壶里的水又沸腾起来。

"还没有伯莎·乔金斯的消息吗,卢多?"巴格曼在他们身边的草地上坐下后,韦斯莱先生问道。

## CHAPTER SEVEN   Bagman and Crouch

'Not a dicky bird,' said Bagman comfortably. 'But she'll turn up. Poor old Bertha ... memory like a leaky cauldron and no sense of direction. Lost, you take my word for it. She'll wander back into the office some time in October, thinking it's still July.'

'You don't think it might be time to send someone to look for her?' Mr Weasley suggested tentatively, as Percy handed Bagman his tea.

'Barty Crouch keeps saying that,' said Bagman, his round eyes widening innocently, 'but we really can't spare anyone at the moment. Oh – talk of the devil! Barty!'

A wizard had just Apparated at their fireside, and he could not have made more of a contrast with Ludo Bagman, sprawled on the grass in his old Wasp robes. Barty Crouch was a stiff, upright, elderly man, dressed in an impeccably crisp suit and tie. The parting in his short grey hair was almost unnaturally straight and his narrow tooth-brush moustache looked as though he trimmed it using a slide-rule. His shoes were very highly polished. Harry could see at once why Percy idolised him. Percy was a great believer in rigidly following rules, and Mr Crouch had complied with the rule about Muggle dressing so thoroughly that he could have passed as a bank manager; Harry doubted even Uncle Vernon would have spotted him for what he really was.

'Pull up a bit of grass, Barty,' said Ludo brightly, patting the ground beside him.

'No, thank you, Ludo,' said Crouch, and there was a bite of impatience in his voice. 'I've been looking for you everywhere. The Bulgarians are insisting we add another twelve seats to the Top Box.'

'Oh, is *that* what they're after?' said Bagman. 'I thought the chap was asking to borrow a pair of tweezers. Bit of a strong accent.'

'Mr Crouch!' said Percy breathlessly, sunk into a kind of half bow which made him look like a hunchback. 'Would you like a cup of tea?'

'Oh,' said Mr Crouch, looking over at Percy in mild surprise. 'Yes – thank you, Weatherby.'

Fred and George choked into their own cups. Percy, very pink around the ears, busied himself with the kettle.

'Oh, and I've been wanting a word with you, too, Arthur,' said Mr

## 第7章 巴格曼和克劳奇

"连影子都没有,"巴格曼大大咧咧地说,"不过放心,她会出现的。可怜的老伯莎……她的记忆力像一只漏底的坩埚,方向感极差。肯定是迷路了,信不信由你。到了十月的某一天,她又会晃晃悠悠地回到办公室,以为还是七月份呢。"

"你不打算派人去找找她吗?"韦斯莱先生试探着提出建议,这时珀西把一杯茶递给了巴格曼。

"巴蒂·克劳奇倒是一直这么说,"巴格曼说,圆溜溜的眼睛睁得很大,露出天真的神情,"可是眼下真是腾不出人手来。呵——正说着他,他就来了!巴蒂!"

一个巫师突然幻影显形出现在他们的篝火旁,他和穿着黄蜂队旧长袍、懒洋洋坐在草地上的卢多·巴格曼相比,形成了十分鲜明的反差。巴蒂·克劳奇是个五十来岁的男人,腰板挺直,动作生硬,穿着一尘不染的挺括西装,打着领带。灰白的短发打理得一丝不乱,中间那道缝直得有点不自然。他那牙刷般狭窄的小胡子,像是比着滑尺修剪过的。他的鞋子也擦得锃亮。哈利一下子就明白珀西为什么崇拜他了。珀西一向主张严格遵守纪律,而克劳奇先生一丝不苟地遵守了麻瓜的着装纪律,他做得太地道了,简直可以冒充一个银行经理。哈利怀疑就连弗农姨父也难以识破他的真实身份。

"坐下歇会儿吧,巴蒂。"卢多高兴地说,拍了拍身边的草地。

"不用,谢谢你,卢多,"克劳奇说,声音里有一丝不耐烦,"我一直在到处找你。保加利亚人坚持要我们在顶层包厢上再加十二个座位。"

"噢,原来他们想要这个!"巴格曼说,"我还以为那家伙要向我借一把镊子呢。口音太重了。"

"克劳奇先生!"珀西激动得气都喘不匀了。他倾着身子,做出鞠躬的姿势,这使他看上去像个驼背,"您想来一杯茶吗?"

"哦,"克劳奇先生说,微微有些吃惊地打量着珀西,"好吧——谢谢你,韦瑟比。"

弗雷德和乔治笑得差点儿把茶水喷在杯子里。珀西耳朵变成了粉红色,假装低头照料茶壶。

"对了,有件事我一直想跟你说,亚瑟。"克劳奇先生说,犀利的

Crouch, his sharp eyes falling upon Mr Weasley. 'Ali Bashir's on the warpath. He wants a word with you about your embargo on flying carpets.'

Mr Weasley heaved a deep sigh. 'I sent him an owl about that just last week. If I've told him once I've told him a hundred times: carpets are defined as a Muggle Artefact by the Registry of Proscribed Charmable Objects, but will he listen?'

'I doubt it,' said Mr Crouch, accepting a cup from Percy. 'He's desperate to export here.'

'Well, they'll never replace brooms in Britain, will they?' said Bagman.

'Ali thinks there's a niche in the market for a family vehicle,' said Mr Crouch. 'I remember my grandfather had an Axminster that could seat twelve – but that was before carpets were banned, of course.'

He spoke as though he wanted to leave nobody in any doubt that all his ancestors had abided strictly by the law.

'So, been keeping busy, Barty?' said Bagman breezily.

'Fairly,' said Mr Crouch drily. 'Organising Portkeys across five continents is no mean feat, Ludo.'

'I expect you'll both be glad when this is over?' said Mr Weasley.

Ludo Bagman looked shocked. 'Glad! Don't know when I've had more fun ... still, it's not as though we haven't got anything to look forward to, eh, Barty? Eh? Plenty left to organise, eh?'

Mr Crouch raised his eyebrows at Bagman. 'We agreed not to make the announcement until all the details –'

'Oh, details!' said Bagman, waving the word away like a cloud of midges. 'They've signed, haven't they? They've agreed, haven't they? I bet you anything these kids'll know soon enough anyway. I mean, it's happening at Hogwarts –'

'Ludo, we need to meet the Bulgarians, you know,' said Mr Crouch sharply, cutting Bagman's remarks short. 'Thank you for the tea, Weatherby.'

He pushed his undrunk tea back at Percy and waited for Ludo to rise; Bagman struggled to his feet again, swigging down the last of his tea, the gold in his pockets chinking merrily.

'See you all later!' he said. 'You'll be up in the Top Box with me – I'm commentating!' He waved, Barty Crouch nodded curtly, and both of them

## 第7章 巴格曼和克劳奇

目光又落到韦斯莱先生身上,"阿里·巴什尔提出挑衅,想找你谈谈有关你们禁运飞毯的规定。"

韦斯莱先生重重地叹了口气。"我上星期派一只猫头鹰送信给他,专门谈了这事。我已经跟他说了一百遍:地毯在禁用魔法物品登记簿上被定义为麻瓜手工艺品,可是他会听吗?"

"我估计他不会,"克劳奇先生说着,接过珀西递给他的一杯茶,"他迫不及待地想往这儿出口飞毯。"

"可是,飞毯在英国永远不可能代替飞天扫帚,是不是?"巴格曼问。

"阿里认为在家庭交通工具的市场里有空子可钻。"克劳奇先生说,"我记得我的祖父当年有一条阿克斯明斯特绒头地毯,上面可以坐十二个人——不过,当然啦,那是在飞毯被禁之前。"

他这么说似乎是想让大家相信,他的祖先都是严格遵守法律的。

"怎么样,忙得够呛吧,巴蒂?"巴格曼轻松愉快地问。

"比较忙,"克劳奇先生干巴巴地说,"在五个大陆上组织和安排门钥匙,这可不是一件容易的事,卢多。"

"我想你们都巴不得这件事赶紧结束吧?"韦斯莱先生问。

卢多·巴格曼似乎大吃一惊。

"巴不得!我从没有这么快活过……不过,前面倒不是没有盼头,是吗,巴蒂?嗯?还要组织许多活动呢,是不是?"

克劳奇先生冲巴格曼扬起眉毛。

"我们保证先不对外宣布,直到所有的细节——"

"哦,细节!"巴格曼说,不以为然地挥了挥手,像驱赶一群飞蚊,"他们签字了,是不是?他们同意了,是不是?我愿意跟你打赌,这些孩子很快就会知道的。我是说,事情就发生在霍格沃茨——"

"卢多,你该知道,我们需要去见那些保加利亚人了。"克劳奇先生严厉地说,打断了巴格曼的话头,"谢谢你的茶水,韦瑟比。"

他把一口没喝的茶杯塞回珀西手里,等着卢多起身。卢多挣扎着站起来,一口喝尽杯里的茶,那些加隆在他口袋里愉快地叮当作响。

"待会儿见!"他说,"你们和我一起在顶层包厢上——我是比赛的解说员!"他挥手告别,巴蒂·克劳奇则淡淡地点了点头,随后两

## CHAPTER SEVEN   Bagman and Crouch

Disapparated.

'What's happening at Hogwarts, Dad?' said Fred at once. 'What were they talking about?'

'You'll find out soon enough,' said Mr Weasley, smiling.

'It's classified information, until such time as the Ministry decides to release it,' said Percy stiffly. 'Mr Crouch was quite right not to disclose it.'

'Oh, shut up, Weatherby,' said Fred.

A sense of excitement rose like a palpable cloud over the campsite as the afternoon wore on. By dusk, the still summer air itself seemed to be quivering with anticipation, and as darkness spread like a curtain over the thousands of waiting wizards, the last vestiges of pretence disappeared: the Ministry seemed to have bowed to the inevitable, and stopped fighting the signs of blatant magic now breaking out everywhere.

Salesmen were Apparating every few feet, carrying trays and pushing carts full of extraordinary merchandise. There were luminous rosettes – green for Ireland, red for Bulgaria – which were squealing the names of the players, pointed green hats bedecked with dancing shamrocks, Bulgarian scarves adorned with lions that really roared, flags from both countries which played their national anthems as they were waved; there were tiny models of Firebolts, which really flew, and collectible figures of famous players, which strolled across the palm of your hand, preening themselves.

'Been saving my pocket money all summer for this,' Ron told Harry, as they and Hermione strolled through the salesmen, buying souvenirs. Though Ron purchased himself a dancing-shamrock hat and a large green rosette, he also bought a small figure of Viktor Krum, the Bulgarian Seeker. The miniature Krum walked backwards and forwards over Ron's hand, scowling up at the green rosette above him.

'Wow, look at these!' said Harry, hurrying over to a cart piled high with what looked like brass binoculars, except that they were covered in all sorts of weird knobs and dials.

'Omnioculars,' said the saleswizard eagerly. 'You can replay action ... slow everything down ... and they flash up a play-by-play breakdown if you need it. Bargain – ten Galleons each.'

## 第7章 巴格曼和克劳奇

人都幻影移形,消失不见了。

"霍格沃茨要发生什么事吗,爸爸?"弗雷德立刻问道,"他们刚才说的是什么?"

"你们很快就会知道的。"韦斯莱先生笑着说。

"这是机密,要等部里决定公开的时候才能知道。"珀西一本正经地说,"克劳奇先生不轻易泄露机密是对的。"

"哦,你闭嘴吧,韦瑟比。"弗雷德说。

随着下午的过去,兴奋的情绪如同一团可以触摸到的云在营地上弥漫开来。黄昏时分,就连寂静的夏日空气似乎也在颤抖地期待着。当夜色像帷幕一样笼罩着成千上万个急切等待的巫师时,最后一丝伪装的痕迹也消失了:魔法部似乎屈服于不可避免的趋势,不再同人们作对,听任那些明显使用魔法的迹象在各处冒出来。

每隔几步,就有幻影显形的小贩从天而降,端着托盘,推着小车,里面装满了稀奇古怪的玩意儿。有发光的玫瑰形徽章——绿色的代表爱尔兰,红色的代表保加利亚——还能尖声喊出队员们的名字;有绿色的高帽子,上面装点着随风起舞的三叶草;有保加利亚的围巾,印在上面的狮子真的会发出吼叫;有两国的国旗,挥舞起来会演奏各自的国歌;还有真的会飞的火弩箭小模型;有供收藏的著名队员塑像,那些小塑像可以在你的手掌上走来走去,一副得意扬扬的派头。

"攒了一夏天的零花钱,就是为了这个。"三个人悠闲地穿过那些小贩时,罗恩一边购买纪念品,一边对哈利说。罗恩买了一顶跳舞三叶草的帽子、一个绿色的玫瑰形大徽章,不过他同时也买了保加利亚找球手威克多尔·克鲁姆的小塑像。那个小型的克鲁姆在罗恩手上来来回回地走,皱着眉头瞪着他上方的绿色徽章。

"哇,快看这些!"哈利说,冲到一辆小推车跟前,那车里高高地堆着许多像是黄铜双筒望远镜的东西,但上面布满各种各样古怪的旋钮和转盘。

"全景望远镜,"巫师小贩热情地推销道,"你可以重放画面……用慢动作放……如果需要的话,它还能迅速闪出赛况分析。成交吧——十个加隆一架。"

## CHAPTER SEVEN  Bagman and Crouch

'Wish I hadn't bought this now,' said Ron, gesturing at his dancing shamrock hat and gazing longingly at the Omnioculars.

'Three pairs,' said Harry firmly to the wizard.

'No – don't bother,' said Ron, going red. He was always touchy about the fact that Harry, who had inherited a small fortune from his parents, had much more money than he did.

'You won't be getting anything for Christmas,' Harry told him, thrusting Omnioculars into his and Hermione's hands. 'For about ten years, mind.'

'Fair enough,' said Ron, grinning.

'Oooh, thanks, Harry,' said Hermione. 'And I'll get us some programmes, look –'

Their money bags considerably lighter, they went back to the tents. Bill, Charlie and Ginny were all sporting green rosettes too, and Mr Weasley was carrying an Irish flag. Fred and George had no souvenirs as they had given Bagman all their gold.

And then a deep, booming gong sounded somewhere beyond the woods, and, at once, green and red lanterns blazed into life in the trees, lighting a path to the pitch.

'It's time!' said Mr Weasley, looking as excited as any of them. 'Come on, let's go!'

## 第7章 巴格曼和克劳奇

"我要是不买这个就好了。"罗恩瞅瞅他那顶跳舞三叶草的帽子，又眼馋地望着全景望远镜。

"买三架。"哈利毫不迟疑地对那巫师说。

"别——你别费心了。"罗恩说着，脸涨得通红。他知道，哈利继承了父母的一小笔遗产，比他有钱得多，他对这一事实总是很敏感。

"圣诞节你就别想收到礼物啦，"哈利对他说，一边把全景望远镜塞进他和赫敏手里，"记住，十年都不给你送礼物啦！"

"够合理的。"罗恩咧嘴一笑，说道。

"嗬，谢谢你，哈利。"赫敏说，"我来给每人买一份比赛说明书，瞧，就在那边……"

现在钱袋空了许多，他们又回到了自己的帐篷。比尔、查理和金妮也戴着绿色徽章，韦斯莱先生举着一面爱尔兰旗子。弗雷德和乔治什么纪念品也没有，他们把金币全部给了巴格曼。

这时，树林远处的什么地方传来低沉浑厚的锣声，立刻，千盏万盏红红绿绿的灯笼在树上绽放光明，照亮了通往赛场的道路。

"时间到了！"韦斯莱先生说，他看上去和大家一样兴奋，"快点儿，我们走吧！"

## CHAPTER EIGHT

# The Quidditch World Cup

Clutching their purchases, Mr Weasley in the lead, they all hurried into the wood, following the lantern-lit trail. They could hear the sounds of thousands of people moving around them, shouts and laughter, snatches of singing. The atmosphere of feverish excitement was highly infectious; Harry couldn't stop grinning. They walked through the wood for twenty minutes, talking and joking loudly, until at last they emerged on the other side, and found themselves in the shadow of a gigantic stadium. Though Harry could see only a fraction of the immense gold walls surrounding the pitch, he could tell that ten cathedrals would fit comfortably inside it.

'Seats a hundred thousand,' said Mr Weasley, spotting the awestruck look on Harry's face. 'Ministry task force of five hundred have been working on it all year. Muggle-Repelling Charms on every inch of it. Every time Muggles have got anywhere near here all year, they've suddenly remembered urgent appointments and had to dash away again … Bless them,' he added fondly, leading the way towards the nearest entrance, which was already surrounded by a swarm of shouting witches and wizards.

'Prime seats!' said the Ministry witch at the entrance, when she checked their tickets. 'Top Box! Straight upstairs, Arthur, and as high as you can go.'

The stairs into the stadium were carpeted in rich purple. They clambered upwards with the rest of the crowd, which slowly filtered away through doors into the stands to their left and right. Mr Weasley's party kept climbing, and at last they reached the top of the staircase, and found themselves in a small box, set at the highest point of the stadium and situated exactly halfway between the golden goal-posts. About twenty purple-and-gilt chairs stood in two rows here, and Harry, filing into the front seats with the Weasleys, looked down upon a scene the like of which he could never have imagined.

## 第8章

## 魁地奇世界杯赛

韦斯莱先生在前面领路,大家手里攥着买来的东西,顺着灯笼照亮的通道快步走进树林。他们可以听见成千上万的人在周围走动,听见喊叫声、欢笑声,还听见断断续续的歌声。这种狂热的兴奋情绪是很有传染性的,哈利也忍不住笑得合不拢嘴。他们在树林里走了二十分钟,边走边高声地谈笑打趣,最后从树林的另一边出来了,发现自己正处在一座巨大的体育场的阴影中。哈利只能看见围住赛场的宏伟金墙的一部分,但他看得出来,里面装十个大教堂都不成问题。

"可以容纳十万观众。"韦斯莱先生看到哈利脸上惊愕的表情,说道,"魔法部五百个工作人员为此忙碌了整整一年。这里的每一寸地方都施了麻瓜驱逐咒。这一年当中,每当有麻瓜接近这里,就会突然想起十万火急的事情,匆匆走开……愿上帝保佑他们。"他慈爱地说,领着大家走向最近的入口处,那里已经围满了许多大喊大叫的巫师。

"一等票!"入口处的那位魔法部女巫师看了看他们的票说道,"顶层包厢!一直往楼上走,亚瑟,走到最顶上。"

通向体育场的楼梯上铺着紫红色的地毯。他们和人群一起拾级而上,那些人流慢慢地分别进了左右两边的看台。韦斯莱先生率领的这一行人一直往上走,最后到了楼梯顶上。他们发现自己来到了一个小包厢里,位置在体育场的最高处,而且正好在两侧金色的球门柱的中间。这里有二十来把紫色镀金的座椅,分成两排。哈利跟着韦斯莱一家排队坐进了前面一排,朝下面望去,那情景是他怎么也想象不到的。

## CHAPTER EIGHT    The Quidditch World Cup

A hundred thousand witches and wizards were taking their places in the seats which rose in levels around the long oval pitch. Everything was suffused with a mysterious golden light that seemed to come from the stadium itself. The pitch looked smooth as velvet from their lofty position. At either end of the pitch stood three goal hoops, fifty feet high; right opposite them, almost at Harry's eye level, was a gigantic blackboard. Gold writing kept dashing across it as though an invisible giant's hand was scrawling upon it and then wiping it off again; watching it, Harry saw that it was flashing advertisements across the pitch.

*The Bluebottle: A Broom for All the Family – safe, reliable and with In-built Anti-Burglar Buzzer ...*
*Mrs Skower's All-Purpose Magical Mess-Remover: No Pain, No Stain! ...*
*Gladrags Wizardwear – London, Paris, Hogsmeade ...*

Harry tore his eyes away from the sign and looked over his shoulder to see who else was sharing the box with them. So far it was empty, except for a tiny creature sitting in the second from last seat at the end of the row behind them. The creature, whose legs were so short they stuck out in front of it on the chair, was wearing a tea-towel draped like a toga, and it had its face hidden in its hands. Yet those long, bat-like ears were oddly familiar ...

'*Dobby?*' said Harry incredulously.

The tiny creature looked up and parted its fingers, revealing enormous brown eyes and a nose the exact size and shape of a large tomato. It wasn't Dobby – it was, however, unmistakeably a house-elf, as Harry's friend Dobby had been. Harry had set Dobby free from his old owners, the Malfoy family.

'Did sir just call me Dobby?' squeaked the elf curiously, from between its fingers. Its voice was higher even than Dobby's had been, a teeny, quivering squeak of a voice, and Harry suspected – though it was very hard to tell with a house-elf – that this one might just be female. Ron and Hermione spun around in their seats to look. Though they had heard a lot about Dobby from Harry, they had never actually met him. Even Mr Weasley looked around in interest.

## 第8章 魁地奇世界杯赛

十万巫师正在陆陆续续地就座，那些座位围绕着椭圆形的体育场，呈阶梯形向上排列。这里的一切都笼罩着一种神秘的金光，这光芒仿佛来自体育场本身。从他们在高处的位置望去，赛场像天鹅绒一样平整光滑。赛场两边分别竖着三个投球的圆环，有五十英尺高；在他们对面，几乎就在与哈利视线平行的位置，是一块巨大的黑板，上面不断闪现出金色的文字，就好像有一只看不见的巨手在黑板上龙飞凤舞地写字，然后又把它们擦去。哈利仔细一看，才知那些闪动的文字都是给赛场观众看的广告。

矢车菊：适合全家的飞天扫帚——安全，可靠，带有内置式防盗蜂音器……

斯科尔夫人牌万能神奇去污剂：轻轻松松，去除污渍！……

风雅牌巫师服——伦敦、巴黎、霍格莫德……

哈利将视线从广告牌上收回，扭过头去，看看还有谁和他们一起坐在这个包厢。包厢里现在还没什么人，只是在他们后面一排的倒数第二个座位上坐着一个小得出奇的家伙。那小家伙的两条腿太短了，只能直直地伸在椅子上。它身上围着一条擦拭茶具的茶巾，像穿着一件宽松的袍子，脸埋在两只手里。可是，那一对长长的、蝙蝠般的大耳朵却那么眼熟……

"多比？"哈利不敢相信地说。

小家伙抬起头来，松开手指，露出一双巨大的棕色眼睛和一只形状和大小都像一个大番茄的鼻子。不是多比——不过，毫无疑问，这也是一个家养小精灵，和哈利的朋友多比以前的身份一样。哈利已经把多比从他先前的主人——马尔福一家手里解放了出来。

"先生刚才叫我多比吗？"小精灵从手指缝间好奇地问，声音很尖，甚至比多比的声音还要尖，是一种微微颤抖的刺耳声音，因此哈利怀疑——尽管家养小精灵很难区分性别——这一个大概是女的。罗恩和赫敏都从座位上回过头来，他们虽然听哈利说过多比的许多事情，但从来没有真的见过他。就连韦斯莱先生也很有兴趣地扭头望着。

## CHAPTER EIGHT  The Quidditch World Cup

'Sorry,' Harry told the elf, 'I just thought you were someone I knew.'

'But I knows Dobby too, sir!' squeaked the elf. She was shielding her face, as though blinded by light, though the Top Box was not brightly lit. 'My name is Winky, sir – and you, sir –' her dark brown eyes widened to the size of side plates as they rested upon Harry's scar, 'you is surely Harry Potter!'

'Yeah, I am,' said Harry.

'But Dobby talks of you all the time, sir!' she said, lowering her hands very slightly and looking awestruck.

'How is he?' said Harry. 'How's freedom suiting him?'

'Ah, sir,' said Winky, shaking her head, 'ah, sir, meaning no disrespect, sir, but I is not sure you did Dobby a favour, sir, when you is setting him free.'

'Why?' said Harry, taken aback. 'What's wrong with him?'

'Freedom is going to Dobby's head, sir,' said Winky sadly. 'Ideas above his station, sir. Can't get another position, sir.'

'Why not?' said Harry.

Winky lowered her voice by a half octave and whispered, '*He is wanting paying for his work, sir.*'

'Paying?' said Harry blankly. 'Well – why shouldn't he be paid?'

Winky looked quite horrified at the idea, and closed her fingers slightly so that her face was half hidden again.

'House-elves is not paid, sir!' she said in a muffled squeak. 'No, no, no. I says to Dobby, I says, go find yourself a nice family and settle down, Dobby. He is getting up to all sorts of high jinks, sir, what is unbecoming to a house-elf. You goes racketing around like this, Dobby, I says, and next thing I hear you's up in front of the Department for the Regulation and Control of Magical Creatures, like some common goblin.'

'Well, it's about time he had a bit of fun,' said Harry.

'House-elves is not supposed to have fun, Harry Potter,' said Winky firmly, from behind her hands. 'House-elves does what they is told. I is not liking heights at all, Harry Potter –' she glanced towards the edge of the box and gulped, '– but my master sends me to the Top Box and I comes, sir.'

'Why's he sent you up here, if he knows you don't like heights?' said

"对不起,"哈利对小精灵说,"我把你当成我以前认识的一个人了。"

"可是我也认识多比啊,先生!"小精灵尖声地说。她用手挡着脸,好像被光刺得睁不开眼睛,其实顶层包厢的光线并不强烈。"我叫闪闪,先生——先生你——"当她的目光落到哈利额头的伤疤上时,那双深棕色的眼睛顿时睁得老大,像两个小菜碟,"你肯定是哈利·波特!"

"是的。"哈利说。

"哎呀,多比一天到晚都在谈你,先生!"她说,把双手稍微放下一些,脸上的表情十分敬畏。

"多比怎么样了?"哈利问,"自由以后过得惯吗?"

"啊,先生,"闪闪摇着头说,"啊,先生,无意冒犯你,先生,你把多比解放出来,恐怕对他并没有什么好处。"

"为什么?"哈利吃惊地问,"他有什么不对劲吗?"

"多比脑子里整天想着自由,先生,"闪闪悲哀地说,"尽是些不切实际的想法,先生。他找不到工作,先生。"

"为什么找不到?"哈利问。

闪闪把声音降低半个八度,悄声说:"他想得到报酬,先生。"

"报酬?"哈利茫然地问,"怎么——他不应该得到报酬吗?"

闪闪似乎被这个想法吓坏了,把手指合拢起来,这样她的脸又被挡住了一半。

"家养小精灵干活是没有报酬的,先生!"她从手指后面尖声说,"不行,这样不行,不行。我对多比说,我说,给自己找一个像样的家庭,好好地安顿下来,多比。他整天就知道寻欢作乐,先生,这对一个家养小精灵来说是不合适的。我说,你这样到处玩耍,接下来我就会听说你像个下贱的妖精一样,被魔法生物管理控制司抓去问罪了。"

"可是,他也应该找点儿乐趣了。"哈利说。

"家养小精灵是不应该有乐趣的,哈利·波特,"闪闪双手捂着脸认真地说,"家养小精灵完全听从主人的吩咐。我有恐高症,哈利·波特——"她朝包厢边缘扫了一眼,吸了口冷气,"——可是我的主人派我到顶层包厢来,我就来了,先生。"

"他明明知道你有恐高症,为什么还要派你到这儿来?"哈利不满

## CHAPTER EIGHT  The Quidditch World Cup

Harry, frowning.

'Master – master wants me to save him a seat, Harry Potter, he is very busy,' said Winky, tilting her head towards the empty space beside her. 'Winky is wishing she is back in master's tent, Harry Potter, but Winky does what she is told, Winky is a good house-elf.'

She gave the edge of the box another frightened look, and hid her eyes completely again. Harry turned back to the others.

'So that's a house-elf?' Ron muttered. 'Weird things, aren't they?'

'Dobby was weirder,' said Harry, fervently.

Ron pulled out his Omnioculars and started testing them, staring down into the crowd on the other side of the stadium.

'Wild!' he said, twiddling the replay knob on the side. 'I can make that old bloke down there pick his nose again … and again … and again …'

Hermione, meanwhile, was skimming eagerly through her velvet-covered, tasselled programme.

'"A display from the team mascots will precede the match",' she read aloud.

'Oh, that's always worth watching,' said Mr Weasley. 'National teams bring creatures from their native land, you know, to put on a bit of a show.'

The box filled gradually around them over the next half hour. Mr Weasley kept shaking hands with people who were obviously very important wizards. Percy jumped to his feet so often that he looked as though he was trying to sit on a hedgehog. When Cornelius Fudge, the Minister for Magic himself, arrived, Percy bowed so low that his glasses fell off and shattered. Highly embarrassed, he repaired them with his wand, and thereafter remained in his seat, throwing jealous looks at Harry, whom Cornelius Fudge had greeted like an old friend. They had met before, and Fudge shook Harry's hand in fatherly fashion, asked how he was, and introduced him to the wizards on either side of him.

'Harry Potter, you know,' he loudly told the Bulgarian Minister, who was wearing splendid robes of black velvet trimmed with gold, and didn't seem to understand a word of English. '*Harry Potter* … oh, come on now, you know who he is … the boy who survived You-Know-Who … you *do* know who he is –'

The Bulgarian wizard suddenly spotted Harry's scar and started gabbling loudly and excitedly, pointing at it.

地皱起眉头，问道。

"主人……主人要我给他占一个座位，哈利·波特，他太忙了。"闪闪侧过脑袋，望了望她旁边的空座位，"闪闪真希望回到主人的帐篷里，哈利·波特，但是闪闪听从吩咐。闪闪是个很乖的家养小精灵。"

她又恐惧地看了看包厢边缘，赶紧把眼睛完全捂住了。哈利回过头来，望着大家。

"那就是家养小精灵？"罗恩小声问，"真是些古怪的家伙，是吗？"

"多比还要古怪呢。"哈利深有感触地说。

罗恩掏出他的全景望远镜，开始调试，望着体育场另一面的人群。

"真棒啊！"他摆弄着望远镜侧面的重放旋钮，说道，"我可以让那边的那个老家伙再掏一遍鼻子……再掏一遍……再掏一遍……"

这时，赫敏正在急切地翻看她那本带流苏的天鹅绒封面的比赛说明书。

"比赛前有球队吉祥物的表演。"她大声念道。

"哦，那永远是值得一看的。"韦斯莱先生说，"你知道，每个国家队都从本国带来一些稀奇的动物，要在这里做一番表演。"

在接下来的半小时里，他们所在的包厢里渐渐坐满了人。韦斯莱先生不停地与人握手，那些人一看就是很有身份的巫师。珀西一次次地匆忙站起，看上去就像坐在满身是刺的刺猬背上。当魔法部部长康奈利·福吉本人驾到时，珀西因鞠躬鞠得太低，眼镜掉在地上，摔得粉碎。他尴尬极了，用魔杖修好镜片，然后就呆呆地坐在座位上。当康奈利·福吉像老朋友一样向哈利打招呼时，珀西朝哈利投去嫉妒的目光。哈利和福吉以前就认识，福吉像父亲一般慈祥地握着哈利的手，向他嘘寒问暖，并把他介绍给坐在旁边的巫师。

"哈利·波特，你知道的，"他大声告诉保加利亚的魔法部部长——那人穿着华丽的镶金边黑色天鹅绒长袍，看样子一句英语也听不懂，"哈利·波特……哦，想一想看，你应该知道他是谁……就是那个从神秘人手中死里逃生的男孩……你一定知道他是谁了吧——"

保加利亚巫师突然看到了哈利额头上的伤疤，立刻兴奋地用手指着，嘴里大声地叽里咕噜说了一串话。

## CHAPTER EIGHT  The Quidditch World Cup

'Knew we'd get there in the end,' said Fudge wearily to Harry. 'I'm no great shakes at languages, I need Barty Crouch for this sort of thing. Ah, I see his house-elf's saving him a seat ... good job too, these Bulgarian blighters have been trying to cadge all the best places ... ah, and here's Lucius!'

Harry, Ron and Hermione turned quickly. Edging along the second row to three still-empty seats right behind Mr Weasley were none other than Dobby the house-elf's old owners – Lucius Malfoy, his son, Draco, and a woman Harry supposed must be Draco's mother.

Harry and Draco Malfoy had been enemies ever since their very first journey to Hogwarts. A pale boy with a pointed face and white-blond hair, Draco greatly resembled his father. His mother was blonde, too; tall and slim, she would have been nice looking if she hadn't been wearing a look that suggested there was a nasty smell under her nose.

'Ah, Fudge,' said Mr Malfoy, holding out his hand as he reached the Minister for Magic. 'How are you? I don't think you've met my wife, Narcissa? Or our son, Draco?'

'How do you do, how do you do?' said Fudge, smiling and bowing to Mrs Malfoy. 'And allow me to introduce you to Mr Oblansk – Obalonsk – Mr – well, he's the Bulgarian Minister for Magic, and he can't understand a word I'm saying anyway, so never mind. And let's see who else – you know Arthur Weasley, I daresay?'

It was a tense moment. Mr Weasley and Mr Malfoy looked at each other and Harry vividly recalled the last time that they had come face to face; it had been in Flourish and Blotts bookshop, and they had had a fight. Mr Malfoy's cold grey eyes swept over Mr Weasley, and then up and down the row.

'Good Lord, Arthur,' he said softly. 'What did you have to sell to get seats in the Top Box? Surely your house wouldn't have fetched this much?'

Fudge, who wasn't listening, said, 'Lucius has just given a *very* generous contribution to St Mungo's Hospital for Magical Maladies and Injuries, Arthur. He's here as my guest.'

'How – how nice,' said Mr Weasley, with a very strained smile.

Mr Malfoy's eyes had returned to Hermione, who went slightly pink, but stared determinedly back at him. Harry knew exactly what was making Mr Malfoy's lip curl. The Malfoys prided themselves on being pure-bloods; in other words, they considered anyone of Muggle descent, like Hermione,

## 第8章 魁地奇世界杯赛

"我就知道总会让他明白的。"福吉疲劳地对哈利说,"我对语言不太擅长,碰到这类事情,就需要巴蒂·克劳奇了。啊,我看见他的家养小精灵给他占了一个座位……想得真周到,保加利亚的这些家伙总想把最好的座位都骗到手……啊,卢修斯来了!"

哈利、罗恩和赫敏立刻转过头去。挤进韦斯莱先生后面第二排仍然空着的三个座位的,正是家养小精灵多比原先的主人:卢修斯·马尔福、他的儿子德拉科,还有一个女人,哈利猜想她一定是德拉科的母亲。

哈利和德拉科·马尔福从第一次去霍格沃茨上学起,就一直是死对头。德拉科是一个肤色苍白的男孩,尖尖的脸,淡金色的头发,和他父亲长得非常像。他母亲也是金头发,又高又苗条,本来长得不算难看,可老是摆出一副厌恶的神情,就好像闻到了什么难闻的气味。

"啊,福吉,"马尔福走过魔法部部长身边时,伸出手去,"你好。我想你还没有见过我的妻子纳西莎吧?还有我们的儿子德拉科。"

"你好,你好,"福吉说,笑着对马尔福夫人鞠了个躬,"请允许我把你介绍给奥伯兰斯克先生——奥巴隆斯克先生——他是保加利亚魔法部的部长,没关系,反正他根本听不懂我在说些什么。让我看看还有谁——你认识亚瑟·韦斯莱吧?"

这一刻真是紧张。韦斯莱先生和马尔福先生互相对视着,哈利清楚地记起他们上次见面的情景:那是在丽痕书店,他们俩打了一架。马尔福先生冷冰冰的灰眼睛越过韦斯莱先生,来回扫视着那排座位。

"天哪,亚瑟,"他轻声说道,"你卖了什么才弄到了这顶层包厢的座位?你的家当肯定不值这么多钱,对吧?"

福吉没有领会马尔福先生在说什么,他说:"卢修斯最近刚给圣芒戈魔法伤病医院捐了很大一笔款子,亚瑟。他是我请来的贵宾。"

"噢——太好了。"韦斯莱先生脸上勉强笑着说。

马尔福先生的目光扫到赫敏身上,赫敏微微涨红了脸,但毫不退缩地与他对视。哈利很清楚马尔福先生的嘴唇为什么会那样皱起来。马尔福一家一向为自己是纯血统巫师而骄傲,也就是说,他们认为麻瓜的后代,比如赫敏,都是低人一等的。不过,在魔法部部长的目光

## CHAPTER EIGHT    The Quidditch World Cup

second-class. However, under the gaze of the Minister for Magic, Mr Malfoy didn't dare say anything. He nodded sneeringly to Mr Weasley, and continued down the line to his seats. Draco shot Harry, Ron and Hermione one contemptuous look, then settled himself between his mother and father.

'Slimy gits,' Ron muttered, as he, Harry and Hermione turned to face the pitch again. Next moment, Ludo Bagman had charged into the box.

'Everyone ready?' he said, his round face gleaming like a great, excited Edam. 'Minister – ready to go?'

'Ready when you are, Ludo,' said Fudge comfortably.

Ludo whipped out his wand, directed it at his own throat and said '*Sonorus!*' and then spoke over the roar of sound that was now filling the packed stadium; his voice echoed over them, booming into every corner of the stands: 'Ladies and gentlemen ... welcome! Welcome to the final of the four hundred and twenty-second Quidditch World Cup!'

The spectators screamed and clapped. Thousands of flags waved, adding their discordant national anthems to the racket. The huge blackboard opposite them was wiped clear of its last message (*Bertie Bott's Every Flavour Beans – a Risk with Every Mouthful!*) and now showed BULGARIA: ZERO, IRELAND: ZERO.

'And now, without further ado, allow me to introduce ... the Bulgarian Team Mascots!'

The right-hand side of the stands, which was a solid block of scarlet, roared its approval.

'I wonder what they've brought?' said Mr Weasley, leaning forwards in his seat. 'Aaah!' He suddenly whipped off his glasses and polished them hurriedly on his robes. '*Veela!*'

'What are Veel–?'

But a hundred Veela were now gliding out onto the pitch, and Harry's question was answered for him. Veela were women ... the most beautiful women Harry had ever seen ... except that they weren't – they couldn't be – human. This puzzled Harry for a moment, while he tried to guess what exactly they could be; what could make their skin shine moon-bright like that, or their white-gold hair fan out behind them without wind ... but then the music started, and Harry stopped worrying about them not being human – in fact, he stopped worrying about anything at all.

## 第8章 魁地奇世界杯赛

注视下,马尔福先生不敢说什么出格的话。他讥讽地对韦斯莱先生点了点头,继续走向自己的座位。德拉科轻蔑地瞪了哈利、罗恩和赫敏一眼,坐在了他父母中间。

"讨厌的家伙。"罗恩嘟哝了一句,他和哈利、赫敏又把视线转向赛场。接着,卢多·巴格曼冲进了包厢。

"大家都准备好了吗?"他说,圆圆的脸像一块巨大的球形干酪一样闪闪发亮,"部长——可以开始了吗?"

"你说开始就开始吧,卢多。"福吉和蔼地说。

卢多抽出他的魔杖,指着自己的喉咙说道:"声音洪亮!"然后他说的话就像雷鸣一样,响彻了整个座无虚席的体育场。他的声音在他们头顶上回荡,响亮地传向看台的每个角落。

"女士们,先生们……欢迎你们的到来!欢迎你们前来观看第422届魁地奇世界杯赛!"

观众们爆发出一阵欢呼和掌声。成千上万面旗帜同时挥舞,还伴有乱七八糟的国歌声,场面真是热闹非凡。他们对面的黑板上,最后那行广告(比比多味豆——每一口都是一次冒险的经历!)被抹去了,现在显示的是:**保加利亚:0,爱尔兰:0**。

"好了,闲话少说,请允许我介绍……保加利亚国家队的吉祥物!"

看台的右侧是一片整齐的鲜红色方阵,此刻爆发出响亮的欢呼声。

"不知道他们带来了什么。"韦斯莱先生说,从座位上探出身子,"啊!"他猛地摘下眼镜,在袍子上匆匆地擦着,"媚娃!"

"什么是媚——"

只见一百个媚娃已经滑向了赛场,哈利的疑问得到了解答。媚娃是女人……是哈利有生以来见过的最漂亮的女人……不过她们不是——不可能是——真人。哈利困惑了片刻,猜不出她们到底是什么:她们的皮肤为什么像月亮一般泛着皎洁的柔光,她们的头发为什么没有风也在脑后飘扬……就在这时,音乐响了起来,哈利不再考虑她们是不是真人了——实际上,他什么也无法考虑了。

## CHAPTER EIGHT   The Quidditch World Cup

The Veela had started to dance, and Harry's mind had gone completely and blissfully blank. All that mattered in the world was that he kept watching the Veela, because if they stopped dancing, terrible things would happen ...

And as the Veela danced faster and faster, wild, half-formed thoughts started chasing through Harry's dazed mind. He wanted to do something very impressive, right now. Jumping from the box into the stadium seemed a good idea ... but would it be good enough?

'Harry, what *are* you doing?' said Hermione's voice from a long way off.

The music stopped. Harry blinked. He was standing up, and one of his legs was resting on the wall of the box. Next to him, Ron was frozen in an attitude that looked as though he was about to dive from a springboard.

Angry yells were filling the stadium. The crowd didn't want the Veela to go. Harry was with them; he would, of course, be supporting Bulgaria, and he wondered vaguely why he had a large green shamrock pinned to his chest. Ron, meanwhile, was absent-mindedly shredding the shamrocks on his hat. Mr Weasley, smiling slightly, leant over to Ron and tugged the hat out of his hands.

'You'll be wanting that,' he said, 'once Ireland have had their say.'

'Huh?' said Ron, staring open-mouthed at the Veela, who had now lined up along one side of the pitch.

Hermione made a loud tutting noise. She reached up and pulled Harry back into his seat. '*Honestly!*' she said.

'And now,' roared Ludo Bagman's voice, 'kindly put your wands in the air ... for the Irish National Team Mascots!'

Next moment, what seemed to be a great green-and-gold comet had come zooming into the stadium. It did one circuit of the stadium, then split into two smaller comets, each hurtling towards the goal-posts. A rainbow arced suddenly across the pitch, connecting the two balls of light. The crowd 'oooohed' and 'aaaaahed', as though at a firework display. Now the rainbow faded and the balls of light reunited and merged; they had formed a great shimmering shamrock, which rose up into the sky and began to soar over the stands. Something like golden rain seemed to be falling from it –

媚娃开始跳舞,哈利的脑子变得一片空白,只感到一种极度的喜悦。世界上的一切都不重要了,只要他能一直看着媚娃就行,因为如果她们停止跳舞,就会发生可怕的事……

随着媚娃的舞姿越来越快,一些疯狂的、不成形的念头开始在哈利晕晕乎乎的脑海里飞旋。他想做一件特别了不起的事情,现在就做。从包厢跳进体育场怎么样?看来不错……可是够不够精彩呢?

"哈利,你在做什么?"从遥远的地方传来赫敏的声音。

音乐停止了。哈利茫然地眨了眨眼睛。他站在那里,一条腿架在包厢的隔墙上。在他旁边,罗恩做出似乎要从跳板上跳水的姿势,呆在那里一动不动。

体育场里充满了愤怒的吼叫。人们不愿意媚娃离开。哈利的想法也和他们一样。他当然要支持保加利亚队,他隐隐地纳闷自己胸前为什么戴着一棵大大的绿色三叶草。与此同时,罗恩正在精神恍惚地撕扯他帽子上的三叶草。韦斯莱先生微笑着探过身来,把帽子从罗恩手里夺了过去。

"待会儿等到爱尔兰队的表演结束后,"韦斯莱先生说,"你就会需要它了。"

"嗯?"罗恩哼了一声,张口结舌地盯着那些媚娃,这时她们已经列队站在赛场一侧。

赫敏发出很响的咂嘴声。她伸手把哈利拉回到座位上。"哎呀,你怎么这样!"她说。

"现在,"卢多·巴格曼的声音如洪钟一般响起,"请把魔杖举向空中……欢迎爱尔兰国家队的吉祥物!"

紧接着,只听嗖的一声,一个巨大的绿色和金色相间的东西飞进体育场,像一颗大彗星。它在馆内飞了一圈,然后分成两颗较小的彗星,分别冲向一组球门柱。整个赛场上突然出现了一道拱形的彩虹,把那两个闪光的大球连接起来。人群中爆发出"哎呀哎呀"的惊叹声,就好像在看焰火表演。这时,彩虹隐去了,闪光的大球互相连接、交融,形成了一棵巨大的、闪亮夺目的三叶草,高高地升向空中,开始在看台上方盘旋。什么东西噼里啪啦地从上面落了下来,像金色的雨点——

## CHAPTER EIGHT  The Quidditch World Cup

'Excellent!' yelled Ron, as the shamrock soared over their heads, and heavy gold coins rained from it, bouncing off their heads and seats. Squinting up at the shamrock, Harry realised that it was actually composed of thousands of tiny little bearded men with red waistcoats, each carrying a minute lamp of gold or green.

'Leprechauns!' said Mr Weasley, over the tumultuous applause of the crowd, many of whom were still fighting and rummaging around under their chairs to retrieve the gold.

'There you go,' Ron yelled happily, stuffing a fistful of gold coins into Harry's hand. 'For the Omnioculars! Now you've got to buy me a Christmas present, ha!'

The great shamrock dissolved, the leprechauns drifted down onto the pitch on the opposite side from the Veela, and settled themselves cross-legged to watch the match.

'And now, ladies and gentlemen, kindly welcome – the Bulgarian National Quidditch Team! I give you – Dimitrov!'

A scarlet-clad figure on a broomstick, moving so fast it was blurred, shot out onto the pitch from an entrance far below, to wild applause from the Bulgarian supporters.

'Ivanova!'

A second scarlet-robed player zoomed out.

'Zograf! Levski! Vulchanov! Volkov! Aaaaaaand – *Krum*!'

'That's him, that's him!' yelled Ron, following Krum with his Omnioculars; Harry quickly focused his own.

Viktor Krum was thin, dark and sallow-skinned, with a large curved nose and thick black eyebrows. He looked like an overgrown bird of prey. It was hard to believe he was only eighteen.

'And now, please greet – the Irish National Quidditch Team!' yelled Bagman. 'Presenting – Connolly! Ryan! Troy! Mullet! Moran! Quigley! Aaaaaaand – *Lynch*!'

Seven green blurs swept onto the pitch; Harry spun a small dial on the side of his Omnioculars, and slowed the players down enough to read the word 'Firebolt' on each of their brooms, and see their names, embroidered in silver, upon their backs.

'And here, all the way from Egypt, our referee, acclaimed Chairwizard of

## 第8章 魁地奇世界杯赛

"太棒了!"罗恩大叫,三叶草在他们头顶上盘旋,不断撒下巨大的金币,落在他们的头上和座位上。哈利眯起眼睛,仔细观察那三叶草,发现它实际上是由无数个穿着红马甲、留着小胡子的小人儿组成的,每个小人儿都提着一盏金色或绿色的小灯。

"是爱尔兰小矮妖!"韦斯莱先生在一片欢呼声中说。人们一边喝彩,一边还在乱哄哄地争抢,或钻到座位下面去捡金币。

"给你,"罗恩高兴地喊道,将一把金币塞进哈利手里,"还你的全景望远镜!现在你必须给我买圣诞礼物了,哈哈!"

巨大的三叶草消逝了,小矮妖们慢慢落到赛场上那些媚娃的对面,盘腿坐下来,准备观看比赛。

"现在,女士们,先生们,请热烈欢迎——保加利亚魁地奇国家队!我给大家介绍——迪米特洛夫!"

一个骑在飞天扫帚上的穿红衣服的身影,从下面的一个入口处飞进赛场,他飞得太快了,简直看不清楚。他赢得了保加利亚队支持者们的狂热喝彩。

"伊万诺瓦!"

第二个穿鲜红色长袍的身影嗖地飞了出来。

"佐格拉夫!莱弗斯基!沃卡诺夫!沃尔科夫!接下来——克鲁姆!"

"是他,是他!"罗恩喊道,用他的全景望远镜追随着克鲁姆。哈利赶紧也把自己的望远镜对准了他。

威克多尔·克鲁姆长得又黑又瘦,皮肤是灰黄色的,一个大鹰钩鼻子,两道黑黑的浓眉,看上去就像一只身材十分巨大的老鹰。真难以相信他只有十八岁。

"现在,请欢迎——爱尔兰魁地奇国家队!"巴格曼响亮地喊道,"出场的是——康诺利!瑞安!特洛伊!马莱特!莫兰!奎格利!还—还—还有——林齐!"

七个模糊的绿色身影飞向了赛场,哈利转了转全景望远镜侧面的一个小钮,把队员的动作放慢,看清了他们的飞天扫帚上都印着火弩箭,还看到他们背上都用银线绣着各自的姓名。

"还有我们今天的裁判,不远万里从埃及飞来的、深受拥护的国际

## CHAPTER EIGHT  The Quidditch World Cup

the International Association of Quidditch, Hassan Mostafa!'

A small and skinny wizard, completely bald but with a moustache to rival Uncle Vernon's, wearing robes of pure gold to match the stadium, strode out onto the pitch. A silver whistle was protruding from under the moustache, and he was carrying a large wooden crate under one arm, his broomstick under the other. Harry spun the speed dial on his Omnioculars back to normal, watching closely as Mostafa mounted his broomstick and kicked the crate open – four balls burst into the air: the scarlet Quaffle, the two black Bludgers and (Harry saw it for the briefest moment, before it sped out of sight) the minuscule, winged, Golden Snitch. With a sharp blast on his whistle, Mostafa shot into the air after the balls.

'Theeeeeeeey're OFF!' screamed Bagman. 'And it's Mullet! Troy! Moran! Dimitrov! Back to Mullet! Troy! Levski! Moran!'

It was Quidditch as Harry had never seen it played before. He was pressing his Omnioculars so hard to his eyes that his glasses were cutting into the bridge of his nose. The speed of the players was incredible – the Chasers were throwing the Quaffle to each other so fast that Bagman only had time to say their names. Harry spun the 'slow' dial on the right of his Omnioculars again, pressed the 'play by play' button on the top and he was immediately watching in slow motion, while glittering purple lettering flashed across the lenses, and the noise of the crowd pounded against his eardrums.

'*Hawkshead Attacking Formation*' he read, as he watched the three Irish Chasers zoom closely together, Troy in the centre, slightly ahead of Mullet and Moran, bearing down upon the Bulgarians. '*Porskoff Ploy*' flashed up next, as Troy made as though to dart upwards with the Quaffle, drawing away the Bulgarian Chaser Ivanova, and dropping the Quaffle to Moran. One of the Bulgarian Beaters, Volkov, swung hard at a passing Bludger with his small club, knocking it into Moran's path; Moran ducked to avoid the Bludger and dropped the Quaffle; and Levski, soaring beneath, caught it –

'TROY SCORES!' roared Bagman, and the stadium shuddered with a roar of applause and cheers. 'Ten – zero to Ireland!'

'What?' Harry yelled, looking wildly around through his Omnioculars. 'But Levski's got the Quaffle!'

'Harry, if you're not going to watch at normal speed, you're going to miss things!' shouted Hermione, who was dancing up and down, waving her arms

## 第8章 魁地奇世界杯赛

魁地奇联合会主席——哈桑·穆斯塔发!"

一个矮小、精瘦的巫师穿着与体育场颜色相配的纯金色长袍,大步走向赛场。他头顶全秃了,但那一把大胡子却可以和弗农姨父的胡子媲美。一只银口哨从胡子下面伸了出来。他一只胳膊底下夹着一只大木箱,另一只胳臂底下夹着他的飞天扫帚。哈利把全景望远镜又调回到正常速度,仔细观看穆斯塔发跨上他的飞天扫帚,一脚把木箱踢开——四只球一下子蹿到空中:鲜红的鬼飞球,两只黑色的游走球,还有那只很小很小、长着翅膀的金色飞贼(哈利只瞥见一眼,它就飞得无影无踪了)。穆斯塔发吹响口哨,也跟着那些球飞向空中。

"啊,他—他—他们**出发了**!"巴格曼尖叫着,"这是马莱特!特洛伊!莫兰!迪米特洛夫!又传给马莱特!特洛伊!莱弗斯基!莫兰!"

哈利从来没见过这样精彩的魁地奇比赛。他把全景望远镜紧紧按在眼镜上,压得眼镜都陷进了鼻梁。队员们的速度简直令人难以置信——追球手不停地把鬼飞球传给其他队员,速度之快,巴格曼只来得及报出他们的名字。哈利又拧了拧全景望远镜右侧的慢速旋钮,再按一下顶部的赛况分析键,立刻就看到了慢动作,镜头上还闪过一些紫色的文字,同时全场观众的喧闹声震击着他的耳膜。

鹰头进攻阵形。他读到这样的文字,同时看见三位爱尔兰追球手紧挨在一起飞驰,特洛伊在中间,稍微后面一点是马莱特和莫兰,三人一起向保加利亚队员逼近。接着,镜头上又闪出波斯科夫战术的字样,只见特洛伊带着鬼飞球假装往上冲,引开保加利亚追球手伊万诺瓦,再把球扔给莫兰。保加利亚的击球手之一沃尔科夫用手里的球棒狠击飞来的游走球,把它击向莫兰那边;莫兰往下一缩,躲开游走球,扔出鬼飞球,在下面盘旋的莱弗斯基一把将球接住——

"**特洛伊进球**!"巴格曼的大嗓门吼道,全场一片欢呼喝彩,震得体育场都在颤动,"10:0,爱尔兰队领先!"

"什么?"哈利着急地通过全景望远镜到处搜索,嘴里大声喊道,"可是鬼飞球被莱弗斯基拿去了呀!"

"哈利,如果你还不用正常速度观看,就要错过精彩的场面了。"赫敏大声说,特洛伊进球后绕赛场一周,赫敏兴奋地跳上跳下,不停

## CHAPTER EIGHT   The Quidditch World Cup

in the air while Troy did a lap of honour of the pitch. Harry looked quickly over the top of his Omnioculars, and saw that the leprechauns watching from the side-lines had all risen into the air again, and formed the great, glittering shamrock. Across the pitch, the Veela were watching them sulkily.

Furious with himself, Harry spun his speed dial back to normal as play resumed.

Harry knew enough about Quidditch to see that the Irish Chasers were superb. They worked as a seamless team, appearing to read each other's minds by the way they positioned themselves, and the rosette on Harry's chest kept squeaking their names: '*Troy – Mullet – Moran!*' and within ten minutes, Ireland had scored twice more, bringing their lead to thirty – zero, and causing a thunderous tide of roars and applause from the green-clad supporters.

The match became still faster, but more brutal. Volkov and Vulchanov, the Bulgarian Beaters, were whacking the Bludgers as fiercely as possible at the Irish Chasers, and were starting to prevent them using some of their best moves; twice they were forced to scatter, and then, finally, Ivanova managed to break through their ranks, dodge the Keeper, Ryan, and score Bulgaria's first goal.

'Fingers in your ears!' bellowed Mr Weasley, as the Veela started to dance in celebration. Harry screwed up his eyes, too; he wanted to keep his mind on the game. After a few seconds, he chanced a glance at the pitch. The Veela had stopped dancing, and Bulgaria were again in possession of the Quaffle.

'Dimitrov! Levski! Dimitrov! Ivanova – oh, I say!' roared Bagman.

One hundred thousand wizards and witches gasped as the two Seekers, Krum and Lynch, plummeted through the centre of the Chasers, so fast that it looked as though they had just jumped from aeroplanes without parachutes. Harry followed their descent through his Omnioculars, squinting to see where the Snitch was –

'They're going to crash!' screamed Hermione next to Harry.

She was half right – at the very last second, Viktor Krum pulled out of the dive and spiralled off. Lynch, however, hit the ground with a dull thud that could be heard throughout the stadium. A huge groan rose from the Irish seats.

'Fool!' moaned Mr Weasley. 'Krum was feinting!'

'It's time out!' yelled Bagman's voice. 'As trained mediwizards hurry onto the pitch to examine Aidan Lynch!'

地挥舞双臂。哈利赶紧把目光从全景望远镜上抬起,看见那些在边线上观看比赛的小矮妖又都升到了空中,再次形成那棵巨大的闪闪发光的三叶草。赛场对面的媚娃脸色阴沉地望着他们。

哈利很生自己的气,他把速度旋钮调回到正常速度,比赛继续进行。

哈利对魁地奇比赛很了解,他看出爱尔兰队的追球手是超一流的。他们配合得天衣无缝,动作十分协调,好像彼此都能看透对方的心思,哈利胸前的徽章不停地尖叫着他们的名字:"特洛伊——马莱特——莫兰!"十分钟内,爱尔兰队又进了两个球,将比分改写成30:0,引起穿绿衣服的支持者们排山倒海般的欢呼和喝彩。

比赛变得更加激烈,也更加残酷。保加利亚的击球手沃尔科夫和沃卡诺夫使出吃奶的力气把游走球击向爱尔兰追球手,并试图阻止他们采用一些最佳攻势。他们两次被追散开,最后,伊万诺瓦终于突破了他们的阵容,躲开守门员瑞安,为保加利亚队进了第一个球。

"快用手指堵住耳朵!"韦斯莱先生看见媚娃开始跳舞庆祝了,赶紧大声喊道。哈利把眼睛也闭上了,他想让自己的注意力集中在比赛上。几秒钟后,他冒险朝赛场扫了一眼。媚娃已经停止跳舞,鬼飞球又在保加利亚队手里了。

"迪米特洛夫!莱弗斯基!迪米特洛夫!伊万诺瓦——哦,天哪!"巴格曼用洪亮的大嗓门说道。

十万巫师屏住呼吸,注视着两位找球手——克鲁姆和林齐——在追球手们中间快速下落,速度真快啊,就好像没带降落伞就从飞机上跳了下来。哈利通过全景望远镜追随着他们的坠落,眯起眼睛寻找金色飞贼——

"他们要摔在地上了!"哈利身边的赫敏惊叫道。

她只说对了一半——在最后一秒钟,威克多尔·克鲁姆停止俯冲,重新上升,盘旋着飞走了。而林齐则重重地摔在地上,砰的一声,整个体育场都能听见。爱尔兰观众的座位席上传来一片哀叹。

"傻瓜!"韦斯莱先生埋怨道,"克鲁姆是在做假动作!"

"比赛暂停,"巴格曼先生吼道,"训练有素的场内医生冲向赛场,检查艾丹·林齐的伤势!"

## CHAPTER EIGHT  The Quidditch World Cup

'He'll be OK, he only got ploughed!' Charlie said reassuringly to Ginny, who was hanging over the side of the box, looking horror-struck. 'Which is what Krum was after, of course ...'

Harry hastily pressed the 'replay' and 'play by play' buttons on his Omnioculars, twiddled the speed dial, and put them back up to his eyes.

He watched as Krum and Lynch dived again in slow motion. *Wronski Feint – dangerous Seeker diversion*' read the shining purple lettering across his lenses. He saw Krum's face contorted with concentration as he pulled out of the dive just in time, while Lynch was flattened, and he understood – Krum hadn't seen the Snitch at all, he was just making Lynch copy him. Harry had never seen anyone fly like that; Krum hardly looked as though he was using a broomstick at all; he moved so easily through the air that it looked as though he was unsupported and weightless. Harry turned his Omnioculars back to normal, and focused them on Krum. He was circling high above Lynch, who was now being revived by mediwizards with cups of potion. Harry, focusing still more closely upon Krum's face, saw his dark eyes darting all over the ground a hundred feet below. He was using the time while Lynch was revived to look for the Snitch without interference.

Lynch got to his feet at last, to loud cheers from the green-clad supporters, mounted his Firebolt and kicked back off into the air. His revival seemed to give Ireland new heart. When Mostafa blew his whistle again, the Chasers moved into action with a skill unrivalled by anything Harry had seen so far.

After fifteen more fast and furious minutes, Ireland had pulled ahead by ten more goals. They were now leading by one hundred and thirty points to ten, and the game was starting to get dirtier.

As Mullet shot towards the goalposts yet again, clutching the Quaffle tightly under her arm, the Bulgarian Keeper, Zograf, flew out to meet her. Whatever happened was over so quickly Harry didn't catch it, but a scream of rage from the Irish crowd, and Mostafa's long, shrill whistle blast, told him it had been a foul.

'And Mostafa takes the Bulgarian Keeper to task for cobbing – excessive use of elbows!' Bagman informed the roaring spectators. 'And – yes, it's a penalty to Ireland!'

The leprechauns, who had risen angrily into the air like a swarm of glittering hornets when Mullet had been fouled, now darted together to form

## 第8章 魁地奇世界杯赛

"他没事,只是用力过猛!"查理安慰金妮道——金妮挪到包厢侧面,脸上一副惊恐的表情,"当然啦,这正是克鲁姆想达到的目的……"

哈利急忙按了按全景望远镜的重放和赛况分析键,调整了一下速度转盘,然后把望远镜重新贴在眼睛上。

他看着克鲁姆和林齐以慢动作再次俯冲下去。镜头上闪过一行发亮的紫色文字:朗斯基假动作——找球手变向,危险。他看见当克鲁姆及时停止俯冲、林齐重重坠地时,克鲁姆的注意力非常集中,脸部肌肉都扭曲了,于是哈利明白了——克鲁姆压根儿就没有看见金色飞贼,只是想让林齐模仿他。哈利从没见过有谁那样飞行,克鲁姆好像根本没有使用飞天扫帚,他自如地在空中飞来飞去,似乎完全不用依靠什么,轻盈得像一根羽毛。哈利把全景望远镜调成正常速度,把镜头对准克鲁姆。场内医生正在喂林齐喝一些魔药,林齐慢慢地恢复了体力,克鲁姆就在林齐的头顶上兜着圈子。哈利更仔细地观察克鲁姆的脸,发现他那双黑眼睛扫视着一百英尺以下的赛场。他正在利用林齐恢复体力的这段时间,不受任何干扰地寻找金色飞贼。

终于,林齐站了起来。在穿绿衣服的支持者们响亮的欢呼声中,他骑上了他的火弩箭,用脚一蹬,蹿向了空中。他的恢复似乎使爱尔兰队有了新的信心。当穆斯塔发再次吹响口哨时,追球手们迅速组织攻势,技术之高超,是哈利从没见过的。

又经过紧张激烈的十五分钟,爱尔兰队又接连攻进十个球。他们现在以130:10领先,比赛开始变得不择手段了。

当马莱特胳膊底下夹着鬼飞球又一次冲向门柱时,保加利亚的守门员佐格拉夫飞出来迎向她。一切都发生得太快,哈利没有看清,但爱尔兰观众中传出一阵愤怒的喊叫,穆斯塔发吹响了一声长长的、刺耳的口哨,他这才明白刚才场上犯规了。

"穆斯塔发斥责保加利亚守门员打人——肘部动作过大!"巴格曼对吵嚷不休的观众们说,"啊——是的,爱尔兰队罚球!"

刚才,马莱特被对方守门员冲撞后,小矮妖们像一群闪闪发亮的大黄蜂一样,气愤地升到空中,现在又迅速组成"哈!哈!哈!"的

the words 'HA HA HA!'. The Veela on the other side of the pitch leapt to their feet, tossed their hair angrily and started to dance again.

As one, the Weasley boys and Harry stuffed their fingers in their ears, but Hermione, who hadn't bothered, was soon tugging on Harry's arm. He turned to look at her, and she pulled his fingers impatiently out of his ears.

'Look at the referee!' she said, giggling.

Harry looked down at the pitch. Hassan Mostafa had landed right in front of the dancing Veela, and was acting very oddly indeed. He was flexing his muscles and smoothing his moustache excitedly.

'Now, we can't have that!' said Ludo Bagman, though he sounded highly amused. 'Somebody slap the referee!'

A mediwizard came tearing across the pitch, his fingers stuffed in his own ears, and kicked Mostafa hard on the shins. Mostafa seemed to come to himself; Harry, watching through the Omnioculars again, saw that he looked exceptionally embarrassed, and was shouting at the Veela, who had stopped dancing and were looking mutinous.

'And unless I'm much mistaken, Mostafa is actually attempting to send off the Bulgarian Team Mascots!' said Bagman's voice. 'Now *there's* something we haven't seen before ... oh, this could turn nasty ...'

It did: the Bulgarian Beaters, Volkov and Vulchanov, had landed either side of Mostafa, and began arguing furiously with him, gesticulating towards the leprechauns, who had now gleefully formed the words 'HEE HEE HEE'. Mostafa was not impressed by the Bulgarians' arguments, however; he was jabbing his finger into the air, clearly telling them to get flying again, and when they refused, he gave two short blasts on his whistle.

'*Two* penalties for Ireland!' shouted Bagman, and the Bulgarian crowd howled with anger. 'And Volkov and Vulchanov had better get back on those brooms ... yes ... there they go ... and Troy takes the Quaffle ...'

Play now reached a level of ferocity beyond anything they had yet seen. The Beaters on both sides were acting without mercy: Volkov and Vulchanov in particular seemed not to care whether their clubs made contact with Bludger or human, as they swung them violently through the air. Dimitrov shot straight at Moran, who had the Quaffle, nearly knocking her off her broom.

'*Foul!*' roared the Irish supporters as one, all standing up in a great wave of

字样。赛场对面的媚娃跳了起来,愤怒地甩着她们的头发,又开始跳舞。

韦斯莱家的男孩和哈利不约而同地用手指堵住耳朵,赫敏则没有这么做。很快,赫敏就使劲拉扯哈利的胳膊。哈利转过脸,赫敏不耐烦地把他的手指从耳朵里抽了出来。

"快看裁判!"她咯咯笑着说。

哈利朝下面的赛场上望去。哈桑·穆斯塔发已经降落到正在跳舞的媚娃面前,行为十分古怪。他屈伸四肢,展示自己的肌肉,并且兴奋地捋着他的大胡子。

"哦,这样可不行!"卢多·巴格曼说,不过听他的口气,他也觉得十分有趣,"有谁上去给裁判一巴掌!"

一个场内医生用手指堵着耳朵,冲进场地,对准穆斯塔发的小腿狠狠踢了几脚。穆斯塔发似乎回过神来了。哈利又举起全景望远镜,看见穆斯塔发显得特别尴尬,冲着媚娃大声嚷嚷,媚娃停止了跳舞,表情似乎很不服气。

"也许我是弄错了,穆斯塔发居然想把保加利亚队的吉祥物打发回家!"巴格曼的声音说道,"哦,这样的情景我们可没有见过……哦,情况可能会变得不好对付了……"

确实,保加利亚队的击球手沃尔科夫和沃卡诺夫一边一个降落在穆斯塔发的两边,开始愤怒地与他争吵,并朝小矮妖们做着手势,小矮妖这时开心地组成"嘿!嘿!嘿!"的字样。然而,穆斯塔发对保加利亚队员的抗议无动于衷。他朝空中举起一根手指,显然是叫他们重新起飞。他们不肯,他就吹了短短两声口哨。

"爱尔兰队两次罚球!"巴格曼喊道——保加利亚观众愤怒地吼开了,"沃尔科夫和沃卡诺夫最好骑到扫帚上去……行了……他们骑上去了……特洛伊拿到了鬼飞球……"

比赛现在达到的凶猛激烈程度,是他们从没见过的。双方的击球手都表现得毫不留情:特别是沃尔科夫和沃卡诺夫,他们根本不管手里的棒子击中的是球还是人,只顾拼命地狂挥乱打。迪米特洛夫径直冲向拿着鬼飞球的莫兰,把她撞得差点从扫帚上摔下去。

"犯规!"爱尔兰队的支持者们齐声喊道。他们全都站了起来,形

green.

'Foul!' echoed Ludo Bagman's magically magnified voice. 'Dimitrov skins Moran – deliberately flying to collide there – and it's got to be another penalty – yes, there's the whistle!'

The leprechauns had risen into the air again and, this time, they formed a giant hand, which was making a very rude sign indeed across the pitch towards the Veela. At this, the Veela lost control. They launched themselves across the pitch, and began throwing what seemed to be handfuls of fire at the leprechauns. Watching through his Omnioculars, Harry saw that they didn't look remotely beautiful now. On the contrary, their faces were elongating into sharp, cruel-beaked bird heads, and long, scaly wings were bursting from their shoulders –

'And *that*, boys,' yelled Mr Weasley over the tumult of the crowd below, 'is why you should never go for looks alone!'

Ministry wizards were flooding onto the field to separate the Veela and the leprechauns, but with little success; meanwhile, the pitched battle below was nothing to the one above. Harry turned this way and that, staring through his Omnioculars, as the Quaffle changed hands with the speed of a bullet –

'Levski – Dimitrov – Moran – Troy – Mullet – Ivanova – Moran again – Moran – MORAN SCORES!'

But the cheers of the Irish supporters were barely heard over the shrieks of the Veela, the blasts now issuing from the Ministry members' wands, and the furious roars of the Bulgarians. The game recommenced immediately; now Levski had the Quaffle, now Dimitrov –

The Irish Beater Quigley swung heavily at a passing Bludger, and hit it as hard as possible towards Krum, who did not duck quickly enough. It hit him hard in the face.

There was a deafening groan from the crowd; Krum's nose looked broken, there was blood everywhere, but Hassan Mostafa didn't blow his whistle. He had become distracted, and Harry couldn't blame him; one of the Veela had thrown a handful of fire and set his broomtail alight.

Harry wanted someone to realise that Krum was injured; even though he was supporting Ireland, Krum was the most exciting player on the pitch. Ron obviously felt the same.

'Time out! Ah, come on, he can't play like that, look at him –'

成一股巨大的绿色波浪。

"犯规!"卢多·巴格曼那被魔法放大的声音也重复着这两个字,"迪米特洛夫碰伤了莫兰——故意飞过去冲撞——肯定会被判罚球——没错,裁判吹哨了!"

小矮妖又全部升到空中,这次他们形成了一只巨手,朝场地那边的媚娃做出一个非常粗鲁的手势。媚娃一看,顿时失去了控制。她们猛扑过赛场,开始将一把一把的火焰般的东西朝小矮妖扔去。哈利通过望远镜看去,发现她们现在一点儿也不美丽了。相反,她们的脸拉长了,变成了尖尖的、长着利喙的鸟头,一对长长的、覆盖着鳞片的翅膀正从她们的肩膀上冒出来——

"明白了吧,孩子们,"韦斯莱先生的声音盖过下面人群的喧哗,"所以你们永远不能只追求外表!"

部里的巫师官员纷纷拥进赛场,试图把媚娃和小矮妖分开,可是收效甚微。不过,此刻下面这场酣战丝毫不能与上面进行的比赛相比。哈利通过望远镜一会儿看这里,一会儿看那里,只见鬼飞球像子弹一样,从这个人手里传到那个人手里。

"莱弗斯基——迪米特洛夫——莫兰——特洛伊——马莱特——伊万诺瓦——又是莫兰——莫兰——**莫兰进球了!**"

可是赛场上充满了媚娃的尖叫声、部里官员的魔杖发出的爆响声,还有保加利亚人愤怒的吼叫声,简直听不见爱尔兰队支持者们的欢呼。比赛立刻继续进行,现在是莱弗斯基拿到了鬼飞球,然后是迪米特洛夫——

爱尔兰队的击球手奎格利使出吃奶的力气,把一只飞来的游走球击向克鲁姆,克鲁姆躲闪不及,被游走球迎面撞上。

观众席里传来震耳欲聋的抱怨声。克鲁姆的鼻子好像撞坏了,血流得到处都是,可是哈桑·穆斯塔发没有吹哨。他注意力不集中了;哈利也没有办法责怪他,一个媚娃朝他扔出一把火,点着了他的扫帚尾巴。

哈利真希望有人发现克鲁姆受伤了,尽管他是支持爱尔兰队的,但克鲁姆是场上最令人激动的队员。罗恩显然也有同感。

"暂停!啊,快点儿,他那个样子不能再比赛了,你看他——"

'*Look at Lynch!*' Harry yelled.

For the Irish Seeker had suddenly gone into a dive, and Harry was quite sure that this was no Wronski Feint; this was the real thing ...

'He's seen the Snitch!' Harry shouted. 'He's seen it! Look at him go!'

Half the crowd seemed to have realised what was happening, the Irish supporters rose in a great wave of green, screaming their Seeker on ... but Krum was on his tail. How he could see where he was going, Harry had no idea; there were flecks of blood flying through the air behind him, but he was drawing level with Lynch now, as the pair of them hurtled towards the ground again –

'They're going to crash!' shrieked Hermione.

'They're not!' roared Ron.

'Lynch is!' yelled Harry.

And he was right – for the second time, Lynch hit the ground with tremendous force, and was immediately stampeded by a horde of angry Veela.

'The Snitch, where's the Snitch?' bellowed Charlie, along the row.

'He's got it – Krum's got it – it's all over!' shouted Harry.

Krum, his red robes shining with blood from his nose, was rising gently into the air, his fist held high, a glint of gold in his hand.

The scoreboard was flashing **BULGARIA: ONE HUNDRED AND SIXTY, IRELAND: ONE HUNDRED AND SEVENTY** across the crowd, who didn't seem to have realised what had happened. Then, slowly, as though a great jumbo jet was revving up, the rumbling from the Ireland supporters grew louder and louder and erupted into screams of delight.

'IRELAND WIN!' shouted Bagman, who, like the Irish, seemed to have been taken aback by the sudden end of the match. 'KRUM GETS THE SNITCH – BUT IRELAND WIN – good Lord, I don't think any of us were expecting that!'

'What did he catch the Snitch for?' Ron bellowed, even as he jumped up and down, applauding with his hands over his head. 'He ended it when Ireland were a hundred and sixty points ahead, the idiot!'

'He knew they were never going to catch up,' Harry shouted back over all the noise, also applauding loudly, 'the Irish Chasers were too good ... he

## 第 8 章 魁地奇世界杯赛

"快看林齐!"哈利大喊。

只见爱尔兰的找球手突然向下俯冲,哈利可以肯定这绝不是朗斯基假动作,这次是真的了……

"他看见金色飞贼了!"哈利高喊,"他看见了!快看他!"

这时,有一半观众意识到了是怎么回事。爱尔兰队的支持者们又纷纷起立,再次掀起一股绿色波浪,尖叫着给他们的找球手加油……可是克鲁姆紧随其后。他怎么能看见前面的路呢,哈利真不明白;血花在他身后的空中飞溅,可是他已经追上了林齐,与他平行了,两人再次向地面俯冲下去——

"他们要摔到地上了!"赫敏尖叫。

"不会的!"罗恩喊道。

"林齐会的!"哈利大嚷。

他说得对——林齐第二次重重地摔在地上,一群愤怒的媚娃立刻一窝蜂似的围了上去。

"金色飞贼呢,金色飞贼在哪里?"坐在那边的查理喊道。

"他抓住了——克鲁姆抓住了——比赛结束了!"哈利大叫。

克鲁姆鲜红的袍子上闪烁着斑斑点点的鼻血。他轻盈地升到空中,高高举起拳头,指缝里露出一道金光。

记分板上闪动着比分,**保加利亚:160,爱尔兰:170**,而观众似乎还没有意识到究竟是怎么回事。然后,慢慢地,就像一架巨型喷气式飞机正在加速,爱尔兰队支持者们的议论声越来越响,最后爆发出无数喜悦的狂喊。

"爱尔兰队获胜了!"巴格曼喊道,似乎和爱尔兰人一样被比赛的突然结束弄得有些茫然,"**克鲁姆抓到了金色飞贼——可是爱尔兰队获胜了**——天哪,我想大家谁也没有料到会是这样的结局!"

"他为什么要这时候去抓金色飞贼呢?"罗恩尽管高举着双手,跳上跳下地欢呼,仍然不解地大声嚷嚷,"他在爱尔兰队领先一百六十分的时候结束比赛,真是太傻了!"

"他知道他们永远也不可能追上来!"哈利也在大声欢呼。他盖过其他声音对罗恩喊道:"爱尔兰队的追球手太棒了……克鲁姆只想根据

wanted to end it on his terms, that's all ...'

'He was very brave, wasn't he?' Hermione said, leaning forward to watch Krum land, and the swarm of mediwizards blasting a path through the battling leprechauns and Veela to get to him. 'He looks a terrible mess ...'

Harry put his Omnioculars to his eyes again. It was hard to see what was happening below, because leprechauns were zooming delightedly all over the pitch, but he could just make out Krum, surrounded by mediwizards. He looked surlier than ever, and refused to let them mop him up. His team-mates were around him, shaking their heads and looking dejected; a short way away, the Irish players were dancing gleefully in a shower of gold descending from their mascots. Flags were waving all over the stadium, the Irish national anthem blared from all sides; the Veela were shrinking back into their usual, beautiful selves now, though looking dispirited and forlorn.

'Vell, ve fought bravely,' said a gloomy voice behind Harry. He looked around; it was the Bulgarian Minister for Magic.

'You can speak English!' said Fudge, sounding outraged. 'And you've been letting me mime everything all day!'

'Vell, it vos very funny,' said the Bulgarian Minister, shrugging.

'And as the Irish team perform a lap of honour, flanked by their mascots, the Quidditch World Cup itself is brought into the Top Box!' roared Bagman.

Harry's eyes were suddenly dazzled by a blinding white light, as the Top Box was magically illuminated so that everyone in the stands could see the inside. Squinting towards the entrance, he saw two panting wizards carrying into the box a vast golden cup, which they handed to Cornelius Fudge, who was still looking very disgruntled that he'd been using sign language all day for nothing.

'Let's have a really loud hand for the gallant losers – Bulgaria!' Bagman shouted.

And up the stairs into the box came the seven defeated Bulgarian players. The crowd below were applauding appreciatively; Harry could see thousands and thousands of Omniocular lenses flashing and winking in their direction.

One by one, the Bulgarians filed between the rows of seats in the box, and Bagman called out the name of each as they shook hands with their

## 第8章 魁地奇世界杯赛

自己的情况结束比赛,就是这样……"

"他真是非常勇敢,是不是?"赫敏探身向前,注视着克鲁姆降落到地面上——一大群场内医生在扭打到一起的小矮妖和媚娃之中劈开一条路,急急忙忙赶到他身边去,"他的样子真狼狈……"

哈利又把全景望远镜贴在眼睛上。很难看清下面的情况,因为小矮妖们欣喜若狂地在赛场上空穿来穿去,但他总算认出了被一群场内医生包围着的克鲁姆。克鲁姆的脸色更阴沉了,他不让医生替他清理伤口,擦洗血迹。他的队友们也都围在他身边,摇着头,一副垂头丧气的样子。就在旁边不远的地方,爱尔兰队的球员们高兴得手舞足蹈,他们的吉祥物向他们抛撒着阵雨般的金币。体育场内到处挥舞着旗子,爱尔兰国歌从四面八方响起。媚娃又恢复了她们原来美丽的样子,不过一个个看上去垂头丧气,愁眉苦脸。

"我说,我们打得很勇敢。"哈利身后一个沉重的声音说。他扭头一看,是保加利亚的魔法部部长。

"你会说英语!"福吉说,语气非常恼火,"可你让我整天在这里比比画画!"

"嘿,那是很好玩的呀。"保加利亚部长耸耸肩膀,说道。

"现在,爱尔兰队的队员在他们吉祥物的陪伴下绕场一周,魁地奇世界杯赛奖杯被送到了顶层包厢!"巴格曼洪钟般的声音说道。

突然一道耀眼的强光刺得哈利睁不开眼睛,顶层包厢被神奇般地照亮了,使所有看台的观众都能看见包厢内的情况。哈利眯起眼睛看着入口处,只见两个气喘吁吁的巫师抬着一只很大的金杯进了包厢,把它递给了康奈利·福吉。福吉仍然一副不高兴的样子,因为他白白比画了一整天,想让保加利亚人听懂他的话。

"让我们热烈鼓掌,欢迎虽败犹荣的保加利亚队员上台!"巴格曼喊道。

七个吃了败仗的保加利亚队员上楼进入了包厢。下面的观众纷纷鼓掌欢呼,表示对他们的赞赏。哈利可以看见无数个全景望远镜的镜片朝他们这边闪烁。

保加利亚队员一个接一个地走进包厢的两排座位之间,轮番与自

## CHAPTER EIGHT  The Quidditch World Cup

own Minister and then with Fudge. Krum, who was last in line, looked a real mess. Two black eyes were blooming spectacularly on his bloody face. He was still holding the Snitch. Harry noticed that he seemed much less co-ordinated on the ground. He was slightly duck-footed and distinctly round-shouldered. But when Krum's name was announced, the whole stadium gave him a resounding, ear-splitting roar.

And then came the Irish team. Aidan Lynch was being supported by Moran and Connolly; the second crash seemed to have dazed him and his eyes looked strangely unfocused. But he grinned happily as Troy and Quigley lifted the Cup into the air and the crowd below thundered their approval. Harry's hands were numb with clapping.

At last, when the Irish team had left the box to perform another lap of honour on their brooms (Aidan Lynch on the back of Connolly's, clutching hard around his waist and still grinning in a bemused sort of way), Bagman pointed his wand at his throat and muttered, '*Quietus*'.

'They'll be talking about this one for years,' he said hoarsely, 'a really unexpected twist, that ... shame it couldn't have lasted longer ... ah yes ... yes, I owe you ... how much?'

For Fred and George had just scrambled over the backs of their seats, and were standing in front of Ludo Bagman with broad grins on their faces, their hands outstretched.

己的部长和福吉握手,巴格曼大声喊出每个人的名字。克鲁姆排在最后,一副很狼狈的样子,血迹斑斑的脸上,两个黑眼圈显得格外醒目。他手里仍然攥着金色飞贼。哈利注意到,他落到地面上之后,动作看上去就不那么协调了。两条腿有点外八字,而且肩膀明显向前拱着。可是当巴格曼报出克鲁姆的名字时,整个体育场给予了他无比热烈的、震耳欲聋的欢呼。

接着上台的是爱尔兰队的队员。艾丹·林齐被莫兰和康诺利扶着,第二次坠地似乎把他摔晕了,他的眼神散乱茫然。可是当特洛伊和奎格利把奖杯高高举起、观众们爆发出雷鸣般的鼓掌欢呼时,林齐也咧嘴露出了笑容。哈利把手掌都拍麻了。

最后,爱尔兰队离开包厢,骑扫帚绕场一周(艾丹·林齐坐在康诺利身后,紧紧抱着康诺利的腰,脸上仍然痴痴地傻笑着)。这时,巴格曼用他的魔杖指着喉咙,低声说:"悄声细语。"

"这场比赛,要被人们议论好几年,"他声音嘶哑地说,"真是一个意想不到的转折……只可惜比赛没有进行得更长一些……啊,对了……对了,我应该给你们……多少钱?"

弗雷德和乔治已经从椅子背上翻过去,站到了卢多·巴格曼面前。他们开心地笑着,伸出摊开的手掌。

## CHAPTER NINE

# The Dark Mark

'Don't tell your mother you've been gambling,' Mr Weasley implored Fred and George, as they all made their way slowly down the purple-carpeted stairs.

'Don't worry, Dad,' said Fred gleefully, 'we've got big plans for this money, we don't want it confiscated.'

Mr Weasley looked for a moment as though he was going to ask what these big plans were, but seemed to decide, upon reflection, that he didn't want to know.

They were soon caught up in the crowds now flooding out of the stadium and back to their campsites. Raucous singing was borne towards them on the night air as they retraced their steps along the lantern-lit path, and leprechauns kept shooting over their heads, cackling and waving their lanterns. When they finally reached the tents, nobody felt like sleeping at all and, given the level of noise around them, Mr Weasley agreed that they could all have one last cup of cocoa together before turning in. They were soon arguing enjoyably about the match; Mr Weasley got drawn into a disagreement about cobbing with Charlie, and it was only when Ginny fell asleep right at the tiny table and spilled hot chocolate all over the floor that Mr Weasley called a halt to the verbal replays, and insisted that everyone went to bed. Hermione and Ginny went into the next tent, and Harry and the rest of the Weasleys changed into pyjamas and clambered into their bunks. From the other side of the campsite they could still hear much singing, and the odd echoing bang.

'Oh, I am glad I'm not on duty,' muttered Mr Weasley sleepily, 'I wouldn't fancy having to go and tell the Irish they've got to stop celebrating.'

Harry, who was on a top bunk above Ron, lay staring up at the canvas ceiling of the tent, watching the glow of an occasional leprechaun lantern

## 第9章

## 黑魔标记

"**你**们赌钱的事可不要告诉你们的妈妈。"在大家慢慢走下铺着紫红色地毯的楼梯时,韦斯莱先生恳求弗雷德和乔治说。

"别担心,爸爸,"弗雷德开心地说,"这笔钱我们有许多宏伟的计划。我们才不想让它被没收呢。"

韦斯莱先生迟疑了一下,大概是想问问他们宏伟的计划是什么,但他转念一想,似乎决定还是不问为好。

很快,离开体育场返回营地的人潮就把他们包围了。他们顺着被灯笼照亮的通道往回走,夜空里传来粗声粗气的歌声,小矮妖们不停地在他们头顶上穿梭飞驰,挥舞着手里的灯笼,嘎嘎欢笑。最后,终于到了帐篷边,可是谁也不想睡觉。考虑到周围实在太喧闹了,韦斯莱先生便同意大家喝完一杯可可奶再进帐篷。大家立刻就为刚才比赛的事争论起来。关于撞人犯规的问题,韦斯莱先生和查理争得不可开交。最后金妮在小桌边睡着了,把一杯热巧克力全洒在了地上,韦斯莱先生才命令大家停止对比赛的争论,进去睡觉。赫敏和金妮钻进了旁边的帐篷,哈利和韦斯莱家的男孩们换上睡衣,爬向他们的铺位。这时,仍能听见营地另一边传来的歌声和奇怪的撞击声,在夜空中久久回响。

"哦,幸亏我没有值班,"韦斯莱先生睡意浓浓地嘟哝说,"幸亏我不用去叫爱尔兰人停止欢庆胜利,不然真是难以想象。"

哈利睡在罗恩的上铺,他躺在床上,眼睛盯着帐篷里的帆布篷顶,看着偶尔有一个小矮妖提着灯笼从上面飞过,掠过一道闪光,他脑海

flying overhead, and picturing again some of Krum's more spectacular moves. He was itching to get back on his own Firebolt and try out the Wronski Feint ... somehow Oliver Wood had never managed to convey with all his wriggling diagrams what that move was supposed to look like ... Harry saw himself in robes that had his name on the back, and imagined the sensation of hearing a hundred-thousand-strong crowd roar, as Ludo Bagman's voice echoed throughout the stadium, 'I give you ... *Potter!*'

Harry never knew whether he had actually dropped off to sleep or not – his fantasies of flying like Krum might well have slipped into actual dreams – all he knew was that, quite suddenly, Mr Weasley was shouting.

'Get up! Ron – Harry – come on now, get up, this is urgent!'

Harry sat up quickly and the top of his head hit canvas.

''S'matter?' he said.

Dimly, he could tell that something was wrong. The noises in the campsite had changed. The singing had stopped. He could hear screams, and the sound of people running.

He slipped down from the bunk, and reached for his clothes, but Mr Weasley, who had pulled on his jeans over his own pyjamas, said, 'No time, Harry – just grab a jacket and get outside – quickly!'

Harry did as he was told, and hurried out of the tent, Ron at his heels.

By the light of the few fires that were still burning, he could see people running away into the woods, fleeing something that was moving across the field towards them, something that was emitting odd flashes of light, and noises like gunfire. Loud jeering, roars of laughter and drunken yells were drifting towards them; then came a burst of strong green light, which illuminated the scene.

A crowd of wizards, tightly packed and moving together with wands pointing straight upwards, was marching slowly across the field. Harry squinted at them ... they didn't seem to have faces ... then he realised that their heads were hooded and their faces masked. High above them, floating along in mid-air, four struggling figures were being contorted into grotesque shapes. It was as though the masked wizards on the ground were puppeteers, and the people above them were marionettes operated by invisible strings that rose from the wands into the air. Two of the figures were very small.

More wizards were joining the marching group, laughing and pointing

## 第9章 黑魔标记

里又浮现出克鲁姆的一些精彩动作。他真渴望骑到自己的火弩箭上，尝试一下朗斯基假动作……奥利弗·伍德虽然设计了那么些动来动去的示意图，但不知怎的，他从来没有传授过这种假动作应该怎么做……哈利仿佛看见自己穿着背后印着他名字的长袍，想象着听见十万观众的震耳欲聋的欢呼，而卢多·巴格曼的声音在整个体育场内回荡："热烈欢迎……波特！"

哈利不知道自己到底有没有睡着——他一直在幻想像克鲁姆那样飞翔，也许就这样不知不觉进入了梦境——他只知道韦斯莱先生突然大喊起来。

"起来！罗恩——哈利——快点儿，起来，有紧急情况！"

哈利猛地坐起身，脑袋撞在了帆布顶上。

"什—什么事？"他问。

隐隐约约地，他觉得事情有点不对劲儿。营地上的声音变了。歌声停止了，他听见了惊叫声和人们慌乱的奔跑声。

他从双层床上滑下来，伸手去拿衣服，可是韦斯莱先生说："来不及了，哈利——随便抓一件外衣就出去吧，快点儿！"韦斯莱先生自己就是把牛仔裤直接套在睡裤上的。

哈利听从吩咐，急急忙忙奔出帐篷，罗恩跟在他身后。

就着仍在燃烧的几堆篝火的火光，哈利看见人们纷纷朝树林里跑去，好像在逃避某个在营地上向他们移动的东西。那东西古怪地闪着光，还发出打枪一般的声音。响亮的讥笑声、狂笑声、醉醺醺的叫嚷声，也都向他们移动过来。接着，一道绿色的强光一闪，照亮了周围的一切。

一群巫师紧紧挤作一团，每个人都把手里的魔杖向上指着，一起向前推进，慢慢地在场地上移动。哈利眯着眼睛仔细打量……这些人似乎没有面孔……接着他才反应过来，他们的脑袋上戴着兜帽，脸上罩着面具。在他们头顶上方，四个挣扎着的人影在空中飘浮，被扭曲成各种怪异的形状，就好像地面上这些蒙面巫师是操纵木偶的人，而他们上方那几个人是牵线木偶，被从魔杖里射向空中的无形的绳子控制着。其中两个人影很小。

更多的巫师加入到前进的队伍中，大声笑着，指着上面飘浮的几

## CHAPTER NINE  The Dark Mark

up at the floating bodies. Tents crumpled and fell as the marching crowd swelled. Once or twice Harry saw one of the marchers blast a tent out of his way with his wand. Several caught fire. The screaming grew louder.

The floating people were suddenly illuminated as they passed over a burning tent, and Harry recognised one of them – Mr Roberts, the campsite manager. The other three looked as though they might be his wife and children. One of the marchers below flipped Mrs Roberts upside-down with his wand; her nightdress fell down to reveal voluminous drawers; she struggled to cover herself up as the crowd below her screeched and hooted with glee.

'That's sick,' Ron muttered, watching the smallest Muggle child, who had begun to spin like a top, sixty feet above the ground, his head flopping limply from side to side. 'That is really sick ...'

Hermione and Ginny came hurrying towards them, pulling coats over their nightdresses, with Mr Weasley right behind them. At the same moment, Bill, Charlie and Percy emerged from the boys' tent, fully dressed, with their sleeves rolled up and their wands out.

'We're going to help the Ministry,' Mr Weasley shouted over all the noise, rolling up his own sleeves. 'You lot – get into the woods, and *stick together*. I'll come and fetch you when we've sorted this out!'

Bill, Charlie and Percy were already sprinting away towards the oncoming marchers; Mr Weasley tore after them. Ministry wizards were dashing from every direction towards the source of the trouble. The crowd beneath the Roberts family was coming ever closer.

'C'mon,' said Fred, grabbing Ginny's hand and starting to pull her towards the wood. Harry, Ron, Hermione and George followed. They all looked back as they reached the trees. The crowd beneath the Roberts family was larger than ever; they could see the Ministry wizards trying to get through it to the hooded wizards in the centre, but they were having great difficulty. It looked as though they were scared to perform any spell that might make the Roberts family fall.

The coloured lanterns that had lit the path to the stadium had been extinguished. Dark figures were blundering through the trees; children were crying; anxious shouts and panicked voices were reverberating around them in the cold night air. Harry felt himself being pushed hither and thither by people whose faces he could not see. Then he heard Ron yell with pain.

'What happened?' said Hermione anxiously, stopping so abruptly that

## 第 9 章 黑魔标记

具躯体。随着游行队伍的不断壮大，帐篷被挤塌了。有一两次，哈利看见一个游行者用魔杖把路边的帐篷点着了。几个帐篷都燃烧起来。尖叫声更响亮了。

当空中飘浮的那几个人从燃烧的帐篷上经过、被火光突然照亮时，哈利认出其中一个是营地管理员罗伯茨先生。另外三个看样子是他的妻子和孩子。下面的一个游行者用魔杖把罗伯茨夫人转成了头朝下。罗伯茨夫人的睡衣垂落下来，露出一大堆松垮的内裤，下面的人群开心地尖叫、起哄，她挣扎着想把自己的身体盖住。

"真恶心。"罗恩嘟哝说，望着那个最小的麻瓜小孩——小孩在离地面六十英尺的半空，开始像陀螺一样旋转起来，脑袋软绵绵地忽而歪向这边，忽而歪向那边，"太不像话了……"

赫敏和金妮匆匆向他们跑来，一边把外衣套在睡衣外面，韦斯莱先生跟在她们后面。就在这时，比尔、查理和珀西也从男孩们的帐篷里出来了。他们穿戴整齐，袖子高高卷起，魔杖拿在手里。

"我们要帮助部里维持秩序！"韦斯莱先生的声音盖过了喧闹声，他卷起了自己的袖子，"你们几个——快进林子里去，走在一起，不要散开。等事情解决后我再去找你们！"

比尔、查理和珀西已经朝迎面过来的游行队伍奔去，韦斯莱先生赶紧追了上去。部里的工作人员从四面八方奔向混乱的源头。罗伯茨一家下面的那群人越走越近了。

"快走。"弗雷德说着，一把抓住金妮的手，把她往树林里拖去。哈利、罗恩、赫敏和乔治在后面跟着。他们钻进树林时，都扭头朝身后望着，只见罗伯茨一家下面的队伍比刚才更庞大了。可以看见部里的巫师工作人员拼命想冲进去，接近中间那些戴兜帽的巫师，可是遇到了很大阻力。看样子他们似乎不敢施什么魔法，生怕会使罗伯茨一家摔下来。

原先照亮通往体育场道路的彩灯现在已经熄灭了。树林里有一些黑乎乎的人影跌跌撞撞地走着，小孩在哭闹，紧张焦虑的叫喊声和说话声在周围寒冷的夜空中回荡。哈利感到自己被人群推来搡去，但看不清这些人的面孔。然后，他听见罗恩痛苦地喊叫起来。

"怎么回事？"赫敏紧张地问，猛地刹住脚步——哈利撞到了她身

## CHAPTER NINE  The Dark Mark

Harry walked into her. 'Ron, where are you? Oh, this is stupid – *Lumos!*'

She illuminated her wand and directed its narrow beam across the path. Ron was lying sprawled on the ground.

'Tripped over a tree-root,' he said angrily, getting to his feet again.

'Well, with feet that size, hard not to,' said a drawling voice from behind them.

Harry, Ron and Hermione turned sharply. Draco Malfoy was standing alone nearby them, leaning against a tree, looking utterly relaxed. His arms folded, he seemed to have been watching the scene on the campsite through a gap in the trees.

Ron told Malfoy to do something that Harry knew he would never have dared say in front of Mrs Weasley.

'Language, Weasley,' said Malfoy, his pale eyes glittering. 'Hadn't you better be hurrying along, now? You wouldn't like *her* spotted, would you?'

He nodded at Hermione, and at the same moment, a blast like a bomb sounded from the campsite, and a flash of green light momentarily lit the trees around them.

'What's that supposed to mean?' said Hermione defiantly.

'Granger, they're after *Muggles*,' said Malfoy. 'D'you want to be showing off your knickers in mid-air? Because if you do, hang around … they're moving this way, and it would give us all a laugh.'

'Hermione's a witch,' Harry snarled.

'Have it your own way, Potter,' said Malfoy, grinning maliciously. 'If you think they can't spot a Mudblood, stay where you are.'

'You watch your mouth!' shouted Ron. Everybody present knew that 'Mudblood' was a very offensive term for a witch or wizard of Muggle parentage.

'Never mind, Ron,' said Hermione quickly, seizing Ron's arm to restrain him as he took a step towards Malfoy.

There came a bang from the other side of the trees that was louder than anything they had heard. Several people nearby screamed.

Malfoy chuckled softly. 'Scare easily, don't they?' he said lazily. 'I suppose your daddy told you all to hide? What's he up to – trying to rescue the Muggles?'

## 第9章 黑魔标记

上,"罗恩,你在哪里?哦,我们太傻了——荧光闪烁!"

她把魔杖点亮了,用那道狭窄的光柱照着小路。罗恩四仰八叉地躺在地上。

"被树根绊倒了。"他气呼呼地说,从地上站了起来。

"哼,长着那样一双脚,很难不被绊倒。"一个拖腔拖调的声音在他们身后响起。

哈利、罗恩和赫敏猛地转过身来。德拉科·马尔福独自一人站在近旁,靠着一棵树,一副悠闲自得的样子。他抱着双臂,看样子刚才一直在透过树间缝隙望着营地上的混乱场面。

罗恩对马尔福说了一句粗话,哈利知道,若是韦斯莱夫人在场,他是绝对不敢说这种话的。

"嘴里干净些,"马尔福说,浅色的眼睛在夜色中闪闪发亮,"我看你们最好还是抓紧时间逃跑吧!你们不希望被人发现吧?"

他冲赫敏点了点头,就在这时,营地那边传来一声巨响,如同扔响了一枚炸弹,一道绿光霎时照亮了他们周围的树木。

"你这是什么意思?"赫敏不服气地问。

"格兰杰,他们找的就是麻瓜。"马尔福说,"难道你愿意在半空中展示你的衬裤?如果你愿意,就在这里待着吧……他们正朝这边走来,我们大家可以大笑一场了。"

"赫敏是个女巫!"哈利愤怒地吼道。

"随你的便吧,波特,"马尔福说,脸上露出了狞笑,"如果你们觉得他们辨认不出泥巴种,就尽管待在这里好了。"

"你说话注意点儿!"罗恩喊道。在场的人都知道,"泥巴种"是一句很难听的话,用来骂那些父母是麻瓜的巫师。

"别理他,罗恩。"赫敏急忙说道,她看见罗恩向马尔福逼近一步,便赶紧抓住罗恩的胳膊阻止了他。

树林的另一边突然传来一声爆响,比他们听见的任何声音都震耳。旁边有几个人尖叫起来。马尔福轻轻地笑出了声。

"太容易受惊吓了,这些人,是吗?"他懒洋洋地说,"我猜你爸爸叫你们都藏起来吧?他准备做什么——去把那些麻瓜救出来?"

## CHAPTER NINE    The Dark Mark

'Where're *your* parents?' said Harry, his temper rising. 'Out there wearing masks, are they?'

Malfoy turned his face to Harry, still smiling. 'Well ... if they were, I wouldn't be likely to tell you, would I, Potter?'

'Oh, come on,' said Hermione, with a disgusted look at Malfoy, 'let's go and find the others.'

'Keep that big bushy head down, Granger,' sneered Malfoy.

'Come *on*,' Hermione repeated, and she pulled Harry and Ron off up the path again.

'I'll bet you anything his dad is one of that masked lot!' said Ron hotly.

'Well, with any luck, the Ministry will catch him!' said Hermione fervently. 'Oh, I can't believe this, where have the others got to?'

Fred, George and Ginny were nowhere to be seen, though the path was packed with plenty of other people, all of them looking nervously over their shoulders towards the commotion back at the campsite.

A huddle of teenagers in pyjamas was arguing vociferously a little way along the path. When they saw Harry, Ron and Hermione, a girl with thick, curly hair turned and said quickly, '*Où est Madame Maxime? Nous l'avons perdue –*'

'Er – what?' said Ron.

'Oh ...' The girl who had spoken turned her back on him, and as they walked on they distinctly heard her say, '"Ogwarts.'

'Beauxbatons,' muttered Hermione.

'Sorry?' said Harry.

'They must go to Beauxbatons,' said Hermione. 'You know ... Beauxbatons Academy of Magic ... I read about it in *An Appraisal of Magical Education in Europe*.'

'Oh ... yeah ... right,' said Harry.

'Fred and George can't have gone that far,' said Ron, pulling out his wand, lighting it like Hermione, and squinting up the path. Harry dug in the pockets of his jacket for his own wand – but it wasn't there. The only things he could find were his Omnioculars.

'Ah, no, I don't believe it ... I've lost my wand!'

'You're kidding?'

Ron and Hermione raised their wands high enough to spread the narrow beams of light further on the ground; Harry looked all around him, but his

## 第9章 黑魔标记

"你的父母呢？"哈利火了，说道，"在那边，蒙着面罩，是不是？"

马尔福把脸转向哈利，脸上仍然微笑着。

"我说……如果是这样，我也不可能告诉你，不是吗，波特？"

"哦，快走吧，"赫敏用厌恶的目光看了马尔福一眼，说道，"我们去找找其他人吧。"

"把你那颗毛蓬蓬的大脑袋低下，格兰杰。"马尔福讥笑道。

"快走。"赫敏又说了一遍，拉着哈利和罗恩继续上路了。

"我敢跟你打赌，他爸爸肯定是那些蒙面家伙当中的一个！"罗恩气愤地说。

"如果运气好，部里会抓住他的！"赫敏激动地说，"哦，我真不敢相信这件事。其他人上哪儿去了？"

弗雷德、乔治和金妮已不见踪影，小路上密密麻麻地挤满了人，一个个都紧张地扭过头，朝营地上发生骚动的方向张望。在小路边，一群身穿睡衣的少男少女挤成一团，吵吵嚷嚷地争论着什么。当他们看见哈利、罗恩和赫敏时，一个有着浓密鬈发的小姑娘转过身，很快地说："马克西姆女士在哪里？我们找不到她了——"

"嗯——什么？"罗恩说。

"噢……"说话的小姑娘又把身子转了回去，他们继续往前走时，清楚地听见她说了一句"霍格沃茨"。

"布斯巴顿。"赫敏低声说。

"对不起，你说什么？"哈利说。

"他们肯定是布斯巴顿的，"赫敏说，"你知道的……布斯巴顿魔法学院……我在《欧洲魔法教育评估》上读到过。"

"哦……原来……是这样。"哈利说。

"弗雷德和乔治不可能走得太远。"罗恩说着，抽出魔杖，也像赫敏一样把它点亮了，然后眯起眼睛顺着小路望去。哈利在外衣的口袋里寻找自己的魔杖——可是魔杖不见了。他找到的只有那架全景望远镜。

"哎呀，糟糕，真不敢相信……我的魔杖丢了！"

"你在开玩笑吧？"

罗恩和赫敏把他们的魔杖高高举起，让细长的光柱照亮更多的地

## CHAPTER NINE  The Dark Mark

wand was nowhere to be seen.

'Maybe it's back in the tent,' said Ron.

'Maybe it fell out of your pocket when we were running?' Hermione suggested anxiously.

'Yeah,' said Harry, 'maybe ...'

He usually kept his wand with him at all times in the wizarding world, and finding himself without it in the midst of a scene like this made him feel very vulnerable.

A rustling noise made all three of them jump. Winky the house-elf was fighting her way out of a clump of bushes nearby. She was moving in a most peculiar fashion, apparently with great difficulty; it was as though someone invisible was trying to hold her back.

'There is bad wizards about!' she squeaked distractedly, as she leant forwards and laboured to keep running. 'People high – high in the air! Winky is getting out of the way!'

And she disappeared into the trees on the other side of the path, panting and squeaking as she fought the force that was restraining her.

'What's up with her?' said Ron, looking curiously after Winky. 'Why can't she run properly?'

'Bet she didn't ask permission to hide,' said Harry. He was thinking of Dobby: every time he had tried to do something the Malfoys wouldn't like, he had been forced to start beating himself up.

'You know, house-elves get a *very* raw deal!' said Hermione indignantly. 'It's slavery, that's what it is! That Mr Crouch made her go up to the top of the stadium, and she was terrified, and he's got her bewitched so she can't even run when they start trampling tents! Why doesn't anyone *do* something about it?'

'Well, the elves are happy, aren't they?' Ron said. 'You heard old Winky back at the match ... "House-elves is not supposed to have fun"... that's what she likes, being bossed around ...'

'It's people like *you*, Ron,' Hermione began hotly, 'who prop up rotten and unjust systems, just because they're too lazy to –'

Another loud bang echoed from the edge of the wood.

'Let's just keep moving, shall we?' said Ron, and Harry saw him glance edgily at Hermione. Perhaps there was truth in what Malfoy had said;

## 第9章 黑魔标记

方。哈利在周围找了又找，可是怎么也找不到他的魔杖。

"也许落在帐篷里了。"罗恩说。

"会不会是刚才奔跑的时候，从你口袋里掉出来了？"赫敏焦急地问道。

"是啊，"哈利说，"很可能……"

在魔法世界里，他总是把魔杖随时带在身上，此刻，在这样的情景下发现魔杖不见了，他感到自己软弱无助。

突然，旁边传来一阵沙沙声，三个人都吓了一跳。家养小精灵闪闪正奋力从灌木丛中钻出来。她的动作非常古怪，似乎特别费劲，就好像有一个看不见的人正在把她拉回去。

"到处都是坏巫师！"她一边探着身子拼命要往前跑，一边慌慌张张地尖叫道，"人在高高的——高高的上面！闪闪要逃走！"

她喘息，尖叫，与那股束缚她的力量搏斗着，钻进了小路另一边的树丛里。

"她是怎么回事？"罗恩好奇地望着闪闪的背影，"为什么不能好好跑步？"

"我猜她没有征得主人同意就擅自躲避了。"哈利说。他想起了多比：每当多比想做什么马尔福一家不喜欢的事情时，身为家养小精灵的他就不得不把自己痛打一顿。

"你们知道吗，家养小精灵受到的是很不公正的待遇！"赫敏气愤地说，"他们完全就是奴隶！克劳奇先生强迫闪闪爬到体育场的最上面，她吓坏了，然后克劳奇先生又给她施了魔法，弄得她在人们开始踩踏帐篷时，也没有办法逃跑！为什么没有人站出来阻止这样的事呢？"

"我说，家养小精灵其实是快活的，是不是？"罗恩说，"你听见刚才比赛时闪闪说的话了吗……'家养小精灵是不应该有乐趣的'……她就喜欢这样，被人使唤来使唤去……"

"正是你们这样的人，罗恩，"赫敏激烈地说，"维护着这种腐朽的不合理的制度，就因为你们太懒惰……"

又是一声惊天动地的爆响从树林边缘传来，在夜空中回荡。

"我们还是走吧，好不好？"罗恩说，哈利看见他紧张地瞟了赫敏

## CHAPTER NINE   The Dark Mark

perhaps Hermione *was* in more danger than they were. They set off again, Harry still searching his pockets, even though he knew his wand wasn't there.

They followed the dark path deeper into the wood, still keeping an eye out for Fred, George and Ginny. They passed a group of goblins, who were cackling over a sack of gold they had undoubtedly won betting on the match, and who seemed quite unperturbed by the trouble on the campsite. Further still along the path, they walked into a patch of silvery light, and when they looked through the trees, they saw three tall and beautiful Veela standing in a clearing, surrounded by a gaggle of young wizards, all of whom were talking very loudly.

'I pull down about a hundred sacks of Galleons a year,' one of them shouted. 'I'm a dragon-killer for the Committee for the Disposal of Dangerous Creatures.'

'No, you're not,' yelled his friend, 'you're a dish-washer at the Leaky Cauldron ... but I'm a Vampire Hunter, I've killed about ninety so far –'

A third young wizard, whose pimples were visible even by the dim, silvery light of the Veela, now cut in, 'I'm about to become the youngest ever Minister for Magic, I am.'

Harry snorted with laughter. He recognised the pimply wizard; his name was Stan Shunpike, and he was in fact a conductor on the triple-decker Knight Bus.

He turned to tell Ron this, but Ron's face had gone oddly slack, and next second Ron was yelling, 'Did I tell you I've invented a broomstick that'll reach Jupiter?'

'*Honestly!*' said Hermione again, and she and Harry grabbed Ron firmly by the arms, wheeled him around and marched him away. By the time the sounds of the Veela and their admirers had faded completely, they were in the very heart of the wood. They seemed to be alone now; everything was much quieter.

Harry looked around. 'I reckon we can just wait here, you know, we'll hear anyone coming a mile off.'

The words were hardly out of his mouth, when Ludo Bagman emerged from behind a tree right ahead of them.

Even by the feeble light of the two wands, Harry could see that a great change had come over Bagman. He no longer looked buoyant and rosy-faced; there was no more spring in his step. He looked very white and strained.

'Who's that?' he said, blinking down at them, trying to make out their

## 第9章 黑魔标记

一眼。也许马尔福的话有一定的道理,也许赫敏的处境比他们更危险。他们又出发了,哈利仍然在口袋里掏来掏去,尽管明知道魔杖不在身上。

他们顺着漆黑的小路走进越来越深的树林,一边继续寻找弗雷德、乔治和金妮。路上,他们看到一群妖精只顾对着一袋金币叽叽呱呱地说笑,仿佛对营地上的骚乱无动于衷,这些金币无疑是他们在比赛中赌博赢来的。他们又往前走了一段,走进了一片银色的柔光中。透过树丛望去,他们看见三个修长美丽的媚娃站在一片空地上,旁边围着一群年轻巫师,都在用很响的声音说话。

"我一年挣一百袋金币!"其中一个喊道,"我在处置危险动物委员会工作,专门屠杀火龙!"

"呸!你才不是呢!"他的朋友嚷道,"你是破釜酒吧洗盘子的……我呢,我是专门猎杀吸血鬼的,已经杀死了九十多个——"

第三个巫师插话了——他脸上的青春痘即使在媚娃发出的微弱银光中也看得很清楚:"我马上就要成为有史以来最年轻的魔法部部长。"

哈利嘲讽地笑了起来。他认出了那个长青春痘的巫师,此人名叫斯坦·桑帕克,实际上是那辆三层骑士公共汽车上的售票员。

他转身正想把这个告诉罗恩,却发现罗恩脸上的肌肉奇怪地耷拉着,接着,罗恩冲着那些人大声叫道:"我有没有告诉你们,我发明了一种飞天扫帚,能一直飞到木星上?"

"哎呀,你怎么这样!"赫敏说。她和哈利使劲抓住罗恩的手臂,拉他转过身来,然后押着他走开了。当媚娃和她们那些崇拜者的声音完全听不见时,他们已经来到了树林的正中央。这里似乎只有他们几个,周围安静多了。

哈利环顾四周。"我想我们不妨就在这里等着,怎么样?有人过来的话,一英里外我们就听得见。"

他的话音刚落,卢多·巴格曼就从他们前面的一棵树后钻了出来。

尽管两根魔杖发出的光线非常微弱,哈利还是看出巴格曼身上起了很大的变化。他看上去不再轻松愉快,脸色不再红润,脚底下也不再装着弹簧。他显得脸色苍白,神情紧张。

"谁在那边?"他说,冲他们使劲眨着眼睛,想辨认出他们的脸,"你

## CHAPTER NINE   The Dark Mark

faces. 'What are you doing in here, all alone?'

They looked at each other, surprised.

'Well – there's a sort of riot going on,' said Ron.

Bagman stared at him. 'What?'

'On the campsite ... some people have got hold of a family of Muggles ...'

Bagman swore loudly. 'Damn them!' he said, looking quite distracted, and without another word, he Disapparated with a small *pop*.

'Not exactly on top of things, Mr Bagman, is he?' said Hermione, frowning.

'He was a great Beater, though,' said Ron, leading the way off the path into a small clearing, and sitting down on a patch of dry grass at the foot of a tree. 'The Wimbourne Wasps won the league three times in a row while he was with them.'

He took his small figure of Krum out of his pocket, set it down on the ground and watched it walk around for a while. Like the real Krum, the model was slightly duck-footed and round-shouldered, much less impressive on his splayed feet than on his broomstick. Harry was listening out for noise from the campsite. Everything still seemed quiet; perhaps the riot was over.

'I hope the others are OK,' said Hermione after a while.

'They'll be fine,' said Ron.

'Imagine if your dad catches Lucius Malfoy,' said Harry, sitting down next to Ron and watching the small figure of Krum slouching over the fallen leaves. 'He's always said he'd like to get something on him.'

'That'd wipe the smirk off old Draco's face, all right,' said Ron.

'Those poor Muggles, though,' said Hermione nervously. 'What if they can't get them down?'

'They will,' said Ron reassuringly, 'they'll find a way.'

'Mad, though, to do something like that when the whole Ministry of Magic's out here tonight!' said Hermione. 'I mean, how do they expect to get away with it? Do you think they've been drinking, or are they just –'

But she broke off abruptly and looked over her shoulder. Harry and Ron looked quickly around, too. It sounded as though someone was staggering towards their clearing. They waited, listening to the sounds of the uneven

## 第9章 黑魔标记

们独自在这里做什么?"

他们互相看着,都很吃惊。

"是这样——那边发生了骚乱。"罗恩说。

巴格曼盯着他。"什么?"

"在营地上……有人抓住了一家麻瓜……"

巴格曼大声骂了一句。

"该死!"他说,一副心烦意乱的样子,然后,没有再说一个字,就噗的一声幻影移形了。

"巴格曼先生对情况一无所知,是吗?"赫敏皱着眉头说。

"可是,他以前是个了不起的击球手呢,"罗恩说,他在前面打头,沿着小路走入一小块空地,然后一屁股坐在树下的一片干草上,"他在温布恩黄蜂队的时候,那个队赢得了三连冠呢。"

他从口袋里掏出克鲁姆的小塑像,放在地上,注视着它走来走去。这个小模型像克鲁姆本人一样,走路也有点外八字,肩膀也有点向前拱着,他的八字脚踩在地面上,比起他骑在飞天扫帚上的样子来大为逊色。哈利倾听着营地那边的声音。一切似乎平静多了,也许骚乱已经结束。

"希望其他人都平安无事。"过了一会儿,赫敏说道。

"他们不会有事的。"罗恩说。

"想象一下吧,如果你爸爸抓住卢修斯·马尔福就好了,"哈利说着,也在罗恩身边坐下,望着克鲁姆的小塑像在落叶上没精打采地走动,"他总是说要抓住马尔福的把柄。"

"没错,那样一来,讨厌的德拉科就再也露不出那种奸笑了。"罗恩说。

"唉,那些麻瓜太可怜了,"赫敏不安地说,"如果人们没法把他们弄下来,怎么办呢?"

"不会的,"罗恩向她保证说,"他们总有办法的。"

"真是疯了,居然做出这样的事,要知道今晚魔法部的所有官员都在这里啊!"赫敏说,"我的意思是,他们难道指望能轻易逃脱?你们说,他们是不是喝多了酒,还是——"

她猛地停住话头,扭头朝身后望去。哈利和罗恩也迅速转过脑袋。听声音,好像有人正高一脚低一脚地向他们这片空地走来。他们等待着,

## CHAPTER NINE   The Dark Mark

steps behind the dark trees. But the footsteps came to a sudden halt.

'Hello?' called Harry.

There was silence. Harry got to his feet and peered around the tree. It was too dark to see very far, but he could sense somebody standing just beyond the range of his vision.

'Who's there?' he said.

And then, without warning, the silence was rent by a voice unlike any they had heard in the wood; and it uttered, not a panicked shout, but what sounded like a spell.

'*MORSMORDRE!*'

And something vast, green and glittering erupted from the patch of darkness Harry's eyes had been struggling to penetrate: it flew up over the treetops and into the sky.

'What the –?' gasped Ron, as he sprang to his feet again, staring up at the thing that had appeared.

For a split second, Harry thought it was another leprechaun formation. Then he realised that it was a colossal skull, composed of what looked like emerald stars, with a serpent protruding from its mouth like a tongue. As they watched, it rose higher and higher, blazing in a haze of greenish smoke, etched against the black sky like a new constellation.

Suddenly, the wood all around them erupted with screams. Harry didn't understand why, but the only possible cause was the sudden appearance of the skull, which had now risen high enough to illuminate the entire wood, like some grisly neon sign. He scanned the darkness for the person who had conjured the skull, but he couldn't see anyone.

'Who's there?' he called again.

'Harry, come on, *move!*' Hermione had seized the back of his jacket, and was tugging him backwards.

'What's the matter?' Harry said, startled to see her face so white and terrified.

'It's the Dark Mark, Harry!' Hermione moaned, pulling him as hard as she could. 'You-Know-Who's sign!'

'*Voldemort's* –?'

'Harry, come *on!*'

Harry turned – Ron was hurriedly scooping up his miniature Krum – the

## 第9章 黑魔标记

听着漆黑的树丛后跌跌撞撞的脚步声。可是,脚步声突然停止了。

"你好?"哈利喊道。

没有声音。哈利站起来,回身望着树后。四下里黑乎乎的,稍远一点就看不见了,但他可以感觉到有人就站在他的视线之外。

"谁在那儿?"他问。

然后,没有一点征兆,一个声音突然划破了寂静。这声音和他们在树林里听见的其他声音都不一样,它发出的不是紧张的喊叫,而像是一句咒语。

"**尸骨再现!**"

接着,从哈利的目光拼命想穿透的那一片黑暗中,冒出一个巨大的绿光闪闪的东西。它一下子跃上树梢,飞到了空中。

"这是什么——"罗恩紧张地说,也赶紧跳了起来,抬头盯着那刚刚出现的东西。

哈利一开始以为又是小矮妖组成的图形,可是紧接着,他发现那是一个硕大无比的骷髅,由无数碧绿色的星星般的东西组成,一条大蟒蛇从骷髅的嘴巴里冒出来,像是一根舌头。就在他们注视的时候,骷髅越升越高,在一团绿莹莹的烟雾中发出耀眼的光,被漆黑的夜空衬托着,就像一个新的星座。

突然,他们周围的树林里爆发出阵阵尖叫声。哈利不明白叫声的由来,唯一可能的原因就是这个骷髅的突然出现。它现在已经升得很高,像一个恐怖的霓虹灯招牌一样,照亮了整个树林。哈利在黑暗中寻找那个变出骷髅的人,可是一个人影也没看见。

"谁在那儿?"他又喊了一声。

"哈利,快点儿,走吧!"赫敏抓住他的衣领,把他往后拖。

"怎么回事?"哈利说,吃惊地看见赫敏脸色煞白,神情极为恐惧。

"这是黑魔标记,哈利!"赫敏呻吟般地说,一边拼命地拉着他,"神秘人的符号!"

"伏地魔的——"

"哈利,快走吧!"

哈利转过身——罗恩赶忙从地上抄起他的克鲁姆小塑像——三个

## CHAPTER NINE  The Dark Mark

three of them started across the clearing – but before they had taken more than a few hurried steps, a series of popping noises announced the arrival of twenty wizards, appearing from thin air, surrounding them.

Harry whirled around, and in a split second, he registered one fact: each of these wizards had his wand out, and every wand was pointing right at himself, Ron and Hermione. Without pausing to think, he yelled, 'DUCK!' He seized the other two and pulled them down onto the ground.

'*STUPEFY!*' roared twenty voices – there was a blinding series of flashes and Harry felt the hair on his head ripple as though a powerful wind had swept the clearing. Raising his head a fraction of an inch he saw jets of fiery red light flying over them from the wizards' wands, crossing each other, bouncing off tree-trunks, rebounding into the darkness –

'Stop!' yelled a voice he recognised. 'STOP! *That's my son!*'

Harry's hair stopped blowing about. He raised his head a little higher. The wizard in front of him had lowered his wand. He rolled over and saw Mr Weasley striding towards them, looking terrified.

'Ron – Harry –' his voice sounded shaky, '– Hermione – are you all right?'

'Out of the way, Arthur,' said a cold, curt voice.

It was Mr Crouch. He and the other Ministry wizards were closing in on them. Harry got to his feet to face them. Mr Crouch's face was taut with rage.

'Which of you did it?' he snapped, his sharp eyes darting between them. 'Which of you conjured the Dark Mark?'

'We didn't do that!' said Harry, gesturing up at the skull.

'We didn't do anything!' said Ron, who was rubbing his elbow, and looking indignantly at his father. 'What did you want to attack us for?'

'Do not lie, sir!' shouted Mr Crouch. His wand was still pointing directly at Ron, and his eyes were popping – he looked slightly mad. 'You have been discovered at the scene of the crime!'

'Barty,' whispered a witch in a long woollen dressing-gown, 'they're kids, Barty, they'd never have been able to –'

'Where did the Mark come from, you three?' said Mr Weasley quickly.

'Over there,' said Hermione shakily, pointing at the place where they had heard the voice, 'there was someone behind the trees … they shouted words – an incantation –'

## 第9章 黑魔标记

人开始穿过空地——可是慌慌张张地才走了几步,就听见一连串噗噗噗的声音,二十个巫师从天而降,把他们团团围住。

哈利转了个圈,立刻就注意到这样一个事实:这些巫师都掏出了自己的魔杖,每根魔杖都指着他、罗恩和赫敏。他没有思索,赶紧喊了一声:"**快躲!**"他一把拉住另外两人,把他们拖倒在地。

"**昏昏倒地!**"二十个声音同时吼道——接着便是一连串耀眼的闪光,哈利感到他的头发在摇摆起伏,如同有一股强劲的风吹过空地。他微微把头抬起一点儿,看见一道道烧灼般的红光从巫师的魔杖里射出,在他们头顶上互相交错,撞在树干上,又被弹到了黑暗中——

"住手!"一个他熟悉的声音喊道,"**住手!那是我儿子!**"

哈利的头发不再波动了,他又把头抬起一点儿,他前面的那个巫师已经放下了手里的魔杖。哈利翻过身,看见韦斯莱先生大步朝他们走来,神情十分惊恐。

"罗恩——哈利——"他的声音有些颤抖,"赫敏——你们都没事吧?"

"闪开,亚瑟。"一个冷冰冰的、不带感情的声音说。

是克劳奇先生。他和部里的其他巫师官员都围了过来。哈利站起来面对他们。克劳奇先生气得板紧了脸。

"这是你们谁干的?"他厉声问道,犀利的眼睛在他们三个人之间扫来扫去,"你们谁变出了黑魔标记?"

"我们没有!"哈利指着上面的骷髅,说道。

"我们什么也没干!"罗恩说,他揉着自己的胳膊肘,气呼呼地望着父亲,"你们为什么要攻击我们?"

"不要撒谎,先生!"克劳奇先生说。他仍然用魔杖指着罗恩,眼珠子瞪得都要暴出来了——他的样子有点疯狂。"你们是在犯罪现场被发现的!"

"巴蒂,"一个穿着长长的羊毛晨衣的女巫小声说,"他们还是孩子,巴蒂,他们决不可能——"

"你们三个,这个标记是从哪儿来的?"韦斯莱先生焦急地问。

"那边,"赫敏用发抖的声音说,指着他们刚才听见声音的地方,"树后面有人……那人大声说话……念了一句咒语……"

## CHAPTER NINE  The Dark Mark

'Oh, stood over there, did they?' said Mr Crouch, turning his popping eyes on Hermione now, disbelief etched all over his face. 'Said an incantation, did they? You seem very well informed about how that Mark is summoned, missy –'

But none of the Ministry wizards apart from Mr Crouch seemed to think it remotely likely that Harry, Ron or Hermione had conjured the skull; on the contrary, at Hermione's words, they had raised all their wands again, and were pointing in the direction she had indicated, squinting through the dark trees.

'We're too late,' said the witch in the woollen dressing-gown, shaking her head. 'They'll have Disapparated.'

'I don't think so,' said a wizard with a scrubby brown beard. It was Amos Diggory, Cedric's father. 'Our Stunners went right through those trees ... there's a good chance we got them ...'

'Amos, be careful!' said a few of the wizards warningly, as Mr Diggory squared his shoulders, raised his wand, marched across the clearing and disappeared into the darkness. Hermione watched him vanish with her hands over her mouth.

A few seconds later, they heard Mr Diggory shout.

'Yes! We got them! There's someone here! Unconscious! It's – but – blimey ...'

'You've got someone?' shouted Mr Crouch, sounding highly disbelieving. 'Who? Who is it?'

They heard snapping twigs, the rustling of leaves, and then crunching footsteps as Mr Diggory re-emerged from behind the trees. He was carrying a tiny, limp figure in his arms. Harry recognised the tea-towel at once. It was Winky.

Mr Crouch did not move or speak as Mr Diggory deposited Mr Crouch's elf on the ground at his feet. The other Ministry wizards were all staring at Mr Crouch. For a few seconds Crouch remained transfixed, his eyes blazing in his white face as he stared down at Winky. Then he appeared to come to life again.

'This – cannot – be,' he said jerkily. 'No –'

He moved quickly around Mr Diggory and strode off towards the place where he had found Winky.

'No point, Mr Crouch,' Mr Diggory called after him. 'There's no one else there.'

But Mr Crouch did not seem prepared to take his word for it. They could

## 第9章 黑魔标记

"哦，那个人就站在那里，是吗？"克劳奇先生说，又把暴突的眼睛转向赫敏，脸上写满了怀疑，"还念了一句咒语，是吗？你似乎对怎么变出标记知道得很清楚啊，小姐——"

可是除了克劳奇先生，那些部里的巫师官员似乎都认为哈利、罗恩和赫敏绝对不可能变出骷髅。他们听了赫敏的话，一个个又把魔杖举了起来，对准她所指的方向，眯着眼朝黑黢黢的树丛中窥视。

"我们来晚了，"那位穿羊毛晨衣的女巫摇了摇头，说道，"他们早就幻影移形了。"

"我不这样认为，"一位留着棕色短胡子的巫师说话了——他正是阿莫斯·迪戈里，塞德里克的父亲，"我们的昏迷咒正好钻进了这片树丛……我们很有可能击中了他们……"

"阿莫斯，小心！"几位巫师提醒道，只见迪戈里先生挺起胸膛，举起魔杖，大步穿过空地，消失在黑暗中。赫敏紧张地用手捂着嘴巴，望着他隐去的背影。

几秒钟后，他们听见了迪戈里先生的喊声。

"成了！抓住了！这儿有人！昏迷不醒！是——哎哟——天哪……"

"你抓住了一个人？"克劳奇先生喊道，完全是一种不相信的语气，"谁？是谁？"

他们听见树枝的折断声，落叶的沙沙声，然后是嘎吱嘎吱的脚步声，迪戈里先生从树丛后出来了。他手臂里抱着一个小小的软绵绵的身体。哈利一眼就认出了那块茶巾。是闪闪。

克劳奇先生看着迪戈里先生把自己的家养小精灵放在自己脚下，他没有动弹，也没有说话。魔法部的其他官员都盯着克劳奇先生。有好几秒钟，克劳奇一动不动地站着，仿佛凝固了一般，苍白的脸上那双喷火的眼睛狠狠盯着地上的闪闪。然后，他似乎又回过神来。

"这——不可能——不可能，"他一顿一顿地说，"不可能——"

他飞快地绕过迪戈里先生，大步朝闪闪被发现的地方走去。

"没用的，克劳奇先生，"迪戈里先生冲着他的背影喊道，"那儿没有别人了。"

可是克劳奇先生似乎不想理睬他的话。他们听见他在那里走来走

hear him moving around, the rustling of leaves as he pushed the bushes aside, searching.

'Bit embarrassing,' Mr Diggory said grimly, looking down at Winky's unconscious form. 'Barty Crouch's house-elf ... I mean to say ...'

'Come off it, Amos,' said Mr Weasley quietly, 'you don't seriously think it was the elf? The Dark Mark's a wizard's sign. It requires a wand.'

'Yeah,' said Mr Diggory, 'and she *had* a wand.'

'*What?*' said Mr Weasley.

'Here, look.' Mr Diggory held up a wand and showed it to Mr Weasley. 'Had it in her hand. So that's clause three of the Code of Wand Use broken for a start. *No non-human creature is permitted to carry or use a wand.*'

Just then there was another *pop*, and Ludo Bagman Apparated right next to Mr Weasley. Looking breathless and disorientated, he spun on the spot, goggling upwards at the emerald green skull.

'The Dark Mark!' he panted, almost trampling Winky as he turned enquiringly to his colleagues. 'Who did it? Did you get them? Barty! What's going on?'

Mr Crouch had returned empty-handed. His face was still ghostly white, and his hands and his toothbrush moustache were both twitching.

'Where have you been, Barty?' said Bagman. 'Why weren't you at the match? Your elf was saving you a seat, too – Gulping gargoyles!' Bagman had just noticed Winky lying at his feet. 'What happened to *her*?'

'I have been busy, Ludo,' said Mr Crouch, still talking in the same jerky fashion, barely moving his lips. 'And my elf has been Stunned.'

'Stunned? By you lot, you mean? But why –?'

Comprehension dawned suddenly on Bagman's round, shiny face; he looked up at the skull, down at Winky and then at Mr Crouch.

'*No!*' he said. 'Winky? Conjure the Dark Mark? She wouldn't know how! She'd need a wand for a start!'

'And she had one,' said Mr Diggory. 'I found her holding one, Ludo. If it's all right with you, Mr Crouch, I think we should hear what she's got to say for herself.'

Crouch gave no sign that he had heard Mr Diggory, but Mr Diggory

## 第9章 黑魔标记

去,还听见他拨开灌木寻找,把树叶弄得沙沙作响。

"有点令人尴尬,"迪戈里先生严厉地说,低头看着闪闪神志不清的身影,"巴蒂·克劳奇的家养小精灵……我的意思是……"

"别胡扯了,阿莫斯,"韦斯莱先生小声说道,"难道你当真认为是小精灵干的?黑魔标记是个巫师符号,是需要用魔杖的。"

"是啊,"迪戈里先生说,"她拿着魔杖呢。"

"什么?"韦斯莱先生说。

"这儿,你们瞧,"迪戈里先生举起一根魔杖,递给韦斯莱先生,"她手里拿着的。这首先就违反了《魔杖使用准则》的第三款:任何非人类的生物都不得携带或使用魔杖。"

就在这时,又是噗的一声,卢多·巴格曼先生幻影显形出现在韦斯莱先生旁边。巴格曼气喘吁吁,一副晕头转向的样子。他原地转着圈儿,瞪眼望着空中那碧绿色的骷髅。

"黑魔标记!"他喘着气说,转身询问地看着他的同事,差点踩在闪闪身上,"是谁做的?你们抓到人了吗?巴蒂!到底是怎么回事?"

克劳奇先生空着手回来了。他的脸仍然惨白得可怕,双手和牙刷状的小胡子都在抽搐。

"你上哪儿去了,巴蒂?"巴格曼问,"为什么没来观看比赛?你的家养小精灵还给你占了个座位呢——贪吃的滴水嘴石兽啊!"巴格曼这才发现闪闪就躺在他脚边,"她怎么啦?"

"我一直忙得要命,卢多。"克劳奇先生说,仍然是那样一字一顿,嘴唇几乎没动,"我的家养小精灵被人施了昏迷咒。"

"被人施了昏迷咒?你是说,被你们这些人?为什么——"

巴格曼那张发亮的圆脸上突然露出恍然大悟的神情。他抬头望望骷髅,又低头看看闪闪,最后目光落在克劳奇先生身上。

"不可能!"他说,"闪闪?变出了黑魔标记?她不知道怎么变呀!首先,她得需要一根魔杖呀!"

"她确实有一根魔杖,"迪戈里先生说,"我发现她手里拿着一根,卢多。如果你没有意见,克劳奇先生,我认为我们应该听听她怎样为自己辩护。"

克劳奇先生毫无反应,仿佛没有听见迪戈里先生的话,而迪戈里先生似

## CHAPTER NINE  The Dark Mark

seemed to take his silence for assent. He raised his own wand, pointed it at Winky and said, '*Rennervate!*'

Winky stirred feebly. Her great brown eyes opened and she blinked several times in a bemused sort of way. Watched by the silent wizards, she raised herself shakily into a sitting position. She caught sight of Mr Diggory's feet, and slowly, tremulously, raised her eyes to stare up into his face; then, more slowly still, she looked up into the sky. Harry could see the floating skull reflected twice in her enormous, glassy eyes. She gave a gasp, looked wildly around the crowded clearing and burst into terrified sobs.

'Elf!' said Mr Diggory sternly. 'Do you know who I am? I'm a member of the Department for the Regulation and Control of Magical Creatures!'

Winky began to rock backwards and forwards on the ground, her breath coming in sharp bursts. Harry was reminded forcibly of Dobby in his moments of terrified disobedience.

'As you see, elf, the Dark Mark was conjured here a short while ago,' said Mr Diggory. 'And you were discovered moments later, right beneath it! An explanation, if you please!'

'I – I – I is not doing it, sir!' Winky gasped. 'I is not knowing how, sir!'

'You were found with a wand in your hand!' barked Mr Diggory, brandishing it in front of her. And as the wand caught the green light that was filling the clearing from the skull above, Harry recognised it.

'Hey – that's mine!' he said.

Everyone in the clearing looked at him.

'Excuse me?' said Mr Diggory, incredulously.

'That's my wand!' said Harry. 'I dropped it!'

'You dropped it?' repeated Mr Diggory in disbelief. 'Is this a confession? You threw it aside after you conjured the Mark?'

'Amos, think who you're talking to!' said Mr Weasley, very angrily. 'Is *Harry Potter* likely to conjure the Dark Mark?'

'Er – of course not,' mumbled Mr Diggory. 'Sorry ... carried away ...'

'I didn't drop it there, anyway,' said Harry, jerking his thumb towards the trees beneath the skull. 'I missed it right after we got into the wood.'

'So,' said Mr Diggory, his eyes hardening as he turned to look at Winky

## 第9章 黑魔标记

乎把他的沉默当成了默许。他举起自己的魔杖,指着闪闪说道:"快快复苏!"

闪闪有气无力地动了起来。那双铜铃般的棕色眼睛睁开了,她使劲眨了眨眼皮,神情一片茫然。在巫师们沉默的目光注视下,她颤巍巍地支撑着坐了起来。她看见了迪戈里先生的脚,然后慢慢地、哆哆嗦嗦地抬起目光,望着他的脸,接着,又更缓慢地把目光投向上面的夜空。哈利可以看见,那飘浮的骷髅形象分别映在她两只呆滞的大眼睛里。她倒吸了一口冷气,目光迷乱地看着围在空地上的人们,然后突然害怕地哭了起来。

"小精灵!"迪戈里先生严厉地问,"你知道我是谁吗?我是魔法生物管理控制司的成员!"

闪闪开始在地上前后摇晃,呼吸不时被强烈的抽泣打断。哈利一下子想起,多比因违抗命令而感到害怕时,也是这个样子。

"你也看见了,小精灵,就在刚才,有人在这里变出了黑魔标记。"迪戈里先生说,"片刻之后,你被我们发现了,就在标记的下面!请你给我们一个解释!"

"我——我——我没有,先生!"闪闪喘着大气说,"我不知道怎么变,先生!"

"你被发现的时候,手里拿着一根魔杖!"迪戈里先生咆哮道,在闪闪面前挥舞着那根魔杖。当骷髅射向空地的绿光照在魔杖上时,哈利认出来了。

"呀——那是我的!"他说。

空地上的人都转过脸来望着他。

"对不起,你说什么?"迪戈里先生不敢相信地问。

"那是我的魔杖!"哈利说,"我把它丢了!"

"你把它丢了?"迪戈里先生怀疑地重复了一句,"你是在坦白吗?你变出标记后,就把魔杖扔掉了?"

"阿莫斯,想想你在跟谁说话!"韦斯莱先生非常生气地说,"难道哈利·波特会变出黑魔标记?"

"呃——当然不会,"迪戈里先生含混地嘟哝道,"对不起……我气昏了头……"

"我没有把它扔在那里,"哈利用大拇指朝骷髅下面的树丛指了指,"我们刚走进树林,我的魔杖就不见了。"

"这么说,"迪戈里先生说着,又把目光投向蜷缩在他脚边的闪闪,

## CHAPTER NINE   The Dark Mark

again, cowering at his feet. 'You found this wand, eh, elf? And you picked it up and thought you'd have some fun with it, did you?'

'I is not doing magic with it, sir!' squealed Winky, tears streaming down the sides of her squashed and bulbous nose. 'I is … I is … I is just picking it up, sir! I is not making the Dark Mark, sir, I is not knowing how!'

'It wasn't her!' said Hermione. She looked very nervous, speaking up in front of all these Ministry wizards, yet determined all the same. 'Winky's got a squeaky little voice and the voice we heard doing the incantation was much deeper!' She looked round at Harry and Ron, appealing for their support. 'It didn't sound anything like Winky, did it?'

'No,' said Harry, shaking his head. 'It definitely didn't sound like an elf.'

'Yeah, it was a human voice,' said Ron.

'Well, we'll soon see,' growled Mr Diggory, looking unimpressed. 'There's a simple way of discovering the last spell a wand performed, elf, did you know that?'

Winky trembled and shook her head frantically, her ears flapping, as Mr Diggory raised his own wand again, and placed it tip to tip with Harry's.

'*Prior Incantato!*' roared Mr Diggory.

Harry heard Hermione gasp, horrified, as a gigantic serpent-tongued skull erupted from the point where the two wands met, but it was a mere shadow of the green skull high above them, it looked as though it was made of thick grey smoke: the ghost of a spell.

'*Deletrius!*' Mr Diggory shouted, and the smoky skull vanished in a wisp of smoke.

'So,' said Mr Diggory with a kind of savage triumph, looking down upon Winky, who was still shaking convulsively.

'I is not doing it!' she squealed, her eyes rolling in terror. 'I is not, I is not, I is not knowing how! I is a good elf, I isn't using wands, I isn't knowing how!'

'You've been caught red-handed, elf!' Mr Diggory roared. '*Caught with the guilty wand in your hand!*'

'Amos,' said Mr Weasley loudly, 'think about it … precious few wizards

## 第9章 黑魔标记

眼神变得冷酷了,"小精灵,是你发现这根魔杖的,是不是?你把它捡起来,以为可以拿它找点乐子,是不是?"

"我没有用它变魔法,先生!"闪闪尖声说道,眼泪像小溪一样,顺着被压扁的球状鼻子的两侧流下来,"我……我……我只是把它捡了起来,先生!我没有变出黑魔标记,先生,我不知道怎么变!"

"不是她!"赫敏说——她在这么些魔法部官员面前说话,显得非常紧张,但毫不退缩——"闪闪说话尖声细气,我们刚才听见的那个念咒语的声音要低沉得多!"她转脸看着哈利和罗恩,请求得到他们的赞同,"根本不像闪闪的声音,对吗?"

"对,"哈利点了点头,说道,"那声音绝对不是一个小精灵的。"

"是啊,那是人的声音。"罗恩说。

"好吧,我们很快就会知道的,"迪戈里先生咆哮着,似乎没有听进他们的话,"有一个简单的办法,可以发现魔杖上一次施的魔咒,小精灵,你知道吗?"

闪闪浑身发抖,拼命摇头,耳朵啪啪地扇动着。迪戈里先生举起自己的魔杖,把它跟哈利的魔杖对接在一起。

"闪回前咒!"迪戈里先生大吼一声。

哈利听见赫敏倒抽了一口冷气,同时看见一个十分恐怖的、吐着蛇芯子的骷髅从两根魔杖相接的地方冒了出来,不过这只是他们头顶上空那个绿色骷髅的影子。它仿佛是由浓浓的灰色烟雾构成的:是一个魔幻的幽灵。

"消隐无踪!"迪戈里先生大喊一声,烟雾构成的骷髅化成一缕轻烟,消失了。

"这怎么说?"迪戈里先生摆出一种残酷的得意神情,望着脚下的闪闪。闪闪仍然在剧烈地颤抖着。

"不是我!"她尖声叫道,眼珠惊恐地转动着,"不是我,不是我,我不知道怎么弄!我是一个好精灵,我没有摆弄魔杖,我不知道怎么弄!"

"你被当场抓住了,小精灵!"迪戈里先生吼道,"被抓时手里拿着这根犯罪的魔杖!"

"阿莫斯,"韦斯莱先生大声说,"你想想吧……会施那个魔咒的巫

## CHAPTER NINE  The Dark Mark

know how to do that spell ... where would she have learnt it?'

'Perhaps Amos is suggesting,' said Mr Crouch, cold anger in every syllable, 'that I routinely teach my servants to conjure the Dark Mark?'

There was a deeply unpleasant silence.

Amos Diggory looked horrified. 'Mr Crouch ... not ... not at all ...'

'You have now come very close to accusing the two people in this clearing who are *least* likely to conjure that Mark!' barked Mr Crouch. 'Harry Potter – and myself! I suppose you are familiar with the boy's story, Amos?'

'Of course – everyone knows –' muttered Mr Diggory, looking highly discomfited.

'And I trust you remember the many proofs I have given, over a long career, that I despise and detest the Dark Arts and those who practise them?' Mr Crouch shouted, his eyes bulging again.

'Mr Crouch, I – I never suggested you had anything to do with it!' muttered Amos Diggory, now reddening behind his scrubby brown beard.

'If you accuse my elf, you accuse me, Diggory!' shouted Mr Crouch. 'Where else would she have learnt to conjure it?'

'She – she might've picked it up anywhere –'

'Precisely, Amos,' said Mr Weasley. '*She might have picked it up anywhere ...* Winky?' he said kindly, turning to the elf, but she flinched as though he, too, was shouting at her. 'Where exactly did you find Harry's wand?'

Winky was twisting the hem of her tea-towel so violently that it was fraying beneath her fingers.

'I – I is finding it ... finding it there, sir ...' she whispered, 'there ... in the trees, sir ...'

'You see, Amos?' said Mr Weasley. 'Whoever conjured the Mark could have Disapparated right after they'd done it, leaving Harry's wand behind. A clever thing to do, not using their own wand, which could have betrayed them. And Winky here had the misfortune to come across the wand moments later and pick it up.'

'But then, she'd have been feet away from the real culprit!' said Mr Diggory impatiently. 'Elf? Did you see anyone?'

## 第9章 黑魔标记

师只是凤毛麟角……她是从哪儿学会的呢？"

"也许迪戈里是在暗示，"克劳奇先生说，每个音节都透着冷冰冰的怒气，"暗示我定期教我的仆人变黑魔标记？"

接着是一阵十分压抑的沉默。

迪戈里先生仿佛吓坏了，"克劳奇先生……不是……绝对不是……"

"到现在为止，你用几乎很明显的语言，无端指控了这片空地上的两个人，而他们是最不可能变出那个标记的！"克劳奇先生怒吼着说，"哈利·波特——还有我！我想你应该熟悉这个男孩的身世吧，阿莫斯？"

"当然——每个人都知道——"迪戈里先生嘟哝着，神情十分惶恐。

"我相信你还记得，在我漫长的职业生涯中，有许多证据表明我一贯厌恶和仇恨黑魔法，以及所有玩弄黑魔法的人，是不是？"克劳奇先生大声喊道，眼珠子又暴突出来。

"克劳奇先生，我—我绝没有暗示你跟这件事有关！"阿莫斯·迪戈里又嘟哝着说，他那棕色短胡子后面的脸已经涨得通红。

"你指控我的小精灵，就等于在指控我，迪戈里！"克劳奇先生嚷道，"不然她能从哪儿学会变这种魔法？"

"她—她也许是偶然从别处学会的……"

"说得对啊，阿莫斯，"韦斯莱先生说，"她也许是偶然从别处学会的……闪闪？"他和气地转向小精灵，可是闪闪畏惧地退缩着，好像他也在冲她嚷嚷似的，"你到底是在哪儿捡到哈利的魔杖的？"

闪闪使劲拧着她身上那块茶巾的贴边，她手指的劲儿太大了，贴边被拧得开了线。

"我—我是在……那儿捡到的，先生……"她低声说道，"那儿……在树林子里，先生……"

"明白了吧，阿莫斯？"韦斯莱先生说，"变出标记的人，不管他们是谁，在完事后就幻影移形了，扔下了哈利的魔杖。干得真聪明，不用自己的魔杖，免得暴露身份。片刻之后，这个倒霉的闪闪无意间看到魔杖，把它捡了起来。"

"这么说，她当时离真正的罪犯只有几步远？"迪戈里先生不耐烦地说，"小精灵，你看见什么人没有？"

## CHAPTER NINE  The Dark Mark

Winky began to tremble worse than ever. Her giant eyes flickered from Mr Diggory to Ludo Bagman, and on to Mr Crouch.

Then she gulped, and said, 'I is seeing no one, sir ... no one...'

'Amos,' said Mr Crouch curtly, 'I am fully aware that, in the ordinary course of events, you would want to take Winky into your department for questioning. I ask you, however, to allow me to deal with her.'

Mr Diggory looked as though he didn't think much of this suggestion at all, but it was clear to Harry that Mr Crouch was such an important member of the Ministry that he did not dare refuse him.

'You may rest assured that she will be punished,' Mr Crouch added coldly.

'M-m-master ...' Winky stammered, looking up at Mr Crouch, her eyes brimming with tears. 'M-m-master, p-p-please ...'

Mr Crouch stared back, his face somehow sharpened, each line upon it more deeply etched. There was no pity in his gaze. 'Winky has behaved tonight in a manner I would not have believed possible,' he said slowly. 'I told her to remain in the tent. I told her to stay there while I went to sort out the trouble. And I find that she disobeyed me. *This means clothes.*'

'No!' shrieked Winky, prostrating herself at Mr Crouch's feet. 'No, master! Not clothes, not clothes!'

Harry knew that the only way to turn a house-elf free was to present it with proper garments. It was pitiful to see the way Winky clutched at her tea-towel as she sobbed over Mr Crouch's feet.

'But she was frightened!' Hermione burst out angrily, glaring at Mr Crouch. 'Your elf's scared of heights, and those wizards in masks were levitating people! You can't blame her for wanting to get out of their way!'

Mr Crouch took a step backwards, freeing himself from contact with the elf, whom he was surveying as though she was something filthy and rotten that was contaminating his over-shined shoes.

'I have no use for a house-elf who disobeys me,' he said coldly, looking up at Hermione. 'I have no use for a servant who forgets what is due to her master, and to her master's reputation.'

Winky was crying so hard that her sobs echoed around the clearing.

There was a very nasty silence, which was ended by Mr Weasley, who said quietly, 'Well, I think I'll take my lot back to the tent, if nobody's got any objections. Amos, that wand's told us all it can – if Harry could have it back,

## 第9章 黑魔标记

闪闪抖得比刚才更厉害了。两个灯泡大的眼睛看看迪戈里先生，又看看卢多·巴格曼，再看看克劳奇先生。

然后她吸了一大口气，说道："我没有看见什么人，先生……一个人也没有……"

"阿莫斯，"克劳奇先生很生硬地说，"我完全知道，按照一般的程序，你要把闪闪带到你的司里审问，不过，我还是请你允许由我来处置她。"

迪戈里先生似乎不太赞成这个建议，但哈利清楚，克劳奇先生是魔法部里举足轻重的大人物，迪戈里先生不敢拒绝他。

"你放心，她会受到惩罚的。"克劳奇先生冷冷地补充道。

"主—主—主人……"闪闪抬头看着克劳奇先生，眼睛里含着泪花，结结巴巴地说，"主—主—主人，求—求—求求你……"

克劳奇先生瞪视着闪闪，脸变得僵硬起来，每条皱纹都深深地陷了进去，目光里没有丝毫怜悯。"闪闪今晚的行为，令我感到十分震惊，"他慢慢地说，"我叫她待在帐篷里。我叫她守在那里，我去解决骚乱。结果发现她违抗了我。这就意味着——衣服！"

"不！"闪闪失声尖叫，一头扑在克劳奇先生脚下，"不，主人！不要衣服，不要衣服！"

哈利知道，释放一个家养小精灵的唯一方式，就是赐给他一件像样的衣服。闪闪紧紧攥住她的茶巾，伏在克劳奇先生的脚上哭泣，那样子真是可怜。

"她当时是吓坏了！"赫敏狠狠地瞪着克劳奇先生，愤慨地说道，"你的家养小精灵有恐高症，而那些蒙面的巫师把人弄到空中悬着！她想逃脱他们也是情有可原的，你不能责怪她！"

克劳奇先生后退一步，摆脱了小精灵的纠缠。他低头审视着闪闪，那神情就好像她是什么肮脏腐烂的东西，正在玷污他擦得锃亮的皮鞋。

"我不需要违抗我命令的家养小精灵，"他望着赫敏，冷冷地说，"我不需要一个忘记听从主人意旨、维护主人名誉的家仆。"

闪闪哭得伤心极了，她的哭声在空地上回荡。

又是一阵令人十分尴尬的沉默，最后韦斯莱先生轻声地说："好吧，如果没有人反对的话，我就把我的人带回帐篷去了。阿莫斯，魔杖已

## CHAPTER NINE  The Dark Mark

please –'

Mr Diggory handed Harry his wand and Harry pocketed it.

'Come on, you three,' Mr Weasley said quietly. But Hermione didn't seem to want to move; her eyes were still upon the sobbing elf. 'Hermione!' Mr Weasley said, more urgently. She turned and followed Harry and Ron out of the clearing and off through the trees.

'What's going to happen to Winky?' said Hermione, the moment they had left the clearing.

'I don't know,' said Mr Weasley.

'The way they were treating her!' said Hermione furiously. 'Mr Diggory, calling her "elf" all the time … and Mr Crouch! He knows she didn't do it and he's still going to sack her! He didn't care how frightened she'd been, or how upset she was – it was like she wasn't even human!'

'Well, she's not,' said Ron.

Hermione rounded on him. 'That doesn't mean she hasn't got feelings, Ron, it's disgusting the way –'

'Hermione, I agree with you,' said Mr Weasley quickly, beckoning her on, 'but now is not the time to discuss elf rights. I want to get back to the tent as fast as we can. What happened to the others?'

'We lost them in the dark,' said Ron. 'Dad, why was everyone so uptight about that skull thing?'

'I'll explain everything back at the tent,' said Mr Weasley tensely.

But when they reached the edge of the wood, their progress was impeded.

A large crowd of frightened-looking witches and wizards was congregated there, and when they saw Mr Weasley coming towards them, many of them surged forwards. 'What's going on in there?' 'Who conjured it?' 'Arthur – it's not – *him*?'

'Of course it's not him,' said Mr Weasley impatiently. 'We don't know who it was, it looks like they Disapparated. Now excuse me, please, I want to get to bed.'

He led Harry, Ron and Hermione through the crowd and back into the campsite. All was quiet now; there was no sign of the masked wizards, though several ruined tents were still smoking.

Charlie's head was poking out of the boys' tent.

## 第9章 黑魔标记

经把它所知道的都告诉我们了——如果你能把它还给哈利，就请——"

迪戈里先生把那根魔杖递给了哈利，哈利把它装进了口袋。

"走吧，你们三个。"韦斯莱先生小声说。可是赫敏似乎不愿动弹，她的目光仍然落在哭泣的小精灵身上。"赫敏！"韦斯莱先生说，口气更急迫了。赫敏转过身，跟着哈利和罗恩走出空地，在树林里穿行。

"闪闪会怎么样呢？"他们一离开空地，赫敏就问道。

"不知道。"韦斯莱先生说。

"他们怎么那样对待她！"赫敏气愤地说，"迪戈里先生一直管她叫'小精灵'……还有克劳奇先生！他明明知道不是闪闪干的，还要把她开除！他根本不管她是多么害怕，多么难过——他根本就不把她当人！"

"咳，她本来就不是人嘛。"罗恩说。

赫敏立刻转过来攻击他。"那并不意味着她就没有感情，罗恩。他们那样真令人恶心，竟然——"

"赫敏，我同意你的看法，"韦斯莱先生赶紧说道，示意她继续往前走，"但现在不是讨论小精灵权益的时候。我希望我们尽快回到帐篷里。其他人怎么样了？"

"我们在黑暗里和他们走散了。"罗恩说，"爸爸，为什么大家都对那个骷髅那么紧张？"

"回到帐篷以后，我再跟你们解释。"韦斯莱先生焦急地说。

可是到达树林边缘时，他们遇到了阻碍。

一大群神色惶恐的巫师聚集在那里，看见韦斯莱先生朝他们走来，许多人便向前推挤。

"那边是怎么回事？"

"那标记是谁变出来的？"

"亚瑟——会不会是——他？"

"当然不是他，"韦斯莱先生不耐烦地说，"我们也不知道是谁，看样子他们幻影移形了。好了，请大家让开，求求你们，我想回去睡觉了。"

他领着哈利、罗恩和赫敏穿过人群，回到营地。现在到处都安静了，再也没有那些蒙面巫师的影子，只有几个被摧毁的帐篷还在冒烟。

查理从男孩的帐篷里伸出脑袋。

## CHAPTER NINE  The Dark Mark

'Dad, what's going on?' he called through the dark. 'Fred, George and Ginny got back OK, but the others –'

'I've got them here,' said Mr Weasley, bending down and entering the tent. Harry, Ron and Hermione entered after him.

Bill was sitting at the small kitchen table, holding a bedsheet to his arm, which was bleeding profusely. Charlie had a large rip in his shirt, and Percy was sporting a bloody nose. Fred, George and Ginny looked unhurt, though shaken.

'Did you get them, Dad?' said Bill sharply. 'The person who conjured the Mark?'

'No,' said Mr Weasley. 'We found Barty Crouch's elf holding Harry's wand, but we're none the wiser about who actually conjured the Mark.'

'*What?*' said Bill, Charlie and Percy together.

'Harry's wand?' said Fred.

'*Mr Crouch's elf?*' said Percy, sounding thunderstruck.

With some assistance from Harry, Ron and Hermione, Mr Weasley explained what had happened in the woods. When they had finished their story, Percy swelled indignantly.

'Well, Mr Crouch is quite right to get rid of an elf like that!' he said. 'Running away when he'd expressly told her not to ... embarrassing him in front of the whole Ministry ... how would that have looked, if she'd been had up in front of the Department for the Regulation and Control –'

'She didn't do anything – she was just in the wrong place at the wrong time!' Hermione snapped at Percy, who looked very taken aback. Hermione had always got on fairly well with Percy – better, indeed, than any of the others.

'Hermione, a wizard in Mr Crouch's position can't afford a house-elf who's going to run amok with a wand!' said Percy pompously, recovering himself.

'She didn't run amok!' shouted Hermione. 'She just picked it up off the ground!'

'Look, can someone just explain what that skull thing was?' said Ron impatiently. 'It wasn't hurting anyone ... why's it such a big deal?'

'I told you, it's You-Know-Who's symbol, Ron,' said Hermione, before anyone else could answer. 'I read about it in *The Rise and Fall of the Dark Arts*.'

## 第9章 黑魔标记

"爸爸，怎么回事？"他在黑暗中喊道，"弗雷德、乔治和金妮都平安回来了，可是他们几个——"

"我把他们都带回来了。"韦斯莱先生说着，弯腰钻进了帐篷。哈利、罗恩和赫敏也跟着他钻了进去。

比尔坐在小餐桌旁，用一条床单捂着手臂，鲜血正从那里不断冒出来。查理的衬衫撕了个大口子，珀西炫耀着他流血的鼻子。弗雷德、乔治和金妮看上去安然无恙，不过都惊魂未定。

"你们抓到人了吗，爸爸？"比尔劈头就问，"变出那个标记的人？"

"没有，"韦斯莱先生说，"我们发现巴蒂·克劳奇的家养小精灵拿着哈利的魔杖，但到底是谁变出了那个标记，我们一点儿也不知道。"

"什么？"比尔、查理和珀西异口同声地问。

"哈利的魔杖？"弗雷德说。

"克劳奇先生的家养小精灵？"珀西问，口气十分震惊。

韦斯莱先生在哈利、罗恩和赫敏的帮助下，把树林里发生的事情原原本本地告诉了大家。他们说完后，珀西气得直喘粗气。

"要我说，克劳奇先生就应该赶走这样一个家养小精灵！"他说，"主人明确告诉她待着别动，她却逃跑了……还在那么多魔法部官员面前让主人难堪……如果她被带到魔法生物管理控制司接受审问，那就太——"

"她什么也没干——她只是不该在那个时候出现在那个地点！"赫敏厉声反击珀西，令珀西大吃一惊。赫敏跟珀西的关系一向是很好的——实际上比其他人都好。

"赫敏，处在克劳奇先生那个位置的巫师，如果他的家养小精灵拿着一根魔杖到处胡作非为，这个责任他可担当不起！"珀西恢复了常态，自负地说。

"她没有到处胡作非为！"赫敏嚷道，"她只是从地上捡了根魔杖！"

"好了，好了，有谁能解释一下那个骷髅是什么东西？"罗恩不耐烦地说，"它并没有伤害什么人……为什么人人都那么大惊小怪？"

"我来告诉你吧，那是神秘人的符号，罗恩，"赫敏赶在别人前面回答道，"我在《黑魔法的兴衰》里读到过。"

'And it hasn't been seen for thirteen years,' said Mr Weasley quietly. 'Of course people panicked ... it was almost like seeing You-Know-Who back again.'

'I don't get it,' said Ron, frowning. 'I mean ... it's still only a shape in the sky ...'

'Ron, You-Know-Who and his followers sent the Dark Mark into the air whenever they killed,' said Mr Weasley. 'The terror it inspired ... you have no idea, you're too young. Just picture coming home, and finding the Dark Mark hovering over your house, and knowing what you're about to find inside ...' Mr Weasley winced. 'Everyone's worst fear ... the very worst ...'

There was silence for a moment.

Then Bill, removing the sheet from his arm to check on his cut, said, 'Well, it didn't help us tonight, whoever conjured it. It scared the Death Eaters away the moment they saw it. They all Disapparated before we'd got near enough to unmask any of them. We caught the Robertses before they hit the ground, though. They're having their memories modified right now.'

'Death Eaters?' said Harry. 'What are Death Eaters?'

'It's what You-Know-Who's supporters called themselves,' said Bill. 'I think we saw what's left of them tonight – the ones who managed to keep themselves out of Azkaban, anyway.'

'We can't prove it was them, Bill,' said Mr Weasley. 'Though it probably was,' he added hopelessly.

'Yeah, I bet it was!' said Ron suddenly. 'Dad, we met Draco Malfoy in the woods, and he as good as told us his dad was one of those nutters in masks! And we all know the Malfoys were right in with You-Know-Who!'

'But what were Voldemort's supporters –' Harry began. Everybody flinched – like most of the wizarding world, the Weasleys always avoided saying Voldemort's name. 'Sorry,' said Harry quickly. 'What were You-Know-Who's supporters up to, levitating Muggles? I mean, what was the point?'

'The point?' said Mr Weasley, with a hollow laugh. 'Harry, that's their idea of fun. Half the Muggle killings back when You-Know-Who was in power were done for fun. I suppose they had a few drinks tonight and couldn't resist reminding us all that lots of them are still at large. A nice little reunion for

## 第9章 黑魔标记

"已经有十三年没看见它了,"韦斯莱先生轻声说,"人们自然很紧张……这简直就像是又看见了神秘人。"

"我不明白,"罗恩皱着眉头说,"我的意思是……说到底,这只是半空中的一个影子……"

"罗恩,神秘人和他的信徒每次杀了人,都要在空中显示黑魔标记。"韦斯莱先生说,"它带来的恐惧……你不知道,你还太小。想象一下,你回到家里,发现黑魔标记就在你家房子上空盘旋,你知道你进去后会看见什么……"韦斯莱先生打了个哆嗦,"这是每个人最恐惧的……最最恐惧的……"

接着是片刻的沉默。

比尔拿开裹在手臂上的床单,查看伤口,说道:"唉,不管这个标记是谁变出来的,今天晚上可给我们帮了倒忙。那些食死徒一看见它就跑了。他们一个个匆匆幻影移形,我们还没来得及接近他们,揭开他们脸上的面具。不过,我们接住了罗伯茨一家,没让他们摔在地上。现在他们的记忆正在被修改。"

"食死徒?"哈利问,"食死徒是什么?"

"这是神秘人的信徒对他们自己的称呼。"比尔说,"我们今晚看见的应该是这些人的残余——他们不知怎的逃脱了,没有被关进阿兹卡班。"

"我们没法证明就是他们,比尔。"韦斯莱先生说,"不过很有可能。"他又无奈地说。

"对,我猜肯定是这样!"罗恩突然说,"爸爸,我们在树林里遇见了德拉科·马尔福,他实际上差不多告诉了我们,他爸爸就是那些蒙面疯子中的一个!我们都知道马尔福一家以前和神秘人很有交情!"

"可是伏地魔的信徒——"哈利说,大家都打了个寒战——韦斯莱一家和魔法世界里的大多数人一样,一向避免说出伏地魔的名字,"对不起,"哈利赶紧说道,"神秘人的信徒想干什么,把麻瓜弄到半空悬着?我的意思是,这有什么意义呢?"

"意义?"韦斯莱先生干笑了一声,说道,"哈利,那就是他们作乐的方式。过去神秘人当道的时候,他们杀害麻瓜多半都是为了取乐。我猜想他们今晚多喝了几杯酒,就忍不住想提醒我们一下:他们还有

## CHAPTER NINE   The Dark Mark

them,' he finished disgustedly.

'But if they *were* the Death Eaters, why did they Disapparate when they saw the Dark Mark?' said Ron. 'They'd have been pleased to see it, wouldn't they?'

'Use your brains, Ron,' said Bill. 'If they really were Death Eaters, they worked really hard to keep out of Azkaban when You-Know-Who lost power, and told all sorts of lies about him forcing them to kill and torture people. I bet they'd be even more frightened than the rest of us to see him come back. They denied they'd ever been involved with him when he lost his powers, and went back to their daily lives ... I don't reckon he'd be over-pleased with them, do you?'

'So ... whoever conjured the Dark Mark ...' said Hermione slowly, 'were they doing it to show support for the Death Eaters, or to scare them away?'

'Your guess is as good as ours, Hermione,' said Mr Weasley. 'But I'll tell you this ... it was only the Death Eaters who ever knew how to conjure it. I'd be very surprised if the person who did it hadn't been a Death Eater once, even if they're not now ... Listen, it's very late, and if your mother hears what's happened she'll be worried sick. We'll get a few more hours' sleep and then try and get an early Portkey out of here.'

Harry got back into his bunk with his head buzzing. He knew he ought to feel exhausted; it was nearly three in the morning, but he felt wide awake – wide awake, and worried.

Three days ago – it felt like much longer, but it had only been three days – he had awoken with his scar burning. And tonight, for the first time in thirteen years, Lord Voldemort's Mark had appeared in the sky. What did these things mean?

He thought of the letter he had written to Sirius before leaving Privet Drive. Would Sirius have got it yet? When would he reply? Harry lay looking up at the canvas, but no flying fantasies came to him now to ease him to sleep, and it was a long time after Charlie's snores filled the tent that Harry finally dozed off.

## 第9章 黑魔标记

很多人在外逍遥。他们搞了一个愉快的小派对。"他厌恶地说。

"可是如果他们是食死徒,为什么一看见黑魔标记就幻影移形了呢?"罗恩问,"他们应该很高兴看见它呀,对不对?"

"你动脑子想一想吧,罗恩,"比尔说,"如果他们真是食死徒,神秘人失势之后,他们千方百计不让自己被关进阿兹卡班,编造了各种谎话,说当初是神秘人强迫他们杀害和折磨别人的。我敢打赌,他们比我们这些人更害怕看见神秘人回来。神秘人倒台后,他们百般否认自己跟他有关系,又重新过上了正常人的生活……我认为神秘人对他们不会很满意,你说呢?"

"那么……变出黑魔标记的人……"赫敏慢慢地说,"这么做到底是为了表示支持食死徒,还是要把他们吓跑呢?"

"我们也不能确定,赫敏,"韦斯莱先生说,"不过我要告诉你们一点……只有食死徒才知道怎样变出那个标记。我可以肯定,变出标记的人以前肯定是食死徒,尽管现在也许不是了……听着,时间已经很晚了,如果你们的妈妈听说了这些事情,准会担心得要命。我们抓紧时间睡几个小时,然后早早地弄到门钥匙,离开这里。"

哈利爬回到他的双层床上,脑袋里嗡嗡作响。他知道他应该感到精疲力竭才是:现在已是凌晨三点,可是他却感到异常清醒——清醒,而且担忧。

三天前——现在感觉已是很久以前,实际上只过去了三天——他醒来时感到额头上的伤疤剧痛难忍。今晚,伏地魔的标记十三年来第一次出现在空中。这一切都意味着什么呢?

他想起了离开女贞路前写给小天狼星的信。小天狼星收到没有?他什么时候会回信?哈利仰面躺在床上,望着帆布篷顶,然而脑子里没有想象出什么东西帮助他入睡。帐篷里早就响起了查理的鼾声,过了很久哈利才终于昏昏沉沉地睡去。

## CHAPTER TEN

# Mayhem at the Ministry

Mr Weasley woke them after only a few hours' sleep. He used magic to pack up the tents, and they left the campsite as quickly as possible, passing Mr Roberts at the door of his cottage. Mr Roberts had a strange, dazed look about him, and he waved them off with a vague 'Merry Christmas'.

'He'll be all right,' said Mr Weasley quietly, as they marched off onto the moor. 'Sometimes, when a person's memory's modified, it makes them a bit disorientated for a while ... and that was a big thing they had to make him forget.'

They heard urgent voices as they approached the spot where the Portkeys lay and, when they reached it, they found a great number of witches and wizards gathered around Basil, the keeper of the Portkeys, all clamouring to get away from the campsite as quickly as possible. Mr Weasley had a hurried discussion with Basil; they joined the queue, and were able to take an old rubber tyre back to Stoatshead Hill before the sun had really risen. They walked back through Ottery St Catchpole towards The Burrow in the dawn light, talking very little because they were so exhausted, and thinking longingly of their breakfast. As they rounded the corner in the lane, and The Burrow came into view, a cry echoed along the damp lane.

'Oh, thank goodness, thank goodness!'

Mrs Weasley, who had evidently been waiting for them in the front yard, came running towards them, still wearing her bedroom slippers, her face pale and strained, a screwed-up copy of the *Daily Prophet* clutched in her hand. 'Arthur – I've been so worried – *so worried* –'

She flung her arms around Mr Weasley's neck, and the *Daily Prophet* fell out of her limp hand onto the ground. Looking down, Harry saw the headline: SCENES OF TERROR AT THE QUIDDITCH WORLD CUP, complete with a twinkling, black-and-white photograph of the Dark Mark over the tree-tops.

# 第 10 章

## 魔法部乱成一团

只睡了几个小时,韦斯莱先生就把他们叫醒了。他用魔法把帐篷收起来装进背包,然后他们尽快离开了营地,路上看见罗伯茨先生站在他小石屋门口。罗伯茨先生样子怪怪的,神情恍惚,他朝他们挥手告别,还含混地说了句"圣诞快乐"。

"他不会有事的,"他们大步向沼泽地走去时,韦斯莱先生小声说道,"有时候,当一个人的记忆被修改时,会暂时有点儿犯糊涂……况且他们想使他忘记的又是那么一件大事。"

他们走近放门钥匙的地方时,听见许多人在急切地吵吵嚷嚷;再走过去一点儿,发现一大堆巫师把门钥匙管理员巴兹尔团团围住,都吵闹着要尽快离开营地。韦斯莱先生和巴兹尔三言两语地商量了一下。大家站进队伍里,最后总算在太阳还没升起前领到了一只旧轮胎,可以靠它返回白鼬山了。在拂晓的微光中,他们穿过奥特里·圣卡奇波尔村,沿着湿漉漉的小路朝陋居走去。一路上大家很少说话,因为都累得要命,一心只想赶紧吃到早饭。他们转了个弯,陋居便赫然出现了,小路上传来一声喊叫。

"哦,谢天谢地,谢天谢地!"

韦斯莱夫人显然一直在前院等他们,这时撒腿向他们奔来,脚上还穿着她在卧室里穿的拖鞋。她脸色苍白,神情紧张,手里攥着一张卷起来的《预言家日报》。"亚瑟……我真是太担心了……太担心了……"

她一把搂住韦斯莱先生的脖子,《预言家日报》从她无力的手中滑落到地上。哈利低头一看,标题是:**魁地奇世界杯赛上的恐怖场面**,还配有黑魔标记悬在树梢上的闪光黑白照片。

## CHAPTER TEN  Mayhem at the Ministry

'You're all right,' Mrs Weasley muttered distractedly, releasing Mr Weasley and staring around at them all with red eyes, 'you're alive ... oh, *boys* ...'

And to everybody's surprise, she seized Fred and George and pulled them both into such a tight hug that their heads banged together.

'*Ouch*! Mum – you're strangling us –'

'I shouted at you before you left!' Mrs Weasley said, starting to sob. 'It's all I've been thinking about! What if You-Know-Who had got you, and the last thing I ever said to you was that you didn't get enough O.W.L.s? Oh, Fred ... George ...'

'Come on, now, Molly, we're all perfectly OK,' said Mr Weasley soothingly, prising her off the twins and leading her back towards the house. 'Bill,' he added in an undertone, 'pick up that paper, I want to see what it says ...'

When they were all crammed into the tiny kitchen, and Hermione had made Mrs Weasley a cup of very strong tea, into which Mr Weasley insisted on pouring a shot of Ogdens Old Firewhisky, Bill handed his father the newspaper. Mr Weasley scanned the front page while Percy looked over his shoulder.

'I knew it,' said Mr Weasley heavily. '*Ministry blunders ... culprits not apprehended ... lax security ... Dark wizards running unchecked ... national disgrace ...* Who wrote this? Ah ... of course ... Rita Skeeter.'

'That woman's got it in for the Ministry of Magic!' said Percy furiously. 'Last week she was saying we're wasting our time quibbling about cauldron thickness, when we should be stamping out vampires! As if it wasn't *specifically* stated in paragraph twelve of the *Guidelines for the Treatment of Non-Wizard Part-Humans* –'

'Do us a favour, Perce,' said Bill, yawning, 'and shut up.'

'I'm mentioned,' said Mr Weasley, his eyes widening behind his glasses as he reached the bottom of the *Daily Prophet* article.

'Where?' spluttered Mrs Weasley, choking on her tea and whisky. 'If I'd seen that, I'd have known you were alive!'

'Not by name,' said Mr Weasley. 'Listen to this: "*If the terrified wizards and witches who waited breathlessly for news at the edge of the wood expected reassurance from the Ministry of Magic, they were sadly disappointed. A Ministry official emerged some time after the appearance of the Dark Mark, alleging that nobody had been hurt, but refusing to give any more information. Whether this statement will be enough to quash the rumours that several bodies were removed from the woods an hour later, remains to be seen.*" Oh, really,'

## 第10章 魔法部乱成一团

"你们都没事,"韦斯莱夫人惊魂未定地念叨着,松开韦斯莱先生,一双红通通的眼睛挨个儿看着他们,"你们都活着……哦,儿子……"

出乎每个人的意料,她一把抓住弗雷德和乔治,狠狠地搂了一下。她用的劲儿太猛了,双胞胎的脑袋咚地撞在一起。

"哎哟!妈妈——你要把我们勒死了——"

"你们走之前我冲你们嚷嚷来着!"韦斯莱夫人说,忍不住哭了起来,"我一直在想这个事!如果神秘人把你们抓去,而我对你们说的最后一句话竟是你们 O.W.L. 证书太少?哦,弗雷德……乔治……"

"好了,好了,莫丽,我们大家都平安无事。"韦斯莱先生安慰着她,从她怀里拽出一对双胞胎,然后领着她向房子里走去,"比尔,"他压低声音说,"把那张报纸捡起来,我想看看上面怎么说的……"

他们都挤进狭小的厨房,赫敏给韦斯莱夫人沏了一杯很浓的茶,韦斯莱先生坚持往里面倒了一点奥格登陈年火焰威士忌,然后,比尔把报纸递给了父亲。韦斯莱先生匆匆浏览着第一版,珀西也从他身后看着。

"我就知道会是这样,"韦斯莱先生沉重地说,"魔法部惊慌失措……罪犯未被抓获……治安松懈……黑巫师逍遥法外……给国家带来耻辱……这是谁写的?啊……自然是她……丽塔·斯基特。"

"那个女人专门同魔法部作对!"珀西气愤地说,"她上个星期说,我们本应该全力以赴去消灭吸血鬼,可却在坩埚的厚度上吹毛求疵,浪费时间!好像《非巫师的半人类待遇准则》的第十二段没有专门指出——"

"行行好吧,珀西,"比尔说着,打了个哈欠,"不要再说了。"

"提到我了。"韦斯莱先生读到《预言家日报》那篇文章的结尾处时,突然瞪大了镜片后面的眼睛。

"哪儿?"韦斯莱夫人呛了一口威士忌茶水,咳喘着问,"我刚才要是看见,就知道你还活着了!"

"没有点名,"韦斯莱先生说,"听听这段:那些巫师惊慌失措,在树林边屏住呼吸等候消息,希望得到魔法部的安慰,可令人遗憾的是,他们大失所望。在黑魔标记出现后不久,一位魔法部官员露面了,宣称没有人受到伤害,但拒绝透露更多情况。究竟他的话是否足以平息那种'一小时后从树林里抬出几具尸体'的谣传,还有待继续观察。哦,

## CHAPTER TEN    Mayhem at the Ministry

said Mr Weasley in exasperation, handing the paper to Percy. 'Nobody *was* hurt, what was I supposed to say? *Rumours that several bodies were removed from the woods* ... well, there certainly will be rumours now she's printed that.'

He heaved a deep sigh. 'Molly, I'm going to have to go into the office, this is going to take some smoothing over.'

'I'll come with you, Father,' said Percy importantly. 'Mr Crouch will need all hands on deck. And I can give him my cauldron report in person.'

He bustled out of the kitchen.

Mrs Weasley looked most upset. 'Arthur, you're supposed to be on holiday! This hasn't got anything to do with your office, surely they can handle this without you?'

'I've got to go, Molly,' said Mr Weasley, 'I've made things worse. I'll just change into my robes and I'll be off ...'

'Mrs Weasley,' said Harry suddenly, unable to contain himself, 'Hedwig hasn't arrived with a letter for me, has she?'

'Hedwig, dear?' said Mrs Weasley distractedly. 'No ... no, there hasn't been any post at all.'

Ron and Hermione looked curiously at Harry.

With a meaningful look at both of them he said, 'All right if I go and dump my stuff in your room, Ron?'

'Yeah ... think I will, too,' said Ron at once. 'Hermione?'

'Yes,' she said quickly, and the three of them marched out of the kitchen and up the stairs.

'What's up, Harry?' said Ron, the moment they had closed the door of the attic room behind them.

'There's something I haven't told you,' Harry said. 'On Saturday morning, I woke up with my scar hurting again.'

Ron and Hermione's reactions were almost exactly as Harry had imagined them back in his bedroom in Privet Drive. Hermione gasped and started making suggestions at once, mentioning a number of reference books, and everybody from Albus Dumbledore to Madam Pomfrey, the Hogwarts matron.

Ron simply looked dumbstruck. 'But – he wasn't there, was he? You-Know-Who? I mean – last time your scar kept hurting, he was at Hogwarts, wasn't he?'

## 第10章 魔法部乱成一团

天哪，"韦斯莱先生恼怒地说，把报纸递给珀西，"确实没有人受到伤害呀。我应该怎么说呢？'从树林里抬出几具尸体'的谣传……好了，现在她写出这种话，肯定会谣言四起的。"

他深深地叹了口气，"莫丽，我得去办公室了，这件事需要澄清一下。"

"我和你一起去，爸爸，"珀西自傲地说，"克劳奇先生肯定需要大家各就各位，而且，我还可以把我的坩埚报告亲自交给他。"

他说完就冲出了厨房。韦斯莱夫人显得非常难过。

"亚瑟，按理说你是在休假啊！这件事跟你们办公室毫无关系；没有你，他们也能处理好的，是不是？"

"我必须去，莫丽，"韦斯莱先生说，"是我把事情搞得更糟糕了。我去换上长袍就走……"

"韦斯莱夫人，"哈利再也控制不住自己，突然说道，"海德薇有没有带信回来给我？"

"海德薇？"韦斯莱夫人神情恍惚地说，"没有，亲爱的……没有，一封信也没有收到。"

罗恩和赫敏好奇地望着哈利。

哈利意味深长地看了他们俩一眼，说道："罗恩，我能不能到你房间去放一下我的东西？"

"好啊……我也去吧。"罗恩毫不迟疑地回答，"赫敏，你呢？"

"好吧。"她立刻说道，于是三个人鱼贯离开厨房，往楼上走去。

"怎么回事，哈利？"他们进到顶楼房间，一关上房门，罗恩就问。

"有件事我没有跟你们说，"哈利说，"星期六早晨我醒过来的时候，我的伤疤又疼了。"

罗恩和赫敏的反应，跟哈利在女贞路卧室里想象的几乎一模一样。赫敏倒吸了一口气，马上提出各种建议，列举了一大堆参考书名，又列举了一大堆人名，从阿不思·邓布利多，到霍格沃茨的校医庞弗雷女士。

罗恩只是一副目瞪口呆的样子，"可是——他当时不在场啊，是不是？那个神秘人？我的意思是——上次你伤疤疼的时候，他是在霍格沃茨的，对不对？"

## CHAPTER TEN    Mayhem at the Ministry

'I'm sure he wasn't in Privet Drive,' said Harry. 'But I was dreaming about him ... him and Peter – you know, Wormtail. I can't remember all of it now, but they were plotting to kill ... someone.'

He had teetered for a moment on the verge of saying 'me', but couldn't bring himself to make Hermione look any more horrified than she already did.

'It was only a dream,' said Ron bracingly. 'Just a nightmare.'

'Yeah, but was it, though?' said Harry, turning to look out of the window at the brightening sky. 'It's weird, isn't it ... my scar hurts, and three days later the Death Eaters are on the march, and Voldemort's sign's up in the sky again.'

'Don't – say – his – name!' Ron hissed through gritted teeth.

'And remember what Professor Trelawney said?' Harry went on, ignoring Ron. 'At the end of last year?'

Professor Trelawney was their Divination teacher at Hogwarts.

Hermione's terrified look vanished as she let out a derisive snort. 'Oh, Harry, you aren't going to pay any attention to anything that old fraud says?'

'You weren't there,' said Harry. 'You didn't hear her. This time was different. I told you, she went into a trance – a real one. And she said the Dark Lord would rise again ... *greater and more terrible than ever before* ... and he'd manage it because his servant was going to go back to him ... and that night Wormtail escaped.'

There was a silence in which Ron fidgeted absent-mindedly with a hole in his Chudley Cannons bedspread.

'Why were you asking if Hedwig had come, Harry?' Hermione asked. 'Are you expecting a letter?'

'I told Sirius about my scar,' said Harry, shrugging. 'I'm waiting for his answer.'

'Good thinking!' said Ron, his expression clearing. 'I bet Sirius'll know what to do!'

'I hoped he'd get back to me quickly,' said Harry.

'But we don't know where Sirius is ... he could be in Africa or somewhere, couldn't he?' said Hermione reasonably. 'Hedwig's not going to manage *that* journey in a few days.'

'Yeah, I know,' said Harry, but there was a leaden feeling in his stomach as

## 第10章 魔法部乱成一团

"我知道他肯定不在女贞路,"哈利说,"可是我在梦里看见他了……他和彼得——你们知道的,就是虫尾巴。梦里的全部情形,我已经记不清了,只记得他们在密谋,要杀……一个人。"

他迟疑了一下,差点说出"要杀我",但是不忍心让赫敏的神情变得更恐惧,因为赫敏已经大惊失色了。

"这只是一场梦,"罗恩鼓励他振作起来,"只是一场噩梦。"

"是啊,但真的是梦吗?"哈利说,转脸望着窗外渐渐明亮起来的天空,"很古怪,是不是?……我的伤疤疼了起来,三天之后,食死徒就游行了,伏地魔的符号就又在空中出现了。"

"不要——说出——他的——名字!"罗恩从紧咬的牙缝里嘶嘶地说。

"还记得特里劳尼教授说的话吗?"哈利没理睬罗恩,继续说道,"就在上学期结束的时候?"

特里劳尼教授是他们在霍格沃茨学校的占卜课老师。

赫敏脸上惊恐的表情消失了,她发出一声短促的嘲笑。"哦,哈利,你该不会把那个老骗子说的话放在心上吧?"

"你们当时不在场,"哈利说,"没有听见她说的话。这一次可不同以往。我告诉你们吧,她进入了催眠状态——是真的催眠状态。她说黑魔头还会卷土重来……比以前更强大、更可怕……黑魔头能够这样,是因为他的仆人会回到他身边……就在那天晚上,虫尾巴逃跑了。"

一时间谁也没有说话,罗恩心不在焉地摆弄着他那条查德里火炮队床单上的一个破洞。

"你为什么要问海德薇有没有回来,哈利?"赫敏问道,"你在等信吗?"

"我把伤疤疼的事告诉了小天狼星,"哈利耸了耸肩膀,说,"我在等他的回信。"

"想得真妙!"罗恩说,脸上顿时多云转晴,"我敢说小天狼星肯定知道该怎么办!"

"真希望他赶快跟我联系。"哈利说。

"可我们不知道小天狼星在哪里……他可能远在非洲呢,是不是?"赫敏很明智地说,"海德薇不可能在几天之内到达那么远的地方。"

"是啊,我知道。"哈利说,可是当他望着窗外的天空,不见海德

## CHAPTER TEN — Mayhem at the Ministry

he looked out of the window at the Hedwig-free sky.

'Come and have a game of Quidditch in the orchard, Harry,' said Ron. 'Come on – three on three, Bill and Charlie and Fred and George will play ... you can try out the Wronski Feint ...'

'Ron,' said Hermione, in an I-don't-think-you're-being-very-sensitive sort of voice, 'Harry doesn't want to play Quidditch right now ... he's worried, and he's tired ... we all need to go to bed ...'

'Yeah, I want to play Quidditch,' said Harry suddenly. 'Hang on, I'll get my Firebolt.'

Hermione left the room, muttering something which sounded very much like '*Boys*'.

Neither Mr Weasley nor Percy was at home much over the following week. Both left the house each morning before the rest of the family got up, and returned well after dinner every night.

'It's been absolute uproar,' Percy told them importantly, the Sunday evening before they were due to return to Hogwarts. 'I've been putting out fires all week. People keep sending Howlers and of course, if you don't open a Howler straight away, it explodes. Scorch marks all over my desk and my best quill reduced to cinders.'

'Why are they all sending Howlers?' asked Ginny, who was mending her copy of *One Thousand Magical Herbs and Fungi* with Spellotape on the rug in front of the living-room fire.

'Complaining about security at the World Cup,' said Percy. 'They want compensation for their ruined property. Mundungus Fletcher's put in a claim for a twelve-bedroomed tent with en-suite jacuzzi, but I've got his number. I know for a fact he was sleeping under a cloak propped on sticks.'

Mrs Weasley glanced at the grandfather clock in the corner. Harry liked this clock. It was completely useless if you wanted to know the time, but otherwise very informative. It had nine golden hands, and each of them was engraved with one of the Weasley family's names. There were no numerals around the face, but descriptions of where each family member might be. 'Home', 'school' and 'work' were there, but there was also 'lost', 'hospital', 'prison' and, in the position where the number twelve would be on a normal clock, 'mortal peril'.

Eight of the hands were currently pointing at the 'home' position, but Mr

薇的影子，心里还是感到沉甸甸的。

"来吧，哈利，我们在果园里来一场魁地奇比赛。"罗恩说，"来吧——三个人对三个人，比尔、查理、弗雷德和乔治都参加进来……你可以试试朗斯基假动作……"

"罗恩，"赫敏说，声音里透着"我认为你太不知趣了"的意思，"哈利现在不想打魁地奇……他心里很乱，很疲倦……我们都需要上床睡觉了……"

"好吧，我愿意打一场魁地奇，"哈利突然说道，"等一下，我要拿上我的火弩箭。"

赫敏离开了房间，嘴里嘀咕着什么，好像是说："这帮男生！"

在以后的一个星期里，韦斯莱先生和珀西都很少在家。每天一早，家里其他人还没有起床，他们俩就离开了家，一直到晚饭以后很久才回来。

"真是乱成了一锅粥，"珀西煞有介事地告诉他们——这是一个星期天的晚上，第二天他们就要返回霍格沃茨了，"整整一个星期，我都像在救火一样。人们不停地寄来吼叫信，如果你不马上把吼叫信拆开，它就会爆炸。我桌子上到处都是烧焦的痕迹，那支最好的羽毛笔也变成了一堆炭渣。"

"他们为什么都寄吼叫信呢？"金妮问。她正坐在客厅炉火前的地毯上，用透明魔法胶带修补她那本《千种神奇药草及蕈类》。

"抱怨世界杯赛的安全问题，"珀西说，"希望对他们被损坏的财物进行赔偿。蒙顿格斯·弗莱奇提出索赔一顶带十二个卧室和配套按摩浴缸的帐篷，可是我摸透了他的底细。我知道他实际上是用棍子支着一件斗篷过的夜。"

韦斯莱夫人瞥了一眼墙角的那座老爷钟。哈利很喜欢这座钟。如果你想知道时间，它是完全不管用的，可它却能向你提供许多其他情况。它有九根金针，每根针上都刻着韦斯莱家一个人的名字。钟面上没有数字，却写着每位家庭成员可能会在的地方。有家、学校和上班，也有路上、失踪、医院、监狱，在普通钟上十二点的地方，标着生命危险。

此刻，八根针都指着家的位置，韦斯莱先生的那根——是九根针

## CHAPTER TEN   Mayhem at the Ministry

Weasley's, which was the longest, was still pointing at 'work'. Mrs Weasley sighed.

'Your father hasn't had to go into the office at weekends since the days of You-Know-Who,' she said. 'They're working him far too hard. His dinner's going to be ruined if he doesn't come home soon.'

'Well, Father feels he's got to make up for his mistake at the match, doesn't he?' said Percy. 'If truth be told, he was a tad unwise to make a public statement without clearing it with his Head of Department first –'

'Don't you dare blame your father for what that wretched Skeeter woman wrote!' said Mrs Weasley, flaring up at once.

'If Dad hadn't said anything, old Rita would just have said it was disgraceful that nobody from the Ministry had commented,' said Bill, who was playing chess with Ron. 'Rita Skeeter never makes anyone look good. Remember, she interviewed all the Gringotts curse breakers once, and called me "a long-haired pillock"?'

'Well, it is a bit long, dear,' said Mrs Weasley gently. 'If you'd just let me –'

'*No*, Mum.'

Rain lashed against the living-room window. Hermione was immersed in *The Standard Book of Spells, Grade 4,* copies of which Mrs Weasley had bought for her, Harry and Ron in Diagon Alley. Charlie was darning a fireproof balaclava. Harry was polishing his Firebolt, the Broomstick Servicing Kit Hermione had given him for his thir-teenth birthday open at his feet. Fred and George were sitting in a far corner, quills out, talking in whispers, their heads bent over a piece of parchment.

'What are you two up to?' said Mrs Weasley sharply, her eyes on the twins.

'Homework,' said Fred vaguely.

'Don't be ridiculous, you're still on holiday,' said Mrs Weasley.

'Yeah, we've left it a bit late,' said George.

'You're not by any chance writing out a new *order form*, are you?' said Mrs Weasley shrewdly. 'You wouldn't be thinking of restarting *Weasleys' Wizard Wheezes*, by any chance?'

'Now, Mum,' said Fred, looking up at her, a pained look on his face. 'If the Hogwarts Express crashed tomorrow, and George and I died, how would you feel knowing that the last thing we ever heard from you was an unfounded accusation?'

## 第10章　魔法部乱成一团

里最长的一根，仍然指着上班。韦斯莱夫人叹了口气。

"从神秘人失势那天起，你爸爸周末一直不需要加班。"她说，"现在他们要把他累坏了。如果他再不赶快回来，他的晚饭就没法吃了。"

"嘿，爸爸觉得必须弥补他在比赛那天犯的过错，是不是？"珀西说，"说老实话，他没有请示他的领导就当众发言，有点不够明智——"

"都是斯基特那个讨厌的女人信笔胡写，你怎么敢因此责怪你爸爸呢！"韦斯莱夫人一下子就火了，说道。

"如果爸爸什么都不说，丽塔那老家伙又会评论说魔法部的人一言不发，有失身份。"正在跟罗恩下棋的比尔说道，"丽塔·斯基特从来不写别人的好话。记得吗，她有一次采访了古灵阁的所有解咒员，然后管我叫'长毛鬼'！"

"我说，你的头发确实有点儿长，亲爱的，"韦斯莱夫人温柔地说，"你只要让我——"

"不行，妈妈。"

雨点啪嗒啪嗒地打在客厅的窗户上。赫敏专心地读着《标准咒语，四级》，韦斯莱夫人在对角巷给她、哈利和罗恩各买了一本。查理在织补一个防火的套头帽兜。哈利在擦拭他的火弩箭，那个飞天扫帚护理工具箱，赫敏在他十三岁生日时送给他的礼物，现在打开了放在他脚边。弗雷德和乔治坐在那边的一个角落里，拿着羽毛笔，脑袋凑在一张羊皮纸上，低声地谈论着什么。

"你们两个在干什么？"韦斯莱夫人严厉地问，一边用眼睛盯着双胞胎兄弟。

"做家庭作业。"弗雷德含糊地回答。

"别丢人现眼了，现在正放假呢。"韦斯莱夫人说。

"是啊，我们有点拖拉了。"乔治说。

"你们该不会又在写订货单吧？"韦斯莱夫人一针见血地指出，"你们该不会又琢磨着要搞什么韦斯莱魔法把戏坊吧？"

"哎呀，妈妈，"弗雷德抬头看着她，脸上露出一副痛苦的表情，"如果明天霍格沃茨特快列车被撞毁，我和乔治都死了，你想到我们从你这儿听到的最后一句话是毫无根据的指责，你心里该是什么滋味啊？"

## CHAPTER TEN — Mayhem at the Ministry

Everyone laughed, even Mrs Weasley.

'Oh, your father's coming!' she said suddenly, looking up at the clock again.

Mr Weasley's hand had suddenly spun from 'work' to 'travelling'; a second later it had shuddered to a halt on 'home' with the others, and they heard him calling from the kitchen.

'Coming, Arthur!' called Mrs Weasley, hurrying out of the room.

A few moments later, Mr Weasley had come into the warm living room, carrying his dinner on a tray. He looked completely exhausted.

'Well, the fat's really in the fire now,' he told Mrs Weasley as he sat down in an armchair near the fire and toyed unenthusiastically with his somewhat shrivelled cauliflower. 'Rita Skeeter's been ferreting around all week, looking for more Ministry mess-ups to report. And now she's found out about poor old Bertha going missing, so that'll be the headline in the *Prophet* tomorrow. I *told* Bagman he should have sent someone to look for her ages ago.'

'Mr Crouch has been saying it for weeks and weeks,' said Percy swiftly.

'Crouch is very lucky Rita hasn't found out about Winky,' said Mr Weasley irritably. 'There'd be a week's worth of headlines in his house-elf being caught holding the wand that conjured the Dark Mark.'

'I thought we were all agreed that that elf, while irresponsible, did *not* conjure the Mark?' said Percy hotly.

'If you ask me, Mr Crouch is very lucky no one at the *Daily Prophet* knows how mean he is to elves!' said Hermione angrily.

'Now, look here, Hermione!' said Percy. 'A high-ranking Ministry official like Mr Crouch deserves unswerving obedience from his servants –'

'His *slave*, you mean!' said Hermione, her voice rising shrilly. 'Because he didn't *pay* Winky, did he?'

'I think you'd all better go upstairs and check that you've packed properly!' said Mrs Weasley, breaking up the argument. 'Come on, now, all of you …'

Harry repacked his Broomstick Servicing Kit, put his Firebolt over his shoulder and went back upstairs with Ron. The rain sounded even louder at the top of the house, accompanied by loud whistlings and moans from the wind, not to mention sporadic howls from the ghoul who lived in the attic.

## 第10章 魔法部乱成一团

大家都笑了起来，韦斯莱夫人也忍俊不禁。

"哦，你们的爸爸回来了！"她又抬头望了望钟，突然说道。

韦斯莱先生的那根针突然从"上班"跳到了"路上"，一秒钟后，它就颤颤巍巍地和其他针一起，停在了"家"的位置上。这时，大家听见厨房里传来韦斯莱先生的喊声。

"来了，亚瑟！"韦斯莱夫人大声说，匆匆出了房间。

片刻之后，韦斯莱先生用托盘端着他的晚饭，走进了温暖的客厅。他一副累坏了的样子。

"唉，事情越发不可收拾了，"他坐在壁炉边的一把扶手椅上，没精打采地摆弄着盘子里有些皱巴巴的花椰菜，一边对韦斯莱夫人说，"丽塔·斯基特整个星期都在四处钻营，搜寻魔法部有没有更多的混乱情况可供报道。现在她发现了可怜的老伯莎失踪的事，看来这就是《预言家日报》明天的大标题了。我对巴格曼说过，他早就应该派人去找伯莎。"

"克劳奇先生好几个星期一直在这么说。"珀西赶紧说道。

"克劳奇还算走运，丽塔没有发现闪闪的事。"韦斯莱先生烦躁地说，"他的家养小精灵被抓，手里拿着变出黑魔标记的魔杖，这件事可以成为整整一星期的头版头条。"

"我想，我们大家都认为，那个小精灵尽管缺乏责任感，却并没有变出黑魔标记，对不对？"珀西激烈地辩论道。

"如果你问我，我倒认为克劳奇先生真是非常走运，《预言家日报》的人竟不知道他是怎样虐待小精灵的！"赫敏气愤地说。

"赫敏，你想想吧！"珀西说，"像克劳奇先生这样的魔法部高级官员，应该得到他仆人的绝对顺从——"

"你是说他的奴隶吧！"赫敏激动地抬高声音，说道，"因为他并不付给闪闪工钱，对不对？"

"我想你们还是都上楼去，看行李是不是都收拾好了！"韦斯莱夫人打断了他们的争论，说道，"快去吧，你们都去吧……"

哈利把飞天扫帚护理工具箱收拾好，扛着他的火弩箭，和罗恩一起回到楼上。雨点砸在房顶上的声音更响了，还夹杂着一阵阵狂风的凄厉呼啸和呻吟，更别提住在阁楼上的食尸鬼发出的零星号叫了。他

## CHAPTER TEN

### Mayhem at the Ministry

Pigwidgeon began twittering and zooming around his cage again when they entered. The sight of the half-packed trunks seemed to have sent him into a frenzy of excitement.

'Bung him some Owl Treats,' said Ron, throwing a packet across to Harry, 'it might shut him up.'

Harry poked a few Owl Treats through the bars of Pigwidgeon's cage, then turned to his trunk. Hedwig's cage stood next to it, still empty.

'It's been over a week,' Harry said, looking at Hedwig's deserted perch. 'Ron, you don't reckon Sirius has been caught, do you?'

'Nah, it would've been in the *Daily Prophet*,' said Ron. 'The Ministry would want to show they'd caught *someone*, wouldn't they?'

'Yeah, I suppose …'

'Look, here's the stuff Mum got for you in Diagon Alley. And she's got some gold out of your vault for you … and she's washed all your socks.'

He heaved a pile of parcels onto Harry's camp bed and dropped the money bag and a load of socks next to it. Harry started unwrapping the shopping. Apart from *The Standard Book of Spells, Grade 4*, by Miranda Goshawk, he had a handful of new quills, a dozen rolls of parchment and refills for his potion-making kit – he had been running low on spine of lionfish and essence of belladonna. He was just piling underwear into his cauldron when Ron made a loud noise of disgust behind him.

'What is *that* supposed to be?'

He was holding up something that looked to Harry like a long, maroon velvet dress. It had a mouldy-looking lace frill at the collar and matching lace cuffs.

There was a knock on the door, and Mrs Weasley entered, carrying an armful of freshly laundered Hogwarts robes.

'Here you are,' she said, sorting them into two. 'Now, mind you pack them properly so they don't crease.'

'Mum, you've given me Ginny's new dress,' said Ron, holding it out to her.

'Of course I haven't,' said Mrs Weasley. 'That's for you. Dress robes.'

'*What?*' said Ron, looking horror-struck.

'Dress robes!' repeated Mrs Weasley. 'It says on your school list that you're

## 第10章 魔法部乱成一团

们进屋后,那只叫小猪的猫头鹰开始吱吱叫着,在笼子里飞来飞去。它看到那些收拾了一半的箱子,似乎兴奋得有些发狂了。

"塞点猫头鹰食给它,"罗恩说着,把一包东西扔给哈利,"就会使它安静下来。"

哈利把几粒猫头鹰食塞进小猪的笼子,然后转过头来望着自己的箱子。海德薇的笼子就在箱子旁边,里面还是空的。

"它已经走了一个多星期了。"哈利看着海德薇的空笼子,说道,"罗恩,你说小天狼星会不会被抓住了?"

"不会,不然《预言家日报》上会有报道的。"罗恩说,"魔法部巴不得显示一下他们抓住了什么人呢,是吧?"

"是啊,我猜是……"

"瞧,这些都是妈妈在对角巷给你买的东西。她还从你的地下金库里给你取了一些金币……还替你把所有的袜子都洗干净了。"

罗恩把一大堆包裹搬到哈利的行军床上,又把钱袋和一大包袜子扔在包裹旁边。哈利开始拆看韦斯莱夫人给他买的东西。除了米兰达·戈沙克所著的《标准咒语,四级》外,还有一把新的羽毛笔、十二卷羊皮纸,以及他调配魔药的原料箱里需要添补的东西——他的狮子鱼脊骨粉和颠茄精快用完了。他刚要把内衣放进他的坩埚,就听见罗恩在后面很厌恶地嚷嚷起来。

"这是什么玩意儿?"

罗恩手里举着个东西,在哈利看来那像是一件酱紫色的天鹅绒长裙,领口镶着仿佛发了霉的荷叶边,袖口上也有相配的花边。

就在这时传来了敲门声,韦斯莱夫人走了进来,怀里抱着刚刚洗净熨平的霍格沃茨校袍。

"给你们的。"她说,把那些长袍分成两堆,"好了,装箱的时候要记住放整齐了,别让它们起皱。"

"妈妈,你把金妮的新衣服给我了。"罗恩说着,把那件衣服递给了她。

"我怎么会弄错呢,"韦斯莱夫人说,"这就是给你的。礼服长袍。"

"什么?"罗恩说,表情很是惊恐。

"礼服长袍!"韦斯莱夫人又说了一遍,"你们学校开出来的单子

## CHAPTER TEN  Mayhem at the Ministry

supposed to have dress robes this year ... robes for formal occasions.'

'You've got to be kidding,' said Ron in disbelief. 'I'm not wearing that, no way.'

'Everyone wears them, Ron!' said Mrs Weasley crossly. 'They're all like that! Your father's got some for smart parties!'

'I'll go starkers before I put that on,' said Ron stubbornly.

'Don't be so silly,' said Mrs Weasley, 'you've got to have dress robes, they're on your list! I got some for Harry, too ... show him, Harry ...'

In some trepidation, Harry opened the last parcel on his camp bed. It wasn't as bad as he had expected, however; his dress robes didn't have any lace on them at all; in fact, they were more or less the same as his school ones, except that they were bottle green instead of black.

'I thought they'd bring out the colour of your eyes, dear,' said Mrs Weasley fondly.

'Well, they're OK!' said Ron angrily, looking at Harry's robes. 'Why couldn't I have some like that?'

'Because ... well, I had to get yours second-hand, and there wasn't a lot of choice!' said Mrs Weasley, flushing.

Harry looked away. He would willingly have split all the money in his Gringotts vault with the Weasleys, but he knew they would never take it.

'I'm never wearing them,' Ron was saying stubbornly. 'Never.'

'Fine,' snapped Mrs Weasley. 'Go naked. And Harry, make sure you get a picture of him. Goodness knows I could do with a laugh.'

She left the room, slamming the door behind her. There was a funny spluttering noise from behind them. Pigwidgeon was choking on an overlarge Owl Treat.

'Why is everything I own rubbish?' said Ron furiously, striding across the room to unstick Pigwidgeon's beak.

## 第 10 章　魔法部乱成一团

上写着，你今年应该准备礼服长袍了……就是正式场合穿的袍子。"

"你一定是在开玩笑吧。"罗恩不敢相信地说，"我决不穿这种衣服，决不！"

"每个人都要穿的，罗恩！"韦斯莱夫人恼火地说，"那些衣服都是这样的！你父亲也有几件，是参加体面的聚会时穿的！"

"我宁可一丝不挂，也不穿它。"罗恩固执地说。

"别犯傻了，"韦斯莱夫人说，"你必须有一件礼服长袍，你的单子上列着呢！我也给哈利买了一件……给他看看，哈利……"

哈利有些惶恐地打开行军床上的最后一个包裹，还好，并不像他料想的那样糟糕。他的礼服长袍上一条花边也没有——实际上，长袍的样子和他的校袍差不多，不过颜色不是黑的，而是深绿色的。

"我想它会把你眼睛的颜色衬托得更漂亮，亲爱的。"韦斯莱夫人慈爱地说。

"这倒挺好！"罗恩看着哈利的长袍，气呼呼地说，"为什么我不能有一件这样的？"

"因为……唉，我不得不给你买二手货，所以就没有多少可选择的了！"韦斯莱夫人说着，脸红了。

哈利移开了目光。他真愿意把他在古灵阁地下金库里的钱都拿出来，分给韦斯莱一家，但他知道他们不会接受的。

"我决不会穿这种衣服，"罗恩还是固执地说，"决不！"

"好吧，"韦斯莱夫人严厉地反驳道，"你就光着身子吧。哈利，别忘了给他拍一张照片。上帝作证，我很愿意大笑一场。"

她走出房间，把门狠狠地关上。喀喀喀，他们身后传来一种很奇怪的声音，小猪被一粒过大的猫头鹰食卡住了喉咙。

"为什么我的东西都是破烂货！"罗恩气愤地说，一边大步走过去掰开小猪的嘴巴。

## CHAPTER ELEVEN

# Aboard the Hogwarts Express

There was a definite end-of-the-holidays gloom in the air when Harry awoke next morning. Heavy rain was still splattering against the window as he got dressed in jeans and a sweatshirt; they would change into their school robes on the Hogwarts Express.

He, Ron, Fred and George had just reached the first-floor landing on their way down to breakfast, when Mrs Weasley appeared at the foot of the stairs, looking harassed.

'Arthur!' she called up the staircase, 'Arthur! Urgent message from the Ministry!'

Harry flattened himself against the wall as Mr Weasley came clattering past with his robes on back-to-front, and hurtled out of sight. When Harry and the others entered the kitchen, they saw Mrs Weasley rummaging anxiously in the dresser drawers – 'I've got a quill here somewhere!' – and Mr Weasley bending over the fire, talking to –

Harry shut his eyes hard and opened them again to make sure that they were working properly.

Amos Diggory's head was sitting in the middle of the flames like a large bearded egg. It was talking very fast, completely unperturbed by the sparks flying around it and the flames licking its ears.

'... Muggle neighbours heard bangs and shouting, so they went and called those what-d'you-call-'ems – please-men. Arthur, you've got to get over there –'

'Here!' said Mrs Weasley breathlessly, pushing a piece of parchment, a bottle of ink and a crumpled quill into Mr Weasley's hands.

'– it's a real stroke of luck I heard about it,' said Mr Diggory's head, 'I had to come into the office early to send a couple of owls, and I found the Improper Use of Magic lot all setting off – if Rita Skeeter gets hold of this one, Arthur –'

# 第 11 章

## 登上霍格沃茨特快列车

第二天早晨,哈利醒来时,家里笼罩着一种假期结束的沉闷气氛。大雨仍然啪啪地敲打着窗户,他穿上牛仔裤和一件运动衫。他们要在霍格沃茨特快列车上再换上校袍。

他和罗恩、弗雷德、乔治下楼吃早饭,刚走到二楼的拐弯处,就见韦斯莱夫人突然出现在楼梯底下,一副心烦意乱的样子。

"亚瑟!"她冲着楼上喊道,"亚瑟!魔法部有紧急口信!"

哈利紧贴在墙上,韦斯莱先生噔噔噔地从他身边跑过,一眨眼就不见了,他的长袍都前后穿反了。哈利和其他人走进厨房时,看见韦斯莱夫人焦急地在抽屉里翻找着什么——"我记得这里有一支羽毛笔的!"——韦斯莱先生探身向着炉火,正在说话——

哈利使劲把眼睛闭上又睁开,还以为自己的眼睛出了毛病。

阿莫斯·迪戈里的头悬在火焰中间,像一个长着胡子的巨大的鸡蛋。它正飞快地说着什么,火苗在它周围飞舞,火舌舔着它的耳朵,但它丝毫不受妨碍。

"……住在附近的麻瓜们听见砰砰的撞击声和喊叫声,就去喊来了——你管他们叫什么来着——金察。亚瑟,你必须去一趟——"

"给你!"韦斯莱夫人上气不接下气地说,把一张羊皮纸、一瓶墨水和一支皱巴巴的羽毛笔塞进韦斯莱先生手里。

"——幸好我听说了这件事,"迪戈里先生的头说道,"我因为要派两只猫头鹰送信,不得不很早就到了办公室,结果发现禁止滥用魔法办公室的人都出动了——如果丽塔·斯基特抓住这件事大做文章,亚瑟——"

## CHAPTER ELEVEN    Aboard the Hogwarts Express

'What does Mad-Eye say happened?' asked Mr Weasley, unscrewing the ink bottle, loading up his quill and preparing to take notes.

Mr Diggory's head rolled its eyes. 'Says he heard an intruder in his yard. Says they were creeping towards the house, but they were ambushed by his dustbins.'

'What did the dustbins do?' asked Mr Weasley, scribbling frantically.

'Made one hell of a noise and fired rubbish everywhere, as far as I can tell,' said Mr Diggory. 'Apparently one of them was still rocketing around when the please-men turned up –'

Mr Weasley groaned. 'And what about the intruder?'

'Arthur, you know Mad-Eye,' said Mr Diggory's head, rolling its eyes again. 'Someone creeping into his yard at the dead of night? More likely there's a very shellshocked cat wandering around somewhere, covered in potato peelings. But if the Improper Use of Magic lot get their hands on Mad-Eye, he's had it – think of his record – we've got to get him off on a minor charge, something in your department – what are exploding dustbins worth?'

'Might be a caution,' said Mr Weasley, still writing very fast, his brow furrowed. 'Mad-Eye didn't use his wand? He didn't actually attack anyone?'

'I'll bet he leapt out of bed and started jinxing everything he could reach through the window,' said Mr Diggory, 'but they'll have a job proving it, there aren't any casualties.'

'All right, I'm off,' Mr Weasley said, and he stuffed the parchment with his notes on it into his pocket and dashed out of the kitchen again.

Mr Diggory's head looked around at Mrs Weasley.

'Sorry about this, Molly,' it said, more calmly, 'bothering you so early and everything … but Arthur's the only one who can get Mad-Eye off, and Mad-Eye's supposed to be starting his new job today. Why he had to choose last night …'

'Never mind, Amos,' said Mrs Weasley. 'Sure you won't have a bit of toast or anything before you go?'

'Oh, go on, then,' said Mr Diggory.

Mrs Weasley took a piece of buttered toast from a stack on the kitchen table, put it into the fire tongs and transferred it into Mr Diggory's mouth.

## 第11章 登上霍格沃茨特快列车

"疯眼汉说发生了什么事?"韦斯莱先生说着,拧开墨水瓶的盖子,让羽毛笔吸足墨水,准备记录。

迪戈里先生的头翻了个白眼。"他说听见有人闯进了他的院子。说他悄悄朝房子走去,可是遭到了他的垃圾箱的伏击。"

"垃圾箱做了什么?"韦斯莱先生问,一边龙飞凤舞地记录着。

"发出一声可怕的巨响,然后把垃圾炸得到处都是,我知道的就是这些。"迪戈里先生说,"显然,当金察赶到的时候,有一个垃圾箱还在到处蹿来蹿去——"

韦斯莱先生发出一声呻吟,"那个闯进院子的人呢?"

"亚瑟,你是了解疯眼汉的。"迪戈里先生的头说着,又翻了翻白眼,"有人会在半夜三更溜进他的院子?没准是一只在外面吃了败仗的野猫,漫无目的地在那里溜达,身上挂着土豆皮。可是如果禁止滥用魔法办公室的人抓住了疯眼汉,他可就倒霉了——想想他的前科记录——我们得想办法给他弄个轻一点的罪名,由你们部门接手——让垃圾箱爆炸会受什么惩罚?"

"大概会受到警告吧。"韦斯莱先生说,一边仍然飞快地做着记录,他的眉头已经皱了起来,"疯眼汉没有使用魔杖吧?他事实上并没有攻击别人吧?"

"我敢说,他当时跳下床来朝窗外看,看到什么就让什么遭了殃。"迪戈里先生说,"可是他们很难证明,因为并没有人员伤亡。"

"好吧,我这就出发,"韦斯莱先生说着,把记录的羊皮纸塞进口袋,转身又冲出了厨房。

迪戈里先生转过头来,望着韦斯莱夫人。

"真是对不起,莫丽,"他说,语调平静多了,"这么早就来打扰你们……可是只有亚瑟才能替疯眼汉开脱,使他免受惩罚,本来疯眼汉今天就要开始新的工作了。真不明白他为什么要选择昨天夜里……"

"没关系,阿莫斯,"韦斯莱夫人说,"你想不想吃一片面包什么的再走?"

"哦,好吧。"迪戈里先生说。

韦斯莱夫人从餐桌上的一摞黄油面包上拿了一片,用火钳夹住,递进迪戈里先生嘴里。

'Fanks,' he said in a muffled voice, and then, with a small *pop*, vanished.

Harry could hear Mr Weasley calling hurried goodbyes to Bill, Charlie, Percy and the girls. Within five minutes, he was back in the kitchen, his robes on the right way now, dragging a comb through his hair.

'I'd better hurry – you have a good term, boys,' said Mr Weasley to Harry, Ron and the twins, dragging a cloak over his shoulders and preparing to Disapparate. 'Molly, are you going to be all right taking the kids to King's Cross?'

'Of course I will,' she said. 'You just look after Mad-Eye, we'll be fine.'

As Mr Weasley vanished, Bill and Charlie entered the kitchen.

'Did someone say Mad-Eye?' Bill asked. 'What's he been up to now?'

'He says someone tried to break into his house last night,' said Mrs Weasley.

'Mad-Eye Moody?' said George thoughtfully, spreading marmalade on his toast. 'Isn't he that nutter –'

'Your father thinks very highly of Mad-Eye Moody,' said Mrs Weasley sternly.

'Yeah, well, Dad collects plugs, doesn't he?' said Fred quietly, as Mrs Weasley left the room. 'Birds of a feather ...'

'Moody was a great wizard in his time,' said Bill.

'He's an old friend of Dumbledore's, isn't he?' said Charlie.

'Dumbledore's not what you'd call *normal*, though, is he?' said Fred. 'I mean, I know he's a genius and everything ...'

'Who *is* Mad-Eye?' asked Harry.

'He's retired, used to work at the Ministry,' said Charlie. 'I met him once when Dad took me into work with him. He was an Auror – one of the best ... a Dark-wizard-catcher,' he added, seeing Harry's blank look. 'Half the cells in Azkaban are full because of him. He made himself loads of enemies, though ... the families of people he caught, mainly ... and I heard he's been getting really paranoid in his old age. Doesn't trust anyone any more. Sees Dark wizards everywhere.'

Bill and Charlie decided to come and see everyone off at King's Cross station, but Percy, apologising most profusely, said that he really needed to get to work.

'I just can't justify taking more time off at the moment,' he told them. 'Mr

## 第11章 登上霍格沃茨特快列车

"谢谢。"他含混地说了一句,然后只听噗的一声轻响,他就消失了。

哈利可以听见韦斯莱先生大声地向比尔、查理、珀西和两个女孩匆匆告别。五分钟后,他又回到厨房,用一把梳子胡乱地划拉着头发,身上的长袍已经正过来了。

"我得赶快走了——祝你们这学期一切都好,孩子们。"韦斯莱先生一边对哈利、罗恩和一对双胞胎说着,一边将一件斗篷披在肩上,准备幻影移形,"莫丽,你送孩子们去国王十字车站没问题吧?"

"当然没问题,"她说,"你去照管疯眼汉吧,我们不会有事的。"

韦斯莱先生刚一消失,比尔、查理就走进了厨房。

"有人提到疯眼汉?"比尔问道,"他又干什么了?"

"他说昨晚有人想闯进他的房子。"韦斯莱夫人说。

"疯眼汉穆迪?"乔治若有所思地说,一边往他的面包片上抹了一层橘子酱,"就是那个疯子——"

"你们的爸爸对疯眼汉穆迪评价很高。"韦斯莱夫人严厉地说。

"是啊,爸爸还收集插头呢,对吧?"等韦斯莱夫人离开房间后,弗雷德小声地说,"他们是同一类人……"

"穆迪当年可是个很了不起的巫师。"比尔说。

"他还是邓布利多的老朋友,是吗?"查理说。

"邓布利多就不是你们所说的正常人,对吧?"弗雷德说,"我的意思是,我知道他是个天才,很了不起……"

"疯眼汉是谁?"哈利问道。

"他现在退休了,以前在魔法部工作,"查理说,"我见过他一次,爸爸和他一起共事时带我去过。他是个傲罗——最好的一个……就是专抓黑巫师的高手。"他看见哈利脸上困惑的神情,说明道,"阿兹卡班里的一半牢房都是被他填满的。不过他也给自己树了很多仇敌……主要是那些被他抓住的人的亲属……我听说,他上了年纪以后,变得越来越多疑,什么人都不相信,走到哪儿都看见黑巫师。"

比尔和查理决定到国王十字车站送一送大家,而珀西一再道歉,说他实在太忙,脱不开身。

"这个时候我没有理由请假,"他对他们说,"克劳奇先生有许多事

## CHAPTER ELEVEN    Aboard the Hogwarts Express

Crouch is really starting to rely on me.'

'Yeah, you know what, Percy?' said George seriously. 'I reckon he'll know your name soon.'

Mrs Weasley had braved the telephone in the village Post Office to order three ordinary Muggle taxis to take them into London.

'Arthur tried to borrow Ministry cars for us,' Mrs Weasley whispered to Harry as they stood in the rain-washed yard, watching the taxi drivers heaving six heavy Hogwarts trunks into their cars. 'But there weren't any to spare ... oh dear, they don't look happy, do they?'

Harry didn't like to tell Mrs Weasley that Muggle taxi drivers rarely transported over-excited owls, and Pigwidgeon was making an ear-splitting racket. Nor did it help that a number of Dr Filibuster's Fabulous Wet-Start, No-Heat Fireworks went off unexpectedly when Fred's trunk sprang open, causing the driver carrying it to yell with fright and pain as Crookshanks clawed his way up the man's leg.

The journey was uncomfortable, owing to the fact that they were jammed in the back of the taxis with their trunks. Crookshanks took quite a while to recover from the fireworks, and by the time they entered London, Harry, Ron and Hermione were all severely scratched. They were very relieved to get out at King's Cross, even though the rain was coming down harder than ever, and they got soaked carrying their trunks across the busy road and into the station.

Harry was used to getting onto platform nine and three-quarters by now. It was a simple matter of walking straight through the apparently solid barrier dividing platforms nine and ten. The only tricky part was doing this in an unobtrusive way, so as to avoid attracting Muggle attention. They did it in groups today; Harry, Ron and Hermione (the most conspicuous, as they were accompanied by Pigwidgeon and Crookshanks) went first; they leant casually against the barrier, chatting unconcernedly, and slid sideways through it ... and as they did so, platform nine and three-quarters materialised in front of them.

The Hogwarts Express, a gleaming scarlet steam engine, was already there, clouds of steam billowing from it, through which the many Hogwarts students and parents on the platform appeared like dark ghosts. Pigwidgeon became noisier than ever in response to the hooting of many owls through the mist. Harry, Ron and Hermione set off to find seats, and were soon stowing their luggage in a compartment halfway along the train. They then

## 第11章 登上霍格沃茨特快列车

情都开始指望我了。"

"是啊，你知道吗，珀西？"乔治一本正经地说，"我猜他很快就会知道你的名字了。"

韦斯莱夫人鼓起勇气，用了一下村邮电所里的电话，预订了三辆普通的麻瓜出租车送他们去伦敦。

"亚瑟本来想借部里的车送我们，"韦斯莱夫人小声对哈利说——这时他们正站在大雨瓢泼的院子里，看着出租车司机把六只沉重的霍格沃茨皮箱搬进车里，"可是部里的车腾不出来……哦，天哪，他们看上去不大高兴，是吗？"

哈利没有告诉韦斯莱夫人，麻瓜出租车司机是很少运送狂躁不安的猫头鹰的，而小猪在那里一个劲儿地吵闹，声音震耳欲聋。更不用说弗雷德的箱子突然弹开，许多费力拔博士见水开花神奇冷烟火出人意料地炸响了，吓得那个搬箱子的司机大叫起来，而这时克鲁克山用尖利的爪子顺着那人的大腿往上爬，使他的喊声里又多了几分痛苦。

大家和那些箱子一起挤坐在出租车后面，一路上很不舒服。克鲁克山受了烟火的惊吓，好半天才恢复过来。当车子驶进伦敦时，哈利、罗恩和赫敏都被严重抓伤了。总算在国王十字车站下车了，大家都松了口气，尽管雨下得比刚才还大，兜头盖脸地朝他们浇来。他们提着箱子穿过繁忙的街道，走进车站，浑身都湿透了。

现在，哈利对登上 $9\frac{3}{4}$ 站台已经习惯了。其实很容易，只要径直穿过第9和第10站台之间的那堵仿佛很坚固的隔墙就行了。唯一需要当心的是，要做得不让人看出来，以免引起麻瓜们的注意。他们今天是分组过去的。首先是哈利、罗恩和赫敏（他们是最显眼的，因为带着猫头鹰小猪和克鲁克山），他们悠闲地靠在隔墙上，漫不经心地聊着天，然后就侧身从墙里钻了过去……一钻过去，$9\frac{3}{4}$ 站台就在他们面前出现了。

霍格沃茨特快列车已经停在那里，这是一辆深红色的蒸汽机车，正在喷出滚滚浓烟。透过浓烟望去，站台上的许多霍格沃茨学生和家长仿佛是黑乎乎的鬼影。小猪听到烟雾中有许多猫头鹰的叫声，也吱吱叫着响应，吵得比刚才更厉害了。哈利、罗恩和赫敏开始寻找座位，很快，他们就把行李搬进了列车中间的一个包厢，然后跳回到站台上，

## CHAPTER ELEVEN   Aboard the Hogwarts Express

hopped back down onto the platform, to say goodbye to Mrs Weasley, Bill and Charlie.

'I might be seeing you all sooner than you think,' said Charlie, grinning, as he hugged Ginny goodbye.

'Why?' said Fred keenly.

'You'll see,' said Charlie. 'Just don't tell Percy I mentioned it ... it's "classified information, until such time as the Ministry sees fit to release it", after all.'

'Yeah, I sort of wish I was back at Hogwarts this year,' said Bill, hands in his pockets, looking almost wistfully at the train.

'*Why?*' said George impatiently.

'You're going to have an interesting year,' said Bill, his eyes twinkling. 'I might even get time off to come and watch a bit of it ...'

'A bit of *what?*' said Ron.

But at that moment, the whistle blew, and Mrs Weasley chivvied them towards the train doors.

'Thanks for having us to stay, Mrs Weasley,' said Hermione, as they climbed on board, closed the door and leant out of the window to talk to her.

'Yeah, thanks for everything, Mrs Weasley,' said Harry.

'Oh, it was my pleasure, dears,' said Mrs Weasley. 'I'd invite you for Christmas, but ... well, I expect you're all going to want to stay at Hogwarts, what with ... one thing and another.'

'Mum!' said Ron irritably. 'What d'you three know that we don't?'

'You'll find out this evening, I expect,' said Mrs Weasley, smiling. 'It's going to be very exciting – mind you, I'm very glad they've changed the rules –'

'What rules?' said Harry, Ron, Fred and George together.

'I'm sure Professor Dumbledore will tell you ... now, behave, won't you? *Won't* you, Fred? And you, George?'

The pistons hissed loudly, and the train began to move.

'Tell us what's happening at Hogwarts!' Fred bellowed out of the window, as Mrs Weasley, Bill and Charlie sped away from them. 'What rules are they changing?'

But Mrs Weasley only smiled and waved. Before the train had rounded the corner, she, Bill and Charlie had Disapparated.

## 第 11 章 登上霍格沃茨特快列车

向韦斯莱夫人、比尔和查理告别。

"我也许很快就能看到你们大家。"查理搂抱金妮跟她告别时，微笑着说。

"为什么？"弗雷德急切地问。

"你会知道的，"查理说，"千万别告诉珀西我提到这事儿……要知道，这是'绝密情报，要等魔法部认为合适的时候才能公布'。"

"啊，真希望我今年能回霍格沃茨上学。"比尔说。他两手插在口袋里，眼睛望着火车，神情有些惆怅。

"为什么？"乔治不耐烦地问。

"你们这一年会过得非常有趣，"比尔说，眼睛里闪着光芒，"我也许会请假来观看一部分……"

"一部分什么？"罗恩问。

可是就在这时，哨子吹响了，韦斯莱夫人把他们赶向车门。

"谢谢你留我们住下，韦斯莱夫人。"赫敏说。这时他们已经登上火车，关好车门，她从窗口探出身子跟韦斯莱夫人说话。

"是啊，谢谢你为我做的一切，韦斯莱夫人。"哈利说。

"哦，我很乐意的，亲爱的，"韦斯莱夫人说，"我想邀请你来过圣诞节，可是……我估计你们都情愿留在霍格沃茨，因为……这样或那样的原因。"

"妈妈！"罗恩烦躁地说，"到底是什么事情，你们三个都知道，就瞒着我们？"

"我估计你们今晚就会弄清楚，"韦斯莱夫人微笑着说，"一定会很刺激的——告诉你们吧，我真高兴他们修改了章程——"

"什么章程？"哈利、罗恩、弗雷德和乔治同时问道。

"我敢肯定邓布利多教授会告诉你们的……好了，表现好些，知道吗？听见没有，弗雷德？还有你，乔治？"

发动机的活塞发出响亮的嘶嘶声，火车开动了。

"快告诉我们霍格沃茨要发生什么事！"弗雷德冲着窗外大喊——韦斯莱夫人、比尔和查理正在急速地远去，"他们修改了什么章程？"

可是韦斯莱夫人只是笑着朝他们挥手。不等火车拐弯，她和比尔、查理就幻影移形了。

### CHAPTER ELEVEN    Aboard the Hogwarts Express

Harry, Ron and Hermione went back to their compartment. The thick rain splattering the windows made it very difficult to see out of them. Ron undid his trunk, pulled out his maroon dress robes, and flung them over Pigwidgeon's cage to muffle his hooting.

'Bagman wanted to tell us what's happening at Hogwarts,' he said grumpily, sitting down next to Harry. 'At the World Cup, remember? But my own mother won't say. Wonder what –'

'Shh!' Hermione whispered suddenly, pressing her finger to her lips and pointing towards the compartment next to theirs. Harry and Ron listened, and heard a familiar drawling voice drifting in through the open door.

'… Father actually considered sending me to Durmstrang rather than Hogwarts, you know. He knows the Headmaster, you see. Well, you know his opinion of Dumbledore – the man's such a Mudblood-lover – and Durmstrang doesn't admit that sort of riff-raff. But Mother didn't like the idea of me going to school so far away. Father says Durmstrang takes a far more sensible line than Hogwarts about the Dark Arts. Durmstrang students actually *learn* them, not just the defence rubbish we do …'

Hermione got up, tiptoed to the compartment door, and slid it shut, blocking out Malfoy's voice.

'So he thinks Durmstrang would have suited him, does he?' she said angrily. 'I wish he *had* gone, then we wouldn't have had to put up with him.'

'Durmstrang's another wizarding school?' said Harry.

'Yes,' said Hermione sniffily, 'and it's got a horrible reputation. According to *An Appraisal of Magical Education in Europe*, it puts a lot of emphasis on the Dark Arts.'

'I think I've heard of it,' said Ron vaguely. 'Where is it? What country?'

'Well, nobody knows, do they?' said Hermione, raising her eyebrows.

'Er – why not?' said Harry.

'There's traditionally been a lot of rivalry between all the magic schools. Durmstrang and Beauxbatons like to conceal their whereabouts so nobody can steal their secrets,' said Hermione matter-of-factly.

'Come off it,' said Ron, starting to laugh. 'Durmstrang's got to be about the same size as Hogwarts, how are you going to hide a dirty great castle?'

'But Hogwarts *is* hidden,' said Hermione, in surprise, 'everyone knows

## 第11章 登上霍格沃茨特快列车

哈利、罗恩和赫敏回到他们的包厢，密集的雨点噼噼啪啪地敲打着玻璃窗，使他们很难看清外面的景物。罗恩打开自己的箱子，抽出他那件酱紫色的礼服长袍，盖在小猪的笼子上，它的叫声太吵人了。

"巴格曼倒愿意告诉我们霍格沃茨发生的事情，"他在哈利身边坐了下来，闷闷不乐地说，"记得吗，就在世界杯赛上？可是我自己的亲妈却不肯说。真不知道——"

"嘘！"赫敏突然小声说，用手指按住嘴唇，指着旁边的包厢。哈利和罗恩仔细一听，一个熟悉的拖腔拖调的声音从敞开的门口飘了进来。

"……你们知道吗，我爸爸真的考虑过要把我送到德姆斯特朗，而不是霍格沃茨。他认识那个学校的校长。唉，你们知道他对邓布利多的看法——那人太喜欢泥巴种了——德姆斯特朗根本不允许那些下三烂的人入学。可是我妈妈不愿意我到那么远的地方上学。爸爸说，德姆斯特朗对黑魔法采取的态度比霍格沃茨合理得多。德姆斯特朗的学生能学习黑魔法，不像我们，学什么破烂的防御术……"

赫敏站起身，踮着脚走到包厢门边，把门轻轻拉上，不让马尔福的声音传进来。

"这么说，他认为德姆斯特朗比较适合他喽？"赫敏气呼呼地说，"我倒希望他去那里上学，我们就用不着忍受他了。"

"德姆斯特朗也是一所魔法学校吗？"哈利问。

"对，"赫敏轻蔑地哼了一声，说道，"它的名声坏透了。照《欧洲魔法教育评估》上的说法，这所学校对黑魔法非常重视。"

"我好像听说过，"罗恩含混地说，"它在哪儿？哪个国家？"

"唉，不会有人知道的，不是吗？"赫敏扬起眉毛，说道。

"哦——为什么呢？"哈利问。

"各个魔法学校之间始终存在着激烈的竞争。德姆斯特朗和布斯巴顿愿意把它们的校址隐蔽起来，这样就没有人能窃取它们的秘密了。"赫敏一本正经地回答。

"别胡扯了，"罗恩说着笑了起来，"德姆斯特朗肯定跟霍格沃茨差不多大——你怎么能把一座大城堡隐蔽起来呢？"

"可霍格沃茨就是隐蔽着的。"赫敏说，显得有些诧异，"大家都知

## CHAPTER ELEVEN  Aboard the Hogwarts Express

that ... well, everyone who's read *Hogwarts: A History*, anyway.'

'Just you, then,' said Ron. 'So go on – how d'you hide a place like Hogwarts?'

'It's bewitched,' said Hermione. 'If a Muggle looks at it, all they see is a mouldering old ruin with a sign over the entrance saying DANGER, DO NOT ENTER, UNSAFE.'

'So Durmstrang'll just look like a ruin to an outsider, too?'

'Maybe,' said Hermione, shrugging, 'or it might have Muggle-Repelling Charms on it, like the World Cup Stadium. And to keep foreign wizards from finding it, they'll have made it Unplottable –'

'Come again?'

'Well, you can enchant a building so it's impossible to plot on a map, can't you?'

'Er ... if you say so,' said Harry.

'But I think Durmstrang must be somewhere in the far north,' said Hermione thoughtfully. 'Somewhere very cold, because they've got fur capes as part of their uniforms.'

'Ah, think of the possibilities,' said Ron dreamily. 'It would've been so easy to push Malfoy off a glacier and make it look like an accident ... shame his mother likes him ...'

The rain became heavier and heavier as the train moved further north. The sky was so dark and the windows so steamy that the lanterns were lit by midday. The lunch trolley came rattling along the corridor, and Harry bought a large stack of Cauldron Cakes for them to share.

Several of their friends looked in on them as the afternoon progressed, including Seamus Finnigan, Dean Thomas and Neville Longbottom, a round-faced, extremely forgetful boy who had been brought up by his formidable witch of a grandmother. Seamus was still wearing his Ireland rosette. Some of its magic seemed to be wearing off now; it was still squeaking '*Troy! Mullet! Moran!*', but in a very feeble and exhausted sort of way. After half an hour or so, Hermione, growing tired of the endless Quidditch talk, buried herself once more in *The Standard Book of Spells, Grade 4*, and started trying to learn a Summoning Charm.

Neville listened jealously to the others' conversation as they relived the Cup match.

## 第11章 登上霍格沃茨特快列车

道啊……噢,凡是读过《霍格沃茨:一段校史》的人都应该知道。"

"那就只有你了。"罗恩说,"你再接着说——你怎么能把霍格沃茨这样一座大城堡隐蔽起来呢?"

"它被施了魔法,"赫敏说,"麻瓜望着它,只能看见一堆破败的废墟,入口处挂着一个牌子,写着**危险,不得进入,不安全**。"

"这么说,在一个外人看来,德姆斯特朗也是一堆废墟?"

"大概是吧,"赫敏耸了耸肩膀,说道,"或者它被施了麻瓜驱逐咒,就像世界杯赛的体育场一样。为了不让外国巫师发现它,还可以使它变得不可标绘——"

"这又是什么意思?"

"是这样,你可以给建筑物施一个魔咒,别人就无法在地图上把它标绘出来了,对吧?"

"嗯……你说是就是吧。"哈利说。

"不过我认为德姆斯特朗大概在北部很远的地方,"赫敏若有所思地说,"一个非常寒冷的地区,因为他们的校服还包括毛皮斗篷呢。"

"啊,设想一下会发生什么事吧,"罗恩很神往地说,"把马尔福从冰川上推下去,弄得就像一次意外事故,这大概不会很难……真遗憾,他妈妈这么舍不得他……"

火车不停地往北行驶,雨下得越来越大,越来越猛。天空一片漆黑,车窗上蒙着水汽,所以大白天也点起了灯笼。嘎啦嘎啦,供应午饭的小推车顺着过道推过来了,哈利买了一大摞坩埚形蛋糕,让大家一起分享。

下午,他们的几位朋友过来看望他们,有西莫·斐尼甘、迪安·托马斯,还有纳威·隆巴顿——这是一个圆圆脸的男孩,记性差得要命,是他那令人敬畏的巫师奶奶把他拉扯大的。西莫还戴着他的爱尔兰徽章,它的一些魔力似乎在慢慢消退。它仍然在尖叫"特洛伊!马莱特!莫兰!"但是声音有气无力,好像已经精疲力竭了。过了半个小时左右,赫敏对他们没完没了地谈论魁地奇感到厌倦了,就又开始埋头阅读《标准咒语,四级》,并试着学习一种召唤咒。

大家兴奋地回顾世界杯赛时,纳威在一旁眼巴巴地听着。

## CHAPTER ELEVEN   Aboard the Hogwarts Express

'Gran didn't want to go,' he said miserably. 'Wouldn't buy tickets. It sounded amazing, though.'

'It was,' said Ron. 'Look at this, Neville ...'

He rummaged in his trunk up in the luggage rack, and pulled out the miniature figure of Viktor Krum.

'Oh, *wow*,' said Neville enviously, as Ron tipped Krum onto his pudgy hand.

'We saw him right up close, as well,' said Ron. 'We were in the Top Box –'

'For the first and last time in your life, Weasley.'

Draco Malfoy had appeared in the doorway. Behind him stood Crabbe and Goyle, his enormous, thuggish cronies, both of whom appeared to have grown at least a foot during the summer. Evidently they had overheard the conversation through the compartment door, which Dean and Seamus had left ajar.

'Don't remember asking you to join us, Malfoy,' said Harry coolly.

'Weasley ... what is *that*?' said Malfoy, pointing at Pigwidgeon's cage. A sleeve of Ron's dress robes was dangling from it, swaying with the motion of the train, the mouldy lace cuff very obvious.

Ron made to stuff the robes out of sight, but Malfoy was too quick for him; he seized the sleeve and pulled.

'Look at this!' said Malfoy in ecstasy, holding up Ron's robes and showing Crabbe and Goyle. 'Weasley, you weren't thinking of *wearing* these, were you? I mean – they were very fashionable in about 1890 ...'

'Eat dung, Malfoy!' said Ron, the same colour as the dress robes as he snatched them back out of Malfoy's grip. Malfoy howled with derisive laughter; Crabbe and Goyle guffawed stupidly.

'So ... going to enter, Weasley? Going to try and bring a bit of glory to the family name? There's money involved as well, you know ... you'd be able to afford some decent robes if you won ...'

'What are you talking about?' snapped Ron.

'*Are you going to enter?*' Malfoy repeated. 'I suppose *you* will, Potter? You never miss a chance to show off, do you?'

"奶奶不想去，"他可怜巴巴地说，"不肯买票。啊，听起来真够刺激的。"

"没错，"罗恩说，"你看看这个，纳威……"

他在行李架上的箱子里翻找了一会儿，抽出那个威克多尔·克鲁姆的小塑像。

"哇，太棒了。"当罗恩把克鲁姆放在纳威胖乎乎的手掌上时，纳威羡慕地说。

"我们在上面看见他了，离得很近，"罗恩说，"我们坐在顶层包厢——"

"你这辈子也就这一次了，韦斯莱。"

德拉科·马尔福出现在门口，身后站着克拉布和高尔，他们是马尔福的两个死党，块头大得吓人，一副凶神恶煞的样子。这个夏天他们俩似乎又长高了至少一英尺。显然，他们通过包厢的门偷听了刚才的谈话，迪安和西莫没有把门关严。

"我们好像并没有邀请你们进来，马尔福。"哈利冷冷地说。

"韦斯莱……那是什么？"马尔福指着小猪的笼子问道。罗恩的礼服长袍的一只袖子从笼子上挂下来，随着火车的运行摇摆不停，袖口上仿佛发了霉的花边非常显眼。

罗恩想把长袍藏起来，可是马尔福的动作比他快，一把抓住袖子，使劲一拉。

"看看这个！"马尔福开心极了，把罗恩的长袍举起来给克拉布和高尔看，"韦斯莱，难道你想穿这样的衣服，嗯？我的意思是——它们在十八世纪九十年代左右还是蛮时髦的……"

"吃屎去吧，马尔福！"罗恩说——他脸涨得跟礼服长袍一个颜色，一把从马尔福手中夺过长袍。马尔福发出一串高声的嘲笑，克拉布和高尔也跟着傻笑起来，声音粗野刺耳。

"怎么……你也想参加，韦斯莱？你也想试试身手，给你的家庭增添一份光荣？你知道，这事儿跟钱也有关系呢……如果你赢了，就有钱买几件体面的长袍了……"

"你在胡扯些什么？"罗恩气恼地问。

"你想参加吗？"马尔福又说了一遍，"我猜你会的，波特？你从不错过一个炫耀自己的机会，是不是？"

## CHAPTER ELEVEN   Aboard the Hogwarts Express

'Either explain what you're on about or go away, Malfoy,' said Hermione testily, over the top of *The Standard Book of Spells, Grade 4*.

A gleeful smile spread across Malfoy's pale face.

'Don't tell me you don't *know*?' he said delightedly. 'You've got a father and brother at the Ministry and you don't even *know*? My god, *my* father told me about it ages ago ... heard it from Cornelius Fudge. But then, father's always associated with the top people at the Ministry ... maybe your father's too junior to know about it, Weasley ... yes ... they probably don't talk about important stuff in front of him ...'

Laughing once more, Malfoy beckoned to Crabbe and Goyle, and the three of them disappeared.

Ron got to his feet and slammed the sliding compartment door so hard behind them that the glass shattered.

'*Ron!*' said Hermione reproachfully, and she pulled out her wand, muttered '*Reparo!*', and the glass shards flew back into a single pane, and back into the door.

'Well ... making it look like he knows everything and we don't ...' Ron snarled. '*Father's always associated with the top people at the Ministry* ... Dad could've got promotion any time ... he just likes it where he is ...'

'Of course he does,' said Hermione quietly. 'Don't let Malfoy get to you, Ron –'

'Him! Get to me! As if!' said Ron, picking up one of the remaining Cauldron Cakes and squashing it into a pulp.

Ron's bad mood continued for the rest of the journey. He didn't talk much as they changed into their school robes, and was still glowering when the Hogwarts Express slowed down at last, and finally stopped in the pitch-darkness of Hogsmeade station.

As the train doors opened, there was a rumble of thunder overhead. Hermione bundled Crookshanks up in her cloak and Ron left his dress robes over Pigwidgeon as they left the train, heads bent and eyes narrowed against the downpour. The rain was now coming down so thick and fast that it was as though buckets of ice-cold water were being emptied repeatedly over their heads.

'Hi, Hagrid!' Harry yelled, seeing a gigantic silhouette at the far end of the platform.

'All righ', Harry?' Hagrid bellowed back, waving. 'See yeh at the feast if we don' drown!'

## 第11章 登上霍格沃茨特快列车

"要么解释一下你的话，要么就走开，马尔福。"赫敏把目光从《标准咒语，四级》上抬起，不耐烦地说道。

一丝喜悦的微笑掠过马尔福苍白的脸。

"莫非你不知道？"他高兴地说，"你爸爸和你哥哥都在魔法部工作，你居然会不知道？我的天哪，我爸爸好久以前就告诉我了……是听康奈利·福吉说的。反正，我爸爸接触的都是魔法部的高层人物……大概你爸爸的级别太低了，没有权利知道，韦斯莱……对，是这样……他们大概从不在他面前谈论重要的话题……"

马尔福又放声大笑起来，一边对克拉布和高尔做了个手势，三个人一起消失了。

罗恩站起来，狠狠地把包厢门关上，他用的力气太大了，门上的玻璃被撞碎了。

"罗恩！"赫敏责备道，抽出自己的魔杖，低声念了一句，"恢复如初！"那些碎玻璃片就自动拼成一块完整的玻璃，重新回到了门框上。

"真倒霉……就好像他什么都知道，我们全蒙在鼓里……"罗恩气愤地吼了起来，"'我爸爸接触的都是魔法部的高层人物'……我爸爸随时都能提升……他只是喜欢现在这个位置……"

"当然是这样，"赫敏轻声说，"别让马尔福影响你的情绪，罗恩——"

"他！影响我的情绪！才不会呢！"罗恩说着，拿起剩下的一块坩埚形蛋糕，一把捏成了泥酱。

在接下来的旅程中，罗恩的情绪一直不好。当他们换上校袍时，他沉默不语；当霍格沃茨特快列车终于放慢速度、停靠在漆黑的霍格莫德车站时，他仍然阴沉着脸。

车门打开了，空中传来隆隆的雷声。赫敏用斗篷兜住克鲁克山，罗恩仍旧把他的礼服长袍罩在小猪的笼子上。他们下了火车，在倾盆大雨中低着头，眯着眼。雨下得又急又猛，就好像一桶桶冰冷的水不断浇在他们头上。

"你好，海格！"哈利看见站台那头一个巨大的身影，大声喊道。

"你好，哈利！"海格粗声大气地回答，挥了挥手，"如果我们没被淹死的话，就在宴会上见吧！"

## CHAPTER ELEVEN — Aboard the Hogwarts Express

First-years traditionally reached Hogwarts castle by sailing across the lake with Hagrid.

'Oooh, I wouldn't fancy crossing the lake in this weather,' said Hermione fervently, shivering as they inched slowly along the dark platform with the rest of the crowd. A hundred horseless carriages stood waiting for them outside the station. Harry, Ron, Hermione and Neville climbed gratefully into one of them, the door shut with a snap, and a few moments later, with a great lurch, the long procession of carriages was rumbling and splashing its way up the track towards Hogwarts castle.

## 第 11 章　登上霍格沃茨特快列车

按照惯例，一年级新生由海格从湖上摆渡过去，进入霍格沃茨城堡。

"哦，我可不会高兴在这样的天气摆渡过湖。"赫敏浑身颤抖，激动地说。这时他们随着人流一点点地挪动脚步，走过漆黑的站台。车站外面，一百辆没有马拉的马车在等候着他们。哈利、罗恩、赫敏和纳威赶紧爬上其中一辆，这才感到松了口气。门砰的一声关上，片刻之后，随着一阵剧烈的颠簸，长长的马车队顺着通往霍格沃茨城堡的小道辘辘出发了，一路噼里啪啦地溅起水花。

# CHAPTER TWELVE

# The Triwizard Tournament

Through the gates, flanked with statues of winged boars, and up the sweeping drive the carriages trundled, swaying dangerously in what was fast becoming a gale. Leaning against the window, Harry could see Hogwarts coming nearer, its many lighted windows blurred and shimmering behind the thick curtain of rain. Lightning flashed across the sky as their carriage came to a halt before the great oak front doors, which stood at the top of a flight of stone steps. People who had occupied the carriages in front were already hurrying up the stone steps into the castle; Harry, Ron, Hermione and Neville jumped down from their carriage and dashed up the steps too, looking up only when they were safely inside the cavernous, torch-lit Entrance Hall, with its magnificent marble staircase.

'Blimey,' said Ron, shaking his head and sending water everywhere, 'if that keeps up, the lake's going to overflow. I'm soak– ARGH!'

A large, red, water-filled balloon had dropped from out of the ceiling onto Ron's head, and exploded. Drenched and spluttering, Ron staggered sideways into Harry, just as a second water bomb dropped – narrowly missing Hermione, it burst at Harry's feet, sending a wave of cold water over his trainers into his socks. People all around them shrieked and started pushing each other in their efforts to get out of the line of fire – Harry looked up, and saw, floating twenty feet above them, Peeves the poltergeist, a little man in a bell-covered hat and orange bow-tie, his wide, malicious face contorted with concentration as he took aim again.

'PEEVES!' yelled an angry voice. 'Peeves, come down here at ONCE!'

Professor McGonagall, deputy headmistress and Head of Gryffindor house, had come dashing out of the Great Hall; she skidded on the wet floor and grabbed Hermione around the neck to stop herself falling. 'Ouch –

第 12 章

三强争霸赛

马车穿过两边有带翅野猪雕塑的大门，顺着宽敞的车道行驶，由于狂风大作，车身剧烈地摇晃着。哈利靠在车窗上，看见霍格沃茨越来越近了，许多亮灯的窗户在厚厚的雨帘后面模模糊糊地闪着光。他们的马车在两扇橡木大门前的石阶下停住了，就在这时，一道闪电划破天空，前面马车里的人已匆匆登上石阶，跑进城堡。哈利、罗恩、赫敏和纳威从马车里跳下来，也三步并作两步地奔上石阶，直到进了洞穴般深邃的门厅里，才把头抬起来。门厅里点着火把，大理石楼梯气派非凡。

"天哪，"罗恩说着，使劲晃了晃脑袋，把水珠洒得到处都是，"如果再这样下个不停，湖里就要发大水了。我成了落汤鸡——**哎呀！**"

一个装满水的大红气球从天花板上落下来，在罗恩的头顶上爆炸。罗恩被浇得浑身透湿，嘴巴里嘟囔着，跌跌撞撞地一闪，倒在旁边的哈利身上。就在这时，第二个水炸弹又落了下来——差一点儿击中赫敏，在哈利脚边爆炸了。冰冷的水喷出来，浇在他的运动鞋上，浸湿了他的袜子。周围的人们失声尖叫，互相推挤着，都想赶快离开这个是非之地。哈利抬头一看，只见在头顶上二十英尺的地方，飘浮着恶作剧精灵皮皮鬼。他个头矮小，戴着一顶有铃铛的帽子，系着橘红色的领结。他又一次瞄准目标，那张调皮的大阔脸上的肌肉紧绷着。

"**皮皮鬼！**"一个愤怒的声音喊道，"皮皮鬼，你**立刻**给我下来！"

副校长兼格兰芬多学院院长麦格教授从礼堂里冲了出来。地上太湿了，她脚下一滑，赶紧抓住赫敏的脖子才没有摔倒。"哎哟——对不起，

## CHAPTER TWELVE    The Triwizard Tournament

sorry, Miss Granger —'

'That's all right, Professor!' Hermione gasped, massaging her throat.

'Peeves, get down here NOW!' barked Professor McGonagall, straightening her pointed hat and glaring upwards through her square-rimmed spectacles.

'Not doing nothing!' cackled Peeves, lobbing a water bomb at several fifth-year girls, who screamed and dived into the Great Hall. 'Already wet, aren't they? Little squirts! Wheeeeeeeeee!' and he aimed another bomb at a group of second-years who had just arrived.

'I shall call the Headmaster!' shouted Professor McGonagall. 'I'm warning you, Peeves —'

Peeves stuck out his tongue, threw the last of his water bombs into the air, and zoomed off up the marble staircase, cackling insanely.

'Well, move along, then!' said Professor McGonagall sharply to the bedraggled crowd. 'Into the Great Hall, come on!'

Harry, Ron and Hermione slipped and slid across the Entrance Hall and through the double doors on the right, Ron muttering furiously under his breath as he pushed his sopping hair off his face.

The Great Hall looked its usual splendid self, decorated for the start-of-term feast. Golden plates and goblets gleamed by the light of hundreds and hundreds of candles, floating over the tables in mid-air. The four long house tables were packed with chattering students; at the top of the Hall, the staff sat along one side of a fifth table, facing their pupils. It was much warmer in here. Harry, Ron and Hermione walked past the Slytherins, the Ravenclaws and the Hufflepuffs, and sat down with the rest of the Gryffindors at the far side of the Hall, next to Nearly Headless Nick, the Gryffindor ghost. Pearly white and semi-transparent, Nick was dressed tonight in his usual doublet, with a particularly large ruff, which served the dual purpose of looking extra festive and ensuring that his head didn't wobble too much on his partially severed neck.

'Good evening,' he said, beaming at them.

'Says who?' said Harry, taking off his trainers and emptying them of water. 'Hope they hurry up with the Sorting, I'm starving.'

The Sorting of the new students into houses took place at the start of

## 第12章 三强争霸赛

格兰杰小姐——"

"没关系，教授！"赫敏喘着气说，一边揉着自己的喉咙。

"皮皮鬼，你**现在**就给我下来！"麦格教授大声吼道，她整了整头上的尖顶高帽，透过方框眼镜朝上面瞪视着。

"我没做什么！"皮皮鬼咯咯地笑着，又把一个水炸弹朝几个五年级女生扔去——女生们吓得尖叫着冲进礼堂，"反正她们身上已经湿了，对吧？喂，小毛孩！吃我一炮！"他又拿起一个水炸弹，瞄准了刚刚进来的一群二年级学生。

"我去叫校长了！"麦格教授大声说，"我警告你，皮皮鬼——"

皮皮鬼伸出舌头，把最后几个水炸弹扔到空中，然后嗖地蹿上大理石楼梯，一边疯狂地嘎嘎怪笑。

"好了，快走吧！"麦格教授严厉地对淋成落汤鸡的学生们说，"进礼堂，快点儿！"

哈利、罗恩和赫敏一步一滑地走过门厅，穿过右边一道双开门。罗恩气呼呼地小声嘟哝着，把湿漉漉的头发从脸上拨开。

礼堂还是那样辉煌气派，为了新学期的宴会又格外装饰了一番。成百上千支蜡烛在桌子上方悬空飘浮，照得金盘子和高脚杯闪闪发亮。四张长长的学院桌子旁已经坐满了叽叽喳喳的学生。在礼堂的顶端还有第五张桌子，教工们挨个儿坐在桌子的一边，面对他们的学生。这里暖和多了。哈利、罗恩和赫敏从斯莱特林、拉文克劳、赫奇帕奇三个学院的学生前走过，然后和其他格兰芬多学院的学生一起，坐在礼堂尽头的那张桌子旁。他们旁边是格兰芬多学院的鬼魂——差点没头的尼克。尼克全身半透明，泛着珍珠白色。今晚他穿着惯常穿的紧身上衣，但戴着特别大的轮状皱领。他戴这个皱领有双重目的，一是为了显得更有喜庆色彩，二是为了保证他的脑袋在被割断了一半的脖子上不会摇晃得太厉害。

"晚上好。"他微笑着对他们说。

"好什么呀？"哈利说着，脱下运动鞋，把里面的水倒出来，"真希望他们快点进行分院。我都快饿死了。"

分院仪式是把新生分到各个学院，在每个新学年开始的时候举行。

## CHAPTER TWELVE   The Triwizard Tournament

every school year, but by an unlucky combination of circumstances, Harry hadn't been present at one since his own. He was quite looking forward to it.

Just then, a highly excited, breathless voice called down the table, 'Hiya, Harry!'

It was Colin Creevey, a third-year to whom Harry was something of a hero.

'Hi, Colin,' said Harry warily.

'Harry, guess what? Guess what, Harry? My brother's starting! My brother Dennis!'

'Er – good,' said Harry.

'He's really excited!' said Colin, practically bouncing up and down in his seat. 'I just hope he's in Gryffindor! Keep your fingers crossed, eh, Harry?'

'Er – yeah, all right,' said Harry. He turned back to Hermione, Ron and Nearly Headless Nick. 'Brothers and sisters usually go in the same houses, don't they?' he said. He was judging by the Weasleys, all seven of whom had been put into Gryffindor.

'Oh, no, not necessarily,' said Hermione. 'Parvati Patil's twin's in Ravenclaw, and they're identical, you'd think they'd be together, wouldn't you?'

Harry looked up at the staff table. There seemed to be rather more empty seats there than usual. Hagrid, of course, was still fighting his way across the lake with the first-years; Professor McGonagall was presumably supervising the drying of the Entrance Hall floor, but there was another empty chair, too, and he couldn't think who else was missing.

'Where's the new Defence Against the Dark Arts teacher?' said Hermione, who was also looking up at the teachers.

They had never yet had a Defence Against the Dark Arts teacher who had lasted more than three terms. Harry's favourite by far had been Professor Lupin, who had resigned last year. He looked up and down the staff table. There was definitely no new face there.

'Maybe they couldn't get anyone!' said Hermione, looking anxious.

Harry scanned the table more carefully. Tiny little Professor Flitwick, the Charms teacher, was sitting on a large pile of cushions beside Professor Sprout, the Herbology teacher, whose hat was askew over her flyaway grey hair. She was talking to Professor Sinistra of the Astronomy department. On Professor Sinistra's other side was the sallow-faced, hook-nosed, greasy-haired Potions master, Snape – Harry's least favourite person at Hogwarts.

## 第12章 三强争霸赛

可是哈利在自己被分进格兰芬多学院以后，由于许多偶然的因素，一直没有现场观看过分院仪式。他一直盼着能再经历一次。

就在这时，一个兴奋得喘不过气来的声音从桌子那头传来："你好，哈利！"

是科林·克里维，一个三年级男生，一直把哈利看作英雄般的人物。

"你好，科林。"哈利很小心地说。

"哈利，你猜怎么着？你猜怎么着，哈利？我弟弟也入学了！我弟弟丹尼斯！"

"哦——太好了。"哈利说。

"他兴奋得要命！"科林说着，居然在长凳上弹跳了一下，"我真希望他被分在格兰芬多！你替他祷告吧，哈利，好吗？"

"噢——好的，没问题。"哈利说，他又转过头来，对赫敏、罗恩和差点没头的尼克说，"兄弟姐妹一般都分在同一个学院，是吗？"他是根据韦斯莱一家的情况来判断的，韦斯莱家的七个孩子都被分在了格兰芬多学院。

"哦，不一定，"赫敏说，"帕瓦蒂·佩蒂尔的双胞胎妹妹就在拉文克劳，她们俩简直一模一样。本来还以为她们会被分在一起呢，是吧？"

哈利朝教工桌子望去。那里的空位子似乎比往常多。当然喽，海格正带着那些一年级新生奋力渡湖呢；麦格教授大概在让人把门厅的地面弄干，可是还空着一个座位呢，哈利想不出还有谁没来。

"怎么不见黑魔法防御术课的新老师？"赫敏说，她也望着那边的教师们。

他们的黑魔法防御术课老师没有一个待到超过三个学期的。迄今为止，哈利最喜欢的是卢平教授，但他去年辞职了。哈利来来回回扫视着教工桌子，毫无疑问，没有一张新面孔。

"也许他们找不到人！"赫敏说，显得有些焦急。

哈利更仔细地审视着教工桌子。教他们魔咒课的小矮个儿弗立维教授坐在一大堆软垫上，旁边是草药课老师斯普劳特教授，帽子斜戴在她飘拂的灰色长发上。她正在跟教天文课的辛尼斯塔教授谈着什么。在辛尼斯塔教授的另一边，坐着灰黄脸、鹰钩鼻、头发油腻腻的魔药

## CHAPTER TWELVE   The Triwizard Tournament

Harry's loathing of Snape was matched only by Snape's hatred of him, a hatred which had, if possible, intensified last year, when Harry had helped Sirius escape right under Snape's overlarge nose – Snape and Sirius had been enemies since their own schooldays.

On Snape's other side was an empty seat, which Harry guessed was Professor McGonagall's. Next to it, and in the very centre of the table, sat Professor Dumbledore, the Headmaster, his sweeping silver hair and beard shining in the candlelight, his magnificent deep-green robes embroidered with many stars and moons. The tips of Dumbledore's long, thin fingers were together and he was resting his chin upon them, staring up at the ceiling through his half-moon spectacles as though lost in thought. Harry glanced up at the ceiling, too.

It was enchanted to look like the sky outside, and he had never seen it look this stormy. Black and purple clouds were swirling across it, and as another thunderclap sounded outside, a fork of lightning flashed across it.

'Oh, hurry up,' Ron moaned, beside Harry. 'I could eat a Hippogriff.'

The words were no sooner out of his mouth than the doors of the Great Hall opened, and silence fell. Professor McGonagall was leading a long line of first-years up to the top of the Hall. If Harry, Ron and Hermione were wet, it was nothing to how these first-years looked. They appeared to have swum across the lake rather than sailing. All of them were shivering with a combination of cold and nerves as they filed along the staff table and came to a halt in a line facing the rest of the school – all of them except the smallest of the lot, a boy with mousey hair, who was wrapped in what Harry recognised as Hagrid's moleskin overcoat. The coat was so big for him that it looked as though he was draped in a furry black marquee. His small face protruded from over the collar, looking almost painfully excited. When he had lined up with his terrified-looking peers, he caught Colin Creevey's eye, gave a double thumbs-up and mouthed, 'I fell in the lake!' He looked positively delighted about it.

Professor McGonagall now placed a three-legged stool on the ground before the first-years and, on top of it, an extremely old, dirty, patched wizard's hat. The first-years stared at it. So did everyone else. For a moment, there was silence. Then a tear near the brim opened wide like a mouth, and the hat broke into song:

## 第12章 三强争霸赛

课老师——斯内普，他是哈利在霍格沃茨最不喜欢的人。哈利讨厌斯内普，斯内普也同样仇恨哈利，去年这种仇恨变得更加强烈了，因为哈利帮助小天狼星在斯内普硕大的鼻子底下逃跑了——而斯内普和小天狼星自学生时代起就是不共戴天的仇敌。

斯内普另一边的座位空着，哈利猜想那是麦格教授的位子。再那边就是桌子的正中间了，坐着校长邓布利多教授。他飘逸的银白色头发和胡须在烛光下闪闪发亮，华贵的深绿色长袍上绣着许多星星和月亮。邓布利多两只修长的手的指尖碰在一起，下巴就放在指尖上，眼睛透过半月形的镜片望着上面的天花板，好像陷入了沉思。哈利也把目光投向天花板。

天花板被施了魔法，看上去和外面的天空一样，哈利从没见过它这样风雨大作。黑色和紫色的云团在上面翻滚，随着外面又响起一阵雷声，一道分叉的闪电在天花板上划过。

"哦，快点儿吧，"哈利旁边的罗恩叹着气说，"我简直吃得下一只鹰头马身有翼兽呢。"

他话音刚落，礼堂的门开了，大家立刻安静下来。麦格教授领着长长一排一年级新生走到礼堂顶端。如果说哈利、罗恩和赫敏浑身湿透的话，和这些一年级新生一比，就根本不算什么了。看他们的样子，就好像不是乘渡船，而是从湖里游过来的。他们顺着教工桌子站成一排，停住脚步，面对着全校同学，因为又冷又紧张，一个个浑身发抖——只有最小的那个男孩子例外。他长着灰褐色的头发，身上裹着一件什么东西，哈利一眼认出那是海格的鼹鼠皮大衣。大衣穿在他身上太大了，他的样子就好像罩在一顶黑色的马戏团毛皮帐篷下。他的小脸从领子上伸出来，神情激动得要命。当他和那些惊恐万状的同伴站成一排时，他的目光和科林·克里维相遇了。他跷起两个大拇指，用口型说道："我掉进湖里了！"看样子，他为这个高兴坏了。

这时，麦格教授把一个三脚凳放在新生前面的地上，又在凳子上放了一顶破破烂烂、脏兮兮、打满补丁的巫师帽。一年级新生们愣愣地望着它。其他人也望着它。一时间，礼堂里一片寂静。然后帽檐附近的一道裂缝像嘴巴一样张开了，帽子突然唱起歌来：

## CHAPTER TWELVE   The Triwizard Tournament

'A thousand years or more ago,
When I was newly sewn,
There lived four wizards of renown,
Whose names are still well known:
Bold Gryffindor, from wild moor,
Fair Ravenclaw, from glen,
Sweet Hufflepuff, from valley broad,
Shrewd Slytherin, from fen.
They shared a wish, a hope, a dream,
They hatched a daring plan
To educate young sorcerers
Thus Hogwarts School began.
Now each of these four founders
Formed their own house, for each
Did value different virtues
In the ones they had to teach.
By Gryffindor, the bravest were
Prized far beyond the rest;
For Ravenclaw, the cleverest
Would always be the best;
For Hufflepuff, hard workers were
Most worthy of admission;
And power-hungry Slytherin
Loved those of great ambition.
While still alive they did divide
Their favourites from the throng,
Yet how to pick the worthy ones
When they were dead and gone?'
Twas Gryffindor who found the way,
He whipped me off his head

## 第12章 三强争霸赛

那是一千多年前的事情，
我刚刚被编织成形，
有四个大名鼎鼎的巫师，
他们的名字流传至今：
勇敢的格兰芬多，来自荒芜的沼泽，
美丽的拉文克劳，来自宁静的河畔，
仁慈的赫奇帕奇，来自开阔的谷地，
精明的斯莱特林，来自那一片泥潭。
他们共有一个梦想、一个心愿，
同时有了一个大胆的打算，
要把年轻的巫师培育成材，
霍格沃茨学校就这样创办。
这四位伟大的巫师
每人都把自己的学院建立，
他们在所教的学生身上
看重的才华想法不一。
格兰芬多认为，最勇敢的人
应该受到最高的奖励；
拉文克劳觉得，头脑最聪明者
总是最有出息；
赫奇帕奇感到，最勤奋努力的
才最有资格入院学习；
而渴望权力的斯莱特林
最喜欢那些有野心的学子。
四大巫师在活着的年月
亲自把得意门生挑选出来，
可是当他们长眠于九泉，
怎样挑出学生中的人才？
是格兰芬多想出了办法，
把我从他头上摘下，

## CHAPTER TWELVE    The Triwizard Tournament

*The founders put some brains in me
So I could choose instead!
Now slip me snug about your ears,
I've never yet been wrong,
I'll have a look inside your mind
And tell where you belong!'*

The Great Hall rang with applause as the Sorting Hat finished.

'That's not the song it sang when it sorted us,' said Harry, clapping along with everyone else.

'Sings a different one every year,' said Ron. 'It's got to be a pretty boring life, hasn't it, being a hat? I suppose it spends all year making up the next one.'

Professor McGonagall was now unrolling a large scroll of parchment.

'When I call out your name, you will put on the Hat and sit on the stool,' she told the first-years. 'When the Hat announces your house, you will go and sit at the appropriate table.

'Ackerley, Stewart!'

A boy walked forward, visibly trembling from head to foot, picked up the Sorting Hat, put it on and sat down on the stool.

'*Ravenclaw!*' shouted the Hat.

Stewart Ackerley took off the Hat and hurried into a seat at the Ravenclaw table, where everyone was applauding him. Harry caught a glimpse of Cho, the Ravenclaw Seeker, cheering Stewart Ackerley as he sat down. For a fleeting second, Harry had a strange desire to join the Ravenclaw table too.

'Baddock, Malcolm!'

'*Slytherin!*'

The table on the other side of the Hall erupted with cheers; Harry could see Malfoy clapping as Baddock joined the Slytherins. Harry wondered whether Baddock knew that Slytherin house had turned out more Dark witches and wizards than any other. Fred and George hissed Malcolm Baddock as he sat down.

'Branstone, Eleanor!'

## 第12章 三强争霸赛

> 四巨头都给我注入了思想，
> 从此就由我来挑选、评价！
> 好了，把我好好地扣在头上，
> 我从来没有看走过眼，
> 我要看一看你的头脑，
> 判断你属于哪个学院！

分院帽唱完后，礼堂里响起了热烈的掌声。

"这首歌不是上次它给我们分院时唱的那首。"哈利和大家一起鼓掌，一边说道。

"每年唱的歌都不一样。"罗恩说，"作为一顶帽子，它的生活一定挺单调的，是不是？我猜它是花了整整一年时间才想出下一首歌的。"

这时，麦格展开一大卷羊皮纸。

"我叫到谁的名字，谁就戴上帽子，坐到凳子上，"她对一年级新生说，"等帽子宣布了学院，就去坐在相应的桌子旁。

"斯图尔特·阿克利！"

一个男孩走上前，可以看出他从头到脚都在发抖。他拿起分院帽，戴在头上，坐在了那张凳子上。

"拉文克劳！"分院帽喊道。

斯图尔特·阿克利摘掉帽子，匆匆跑到拉文克劳桌子旁的一个座位上坐下，桌旁的每个人都鼓掌欢迎他。哈利无意间看见了拉文克劳队的找球手秋·张，她在斯图尔特·阿克利坐下时高兴地欢呼着。一时间，哈利产生了一个奇怪的冲动，希望自己也坐到拉文克劳桌子边上去。

"马尔科姆·巴多克！"

"斯莱特林！"

礼堂另一边的桌旁传来响亮的欢呼声。哈利看见当巴多克加入到斯莱特林的行列中时，马尔福也在拼命鼓掌。哈利心想，不知巴多克是否知道，从斯莱特林学院出来的黑巫师比其他学院都多。马尔科姆·巴多克坐下时，弗雷德和乔治嘘嘘地喝着倒彩。

"埃莉诺·布兰斯通！"

## CHAPTER TWELVE   The Triwizard Tournament

'*Hufflepuff!*'

'Cauldwell, Owen!'

'*Hufflepuff!*'

'Creevey, Dennis!'

Tiny Dennis Creevey staggered forward, tripping over Hagrid's moleskin, just as Hagrid himself sidled into the Hall through a door behind the teachers' table. About twice as tall as a normal man, and at least three times as broad, Hagrid, with his long, wild, tangled black hair and beard, looked slightly alarming – a misleading impression, for Harry, Ron and Hermione knew Hagrid to possess a very kind nature. He winked at them as he sat down at the end of the staff table, and watched Dennis Creevey putting on the Sorting Hat. The rip at the brim opened wide –

'*Gryffindor!*' the Hat shouted.

Hagrid clapped along with the Gryffindors, as Dennis Creevey, beaming widely, took off the Hat, placed it back on the stool, and hurried over to join his brother.

'Colin, I fell in!' he said shrilly, throwing himself into an empty seat. 'It was brilliant! And something in the water grabbed me and pushed me back in the boat!'

'Cool!' said Colin, just as excitedly. 'It was probably the giant squid, Dennis!'

'*Wow!*' said Dennis, as though nobody in their wildest dreams could hope for more than being thrown into a storm-tossed, fathoms-deep lake, and pushed out of it again by a giant sea-monster.

'Dennis! Dennis! See that boy down there? The one with the black hair and glasses? See him? *Know who he is, Dennis?*'

Harry looked away, staring very hard at the Sorting Hat, now sorting Emma Dobbs.

The Sorting continued; boys and girls with varying degrees of fright on their faces moving, one by one, to the three-legged stool, the line dwindling slowly as Professor McGonagall passed the 'L's.

'Oh, hurry up,' Ron moaned, massaging his stomach.

'Now, Ron, the Sorting's much more important than food,' said Nearly Headless Nick, as 'Madley, Laura!' became a Hufflepuff.

"赫奇帕奇!"

"欧文·考德韦尔!"

"赫奇帕奇!"

"丹尼斯·克里维!"

小不点儿丹尼斯·克里维跌跌撞撞地往前走,老是被海格的鼹鼠皮大衣绊住,恰巧就在这时,海格本人从教工桌子后面的一扇门外偷偷溜进了礼堂。海格个子是常人的两倍,块头至少是常人的三倍,长长的黑头发和黑胡子乱蓬蓬地纠结在一起,样子有些吓人——经常会使人产生错误的印象,而哈利、罗恩和赫敏知道,海格实际上有一颗非常慈善的心。他朝他们眨眨眼睛,在教工桌子的末端坐了下来,看着丹尼斯·克里维戴上分院帽。帽檐上的裂缝张开了——

"格兰芬多!"帽子大声说道。

丹尼斯·克里维高兴得满脸放光,他摘掉帽子,把它放回到凳子上,然后匆匆跑过来和他哥哥坐到一起。这时,海格也和格兰芬多的同学一起鼓起掌来。

"科林,我掉进了湖里!"他一屁股坐在一个空位子上,尖着嗓子说道,"太精彩了!水里有个东西抓住了我,把我推回到船上!"

"真酷!"科林说,也和弟弟一样兴奋,"大概是巨乌贼,丹尼斯!"

"哇!"丹尼斯叫了起来。刚才被抛进一个风高浪急、深不可测的湖里,又被一个巨大的湖怪推出来,他好像觉得这是任何人连做梦也不敢向往的经历。

"丹尼斯!丹尼斯!看见那边那个男孩了吗?长着黑头发、戴着眼镜的那个?看见了吗?你知道他是谁吗,丹尼斯?"

哈利移开了目光,使劲盯着分院帽,现在轮到埃玛·多布斯了。

分院仪式继续进行,那些男男女女的新生们脸上带着不同程度的恐惧,一个接一个地走向三脚凳。队伍在慢慢缩短,麦格教授已经念完了名单上以L开头的名字。

"哦,快点吧。"罗恩呻吟道,用手揉着肚子。

"我说,罗恩,分院仪式比吃饭重要得多。"差点没头的尼克说。这时,劳拉·马德莱被分到了赫奇帕奇。

## CHAPTER TWELVE   The Triwizard Tournament

''Course it is, if you're dead,' snapped Ron.

'I do hope this year's batch of Gryffindors are up to scratch,' said Nearly Headless Nick, applauding as 'McDonald, Natalie!' joined the Gryffindor table. 'We don't want to break our winning streak, do we?'

Gryffindor had won the Inter-House Championship for the last three years in a row.

'Pritchard, Graham!'

'*Slytherin!*'

'Quirke, Orla!'

'*Ravenclaw!*'

And finally, with 'Whitby, Kevin!' ('*Hufflepuff!*') the Sorting ended. Professor McGonagall picked up the Hat and the stool, and carried them away.

'About time,' said Ron, seizing his knife and fork and looking expectantly at his golden plate.

Professor Dumbledore had got to his feet. He was smiling around at the students, his arms opened wide in welcome.

'I have only two words to say to you,' he told them, his deep voice echoing around the Hall. '*Tuck in.*'

'Hear, hear!' said Harry and Ron loudly, as the empty dishes filled magically before their eyes.

Nearly Headless Nick watched mournfully as Harry, Ron and Hermione loaded their plates.

'Aaah, 'at's be'er,' said Ron, with his mouth full of mashed potato.

'You're lucky there's a feast at all tonight, you know,' said Nearly Headless Nick. 'There was trouble in the kitchens earlier.'

'Why? Wha' 'appened?' said Harry, through a sizeable chunk of steak.

'Peeves, of course,' said Nearly Headless Nick, shaking his head, which wobbled dangerously. He pulled his ruff a little higher up his neck. 'The usual argument, you know. He wanted to attend the feast – well, it's quite out of the question, you know what he's like, utterly uncivilised, can't see a plate of food without throwing it. We held a ghosts' council – the Fat Friar was all for giving him the chance – but most wisely, in my opinion, the Bloody Baron put his foot down.'

The Bloody Baron was the Slytherin ghost, a gaunt and silent spectre

## 第12章 三强争霸赛

"你是死人,当然会这么说。"罗恩反驳道。

"我希望今年格兰芬多的新生都是优秀的人才。"差点没头的尼克说——这时纳塔丽·麦克唐纳加入了格兰芬多餐桌,尼克热情鼓掌,"我们可不愿意打破我们获胜的势头,是吧?"

格兰芬多已经连续三年赢得了学院杯冠军。

"格雷厄姆·普里查德!"

"斯莱特林!"

"奥拉·奎尔克!"

"拉文克劳!"

最后,随着凯文·威特比被分到赫奇帕奇的叫声响起,分院仪式结束了。麦格教授收拾起分院帽和小凳子,把它们拿走了。

"是时候了。"罗恩说着抓起刀叉,眼巴巴地望着面前的金菜盘。

邓布利多教授站了起来。他笑吟吟地望着所有的同学,张开双臂,做出欢迎的姿势。

"我只有两个字要对你们说,"他说,浑厚的声音在礼堂里回响,"吃吧!"

"好啊,好啊!"哈利和罗恩大声说,眼睁睁地看着那些空盘子里突然神奇地堆满了食物。

差点没头的尼克悲哀地瞅着哈利、罗恩和赫敏把食物盛进各自的盘子。

"啊,这下好多了。"罗恩塞了一嘴土豆泥,含混不清地说。

"要知道,你们还算走运,今天晚上的宴会差点泡汤了,"差点没头的尼克说,"早些时候厨房里出了乱子。"

"为什么?怎么回事?"哈利嘴里含着一块很大的牛排,嘟嘟囔囔地问。

"自然是皮皮鬼在捣乱,"尼克说着,摇了摇头,这使他的脑袋很危险地摇晃起来——他赶紧把轮状皱领拉上去一点,护住脖子,"又为那件事争吵不休,你们知道的,他想参加宴会——唉,这根本不可能,你们知道他那副德行,完全没有教养,看见吃的东西就到处乱扔。我们召开了一个幽灵会议——胖修士倒是主张给他这次机会——可是血人巴罗坚决不同意,我认为他这样做是十分明智的。"

血人巴罗是斯莱特林学院的幽灵,长得瘦巴巴,总是沉默寡言,

covered in silver bloodstains. He was the only person at Hogwarts who could really control Peeves.

'Yeah, we thought Peeves seemed hacked off about something,' said Ron darkly. 'So what did he do in the kitchens?'

'Oh, the usual,' said Nearly Headless Nick, shrugging. 'Wreaked havoc and mayhem. Pots and pans everywhere. Place swimming in soup. Terrified the house-elves out of their wits –'

*Clang.* Hermione had knocked over her golden goblet. Pumpkin juice spread steadily over the tablecloth, staining several feet of white linen orange, but Hermione paid no attention.

'There are house-elves *here*?' she said, staring, horror-struck, at Nearly Headless Nick. 'Here at *Hogwarts*?'

'Certainly,' said Nearly Headless Nick, looking surprised at her reaction. 'The largest number in any dwelling in Britain, I believe. Over a hundred.'

'I've never seen one!' said Hermione.

'Well, they hardly ever leave the kitchen by day, do they?' said Nearly Headless Nick. 'They come out at night to do a bit of cleaning ... see to the fires and so on ... I mean, you're not supposed to see them, are you? That's the mark of a good house-elf, isn't it, that you don't know it's there?'

Hermione stared at him.

'But they get *paid*?' she said. 'They get *holidays*, don't they? And – and sick leave, and pensions and everything?'

Nearly Headless Nick chortled so much that his ruff slipped and his head flopped off, dangling on the inch or so of ghostly skin and muscle that still attached it to his neck.

'Sick leave and pensions?' he said, pushing his head back onto his shoulders and securing it once more with his ruff. 'House-elves don't want sick leave and pensions!'

Hermione looked down at her hardly touched plate of food, then put her knife and fork down upon it and pushed it away from her.

'Oh, c'mon, 'Er-my-knee,' said Ron, accidentally spraying Harry with bits of Yorkshire pudding. 'Oops – sorry, 'Arry –' He swallowed. 'You won't get them sick leave by starving yourself!'

'Slave labour,' said Hermione, breathing hard through her nose. 'That's

## 第 12 章　三强争霸赛

身上布满银色的血迹。在霍格沃茨，只有他才能真正管住皮皮鬼。

"怪不得呢，我们就觉得皮皮鬼好像在为什么事儿生气。"罗恩闷闷不乐地说，"他在厨房里做了什么？"

"哦，还是老一套，"尼克耸了耸肩膀说，"大搞破坏，弄得一片混乱。锅碗瓢盆扔得到处都是，整个厨房都被汤淹了。家养小精灵们吓得六神无主——"

当啷。赫敏打翻了她的高脚金酒杯，南瓜汁不断地倾洒在桌布上，给白色的亚麻布染上了一片橘黄色，漫延好几英尺，可是赫敏不予理会。

"这里也有家养小精灵？"她神色惊恐地瞪着尼克，问道，"就在霍格沃茨？"

"那还用说，"差点没头的尼克说，对她的反应感到有些惊讶，"我相信，英国任何一处住宅里的家养小精灵都没有这里的多。有一百多个呢。"

"我一个都没看见过！"赫敏说。

"噢，他们白天很少离开厨房的，不是吗？"尼克说，"晚上出来打扫打扫卫生……照看一下炉子什么的……我的意思是，你是不应该看见他们的，对不对？一个好的家养小精灵的标志就是你根本不知道他的存在，对不对？"

赫敏瞪着他。

"可是他们拿工钱吗？"她问，"他们有假期吗？还有——他们有病假，有津贴，有种种的一切吗？"

尼克咯咯笑了起来，他笑得太厉害了，轮状皱领一歪，脑袋滚落下来，被仍然连着脖子的一两英寸死皮和肌肉挂着，晃悠悠地悬在那里。

"病假和津贴？"他说，把脑袋重新扶到脖子上，用轮状皱领重新固定好，"家养小精灵是不需要病假和津贴的！"

赫敏低头望着自己盘子里几乎没有动过的食物，把刀叉放在盘子上，把盘子推开了。

"哦，得了吧，厄敏。"罗恩说，不小心把一些约克郡布丁的碎屑喷到了哈利身上，"哎哟——对不起，阿利——"他使劲咽了一口，"你把自己饿死，也不会为他们争取到病假的！"

"奴隶劳动，"赫敏说，呼吸变得非常粗重，"这顿晚饭就是这么来的。

what made this dinner. *Slave labour.*'

And she refused to eat another bite.

The rain was still drumming heavily against the high, dark windows. Another clap of thunder shook the windows, and the stormy ceiling flashed, illuminating the golden plates as the remains of the first course vanished and were replaced, instantly, with puddings.

'Treacle tart, Hermione!' said Ron, deliberately wafting its smell towards her. 'Spotted dick, look! Chocolate gateau!'

But Hermione gave him a look so reminiscent of Professor McGonagall that he gave up.

When the puddings, too, had been demolished, and the last crumbs had faded off the plates, leaving them sparkling clean, Albus Dumbledore got to his feet again. The buzz of chatter filling the Hall ceased almost at once, so that only the howling wind and pounding rain could be heard.

'So!' said Dumbledore, smiling around at them all. 'Now that we are all fed and watered' ('Hmph!' said Hermione), 'I must once more ask for your attention, while I give out a few notices.

'Mr Filch, the caretaker, has asked me to tell you that the list of objects forbidden inside the castle has this year been extended to include Screaming Yo-yos, Fanged Frisbees and Ever-Bashing Boomerangs. The full list comprises some four hundred and thirty-seven items, I believe, and can be viewed in Mr Filch's office, if anybody would like to check it.'

The corners of Dumbledore's mouth twitched.

He continued, 'As ever, I would like to remind you all that the Forest in the grounds is out-of-bounds to students, as is the village of Hogsmeade to all below third year.

'It is also my painful duty to inform you that the inter-house Quidditch Cup will not take place this year.'

'*What?*' Harry gasped. He looked around at Fred and George, his fellow members of the Quidditch team. They were mouthing soundlessly at Dumbledore, apparently too appalled to speak.

Dumbledore continued, 'This is due to an event that will be starting in October, and continuing throughout the school year, taking up much of the teachers' time and energy – but I am sure you will all enjoy it immensely. I have great pleasure in announcing that this year at Hogwarts –'

## 第12章 三强争霸赛

奴隶劳动。"

她一口也不肯再吃了。

大雨仍然密集地敲打着高高的、黑乎乎的窗户。又一阵雷声炸起，震得玻璃窗咔咔作响，阴霾的天花板上划过一道闪电，照亮了金色的盘子，盘子里剩下的第一道食品消失了，眨眼间又装满了甜点。

"糖浆水果馅饼，赫敏！"罗恩说着，故意把香喷喷的馅饼送到赫敏面前，"葡萄干布丁，你看！还有巧克力蛋糕！"

赫敏瞪了罗恩一眼，那目光一下子使他想起了麦格教授，罗恩顿时就收敛了。

最后，甜点也被扫荡一空，盘子里最后剩下的碎屑消失了，盘子又变得干干净净，闪闪发亮，这时，阿不思·邓布利多再次站起身来。大厅里嗡嗡的说话声顿时停止，只能听见狂风的呼啸和大雨的敲击。

"好了！"邓布利多笑眯眯地望着大家，说道，"既然我们都吃饱喝足了，（'哼！'赫敏说）我必须再次请大家注意，我要宣布几条通知。

"管理员费尔奇先生希望我告诉大家，今年，城堡内禁止使用的物品又增加了几项，它们是尖叫悠悠球、狼牙飞碟和连击回飞镖。整个清单大概包括四百三十七项，在费尔奇先生的办公室可以看到，有兴趣的人可以去核对一下。"

邓布利多的嘴角抽动了几下。

他继续说道："和以前一样，我要提醒大家，场地那边的禁林是学生不能进入的，而霍格莫德村，凡是三年级以下的学生都不许光顾。

"我还要非常遗憾地告诉大家，今年将不举办学院杯魁地奇赛了。"

"什么？"哈利惊讶得喘不过气来。他扭头看着他的魁地奇队友弗雷德和乔治。他们都张大嘴巴，无声地瞪着邓布利多，仿佛吃惊得说不出话来。

邓布利多继续说道："这是因为一个大型活动将于十月开始，持续整个学年，将占据老师们许多时间和精力——但是我相信，你们都能从中得到很大的乐趣。我非常高兴地向大家宣布，今年在霍格沃茨——"

## CHAPTER TWELVE   The Triwizard Tournament

But at that moment, there was a deafening rumble of thunder, and the doors of the Great Hall banged open.

A man stood in the doorway, leaning upon a long staff, shrouded in a black travelling cloak. Every head in the Great Hall swivelled towards the stranger, suddenly brightly illuminated by a fork of lightning that flashed across the ceiling. He lowered his hood, shook out a long mane of grizzled, dark grey hair, then began to walk up towards the teachers' table.

A dull *clunk* echoed through the Hall on his every other step. He reached the end of the top table, turned right and limped heavily towards Dumbledore. Another flash of lightning crossed the ceiling. Hermione gasped.

The lightning had thrown the man's face into sharp relief, and it was a face unlike any Harry had ever seen. It looked as though it had been carved out of weathered wood by someone who had only the vaguest idea of what human faces were supposed to look like, and was none too skilled with a chisel. Every inch of skin seemed to be scarred. The mouth looked like a diagonal gash, and a large chunk of the nose was missing. But it was the man's eyes that made him frightening.

One of them was small, dark and beady. The other was large, round as a coin, and a vivid, electric blue. The blue eye was moving ceaselessly, without blinking, and was rolling up, down and from side to side, quite independently of the normal eye – and then it rolled right over, pointing into the back of the man's head, so that all they could see was whiteness.

The stranger reached Dumbledore. He stretched out a hand that was as badly scarred as his face, and Dumbledore shook it, muttering words Harry couldn't hear. He seemed to be making some enquiry of the stranger, who shook his head unsmilingly and replied in an undertone. Dumbledore nodded, and gestured the man to the empty seat on his right-hand side.

The stranger sat down, shook his mane of dark grey hair out of his face, pulled a plate of sausages towards him, raised it to what was left of his nose and sniffed it. He then took a small knife out of his pocket, speared a sausage on the end of it, and began to eat. His normal eye was fixed upon the sausages, but the blue eye was still darting restlessly around in its socket, taking in the Hall and the students.

'May I introduce our new Defence Against the Dark Arts teacher,' said Dumbledore brightly, into the silence. 'Professor Moody.'

## 第12章　三强争霸赛

就在这时，一阵震耳欲聋的雷声响起，礼堂的门被砰地撞开了。

一个男人站在门口，拄着一根长长的拐杖，身上裹着一件黑色的旅行斗篷。礼堂里的人都转过头去望着他，突然，一道分叉的闪电划过天花板，把陌生人照亮了。他摘下兜帽，抖出一头长长的灰白头发，开始朝教工桌子走去。

噔，噔，他每走两步，都有一个沉闷的声音在礼堂里回响。他径直走到主宾席的尽头，向右一转，一瘸一拐地朝邓布利多走去。又一道闪电划过天花板，赫敏倒吸了一口冷气。

闪电把那人的脸照得无比鲜明，哈利从来没有见过这样的一张脸。它就像是在一块腐朽的木头上雕刻出来的，而雕刻者对人脸应该是怎么样只有一个模糊的概念，对刻刀的使用也不太在行。那脸上的每一寸皮肤似乎都伤痕累累，嘴巴像一个歪斜的大口子，鼻子应该隆起的地方却不见了。而这个男人最令人恐怖的是他的眼睛。

他的一只眼睛很小，黑黑的，亮晶晶的；另一只眼睛却很大，圆圆的像一枚硬币，而且是鲜明的亮蓝色。那只蓝眼睛一眨不眨地动个不停，上下左右地转来转去，完全与那只正常的眼睛不相干——后来，那蓝眼珠一翻，钻进那人的脑袋里面，大家只能看见一个大白眼球。

陌生人走到邓布利多身边。他伸出一只手，那只手也像他的脸一样伤痕累累。邓布利多和他握了握手，小声说了几句什么，哈利没有听清。他好像在向陌生人询问什么事情，陌生人面无笑容地摇摇头，压低声音做了回答。邓布利多点点头，示意那人坐在他右边的一个空座位上。

陌生人坐下了，晃了晃脑袋，把灰白色的长发从脸上晃开，然后拉过一盘香肠，举到残缺不全的鼻子跟前闻了闻。他从自己的口袋里掏出一把小刀，从一根香肠的一端戳进去，吃了起来。他那只正常的眼睛盯着香肠，但那只蓝眼睛仍然一刻不停地在眼窝里转来转去，打量着礼堂和同学们。

"请允许我介绍一下我们新来的黑魔法防御术课老师，"邓布利多愉快地打破沉默，"穆迪教授。"

## CHAPTER TWELVE  The Triwizard Tournament

It was usual for new staff members to be greeted with applause, but none of the staff or students clapped except Dumbledore and Hagrid. Both put their hands together and applauded, but the sound echoed dismally into the silence, and they stopped fairly quickly. Everyone else seemed too transfixed by Moody's bizarre appearance to do more than stare at him.

'Moody?' Harry muttered to Ron. '*Mad-Eye Moody*? The one your dad went to help this morning?'

'Must be,' said Ron, in a low, awed voice.

'What happened to him?' Hermione whispered. 'What happened to his *face?*'

'Dunno,' Ron whispered back, watching Moody with fascination.

Moody seemed totally indifferent to his less-than-warm welcome. Ignoring the jug of pumpkin juice in front of him, he reached again into his travelling cloak, pulled out a hip-flask, and took a long draught from it. as he lifted his arm to drink, his cloak was pulled a few inches from the ground, and Harry saw, below the table, several inches of carved wooden leg, ending in a clawed foot.

Dumbledore cleared his throat again.

'As I was saying,' he said, smiling at the sea of students before him, all of whom were still gazing transfixed at Mad-Eye Moody, 'we are to have the honour of hosting a very exciting event over the coming months, an event which has not been held for over a century. It is my very great pleasure to inform you that the Triwizard Tournament will be taking place at Hogwarts this year.'

'You're JOKING!' said Fred Weasley loudly.

The tension that had filled the Hall ever since Moody's arrival suddenly broke.

Nearly everyone laughed, and Dumbledore chuckled appreciatively.

'I am *not* joking, Mr Weasley,' he said, 'though, now you mention it, I did hear an excellent one over the summer about a troll, a hag and a leprechaun who all go into a bar –'

Professor McGonagall cleared her throat loudly.

'Er – but maybe this is not the time ... no ...' said Dumbledore. 'Where was I? Ah yes, the Triwizard Tournament ... well, some of you will not know what this Tournament involves, so I hope those who *do* know will forgive me for giving a short explanation, and allow their attention to wander freely.

## 第12章 三强争霸赛

一般情况下，新老师与大家见面，大家都会鼓掌欢迎，可是现在除了邓布利多和海格，没有一个教师或学生鼓掌。邓布利多和海格拍了几下巴掌，发现掌声在寂静的礼堂里显得孤零零的，便很快地放下了手。其他人似乎都被穆迪古怪的相貌惊呆了，只管目不转睛地盯着他。

"穆迪？"哈利低声对罗恩说，"疯眼汉穆迪？就是你爸爸今天早晨去帮助的那个人？"

"肯定是他。"罗恩畏惧地低声说道。

"他怎么了？"赫敏压低声音问，"他的脸是怎么回事？"

"不知道。"罗恩小声回答，着了迷似的望着穆迪。

穆迪似乎对大家的冷淡反应无动于衷。他没有理睬面前的那一大罐南瓜汁，而是把手伸进了自己的旅行斗篷，掏出一只弧形酒瓶，喝了一大口。当他抬起手臂喝酒时，拖在地上的斗篷被拽起了几寸，哈利看见桌子底下露出几寸木雕的假腿，下面是一只爪形的脚。

邓布利多清了清喉咙。

"正如我刚才说的，"他笑眯眯地望着面前众多的学生，说道——学生们仍呆呆地盯着疯眼汉穆迪，"在接下来的几个月里，我们将十分荣幸地主办一项非常精彩的活动，这项活动已有一个多世纪没有举办了。我十分愉快地告诉大家，三强争霸赛今年将在霍格沃茨举行。"

"你在**开玩笑**吧！"弗雷德·韦斯莱大声说。

自从穆迪进门后就一直笼罩着礼堂的紧张气氛一下子被打破了。

几乎每个人都笑出了声，邓布利多也赞赏地轻轻笑了起来。

"我没有开玩笑，韦斯莱先生，"他说，"不过你既然提到开玩笑，我暑假时倒是听到一个很有趣的笑话，讲的是一个巨怪、一个女妖和一个小矮妖，他们进了同一家酒馆……"

麦格教授很响地清了清嗓子。

"噢——现在说这个大概不太合适……不太合适……"邓布利多说，"我刚才说到哪儿了？啊，对了，三强争霸赛……你们中间有些人还不知道这场争霸赛是怎么回事，所以我希望那些了解情况的人能原谅我在此稍微解释一下，我允许他们的思想开一会儿小差。

## CHAPTER TWELVE  The Triwizard Tournament

'The Triwizard Tournament was first established some seven hundred years ago, as a friendly competition between the three largest European schools of wizardry – Hogwarts, Beauxbatons and Durmstrang. A champion was selected to represent each school, and the three champions competed in three magical tasks. The schools took it in turns to host the Tournament once every five years, and it was generally agreed to be a most excellent way of establishing ties between young witches and wizards of different nationalities – until, that is, the death toll mounted so high that the Tournament was discontinued.'

'*Death toll?*' Hermione whispered, looking alarmed. But her anxiety did not seem to be shared by the majority of students in the Hall; many of them were whispering excitedly with each other, and Harry himself was far more interested in hearing more about the Tournament than in worrying about deaths that had happened hundreds of years ago.

'There have been several attempts over the centuries to reinstate the Tournament,' Dumbledore continued, 'none of which have been very successful. However, our own Departments of International Magical Co-operation and Magical Games and Sports have decided the time is ripe for another attempt. We have worked hard over the summer to ensure that, this time, no champion will find himself or herself in mortal danger.

'The Heads of Beauxbatons and Durmstrang will be arriving with their short-listed contenders in October, and the selection of the three champions will take place at Hallowe'en. An impartial judge will decide which students are most worthy to compete for the Triwizard Cup, the glory of their school, and a thousand Galleons personal prize money.'

'I'm going for it!' Fred Weasley hissed down the table, his face lit with enthusiasm at the prospect of such glory and riches. He was not the only person who seemed to be visualising themself as Hogwarts champion. At every house table, Harry could see people either gazing raptly at Dumbledore, or else whispering fervently to their neighbours. But then Dumbledore spoke again, and the Hall quietened once more.

'Eager though I know all of you will be to bring the Triwizard Cup to Hogwarts,' he said, 'the Heads of the participating schools, along with the Ministry of Magic, have agreed to impose an age restriction on contenders this year. Only students who are of age – that is to say, seventeen years or older – will be allowed to put forward their names for consideration. This' – Dumbledore raised his voice slightly, for several people had made noises of

## 第12章 三强争霸赛

"三强争霸赛创立于大约七百多年前,是欧洲三所最大的魔法学校之间的一种友谊竞争。这三所学校是:霍格沃茨、布斯巴顿和德姆斯特朗。每所学校选出一名勇士,然后三名勇士比试三种魔法项目。三强争霸赛每五年举行一次,三个学校轮流主办,大家一致认为,这是不同国家之间年轻巫师们建立友谊的绝好方式——可是后来,死亡人数实在太多,三强争霸赛就中断了。"

"死亡人数?"赫敏小声说,惊愕地四下张望。但是礼堂里的大多数学生都不像她这样紧张,许多人兴奋地交头接耳。哈利也急于想听到更多三强争霸赛的具体细节,对一百多年前死去的那些人不感兴趣。

"几个世纪以来,人们几次尝试恢复争霸赛,"邓布利多继续说道,"但没有一次成功。不过,我们魔法部的国际魔法合作司和魔法体育运动司认为,再做一次尝试的时机已经成熟。这个夏天我们做了许多工作,以确保每位勇士都不会遭遇生命危险。

"十月份,布斯巴顿和德姆斯特朗的校长将率领他们精心筛选的竞争者前来,挑选勇士的仪式将于万圣节前夕举行。一位公正的裁判员将决定哪些学生最有资格参加争夺三强杯,为自己的学校赢得荣誉,个人还能获得一千加隆的奖金。"

"我要参加!"弗雷德·韦斯莱在桌子那边压低声音说,想到有可能获得这样的荣誉和财富,他兴奋得满脸放光。看来,像他这样幻想成为霍格沃茨勇士的不止他一个。在每个学院的桌子前,哈利都能看见有人或者狂热地注视着邓布利多,或者激动地与邻座窃窃私语。可是邓布利多又说话了,礼堂里再次安静下来。

"我知道你们都渴望为霍格沃茨赢得三强争霸赛的奖杯,"他说,"但是,参赛学校和魔法部一致认为,要对今年的竞争者规定一个年龄界限。只有年满十七岁——也就是说,十七岁以上——的学生,才允许报名,以备考虑。我们觉得,"——邓布利多微微抬高了声音,因为有些人听了他的话后发出愤怒的抗议,韦斯莱孪生兄弟突然变得怒气冲冲——"这一措施是很有必要的,因为争霸赛的项目仍然很艰巨很危险,不管我们采取多少预防措施,六七年级以下的学生是根本不可能对付得了

## CHAPTER TWELVE  The Triwizard Tournament

outrage at these words, and the Weasley twins were suddenly looking furious – 'is a measure we feel is necessary, given that the Tournament tasks will still be difficult and dangerous, whatever precautions we take, and it is highly unlikely that students below sixth and seventh year will be able to cope with them. I will personally be ensuring that no underage student hoodwinks our impartial judge into making them Hogwarts champion.' His light-blue eyes twinkled as they flickered over Fred and George's mutinous faces. 'I therefore beg you not to waste your time submitting yourself if you are under seventeen.

'The delegations from Beauxbatons and Durmstrang will be arriving in October, and remaining with us for the greater part of this year. I know that you will all extend every courtesy to our foreign guests while they are with us, and will give your whole-hearted support to the Hogwarts champion when he or she is selected. And now, it is late, and I know how important it is to you all to be alert and rested as you enter your lessons tomorrow morning. Bedtime! Chop chop!'

Dumbledore sat down again and turned to talk to Mad-Eye Moody. There was a great scraping and banging as all the students got to their feet, and swarmed towards the double doors into the Entrance Hall.

'They can't do that!' said George Weasley, who had not joined the crowd moving towards the door, but was standing up and glaring at Dumbledore. 'We're seventeen in April, why can't we have a shot?'

'They're not stopping me entering,' said Fred stubbornly, also scowling at the top table. 'The champions'll get to do all sorts of stuff you'd never be allowed to do normally. And a thousand Galleons prize money!'

'Yeah,' said Ron, a faraway look on his face. 'Yeah, a thousand Galleons ...'

'Come on,' said Hermione, 'we'll be the only ones left here if you don't move.'

Harry, Ron, Hermione, Fred and George set off for the Entrance Hall, Fred and George debating the ways in which Dumbledore might stop those who were under seventeen entering the Tournament.

'Who's this impartial judge who's going to decide who the champions are?' said Harry.

'Dunno,' said Fred, 'but it's them we'll have to fool. I reckon a couple of drops of Ageing Potion might do it, George ...'

'Dumbledore knows you're not of age, though,' said Ron.

'Yeah, but he's not the one who decides who the champion is, is he?' said

## 第12章 三强争霸赛

的。我本人将保证没有一个不够年龄的学生能够蒙骗我们公正的裁判员，成为霍格沃茨的勇士。"他的目光掠过弗雷德和乔治叛逆的面孔时，一双蓝眼睛闪着意味深长的光，"因此，如果你不满十七岁，我请求你不要浪费时间提出申请。

"布斯巴顿和德姆斯特朗的代表团将于十月份到达，并和我们共同度过这一学年的大部分时光。我相信，这些外国贵宾在此逗留期间，你们都会表现得热情友好，而且，霍格沃茨的勇士一旦最后选定，你们都会全心全意地给予支持。好了，现在时间已经不早，让你们明天早晨精神抖擞、头脑清醒地走进课堂非常重要。去上床睡觉吧！赶快！"

邓布利多坐了下来，转脸跟疯眼汉穆迪谈话。礼堂里咔嚓咔嚓、乒乒乓乓响成一片，学生们纷纷站起来，拥向一道双开门，进入了门厅。

"他们不能这样做！"乔治·韦斯莱没有随着人流走向门口，而是站在那里气呼呼地瞪着邓布利多，说道，"我们明年四月就满十七岁了，凭什么不让我们试一试？"

"他们不能阻止我参加，"弗雷德偏头偏脑地说，也生气地瞪着主宾席，"当了勇士，就能做许多平常不让你做的事情，而且还有一千加隆的奖金呢！"

"是啊，"罗恩说，脸上露出恍惚的神情，"是啊，那可是一千加隆呢……"

"快走吧，"赫敏说，"要是再不走，这里可就只剩下我们几个人了。"

哈利、罗恩、赫敏、弗雷德和乔治开始朝门厅走去，一路上弗雷德和乔治还在不停地争论，邓布利多会采取什么办法阻止不满十七岁的学生参加争霸赛。

"评判谁是勇士的那个公正裁判员会是谁呢？"哈利问。

"不知道，"弗雷德说，"不过他就是我们要蒙骗的人。我认为一两滴增龄剂就管用，乔治……"

"可是邓布利多知道你们不够年龄。"罗恩说。

"是啊，不过谁当勇士并不由他决定，对吗？"弗雷德机灵地说，"在

## CHAPTER TWELVE  The Triwizard Tournament

Fred shrewdly. 'Sounds to me like once this judge knows who wants to enter, he'll choose the best from each school and never mind how old they are. Dumbledore's trying to stop us giving our names.'

'People have died, though!' said Hermione in a worried voice, as they walked through a door concealed behind a tapestry and started up another, narrower staircase.

'Yeah,' said Fred airily, 'but that was years ago, wasn't it? Anyway, where's the fun without a bit of risk? Hey, Ron, what if we find out how to get round Dumbledore? Fancy entering?'

'What d'you reckon?' Ron asked Harry. 'Be cool to enter, wouldn't it? But I s'pose they might want someone older … dunno if we've learnt enough …'

'I definitely haven't,' came Neville's gloomy voice from behind Fred and George. 'I expect my gran'd want me to try, though, she's always going on about how I should be upholding the family honour. I'll just have to – ooops …'

Neville's foot had sunk right through a step halfway up the staircase. There were many of these trick stairs at Hogwarts; it was second nature to most of the older students to jump this particular step, but Neville's memory was notoriously poor. Harry and Ron seized him under the armpits and pulled him out, while a suit of armour at the top of the stairs creaked and clanked, laughing wheezily.

'Shut it, you,' said Ron, banging down its visor as they passed.

They made their way up to the entrance to Gryffindor Tower, which was concealed behind a large portrait of a fat lady in a pink silk dress.

'Password?' she said, as they approached.

'Balderdash,' said George, 'a Prefect downstairs told me.'

The portrait swung forwards to reveal a hole in the wall, through which they all climbed. A crackling fire was warming the circular common room, which was full of squashy armchairs and tables. Hermione cast the merrily dancing flames a dark look, and Harry distinctly heard her mutter '*slave labour*', before bidding them goodnight, and disappearing through the doorway to the girls' dormitories.

Harry, Ron and Neville climbed up the last, spiral staircase until they reached their own dormitory, which was situated at the top of the Tower. Five four-poster beds with deep crimson hangings stood against the walls, each with its owner's trunk at the foot. Dean and Seamus were already

## 第12章 三强争霸赛

我听来,似乎这位裁判员只要知道谁想参加,就从每个学校挑出最优秀的,才不管他们多大年龄呢。邓布利多是想阻止我们报名。"

"可是死了好多人哪!"赫敏用很担忧的语气说。他们穿过一道隐藏在挂毯后面的门,顺着更狭窄的楼梯往上走。

"是啊,"弗雷德满不在乎地说,"但那是好多年以前的事,对吗?而且,如果没有一点冒险,又有什么乐趣呢?喂,罗恩,如果我们有办法骗过邓布利多,你想参加吗?"

"你是怎么想的?"罗恩问哈利,"要是能参加就太棒了,是不是?可是我猜他们大概想要年龄大一点的……不知道我们学的东西够不够……"

"我学的东西肯定不够。"弗雷德和乔治身后传来纳威闷闷不乐的声音,"不过我想我奶奶肯定要我参加的。她总是念叨我应该维护家族的荣誉。我只要——哎哟……"

纳威的脚陷进了楼梯中间的一个台阶。霍格沃茨有许多这样捉弄人的楼梯。对于大多数老生来说,跳过这种特殊台阶已经成为一种本能,可是纳威记性差是出了名的。哈利和罗恩架住他的胳膊把他拉了出来,楼梯顶上的一套盔甲发出吱吱嘎嘎、丁零当啷的声音,笑得喘不过气来。

"闭嘴吧,你。"罗恩说道,在他们路过盔甲时,他给了那家伙一拳。

他们来到上面格兰芬多塔楼的入口处,入口隐藏在一幅巨大的肖像后面,画上有一位穿粉红色丝裙的胖夫人。

"口令?"他们走近时,胖夫人问道。

"胡言乱语。"乔治说,"楼下一个级长告诉我的。"

肖像一下子向前弹开,露出墙上的一个大洞,他们都从这里爬了进去。圆形的公共休息室里摆满了桌子和软塌塌的扶手椅,炉火噼噼啪啪燃得正旺。赫敏用愁闷的目光扫了一眼欢快跳跃的火苗,哈利清楚地听见她嘀咕了一声"奴隶劳动",然后她就向他们告别,出门回女生宿舍去了。

哈利、罗恩和纳威爬上最后一道螺旋形楼梯,来到他们位于塔楼顶部的宿舍。五张四柱床贴墙立着,上面垂挂着深红色帷帐,每个人的箱子都已放在各自的床脚。迪安和西莫已经准备上床了。西莫把他

## CHAPTER TWELVE  The Triwizard Tournament

getting into bed; Seamus had pinned his Ireland rosette to his headboard, and Dean had tacked up a poster of Viktor Krum over his bedside table. His old poster of West Ham football team was pinned right next to it.

'Mental,' Ron sighed, shaking his head at the completely stationary soccer players.

Harry, Ron and Neville got into their pyjamas and into bed. Someone – a house-elf, no doubt – had placed warming pans between the sheets. It was extremely comfortable, lying there in bed and listening to the storm raging outside.

'I might go in for it, you know,' Ron said sleepily through the darkness, 'if Fred and George find out how to … the Tournament … you never know, do you?'

'S'pose not …' Harry rolled over in bed, a series of dazzling new pictures forming in his mind's eye … he had hoodwinked the impartial judge into believing he was seventeen … he had become Hogwarts champion … he was standing in the grounds, his arms raised in triumph in front of the whole school, all of whom were applauding and screaming … he had just won the Triwizard Tournament … Cho's face stood out particularly clearly in the blurred crowd, her face glowing with admiration …

Harry grinned into his pillow, exceptionally glad that Ron couldn't see what he could.

的爱尔兰徽章别在了床头板上，迪安则在他床头柜上方贴了一张威克多尔·克鲁姆的招贴画，原来那张西汉姆联足球队的海报紧挨在它旁边。

"神经。"罗恩叹了口气，冲着那些静止的足球队员摇了摇头。

哈利、罗恩和纳威换上睡衣，爬上床去。有人——肯定是一个家养小精灵——已经把暖床用的长柄炭炉放在了被褥中间。躺在床上，听着风暴在外面肆虐，真是太舒服了。

"你知道，我也许会参加呢，"罗恩在黑暗中昏昏欲睡地说，"如果弗雷德和乔治想出了办法……参加争霸赛……谁也说不准，对吧？"

"说不准……"哈利在床上翻了个身，脑海中浮现出许多灿烂的画面，都是以前从没出现过的……他蒙骗了公正的裁判员，使他相信自己已经十七岁……他成了霍格沃茨的勇士……他站在场地上喜悦地举起双手，面对全校师生，他们都在欢呼尖叫……他刚刚赢了三强争霸赛……秋·张的脸在模糊的人群中显得格外清晰，她脸上红扑扑的，满是钦佩和赞赏……

哈利把脸埋在枕头里笑了，他特别感到欣慰的是罗恩没有看见他看见的东西。

## CHAPTER THIRTEEN

# Mad-Eye Moody

The storm had blown itself out by the following morning, though the ceiling in the Great Hall was still gloomy; heavy clouds of pewter grey swirled overhead as Harry, Ron and Hermione examined their new timetables at breakfast. A few seats along, Fred, George and Lee Jordan were discussing magical methods of ageing themselves and bluffing their way into the Triwizard Tournament.

'Today's not bad ... outside all morning,' said Ron, who was running his finger down his timetable, 'Herbology with the Hufflepuffs and Care of Magical Creatures ... damn it, we're still with the Slytherins ...'

'Double Divination this afternoon,' Harry groaned, looking down. Divination was his least favourite subject, apart from Potions. Professor Trelawney kept predicting Harry's death, which he found extremely annoying.

'You should have given it up like me, shouldn't you?' said Hermione briskly, buttering herself some toast. 'Then you'd be doing something sensible like Arithmancy.'

'You're eating again, I notice,' said Ron, watching Hermione add liberal amounts of jam to her buttered toast.

'I've decided there are better ways of making a stand about elf rights,' said Hermione haughtily.

'Yeah ... and you were hungry,' said Ron, grinning.

There was a sudden rustling noise above them, and a hundred owls came soaring through the open windows, carrying the morning mail. Instinctively, Harry looked up, but there was no sign of white among the mass of brown and grey. The owls circled the tables, looking for the people to whom their letters and packages were addressed. A large tawny owl soared down to

# 第 13 章

# 疯眼汉穆迪

第二天早晨，风暴停息了，不过礼堂的天花板上仍然一片愁云惨雾。哈利、罗恩和赫敏一边吃早饭一边研究这学期的课程表，他们的头顶上空翻滚着大团大团青灰色的浓云。在同一张桌上，弗雷德、乔治和李·乔丹与他们隔着几个座位，正在讨论用什么神奇的法子使自己年龄变大，然后蒙混过关，参加三强争霸赛。

"今天倒不错……整个上午都在户外，"罗恩的手指滑过课程表，说道，"草药课，和赫奇帕奇的学生一起上，保护神奇动物课……倒霉，又和斯莱特林一起……"

"今天下午有两节占卜课。"哈利低着头，叹了口气。占卜课是除魔药课外他最不喜欢的科目。特里劳尼教授总是预言说哈利快要死了，这使他感到特别烦恼。

"你就应该像我一样放弃这门课，不是吗？"赫敏一边往她的面包片上涂黄油，一边轻快地说，"然后可以上一门更有学问的课，比如算术占卜。"

"我发现你又开始吃东西了。"罗恩看着赫敏又往面包片上涂抹大量的果酱，说道。

"我已经想明白了，可以用更好的办法表明对小精灵权益的立场。"赫敏高傲地说。

"是啊……而且你也饿坏了。"罗恩嬉皮笑脸地说。

就在这时，头顶上突然传来一阵瑟瑟的声音，一百只猫头鹰从敞开的窗口飞进来，给大家捎来了早上的邮件。哈利本能地抬起头，然而在一大堆棕色和灰色之间，看不见丝毫白色的影子。猫头鹰们在桌

## CHAPTER THIRTEEN    Mad-Eye Moody

Neville Longbottom and deposited a parcel in his lap – Neville almost always forgot to pack something. On the other side of the Hall Draco Malfoy's eagle owl had landed on his shoulder, carrying what looked like his usual supply of sweets and cakes from home. Trying to ignore the sinking feeling of disappointment in his stomach, Harry returned to his porridge. Was it possible that something had happened to Hedwig, and that Sirius hadn't even got his letter?

His preoccupation lasted all the way across the sodden vegetable path until they arrived in greenhouse three, but here he was distracted by Professor Sprout showing the class the ugliest plants Harry had ever seen. Indeed, they looked less like plants than thick black giant slugs, protruding vertically out of the soil. Each was squirming slightly, and had a number of large, shiny swellings upon it, which appeared to be full of liquid.

'Bubotubers,' Professor Sprout told them briskly. 'They need squeezing. You will collect the pus –'

'The *what*?' said Seamus Finnigan, sounding revolted.

'Pus, Finnigan, pus,' said Professor Sprout, 'and it's extremely valuable, so don't waste it. You will collect the pus, I say, in these bottles. Wear your dragon-hide gloves, it can do funny things to the skin when undiluted, Bubotuber pus.'

Squeezing the Bubotubers was disgusting, but oddly satisfying. As each swelling was popped, a large amount of thick yellowish green liquid burst forth, which smelled strongly of petrol. They caught it in the bottles as Professor Sprout had indicated, and by the end of the lesson had collected several pints.

'This'll keep Madam Pomfrey happy,' said Professor Sprout, stoppering the last bottle with a cork. 'An excellent remedy for the more stubborn forms of acne, Bubotuber pus. Should stop students resorting to desperate measures to rid themselves of pimples.'

'Like poor Eloise Midgen,' said Hannah Abbott, a Hufflepuff, in a hushed voice. 'She tried to curse hers off.'

'Silly girl,' said Professor Sprout, shaking her head. 'But Madam Pomfrey fixed her nose back on in the end.'

A booming bell echoed from the castle across the wet grounds, signalling

## 第13章 疯眼汉穆迪

子上方盘旋，寻找信件和包裹的接收人。一只黄褐色的大猫头鹰朝纳威·隆巴顿这边落下来，把一个包裹扔到他的膝盖上——纳威几乎每次收拾行李都丢三落四。在礼堂的另一边，德拉科·马尔福的雕枭降落在他肩膀上，看样子又从家里给他带来了糖果、蛋糕。哈利竭力摆脱内心沉甸甸的失望感，埋下头去继续喝粥。难道海德薇出了意外，小天狼星没有收到他的信？

哈利一直心事重重，当同学们走过潮湿的菜地，来到三号温室时，他还是愁眉不展。不过他终于回过神来了，因为斯普劳特教授给全班同学看一种植物，哈利还没见过这么丑陋的东西呢。实际上，它们不像植物，倒更像是黑黢黢、黏糊糊的大鼻涕虫，笔直地从土壤里冒出来。而且一个个都在微微蠕动，身上还有许多闪闪发亮的大鼓包，里面似乎都是液体。

"巴波块茎。"斯普劳特教授欢快地告诉大家，"需要用手去挤，你们要收集它的脓液——"

"什么？"西莫·斐尼甘用厌恶的口气问道。

"脓液，斐尼甘，脓液，"斯普劳特教授说，"它有极高的价值，千万不要浪费。听着，你们要把脓液收集到这些瓶子里。戴上你们的龙皮手套，未经稀释的巴波块茎脓液，会对皮肤造成不同寻常的伤害。"

挤块茎的过程令人恶心，却也使人产生一种奇怪的满足感。每当一个鼓包被挤破时，都会喷出一大股黏稠的黄绿色液体，并发出一种刺鼻的汽油味。他们按照斯普劳特教授的吩咐，把这些液体收集在瓶子里，到了快下课时，已经收集了好几瓶。

"这下庞弗雷女士该高兴了。"斯普劳特教授用塞子堵住最后一个瓶子，说道，"巴波块茎的脓液，是治疗顽固性粉刺的最好药物。这样就可以阻止学生用过激手段去除他们的青春痘了。"

"比如可怜的爱洛伊丝·米德根，"赫奇帕奇的学生汉娜·艾博压低声音说，"她想用咒语把青春痘去掉。"

"傻姑娘，"斯普劳特教授摇了摇头，说道，"不过庞弗雷女士最后替她把鼻子又安上去了。"

一阵低沉浑厚的钟声越过潮湿的场地，从城堡传来，下课了，同学

## CHAPTER THIRTEEN  Mad-Eye Moody

the end of the lesson, and the class separated; the Hufflepuffs climbing the stone steps for Transfiguration, and the Gryffindors heading in the other direction, down the sloping lawn towards Hagrid's small wooden cabin, which stood on the edge of the Forbidden Forest.

Hagrid was standing outside his hut, one hand on the collar of his enormous black boarhound, Fang. There were several open wooden crates on the ground at his feet, and Fang was whimpering and straining at his collar, apparently keen to investigate the contents more closely. As they drew nearer, an odd rattling noise reached their ears, punctuated by what sounded like minor explosions.

'Mornin'!' Hagrid said, grinning at Harry, Ron and Hermione. 'Be'er wait fer the Slytherins, they won' want ter miss this – Blast-Ended Skrewts!'

'Come again?' said Ron.

Hagrid pointed down into the crates.

'Eurgh!' squealed Lavender Brown, jumping backwards.

'Eurgh' just about summed up the Blast-Ended Skrewts, in Harry's opinion. They looked like deformed, shell-less lobsters, horribly pale and slimy-looking, with legs sticking out in very odd places and no visible heads. There were about a hundred of them in each crate, each about six inches long, crawling over each other, bumping blindly into the sides of the boxes. They were giving off a very powerful smell of rotting fish. Every now and then, sparks would fly out of the end of a Skrewt and, with a small *phut*, it would be propelled forwards several inches.

'On'y jus' hatched,' said Hagrid proudly, 'so yeh'll be able ter raise 'em yerselves! Thought we'd make a bit of a project of it!'

'And why would we *want* to raise them?' said a cold voice.

The Slytherins had arrived. The speaker was Draco Malfoy. Crabbe and Goyle were chuckling appreciatively at his words.

Hagrid looked stumped at the question.

'I mean, what do they *do*?' asked Malfoy. 'What is the *point* of them?'

Hagrid opened his mouth, apparently thinking hard; there was a few seconds' pause, then he said roughly, 'Tha's next lesson, Malfoy. Yer jus' feedin' 'em today. Now, yeh'll wan' ter try 'em on a few diff'rent things – I've never had 'em before, not sure what they'll go fer – I got ant eggs an' frog livers an' a bit o' grass-snake – just try 'em out with a bit of each.'

## 第13章 疯眼汉穆迪

们纷纷散去。赫奇帕奇的学生走上石阶，去上变形课。格兰芬多的学生去往另一个方向，顺着缓缓下坡的草坪，走向禁林边缘的海格的小木屋。

海格站在小屋门外，一只手牵着他那条巨大的猎狗牙牙的颈圈。他脚边的地上，放着几只敞开的木箱，牙牙呜呜叫着，使劲地挣着颈圈，似乎想仔细调查一下箱子里的东西。他们走近时，一种很奇怪的咔啦咔啦声传入耳中，间或还有微弱的爆炸声。

"上午好！"海格说，朝哈利、罗恩和赫敏露出了微笑，"最好等一等斯莱特林的同学们，他们肯定不想错过这个——炸尾螺！"

"再说一遍？"罗恩说。

海格指了指脚边的箱子。

"恶心！"拉文德·布朗尖叫一声，向后跳了几步。

"恶心"一词正好也概括了哈利对这种炸尾螺的印象。它们活像是变了形、去了壳的大龙虾，白灰灰黏糊糊的，模样非常可怕，许多只脚横七竖八地伸出来，看不见脑袋在哪里。每只箱子里大约有一百条，每条都有六英寸左右，互相叠在一起爬来爬去，昏头昏脑地撞在箱子壁上。它们还发出一股非常强烈的臭鱼烂虾的气味。时不时地，一条炸尾螺的尾部会射出一些火花，然后随着啪的一声轻响，炸尾螺就会向前推进几英寸。

"刚刚孵出来的，"海格骄傲地说，"你们可以亲自把它们养大！我们可以搞一个课题什么的！"

"我们为什么要把它们养大？"一个冷冰冰的声音说。

斯莱特林的学生来了，刚才说话的是德拉科·马尔福。克拉布和高尔哧哧地笑着，对他的话表示赞赏。

海格似乎被这个问题难住了。

"我的意思是，它们能做什么？"马尔福问，"它们有什么用？"

海格张着嘴巴，似乎在拼命思索。停了几秒钟后，他粗声粗气地说："那是下一节课的内容，马尔福。你们今天只管喂它们。好了，要试着喂它们吃几种不同的东西——我以前没有养过炸尾螺，也拿不准它们喜欢吃什么——我准备了蚂蚁蛋、青蛙肝和翠青蛇——每样都拿一点试试，看它们吃不吃。"

## CHAPTER THIRTEEN  Mad-Eye Moody

'First pus and now this,' muttered Seamus.

Nothing but deep affection for Hagrid could have made Harry, Ron and Hermione pick up squelchy handfuls of frog liver and lower them into the crates to tempt the Blast-Ended Skrewts. Harry couldn't suppress the suspicion that the whole thing was entirely pointless, because the Skrewts didn't seem to have mouths.

'*Ouch!*' yelled Dean Thomas, after about ten minutes. 'It got me!'

Hagrid hurried over to him, looking anxious.

'Its end exploded!' said Dean angrily, showing Hagrid a burn on his hand.

'Ah, yeah, that can happen when they blast off,' said Hagrid, nodding.

'Eurgh!' said Lavender Brown again. 'Eurgh, Hagrid, what's that pointy thing on it?'

'Ah, some of 'em have got stings,' said Hagrid enthusiastically (Lavender quickly withdrew her hand from the box). 'I reckon they're the males ... the females've got sorta sucker things on their bellies ... I think they might be ter suck blood.'

'Well, I can certainly see why we're trying to keep them alive,' said Malfoy sarcastically. 'Who wouldn't want pets that can burn, sting and bite all at once?'

'Just because they're not very pretty, it doesn't mean they're not useful,' Hermione snapped. 'Dragon blood's amazingly magical, but you wouldn't want a dragon for a pet, would you?'

Harry and Ron grinned at Hagrid, who gave them a furtive smile from behind his bushy beard. Hagrid would have liked nothing better than a pet dragon, as Harry, Ron and Hermione knew only too well – he had owned one for a brief period during their first year, a vicious Norwegian Ridgeback by the name of Norbert. Hagrid simply loved monstrous creatures – the more lethal, the better.

'Well, at least the Skrewts are small,' said Ron, as they made their way back up to the castle for lunch an hour later.

'They are *now*,' said Hermione in an exasperated voice, 'but once Hagrid's found out what they eat, I expect they'll be six feet long.'

'Well, that won't matter if they turn out to cure sea sickness or something, will it?' said Ron, grinning slyly at her.

'You know perfectly well I only said that to shut Malfoy up,' said

## 第13章 疯眼汉穆迪

"先是块茎的脓液,现在又是这个。"西莫嘟哝道。

哈利、罗恩和赫敏完全是出于对海格的深厚感情,才抓起一把把滑腻腻的青蛙肝,放到箱子里去引诱炸尾螺。哈利不禁怀疑整个这件事都毫无意义,因为炸尾螺似乎根本没有嘴巴。

"哎哟!"大约十分钟后,迪安·托马斯惨叫一声,"它弄疼我了!"

海格赶紧走到迪安身边,神色有些慌张。

"它的尾巴爆炸了!"迪安气呼呼地说,给海格看他手上被烧伤的一块。

"啊,是啊,它们炸响时就可能发生这样的事。"海格点着头说道。

"恶心!"拉文德·布朗又抱怨开了,"真恶心,海格,它身上尖尖的东西是什么?"

"啊,它们有的身上有刺,"海格兴奋地说(拉文德赶紧把手从箱子边缩了回去),"我猜想那些带刺的是公的……母的肚子上有吸盘一样的东西……我认为它们大概会吸血。"

"噢,我当然明白为什么要想办法让它们活着了,"马尔福讽刺地说,"又能烧人,又能蜇人,还能咬人,这样的宠物谁不想要呢?"

"它们的模样不太中看,并不意味着没有用处。"赫敏反驳道,"火龙血具有神奇的功效,可是你愿意养一条火龙作为宠物吗,啊?"

哈利和罗恩朝海格咧嘴笑了,海格也从毛蓬蓬的胡子后面偷偷朝他们笑了笑。海格最大的愿望就是养一条宠物火龙,这一点哈利、罗恩和赫敏太了解了——他们上一年级的时候,海格养过一条火龙,但只养了很短一段时间,那是一条名叫诺伯的凶狠的挪威脊背龙。海格专门喜欢庞大凶狠的动物,越危险越好。

"还好,至少这些炸尾螺还很小。"一小时后,他们返回城堡吃午饭时,罗恩说道。

"它们现在很小,"赫敏用一种恼怒的声音说,"可是一旦海格弄清它们爱吃什么,我猜它们一下子就会变成六英尺长。"

"可是,如果最后发现它们能治疗晕船什么的,就没有关系了,对吧?"罗恩说,一边俏皮地朝赫敏笑着。

"你心里很清楚,我刚才那么说只是为了堵住马尔福的嘴。"赫敏说,

## CHAPTER THIRTEEN  Mad-Eye Moody

Hermione. 'As a matter of fact I think he's right. The best thing to do would be to stamp on the lot of them before they start attacking us all.'

They sat down at the Gryffindor table and helped themselves to lamb chops and potatoes. Hermione began to eat so fast that Harry and Ron stared at her.

'Er – is this the new stand on elf rights?' said Ron. 'You're going to make yourself puke instead?'

'No,' said Hermione, with as much dignity as she could muster with her mouth bulging with sprouts. 'I just want to get to the library.'

'*What?*' said Ron in disbelief. 'Hermione – it's the first day back! We haven't even got homework yet!'

Hermione shrugged and continued to shovel down her food as though she had not eaten for days. Then she leapt to her feet, said, 'See you at dinner!' and departed at high speed.

When the bell rang to signal the start of afternoon lessons, Harry and Ron set off for North Tower where, at the top of a tightly spiralling staircase, a silver stepladder led to a circular trapdoor in the ceiling, and the room where Professor Trelawney lived.

The familiar sweet perfume emanating from the fire met their nostrils as they emerged at the top of the stepladder. As ever, the curtains were all closed; the circular room was bathed in a dim reddish light cast by the many lamps, which were all draped with scarves and shawls. Harry and Ron walked through the mass of occupied chintz chairs and pouffes that cluttered the room, and sat down at the same small circular table.

'Good day,' said the misty voice of Professor Trelawney right behind Harry, making him jump.

A very thin woman with enormous glasses that made her eyes appear far too large for her face, Professor Trelawney was peering down at Harry with the tragic expression she always wore whenever she saw him. The usual large amount of beads, chains and bangles glittered upon her person in the firelight.

'You are preoccupied, my dear,' she said mournfully to Harry. 'My Inner Eye sees past your brave face to the troubled soul within. And I regret to say that your worries are not baseless. I see difficult times ahead for you, alas ... most difficult ... I fear the thing you dread will indeed come to pass ... and perhaps sooner than you think ...'

## 第13章 疯眼汉穆迪

"实际上，我认为马尔福说得对。最明智的做法就是在炸尾螺向我们发起进攻前，就把它们扼杀在摇篮里。"

他们在格兰芬多的餐桌旁坐下，吃起了羊排和土豆。赫敏狼吞虎咽，吃得飞快，哈利和罗恩惊奇地望着她。

"噢——这就是你对小精灵权益的新立场？"罗恩问，"你想把自己撑得呕吐吗？"

"不是，"赫敏说，嘴里鼓鼓囊囊地塞满了豆芽，但还是尽量端起架子，高傲地说，"我只是想去图书馆。"

"什么？"罗恩不敢相信地说，"赫敏——这是开学的第一天啊！还没有布置家庭作业呢！"

赫敏耸了耸肩膀，继续风卷残云地吃着，就好像已经好几天没吃东西似的。然后，她一跃而起，说了一句"晚饭见！"就撒腿跑走了。

下午上课的铃响了，哈利和罗恩向北塔楼走去，就在一道很窄的螺旋形楼梯的顶部，有一架银色的活梯通向天花板上的一扇活板门，那就是特里劳尼教授住的地方。

他们来到活梯顶上，一股从火上发出的熟悉的甜香气味扑鼻而来。这里的一切都和以前一样，窗帘拉得严严实实，圆形的房间里点了许多盏灯，灯上都遮着围巾和披巾，整个房间笼罩在一种朦朦胧胧的红光中。哈利和罗恩穿过房间里乱糟糟的一大堆印花布座椅和蒲团，在原来的那张小圆桌旁坐了下来。

"你们好。"哈利身后突然传来特里劳尼教授虚无缥缈的、空灵的声音，把他吓了一跳。

特里劳尼教授是一个很瘦的女人，戴着一副巨大的眼镜，使两只眼睛在她的那张瘦脸上大得吓人。此刻她正低头盯着哈利，脸上带着悲哀的表情——她每次看见哈利都是这种表情。她身上的一串串念珠、项链、手镯和往常一样在火光下闪闪发亮。

"你有心事，我亲爱的，"她悲戚戚地对哈利说，"我的天目穿透你勇敢的脸，看到了你内心烦躁不安的灵魂。我很遗憾地告诉你，你的担心不是毫无根据的。我看到你前面的日子充满艰辛……非常艰难……我担心你害怕的东西真的会到来……也许比你想象的还要快……"

## CHAPTER THIRTEEN  Mad-Eye Moody

Her voice dropped almost to a whisper. Ron rolled his eyes at Harry, who looked stonily back. Professor Trelawney swept past them and seated herself in a large winged armchair before the fire, facing the class. Lavender Brown and Parvati Patil, who deeply admired Professor Trelawney, were sitting on pouffes very close to her.

'My dears, it is time for us to consider the stars,' she said. 'The movements of the planets and the mysterious portents they reveal only to those who understand the steps of the celestial dance. Human destiny may be deciphered by the planetary rays, which intermingle …'

But Harry's thoughts had drifted. The perfumed fire always made him feel sleepy and dull-witted, and Professor Trelawney's rambling talks on fortune-telling never held him exactly spellbound – though he couldn't help thinking about what she had just said to him. '*I fear the thing you dread will indeed come to pass …*'

But Hermione was right, Harry thought irritably, Professor Trelawney really was an old fraud. He wasn't dreading anything at the moment at all … well, unless you counted his fears that Sirius had been caught … but what did Professor Trelawney know? He had long since come to the conclusion that her brand of fortune-telling was really no more than lucky guesswork and a spooky manner.

Except, of course, for that time at the end of last term, when she had made the prediction about Voldemort rising again … and Dumbledore himself had said that he thought that trance had been genuine, when Harry had described it to him …

'*Harry!*' Ron muttered.

'What?'

Harry looked around; the whole class was staring at him. He sat up straight; he had been almost dozing off, lost in the heat and his thoughts.

'I was saying, my dear, that you were clearly born under the baleful influence of Saturn,' said Professor Trelawney, a faint note of resentment in her voice at the fact that he had obviously not been hanging on her words.

'Born under – what, sorry?' said Harry.

'Saturn, dear, the planet Saturn!' said Professor Trelawney, sounding definitely irritated that he wasn't riveted by this news. 'I was saying that Saturn was surely in a position of power in the heavens at the moment of

## 第13章 疯眼汉穆迪

她的声音渐渐低了下去，最后变得如同耳语一般。罗恩朝哈利翻了翻眼睛，哈利面无表情地望着他。特里劳尼教授轻飘飘地从他们身边掠过，坐在炉火前一把很大的高背扶手椅上，面对着全班同学。拉文德·布朗和帕瓦蒂·佩蒂尔特别崇拜特里劳尼教授，都坐在离她很近的蒲团上。

"亲爱的，我们应该来研究星星了。"特里劳尼教授说，"行星的运行及其所显示的神秘征兆，只有那些懂得天际舞蹈的舞步规则的人，才能参透其中奥秘。人类命运可以通过行星的辐射光来破译，这些光互相交融……"

然而哈利的思绪飘到了别处。发出香味的炉火总是使他感到昏昏欲睡，特里劳尼教授翻来覆去地念叨那些算命的话，从来没有真正把他吸引住——不过他忍不住想起她刚才对自己说的话："我担心你害怕的东西真的会到来……"

赫敏说得对，哈利烦躁地想，特里劳尼教授其实是一个老骗子。他眼下根本没有什么可害怕的……最多只是有些担心小天狼星被抓……可是特里劳尼教授能知道什么？哈利早就得出结论，她那一套算命的伎俩充其量只是侥幸的猜测和一些装神弄鬼的花招。

不过，上学期结束时倒有些例外。她预言说伏地魔还会卷土重来……当哈利向邓布利多描绘当时的情景时，就连邓布利多本人也说，他认为特里劳尼教授的那种催眠状态不是假装的……

"哈利！"罗恩低声说。

"怎么啦？"

哈利环顾四周，发现全班同学都在盯着他。他赶紧坐直身子。由于房间里太热，而且脑子在胡思乱想，他刚才差点儿睡着了。

"亲爱的，我刚才在说，你出生的时候，显然受到土星的不祥影响。"特里劳尼教授说，语气里带着淡淡的不满，因为哈利显然没有专心听她讲课。

"对不起，受到什么——？"哈利问。

"土星，亲爱的，土星！"特里劳尼教授说，看到哈利听了这个消息无动于衷，她的语气明显有些恼怒，"我刚才说，在你出生的那一刻，

## CHAPTER THIRTEEN   Mad-Eye Moody

your birth ... your dark hair ... your mean stature ... tragic losses so young in life ... I think I am right in saying, my dear, that you were born in mid-winter?'

'No,' said Harry, 'I was born in July.'

Ron hastily turned his laugh into a hacking cough.

Half an hour later, each of them had been given a complicated circular chart, and was attempting to fill in the position of the planets at their moment of birth. It was dull work, requiring much consultation of timetables and calculation of angles.

'I've got two Neptunes here,' said Harry after a while, frowning down at his piece of parchment, 'that can't be right, can it?'

'Aaaaah,' said Ron, imitating Professor Trelawney's mystical whisper, 'when two Neptunes appear in the sky, it is a sure sign that a midget in glasses is being born, Harry ...'

Seamus and Dean, who were working nearby, sniggered loudly, though not loudly enough to mask the excited squeals from Lavender Brown – 'Oh, Professor, look! I think I've got an unaspected planet! Oooh, which one's that, Professor?'

'It is Uranus, my dear,' said Professor Trelawney, peering down at the chart.

'Can I have a look at Uranus, too, Lavender?' said Ron.

Most unfortunately, Professor Trelawney heard him, and it was this, perhaps, which made her give them so much homework at the end of the class.

'A detailed analysis of the way the planetary movements in the coming month will affect you, with reference to your personal chart,' she snapped, sounding much more like Professor McGonagall than her usual airy-fairy self. 'I want it ready to hand in next Monday, and no excuses!'

'Miserable old bat,' said Ron bitterly, as they joined the crowds descending the staircases back to the Great Hall and dinner. 'That'll take all weekend, that will ...'

'Lots of homework?' said Hermione brightly, catching up with them. 'Professor Vector didn't give *us* any at all!'

'Well, bully for Professor Vector,' said Ron moodily.

They reached the Entrance Hall, which was packed with people queuing for dinner. They had just joined the end of the line, when a loud voice rang out behind them.

## 第13章 疯眼汉穆迪

土星肯定在天空中占统治地位……你的黑头发……你瘦削的体形……还有你在襁褓中就失去父母……我可以断言，亲爱的，你出生在冬天吧？"

"不是，"哈利说，"我的生日是在七月。"

罗恩忍不住要笑，但赶紧把笑声变成一阵干咳。

半小时后，特里劳尼教授发给每人一张复杂的圆形图表，要他们在上面填写自己出生时的行星位置。这项工作枯燥乏味，需要计算许多烦琐的时间和角度。

"我这里有两颗海王星，"过了一会儿，哈利看着他的那张羊皮纸，皱起了眉头，"这肯定不对，是吗？"

"啊呀，"罗恩模仿特里劳尼教授悄声细气、神秘兮兮的口吻说道，"当天空中出现两颗海王星时，肯定预示着有一个戴眼镜的小人儿要出生了，哈利……"

西莫和迪安在旁边画图，听了这话咯咯地大笑起来，不过他们的笑声还不足以盖过拉文德·布朗兴奋的尖叫——"哦，教授，快看！我想我有一颗没有相位的行星！哎呀，这是什么星，教授？"

"是天王星，亲爱的。"特里劳尼教授低头看着图表，说道。

"可以也让我看一眼天王星吗，拉文德？"罗恩说。

真是倒霉，特里劳尼教授听见了他的话，也许正因为这个，她在下课前给他们布置了那么多家庭作业。

"参照你们各自的图表，详细分析下个月将对你们产生影响的行星运行方式，"她严厉地说——声音不像平时那个空灵虚幻的她，倒更像麦格教授了，"下星期一必须交上来，不得以任何借口推托！"

"讨厌的老蝙蝠，"他们融入下楼的人流，回礼堂吃饭时，罗恩恨恨地说，"整个周末都要搭进去了，这……"

"一大堆家庭作业？"赫敏从后面赶上他们，兴高采烈地问，"维克多教授什么作业都没留！"

"唉，维克多教授太好了。"罗恩心情沉重地说。

他们来到门厅，里面挤满了排队等候吃饭的人。他们刚站到队尾，后面突然响起一个刺耳的声音。

# CHAPTER THIRTEEN    Mad-Eye Moody

'Weasley! Hey, Weasley!'

Harry, Ron and Hermione turned. Malfoy, Crabbe and Goyle were standing there, each looking thoroughly pleased about something.

'What?' said Ron shortly.

'Your dad's in the paper, Weasley!' said Malfoy, brandishing a copy of the *Daily Prophet*, and speaking very loudly, so that everyone in the packed Entrance Hall could hear. 'Listen to this!'

## FURTHER MISTAKES
## AT THE MINISTRY OF MAGIC

It seems as though the Ministry of Magic's troubles are not yet at an end, *writes Rita Skeeter, Special Correspondent.* Recently under fire for its poor crowd control at the Quidditch World Cup, and still unable to account for the disappearance of one of its witches, the Ministry was plunged into fresh embarrassment yesterday by the the antics of Arnold Weasley, of the Misuse of Muggle Artefacts Office.

Malfoy looked up.

'Imagine them not even getting his name right, Weasley, it's almost as though he's a complete nonentity, isn't it?' he crowed.

Everyone in the Entrance Hall was listening now. Malfoy straightened the paper with a flourish, and read on:

Arnold Weasley, who was charged with possession of a flying car two years ago, was yesterday involved with a tussle with several Muggle law-keepers ('policemen') over a number of highly aggressive dustbins. Mr Weasley appears to have rushed to the aid of 'Mad-Eye' Moody, the aged ex-Auror who retired from the Ministry when no longer able to tell the difference between a handshake and attempted murder. Unsurprisingly, Mr Weasly found, unpon arrival at Mr Moody's heavily guarded house, that Mr Moody had once again raised a false alarm. Mr Weasly was forced to modify several memories before he could escape from the policemen,

## 第13章 疯眼汉穆迪

"韦斯莱！喂，韦斯莱！"

哈利、罗恩和赫敏转身望去。马尔福、克拉布和高尔站在那里，好像都为什么事儿高兴得要命似的。

"干吗？"罗恩没好气地问。

"你爸爸上报纸了，韦斯莱！"马尔福说，他挥舞着一份《预言家日报》，说话声故意放得很响，使拥挤在门厅里的每个人都能听见，"听听这个吧！"

### 魔法部又出新乱子

看来魔法部的麻烦还没有完，本报特约记者丽塔·斯基特这样写道。最近，魔法部因在魁地奇世界杯赛中未能有效维持秩序，以及仍未能对其一位女巫师官员的失踪做出解释，一直受到人们的批评。昨天，由于禁止滥用麻瓜物品办公室的阿诺德·韦斯莱的怪异行为，又使魔法部陷入新的尴尬境地。

马尔福抬起头来。

"想想吧，韦斯莱，他们连你父亲的名字都没有写对。他简直就是个无足轻重的小人物，是吧？"他幸灾乐祸地大声说。

此时门厅里的每个人都在听他说话。马尔福像演戏一样竖起报纸，继续念道：

阿诺德·韦斯莱两年前被指控拥有一辆会飞的汽车，昨天又卷入一场与几位麻瓜执法者（"警察"）的争执，起因是为了一大批极具进攻性的垃圾箱。韦斯莱先生似乎是赶来援助疯眼汉穆迪的，此人是一名上了年纪的前傲罗。当疯眼汉穆迪再也不能区分普通握手和蓄意谋杀之间的差别时，就从魔法部退休了。果然，当韦斯莱先生赶到穆迪先生重兵把守的住宅时，发现穆迪先生又是虚惊一场，误发了一个假警报。韦斯莱先生不得不将几个警察的记忆做了修改，才得以从他们那里脱身。但当《预言家日报》记者问韦斯莱先生为何要使魔法部卷入这场毫无意义，而且可能十分

## CHAPTER THIRTEEN   Mad-Eye Moody

but refused to answer Daily Prophet questions about why he had involved the Ministry in such an undignified and potentially embarrassing scene.

'And there's a picture, Weasley!' said Malfoy, flipping the paper over and holding it up. 'A picture of your parents outside their house – if you can call it a house! Your mother could do with losing a bit of weight, couldn't she?'

Ron was shaking with fury. Everyone was staring at him.

'Get stuffed, Malfoy,' said Harry. 'C'mon, Ron ...'

'Oh yeah, you were staying with them this summer, weren't you, Potter?' sneered Malfoy. 'So tell me, is his mother really that porky, or is it just the picture?'

'You know *your* mother, Malfoy?' said Harry – both he and Hermione had grabbed the back of Ron's robes to stop him launching himself at Malfoy – 'That expression she's got, like she's got dung under her nose? Has she always looked like that, or was it just because you were with her?'

Malfoy's pale face went slightly pink. 'Don't you dare insult my mother, Potter.'

'Keep your fat mouth shut, then,' said Harry, turning away.

BANG!

Several people screamed – Harry felt something white hot graze the side of his face – he plunged his hand into his robes for his wand, but before he'd even touched it, he heard a second loud BANG, and a roar which echoed through the Entrance Hall.

'OH NO YOU DON'T, LADDIE!'

Harry spun around. Professor Moody was limping down the marble staircase. His wand was out and it was pointing right at a pure white ferret, which was shivering on the stone-flagged floor, exactly where Malfoy had been standing.

There was a terrified silence in the Entrance Hall. Nobody but Moody was moving a muscle. Moody turned to look at Harry – at least, his normal eye was looking at Harry; the other one was pointing into the back of his head.

'Did he get you?' Moody growled. His voice was low and gravelly.

'No,' said Harry, 'missed.'

'LEAVE IT!' Moody shouted.

## 第13章 疯眼汉穆迪

棘手的事件时，他拒绝回答。

"还有一张照片呢，韦斯莱！"马尔福说着，把报纸翻过来，高高举起，"一张你父母的照片，站在你们家房子门口——你居然管这也叫房子！你妈妈要是能减点儿肥，模样还算凑合，是吧？"

罗恩气得浑身发抖。门厅里的人都看着他。

"滚开，马尔福。"哈利说，"别生气，罗恩……"

"哦，对了，波特，你今年夏天跟他们住在一起的，是吧？"马尔福讥讽地说，"那么请你告诉我，他妈妈是不是真有这么胖，还是照片照得有些失真？"

"那么你妈妈呢，马尔福？"哈利说——他和赫敏都抓住罗恩的长袍后背，不让他朝马尔福扑去——"瞧她脸上的那副表情，就好像她鼻子底下有大粪似的！她总是那副表情吗，还是因为跟你在一起才那样？"

马尔福苍白的脸变得微微泛红。"你竟敢侮辱我妈妈，波特。"

"那就闭上你的肥嘴。"哈利说着，转过身去。

**砰！**

几个人失声尖叫——哈利感到有个白热的东西擦过他的脸颊——他赶紧伸手到长袍里去掏魔杖，可是没等他碰到魔杖，就又听见一声巨响。**砰！**接着一个吼声在门厅里回荡。

"**哦，不许这样，小子！**"

哈利猛地转过身，看见穆迪教授一瘸一拐地走下大理石楼梯。他手里拿着魔杖，直指一只浑身雪白的白鼬，白鼬在石板铺的地上瑟瑟发抖，那正是刚才马尔福站的地方。

门厅里一片可怕的寂静。除了穆迪，谁都不敢动弹。穆迪转脸看着哈利——至少，他那只正常的眼睛是看着哈利的，另一只眼睛则钻进了脑袋里。

"他伤着你了吗？"穆迪怒冲冲地问，声音低沉、沙哑。

"没有，"哈利说，"没有击中。"

"**别碰它！**"穆迪大喊一声。

## CHAPTER THIRTEEN  Mad-Eye Moody

'Leave – what?' Harry said, bewildered.

'Not you – him!' Moody growled, jerking his thumb over his shoulder at Crabbe, who had just frozen, about to pick up the white ferret. It seemed that Moody's rolling eye was magical and could see out of the back of his head.

Moody started to limp towards Crabbe, Goyle and the ferret, which gave a terrified squeak and took off, streaking towards the dungeons.

'I don't think so!' roared Moody, pointing his wand at the ferret again – it flew ten feet into the air, fell with a smack to the floor, and then bounced upwards once more.

'I don't like people who attack when their opponent's back's turned,' growled Moody, as the ferret bounced higher and higher, squealing in pain. 'Stinking, cowardly, scummy thing to do ...'

The ferret flew through the air, its legs and tail flailing helplessly.

'Never – do – that – again –' said Moody, speaking each word as the ferret hit the stone floor and bounced upwards again.

'Professor Moody!' said a shocked voice.

Professor McGonagall was coming down the marble staircase with her arms full of books.

'Hello, Professor McGonagall,' said Moody calmly, bouncing the ferret still higher.

'What – what are you doing?' said Professor McGonagall, her eyes following the bouncing ferret's progress through the air.

'Teaching,' said Moody.

'Teach– Moody, *is that a student?*' shrieked Professor McGonagall, the books spilling out of her arms.

'Yep,' said Moody.

'No!' cried Professor McGonagall, running down the stairs and pulling out her wand; a moment later, with a loud snapping noise, Draco Malfoy had reappeared, lying in a heap on the floor with his sleek blond hair all over his now brilliantly pink face. He got to his feet, wincing.

'Moody, we *never* use Transfiguration as a punishment!' said Professor McGonagall weakly. 'Surely Professor Dumbledore told you that?'

'He might've mentioned it, yeah,' said Moody, scratching his chin unconcernedly, 'but I thought a good sharp shock –'

## 第13章 疯眼汉穆迪

"别碰——什么？"哈利莫名其妙地问。

"不是说你——是说他！"穆迪又吼道，竖起拇指，指了指身后的克拉布，克拉布正要去抱起白鼬，但吓得呆在原地不敢动了。穆迪那只滴溜溜转来转去的眼睛仿佛具有魔力，能看到脑袋后面的东西。

穆迪开始一瘸一拐地朝克拉布、高尔和那只白鼬走去，白鼬惊恐地叫了一声，躲开了，朝地下教室的方向跑去。

"别以为你能跑！"穆迪大吼一声，又把魔杖指向白鼬——白鼬忽地升到十英尺高的半空，啪的一声摔在地上，随即又忽地升了上去。

"我最看不惯在背后攻击别人的人，"穆迪粗声粗气地说——这时白鼬越蹦越高，痛苦地尖叫着，"这种做法最肮脏、卑鄙，是胆小鬼的行为……"

白鼬蹿到半空，四条腿和尾巴无助地胡乱摆动。

"再也——不许——这样——做——"穆迪说，每次白鼬掉在石板地上又忽地蹦起来，他就迸出一个词。

"穆迪教授！"一个吃惊的声音说道。

麦格教授正从大理石楼梯上下来，怀里抱着一摞书。

"你好，麦格教授。"穆迪平静地说，一边使白鼬蹦得更高了。

"你——你在做什么？"麦格教授问道，目光跟着在半空蹦跳的白鼬移动。

"给他个教训。"穆迪说。

"教训——怎么，穆迪，难道那是个学生？"麦格教授惊叫道，怀里的书散落到了地上。

"没错。"穆迪说。

"天哪！"麦格教授叫了一声，匆匆走下楼梯，抽出自己的魔杖。片刻之后，随着噼啪一声巨响，德拉科·马尔福复原了。他缩成一团，躺在石板地上，滑溜溜的淡金色头发披散在此刻红得耀眼的脸上。过了一会儿，他才站了起来，一副哆哆嗦嗦的样子。

"穆迪，我们从不使用变形作为惩罚！"麦格教授有气无力地说，"邓布利多教授肯定告诉过你吧？"

"他大概提到过吧，"穆迪漫不经心地挠着下巴说，"可是我认为需要狠狠地吓唬一下——"

## CHAPTER THIRTEEN  Mad-Eye Moody

'We give detentions, Moody! Or speak to the offender's Head of house!'

'I'll do that, then,' said Moody, staring at Malfoy with great dislike.

Malfoy, whose pale eyes were still watering with pain and humiliation, looked malevolently up at Moody and muttered something in which the words 'my father' were distinguishable.

'Oh yeah?' said Moody quietly, limping forward a few steps, the dull *clunk* of his wooden leg echoing around the hall. 'Well, I know your father of old, boy ... you tell him Moody's keeping a close eye on his son ... you tell him that from me ... now, your Head of house'll be Snape, will it?'

'Yes,' said Malfoy resentfully.

'Another old friend,' growled Moody. 'I've been looking forward to a chat with old Snape ... come on, you ...' and he seized Malfoy's upper arm and marched him off towards the dungeons.

Professor McGonagall stared anxiously after them for a few moments, then waved her wand at her fallen books, causing them to soar up into the air and back into her arms.

'Don't talk to me,' Ron said quietly to Harry and Hermione, as they sat down at the Gryffindor table a few minutes later, surrounded by excited talk on all sides about what had just happened.

'Why not?' said Hermione in surprise.

'Because I want to fix that in my memory for ever,' said Ron, his eyes closed and an uplifted expression on his face. 'Draco Malfoy, the amazing bouncing ferret ...'

Harry and Hermione both laughed, and Hermione began doling beef casserole onto each of their plates.

'He could have really hurt Malfoy, though,' she said. 'It was good, really, that Professor McGonagall stopped it –'

'Hermione!' said Ron furiously, his eyes snapping open again. 'You're ruining the best moment of my life!'

Hermione made an impatient noise and began to eat at top speed again.

'Don't tell me you're going back to the library this evening?' said Harry, watching her.

'Got to,' said Hermione thickly. 'Loads to do.'

'But you told us Professor Vector –'

## 第13章 疯眼汉穆迪

"我们可以关禁闭，穆迪！或者报告当事人所在学院的院长。"

"我会那么做的。"穆迪十分厌恶地瞪着马尔福，说道。

马尔福浅色的眼睛里仍然汪着痛苦和耻辱的泪水，这时他恶毒地抬头望着穆迪，嘴里嘟哝着什么，其中几个词听得很清楚，是"我爸爸"。

"哦，是吗？"穆迪瘸着腿向前走了几步，那条木腿噔噔撞击地面的声音在门厅里回响，"没错，我以前就认识你爸爸，孩子……你告诉他，穆迪正在密切注意他的儿子……你就这样替我告诉他……好了，你们学院的院长是斯内普，是吗？"

"是。"马尔福怨恨地说。

"也是一个老朋友，"穆迪咆哮着说，"我一直盼着跟老伙计斯内普好好聊聊呢……走吧，小子……"说着，他一把抓住马尔福的手臂，拽着他朝地下教室走去。

麦格教授不安地望着他们的背影，好一会儿，她才用魔杖指着掉在地上的书，使它们都升到半空，重新回到她的怀里。

"不要跟我说话。"罗恩小声地对哈利和赫敏说。这已是几分钟后，他们坐在格兰芬多的桌子旁，周围的人都在兴奋地议论刚才发生的事。

"为什么？"赫敏惊奇地问。

"因为我想把这件事永远铭刻在我的记忆里，"罗恩说——他闭着眼睛，脸上是一种十分喜悦的表情，"德拉科·马尔福，那只不同寻常的跳啊跳的大白鼬……"

哈利和赫敏都笑了起来，然后赫敏开始把牛肉大杂烩分在每人的盘子里。

"不过，他真的可能会把马尔福弄伤的，"她说，"幸好麦格教授及时制止了这件事——"

"赫敏！"罗恩猛地睁开眼睛，气呼呼地说，"你在破坏我这辈子最快活的时光！"

赫敏不耐烦地嘟哝了一声，开始吃饭，还是以那种狼吞虎咽的速度。

"你今晚不会又去图书馆吧？"哈利望着她，问道。

"当然去啦，"赫敏嘴里塞着东西，含混不清地说，"一大堆活儿要干呢。"

"可是你对我们说，维克多教授——"

## CHAPTER THIRTEEN  Mad-Eye Moody

'It's not schoolwork,' she said. Within five minutes, she had cleared her plate and departed.

No sooner had she gone than her seat was taken by Fred Weasley. 'Moody!' he said. 'How cool is he?'

'Beyond cool,' said George, sitting down opposite Fred.

'Supercool,' said the twins' best friend, Lee Jordan, sliding into the seat beside George. 'We had him this afternoon,' he told Harry and Ron.

'What was it like?' said Harry eagerly.

Fred, George and Lee exchanged looks full of meaning.

'Never had a lesson like it,' said Fred.

'He *knows*, man,' said Lee.

'Knows what?' said Ron, leaning forwards.

'Knows what it's like to be out there *doing it*,' said George impressively.

'Doing what?' said Harry.

'Fighting the Dark Arts,' said Fred.

'He's seen it all,' said George.

''Mazing,' said Lee.

Ron dived into his bag for his timetable.

'We haven't got him 'til Thursday!' he said in a disappointed voice.

"不是学校的功课。"赫敏说。五分钟后,她就吃完了盘里的东西,匆匆离开了。

她刚走,她的座位就被弗雷德·韦斯莱占据了。"穆迪!"他说,"他真酷啊,是吗?"

"岂止是酷!"乔治说着,在弗雷德对面坐了下来。

"酷毙了!"双胞胎的朋友李·乔丹坐在了乔治旁边的座位上,"我们今天下午上了他的课。"他对哈利和罗恩说。

"怎么样?"哈利急切地问。

弗雷德、乔治和李意味深长地交换了一下目光。

"从没上过这样的课。"弗雷德说。

"他真懂啊,伙计。"李说。

"懂什么?"罗恩探着身子,问道。

"懂在外面做活是怎么回事。"乔治郑重其事地说。

"做什么活?"哈利问。

"打击黑魔法啊。"弗雷德说。

"他什么都见识过。"乔治说。

"太了不起了。"李说。

罗恩埋头在他的书包里翻找课程表。

"我们要到星期四才有他的课呢!"他用失望的口气说。

## CHAPTER FOURTEEN

# The Unforgivable Curses

The next two days passed without great incident, unless you counted Neville melting his sixth cauldron in Potions. Professor Snape, who seemed to have attained new levels of vindictiveness over the summer, gave Neville detention, and Neville returned from it in a state of nervous collapse, having been made to disembowel a barrelful of horned toads.

'You know why Snape's in such a foul mood, don't you?' said Ron to Harry, as they watched Hermione teaching Neville a Scouring Charm to remove the toad guts from under his fingernails.

'Yeah,' said Harry. 'Moody.'

It was common knowledge that Snape really wanted the Dark Arts job, and he had now failed to get it for the fourth year running. Snape had disliked all of their previous Dark Arts teachers, and shown it – but he seemed strangely wary of displaying overt animosity to Mad-Eye Moody. Indeed, whenever Harry saw the two of them together – at mealtimes, or when they passed in the corridors – he had the distinct impression that Snape was avoiding Moody's eye, whether magical or normal.

'I reckon Snape's a bit scared of him, you know,' Harry said thoughtfully.

'Imagine if Moody turned Snape into a horned toad,' said Ron, his eyes misting over, 'and bounced him all around his dungeon ...'

The Gryffindor fourth-years were looking forward to Moody's first lesson so much that they arrived early after lunch on Thursday and queued up outside his classroom before the bell had even rung.

The only person missing was Hermione, who turned up just in time for the lesson.

'Been in the –'

# 第 14 章

## 不可饶恕咒

**接**下来的两天平平淡淡,没出什么状况,除非算上纳威在魔药课上把坩埚烧化的事,这已经是他烧化的第六只坩埚了。斯内普教授的报复心理似乎在暑假里又创新高,他毫不客气地罚纳威关禁闭。纳威只好去给一大桶长角的癞蛤蟆开膛破肚,回来的时候,神经几乎要崩溃了。

"你知道斯内普的脾气为什么这样糟糕,是吧?"罗恩对哈利说,这时他们正看着赫敏教纳威念一种除垢咒,可以清除他指甲缝里的癞蛤蟆内脏。

"是啊,"哈利说,"是因为穆迪。"

大家都知道,斯内普特别想教黑魔法防御术这门课,可是连续四年都没能得到这份工作。对以前的几位黑魔法防御术课的老师,斯内普都心怀不满,而且把这种情绪写在了脸上——不过对于疯眼汉穆迪,他似乎格外小心,不让这种敌意表露出来。确实,每当哈利看见他们俩在一起——在吃饭时或在走廊上擦肩而过时——都明显感到斯内普在躲避穆迪的眼睛,不论是那只魔眼,还是那只正常的眼睛。

"我认为斯内普有点儿怕他。"哈利若有所思地说。

"想象一下吧,如果穆迪把斯内普变成一只长角的癞蛤蟆,"罗恩说——眼睛里蒙蒙眬眬,充满神往,"并指挥他在地下教室里跳来跳去……"

格兰芬多四年级的学生们都眼巴巴地盼着上穆迪的第一节课。星期四吃过午饭,上课铃还没有响,他们就早早地在穆迪的教室外面排队等候了。

唯一没来的是赫敏,她直到快上课了才赶来。

"我去了——"

## CHAPTER FOURTEEN  The Unforgivable Curses

'– library,' Harry finished her sentence for her. 'C'mon, quick, or we won't get decent seats.'

They hurried into three chairs right in front of the teacher's desk, took out their copies of *The Dark Forces: A Guide to Self-Protection*, and waited, unusually quiet. Soon they heard Moody's distinctive clunking footsteps coming down the corridor, and he entered the room, looking as strange and frightening as ever. They could just see his clawed, wooden foot protruding from underneath his robes.

'You can put those away,' he growled, stumping over to his desk and sitting down, 'those books. You won't need them.'

They returned the books to their bags, Ron looking excited.

Moody took out a register, shook his long mane of grizzled grey hair out of his twisted and scarred face and began to call out names, his normal eye moving steadily down the list while his magical eye swivelled around, fixing upon each student as he or she answered.

'Right then,' he said, when the last person had declared themselves present, 'I've had a letter from Professor Lupin about this class. Seems you've had a pretty thorough grounding in tackling Dark creatures – you've covered Boggarts, Red Caps, Hinkypunks, Grindylows, Kappas and werewolves, is that right?'

There was a general murmur of assent.

'But you're behind – very behind – on dealing with curses,' said Moody. 'So I'm here to bring you up to scratch on what wizards can do to each other. I've got one year to teach you how to deal with Dark –'

'What, aren't you staying?' Ron blurted out.

Moody's magical eye spun around to stare at Ron; Ron looked extremely apprehensive, but after a moment Moody smiled – the first time Harry had seen him do so. The effect was to make his heavily scarred face look more twisted and contorted than ever, but it was nevertheless a relief to know that he ever did anything as friendly as smile. Ron looked deeply relieved.

'You'll be Arthur Weasley's son, eh?' Moody said. 'Your father got me out of a very tight corner a few days ago ... yeah, I'm staying just the one year. Special favour to Dumbledore ... one year, and then back to my quiet retirement.'

He gave a harsh laugh, and then clapped his gnarled hands together.

'So – straight into it. Curses. They come in many strengths and forms.

## 第14章 不可饶恕咒

"图书馆。"哈利替她把话说完,"走吧,快点儿,不然就没有好位子了。"

他们急急忙忙地坐到讲台正前的三把椅子上,拿出各自的《黑魔法:自卫指南》等待着,气氛格外肃静。很快,就听见穆迪那很有特色的噔噔的脚步声顺着走廊过来了。他走进教室,样子和平常一样古怪吓人。他们正好可以看见他那只爪子状的木脚从长袍下露出来。

"把这些东西收起来,"他粗声粗气地说,一边拄着拐杖艰难地走到讲台边坐了下来,"这些课本。你们用不着。"

同学们把书收进书包,罗恩显得很兴奋。

穆迪拿出名册,晃了晃脑袋,把花白的长头发从扭曲的、伤痕累累的脸上甩开,开始点名。他那只正常的眼睛顺着名单往下移动,那只魔眼不停地转来转去,盯着每一位应答的学生。

"好了,"当最后一位同学应答结束后,他说,"我收到卢平教授的一封信,介绍了这门课的情况。看起来,对于如何对付黑魔法动物,你们已经掌握了不少基础知识——你们学会了对付博格特、红帽子、欣克庞克、格林迪洛、卡巴和狼人,对吗?"

同学们低声表示赞同。

"可是在如何对付咒语方面,你们学得还很不够——很不够,"穆迪说,"因此,我准备让你们领略一下巫师们之间的做法。我有一年的时间教你们如何对付黑魔——"

"什么,你不留下来吗?"罗恩脱口而出,问道。

穆迪的那只魔眼转了过来,盯住罗恩。罗恩看上去害怕极了,可是很快穆迪就笑了——这是哈利第一次看见穆迪露出笑容。他一笑,那布满伤疤的脸显得更扭曲更怪异了,不过知道他还能露出友好的微笑,总是令人欣慰的。罗恩仿佛大松了一口气。

"你是亚瑟·韦斯莱的儿子吧,嗯?"穆迪说,"几天前,你父亲帮我摆脱了一个很棘手的困境……是啊,我只教一年。帮邓布利多一个忙……只教一年,然后重新过我平静的退休生活。"

他哑着嗓子笑了,然后拍了拍粗糙的大手。

"好了——言归正传。咒语,它们有许多种形态,其魔力各不相同。

## CHAPTER FOURTEEN  The Unforgivable Curses

Now, according to the Ministry of Magic, I'm supposed to teach you counter-curses and leave it at that. I'm not supposed to show you what illegal Dark curses look like until you're in the sixth year. You're not supposed to be old enough to deal with it 'til then. But Professor Dumbledore's got a higher opinion of your nerves, he reckons you can cope, and I say, the sooner you know what you're up against, the better. How are you supposed to defend yourself against something you've never seen? A wizard who's about to put an illegal curse on you isn't going to tell you what he's about to do. He's not going to do it nice and polite to your face. You need to be prepared. You need to be alert and watchful. You need to put that away, Miss Brown, when I'm talking.'

Lavender jumped and blushed. She had been showing Parvati her completed horoscope under the desk. Apparently Moody's magical eye could see through solid wood, as well as out of the back of his head.

'So ... do any of you know which curses are most heavily punished by wizarding law?'

Several hands rose tentatively into the air, including Ron's and Hermione's. Moody pointed at Ron, though his magical eye was still fixed on Lavender.

'Er,' said Ron tentatively, 'my dad told me about one ... is it called the Imperius Curse, or something?'

'Ah, yes,' said Moody appreciatively. 'Your father *would* know that one. Gave the Ministry a lot of trouble at one time, the Imperius Curse.'

Moody got heavily to his mismatched feet, opened his desk drawer, and took out a glass jar. Three large, black spiders were scuttling around inside it. Harry felt Ron recoil slightly next to him – Ron hated spiders.

Moody reached into the jar, caught one of the spiders and held it in the palm of his hand so that they could all see it.

He then pointed his wand at it, and muttered, '*Imperio!*'

The spider leapt from Moody's hand on a fine thread of silk, and began to swing backwards and forwards as though on a trapeze. It stretched out its legs rigidly, then did a backflip, breaking the thread and landing on the desk, where it began to cartwheel in circles. Moody jerked his wand, and the spider rose onto two of its hind legs and went into what was unmistakeably a tap dance.

Everyone was laughing – everyone except Moody.

'Think it's funny, do you?' he growled. 'You'd like it, would you, if I did it

# 第14章 不可饶恕咒

现在，根据魔法部的规定，我应该教你们各种破解咒，仅此而已。照理来说，你们不到六年级，我不应该告诉你们非法的黑魔咒是什么样子，因为你们现在年纪还小，对付不了这套东西。可是邓布利多教授大大夸赞了一番你们的勇气，认为你们能够对付，而在我看来，你们越早了解要对付的东西越好。如果一样东西你从没见过，又怎么在它面前保护自己呢？某个巫师要给你念一个非法的咒语，他是不会把自己的打算告诉你的。他不会坦率、公道、礼貌地给你念咒。你必须做好准备，提高警惕。我说话的时候，你最好把那玩意儿拿开，布朗小姐。"

拉文德吓了一跳，脸涨得通红。刚才，她在桌子底下把画好的天宫算命图拿给帕瓦蒂看。显然，穆迪的那只魔眼不仅能穿透他自己的后脑勺，还能穿透坚硬的木头。

"那么……有谁知道，哪些咒语会受到巫师法最严厉的惩罚？"

几只手战战兢兢地举了起来，其中有罗恩的和赫敏的。穆迪指了指罗恩，不过他那只魔眼仍然盯着拉文德。

"呃，是这样，"罗恩没有把握地说，"我爸爸对我说过一个……名字叫夺魂咒什么的，是吗？"

"啊，是的，"穆迪赞赏地说，"你父亲肯定知道那个咒语。想当年，夺魂咒给魔法部惹了不少麻烦。"

穆迪艰难地支着假腿站起来，打开讲台的抽屉，拿出一个玻璃瓶。三只大黑蜘蛛在里面爬个不停。哈利感到罗恩在他身边微微缩了缩身子——罗恩最讨厌蜘蛛了。

穆迪把手伸进瓶子，抓起一只蜘蛛，放在摊开的手掌上，让大家都能看见。

然后他用魔杖指着蜘蛛，喃喃地念道："魂魄出窍！"

蜘蛛从穆迪手掌上跳开了，悬着一根细丝，开始前后荡来荡去，就像坐在高高的秋千上一样。它僵硬地伸直了腿，然后回身翻了个跟头，细丝被拉断了。它摔在桌上，开始绕着圈子翻跟头。穆迪一抖魔杖，它又支着两条后腿站起来，跳起了一种踢踏舞，没错，就是踢踏舞。

大家都笑了起来——只有穆迪没笑。

"你们觉得很好玩，是吗？"他粗着嗓子问，"如果我对你们来这

### CHAPTER FOURTEEN   The Unforgivable Curses

to you?'

The laughter died away almost instantly.

'Total control,' said Moody quietly, as the spider balled itself up and began to roll over and over. 'I could make it jump out of the window, drown itself, throw itself down one of your throats ...'

Ron gave an involuntary shudder.

'Years back, there were a lot of witches and wizards being controlled by the Imperius Curse,' said Moody, and Harry knew he was talking about the days in which Voldemort had been all-powerful. 'Some job for the Ministry, trying to sort out who was being forced to act, and who was acting of their own free will.

'The Imperius Curse can be fought, and I'll be teaching you how, but it takes real strength of character, and not everyone's got it. Better avoid being hit with it if you can. CONSTANT VIGILANCE!' he barked, and everyone jumped.

Moody picked up the somersaulting spider and threw it back into the jar. 'Anyone else know one? Another illegal curse?'

Hermione's hand flew into the air again and so, to Harry's slight surprise, did Neville's. The only class in which Neville usually volunteered information was Herbology, which was easily his best subject. Neville looked surprised at his own daring.

'Yes?' said Moody, his magical eye rolling right over to fix on Neville.

'There's one – the Cruciatus Curse,' said Neville, in a small but distinct voice.

Moody was looking very intently at Neville, this time with both eyes.

'Your name's Longbottom?' he said, his magical eye swooping down to check the register again.

Neville nodded nervously, but Moody made no further enquiries. Turning back to the class at large, he reached into the jar for the next spider and placed it upon the desktop, where it remained motionless, apparently too scared to move.

'The Cruciatus Curse,' said Moody. 'Needs to be a bit bigger for you to get the idea,' he said, pointing his wand at the spider. '*Engorgio!*'

The spider swelled. It was now larger than a tarantula. Abandoning all pretence, Ron pushed his chair backwards, as far away from Moody's desk as possible.

Moody raised his wand again, pointed it at the spider, and muttered: '*Crucio!*'

At once, the spider's legs bent in upon its body; it rolled over and began to

## 第14章 不可饶恕咒

么一下，你们会喜欢吗？"

笑声几乎立刻就消失了。

"完全受我控制，"穆迪轻声说——这时蜘蛛团起身子，开始不停地滚来滚去，"我可以让它从窗口跳出去，或把自己淹死，或跳进你们哪一位同学的喉咙……"

罗恩不由自主地抖了一下。

"多年以前，许多巫师都受到夺魂咒的控制，"穆迪说——哈利知道他说的是伏地魔势力最强大的那些日子，"真把魔法部忙坏了。他们要分清谁是被迫行事，谁是按自己的意愿行事。

"夺魂咒是可以抵御的，我会把方法教给你们，但是这需要很强的人格力量，不是每个人都能掌握的。你们最好尽量避免被它击中。**时刻保持警惕！**"他突然大吼起来，把大家都吓了一跳。

穆迪抓起翻跟头的蜘蛛，扔回玻璃瓶里。

"还有谁知道什么咒语吗？非法咒语？"

赫敏又把手高高地举了起来，而且纳威也举起了手，这使哈利感到有些吃惊。纳威只有在草药课上才主动发言，那是他最拿手的一门课。纳威似乎对自己的大胆举动也感到意外。

"说吧。"穆迪说，那只魔眼骨碌碌一转，盯住了纳威。

"有一个——钻心咒。"纳威声音很轻但很清晰地说。

穆迪非常专注地望着纳威，这次是两只眼睛同时望着。

"你是隆巴顿吧？"他说，那只魔眼垂下去查看名册。

纳威紧张地点了点头，不过穆迪并没有再问别的。他转身对着全班同学，从玻璃瓶里掏出第二只蜘蛛，放在讲台上。蜘蛛一动不动，看样子是吓坏了。

"钻心咒。"穆迪说，"需要放大一些，你们才能看清，"说着，他用魔杖一指蜘蛛，"速速变大！"

蜘蛛鼓胀起来。现在已经比狼蛛还大了。罗恩顾不得掩饰，把椅子往后挪了挪，尽量离穆迪的讲台远一些。

穆迪又举起魔杖，指着蜘蛛，轻轻地说："钻心剜骨！"

立刻，蜘蛛的腿全部缩了起来，紧贴在身上。它翻转着，同时身

## CHAPTER FOURTEEN   The Unforgivable Curses

twitch horribly, rocking from side to side. No sound came from it, but Harry was sure that if it could have given voice, it would have been screaming. Moody did not remove his wand, and the spider started to shudder and jerk more violently –

'Stop it!' Hermione said shrilly.

Harry looked around at her. She was looking, not at the spider, but at Neville, and Harry, following her gaze, saw that Neville's hands were clenched upon the desk in front of him, his knuckles white, his eyes wide and horrified.

Moody raised his wand. The spider's legs relaxed, but it continued to twitch.

'*Reducio*,' Moody muttered, and the spider shrank back to its proper size. He put it back into the jar.

'Pain,' said Moody softly. 'You don't need thumbscrews or knives to torture someone if you can perform the Cruciatus Curse ... that one was very popular once, too.

'Right ... anyone know any others?'

Harry looked around. From the looks on everyone's faces, he guessed they were all wondering what was going to happen to the last spider. Hermione's hand shook slightly as, for the third time, she raised it into the air.

'Yes?' said Moody, looking at her.

'*Avada Kedavra*,' Hermione whispered.

Several people looked uneasily around at her, including Ron.

'Ah,' said Moody, another slight smile twisting his lop-sided mouth. 'Yes, the last and worst. *Avada Kedavra* ... the killing curse.'

He put his hand into the glass jar, and almost as though it knew what was coming, the third spider scuttled frantically around the bottom of the jar, trying to evade Moody's fingers, but he trapped it, and placed it upon the desktop. It started to scuttle frantically across the wooden surface.

Moody raised his wand, and Harry felt a sudden thrill of foreboding.

'*Avada Kedavra!*' Moody roared.

There was a flash of blinding green light and a rushing sound, as though a vast, invisible something was soaring through the air – instantaneously the spider rolled over onto its back, unmarked, but unmistakeably dead. Several of the girls stifled cries; Ron had thrown himself backwards and almost toppled off his seat as the spider skidded towards him.

## 第14章 不可饶恕咒

体剧烈地抽搐起来,左右晃动。它没有发出声音,但是哈利相信,如果它有发音器官,此刻肯定在拼命尖叫。穆迪没有拿开魔杖,蜘蛛开始浑身发抖,抽动得更厉害了——

"停下!"赫敏尖声喊道。

哈利扭过头去看赫敏。赫敏没有看着蜘蛛,而是看着纳威。哈利顺着她的目光望去,只见纳威双手紧紧攥住面前的桌子,骨节都发白了,眼睛睁得大大的,里面满是恐惧。

穆迪举起魔杖,蜘蛛的腿松弛下来,但仍在抽搐。

"速速缩小。"穆迪喃喃地说。蜘蛛缩回到原来的大小,穆迪把它重新放进瓶里。

"极度痛苦。"穆迪轻声说,"如果你会念钻心咒,你折磨别人就不需要用拇指夹或刀子了……这个咒语一度也非常流行。

"好了……还有谁知道什么咒语吗?"

哈利环顾四周。从大家的面部表情看,似乎都在猜测最后一只蜘蛛会遭遇什么。赫敏第三次把手举起,但她的手微微有些颤抖。

"你说吧。"穆迪望着她,说道。

"阿瓦达索命咒。"赫敏小声说。

几个人不安地扭头看着她,其中包括罗恩。

"啊,"穆迪说——歪斜的嘴又抽动着,露出一丝微笑,"是的,这是最后一个,也是最厉害的一个咒语。阿瓦达索命咒……杀戮咒。"

他把手伸进玻璃瓶,第三只蜘蛛仿佛知道即将到来的厄运,拼命地绕着瓶底爬来爬去,想躲开穆迪的手指,但穆迪还是把它抓住了,放在讲台上。蜘蛛又开始不顾一切地在木头桌面上爬动。

穆迪举起魔杖,哈利突然产生了一种不祥的预感。

"阿瓦达索命!"穆迪吼道。

一道耀眼的绿光刺得人睁不开眼睛,同时伴有一阵杂乱的声音,仿佛一个看不见的庞然大物从空中飞过——与此同时,那蜘蛛翻了过来,仰面躺在桌上,身上并无半点伤痕,但无疑已经死了。几个学生使劲忍住想要发出的喊叫;刚才蜘蛛朝罗恩这边爬来时,罗恩猛地往后一仰,差点从座位上摔下去。

## CHAPTER FOURTEEN  The Unforgivable Curses

Moody swept the dead spider off the desk onto the floor.

'Not nice,' he said calmly. 'Not pleasant. And there's no counter-curse. There's no blocking it. Only one known person has ever survived it, and he's sitting right in front of me.'

Harry felt his face redden as Moody's eyes (both of them) looked into his own. He could feel everyone else looking around at him, too. Harry stared at the blank blackboard as though fascinated by it, but not really seeing it at all ...

So that was how his parents had died ... exactly like that spider. Had they been unblemished and unmarked, too? Had they simply seen the flash of green light and heard the rush of speeding death, before life was wiped from their bodies?

Harry had been picturing his parents' deaths over and over again for three years now, ever since he had found out they had been murdered, ever since he'd found out what had happened that night: how Wormtail had betrayed his parents' whereabouts to Voldemort, who had come to find them at their cottage. How Voldemort had killed Harry's father first. How James Potter had tried to hold him off, while he shouted at his wife to take Harry and run ... and Voldemort had advanced on Lily Potter, told her to move aside so that he could kill Harry ... how she had begged him to kill her instead, refused to stop shielding her son ... and so Voldemort had murdered her, too, before turning his wand on Harry ...

Harry knew these details because he had heard his parents' voices when he had fought the Dementors last year – for that was the terrible power of the Dementors: to force their victim to relive the worst memories of their life, and drown, powerless, in their own despair ...

Moody was speaking again, from a great distance, it seemed to Harry. With a massive effort, he pulled himself back to the present, and listened to what Moody was saying.

'Avada Kedavra's a curse that needs a powerful bit of magic behind it – you could all get your wands out now and point them at me and say the words, and I doubt I'd get so much as a nose-bleed. But that doesn't matter. I'm not here to teach you how to do it.

'Now, if there's no counter-curse, why am I showing you? *Because you've got to know.* You've got to appreciate what the worst is. You don't want to find yourself in a situation where you're facing it. CONSTANT VIGILANCE!'

## 第14章 不可饶恕咒

穆迪把死蜘蛛从桌上扫到地板上。

"很不美好,"他平静地说,"令人很不愉快。而且没有破解咒。无法抵御。据人们所知,只有一个人逃脱了这种咒语,他此刻就坐在我的面前。"

穆迪的眼睛(两只同时)注视着哈利的眼睛,哈利觉得自己的脸红了。他可以感觉到全班同学都扭过头来望着他。哈利盯着空无一物的黑板,似乎对黑板着了迷,实际上他什么也没有看见……

原来,他父母就是这样死去的……和那只蜘蛛一模一样。他们也是毫发无损,没有一点创伤吗?他们也是看见一道绿光一闪,听见死神匆匆赶来,然后生命就从他们的身体里消失了吗?

三年来,自从哈利得知父母是被人杀害的,自从他弄清那天夜里发生的事情:虫尾巴向伏地魔泄漏了他父母的下落,伏地魔在他父母的木屋里找到了他们。自从哈利明白了这一切,就不止一遍地想象父母死亡的情景。他想象伏地魔怎样先害死了他父亲。詹姆·波特怎样拼命抵挡,一边喊妻子带着哈利逃跑……伏地魔怎样朝莉莉·波特逼近,叫她闪到一旁,他要加害哈利……她怎样请求伏地魔杀死自己,不要碰她的儿子,她至死都在护着自己的儿子……于是,伏地魔把她也害死了,然后把魔杖指向了哈利……

哈利知道这些细节,因为他去年与摄魂怪搏斗时,曾经听见过父母的声音。摄魂怪具有那种可怕的魔力,能迫使别人想起一生中最痛苦的往事,陷入绝望的情绪中,瘫软无力,不能自拔……

穆迪又在说话了,哈利觉得他的声音来自一个很远很远的地方。哈利用了很大的努力,才使自己的注意力回到眼前的现实中,听穆迪说话。

"阿瓦达索命咒需要很强大的魔法力量作为基础——你们都可以把魔杖拿出来,对准我,念出这句咒语,我怀疑我最多只会流点鼻血。可是那没有关系。我来不是为了教你们用这个咒语的。

"那么,既然没有破解咒,我为什么要向你们展示这些呢?因为你们必须有所了解。你们必须充分意识到什么是最糟糕的。你们不希望发现自己遇到现在面对的情形吧。**时刻保持警惕!**"他吼道,又把全

## CHAPTER FOURTEEN    The Unforgivable Curses

he roared, and the whole class jumped again.

'Now ... those three curses – Avada Kedavra, Imperius and Cruciatus – are known as the Unforgivable Curses. The use of any one of them on a fellow human being is enough to earn a life sentence in Azkaban. That's what you're up against. That's what I've got to teach you to fight. You need preparing. You need arming. But most of all, you need to practise *constant, never-ceasing vigilance.* Get out your quills ... copy this down ...'

They spent the rest of the lesson taking notes on each of the Unforgivable Curses. No one spoke until the bell rang – but when Moody had dismissed them and they had left the classroom, a torrent of talk burst forth. Most people were discussing the curses in awed voices – 'Did you see it twitch?' '– and when he killed it – just like that!'

They were talking about the lesson, Harry thought, as though it had been some sort of spectacular show, but he hadn't found it very entertaining – and nor, it seemed, had Hermione.

'Hurry up,' she said tensely to Harry and Ron.

'Not the ruddy library again?' said Ron.

'No,' said Hermione curtly, pointing up a side passage. 'Neville.'

Neville was standing alone, halfway up the passage, staring at the stone wall opposite him with the same horrified, wide-eyed look he had worn when Moody had demonstrated the Cruciatus Curse.

'Neville?' Hermione said gently.

Neville looked around.

'Oh, hello,' he said, his voice much higher than usual. 'Interesting lesson, wasn't it? I wonder what's for dinner, I'm – I'm starving, aren't you?'

'Neville, are you all right?' said Hermione.

'Oh, yes, I'm fine,' Neville gabbled, in the same unnaturally high voice. 'Very interesting dinner – I mean lesson – what's for eating?'

Ron gave Harry a startled look.

'Neville, what –?'

But an odd clunking noise sounded behind them, and they turned to see Professor Moody limping towards them. All four of them fell silent, watching him apprehensively, but when he spoke, it was in a much lower and gentler growl than they had yet heard.

## 第14章 不可饶恕咒

班同学吓了一跳。

"好了……这三个咒语——阿瓦达索命咒、夺魂咒、钻心咒——都被称为不可饶恕咒。把其中任何一个咒语用在人类身上,都足够在阿兹卡班坐一辈子监牢。这就是你们要抵御的东西。这就是我要教你们抵御的东西。你们需要做好准备。你们需要有所戒备。不过最重要的,你们需要时刻保持警惕,永远不能松懈。拿出羽毛笔……把这些记下来……"

在这堂课剩下来的时间里,同学们都忙着做笔记,记录这三种不可饶恕咒。教室里静悄悄的,没有人说话,直到下课铃响起——可是当穆迪宣布下课,同学们刚一离开教室,各种议论顿时像决堤的洪水,汹涌而起。大多数同学都用敬畏的口气谈论着那些咒语——"你看见蜘蛛抽搐的样子了吗?""——他一下就把蜘蛛杀死了——就么简单!"

哈利心想,听他们谈论这堂课的口气,就好像观看了一场精彩的滑稽表演,而他觉得这并不怎么有趣——赫敏对此也有同感。

"快走。"赫敏紧张地对哈利和罗恩说。

"又去该死的图书馆?"罗恩说。

"不是,"赫敏简洁地说,指着旁边的一条走廊,"纳威。"

纳威独自站在走廊中间,盯着对面的石墙,还是那样睁大了眼睛,满脸惊恐,跟穆迪演示钻心咒时他的表情一样。

"纳威?"赫敏轻声地说。

纳威转过脸来。

"噢,你们好,"他说,声调比平常高得多,"这堂课真有趣,是吗?不知道晚饭有什么吃的。我——我饿坏了,你们呢?"

"纳威,你没事吧?"赫敏问。

"噢,没事,我很好。"纳威还是用那种高得不正常的声音急促地说,"多么有趣的晚饭——噢,我是说这节课——有什么吃的?"

罗恩惊讶地望了哈利一眼。

"纳威,你怎么——?"

就在这时,他们身后传来一阵噔噔噔的奇怪声音。他们转过身,看见穆迪教授一瘸一拐地朝这边走来。他们四个顿时都不作声了,有点害怕地望着他。可是当他开口说话时,声音尽管粗哑,却比他们以

## CHAPTER FOURTEEN  The Unforgivable Curses

'It's all right, sonny,' he said to Neville. 'Why don't you come up to my office? Come on ... we can have a cup of tea ...'

Neville looked even more frightened at the prospect of tea with Moody. He neither moved nor spoke.

Moody turned his magical eye upon Harry. 'You all right, are you, Potter?'

'Yes,' said Harry, almost defiantly.

Moody's blue eye quivered slightly in its socket as it surveyed Harry.

Then he said, 'You've got to know. It seems harsh, maybe, *but you've got to know*. No point pretending ... well ... come on, Longbottom, I've got some books that might interest you.'

Neville looked pleadingly at Harry, Ron and Hermione, but they didn't say anything, so Neville had no choice but to allow himself to be steered away, one of Moody's gnarled hands on his shoulder.

'What was that about?' said Ron, watching Neville and Moody turn the corner.

'I don't know,' said Hermione, looking pensive.

'Some lesson, though, eh?' said Ron to Harry, as they set off for the Great Hall. 'Fred and George were right, weren't they? He really knows his stuff, Moody, doesn't he? When he did Avada Kedavra, the way that spider just *died*, just snuffed it right –'

But Ron fell suddenly silent at the look on Harry's face, and didn't speak again until they reached the Great Hall, when he said he supposed they had better make a start on Professor Trelawney's predictions tonight, as they would take hours.

Hermione did not join in with Harry and Ron's conversation during dinner, but ate furiously fast, and then left for the library again. Harry and Ron walked back to Gryffindor Tower, and Harry, who had been thinking of nothing else all through dinner, now raised the subject of the Unforgivable Curses himself.

'Wouldn't Moody and Dumbledore be in trouble with the Ministry if they knew we'd seen the curses?' Harry asked, as they approached the Fat Lady.

'Yeah, probably,' said Ron. 'But Dumbledore's always done things his way, hasn't he, and Moody's been getting in trouble for years, I reckon. Attacks first and asks questions later – look at his dustbins. Balderdash.'

The Fat Lady swung forwards to reveal the entrance hole, and they

## 第14章 不可饶恕咒

前听到的低沉柔和多了。

"没关系，孩子，"他对纳威说，"你到我办公室来一趟好吗？来吧……我们可以一起喝一杯茶……"

纳威想到要和穆迪一起喝茶，似乎更害怕了。他没有动，也没有说话。

穆迪把他那只魔眼转向了哈利。"你没事吧，波特？"

"没事。"哈利回答，几乎带着点儿反抗的情绪。

穆迪的蓝眼睛打量着哈利，眼珠在眼窝里微微颤动。

然后他说："你们必须有所了解。也许看起来很残酷，可是你们必须有所了解。没必要掩饰……好了……走吧，隆巴顿，我那儿有几本书，你可能会感兴趣的。"

纳威哀求地望着哈利、罗恩和赫敏，但他们谁也没有说话。纳威别无选择，只好由着穆迪把一只粗糙的大手放在他肩膀上，领着他走开了。

"这是什么意思？"罗恩望着纳威和穆迪拐过墙角，问道。

"我不知道。"赫敏说，显得忧心忡忡。

"不过他教得确实不错，嗯？"他们朝礼堂走去时，罗恩问哈利，"弗雷德和乔治说得对，是吧？穆迪他确实很在行，是吧？他一念阿瓦达索命咒，那只蜘蛛就死了，就那样立刻断了气儿——"

罗恩一看见哈利脸上的表情，赶紧闭口不说了，而且一路上都没有吭声，直到进入礼堂他才说，他觉得他们最好今晚就开始做特里劳尼教授布置的预言作业，那要花好几个小时呢。

赫敏没有参加哈利和罗恩在饭桌上的谈话，她狼吞虎咽地吃得飞快，然后又上图书馆去了。哈利和罗恩走回格兰芬多塔楼，这时，哈利自己又挑起话头，谈起了不可饶恕咒——他刚才在饭桌上一直在想这件事。

"如果魔法部知道我们看见了念咒的情景，会不会找穆迪和邓布利多的麻烦？"他们走近胖夫人肖像时，哈利问道。

"啊，大概会吧，"罗恩说，"不过邓布利多做事就是这样的性格，是吧？而且穆迪许多年来都是麻烦不断。总是不分青红皂白，先动手再说——看看他那些垃圾箱吧。胡言乱语。"

胖夫人向前荡开，露出那个洞口。他们爬进了格兰芬多的公共休

## CHAPTER FOURTEEN  The Unforgivable Curses

climbed into Gryffindor common room, which was crowded and noisy.

'Shall we get our Divination stuff, then?' said Harry.

'I s'pose,' Ron groaned.

They went up to the dormitory to fetch their books and charts, and found Neville there alone, sitting on his bed, reading. He looked a good deal calmer than at the end of Moody's lesson, though still not entirely normal. His eyes were rather red.

'You all right, Neville?' Harry asked him.

'Oh yes,' said Neville, 'I'm fine, thanks. Just reading this book Professor Moody lent me ...'

He held up the book: *Magical Mediterranean Water-Plants and Their Properties.*

'Apparently, Professor Sprout told Professor Moody I'm really good at Herbology,' Neville said. There was a faint note of pride in his voice that Harry had rarely heard there before. 'He thought I'd like this.'

Telling Neville what Professor Sprout had said, Harry thought, had been a very tactful way of cheering Neville up, for Neville very rarely heard that he was good at anything. It was the sort of thing Professor Lupin would have done.

Harry and Ron took their copies of *Unfogging the Future* back down to the common room, found a table and set to work on their predictions for the coming month. An hour later, they had made very little progress, though their table was littered with bits of parchment bearing sums and symbols, and Harry's brain was as fogged as though it had been filled with the fumes from Professor Trelawney's fire.

'I haven't got a clue what this lot's supposed to mean,' he said, staring down at a long list of calculations.

'You know,' said Ron, whose hair was on end because of all the times he had run his fingers through it in frustration, 'I think it's back to the old Divination standby.'

'What – make it up?'

'Yeah,' said Ron, sweeping the jumble of scrawled notes off the table, dipping his pen into some ink and starting to write.

'Next Monday,' he said, as he scribbled, 'I am likely to develop a cough, owing to the unlucky conjunction of Mars and Jupiter.' He looked up at Harry. 'You know her – just put in loads of misery, she'll lap it up.'

## 第14章 不可饶恕咒

息室，里面挤满了人，声音嘈杂。

"我们去拿占卜课的东西，好吗？"哈利问。

"好吧。"罗恩没精打采地说。

他们到楼上的宿舍去拿课本和图表，却发现纳威独自待在屋里，坐在床上看书。他的样子比刚上完穆迪的课时平静多了，不过仍然没有完全恢复正常。他的眼睛红通通的。

"你没事吧，纳威？"哈利问他。

"噢，没事，"纳威回答，"我很好，谢谢你。我在看穆迪教授借给我的这本书……"

他举起手里的书：《地中海神奇水生植物及其特性》。

"看样子是斯普劳特教授告诉了穆迪教授，说我在草药学方面非常棒。"纳威说——声音里有一丝淡淡的骄傲，这是哈利以前很少听到的，"穆迪教授认为我会喜欢这本书。"

哈利心想，把斯普劳特教授的话告诉纳威，这是让纳威高兴起来的一种很聪明的办法，因为纳威很少听人夸奖他有什么长处。这种事情像是卢平教授才做得出来的。

哈利和罗恩拿着他们的《拨开迷雾看未来》回到公共休息室，找了一张桌子，开始预测自己下一个月的命运。一小时后，他们毫无进展，桌上胡乱扔着许多写满数字和符号的羊皮纸片。哈利脑子里仍然迷雾重重，好像被特里劳尼教授炉火里冒出的烟雾填满了。

"这玩意儿到底是什么意思，我一点头绪都没有。"他低头望着长长一排计算公式，说道。

"怎么样，"罗恩说——脑袋上的头发都竖了起来，因为他一直在苦恼地挠头，"我们还是采用占卜课的保留节目吧。"

"你是说——胡编乱造？"

"是啊。"罗恩说着，把桌上乱糟糟的一堆草稿纸扫到地上，让羽毛笔蘸满墨水，埋头写了起来。

"下星期一，"他一边潦草地写，一边说道，"我可能会咳嗽，因为火星和木星不幸相合。"他抬头望着哈利，"你了解她的——我们尽量编一些倒霉事儿，她就爱看这个。"

## CHAPTER FOURTEEN   The Unforgivable Curses

'Right,' said Harry, crumpling up his first attempt and lobbing it over the heads of a group of chattering first-years into the fire. 'OK ... on Monday, I will be in danger of – er – burns.'

'Yeah, you will be,' said Ron darkly, 'we're seeing the Skrewts again on Monday. OK, Tuesday, I'll ... erm ...'

'Lose a treasured possession,' said Harry, who was flicking through *Unfogging the Future* for ideas.

'Good one,' said Ron, copying it down. 'Because of ... erm ... Mercury. Why don't you get stabbed in the back by someone you thought was a friend?'

'Yeah ... cool ...' said Harry, scribbling it down, 'because ... Venus is in the twelfth house.'

'And on Wednesday, I think I'll come off worst in a fight.'

'Aaah, I was going to have a fight. OK, I'll lose a bet.'

'Yeah, you'll be betting I'll win my fight ...'

They continued to make up predictions (which grew steadily more tragic) for another hour, while the common room around them slowly emptied as people went up to bed. Crookshanks wandered over to them, leapt lightly into an empty chair, and stared inscrutably at Harry, rather as Hermione might look if she knew they weren't doing their homework properly.

Staring around the room, trying to think of a kind of misfortune he hadn't yet used, Harry saw Fred and George sitting together against the opposite wall, heads together, quills out, poring over a single piece of parchment. It was most unusual to see Fred and George hidden away in a corner and working silently; they usually liked to be in the thick of things, and the noisy centre of attention. There was something secretive about the way they were working on the piece of parchment, and Harry was reminded of how they had sat together writing something back at The Burrow. He had thought then that it was another order form for *Weasleys' Wizard Wheezes*, but it didn't look like that this time; if it had been, they would surely have let Lee Jordan in on the joke. He wondered whether it had anything to do with entering the Triwizard Tournament.

As Harry watched, George shook his head at Fred, scratched something out with his quill and said, in a very quiet voice that never-theless carried across the almost deserted room, 'No – that sounds like we're accusing him.

## 第14章 不可饶恕咒

"对极了。"哈利说——他把刚才绞尽脑汁思索的成果揉成一团，然后越过一群叽叽喳喳的一年级新生的头顶，把纸团投进了炉火，"好吧……星期一，我会遇到——嗯——被烧伤的危险。"

"对啊，你是有这样的危险，"罗恩愁眉苦脸地说，"我们星期一又要见到炸尾螺了。好了，星期二，我会……嗯……"

"你会破财。"哈利说道，他正在翻着《拨开迷雾看未来》寻找思路。

"好主意，"罗恩说，赶紧把这一条写下来，"因为……嗯……因为水星。你呢，你被一个你以为是朋友的人背叛，怎么样？"

"好啊……太棒了……"哈利草草地记录着，说道，"因为……金星在黄道第十二宫。"

"然后，在星期三，我跟人打架打输了。"

"啊，我刚才也想写打架呢。好吧，我就写打赌输了钱吧。"

"对，就说你赌我打架会赢……"

他们编造着预言（悲剧的色彩越来越浓），就这样又过了一小时，公共休息室里的人陆续回去睡觉了，周围慢慢冷清下来。克鲁克山溜达着走过来，轻巧地跳上一把空椅子，用深奥莫测的目光望着哈利，那神情很像赫敏——如果赫敏知道他们做家庭作业时投机取巧，也会露出这样的神情。

哈利四下张望，苦苦思索一桩他还没有用过的倒霉事件，无意间看见弗雷德和乔治坐在对面的墙边，头碰着头，手里拿着羽毛笔，埋头研究着一张羊皮纸。弗雷德和乔治居然躲在角落里，安安静静地钻研什么，这可真是件稀罕事儿。他们一向都喜欢热闹，喜欢咋咋呼呼，成为大家注意的中心。此刻看他们研究那张羊皮纸的样子，似乎有点鬼鬼祟祟，哈利想起了他们在陋居时坐在一起写东西的情景。于是猜想他们大概又在琢磨一份韦斯莱魔法把戏坊的订货单。可是看看又不像，如果是订货单，他们一定会让李·乔丹参加进来，一块儿乐一乐的。哈利想，这会不会与参加三强争霸赛有关呢？

哈利望着他们，只见乔治朝弗雷德摇了摇头，用羽毛笔划去了纸上的什么东西，然后说了一句话，尽管声音很低，却仍然传到了几乎空无一人的休息室的这头。他说："不行——那会显得我们是在指责他。

got to be careful ...'

Then George looked over and saw Harry watching him. Harry grinned, and quickly returned to his predictions – he didn't want George to think he was eavesdropping. Shortly after that, the twins rolled up their parchment, said goodnight and went off to bed.

Fred and George had been gone ten minutes or so when the portrait hole opened and Hermione climbed into the common room, carrying a sheaf of parchment in one hand and a box whose contents rattled as she walked, in the other. Crookshanks arched his back, purring.

'Hello,' she said, 'I've just finished!'

'So have I!' said Ron triumphantly, throwing down his quill.

Hermione sat down, laid the things she was carrying in an empty armchair and pulled Ron's predictions towards her.

'Not going to have a very good month, are you?' she said sardonically, as Crookshanks curled up in her lap.

'Ah well, at least I'm forewarned,' Ron yawned.

'You seem to be drowning twice,' said Hermione.

'Oh, am I?' said Ron, peering down at his predictions. 'I'd better change one of them to getting trampled by a rampaging Hippogriff.'

'Don't you think it's a bit obvious you've made these up?' said Hermione.

'How dare you!' said Ron, in mock outrage. 'We've been working like house-elves here!'

Hermione raised her eyebrows.

'It's just an expression,' said Ron hastily.

Harry laid down his quill, too, having just finished predicting his own death by decapitation.

'What's in the box?' he asked, pointing at it.

'Funny you should ask,' said Hermione, with a nasty look at Ron. She took off the lid, and showed them the contents.

Inside were about fifty badges, all of different colours, but all bearing the same letters: S.P.E.W.

'"Spew"?' said Harry, picking up a badge and looking at it. 'What's this about?'

## 第14章 不可饶恕咒

必须小心点儿……"

这时弗雷德抬起头,看见哈利正望着他们。哈利咧嘴一笑,赶紧低下头看自己的预言——他不想让乔治认为他在偷听。在这之后不久,双胞胎兄弟卷起羊皮纸,道了声晚安,就回去睡觉了。

弗雷德和乔治走后十分钟左右,肖像后的洞口打开了,赫敏爬进公共休息室,一只手里拿着一卷羊皮纸,另一只手里捧着一个盒子。她一走路,盒子里的东西就咔嗒咔嗒响个不停。克鲁克山拱起后背,呼噜呼噜叫着。

"你们好,"她说,"我忙完了!"

"我也忙完了!"罗恩得意地说,扔下了羽毛笔。

赫敏坐下来,把手里的东西放到一把空椅子上,把罗恩写的预言拉到面前。

"你下个月可够倒霉的,是吧?"她讽刺地说,克鲁克山蜷缩在她的膝盖上。

"是啊,至少我预先得到警告了。"罗恩打着哈欠说。

"你似乎要淹死两次。"赫敏说。

"是吗?"罗恩说,赶紧低头看自己的预言,"我最好把其中一次改成被一头横冲直撞的鹰头马身有翼兽踩死。"

"这不是一眼就能看出都是你胡编乱造的吗?"赫敏说。

"你竟敢这么说!"罗恩假装气愤地说,"我们在这里忙了一个晚上,辛苦得像家养小精灵!"

赫敏扬起了眉毛。

"对不起,措辞不当。"罗恩赶紧说道。

哈利也放下了羽毛笔,他刚刚预言自己将被砍头。

"盒子里是什么?"他指着盒子问道。

"你问得正好。"赫敏不悦地瞪了罗恩一眼,说道。她揭开盒盖,给他们看里面的东西。

盒子里大约有五十枚徽章,颜色各不相同,上面都写着同样的字母:S.P.E.W.。

"呕吐?"哈利拿起一枚徽章,仔细看着,问道,"这是什么意思?"

'Not *spew*,' said Hermione impatiently. 'It's S – P – E – W. Stands for the Society for the Promotion of Elfish Welfare.'

'Never heard of it,' said Ron.

'Well, of course you haven't,' said Hermione briskly, 'I've only just started it.'

'Yeah?' said Ron in mild surprise. 'How many members have you got?'

'Well – if you two join – three,' said Hermione.

'And you think we want to walk around wearing badges saying "spew", do you?' said Ron.

'S – P – E – W!' said Hermione hotly. 'I was going to put Stop the Outrageous Abuse of Our Fellow Magical Creatures and Campaign for a Change in Their Legal Status – but it wouldn't fit. So that's the heading of our manifesto.'

She brandished the sheaf of parchment at them. 'I've been researching it thoroughly in the library. Elf enslavement goes back centuries. I can't believe no one's done anything about it before now.'

'Hermione – open your ears,' said Ron loudly. 'They. Like. It. They *like* being enslaved!'

'Our short-term aims,' said Hermione, speaking even more loudly than Ron, and acting as though she hadn't heard a word, 'are to secure house-elves fair wages and working conditions. Our long-term aims include changing the law about non-wand-use, and trying to get an elf into the Department for the Regulation and Control of Magical Creatures, because they're shockingly under-represented.'

'And how do we do all this?' Harry asked.

'We start by recruiting members,' said Hermione happily. 'I thought two Sickles to join – that buys a badge – and the proceeds can fund our leaflet campaign. You're treasurer, Ron – I've got you a collecting tin upstairs – and Harry, you're secretary, so you might want to write down everything I'm saying now, as a record of our first meeting.'

There was a pause in which Hermione beamed at the pair of them, and Harry sat, torn between exasperation at Hermione, and amusement at the look on Ron's face. The silence was broken, not by Ron, who in any case looked as though he was temporarily dumbstruck, but by a soft *tap, tap* on the window. Harry looked across the now empty common room, and saw,

## 第14章 不可饶恕咒

"不是呕吐，"赫敏不耐烦地说，"是S－P－E－W。意思是家养小精灵权益促进会。"

"没听说过。"罗恩说。

"你当然没听说过，"赫敏干脆利落地说，"是我刚刚创办的。"

"啊？"罗恩略微有些惊讶地问，"你们有多少会员？"

"嗯——如果你们俩也参加——就有三个。"赫敏说。

"你以为我们愿意戴着徽章走来走去，上面写着呕吐？"罗恩说。

"是S－P－E－W！"赫敏恼火地说，"我本来想命名为'禁止残酷虐待我们的神奇动物朋友和改善其法律地位的运动'——可是不太合适。所以我把那个作为我们协会宣言的标题了。"

她朝他们挥舞着那卷羊皮纸。"我一直在图书馆深入研究这个问题。小精灵的奴隶身份可以追溯到好几个世纪以前。我无法相信居然一直没有人对此采取措施。"

"赫敏——你听好了，"罗恩大声说，"他们、喜欢、这样。他们喜欢做别人的奴隶！"

"我们的短期目标，"赫敏说，声音比罗恩还大，好像根本没听见罗恩的话，"是保证家养小精灵获得合理的工钱和良好的工作环境。我们的长远目标包括修改小精灵不得使用魔杖的法律，还要争取让一位小精灵进入魔法生物管理控制司，因为小精灵权益未被充分体现的情况着实令人震惊。"

"我们怎么能做到这些呢？"哈利问。

"首先，我们要发展会员。"赫敏情绪高昂地说，"我认为参加者要付两个银西可——用于购买徽章——这笔收入可供我们印发传单。你是财务总管，罗恩——我在楼上给你准备了一个储钱罐——哈利，你是秘书，你需要把我现在说的每一句话都写下来，作为我们第一次会议的记录。"

一时间，谁也没有说话，赫敏喜滋滋地看着他们俩。哈利坐在那里，既为赫敏的表现感到气恼，又被罗恩脸上的表情逗得想笑。最后沉默被打破了，但出声的不是罗恩，看他的样子，好像暂时还说不出话来。他们听见窗户上传来轻轻的敲打声，啪，啪。哈利的目光越过此刻空荡荡的公共休息室，看见在月光的映照下，一只雪白的猫头鹰栖息在

## CHAPTER FOURTEEN  The Unforgivable Curses

illuminated by the moonlight, a snowy owl perched on the window-sill.

'Hedwig!' he shouted, and he launched himself out of his chair and across the room to pull open the window.

Hedwig flew inside, soared across the room and landed on the table on top of Harry's predictions.

'About time!' said Harry, hurrying after her.

'She's got an answer!' said Ron excitedly, pointing at the grubby piece of parchment tied to Hedwig's leg.

Harry hastily untied it and sat down to read it, whereupon Hedwig fluttered onto his knee, hooting softly.

'What does it say?' Hermione asked breathlessly.

The letter was very short, and looked as though it had been scrawled in a great hurry. Harry read it aloud:

> *Harry –*
>
> *I'm flying north immediately. This news about your scar is the latest in a series of strange rumours that have reached me here. If it hurts again, go straight to Dumbledore – they're saying he's got Mad-Eye out of retirement, which means he's reading the signs, even if no one else is.*
>
> *I'll be in touch soon. My best to Ron and Hermione. Keep your eyes open, Harry.*
>
> *Sirius*

Harry looked up at Ron and Hermione, who stared back at him.

'He's flying north?' Hermione whispered. 'He's coming *back*?'

'Dumbledore's reading what signs?' said Ron, looking perplexed. 'Harry – what's up?'

For Harry had just hit himself in the forehead with his fist, jolting Hedwig out of his lap.

'I shouldn't've told him!' Harry said furiously.

'What are you on about?' said Ron, in surprise.

'It's made him think he's got to come back!' said Harry, now slamming his fist on the table so that Hedwig landed on the back of Ron's chair, hooting indignantly. 'Coming back, because he thinks I'm in trouble! And there's

窗台上。

"海德薇！"他喊道，猛地从椅子上跃起，三步并作两步穿过房间，拉开窗户。

海德薇飞了进来，掠过房间，落在桌上哈利的预言作业上。

"来得正是时候！"哈利说着，匆匆跟了过去。

"它送来了回信！"罗恩激动地说，指着拴在海德薇脚上的一片皱巴巴的羊皮纸。

哈利赶紧把信解下来，坐下看信，海德薇扑扇着翅膀落到他膝盖上，轻轻鸣叫。

"上面怎么说？"赫敏屏住呼吸问。

信很短，好像是在匆忙中草草写就。哈利大声读道：

哈利：

  我马上就飞到北方来。最近听到一系列奇怪的传闻，刚又得知关于你伤疤的这个消息。如果伤疤再疼，请直接去找邓布利多——听说他又起用了已退休的疯眼汉，这就意味着他领会到了那些预兆，尽管别人都还蒙在鼓里。

  我很快就跟你联系。向罗恩和赫敏问好。保持警惕，哈利。

小天狼星

哈利抬头望着罗恩和赫敏，他们也望着他。

"他要飞到北方来？"赫敏小声问，"他要回来？"

"邓布利多领会到了什么预兆？"罗恩一脸困惑地问道，"哈利——怎么啦？"

哈利用拳头猛地敲了一下自己的前额，惊得海德薇从他膝盖上跳开了。

"我不应该告诉他的！"哈利恼怒地说。

"你在说什么呀？"罗恩惊讶地问。

"我的信让他认为他必须赶回来！"哈利说着，又用拳头使劲敲打桌子——海德薇只好落在罗恩的椅子背上，气愤地鸣叫着，"赶回来，因为他以为我遇到了麻烦！其实我一点事儿也没有！我没有东西给你

## CHAPTER FOURTEEN  The Unforgivable Curses

nothing wrong with me! And I haven't got anything for you,' Harry snapped at Hedwig, who was clicking her beak expectantly, 'you'll have to go up to the Owlery if you want food.'

Hedwig gave him an extremely offended look and took off for the open window, cuffing him around the head with her outstretched wing as she went.

'Harry,' Hermione began, in a pacifying sort of voice.

'I'm going to bed,' said Harry shortly. 'See you in the morning.'

Upstairs in the dormitory he pulled on his pyjamas and got into his four-poster, but he didn't feel remotely tired.

If Sirius came back and got caught, it would be his, Harry's, fault. Why hadn't he kept his mouth shut? A few seconds' pain and he'd had to blab ... if he'd just had the sense to keep it to himself ...

He heard Ron come up into the dormitory a short while later, but did not speak to him. For a long time, Harry lay staring up at the dark canopy of his bed. The dormitory was completely silent, and, had he been less preoccupied, Harry would have realised that the absence of Neville's usual snores meant that he was not the only one lying awake.

## 第14章 不可饶恕咒

吃,"哈利没好气地对满怀希望咂着嘴巴的海德薇说,"如果你想吃东西,只好去猫头鹰棚屋了。"

海德薇非常生气地看了他一眼,朝敞开的窗户飞去,用伸展的翅膀拍打了一下哈利的脑袋。

"哈利。"赫敏用安慰的口气说道。

"我要去睡觉了,"哈利不愿多说,"明天见。"

来到楼上的宿舍,哈利穿上睡衣,爬上他那张四柱床,但觉得一点也不累。

如果小天狼星回来后被抓住,那就是他——哈利的过错了。他为什么就不能闭紧嘴巴呢?不过是几秒钟的疼痛,他就唠叨个没完……他为什么不能明智一些,把这件事埋在心里……

片刻之后,他听见罗恩进了宿舍,但他没有跟罗恩说话。哈利久久地躺在床上,瞪着漆黑的帐顶发愣。宿舍里一片寂静,如果哈利不是这样心事重重,就会意识到宿舍里没有响起纳威惯常的鼾声,这说明今夜辗转难眠的不止他一个人。

# CHAPTER FIFTEEN

# Beauxbatons and Durmstrang

Early next morning, Harry woke with a plan fully formed in his mind, as though his sleeping brain had been working on it all night. He got up, dressed in the pale dawn light, left the dormitory without waking Ron and went back down to the deserted common room. Here he took a piece of parchment from the table upon which his Divination homework still lay, and wrote the following letter:

> Dear Sirius,
>
> I reckon I just imagined my scar hurting, I was half-asleep when I wrote to you last time. There's no point coming back, everything's fine here. Don't worry about me, my head feels completely normal.
>
> Harry

He then climbed out of the portrait hole, up through the silent castle (held up only briefly by Peeves, who tried to overturn a large vase on him halfway along the fourth-floor corridor), finally arriving at the Owlery, which was situated at the top of West Tower.

The Owlery was a circular stone room; rather cold and draughty, because none of the windows had glass in them. The floor was entirely covered in straw, owl droppings and the regurgitated skeletons of mice and voles. Hundreds upon hundreds of owls of every breed imaginable were nestled here on perches that rose right up to the top of the tower, nearly all of them asleep, though here and there a round amber eye glared at Harry. He spotted Hedwig nestled between a barn owl and a tawny, and hurried over to her, sliding a little on the dropping-strewn floor.

# 第 15 章

# 布斯巴顿和德姆斯特朗

第二天一早,哈利醒来时,脑子里已经形成了一个完整的计划,就好像他睡着时脑子没有休息,整夜都在盘算这件事。他从床上起来,在黎明苍白的微光中穿好衣服,没有唤醒罗恩,独自离开宿舍,来到空无一人的公共休息室。昨晚的占卜课家庭作业还留在桌上,他拿起一张羊皮纸,写了下面这封信:

亲爱的小天狼星:

    我想,我的伤疤疼大概是心理作用,我上次给你写信时还没有完全睡醒。你没有必要回来,这里一切都好。不要为我担心,我的头一点也不疼了。

哈 利

随即,他从肖像后的洞口爬出去,在寂静的城堡里一直往上走(只被皮皮鬼阻挡了片刻,在五楼的走廊上,皮皮鬼想把一只大花瓶推到他身上),最后来到位于西塔楼最顶层的猫头鹰棚屋。

猫头鹰棚屋是一个圆形的石头房间,非常阴冷,刮着穿堂风,因为那里的窗户上都没有安玻璃。地板上到处都是稻草和猫头鹰粪便,以及猫头鹰吐出的老鼠和田鼠骨头。在直达塔楼最顶处的栖枝上,栖息着成百上千只猫头鹰,各个品种应有尽有。它们几乎都在睡觉,不过时不时地,会有一只圆溜溜的琥珀色眼睛瞪视着哈利。哈利看见海德薇栖息在一只谷仓猫头鹰和一只黄褐色猫头鹰之间,便匆匆走过去,脚踩在洒满鸟粪的地上差点儿滑倒。

## CHAPTER FIFTEEN  Beauxbatons and Durmstrang

It took him a little while to persuade her to wake up and then to look at him as she kept shuffling around on her perch, showing him her tail. She was evidently still furious about his lack of gratitude the previous night. In the end, it was Harry suggesting she might be too tired, and that perhaps he would ask Ron to borrow Pigwidgeon, that made her stick out her leg and allow him to tie the letter to it.

'Just find him, all right?' Harry said, stroking her back as he carried her on his arm to one of the holes in the wall. 'Before the Dementors do.'

She nipped his finger, perhaps rather harder than she would ordinarily have done, but hooted softly in a reassuring sort of way all the same. Then she spread her wings and took off into the sunrise. Harry watched her out of sight with the familiar feeling of unease back in his stomach. He had been so sure that Sirius' reply would alleviate his worries rather than increasing them.

'That was a *lie*, Harry,' said Hermione sharply over breakfast, when he told her and Ron what he had done. 'You *didn't* imagine your scar hurting and you know it.'

'So what?' said Harry. 'He's not going back to Azkaban because of me.'

'Drop it,' said Ron sharply to Hermione, as she opened her mouth to argue some more, and for once, Hermione heeded him, and fell silent.

Harry did his best not to worry about Sirius over the next couple of weeks. True, he could not stop himself looking anxiously around every morning when the post owls arrived, nor, late at night before he went to sleep, prevent himself seeing horrible visions of Sirius, cornered by Dementors down some dark London street, but between times he tried to keep his mind off his godfather. He wished he still had Quidditch to distract him; nothing worked so well on a troubled mind as a good, hard training session. On the other hand, their lessons were becoming more difficult and demanding than ever before, particularly Defence Against the Dark Arts.

To their surprise, Professor Moody had announced that he would be putting the Imperius Curse on each of them in turn, to demonstrate its power and to see whether they could resist its effects.

'But – but you said it's illegal, Professor,' said Hermione uncertainly, as Moody cleared away the desks with a sweep of his wand, leaving a large clear space in the middle of the room. 'You said – to use it against another human was –'

## 第15章 布斯巴顿和德姆斯特朗

他磨了半天嘴皮子，才说服海德薇醒过来望着自己，因为海德薇不停地在栖枝上移来移去，把尾巴冲着哈利。显然，它还在因为哈利昨晚不知好歹的表现而生气。最后，哈利说它大概太累了，他最好去向罗恩借来小猪用一下，海德薇这才伸出腿来，让哈利把信拴上。

"一定要找到他，好吗？"哈利说，抱着海德薇走向墙上的一个洞口，一边抚摸着它的后背，"要赶在摄魂怪前面。"

海德薇咬了咬哈利的手指，也许比平时咬得更用力一些，但它仍然轻轻叫了几声，仿佛是叫他放心。然后，海德薇展开双翅，飞进了晨曦中。哈利望着它飞得看不见了，内心又产生了那种很不踏实的感觉。他一直以为小天狼星的回信肯定会减轻他的担忧，没想到他的担忧反倒增加了。

"你在撒谎，哈利，"早饭桌上，当哈利把他做的事情告诉赫敏和罗恩后，赫敏尖锐地指出，"你的伤疤疼根本不是心理作用，你知道的。"

"那又怎么样？"哈利说，"他不能因为我而再回到阿兹卡班。"

"别说了。"赫敏张嘴还要辩论，罗恩很不客气地阻止了她。赫敏破天荒第一次听从了罗恩，没有再说什么。

在接下来的两个星期里，哈利尽量不去为小天狼星担心。诚然，当每天早晨送信的猫头鹰到来时，他还是忍不住焦虑地东张西望。而每天深夜入睡前，他也无法不让自己幻想小天狼星在伦敦某条阴暗的街道上，被摄魂怪们逼得走投无路的可怕情景。不过在整个白天，他还是尽量不去牵挂自己的教父。他真希望仍然能靠魁地奇转移注意力，没有什么比健康的、大运动量的训练更能排解内心的烦恼焦虑了。另一方面，他们的功课越来越难，要求越来越高，特别是穆迪的黑魔法防御术课。

令他们吃惊的是，穆迪教授宣布说他要轮流对每个同学念夺魂咒，以演示这个咒语的魔力，看他们能不能抵御它的影响。

"可是……可是你说过它是非法的，教授，"当穆迪一挥魔杖，让课桌纷纷靠边，在教室中央留出一大片空地时，赫敏没有把握地说，"你说过……把它用在别人身上是……"

## CHAPTER FIFTEEN   Beauxbatons and Durmstrang

'Dumbledore wants you taught what it feels like,' said Moody, his magical eye swivelling onto Hermione and fixing her with an eerie, unblinking stare. 'If you'd rather learn the hard way – when someone's putting it on you so they can control you completely – fine by me. You're excused. Off you go.'

He pointed one gnarled finger towards the door. Hermione went very pink, and muttered something about not meaning that she wanted to leave. Harry and Ron grinned at each other. They knew Hermione would rather eat Bubotuber pus than miss such an important lesson.

Moody began to beckon students forwards in turn and put the Imperius Curse upon them. Harry watched as, one by one, his classmates did the most extraordinary things under its influence. Dean Thomas hopped three times around the room, singing the national anthem. Lavender Brown imitated a squirrel. Neville performed a series of quite astonishing gymnastics he would certainly not have been capable of in his normal state. Not one of them seemed to be able to fight the curse off, and each of them recovered only when Moody had removed it.

'Potter,' Moody growled, 'you next.'

Harry moved forward into the middle of the classroom, into the space that Moody had cleared of desks. Moody raised his wand, pointed it at Harry, and said, '*Imperio.*'

It was the most wonderful feeling. Harry felt a floating sensation as every thought and worry in his head was wiped gently away, leaving nothing but a vague, untraceable happiness. He stood there feeling immensely relaxed, only dimly aware of everyone watching him.

And then he heard Mad-Eye Moody's voice, echoing in some distant chamber of his empty brain: *Jump onto the desk … jump onto the desk …*

Harry bent his knees obediently, preparing to spring.

*Jump onto the desk …*

Why, though?

Another voice had awoken in the back of his brain. Stupid thing to do, really, said the voice.

*Jump onto the desk …*

No, I don't think I will, thanks, said the other voice, a little more firmly … no, I don't really want to …

*Jump! NOW!*

## 第15章 布斯巴顿和德姆斯特朗

"邓布利多希望让你们感受一下，"穆迪说——那只魔眼转过来，阴森森地、一眨不眨地盯着赫敏，"如果你愿意通过更残酷的方式学习——等着别人给你念这个咒语，把你完全控制在手心里——那很好。我同意。你可以走了。"

他伸出一根粗糙的手指，指着教室的门。赫敏满脸涨得通红，喃喃地嘀咕了一句什么，好像是说她并不想离开。哈利和罗恩相视笑了一下。他们知道赫敏宁可去吃巴波块茎的脓液，也不愿错过这样重要的一课。

穆迪开始招呼同学们轮流上前，给他们念夺魂咒。哈利看到，在咒语的影响下，同学们一个接一个做出最反常的举动。迪安·托马斯一蹦一跳地在教室里转了三圈，嘴里唱着国歌。拉文德·布朗模仿了一只松鼠。纳威表演了一系列十分惊人的体操动作，这是他在正常状态下绝对做不到的。似乎没有一个同学能够抵挡这个咒语，都是在穆迪消除咒语后才恢复了正常。

"波特，"穆迪声音隆隆地说，"轮到你了。"

哈利上前走到教室中央，走到穆迪刚才挪开课桌腾出的空地上。穆迪举起魔杖，指着哈利，说道："魂魄出窍！"

那真是一种最奇妙的感觉。哈利觉得自己轻飘飘的，脑海里的思想和忧虑一扫而光，只留下一片朦朦胧胧的、看不见摸不着的喜悦。他站在那里，感到特别轻松，无忧无虑，只模模糊糊地意识到大家都在注视着自己。

然后，他听见了疯眼汉穆迪的声音，在他空荡荡的脑袋里的某个遥远的角落里回响：跳到桌子上去……跳到桌子上去……

哈利顺从地弯下膝盖，准备跳了。

跳到桌子上去……

可是为什么呢？

他脑袋后面又有一个声音苏醒了。这么做太傻了，那个声音说。

跳到桌子上去……

不，我不想跳，谢谢，另外那个声音说，语气更坚定了一些……不，我真的不想跳……

跳！**快跳！**

## CHAPTER FIFTEEN    Beauxbatons and Durmstrang

The next thing Harry felt was considerable pain. He had both jumped and tried to prevent himself from jumping – the result was that he'd smashed headlong into the desk, knocking it over, and, by the feeling in his legs, fractured both his kneecaps.

'Now, *that's* more like it!' growled Moody's voice, and suddenly Harry felt the empty, echoing feeling in his head disappear. He remembered exactly what was happening, and the pain in his knees seemed to double.

'Look at that, you lot ... Potter fought! He fought it, and he damn near beat it! We'll try that again, Potter, and the rest of you, pay attention – watch his eyes, that's where you see it – very good, Potter, very good indeed! They'll have trouble controlling *you*!'

'The way he talks,' Harry muttered, as he hobbled out of the Defence Against the Dark Arts class an hour later (Moody had insisted on putting Harry through his paces four times in a row, until Harry could throw the curse off entirely), 'you'd think we were all going to be attacked any second.'

'Yeah, I know,' said Ron, who was skipping on every alternate step. He had had much more difficulty with the curse than Harry, though Moody assured him the effects would have worn off by lunchtime. 'Talk about paranoid ...' Ron glanced nervously over his shoulder to check that Moody was definitely out of earshot, and went on, 'No wonder they were glad to get shot of him at the Ministry, did you hear him telling Seamus what he did to that witch who shouted "boo" behind him on April Fools' Day? And when are we supposed to read up on resisting the Imperius Curse with everything else we've got to do?'

All the fourth-years had noticed a definite increase in the amount of work they were required to do this term. Professor McGonagall explained why, when the class gave a particularly loud groan at the amount of Transfiguration homework she had set.

'You are now entering a most important phase of your magical education!' she told them, her eyes glinting dangerously behind her square spectacles. 'Your Ordinary Wizarding Levels are drawing closer –'

'We don't take O.W.L.s 'til fifth year!' said Dean Thomas indignantly.

'Maybe not, Thomas, but believe me, you need all the preparation you can get! Miss granger remains the only person in this class who has managed to turn a hedgehog into a satisfactory pincushion. I might remind you that *your* pincushion, Thomas, still curls up in fright if anyone approaches it with a pin!'

## 第15章 布斯巴顿和德姆斯特朗

接下来，哈利便感到一阵剧痛。他跳了，同时又试图不让自己跳——结果一头撞在桌子上，把桌子撞翻了，腿上钻心地疼，看来他的两个膝盖骨都摔裂了。

"好，这才像话！"穆迪用隆隆的声音说。忽地，哈利觉得脑海里那种空谷回音般的空洞感消失了。他十分清楚地记得刚才发生的事，膝盖越发疼痛难忍。

"看看吧，你们大家……波特抵挡了！他抵挡了，差点儿打败了它！我们再试一次，波特，你们其他人注意看好——盯着他的眼睛，那是关键所在——很好，波特，非常好！他们别想轻易控制你！"

"听他说话的口气，"一小时后（穆迪坚持让哈利连续测试了四次，直到哈利能够完全摆脱那个咒语），哈利一瘸一拐地走出黑魔法防御术课的教室，嘴里嘀咕道，"你还以为我们随时都会受到攻击呢。"

"是啊，没错。"罗恩说，他每走一步就抬脚一跳。他在对付这个咒语时的困难比哈利大得多，不过穆迪向他保证，咒语的影响到吃午饭时就会消失。"说起他的偏执……"罗恩扭头望望，确信穆迪肯定听不见了，才接着说下去，"难怪他们巴不得把他从魔法部赶出去呢。你有没有听见他告诉西莫，愚人节那天一个女巫在他后面喝了个倒彩，他是怎么对付那个女巫的？我们要做的事情那么多，哪有时间研究怎样抵挡夺魂咒啊？"

所有四年级的同学都注意到，他们这学期要做的功课明显增加了。当同学们格外大声地抱怨麦格教授布置的变形课家庭作业太多时，麦格教授解释了原因。

"你们正在进入魔法教育的一个重要时期！"她告诉他们，两只眼睛在方方的镜片后面威严地闪着光，"你们的O.W.L.考试就要临近了——"

"我们要到五年级才参加O.W.L.考试呢！"迪安·托马斯气愤地说。

"也许是这样，托马斯，不过请相信我，你们需要做好充分的准备！在这个班里，始终只有格兰杰小姐一个人能把刺猬变成一只令人满意的针垫。托马斯，我应该提醒你一句，你的针垫在有人拿着针靠近它时，仍然会害怕得蜷缩起来！"

## CHAPTER FIFTEEN · Beauxbatons and Durmstrang

Hermione, who had turned rather pink again, seemed to be trying not to look too pleased with herself.

Harry and Ron were deeply amused when Professor Trelawney told them that they had received top marks for their homework in their next Divination class. She read out large portions of their predictions, commending them for their unflinching acceptance of the horrors in store for them – but they were less amused when she asked them to do the same thing for the month after next; both of them were running out of ideas for catastrophes.

Meanwhile Professor Binns, the ghost who taught History of Magic, had them writing weekly essays on the Goblin Rebellions of the eighteenth century. Professor Snape was forcing them to research antidotes. They took this seriously, as he had hinted that he might be poisoning one of them before Christmas to see if their antidote worked. Professor Flitwick had asked them to read three extra books in preparation for their lesson on Summoning Charms.

Even Hagrid was adding to their workload. The Blast-Ended Skrewts were growing at a remarkable pace, given that nobody had yet discovered what they ate. Hagrid was delighted and, as part of their 'project', suggested that they come down to his hut on alternate evenings to observe the Skrewts and make notes on their extraordinary behaviour.

'I will not,' said Draco Malfoy flatly, when Hagrid had proposed this with the air of Father Christmas pulling an extra large toy out of his sack. 'I see enough of these foul things during lessons, thanks.'

Hagrid's smile faded from his face.

'Yeh'll do wha' yer told,' he growled, 'or I'll be takin' a leaf outta Professor Moody's book ... I hear yeh made a good ferret, Malfoy.'

The Gryffindors roared with laughter. Malfoy flushed with anger, but apparently the memory of Moody's punishment was still sufficiently painful to stop him retorting. Harry, Ron and Hermione returned to the castle at the end of the lesson in high spirits; seeing Hagrid put down Malfoy was particularly satisfying, especially because Malfoy had done his very best to get Hagrid sacked the previous year.

When they arrived in the Entrance Hall, they found themselves unable to proceed owing to the large crowd of students congregated there, all milling around a large sign which had been erected at the foot of the marble staircase. Ron, the tallest of the three, stood on tiptoe to see over the heads in front of them and read the sign aloud to the other two.

## 第15章 布斯巴顿和德姆斯特朗

赫敏的脸又涨得通红，她竭力不让自己表现出太得意的样子。

哈利和罗恩没想到，在接下来的占卜课上，特里劳尼教授居然对他们说，他们的家庭作业获得了高分，这使他们觉得特别可笑。她高声选读了他们预言的许多部分，并表扬他们能够勇敢地接受即将发生的可怕事情——可是，当她要求他们再对下下个月的命运做出预测时，他们就觉得不怎么可笑了。他们俩再也想不出新的灾难事件了。

另一方面，宾斯教授——教他们魔法史的幽灵，这周布置他们写一篇关于十八世纪妖精叛乱的论文。斯内普教授逼着他们研究解药。谁都不敢掉以轻心，因为斯内普教授暗示说，他将在圣诞节前给他们中间的一个人下毒，看看他们的解药是否管用。弗立维教授要求同学们另外再读三本书，为学习召唤咒做准备。

就连海格也给他们增加了负担。炸尾螺长得很快，尽管谁都没有弄清它们到底喜欢吃什么。海格非常高兴，作为"课题"的一部分，他建议他们每隔一天到他的小屋来观察一次炸尾螺，并记录下它们不同寻常的行为。

"我不来，"当海格以圣诞老人从口袋里掏出一只特大玩具的神情提出这个建议时，德拉科·马尔福毫不迟疑地说，"我在课堂上就看够了这些讨厌的东西，谢谢。"

海格脸上的微笑隐去了。

"按我说的办，"他咆哮道，"不然我就学穆迪教授的样儿……我听说你变成白鼬还蛮不错的，马尔福。"

格兰芬多的学生们哄堂大笑。马尔福气红了脸，但他显然对穆迪惩罚他的那一幕记忆犹新，不敢再顶嘴了。下课后，哈利、罗恩和赫敏兴高采烈地回到城堡。看到海格镇压了马尔福的嚣张气焰，真是大快人心，更何况马尔福去年曾千方百计想弄得海格被学校开除。

他们来到门厅，发现再也无法前进，因为一大群学生都挤在大理石楼梯脚下竖起的一则大启事周围。罗恩是他们三个人中最高的，他踮起脚尖，越过前面人的头顶，把启事上的文字大声地念给他们两个听：

## CHAPTER FIFTEEN    Beauxbatons and Durmstrang

### TRIWIZARD TOURNAMENT

The delegations from Beauxbatons and Durmstrang will be arriving at 6 o'clock on Friday 30th of October. Lessons will end half an hour early –

'Brilliant!' said Harry. 'It's Potions last thing on Friday! Snape won't have time to poison us all!'

Students will return their bags and books to their dormitories and assemble in front of the castle to greet our guests before the Welcoming Feast.

'Only a week away!' said Ernie Macmillan of Hufflepuff, emerging from the crowd, his eyes gleaming. 'I wonder if Cedric knows? Think I'll go and tell him ...'

'Cedric?' said Ron blankly, as Ernie hurried off.

'Diggory,' said Harry. 'He must be entering the Tournament.'

'That idiot, Hogwarts champion?' said Ron, as they pushed their way through the chattering crowd towards the staircase.

'He's not an idiot, you just don't like him because he beat Gryffindor at Quidditch,' said Hermione. 'I've heard he's a really good student – *and* he's a Prefect.'

She spoke as though this settled the matter.

'You only like him because he's *handsome*,' said Ron scathingly.

'Excuse me, I don't like people just because they're handsome!' said Hermione indignantly.

Ron gave a loud false cough, which sounded oddly like 'Lockhart!'.

The appearance of the sign in the Entrance Hall had a marked effect upon the inhabitants of the castle. During the following week, there seemed to be only one topic of conversation, no matter where Harry went: the Triwizard Tournament. Rumours were flying from student to student like highly contagious germs: who was going to try for Hogwarts champion, what the Tournament would involve, how the students from Beauxbatons and Durmstrang differed from themselves.

Harry noticed, too, that the castle seemed to be undergoing an extra-

# 第15章 布斯巴顿和德姆斯特朗

## 三强争霸赛

布斯巴顿和德姆斯特朗的代表将于十月三十日星期五傍晚六时抵达。下午的课程提前半小时结束——

"太棒了！"哈利说，"星期五的最后一堂课是魔药课！斯内普来不及给我们大家下毒了！"

届时请同学们把书包和课本送回宿舍，到城堡前面集合，迎接我们的客人，然后参加欢迎宴会。

"只有一个星期了！"赫奇帕奇学院的厄尼·麦克米兰从人群里挤出来，两眼闪闪发光，说道，"也不知塞德里克是不是知道了。我去告诉他一声……"

"塞德里克？"厄尼匆匆走开后，罗恩有些茫然地说。

"就是迪戈里，"哈利说，"他肯定准备参加争霸赛。"

"那个白痴，也想当霍格沃茨的勇士？"罗恩说。他们推开叽叽喳喳的人群，朝楼梯走去。

"他可不是白痴。你只是因为他在魁地奇比赛中打败了格兰芬多才不喜欢他的。"赫敏说，"我听说他是个很出色的学生——还是级长呢。"

听她的口气，好像这就说明了一切。

"你是因为他长得帅才喜欢他的。"罗恩尖刻地说。

"对不起，我不会仅仅因为别人长得帅就喜欢他们！"赫敏气愤地说。

罗恩假装大咳一声，声音怪怪的，听起来很像"洛哈特"。

门厅里出现的这则启事，对住在城堡里的人产生了明显的影响。在接下来的一星期里，哈利不管走到哪里，人们似乎都只谈论一个话题：三强争霸赛。谣言在学生中间迅速流传，像传染性很强的细菌：谁会争当霍格沃茨的勇士，争霸赛会有哪些项目，布斯巴顿和德姆斯特朗的学生与他们有什么不同。

哈利还注意到，城堡似乎正在进行彻底的打扫。几幅肮脏的肖像

## CHAPTER FIFTEEN  Beauxbatons and Durmstrang

thorough cleaning. Several grimy portraits had been scrubbed, much to the displeasure of their subjects, who sat huddled in their frames muttering darkly and wincing as they felt their raw pink faces. The suits of armour were suddenly gleaming and moving without squeaking, and Argus Filch, the caretaker, was behaving so ferociously to any student who forgot to wipe their shoes that he terrified a pair of first-year girls into hysterics.

Other members of staff seemed oddly tense, too.

'Longbottom, kindly do *not* reveal that you can't even perform a simple Switching Spell in front of anyone from Durmstrang!' Professor McGonagall barked at the end of one particularly difficult lesson, during which Neville had accidentally transplanted his own ears onto a cactus.

When they went down to breakfast on the morning of the thirtieth of October, they found that the Great Hall had been decorated overnight. Enormous silk banners hung from the walls, each of them representing a Hogwarts house – red with a gold lion for Gryffindor, blue with a bronze eagle for Ravenclaw, yellow with a black badger for Hufflepuff, and green with a silver serpent for Slytherin. Behind the teachers' table, the largest banner of all bore the Hogwarts coat of arms: lion, eagle, badger and snake united around a large letter 'H'.

Harry, Ron and Hermione spotted Fred and George at the Gryffindor table. Once again, and most unusually, they were sitting apart from everyone else and conversing in low voices. Ron led the way over to them.

'It's a bummer all right,' George was saying gloomily to Fred. 'But if he won't talk to us in person, we'll have to send him the letter after all. Or we'll stuff it into his hand, he can't avoid us for ever.'

'Who's avoiding you?' said Ron, sitting down next to them.

'Wish you would,' said Fred, looking irritated at the interruption.

'What's a bummer?' Ron asked George.

'Having a nosy git like you for a brother,' said George.

'You two got any ideas on the Triwizard Tournament yet?' Harry asked. 'Thought any more about trying to enter?'

'I asked McGonagall how the champions are chosen but she wasn't telling,' said George bitterly. 'She just told me to shut up and get on with Transfiguring my raccoon.'

'Wonder what the tasks are going to be?' said Ron thoughtfully. 'You know,

## 第15章 布斯巴顿和德姆斯特朗

被擦洗干净了，那些被擦洗的人物对此十分不满。他们缩着身子坐在相框里，闷闷不乐地嘟哝，每次一摸到脸上新露出的粉红色嫩肉，就疼得龇牙咧嘴。那些盔甲突然变得锃光瓦亮，活动的时候也不再嘎吱嘎吱响了。管理员阿格斯·费尔奇一看到有学生忘记把鞋擦干净，就凶狠地大发雷霆，吓得两个一年级的女生犯了歇斯底里症。

其他教工也显得格外紧张。

"隆巴顿，拜托，千万别在德姆斯特朗的人面前露馅儿，让他们看出你连一个简单的转换咒都没掌握！"快下课时，麦格教授厉声吼道。那节课上得特别不顺利，纳威无意中把自己的耳朵嫁接到了一棵仙人掌上。

十月三十日那天早晨，他们下楼吃早饭时，发现礼堂在一夜之间被装饰一新。墙上挂着巨大的丝绸横幅，每一条都代表着霍格沃茨的一个学院：红底配一头金色狮子的是格兰芬多，蓝底配一只古铜色老鹰的是拉文克劳，黄底配一只黑獾的是赫奇帕奇，绿底配一条银色蟒蛇的是斯莱特林。在教工桌子的后面，挂着那条最大的横幅，上面是霍格沃茨的饰章：狮、鹰、獾、蛇联在一起，环绕着一个巨大的字母H。

哈利、罗恩和赫敏看见弗雷德和乔治正坐在格兰芬多的餐桌旁。这次两个双胞胎又是很反常地避开众人，压低声音商量着什么。罗恩领头朝他们走去。

"这确实不太愉快，我承认，"乔治沮丧地对弗雷德说，"可是如果他不当面跟我们谈，我们就只好把信寄给他了，或者直接塞进他手里。他不可能永远躲着我们。"

"谁在躲着你们？"罗恩说着，在他们旁边坐了下来。

"希望你能躲着我们。"弗雷德说，似乎很不高兴受到打扰。

"什么事情不太愉快？"罗恩问乔治。

"有你这样一个好管闲事的傻弟弟。"乔治说。

"你们俩对三强争霸赛有办法了吗？"哈利问道，"还想混进去参加吗？"

"我去问过麦格教授：勇士是怎么选出来的，可是她不肯告诉我，"乔治怨恨地说，"她只是叫我闭上嘴巴，专心给我的浣熊变形。"

"不知道争霸赛都有哪些项目？"罗恩若有所思地说，"我敢打赌

## CHAPTER FIFTEEN    Beauxbatons and Durmstrang

I bet we could do them, Harry, we've done dangerous stuff before ...'

'Not in front of a panel of judges, you haven't,' said Fred. 'McGonagall says the champions get awarded points according to how well they've done the tasks.'

'Who are the judges?' Harry asked.

'Well, the Heads of the participating schools are always on the panel,' said Hermione, and everyone looked around at her, rather surprised, 'because all three of them were injured during the Tournament of 1792, when a cockatrice the champions were supposed to be catching went on the rampage.'

She noticed them all looking at her and said, with her usual air of impatience that nobody else had read all the books she had, 'It's all in *Hogwarts: A History*. Though, of course, that book's not *entirely* reliable. "A *Revised* History of Hogwarts" would be a more accurate title. Or "A Highly Biased and *Selective* History of Hogwarts, Which Glosses Over the Nastier Aspects of the School".'

'What are you on about?' said Ron, though Harry thought he knew what was coming.

'*House-elves!*' said Hermione loudly and proving Harry right. 'Not once, in over a thousand pages, does *Hogwarts: A History* mention that we are all colluding in the oppression of a hundred slaves!'

Harry shook his head, and applied himself to his scrambled eggs. His and Ron's lack of enthusiasm had done nothing whatsoever to curb Hermione's determination to pursue justice for house-elves. True, both of them had paid two Sickles for a S.P.E.W. badge, but they had only done it to keep her quiet. Their Sickles had been wasted, however; if anything, they seemed to have made Hermione more vociferous. She had been badgering Harry and Ron ever since, firstly to wear the badges, then to persuade others to do the same, and she had also taken to rattling around the Gryffindor common room every evening, cornering people and shaking the collecting tin under their noses.

'You do realise that your sheets are changed, your fires lit, your classrooms cleaned and your food cooked by a group of magical creatures who are unpaid and enslaved?' she kept saying fiercely.

Some people, like Neville, had paid up just to stop Hermione glowering at them. A few seemed mildly interested in what she had to say, but were

我们也能行，哈利。我们以前做过那么危险的事……"

"但是你们没有当着裁判团的面，不是吗？"弗雷德说，"麦格说，裁判将根据勇士们完成项目的质量给他们评分。"

"谁是裁判？"哈利问。

"噢，参赛学校的校长肯定是裁判团成员，"赫敏说——大家都十分吃惊地扭过头来望着她，"因为在一七九二年的争霸赛中，勇士们要抓的一头鸡身蛇尾怪不受控制，横冲直撞，三位校长都受了伤。"

她注意到大家都在盯着她，便又摆出那副不耐烦的表情，因为居然没有一个人像她一样读过那么多书。她说："这些都写在《霍格沃茨：一段校史》里呢。不过，当然啦，那本书并不完全可靠。也许叫它'一段被修改的霍格沃茨校史'更合适，或者叫它'一段带有高度偏见和有所选择的霍格沃茨校史，学校的阴暗面被掩盖'。"

"你在说什么呀？"罗恩说，不过哈利仿佛知道她接下来要说什么了。

"家养小精灵！"赫敏说，两眼灼灼放光，"在长达一千多页的《霍格沃茨：一段校史》这本书里，竟然只字没提我们在共同压迫一百个奴隶！"

哈利摇了摇头，低头给自己盛炒鸡蛋。他和罗恩的消极态度丝毫没有动摇赫敏为家养小精灵追求公正待遇的决心。诚然，他们俩都付了两个银西可购买了S.P.E.W.徽章，但他们这么做只是为了使赫敏闭嘴。然而，他们的银西可是白白浪费了，赫敏不仅没有因此安静下来，反而吵闹得更厉害了。从那以后，她就一直缠着哈利和罗恩，先是要求他们佩戴徽章，接着又要求他们去说服别人这么做。她还养成了一个习惯，每天晚上在格兰芬多的公共休息室里喋喋不休、不依不饶地缠着别人，拿着储钱罐在别人鼻子底下使劲摇晃。

"你有没有意识到，给你换床单，给你生火，给你打扫教室，给你煮饭烧菜的，都是一群没有工钱、受到奴役的神奇动物啊！"她言辞激烈地缠着别人说。

有一些人，比如纳威，无奈地付了钱，只是为了让赫敏别再恶狠狠地瞪着自己。也有个别人似乎对赫敏说的话略有兴趣，但也不愿意

## CHAPTER FIFTEEN  Beauxbatons and Durmstrang

reluctant to take a more active role in campaigning. Many regarded the whole thing as a joke.

Ron now rolled his eyes at the ceiling, which was flooding them all in autumn sunlight, and Fred became extremely interested in his bacon (both twins had refused to buy a S.P.E.W. badge). George, however, leant towards Hermione.

'Listen, have you ever been down in the kitchens, Hermione?'

'No, of course not,' said Hermione curtly, 'I hardly think students are supposed to –'

'Well, we have,' said George, indicating Fred, 'loads of times, to nick food. And we've met them, and they're *happy*. They think they've got the best job in the world –'

'That's because they're uneducated and brainwashed!' Hermione began hotly, but her next few words were drowned by the sudden whooshing noise from overhead which announced the arrival of the post owls. Harry looked up at once, and saw Hedwig soaring towards him. Hermione stopped talking abruptly; she and Ron watched Hedwig anxiously, as she fluttered down onto Harry's shoulder, folded her wings and held out her leg wearily.

Harry pulled off Sirius' reply and offered Hedwig his bacon rinds, which she ate gratefully. Then, checking that Fred and George were safely immersed in further discussions about the Triwizard Tournament, Harry read out Sirius' letter in a whisper to Ron and Hermione.

> *Nice try, Harry.*
> *I'm back in the country and well hidden. I want you to keep me posted on everything that's going on at Hogwarts. Don't use Hedwig, keep changing owls, and don't worry about me, just watch out for yourself. Don't forget what I said about your scar.*
> *Sirius*

'Why d'you have to keep changing owls?' Ron asked in a low voice.

'Hedwig'll attract too much attention,' said Hermione at once. 'She stands out. A snowy owl that keeps returning to wherever he's hiding … I mean, they're not native birds, are they?'

Harry rolled up the letter and slipped it inside his robes, wondering

## 第15章 布斯巴顿和德姆斯特朗

积极参加活动、为此奔走游说。许多人把整个这件事只当作了一个玩笑。

此刻，罗恩冲着向他们洒下秋日阳光的天花板翻起眼睛，弗雷德突然对他的熏咸肉产生了浓厚的兴趣（双胞胎兄弟都不肯买S.P.E.W.徽章）。乔治则朝赫敏探过身子。

"听我说，赫敏，你有没有到下面的厨房里去过？"

"没有，当然没有，"赫敏干脆地说，"我认为学生是不应该——"

"噢，我们去过，"乔治说，指了指弗雷德，"去过好多次，为了偷点东西吃。我们遇见过他们，他们很开心。他们认为自己得到了世界上最好的工作——"

"那是因为他们没有受过教育，并被灌输了一些错误思想！"赫敏激动地说，可是她下面的话被头顶上一阵突如其来的嗖嗖声淹没了，这声音说明猫头鹰们送信来了。哈利立刻抬起头，看见海德薇正朝他飞来。赫敏也马上停止了说话，和罗恩一起焦虑地望着海德薇，只见它扑棱棱地落到哈利肩膀上，收起双翅，疲倦地伸出一条腿。

哈利抽出小天狼星的回信，然后把他那份熏咸肉的皮递到海德薇嘴里，海德薇感激地吃着。哈利张望了一下，确信弗雷德和乔治又在埋头商量三强争霸赛的事了，便把小天狼星的信小声地念给罗恩和赫敏听。

> 哈利，我理解你的苦心。
>
> 　我回国了，隐蔽得很安全。我希望你把霍格沃茨发生的每件事都写信告诉我。不要用海德薇，要不停地换其他猫头鹰。别为我担忧，你自己多加小心。别忘了我说的关于你伤疤的话。
>
> 　　　　　　　　　　　　　　　　　　　　　　　小天狼星

"为什么要不停地换猫头鹰？"罗恩低声问。

"海德薇会引人注目的，"赫敏立刻说道，"它太显眼了。一只雪白的猫头鹰一而再、再而三地回到他的藏身之处……我的意思是，它可不是当地普通的鸟类，对吧？"

哈利把信卷起来，塞进了他的长袍里面。他不知道自己是放心了，

## CHAPTER FIFTEEN  Beauxbatons and Durmstrang

whether he felt more or less worried than before. He supposed that Sirius managing to get back without being caught was something. He couldn't deny, either, that the idea that Sirius was much nearer was reassuring; at least he wouldn't have to wait so long for a response every time he wrote.

'Thanks, Hedwig,' he said, stroking her. She hooted sleepily, dipped her beak briefly into his goblet of orange juice, then took off again, clearly desperate for a good long sleep in the Owlery.

There was a pleasant feeling of anticipation in the air that day. Nobody was very attentive in lessons, being much more interested in the arrival that evening of the people from Beauxbatons and Durmstrang; even Potions was more bearable than usual, as it was half an hour shorter. When the bell rang early, Harry, Ron and Hermione hurried up to Gryffindor Tower, deposited their bags and books as they had been instructed, pulled on their cloaks and rushed back downstairs into the Entrance Hall.

The Heads of houses were ordering their students into lines.

'Weasley, straighten your hat,' Professor McGonagall snapped at Ron. 'Miss Patil, take that ridiculous thing out of your hair.'

Parvati scowled and removed a large ornamental butterfly from the end of her plait.

'Follow me, please,' said Professor McGonagall, 'first-years in front ... no pushing ...'

They filed down the front steps and lined up in front of the castle. It was a cold, clear evening; dusk was falling and a pale, transparent-looking moon was already shining over the Forbidden Forest. Harry, standing between Ron and Hermione in the fourth row from the front, saw Dennis Creevey positively shivering with anticipation among the other first-years.

'Nearly six,' said Ron, checking his watch and then staring down the drive which led to the front gates. 'How d'you reckon they're coming? The train?'

'I doubt it,' said Hermione.

'How, then? Broomsticks?' Harry suggested, looking up at the starry sky.

'I don't think so ... not from that far away ...'

'A Portkey?' Ron suggested. 'Or they could Apparate – maybe you're allowed to do it under seventeen wherever they come from?'

'You can't Apparate inside the Hogwarts grounds, how often do I have to tell you?' said Hermione impatiently.

## 第15章 布斯巴顿和德姆斯特朗

还是比以前更担心了。他想，小天狼星能够顺利回来而没被抓住，总是一件好事。同时他也无法否认，一想到小天狼星现在离他近了许多，确实感到十分宽慰，至少他每次写信用不着等待那么久才收到回信了。

"谢谢，海德薇。"哈利抚摸着它说道。海德薇困倦地叫了几声，把它的喙伸进哈利盛橘子汁的高脚酒杯里蘸了蘸，然后又起飞了，看样子是急着赶回猫头鹰棚屋好好地睡一觉。

那天，空气里弥漫着一种有所期待的喜悦情绪。课堂上，没有人专心听课，大家都想着今天晚上布斯巴顿和德姆斯特朗的人就要来了。就连魔药课也不像平常那样难以忍受了，因为要提前半小时下课。当铃声早早地敲响后，哈利、罗恩和赫敏匆匆赶到格兰芬多塔楼，按吩咐放下他们的书包和课本，穿上斗篷，然后三步并作两步地冲下楼梯，来到门厅。

学院院长们正在命令自己的学生排队。

"韦斯莱，把帽子戴正。"麦格教授严厉地对罗恩说，"佩蒂尔小姐，把头发上那个荒唐可笑的东西拿掉。"

帕瓦蒂不高兴地皱着眉头，把一只大蝴蝶头饰从辫梢上取了下来。

"请大家跟我来，"麦格教授说，"一年级的同学在前面……不要拥挤……"

他们鱼贯走下台阶，排着队站在城堡前。这是一个寒冷的、空气清新的傍晚，夜幕正在降临，一轮洁白的、半透明的月亮已经挂在了禁林上空。哈利站在罗恩和赫敏中间，在正数第四排，他看见丹尼斯·克里维和其他一年级新生站在一起，激动得浑身颤抖。

"快六点了，"罗恩看了看手表，望着通向前门的车道，说，"你说他们会怎么来？乘火车吗？"

"我想不会。"赫敏说。

"那怎么来？飞天扫帚？"哈利抬头望着星光闪烁的天空，猜测道。

"我认为也不会……从那么远的地方……"

"门钥匙？"罗恩猜道，"或者可以幻影显形——也许在他们那个地方，不满十七岁的人也允许幻影显形？"

"在霍格沃茨的场地内不许幻影显形，我还要对你说多少遍？"赫敏不耐烦地说。

## CHAPTER FIFTEEN  Beauxbatons and Durmstrang

They scanned the darkening grounds excitedly, but nothing was moving; everything was still, silent and quite as usual. Harry was starting to feel cold. He wished they'd hurry up ... maybe the foreign students were preparing a dramatic entrance ... he remembered what Mr Weasley had said back on the campsite before the Quidditch World Cup – 'Always the same, we can't resist showing off when we get together ...'

And then Dumbledore called out from the back row, where he stood with the other teachers – 'Aha! Unless I am very much mistaken, the delegation from Beauxbatons approaches!'

'Where?' said many students eagerly, all looking in different directions.

'*There!*' yelled a sixth-year, pointing over the Forest.

Something large, much larger than a broomstick – or, indeed, a hundred broomsticks – was hurtling across the deep blue sky towards the castle, growing larger all the time.

'It's a dragon!' shrieked one of the first-years, losing her head completely.

'Don't be stupid ... it's a flying house!' said Dennis Creevey.

Dennis's guess was closer ... as the gigantic black shape skimmed over the treetops of the Forbidden Forest, and the lights shining from the castle windows hit it, they saw a gigantic, powder-blue, horse-drawn carriage, the size of a large house, soaring towards them, pulled through the air by a dozen winged horses, all palominos, and each the size of an elephant.

The front three rows of students drew backwards as the carriage hurtled ever lower, coming in to land at a tremendous speed – then, with an almighty crash that made Neville jump backwards onto a Slytherin fifth-year's foot – the horses' hooves, larger than dinner plates, hit the ground. A second later, the carriage landed too, bouncing upon its vast wheels, while the golden horses tossed their enormous heads and rolled large, fiery red eyes.

Harry just had time to see that the door of the carriage bore a coat of arms (two crossed, golden wands, each emitting three stars) before it opened.

A boy in pale blue robes jumped down from the carriage, bent forwards, fumbled for a moment with something on the carriage floor and unfolded a set of golden steps. He sprang back respectfully. Then Harry saw a shining, high-heeled black shoe emerging from the inside of the carriage – a shoe the size of a child's sled – followed, almost immediately, by the largest woman he had ever seen in his life. The size of the carriage, and of the horses, was

## 第15章 布斯巴顿和德姆斯特朗

他们兴奋地扫视着渐渐黑下来的场地,可是不见任何动静。一切都是沉寂、宁静的,和平常没什么两样。哈利开始感到冷了。他真希望他们能快一点儿……也许外国学生正在准备一次富有戏剧性的入场式……他想起了在魁地奇世界杯赛前,韦斯莱先生在营地上说的话:"总是这样——大家聚到一起时,就忍不住想炫耀一番……"

就在这时,和其他教师一起站在后排的邓布利多喊了起来——

"啊!如果我没有弄错的话,布斯巴顿的代表已经来了!"

"在哪儿?"许多学生急切地问,朝不同方向张望着。

"那儿!"一个六年级学生喊道,指着禁林上空。

一个庞然大物,比一把飞天扫帚——或者说比一百把飞天扫帚——还要大得多,正急速地掠过深蓝色的天空,朝城堡飞来,渐渐地越来越大。

"是一条火龙!"一个一年级新生尖叫道,激动得不知该怎么办了。

"别说傻话了……是一座房子在飞!"丹尼斯·克里维说。

丹尼斯的猜测更接近一些……当那个黑乎乎的庞然大物从禁林的树梢上掠过,被城堡窗口的灯光照着时,他们看见一辆巨大的粉蓝色马车朝他们飞来。它有一座房子那么大,十二匹长着翅膀的马拉着它腾空飞翔,都是银鬃马,每匹马都和大象差不多大。

马车飞得更低了,正以无比迅疾的速度降落,站在前三排的同学急忙后退——然后,一阵惊天动地的巨响,吓得纳威往后一跳,踩到了一个斯莱特林五年级同学的脚——只见那些马蹄砰砰地落到地面上,个个都有菜盘子那么大。眨眼之间,马车也降落到地面,在巨大的轮子上震动着,同时那些金色的马抖动着它们硕大的脑袋,火红的大眼睛滴溜溜地转。

哈利刚来得及看见车门上印着的一个饰章(两根十字交叉的金灿灿的魔杖,每根上都冒出三颗星星),车门就打开了。

一个穿着浅蓝色长袍的男孩跳下马车,弯下身子,在马车的地板上摸索着什么,然后打开一个金色的旋梯。他毕恭毕敬地往后一跳,哈利看见一只闪亮的黑色高跟鞋从马车里伸了出来——这只鞋就有儿童用的小雪橇那么大——紧跟着出现了一个女人,块头之大,是他这

## CHAPTER FIFTEEN    Beauxbatons and Durmstrang

immediately explained. A few people gasped.

Harry had only ever seen one person as large as this woman in his life, and that was Hagrid; he doubted whether there was an inch difference in their heights. Yet somehow – maybe simply because he was used to Hagrid – this woman (now at the foot of the steps, and looking around at the waiting, wide-eyed crowd) seemed even more unnaturally large. As she stepped into the light flooding from the Entrance Hall, she was revealed to have a handsome, olive-skinned face, large, black, liquid-looking eyes and a rather beaky nose. Her hair was drawn back in a shining knob at the base of her neck. She was dressed from head to foot in black satin, and many magnificent opals gleamed at her throat and on her thick fingers.

Dumbledore started to clap; the students, following his lead, broke into applause too, many of them standing on tiptoe, the better to look at this woman.

Her face relaxed into a gracious smile, and she walked forwards towards Dumbledore, extending a glittering hand. Dumbledore, though tall himself, had barely to bend to kiss it.

'My dear Madame Maxime,' he said. 'Welcome to Hogwarts.'

'Dumbly-dorr,' said Madame Maxime, in a deep voice. 'I 'ope I find you well?'

'On excellent form, I thank you,' said Dumbledore.

'My pupils,' said Madame Maxime, waving one of her enormous hands carelessly behind her.

Harry, whose attention had been focused completely upon Madame Maxime, now noticed that around a dozen boys and girls – all, by the look of them, in their late teens – had emerged from the carriage and were now standing behind Madame Maxime. They were shivering, which was unsurprising, given that their robes seemed to be made of fine silk, and none of them were wearing cloaks. A few of them had wrapped scarves and shawls around their heads. From what Harry could see of their faces (they were standing in Madame Maxime's enormous shadow), they were staring up at Hogwarts with apprehensive looks on their faces.

''As Karkaroff arrived yet?' Madame Maxime asked.

'He should be here any moment,' said Dumbledore. 'Would you like to wait here and greet him or would you prefer to step inside and warm up a trifle?'

## 第15章 布斯巴顿和德姆斯特朗

辈子从没见过的。这样，马车和那些银鬃马为什么这么大就不言自明了。几个人惊得倒吸一口冷气。

哈利这辈子只见过一个人的块头能跟这个女人相比，那就是海格，他怀疑他们俩的身高几乎没有差别。然而不知怎的——也许只是因为他已经习惯了海格——这个女人（此刻已到了台阶下，正转过身来看着睁大眼睛静候的人群）似乎更加大得离奇。当她走进从门厅泄出的灯光中时，大家发现她有着一张很俊秀的橄榄色的脸，一双水汪汪的又黑又大的眼睛，还有一个尖尖的鼻子，头发梳在脑后，在脖子根部绾成一个闪亮的髻。她从头到脚裹着一件黑缎子衣服，脖子上和粗大的手指上都闪耀着许多华贵的蛋白石。

邓布利多开始鼓掌，同学们也跟着拍起了巴掌，好些人踮着脚尖，想把这个女人看得更清楚些。

她的脸松弛下来，绽开一个优雅的微笑，她伸出一只闪闪发光的手，朝邓布利多走去。邓布利多虽然也是高个子，但吻这只手时几乎没有弯腰。

"亲爱的马克西姆女士，"他说，"欢迎您来到霍格沃茨。"

"邓布利多，"马克西姆女士用低沉的声音说，"我希望您一切都好。"

"非常好，谢谢您。"邓布利多说。

"我的学生。"马克西姆女士说着，抬起一只巨大的手，漫不经心地朝身后挥了挥。

哈利刚才只顾盯着马克西姆女士，这时才注意到大约十二三个男女学生已从马车上下来，此刻正站在马克西姆女士身后。从他们的模样看，年龄大概都在十八九岁左右，一个个都在微微颤抖。这不奇怪，因为他们身上的长袍似乎是精致的丝绸做成，而且谁也没有穿斗篷。有几个学生用围巾或头巾裹住了脑袋。从哈利可以望见的情形看（他们都站在马克西姆女士投下的巨大阴影里），他们都抬头望着霍格沃茨，脸上带着不安的神情。

"卡卡洛夫来了吗？"马克西姆女士问道。

"他随时都会来。"邓布利多说，"您是愿意在这里等着迎接他，还是愿意先进去暖和暖和？"

## CHAPTER FIFTEEN   Beauxbatons and Durmstrang

'Warm up, I think,' said Madame Maxime. 'But ze 'orses –'

'Our Care of Magical Creatures teacher will be delighted to take care of them,' said Dumbledore, 'the moment he has returned from dealing with a slight situation which has arisen with some of his other – er – charges.'

'Skrewts,' Ron muttered to Harry, grinning.

'My steeds require – er – forceful 'andling,' said Madame Maxime, looking as though she doubted whether any Care of Magical Creatures teacher at Hogwarts could be up to the job. 'Zey are very strong …'

'I assure you that Hagrid will be well up to the job,' said Dumbledore, smiling.

'Very well,' said Madame Maxime, bowing slightly, 'will you please inform zis 'Agrid zat ze 'orses drink only single-malt whisky?'

'It will be attended to,' said Dumbledore, also bowing.

'Come,' said Madame Maxime imperiously to her students, and the Hogwarts crowd parted to allow her and her students to pass up the stone steps.

'How big d'you reckon Durmstrang's horses are going to be?' Seamus Finnigan said, leaning around Lavender and Parvati to address Harry and Ron.

'Well, if they're any bigger than this lot, even Hagrid won't be able to handle them,' said Harry. 'That's if he hasn't been attacked by his Skrewts. Wonder what's up with them?'

'Maybe they've escaped,' said Ron hopefully.

'Oh, don't say that,' said Hermione, with a shudder. 'Imagine that lot loose in the grounds …'

They stood, shivering slightly now, waiting for the Durmstrang party to arrive. Most people were gazing hopefully up at the sky. For a few minutes, the silence was broken only by Madame Maxime's huge horses snorting and stamping. But then –

'Can you hear something?' said Ron suddenly.

Harry listened; a loud and oddly eerie noise was drifting towards them from out of the darkness; a muffled rumbling and sucking sound, as though an immense vacuum cleaner was moving along a riverbed …

'The lake!' yelled Lee Jordan, pointing down at it. 'Look at the lake!'

From their position at the top of the lawns overlooking the grounds, they

## 第15章 布斯巴顿和德姆斯特朗

"还是暖和一下吧。"马克西姆女士说,"可是那些马——"

"我们的保护神奇动物老师会很乐意照料它们的,"邓布利多说,"他处理完一个小乱子就回来,是他的——嗯——他要照管的另外一些东西出了乱子。"

"是炸尾螺。"罗恩嘻嘻笑着对哈利小声说。

"我的骏马需要——嗯——力气很大的人才能照料好,"马克西姆女士说,似乎怀疑霍格沃茨的保护神奇动物老师能否胜任这项工作,"它们性子很烈……"

"我向您保证,海格完全能够干好这项工作。"邓布利多微笑着说。

"很好。"马克西姆女士说,微微鞠了一躬,"您能否告诉这个海格一声,这些马只喝纯麦芽威士忌?"

"我会关照的。"邓布利多说,也鞠了一躬。

"来吧。"马克西姆女士威严地对她的学生们说。霍格沃茨的人群闪开一条通道,让她和她的学生走上石阶。

"你认为德姆斯特朗的马会有多大?"西莫·斐尼甘探过身子,隔着拉文德和帕瓦蒂问哈利和罗恩。

"啊,如果它们比这些马还大,那恐怕连海格也摆弄不了啦,"哈利说,"我是说如果海格没有被他那些炸尾螺咬伤的话。不知道它们出了什么乱子?"

"大概是逃跑了。"罗恩满怀希望地说。

"哦,千万别这么说,"赫敏打了个冷战,说道,"想想吧,这些家伙在场地上到处乱爬……"

他们站在那里,等候德姆斯特朗一行人的到来,已经冻得微微有些发抖了。大多数人都眼巴巴地抬头望着天空。一时间四下里一片寂静,只听见马克西姆女士的巨马喷鼻息、跺蹄子的声音。就在这时——

"你听见什么没有?"罗恩突然问道。

哈利仔细倾听。一个很响很古怪的声音从黑暗中向他们飘来:是一种被压抑的隆隆声和吮吸声,就像一个巨大的吸尘器在沿着河床移动……

"在湖里!"李·乔丹大喊一声,指着湖面,"快看湖上!"

他们站在俯瞰场地的草坡上,可以清楚地看到那片平静的黑乎乎

had a clear view of the smooth black surface of the water – except that the surface was suddenly not smooth at all. Some disturbance was taking place deep in the centre; great bubbles were forming on the surface, waves were now washing over the muddy banks – and then, out in the very middle of the lake, a whirlpool appeared, as if a giant plug had just been pulled out of the lake's floor ...

What seemed to be a long, black pole began to rise slowly out of the heart of the whirlpool ... and then Harry saw the rigging ...

'It's a mast!' he said to Ron and Hermione.

Slowly, magnificently, the ship rose out of the water, gleaming in the moonlight. It had a strangely skeletal look about it, as though it was a resurrected wreck, and the dim, misty lights shimmering at its portholes looked like ghostly eyes. Finally, with a great sloshing noise, the ship emerged entirely, bobbing on the turbulent water, and began to glide towards the bank. A few moments later, they heard the splash of an anchor being thrown down in the shallows, and the thud of a plank being lowered onto the bank.

People were disembarking; they could see their silhouettes passing the lights in the ship's portholes. All of them, Harry noticed, seemed to be built along the lines of Crabbe and Goyle ... but then, as they drew nearer, walking up the lawns into the light streaming from the Entrance Hall, he saw that their bulk was really due to the fact that they were wearing cloaks of some kind of shaggy, matted fur. But the man who was leading them up to the castle was wearing furs of a different sort; sleek and silver, like his hair.

'Dumbledore!' he called heartily, as he walked up the slope. 'How are you, my dear fellow, how are you?'

'Blooming, thank you, Professor Karkaroff,' Dumbledore replied.

Karkaroff had a fruity, unctuous voice; when he stepped into the light pouring from the front doors of the castle, they saw that he was tall and thin like Dumbledore, but his white hair was short, and his goatee (finishing in a small curl) did not entirely hide his rather weak chin. When he reached Dumbledore, he shook hands with both of his own.

'Dear old Hogwarts,' he said, looking up at the castle and smiling; his teeth were rather yellow, and Harry noticed that his smile did not extend to his eyes, which remained cold and shrewd. 'How good it is to be here, how good ... Viktor, come along, into the warmth ... you don't mind, Dumbledore? Viktor

## 第15章 布斯巴顿和德姆斯特朗

的水面——不过那水面突然变得不再平静。湖中央的水下起了骚动，水面上翻起巨大的气泡，波浪冲打着泥泞的湖岸——然后，就在湖面的正中央，出现了一个大漩涡，就好像一个巨大的塞子突然从湖底被拔了出来……

一个黑黑的长杆似的东西从漩涡中心慢慢升起……接着哈利看见了船帆索具……

"是一根桅杆！"他对罗恩和赫敏说。

慢慢地，气派非凡地，那艘大船升出了水面，在月光下闪闪发亮。它的样子很怪异，如同一具骷髅，就好像是一艘刚被打捞上来的沉船遗骸，舷窗闪烁着昏暗的、雾蒙蒙的微光，看上去就像幽灵的眼睛。最后，随着一阵稀里哗啦的水声，大船完全冒了出来，在波涛起伏的水面上颠簸，开始朝着湖岸驶来。片刻之后，他们听见扑通一声，一只铁锚扔进了浅水里，然后又是啪的一声，一块木板搭在了湖岸上。

船上的人正在上岸，哈利他们可以看见这些人经过舷窗灯光时的剪影。哈利注意到，他们的身架都跟克拉布和高尔差不多……然而当他们更走近些，顺着草坪走进门厅投出的光线中时，哈利才发现他们之所以显得块头很大，是因为都穿着一种毛皮斗篷，上面的毛蓬乱纠结。不过领着他们走向城堡的那个男人，身上穿的皮毛却是另外一种：银白色的，又柔又滑，很像他的头发。

"邓布利多！"那男人走上斜坡时热情地喊道，"我亲爱的老伙计，你怎么样？"

"好极了，谢谢你，卡卡洛夫教授。"邓布利多回答。

卡卡洛夫的声音圆润润甜腻腻的。当他走进从城堡正门射出的灯光中时，他们看见他像邓布利多一样又高又瘦，但白色的头发很短，山羊胡子（末梢上打着小卷儿）没有完全遮住他瘦削的下巴。他走到邓布利多面前，用两只手同邓布利多握手。

"亲爱的老伙计霍格沃茨，"他抬头望着城堡，微笑着说——他的牙齿很黄，哈利还注意到他尽管脸上笑着，眼睛里却无笑意，依然是冷漠和犀利的，"来到这里真好啊，真好啊……威克多尔，快过来，暖

### CHAPTER FIFTEEN    Beauxbatons and Durmstrang

has a slight head cold ...'

Karkaroff beckoned forwards one of his students. As the boy passed, Harry caught a glimpse of a prominent, curved nose and thick black eyebrows. He didn't need the punch on the arm Ron gave him, or the hiss in his ear, to recognise that profile.

'Harry – *it's Krum!*'

## 第 15 章　布斯巴顿和德姆斯特朗

和一下……你不介意吧，邓布利多？威克多尔有点感冒了……"

卡卡洛夫示意他的一个学生上前。当那男孩走过时，哈利瞥见了一个引人注目的鹰钩鼻和两道又粗又黑的眉毛。他不需要罗恩那样使劲地捅他的胳膊，也不需要别人在周围窃窃私语，就已认出了那个身影。

"哈利——是克鲁姆！"

## CHAPTER SIXTEEN

# The Goblet of Fire

'I don't believe it!' Ron said, in a stunned voice, as the Hogwarts students filed back up the steps behind the party from Durmstrang. 'Krum, Harry! *Viktor Krum!*'

'For heaven's sake, Ron, he's only a Quidditch player,' said Hermione.

'*Only a Quidditch player?*' Ron said, looking at her as though he couldn't believe his ears. 'Hermione – he's one of the best Seekers in the world! I had no idea he was still at school!'

As they recrossed the Entrance Hall with the rest of the Hogwarts students, heading for the Great Hall, Harry saw Lee Jordan jumping up and down on the soles of his feet to get a better look at the back of Krum's head. Several sixth-year girls were frantically searching their pockets as they walked – 'Oh, I don't believe it, I haven't got a single quill on me –' 'D'you think he'd sign my hat in lipstick?'

'*Really*,' Hermione said loftily, as they passed the girls, now squabbling over the lipstick.

'*I'm* getting his autograph if I can,' said Ron, 'you haven't got a quill, have you, Harry?'

'Nope, they're upstairs in my bag,' said Harry.

They walked over to the Gryffindor table and sat down. Ron took care to sit on the side facing the doorway, because Krum and his fellow Durmstrang students were still gathered around it, apparently unsure about where they should sit. The students from Beauxbatons had chosen seats at the Ravenclaw table. They were looking around the Great Hall with glum expressions on their faces. Three of them were still clutching scarves and shawls around their heads.

## 第 16 章

## 火 焰 杯

"**真**不敢相信！"罗恩用一种大为震惊的口吻说——这时霍格沃茨的学生正跟在德姆斯特朗一行人的后面，排队登上石阶，"是克鲁姆，哈利！威克多尔·克鲁姆！"

"看在老天的分上，罗恩，他只是个魁地奇球员罢了。"赫敏说。

"只是个魁地奇球员罢了？"罗恩愣愣地看着她，似乎不敢相信自己的耳朵，"赫敏——他是世界上最棒的找球手之一啊！真没想到他还是个学生！"

当他们和霍格沃茨的其他学生一起再次穿过门厅朝礼堂走去时，哈利看见李·乔丹踮着脚跳上跳下，想把克鲁姆的背影看得更清楚一些。几个六年级女生一边走，一边发疯似的在口袋里翻找着什么——

"唉，真不敢相信，我身上怎么一支羽毛笔也没带——"

"你说，他会用口红在我帽子上签名吗？"

"太荒唐了！"赫敏高傲地说，他们三人从那几个为一支口红争来吵去的女生身边走过。

"如果可能的话，我要得到他的签名照片。"罗恩说，"你没带羽毛笔吧，哈利？"

"没有，都在楼上我的书包里呢。"哈利说。

他们走到格兰芬多的桌子旁坐了下来。罗恩特意坐在朝着门口的那一边，因为克鲁姆和他那些德姆斯特朗的校友还聚集在门口，似乎拿不准应该坐在哪里。布斯巴顿的同学已经选择了拉文克劳桌子旁的座位。他们坐下后，东张西望地打量着礼堂，脸上带着闷闷不乐的表情。其中三个同学仍然用围巾和头巾紧紧裹着脑袋。

## CHAPTER SIXTEEN   The Goblet of Fire

'It's not *that* cold,' said Hermione irritably, who was watching them. 'Why didn't they bring cloaks?'

'Over here! Come and sit over here!' Ron hissed. 'Over here! Hermione, budge up, make a space –'

'What?'

'Too late,' said Ron bitterly.

Viktor Krum and his fellow Durmstrang students had settled themselves at the Slytherin table. Harry could see Malfoy, Crabbe and Goyle looking very smug about this. As he watched, Malfoy bent forwards to speak to Krum.

'Yeah, that's right, smarm up to him, Malfoy,' said Ron scathingly. 'I bet Krum can see right through him, though … bet he gets people fawning over him all the time … where d'you reckon they're going to sleep? We could offer him a space in our dormitory, Harry … I wouldn't mind giving him my bed, I could kip on a camp-bed.'

Hermione snorted.

'They look a lot happier than the Beauxbatons lot,' said Harry.

The Durmstrang students were pulling off their heavy furs and looking up at the starry black ceiling with expressions of interest; a couple of them were picking up the golden plates and goblets and examining them, apparently impressed.

Up at the staff table, Filch, the caretaker, was adding chairs. He was wearing his mouldy old tail coat in honour of the occasion. Harry was surprised to see that he added four chairs, two on either side of Dumbledore's.

'But there are only two extra people,' Harry said. 'Why's Filch putting out four chairs? Who else is coming?'

'Eh?' said Ron vaguely. He was still staring avidly at Krum.

When all the students had entered the Hall and settled down at their house tables, the staff entered, filing up to the top table and taking their seats. Last in line were Professor Dumbledore, Professor Karkaroff and Madame Maxime. When their Headmistress appeared, the pupils from Beauxbatons leapt to their feet. A few of the Hogwarts students laughed. The Beauxbatons party appeared quite unembarrassed, and did not resume their seats until Madame Maxime had sat down on Dumbledore's left-hand side. Dumbledore, however, remained standing, and a silence fell over the Great

## 第16章 火焰杯

"没有那么冷吧,"赫敏不满地说,"他们为什么不带上斗篷呢?"

"在这儿!快过来坐在这儿!"罗恩嘶哑着声音说,"这儿!赫敏,挪过去一点儿,腾出空来——"

"什么?"

"唉,来不及了!"罗恩遗憾地说。

威克多尔·克鲁姆和他那些德姆斯特朗的校友已经在斯莱特林桌子旁落座了。哈利可以看见,马尔福、克拉布和高尔因此而得意扬扬。他看见马尔福倾着身子在跟克鲁姆说话。

"啊,没错,马尔福在巴结他呢。"罗恩尖刻地说,"我敢打赌,克鲁姆一眼就看透了他是个什么货色……我敢说克鲁姆走到哪儿都有人在讨好他、奉承他……你们说,他们会睡在什么地方?我们可以在宿舍里给他提供一个床位,哈利……我愿意把我的床让给他睡,我睡在行军床上。"

赫敏的鼻子里哼了一声。

"他们看上去可比布斯巴顿那伙人开心多了。"哈利说。

德姆斯特朗的学生们一边脱下身上沉重的毛皮斗篷,一边饶有兴致地抬头望着漆黑的、星光闪烁的天花板。其中两个学生还拿起金色的盘子和高脚酒杯,仔细端详,显然很感兴趣。

在那边的教工桌子旁,管理员费尔奇正在添加几把椅子。为了今天这个隆重的场面,他穿上了那件发霉的旧燕尾服。哈利惊讶地看到他加了四把椅子,在邓布利多两边各加了两把。

"可是只多出了两个人哪,"哈利说,"费尔奇为什么要搬出四把椅子,还有谁会来呢?"

"嗯?"罗恩含含糊糊地回答,仍然眼巴巴地盯着克鲁姆。

等所有的学生都进入礼堂、在各自学院的桌子旁落座之后,教工们进来了,他们鱼贯走到主宾席上坐了下来。走在最后的是邓布利多教授、卡卡洛夫教授和马克西姆女士。布斯巴顿的学生一看见他们的校长出现,赶紧站了起来。几个霍格沃茨学生忍不住笑了。但布斯巴顿的学生丝毫没有显得难为情,直到马克西姆女士在邓布利多的左手边坐下后,他们才又重新坐下。邓布利多则一直站着,礼堂里渐渐安

## CHAPTER SIXTEEN   The Goblet of Fire

Hall.

'Good evening, ladies and gentlemen, ghosts and – most particularly – guests,' said Dumbledore, beaming around at the foreign students. 'I have great pleasure in welcoming you all to Hogwarts. I hope and trust that your stay here will be both comfortable and enjoyable.'

One of the Beauxbatons girls still clutching a muffler around her head gave what was unmistakeably a derisive laugh.

'No one's making you stay!' Hermione whispered, bristling at her.

'The Tournament will be officially opened at the end of the feast,' said Dumbledore. 'I now invite you all to eat, drink, and make yourselves at home!'

He sat down, and Harry saw Karkaroff lean forward at once and engage him in conversation.

The dishes in front of them filled with food as usual. The house-elves in the kitchen seemed to have pulled out all the stops; there was a greater variety of dishes in front of them than Harry had ever seen, including several that were definitely foreign.

'What's *that*?' said Ron, pointing at a large dish of some sort of shellfish stew that stood beside a large steak-and-kidney pudding.

'Bouillabaisse,' said Hermione.

'Bless you,' said Ron.

'It's *French*,' said Hermione. 'I had it on holiday, summer before last, it's very nice.'

'I'll take your word for it,' said Ron, helping himself to black pudding.

The Great Hall seemed somehow much more crowded than usual, even though there were barely twenty additional students there; perhaps it was because their differently coloured uniforms stood out so clearly against the black of the Hogwarts robes. Now that they had removed their furs, the Durmstrang students were revealed to be wearing robes of a deep, blood red.

Hagrid sidled into the Hall through a door behind the staff table twenty minutes after the start of the feast. He slid into his seat at the end and waved at Harry, Ron and Hermione with a very heavily bandaged hand.

'Skrewts doing all right, Hagrid?' Harry called.

'Thrivin',' Hagrid called back happily.

'Yeah, I'll just bet they are,' said Ron quietly. 'Looks like they've finally found a food they like, doesn't it? Hagrid's fingers.'

## 第16章 火焰杯

静下来。

"晚上好,女士们,先生们,幽灵们,还有——特别是——贵宾们,"邓布利多说,笑眯眯地望着那些外国学生,"我怀着极大的喜悦,欢迎你们来到霍格沃茨。我希望并且相信,你们会在这里感到舒适愉快。"

一个布斯巴顿的女生仍然用围巾紧紧裹着脑袋,发出一声无疑是讥讽的冷笑。

"又没有人强迫你们留下来!"赫敏小声说,她被那个女生惹恼了。

"争霸赛将于宴会结束时正式开始。"邓布利多说,"我现在邀请大家尽情地吃喝,就像在自己家里一样!"

他坐下了,哈利看见卡卡洛夫立刻靠上前去,跟他交谈。

大家面前的盘子里又像往常一样堆满了食物。厨房里的那些家养小精灵似乎使出了浑身解数。哈利从没见过这么丰盛的菜肴,五花八门地摆在他们面前,其中有几样肯定是外国风味的。

"那是什么?"罗恩问,指着大块牛排腰子布丁旁边的一大盘东西,看样子像是海鲜大杂烩。

"法式杂鱼汤。"赫敏说。

"听不懂。"罗恩说。

"这是法国菜,"赫敏说,"我前年暑假吃过。味道很鲜美的。"

"我就相信你吧。"罗恩说着,给自己盛了一些黑布丁。

不知怎的,礼堂似乎比往常拥挤多了,尽管只多了不到二十个学生,也许是因为他们不同颜色的校服与霍格沃茨的黑袍服相比,显得特别突出。德姆斯特朗的学生脱去了毛皮斗篷,露出里面穿着的血红色长袍。

宴会开始二十分钟后,海格从教工桌子后面的一道门中溜进礼堂。他坐到桌子末端他的座位上,举起一只缠着许多绷带的手,朝哈利、罗恩和赫敏挥了挥。

"炸尾螺怎么样啊,海格?"哈利大声问道。

"长势喜人。"海格高兴地回答。

"是啊,我猜肯定是这样,"罗恩小声说,"看来它们终于找到了一种爱吃的东西了,是吧?那就是海格的手指。"

## CHAPTER SIXTEEN  The Goblet of Fire

At that moment, a voice said, 'Excuse me, are you wanting ze bouillabaisse?'

It was the girl from Beauxbatons who had laughed during Dumbledore's speech. She had finally removed her muffler. A long sheet of silvery blonde hair fell almost to her waist. She had large, deep blue eyes, and very white, even teeth.

Ron went purple. He stared up at her, opened his mouth to reply, but nothing came out except a faint gurgling noise.

'Yeah, have it,' said Harry, pushing the dish towards the girl.

'You 'ave finished wiz it?'

'Yeah,' Ron said breathlessly. 'Yeah, it was excellent.'

The girl picked up the dish and carried it carefully off to the Ravenclaw table. Ron was still goggling at the girl as though he had never seen one before. Harry started to laugh. The sound seemed to jog Ron back to his senses.

'She's a *Veela*!' he said hoarsely to Harry.

'Of course she isn't!' said Hermione tartly. 'I don't see anyone else gaping at her like an idiot!'

But she wasn't entirely right about that. As the girl crossed the Hall, many boys' heads turned, and some of them seemed to have become temporarily speechless, just like Ron.

'I'm telling you, that's not a normal girl!' said Ron, leaning sideways so he could keep a clear view of her. 'They don't make them like that at Hogwarts!'

'They make them OK at Hogwarts,' said Harry, without thinking. Cho Chang happened to be sitting only a few places away from the girl with the silvery hair.

'When you've both put your eyes back in,' said Hermione briskly, 'you'll be able to see who's just arrived.'

She was pointing up at the staff table. The two remaining empty seats had just been filled. Ludo Bagman was now sitting on Professor Karkaroff's other side, while Mr Crouch, Percy's boss, was next to Madame Maxime.

'What are they doing here?' said Harry in surprise.

'They organised the Triwizard Tournament, didn't they?' said Hermione. 'I suppose they wanted to be here to see it start.'

When the second course arrived they noticed a number of unfamiliar

## 第16章 火焰杯

就在这时,一个声音说道:"请原谅,这盘杂鱼汤你们还吃吗?"

正是刚才邓布利多说话时发笑的那个布斯巴顿女生。她终于把围巾摘掉了。一头长长的瀑布般的银亮秀发垂到她的腰际。她有着一双湛蓝色的大眼睛和一口洁白整齐的牙齿。

罗恩的脸一下子涨得通红。他呆呆地望着对方,张开嘴巴想回答,可是只发出了一些奇怪的小声音,好像喉咙被卡住了似的。

"好吧,你端去吧。"哈利说,把盘子推给了那个女生。

"你们吃完了吗?"

"吃完了,"罗恩喘不过气来地说,"吃完了,好吃极了。"

那女生小心翼翼地端着盘子,走向拉文克劳的桌子。罗恩仍然睁大眼睛盯着她,好像以前从没见过女生一样。哈利笑了起来。这声音似乎使罗恩突然醒过神来。

"她是个媚娃!"他嘶哑着声音对哈利说。

"肯定不是!"赫敏尖刻地说,"我没看见别人像白痴一样瞪着她!"

她说得并不完全正确。当那个女生在礼堂里走过时,许多男生都转过脑袋望着她,有几个似乎一时间变得不会说话了,正和罗恩一模一样。

"我说,那女生真是不一般!"罗恩说,一边侧过身子,使自己仍然可以清楚地看见她,"霍格沃茨就没有这样的人物!"

"霍格沃茨的女生也不错。"哈利不假思索地说。秋·张正巧与那个银色头发的女生隔着几个座位。

"等你们俩都把目光收回来以后,"赫敏很不客气地说,"就可以看见刚才是谁进来了。"

她指着教工桌子。两个一直空着的座位刚刚被填满了。卢多·巴格曼坐在卡卡洛夫教授的另一边,珀西的顶头上司克劳奇先生则坐在马克西姆女士的旁边。

"他们来做什么?"哈利惊讶地问。

"三强争霸赛是他们组织的,是不是?"赫敏说,"我猜他们是想亲眼目睹争霸赛的开幕式。"

第二道菜上来了,他们注意到有许多甜食也是从来没见过的。罗

## CHAPTER SIXTEEN   The Goblet of Fire

puddings, too. Ron examined an odd sort of pale blancmange closely, then moved it carefully a few inches to his right, so that it would be clearly visible from the Ravenclaw table. The girl who looked like a Veela appeared to have eaten enough, however, and did not come over to get it.

Once the golden plates had been wiped clean, Dumbledore stood up again. A pleasant sort of tension seemed to fill the Hall now. Harry felt a slight thrill of excitement, wondering what was coming. Several seats along from them, Fred and George were leaning forwards, staring at Dumbledore with great concentration.

'The moment has come,' said Dumbledore, smiling around at the sea of upturned faces. 'The Triwizard Tournament is about to start. I would like to say a few words of explanation before we bring in the casket –'

'The what?' Harry muttered.

Ron shrugged.

'– just to clarify the procedure which we will be following this year. But firstly, let me introduce, for those who do not know them, Mr Bartemius Crouch, Head of the Department of International Magical Co-operation' – there was a smattering of polite applause – 'and Mr Ludo Bagman, Head of the Department of Magical games and Sports.'

There was a much louder round of applause for Bagman than for Crouch, perhaps because of his fame as a Beater, or simply because he looked so much more likeable. He acknowledged it with a jovial wave of his hand. Bartemius Crouch did not smile or wave when his name was announced. Remembering him in his neat suit at the Quidditch World Cup, Harry thought he looked strange in wizard's robes. His toothbrush moustache and severe parting looked very odd next to Dumbledore's long white hair and beard.

'Mr Bagman and Mr Crouch have worked tirelessly over the last few months on the arrangements for the Triwizard Tournament,' Dumbledore continued, 'and they will be joining myself, Professor Karkaroff and Madame Maxime on the panel which will judge the champions' efforts.'

At the mention of the word 'champions', the attentiveness of the listening students seemed to sharpen.

Perhaps Dumbledore had noticed their sudden stillness, for he smiled as he said, 'The casket, then, if you please, Mr Filch.'

## 第 16 章 火焰杯

恩仔细端详了一番，那是一种古怪的、白生生的牛奶冻，他把它小心地挪到离他右手几英寸的地方，这样从拉文克劳桌子上就能清楚地看见它了。可是，那个模样酷似媚娃的女生似乎已经吃饱，没有过来端这盘甜食。

当一个个金色的盘子又被擦洗一新时，邓布利多再次站了起来。一种既兴奋又紧张的情绪似乎在礼堂里弥漫。哈利也感到一阵激动，不知道下面是什么节目。在与他隔几个座位的地方，弗雷德和乔治探着身子，十分专注地盯着邓布利多。

"这个时刻终于到来了，"邓布利多说，微笑地看着一张张仰起的脸，"三强争霸赛就要开始了。我想先解释几句，再把盒子拿进来——"

"把什么拿进来？"哈利小声问。

罗恩耸了耸肩膀。

"——我要说明我们这一学年的活动程序。不过首先请允许我介绍两位来宾，因为有人还不认识他们，这位是巴蒂·克劳奇先生，魔法部国际合作司司长，"——礼堂里响起了稀稀落落的掌声——"这位是卢多·巴格曼先生，魔法部体育运动司司长。"

给巴格曼的掌声要比给克劳奇的响亮得多，也许是因为他作为一名击球手小有名气，也许只是因为他的模样亲切得多。他愉快地挥挥手表示感谢。刚才介绍巴蒂·克劳奇的名字时，克劳奇既没有微笑，也没有挥手。哈利想起了他在魁地奇世界杯赛上一尘不染的西服革履，觉得他此刻穿着巫师长袍的样子有些怪异。和身边邓布利多长长的白发和白胡子相比，克劳奇那牙刷般的短胡髭和一丝不乱的分头显得非常别扭。

"在过去的几个月里，巴格曼先生和克劳奇先生一直在不知疲倦地为安排三强争霸赛辛勤工作，"邓布利多继续说道，"他们将和我、卡卡洛夫教授及马克西姆女士一起，组成裁判团，对勇士们的努力做出评判。"

一听到"勇士"这个词，同学们似乎更专心了。

邓布利多似乎也注意到大家突然静默下来，只见他微微一笑，说道："费尔奇先生，请把盒子拿上来。"

## CHAPTER SIXTEEN    The Goblet of Fire

Filch, who had been lurking unnoticed in a far corner of the Hall, now approached Dumbledore, carrying a great wooden chest, encrusted with jewels. It looked extremely old. A murmur of excited interest rose from the watching students; Dennis Creevey actually stood on his chair to see it properly, but, being so tiny, his head hardly rose above anyone else's.

'The instructions for the tasks the champions will face this year have already been examined by Mr Crouch and Mr Bagman,' said Dumbledore, as Filch placed the chest carefully on the table before him, 'and they have made the necessary arrangements for each challenge. There will be three tasks, spaced throughout the school year, and they will test the champions in many different ways ... their magical prowess – their daring – their powers of deduction – and, of course, their ability to cope with danger.'

At this last word, the Hall was filled with a silence so absolute that nobody seemed to be breathing.

'As you know, three champions compete in the Tournament,' Dumbledore went on calmly, 'one from each of the participating schools. They will be marked on how well they perform each of the Tournament tasks and the champion with the highest total after task three will win the Triwizard Cup. The champions will be chosen by an impartial selector ... the Goblet of Fire.'

Dumbledore now took out his wand, and tapped three times upon the top of the casket. The lid creaked slowly open. Dumbledore reached inside it, and pulled out a large, roughly hewn wooden cup. It would have been entirely unremarkable, had it not been full to the brim with dancing, blue-white flames.

Dumbledore closed the casket and placed the Goblet carefully on top of it, where it would be clearly visible to everyone in the Hall.

'Anybody wishing to submit themselves as champion must write their name and school clearly upon a slip of parchment, and drop it into the Goblet,' said Dumbledore. 'Aspiring champions have twenty-four hours in which to put their names forward. Tomorrow night, Hallowe'en, the Goblet will return the names of the three it has judged most worthy to represent their schools. The Goblet will be placed in the Entrance Hall tonight, where it will be freely accessible to all those wishing to compete.

'To ensure that no underage student yields to temptation,' said Dumbledore, 'I will be drawing an Age Line around the Goblet of Fire once

## 第 16 章 火焰杯

没有人注意到费尔奇刚才一直潜伏在礼堂的一个角落里，此刻他朝邓布利多走去，手里捧着一个镶嵌珠宝、看上去已经很旧的大木盒。学生们出神地看着，兴致勃勃地议论着。丹尼斯·克里维为了看得更清楚些，索性站到了椅子上，可是他的个头实在太小，即使站着，脑袋也比别人高出不了多少。

"今年勇士们比赛的具体项目，克劳奇先生和巴格曼先生已经仔细审查过了，"邓布利多说——这时费尔奇小心地把盒子放在他面前的桌子上，"他们还给每个项目做了许多必要的安排。项目一共有三个，分别在整个学年的不同时间进行，它们将从许多不同方面考验勇士……考验他们在魔法方面的才能——他们的胆量和他们的推理能力——当然啦，还有他们战胜危险的能力。"

听到最后这句话，礼堂里变得鸦雀无声，似乎每一个人都屏住了呼吸。

"你们已经知道，将有三位勇士参加比赛，"邓布利多继续平静地说，"分别代表不同的参赛学校。我们将根据他们完成每个比赛项目的质量给他们评分，三个项目结束后，得分最高的勇士将赢得三强杯。负责挑选勇士的是一位公正的选拔者，它就是火焰杯。"

说到这里，邓布利多拔出魔杖，在盒子盖上敲了三下。盒盖慢慢地、吱吱嘎嘎地打开了。邓布利多把手伸进去，掏出一只削刻得很粗糙的大大的木头高脚杯。杯子本身一点儿也不起眼，但里面却满是跳动着的蓝白色火焰。

邓布利多关上盒子，把杯子放在盒盖上，让礼堂里的每个人都能清楚地看到它。

"每一位想要竞选勇士的同学，都必须将他的姓名和学校清楚地写在一片羊皮纸上，扔进这只高脚杯，"邓布利多说，"有志成为勇士者可在二十四小时内报名。明天晚上，也就是万圣节的晚上，高脚杯将选出它认为最能够代表三个学校的三位同学的姓名。今晚，高脚杯就放在门厅里，所有愿意参加竞选的同学都能接触到它。

"为了避免不够年龄的同学经不起诱惑，"邓布利多说，"等高脚杯放在门厅后，我要在它周围画一条年龄线。任何不满十七周岁的人都

## CHAPTER SIXTEEN   The Goblet of Fire

it has been placed in the Entrance Hall. Nobody under the age of seventeen will be able to cross this line.

'Finally, I wish to impress upon any of you wishing to compete that this Tournament is not to be entered into lightly. Once a champion has been selected by the Goblet of Fire, he or she is obliged to see the Tournament through to the end. The placing of your name in the Goblet constitutes a binding, magical contract. There can be no change of heart once you have become champion. Please be very sure, therefore, that you are wholeheartedly prepared to play, before you drop your name into the Goblet. Now, I think it is time for bed. Goodnight to you all.'

'An Age Line!' Fred Weasley said, his eyes glinting, as they all made their way across the Hall to the doors into the Entrance Hall. 'Well, that should be fooled by an Ageing Potion, shouldn't it? And once your name's in that Goblet, you're laughing – it can't tell whether you're seventeen or not!'

'But I don't think anyone under seventeen will stand a chance,' said Hermione, 'we just haven't learnt enough ...'

'Speak for yourself,' said George shortly. 'You'll try and get in, won't you, Harry?'

Harry thought briefly of Dumbledore's insistence that nobody under seventeen should submit their name, but then the wonderful picture of himself winning the Triwizard Cup filled his mind again ... he wondered how angry Dumbledore would be if someone younger than seventeen *did* find a way to get over the Age Line ...

'Where is he?' said Ron, who wasn't listening to a word of this conversation, but looking through the crowd to see what had become of Krum. 'Dumbledore didn't say where the Durmstrang people are sleeping, did he?'

But this query was answered almost instantly; they were level with the Slytherin table now, and Karkaroff had just bustled up to his students.

'Back to the ship, then,' he was saying. 'Viktor, how are you feeling? Did you eat enough? Should I send for some mulled wine from the kitchens?'

Harry saw Krum shake his head as he pulled his furs back on.

'Professor, *I* vood like some vine,' said one of the other Durmstrang boys hopefully.

'I wasn't offering it to *you*, Poliakoff,' snapped Karkaroff, his warmly

## 第 16 章 火焰杯

无法越过这条线。

"最后,我想提醒每一位想参加竞选的同学注意,这场争霸赛不是儿戏,千万不要冒冒失失地参加。一旦勇士被火焰杯选定,就必须将比赛坚持到底。谁把自己的名字投进杯子,实际上就形成了一道必须遵守的、神奇的契约。一旦成为勇士,就不允许再改变主意。因此,请千万三思而行,弄清自己确实一心一意想参加比赛,再把名字投进杯子。好了,我认为大家该睡觉了。祝大家晚安。"

"年龄线!"弗雷德·韦斯莱说,两只眼睛闪闪发光,"那好办,肯定能被增龄剂蒙骗住的,是不是?只要你的名字进了那个杯子,你就开心地笑吧——它可分不出谁满十七岁,谁不满十七岁!"这时学生们都穿过礼堂,朝通往门厅的那道对开门走去。

"但我认为不满十七岁的人是不可能获胜的,"赫敏说,"我们学的东西还不够……"

"那是说你自己吧。"乔治不耐烦地说,"你也会争取参加的,是吗,哈利?"

哈利想起邓布利多坚持说不满十七周岁的同学不能报名,但随即脑海里又浮想起他赢得三强杯时的辉煌场面……他想,如果某个不满十七岁的人真的想出办法,越过了年龄线,邓布利多不知该有多生气呢……

"他在哪儿?"罗恩说,"邓布利多没说德姆斯特朗的人睡在哪里吧?"他们的话他一个字也没有听进去,只顾在人群中搜寻克鲁姆的身影。

然而他的疑问几乎立刻就得到了回答。这时,他们已经走到斯莱特林的桌子旁,只见卡卡洛夫匆匆地走到他的学生面前。

"好了,回船上去吧。"他说,"威克多尔,你感觉怎么样啦?吃饱了吗?要不要我派人从厨房里端一些热葡萄酒来?"

哈利看见克鲁姆摇了摇头,把毛皮斗篷重新穿上了。

"教授,我想喝点儿葡萄酒。"德姆斯特朗的另一位男生垂涎欲滴地说。

"我没有问你,波利阿科,"卡卡洛夫严厉地说——慈父般的温和

## CHAPTER SIXTEEN  The Goblet of Fire

paternal air vanishing in an instant. 'I notice you have dribbled food all down the front of your robes again, disgusting boy –'

Karkaroff turned and led his students towards the doors, reaching them at exactly the same moment as Harry, Ron and Hermione. Harry stopped to let him walk through first.

'Thank you,' said Karkaroff carelessly, glancing at him.

And then Karkaroff froze. He turned his head back to Harry, and stared at him as though he couldn't believe his eyes. Behind their Headmaster, the students from Durmstrang came to a halt, too. Karkaroff's eyes moved slowly up Harry's face, and fixed upon his scar. The Durmstrang students were staring curiously at Harry, too. Out of the corner of his eye, Harry saw comprehension dawn on a few of their faces. The boy with food all down his front nudged the girl next to him and pointed openly at Harry's forehead.

'Yeah, that's Harry Potter,' said a growling voice from behind them.

Professor Karkaroff spun around. Mad-Eye Moody was standing there, leaning heavily on his staff, his magical eye glaring unblinkingly at the Durmstrang Headmaster.

The colour drained from Karkaroff's face as Harry watched. A terrible look of mingled fury and fear came over his face.

'You!' he said, staring at Moody as though unsure he was really seeing him.

'Me,' said Moody grimly. 'And unless you've got anything to say to Potter, Karkaroff, you might want to move. You're blocking the doorway.'

It was true; half the students in the Hall were now waiting behind them, looking over each other's shoulders to see what was causing the hold-up.

Without another word, Professor Karkaroff swept his students away with him. Moody watched him out of sight, his magical eye fixed upon his back, a look of intense dislike upon his mutilated face.

As the next day was Saturday, most students would normally have breakfasted late. Harry, Ron and Hermione, however, were not alone in rising much earlier than they usually did at weekends. When they went down into the Entrance Hall, they saw about twenty people milling around it, some of them eating toast, all examining the Goblet of Fire. It had been placed in the centre of the hall on the stool that normally bore the Sorting Hat. A thin golden line had been traced on the floor, forming a circle ten feet around it in every direction.

## 第16章 火焰杯

表情一下子就消失了,"我注意到你又把食物滴在你袍子的前襟上了,你这个讨厌的男孩……"

卡卡洛夫转过身,领着学生朝门口走去,他们正好和哈利、罗恩、赫敏同时走到门边。哈利停下来,让卡卡洛夫先过去。

"谢谢。"卡卡洛夫漫不经心地说,朝哈利扫了一眼。

顿时,卡卡洛夫完全呆住了。他把脑袋重新转向哈利,死死地盯住他,仿佛不敢相信自己的眼睛。德姆斯特朗的学生跟在校长身后,也都停住脚步。卡卡洛夫的目光慢慢移到哈利脸上,盯住了那道伤疤。德姆斯特朗的学生也好奇地望着哈利。哈利从眼角看到几个人脸上露出了若有所悟的神情。那个胸前滴满汤渍的男生捅了捅旁边的女生,毫不掩饰地指着哈利的额头。

"没错,那就是哈利·波特。"他们身后传来了一个怒气冲冲的声音。

卡卡洛夫猛地转过身。疯眼汉穆迪站在那里,沉重的身体倚在拐杖上,那只魔眼一眨不眨地瞪着德姆斯特朗的校长。

哈利眼看着卡卡洛夫的脸变得煞白,显出一种愤恨和恐惧混杂的可怕表情。

"是你!"他说,呆呆地瞪着穆迪,似乎不能确定自己真的看见了他。

"是我,"穆迪阴沉地说,"除非你有话要对波特说,卡卡洛夫,不然就赶紧往前走。你们把门口都堵住了。"

真的,礼堂里半数的学生都在他们身后等着,争相越过前面人的肩头,想看看是什么造成了阻塞。

卡卡洛夫教授没有再说什么,他一挥手,带着他的学生走开了。穆迪一直瞪着他,直到看不见为止。他那只魔眼死死盯着卡卡洛夫的背影,残缺不全的脸上露出一种极端反感的表情。

第二天是星期六,一般来说,同学们都很晚才去吃早饭。但今天起得比平常周末早得多的并不只有哈利、罗恩和赫敏。当他们下楼进入门厅时,看见二十多个人围在那里,有几个还在吃面包,大家都在仔细打量着火焰杯。杯子放在门厅中央,放在惯常放分院帽的那个凳子上。地板上画了一圈细细的金线,半径十英尺,把杯子围在中间。

## CHAPTER SIXTEEN  The Goblet of Fire

'Anyone put their name in yet?' Ron asked a third-year girl eagerly.

'All the Durmstrang lot,' she replied. 'But I haven't seen anyone from Hogwarts yet.'

'Bet some of them put in last night after we'd all gone to bed,' said Harry. 'I would've done if it had been me ... wouldn't have wanted everyone watching. What if the Goblet just gobbed you right back out again?'

Someone laughed behind Harry. Turning, he saw Fred, George and Lee Jordan hurrying down the staircase, all three of them looking extremely excited.

'Done it,' Fred said in a triumphant whisper to Harry, Ron and Hermione. 'Just taken it.'

'What?' said Ron.

'The Ageing Potion, dungbrains,' said Fred.

'One drop each,' said George, rubbing his hands together with glee. 'We only need to be a few months older.'

'We're going to split the thousand Galleons between the three of us if one of us wins,' said Lee, grinning broadly.

'I'm not sure this is going to work, you know,' said Hermione warningly. 'I'm sure Dumbledore will have thought of this.'

Fred, George and Lee ignored her.

'Ready?' Fred said to the other two, quivering with excitement. 'C'mon, then – I'll go first –'

Harry watched, fascinated, as Fred pulled a slip of parchment out of his pocket, bearing the words 'Fred Weasley – Hogwarts'. Fred walked right up to the edge of the line, and stood there, rocking on his toes like a diver preparing for a fifty-foot drop. Then, with the eyes of every person in the Entrance Hall upon him, he took a great breath and stepped over the line.

For a split second, Harry thought it had worked – George certainly thought so, for he let out a yell of triumph and leapt after Fred – but next moment, there was a loud sizzling sound, and both twins were hurled out of the golden circle as though they had been thrown by an invisible shot-putter. They landed painfully, ten feet away on the cold stone floor, and to add

## 第16章 火焰杯

"有人把名字投进去了吗？"罗恩急切地问一个三年级女生。

"有，德姆斯特朗的那伙人都投了，"女生回答，"但还没有看见霍格沃茨有谁报名。"

"准是有人趁我们昨晚睡觉时把名字投了进去。"哈利说，"如果是我，就会这么做的……不想让别人看见。如果杯子把你的名字揉成一团扔出来，那多丢脸啊！"

哈利身后的什么人大笑起来。他回头一看，只见弗雷德、乔治和李·乔丹匆匆走下楼梯，三个人都显得极为兴奋。

"成了，"弗雷德以一种得意的口吻小声对哈利、罗恩和赫敏说，"刚喝下去。"

"什么？"罗恩问。

"增龄剂啊，笨蛋。"弗雷德说。

"每人喝了一滴，"乔治喜悦地搓着双手，说道，"我们只需要再长大几个月。"

"如果我们有谁赢了，那一千加隆得三个人平分。"李说，脸上笑得开心极了。

"我觉得这不一定会成功，"赫敏提醒道，"邓布利多肯定会考虑到这一点的。"

弗雷德、乔治和李没有理睬她。

"准备好了吗？"弗雷德激动得浑身颤抖，对另外两个人说，"那么，来吧——我先进去——"

哈利着迷般地看着弗雷德从口袋里掏出一张羊皮纸条，上面写着弗雷德·韦斯莱——霍格沃茨的字样。弗雷德径直走到年龄线的边缘，站在那里，踮着脚尖摇摆着，就像跳水运动员准备从五十英尺的高台跳下去一样。然后，在门厅里每一双眼睛的注视下，他深深吸了口气，跨过了那道线。

一刹那间，哈利以为弗雷德成功了——乔治肯定也这样以为，他得意地大喊一声，跟着弗雷德往前一跳——可是，紧接着就听见一阵嘶嘶的响声，一对双胞胎被抛到了金线圈外面，就好像有一个看不见的铅球运动员把他们扔了出来似的。他们痛苦地摔在十英尺之外冰冷

insult to injury, there was a loud popping noise, and both of them sprouted identical, long white beards.

The Entrance Hall rang with laughter. Even Fred and George joined in, once they had got to their feet, and taken a good look at each other's beards.

'I did warn you,' said a deep, amused voice, and everyone turned to see Professor Dumbledore coming out of the Great Hall. He surveyed Fred and George, his eyes twinkling. 'I suggest you both go up to Madam Pomfrey. She is already tending to Miss Fawcett, of Ravenclaw, and Mr Summers, of Hufflepuff, both of whom decided to age themselves up a little, too. Though I must say, neither of their beards is anything like as fine as yours.'

Fred and George set off for the hospital wing, accompanied by Lee, who was howling with laughter, and Harry, Ron and Hermione, also chortling, went in to breakfast.

The decorations in the Great Hall had changed this morning. As it was Hallowe'en, a cloud of live bats was fluttering around the enchanted ceiling, while hundreds of carved pumpkins leered from every corner. Harry led the way over to Dean and Seamus, who were discussing those Hogwarts students of seventeen or over who might be entering.

'There's a rumour going round, Warrington got up early and put his name in,' Dean told Harry. 'That big bloke from Slytherin who looks like a sloth.'

Harry, who had played Quidditch against Warrington, shook his head in disgust. 'We can't have a Slytherin champion!'

'And all the Hufflepuffs are talking about Diggory,' said Seamus contemptuously. 'But I wouldn't have thought he'd have wanted to risk his good looks.'

'Listen!' said Hermione suddenly.

People were cheering out in the Entrance Hall. They all swivelled around in their seats, and saw Angelina Johnson coming into the Hall, grinning in an embarrassed sort of way. A tall black girl who played Chaser on the Gryffindor Quidditch team, Angelina came over to them, sat down and said, 'Well, I've done it! Just put my name in!'

'You're kidding!' said Ron, looking impressed.

'Are you seventeen, then?' asked Harry.

'"Course she is. Can't see a beard, can you?' said Ron.

## 第16章 火焰杯

的石头地面上，而且在肉体的疼痛之外还受到了羞辱。随着一声很响的爆裂声，两个人的下巴上冒出了一模一样的白色长胡子。

门厅里的人哄堂大笑。就连弗雷德和乔治爬起来，看到对方的白胡子后，也忍不住哈哈大笑起来。

"我提醒过你们。"一个低沉的、被逗乐了的声音说道，大家转过头来，看见邓布利多教授正从礼堂里走出来。他打量着弗雷德和乔治，眼睛里闪着光芒："我建议你们俩都到庞弗雷女士那里去一趟。她已经在护理拉文克劳的福西特小姐和赫奇帕奇的萨默斯先生了，他们俩也是打定主意要让自己的年龄增加一点儿。不过我必须说一句，他们俩的胡子可远远不如你们的漂亮。"

弗雷德和乔治动身去医院了，李·乔丹也陪着去了，他仍然嘀嘀地笑个不停，哈利、罗恩和赫敏也咯咯笑着，进礼堂吃早饭了。

这天早晨，礼堂的装饰又有了变化。因为是万圣节，一大群活蝙蝠绕着施了魔法的天花板飞来飞去，同时还有几百个雕刻出五官的南瓜在每个角落斜眼望着大家。哈利在前面领路，朝迪安和西莫走去，他们俩正在议论那些可能参加争霸赛的十七周岁以上的霍格沃茨同学。

"有人说，沃林顿一大早就起来了，把他的名字投了进去。"迪安告诉哈利，"就是斯莱特林的那个大块头家伙，长得活像只树懒。"

哈利曾经跟沃林顿交手打过魁地奇球，听了这话，厌恶地摇了摇头。"我们可不能让一个斯莱特林的同学当勇士！"

"赫奇帕奇的同学们都在议论迪戈里，"西莫轻蔑地说，"不过在我看来，他大概不会愿意拿自己的俊模样儿冒险。"

"快听！"赫敏突然说道。

外面的门厅里突然传来大声喝彩。大家都在座位上转过身，只见安吉利娜·约翰逊走进礼堂，有点不好意思地咧嘴笑着。她是一个高挑个儿的黑皮肤姑娘，在格兰芬多魁地奇队当追球手。安吉利娜走到他们这边，坐下来说道："呀，我办成了！我把我的名字投进去了！"

"你在开玩笑吧！"罗恩说，显得非常惊讶。

"那么，你满十七岁了吗？"哈利问。

"那还用说。没看见胡子，是不是？"罗恩说。

## CHAPTER SIXTEEN  The Goblet of Fire

'I had my birthday last week,' said Angelina.

'Well, I'm glad someone from Gryffindor's entering,' said Hermione. 'I really hope you get it, Angelina!'

'Thanks, Hermione,' said Angelina, smiling at her.

'Yeah, better you than Pretty-Boy Diggory,' said Seamus, causing several Hufflepuffs passing their table to scowl heavily at him.

'What're we going to do today, then?' Ron asked Harry and Hermione, when they had finished breakfast and were leaving the Great Hall.

'We haven't been down to visit Hagrid yet,' said Harry.

'OK,' said Ron, 'just as long as he doesn't ask us to donate a few fingers to the Skrewts.'

A look of great excitement suddenly dawned on Hermione's face.

'I've just realised – I haven't asked Hagrid to join S.P.E.W. yet!' she said brightly. 'Wait for me, will you, while I nip upstairs and get the badges?'

'What's she like?' said Ron, exasperated, as Hermione ran away up the marble staircase.

'Hey, Ron,' said Harry suddenly. 'It's your friend ...'

The students from Beauxbatons were coming through the front doors from the grounds, among them, the Veela girl. Those gathered around the Goblet of Fire stood back to let them pass, watching eagerly.

Madame Maxime entered the hall behind her students and organised them into a line. One by one, the Beauxbatons students stepped across the Age Line and dropped their slips of parchment into the blue-white flames. As each name entered the fire, it turned briefly red and emitted sparks.

'What d'you reckon'll happen to the ones that aren't chosen?' Ron muttered to Harry, as the Veela girl dropped her parchment into the Goblet of Fire. 'Reckon they'll go back to school, or hang around to watch the Tournament?'

'Dunno,' said Harry. 'Hang around, I suppose ... Madame Maxime's staying to judge, isn't she?'

When all the Beauxbatons students had submitted their names, Madame Maxime led them back out of the hall and into the grounds again.

'Where are *they* sleeping, then?' said Ron, moving towards the front doors and staring after them.

## 第16章 火焰杯

"我上星期过的生日。"安吉利娜说。

"啊,我真高兴格兰芬多终于有人参加了。"赫敏说,"真心希望你能成功,安吉利娜!"

"谢谢,赫敏。"安吉利娜说着,朝赫敏微微一笑。

"是啊,宁愿是你,也不要那个奶油小生迪戈里。"西莫说,他的话引得经过他们桌子的几个赫奇帕奇学生怒气冲冲地瞪着他。

"那么我们今天干什么呢?"罗恩问哈利和赫敏。这时他们已经吃完早饭,正要离开礼堂。

"我们还没有去看望海格呢。"哈利说。

"好吧,"罗恩说,"但愿他不要叫我们也捐献几根手指给炸尾螺。"

赫敏脸上突然露出极为兴奋的表情。

"我刚想起来——我还没有动员海格加入S.P.E.W.呢!"她高兴地说,"你们等一等,我到楼上去拿徽章,好吗?"

"她这是什么毛病?"罗恩恼火地说,眼看着赫敏奔上大理石楼梯。

"快看,罗恩,"哈利突然说道,"是你的那位朋友……"

布斯巴顿的学生正从场地上穿过前门进来,其中就有那个很像媚娃的姑娘。火焰杯周围的那些人往后退了退,让他们通过,同时热切地注视着。

马克西姆女士跟着她的学生走进门厅,吩咐他们排成一队。布斯巴顿的学生一个接一个地跨过年龄线,把羊皮纸条投进蓝白色的火焰。每个名字扔进火里时,火焰都迅速转成红色,并且迸出点点火星。

"你说,那些没被选中的人会怎么样?"当那个很像媚娃的姑娘把她的羊皮纸条投进火焰杯时,罗恩小声问哈利,"是返回自己的学校,还是留在这里观看比赛?"

"不知道,"哈利说,"我猜大概是留下来吧……马克西姆女士还要在这里当裁判呢,是不是?"

当布斯巴顿的学生一个个都报了名后,马克西姆女士领着他们出了门厅,又回到外面的场地上。

"那么,他们在哪儿睡觉呢?"罗恩说,朝前门走了几步,望着他们的背影。

## CHAPTER SIXTEEN   The Goblet of Fire

A loud rattling noise behind them announced Hermione's reappearance with the box of S.P.E.W. badges.

'Oh, good, hurry up,' said Ron, and he jumped down the stone steps, keeping his eyes on the back of the Veela girl, who was now halfway across the lawn with Madame Maxime.

As they neared Hagrid's cabin on the edge of the Forbidden Forest, the mystery of the Beauxbatons' sleeping quarters was solved. The gigantic powder-blue carriage in which they had arrived had been parked two hundred yards from Hagrid's front door, and the students were climbing back inside it. The elephantine flying horses that had pulled the carriage were now grazing in a makeshift paddock alongside it.

Harry knocked on Hagrid's door, and Fang's booming barks answered instantly.

"Bout time!' said Hagrid, when he'd flung open the door and seen who was knocking. 'Thought you lot'd forgotten where I live!'

'We've been really busy, Hag–' Hermione started to say, but then she stopped dead, looking up at Hagrid, apparently lost for words.

Hagrid was wearing his best (and very horrible) hairy brown suit, plus a checked yellow-and-orange tie. This wasn't the worst of it, though; he had evidently tried to tame his hair, using large quantities of what appeared to be axle grease. It was now slicked down into two bunches – perhaps he had tried a ponytail like Bill's, but found he had too much hair. The look didn't really suit Hagrid at all. For a moment, Hermione goggled at him, then, obviously deciding not to comment, she said, 'Erm – where are the Skrewts?'

'Out by the pumpkin patch,' said Hagrid happily. 'They're gettin' massive, mus' be nearly three foot long now. On'y trouble is, they've started killin' each other.'

'Oh, no, really?' said Hermione, shooting a repressive look at Ron, who, staring at Hagrid's odd hairstyle, had just opened his mouth to say something about it.

'Yeah,' said Hagrid sadly. "S'OK, though, I've got 'em in separate boxes now. Still got abou' twenty.'

'Well, that's lucky,' said Ron. Hagrid missed the sarcasm.

Hagrid's cabin comprised a single room, in one corner of which was a gigantic bed covered in a patchwork quilt. A similarly enormous wooden

## 第16章 火焰杯

后面一阵哐啷哐啷的声音,说明赫敏已经拿着那盒 S.P.E.W. 徽章回来了。

"哦,好了,快走吧。"罗恩说。他三步并作两步跳下石阶,可眼睛仍然盯着那个很像媚娃的姑娘的背影,那姑娘正和马克西姆女士一起穿过草坪。

当他们走近位于禁林边缘的海格的小屋时,布斯巴顿的学生在哪里睡觉的秘密一下子就被揭开了。他们来时乘坐的那辆巨大的粉蓝色马车已经停在离海格小屋正门二百码的地方,布斯巴顿的学生正在往里面钻。拉马车的那几匹大象般巨大的飞马正在马车旁边一个临时圈起的围场里吃草。

哈利敲了敲海格的门,屋里立刻传出牙牙低沉的吠叫。

"总算来了!"海格打开房门,说道,"我还以为你们这些小家伙忘记我住在什么地方了呢!"

"我们实在是太忙了,海——"赫敏刚说了一半,突然顿住了,抬头望着海格,显然是惊讶得说不出话来。

海格穿着他那件最好的(同时也是非常难看的)毛茸茸的棕色西装,配着一条黄色和橘红色相间的格子花纹领带。不过,这还不是最糟糕的:他显然尝试过把头发理顺,用了大量的机器润滑油一类的东西。现在他的头发光溜溜地梳成两束——也许他本来打算扎一条比尔那样的马尾巴,结果发现自己头发太多。这副打扮并不适合海格。赫敏呆呆地望了他片刻,然后显然决定不做任何评论,她说:"嗯——炸尾螺在哪里?"

"在外面的南瓜地里,"海格愉快地说,"它们长得大极了,现在每条准有三英尺长呢。只有一个问题,它们开始互相残杀了。"

"哦,真糟糕,不是吗?"赫敏说,同时瞪了罗恩一眼,制止他开口说话。罗恩一直盯着海格古怪的发型,刚想张开嘴巴做一番评论。

"是啊,"海格悲哀地说,"不过没关系,现在我把它们分开来放在箱子里。大概只有二十来条了。"

"啊,幸亏如此。"罗恩说。海格没有听出这句话里的讽刺意味。

海格的小屋只有一个房间,一张巨大的床放在一个角落里,上面铺着碎布拼接成的被子。炉火前面放着同样巨大的木桌和木椅,炉火

## CHAPTER SIXTEEN  The Goblet of Fire

table and chairs stood in front of the fire, beneath the quantity of cured hams and dead birds hanging from the ceiling. They sat down at the table while Hagrid started to make tea, and were soon immersed in yet more discussion of the Triwizard Tournament. Hagrid seemed quite as excited about it as they were.

'You wait,' he said, grinning. 'You jus' wait. Yer going ter see some stuff yeh've never seen before. Firs' task ... ah, but I'm not supposed ter say.'

'Go on, Hagrid!' Harry, Ron and Hermione urged him, but he just shook his head, grinning.

'I don' want ter spoil it fer yeh,' said Hagrid. 'But it's gonna be spectacular, I'll tell yeh that. Them champions're going ter have their work cut out. Never thought I'd live ter see the Triwizard Tournament played again!'

They ended up having lunch with Hagrid, though they didn't eat much – Hagrid had made what he said was a beef casserole, but after Hermione unearthed a large talon in hers, she, Harry and Ron rather lost their appetites. They enjoyed themselves trying to make Hagrid tell them what the tasks in the Tournament were going to be, however, speculating which of the entrants were likely to be selected as champions, and wondering whether Fred and George were beardless yet.

A light rain had started to fall by mid-afternoon; it was very cosy sitting by the fire, listening to the gentle patter of the drops on the window, watching Hagrid darning his socks and arguing with Hermione about house-elves – for he flatly refused to join S.P.E.W. when she showed him her badges.

'It'd be doin' 'em an unkindness, Hermione,' he said gravely, threading a massive bone needle with thick yellow yarn. 'It's in their nature ter look after humans, that's what they like, see? Yeh'd be makin' 'em unhappy ter take away their work, an' insultin' 'em if yeh tried ter pay 'em.'

'But Harry set Dobby free, and he was over the moon about it!' said Hermione. '*And* we heard he's asking for wages now!'

'Yeah, well, yeh get weirdos in every breed. I'm not sayin' there isn't the odd elf who'd take freedom, but yeh'll never persuade most of 'em ter do it – no, nothin' doin', Hermione.'

Hermione looked very cross indeed, and stuffed her box of badges back into her cloak pocket.

By half past five it was growing dark, and Ron, Harry and Hermione

## 第16章 火焰杯

上面的天花板上挂着一大堆腌火腿和死鸟。海格开始沏茶，他们在桌边坐下，很快就又开始议论三强争霸赛的事。海格对这件事似乎和他们一样兴奋。

"你们等着吧，"他咧嘴笑着说，"你们等着瞧吧。会看到以前从没看到过的东西。第一个项目是……啊，我不应该说的。"

"说下去，海格！"哈利、罗恩和赫敏催促道，可是海格摇了摇头，咧开嘴笑了。

"我不想破坏你们的兴致，"海格说，"不过我告诉你们吧，会很精彩的。那些勇士可有事情要做呢。真没想到我这辈子还能看到三强争霸赛又恢复了！"

他们最后和海格一起吃了午饭，不过没吃多少——海格做了一锅东西，据他说是牛肉大杂烩，结果赫敏从她那份里挖出了一个大爪子，此后她、哈利和罗恩就没有了食欲。不过，在这里过得还是很愉快的，他们千方百计地哄海格告诉他们比赛都有哪些项目，推测哪几个参加者有可能被选为勇士，还好奇弗雷德和乔治脸上的胡子是不是褪掉了。

下午三四点钟的时候，天下起了小雨，他们觉得好舒服啊——坐在温暖的炉火边，听着雨点轻轻敲打玻璃窗，看着海格一边织补他的袜子，一边和赫敏辩论家养小精灵的问题——因为当赫敏把徽章拿给他看时，他断然拒绝加入 S.P.E.W.。

"这对他们来说不是一件好事，赫敏，"他严肃地说，用黄色粗纱线穿过一根粗大的骨针，"他们的天性就是照顾人类，他们喜欢这样，明白吗？如果不让他们工作，他们会感到悲哀的，而给他们付工钱对他们来说是一种侮辱。"

"可是哈利解放了多比，多比别提多高兴了！"赫敏说，"而且我们听说，多比现在正要求别人付他工钱呢！"

"是啊，是啊，每一种生物里都有一些怪胎。我并不否认有个别古怪的小精灵愿意获得自由，但你永远不可能说服大多数小精灵去争取自由——真的，这不可能，赫敏。"

赫敏显得非常恼火，把装徽章的盒子塞进了斗篷的口袋里。

五点半钟时，天渐渐黑了，罗恩、哈利和赫敏觉得应该返回

decided it was time to get back up to the castle for the Hallowe'en feast – and, more importantly, the announcement of the school champions.

'I'll come with yeh,' said Hagrid, putting away his darning. 'Jus' give us a sec.'

Hagrid got up, went across to the chest of drawers beside his bed and began searching for something inside it. They didn't pay too much attention, until a truly horrible smell reached their nostrils.

Coughing, Ron said, 'Hagrid, what's that?'

'Eh?' said Hagrid, turning around with a large bottle in his hand. 'Don' yeh like it?'

'Is that aftershave?' said Hermione, in a slightly choked voice.

'Er – eau-de-Cologne,' Hagrid muttered. He was blushing. 'Maybe it's a bit much,' he said gruffly. 'I'll go take it off, hang on ...'

He stumped out of the cabin, and they saw him washing himself vigorously in the water barrel outside the window.

'Eau-de-Cologne?' said Hermione in amazement. '*Hagrid?*'

'And what's with the hair and the suit?' said Harry in an undertone.

'Look!' said Ron suddenly, pointing out of the window.

Hagrid had just straightened up and turned round. If he had been blushing before, it was nothing to what he was doing now. Getting to their feet very cautiously, so that Hagrid wouldn't spot them, Harry, Ron and Hermione peered through the window and saw that Madame Maxime and the Beauxbatons students had just emerged from their carriage, clearly about to set off for the feast, too. They couldn't hear what Hagrid was saying, but he was talking to Madame Maxime with a rapt, misty-eyed expression Harry had only ever seen him wear once before – when he had been looking at the baby dragon, Norbert.

'He's going up to the castle with her!' said Hermione indignantly. 'I thought he was waiting for us?'

Without so much as a backward glance at his cabin, Hagrid was trudging off up the grounds with Madame Maxime, the Beauxbatons students following in their wake, jogging to keep up with their enormous strides.

'He fancies her!' said Ron incredulously. 'Well, if they end up having children, they'll be setting a world record – bet any baby of theirs would weigh about a ton.'

They let themselves out of the cabin and shut the door behind them. It

## 第16章 火焰杯

城堡参加万圣节前夕的宴会——更重要的是参加学校勇士的宣布仪式。

"我和你们一起去,"海格说,把他织补的东西放在一边,"等我一会儿。"

海格站起身,走到床边的五斗橱边,开始在里面寻找什么。他们起先没怎么注意,直到一股特别难闻的气味钻入鼻孔。

罗恩咳嗽起来,问道:"海格,那是什么呀?"

"嗯?"海格转过身,手里拿着一个大瓶子,"你们不喜欢吗?"

"是刮完胡子后搽的润肤香水吗?"赫敏用有点窒息的声音问。

"嗯——是古龙香水。"海格嘟哝道,脸涨得通红,"大概洒得太多了,"他声音沙哑地说,"我把它洗掉,等一等……"

他脚步沉重地走出小屋,他们看见他在窗外的水桶里拼命地洗脸。

"古龙香水?"赫敏惊奇地问,"海格?"

"还有那头发和西装又是怎么回事?"哈利压低声音问。

"瞧!"罗恩突然说,指着窗外。

海格已经直起腰,转过身去。如果说刚才他是涨红了脸,那么和他此刻的脸色相比,就根本不算什么了。哈利、罗恩和赫敏小心翼翼地站起身,不让海格看见,偷偷朝窗外望去,看见马克西姆女士和布斯巴顿的学生刚从马车里出来,看样子是准备去参加宴会。他们听不见海格在说什么,但他与马克西姆女士谈话时,表情如痴如醉,眼睛里雾蒙蒙的,他的这种表情哈利只见过一次——那是他望着刚出生的小火龙诺伯的时候。

"他要和那女人一起去城堡!"赫敏气愤地说,"我还以为他在等我们呢!"

海格甚至没有回头望一眼他的小屋,就迈着重重的脚步,和马克西姆女士一起走过场地。布斯巴顿的学生跟在后面,小跑着才能跟上他们的大步子。

"他爱上她了!"罗恩不敢相信地说,"啊,如果他们以后有了孩子,肯定会创造一个世界纪录——我敢说他们的每个孩子都有一吨重。"

他们自己出了小屋,关好房门。没想到外面这么黑了。他们把斗

## CHAPTER SIXTEEN  The Goblet of Fire

was surprisingly dark outside. Drawing their cloaks more closely around themselves, they set off up the sloping lawns.

'Ooh, it's them, look!' Hermione whispered.

The Durmstrang party were walking up towards the castle from the lake. Viktor Krum was walking side by side with Karkaroff, and the other Durmstrang students were straggling along behind them. Ron watched Krum excitedly, but Krum did not look around as he reached the front doors a little ahead of Hermione, Ron and Harry, and proceeded through them.

When they entered the candlelit Great Hall it was almost full. The Goblet of Fire had been moved; it was now standing in front of Dumbledore's empty chair at the teachers' table. Fred and George – clean shaven again – seemed to have taken their disappointment fairly well.

'Hope it's Angelina,' said Fred, as Harry, Ron and Hermione sat down.

'So do I!' said Hermione breathlessly. 'Well, we'll soon know!'

The Hallowe'en feast seemed to take much longer than usual. Perhaps because it was their second feast in two days, Harry didn't seem to fancy the extravagantly prepared food as much as he would normally have done. Like everyone else in the Hall, judging by the constantly craning necks, the impatient expressions on every face, the fidgeting and the standing up to see whether Dumbledore had finished eating yet, Harry simply wanted the plates to clear, and to hear who had been selected as champions.

At long last, the golden plates returned to their original spotless state; there was a sharp upswing in the level of noise within the Hall, which died away almost instantly as Dumbledore got to his feet. On either side of him, Professor Karkaroff and Madame Maxime looked as tense and expectant as anyone. Ludo Bagman was beaming and winking at various students. Mr Crouch, however, looked quite uninterested, almost bored.

'Well, the Goblet is almost ready to make its decision,' said Dumbledore. 'I estimate that it requires one more minute. Now, when the champions' names are called, I would ask them please to come up to the top of the Hall, walk along the staff table, and go through into the next chamber' – he indicated the door behind the staff table – 'where they will be receiving their first instructions.'

He took out his wand and gave a great sweeping wave with it; at once, all the candles except those inside the carved pumpkins were extinguished, plunging them all into a state of semi-darkness. The Goblet of Fire now

## 第16章 火焰杯

篷裹得更紧一些，顺着草坪的斜坡往上走。

"噢，他们来了，快看！"赫敏小声说。

德姆斯特朗一行人正从湖边朝城堡走来。威克多尔·克鲁姆和卡卡洛夫并排走在前面，其他德姆斯特朗的学生稀稀落落地跟在后面。罗恩激动地望着克鲁姆，然而克鲁姆目不斜视地在赫敏、罗恩和哈利前面到达正门，进去了。

当他们走进烛光映照的礼堂时，里面几乎坐满了人。火焰杯已经被挪了地方。它此刻立在教工桌子上邓布利多的那把空椅子前面。弗雷德和乔治——下巴又光溜溜的了——似乎已经欣然接受了他们的失败。

"真希望是安吉利娜。"当哈利、罗恩和赫敏坐下时，弗雷德说。

"我也是！"赫敏屏住呼吸说道，"啊，我们很快就会知道了！"

万圣节前夕晚宴的时间似乎比往常长得多。也许因为接连两天都是宴会，哈利似乎不像平常那样喜欢那些精心准备的丰盛菜肴了。礼堂里的人不断引颈眺望，每一张面孔上都露出焦急的神情。大家坐立不安，不时站起来看看邓布利多是不是吃完了。哈利也和他们一样，恨不得快点消灭盘子里的食物，赶紧知道究竟是谁被选为勇士了。

终于，金色的盘子又恢复到原来一尘不染的状态，礼堂里的声音突然升高了许多。随即，邓布利多站了起来，礼堂里顿时变得鸦雀无声。邓布利多两边的卡卡洛夫教授和马克西姆女士看上去和大家一样紧张、满怀期待。卢多·巴格曼满脸带笑，朝各个学校的学生眨着眼睛，克劳奇先生则是一副兴味索然的样子，简直可以说是有些厌烦。

"好了，高脚杯就要做出决定了，"邓布利多说，"我估计还需要一分钟。听着，勇士的名字被宣布后，我希望他们走到礼堂前面，再沿着教工桌子走过去，进入隔壁的那个房间——"他指了指教工桌子后面的那扇门，"——他们将在那里得到初步指导。"

他掏出魔杖，大幅度地挥了一下。即刻，除了南瓜灯里的那些蜡烛，其余的蜡烛都熄灭了，礼堂顿时陷入了一种半明半暗的状态。火焰杯现在放出夺目的光芒，比整个礼堂里的任何东西都明亮，那迸射着火

## CHAPTER SIXTEEN  The Goblet of Fire

shone more brightly than anything in the whole Hall, the sparkling bright, bluey-whiteness of the flames almost painful on the eyes. Everyone watched, waiting ... a few people kept checking their watches ...

'Any second,' Lee Jordan whispered, two seats away from Harry.

The flames inside the Goblet turned suddenly red again. Sparks began to fly from it. Next moment, a tongue of flame shot into the air, a charred piece of parchment fluttered out of it – the whole room gasped.

Dumbledore caught the piece of parchment and held it at arm's length, so that he could read it by the light of the flames, which had turned back to blue white.

'The champion for Durmstrang,' he read, in a strong, clear voice, 'will be Viktor Krum.'

'No surprises there!' yelled Ron, as a storm of applause and cheering swept the Hall. Harry saw Viktor Krum rise from the Slytherin table, and slouch up towards Dumbledore; he turned right, walked along the staff table, and disappeared through the door into the next chamber.

'Bravo, Viktor!' boomed Karkaroff, so loudly that everyone could hear him, even over all the applause. 'Knew you had it in you!'

The clapping and chatting died down. Now everyone's attention was focused again on the Goblet, which, seconds later, turned red once more. A second piece of parchment shot out of it, propelled by the flames.

'The champion for Beauxbatons,' said Dumbledore, 'is Fleur Delacour!'

'It's her, Ron!' Harry shouted, as the girl who so resembled a Veela got gracefully to her feet, shook back her sheet of silvery blonde hair and swept up between the Ravenclaw and Hufflepuff tables.

'Oh, look, they're all disappointed,' Hermione said over the noise, nodding towards the remainder of the Beauxbatons party. 'Disappointed' was a bit of an understatement, Harry thought. Two of the girls who had not been selected had dissolved into tears, and were sobbing with their heads on their arms.

When Fleur Delacour, too, had vanished into the side chamber, silence fell again, but this time it was a silence so stiff with excitement you could almost taste it. The Hogwarts champion next ...

And the Goblet of Fire turned red once more; sparks showered out of it; the tongue of flame shot high into the air, and from its tip Dumbledore

## 第16章 火焰杯

星的蓝白色火焰简直有些刺眼。大家都注视着，等待着……几个人不停地看表……

"快了。"李·乔丹小声地说，他和哈利隔着两个座位。

高脚杯里的火焰突然又变成了红色，火星噼噼啪啪迸溅出来。接着，一道火舌蹿到空中，从里面飞出一张被烧焦的羊皮纸——礼堂里的人全都屏住了呼吸。

邓布利多接住那张羊皮纸，举得远远的，这样他才能就着火焰的光看清上面的字。火焰这时又恢复了蓝白色。

"德姆斯特朗的勇士，"他用清楚而有力的口吻说，"是威克多尔·克鲁姆。"

"一点儿也不奇怪！"罗恩大喊，掌声和欢呼声席卷了整个礼堂。哈利看见威克多尔·克鲁姆从斯莱特林的桌子旁站起来，没精打采地朝邓布利多走去。他向右一转，顺着教工桌子往前走，从那扇门进了隔壁的房间。

"太棒了，威克多尔！"卡卡洛夫声如洪钟地吼道，尽管礼堂里掌声很响，大家也能听见他的声音，"我知道你注定就是勇士！"

掌声和交谈声渐渐平息了。现在每个人的注意力再次集中在高脚杯上，几秒钟后，火苗又变红了。第二张羊皮纸在火焰的推动下，从杯子里蹿了出来。

"布斯巴顿的勇士，"邓布利多说，"是芙蓉·德拉库尔！"

"是她，罗恩！"哈利喊道，只见那个酷似媚娃的姑娘优雅地站起来，甩动了一下银亮的秀发，轻盈地从拉文克劳和赫奇帕奇的桌子之间走了过去。

"哦，瞧，他们都很失望呢。"赫敏在一片喧哗声中说道，一边朝布斯巴顿的其他学生点了点头。哈利认为，"失望"这个词用得太轻了。两个没被选中的姑娘泪流满面，把脑袋埋在臂弯里，伤心地哭了。

芙蓉·德拉库尔也进了隔壁的房间，礼堂里又安静下来，这次的寂静里涌动着简直可以品尝到的强烈兴奋。下面就要轮到霍格沃茨的勇士了……

这时，火焰杯再次变成红色，火星迸溅，火舌高高地蹿入空中，

## CHAPTER SIXTEEN  The Goblet of Fire

pulled the third piece of parchment.

'The Hogwarts champion,' he called, 'is Cedric Diggory!'

'No!' said Ron loudly, but nobody heard him except Harry; the uproar from the next table was too great. Every single Hufflepuff had jumped to his or her feet, screaming and stamping, as Cedric made his way past them, grinning broadly, and headed off towards the chamber behind the teachers' table. Indeed, the applause for Cedric went on so long that it was some time before Dumbledore could make himself heard again.

'Excellent!' Dumbledore called happily, as at last the tumult died down. 'Well, we now have our three champions. I am sure I can count upon all of you, including the remaining students from Beauxbatons and Durmstrang, to give your champions every ounce of support you can muster. By cheering your champion on, you will contribute in a very real –'

But Dumbledore suddenly stopped speaking, and it was apparent to everybody what had distracted him.

The fire in the Goblet had just turned red again. Sparks were flying out of it. A long flame shot suddenly into the air, and borne upon it was another piece of parchment.

Automatically, it seemed, Dumbledore reached out a long hand and seized the parchment. He held it out and stared at the name written upon it. There was a long pause, during which Dumbledore stared at the slip in his hands, and everyone in the room stared at Dumbledore. And then Dumbledore cleared his throat, and read out –

'*Harry Potter.*'

## 第 16 章 火焰杯

邓布利多从火舌尖上抽出第三张羊皮纸。

"霍格沃茨的勇士，"他大声说道，"是塞德里克·迪戈里！"

"倒霉！"罗恩大声说，可是除了哈利，谁也没有听见，旁边桌子上的欢呼声简直震耳欲聋。每个赫奇帕奇同学都在跳上跳下，都在尖叫、跺脚，这时塞德里克从他们身边走过，脸上灿烂地笑着，走向教工桌子后面的那个房间。确实，给塞德里克的喝彩持续了很长时间，过了好久，邓布利多才使大家安静下来，听他说话。

"太好了！"当喧闹声终于平息后，邓布利多愉快地大声说道，"好了，现在我们的三位勇士都选出来了。我知道，我完全可以信赖你们大家，包括布斯巴顿和德姆斯特朗的其他同学，你们一定会全力以赴地支持你们的勇士。通过给勇士加油，你们也会为这次活动做出很大的贡献——"

可是邓布利多突然打住了话头，大家也看出是什么吸引了他的注意力。

高脚杯里的火焰又变红了。火星噼噼啪啪地迸溅出来。一道长长的火舌突然蹿到半空，又托出一张羊皮纸。

邓布利多仿佛是下意识地伸出一只修长的手，抓住了那张羊皮纸。他把它举得远远的，瞪着上面写的名字。长时间的肃静，邓布利多瞪着手里的纸条，礼堂里的每个人都瞪着邓布利多。然后，邓布利多清了清嗓子，大声念道——

"哈利·波特。"

# CHAPTER SEVENTEEN

# The Four Champions

Harry sat there, aware that every head in the Great Hall had turned to look at him. He was stunned. He felt numb. He was surely dreaming. He had not heard correctly.

There was no applause. A buzzing, as though of angry bees, was starting to fill the Hall; some students were standing up to get a better look at Harry as he sat, frozen, in his seat.

Up at the top table, Professor McGonagall had got to her feet and swept past Ludo Bagman and Professor Karkaroff to whisper urgently to Professor Dumbledore, who bent his ear towards her, frowning slightly.

Harry turned to Ron and Hermione; beyond them, he saw the long Gryffindor table all watching him, open mouthed.

'I didn't put my name in,' Harry said blankly. 'You know I didn't.'

Both of them stared just as blankly back.

At the top table, Professor Dumbledore had straightened up, nodding to Professor McGonagall.

'Harry Potter!' he called again. 'Harry! Up here, if you please!'

'Go on,' Hermione whispered, giving Harry a slight push.

Harry got to his feet, trod on the hem of his robes and stumbled slightly. He set off up the gap between the Gryffindor and Hufflepuff tables. It felt like an immensely long walk; the top table didn't seem to be getting any nearer at all, and he could feel hundreds and hundreds of eyes upon him, as though each was a searchlight. The buzzing grew louder and louder. After what seemed like an hour, he was right in front of Dumbledore, feeling the stares of all the teachers upon him.

'Well ... through the door, Harry,' said Dumbledore. He wasn't smiling.

# 第 17 章

## 四位勇士

哈利坐在那里,意识到礼堂里的每个人都转过头望着他。他呆住了,脑子里一片空白。他肯定是在做梦。他刚才肯定听错了。

没有掌声。一阵嗡嗡声开始在礼堂里弥漫,好像无数只愤怒的蜜蜂在鸣叫。有些学生还站起来,为了把哈利看得更清楚些,而哈利僵坐在座位上,就像凝固了一样。

麦格教授从主宾席上站了起来,快步从卢多·巴格曼和卡卡洛夫教授身边走过,在邓布利多教授耳边急切地低语,邓布利多侧耳倾听,微微皱起了眉头。

哈利转脸望着罗恩和赫敏。他看见,他们后面长长的格兰芬多桌子旁的同学们都张大嘴巴,注视着自己。

"我没有把我的名字投进去。"哈利茫然地说,"你们知道我没有。"

他们俩也一脸茫然,呆呆地望着他。

在主宾席上,邓布利多教授直起身子,朝麦格教授点了点头。

"哈利·波特!"他再一次大声喊道,"哈利!请你上这儿来!"

"去吧。"赫敏小声催促道,轻轻推了推哈利。

哈利站了起来,踩在长袍的底边上,稍稍绊了一下。他顺着格兰芬多和赫奇帕奇桌子之间的通道往前走。这条路似乎显得格外漫长,主宾席似乎永远是那么遥不可及。他可以感觉到成百上千双眼睛都盯在自己身上,每只眼睛都像是一盏探照灯。嗡嗡的议论声越来越响。仿佛过了整整一小时,哈利才终于走到邓布利多面前,感到所有教师的目光都在他身上。

"好吧……到那扇门里去,哈利。"邓布利多说,脸上没有笑容。

## CHAPTER SEVENTEEN  The Four Champions

Harry moved off along the teachers' table. Hagrid was sat right at the end. He did not wink at Harry, or wave, or give any of his usual signs of greeting. He looked completely astonished, and stared at Harry as he passed, like everyone else. Harry went through the door out of the Great Hall, and found himself in a smaller room, lined with paintings of witches and wizards. A handsome fire was roaring in the fireplace opposite him.

The faces in the portraits turned to look at him as he entered. He saw a wizened witch flit out of the frame of her picture and into the one next to it, which contained a wizard with a walrus moustache. The wizened witch started whispering in his ear.

Viktor Krum, Cedric Diggory and Fleur Delacour were grouped around the fire. They looked strangely impressive, silhouetted against the flames. Krum, hunched up and brooding, was leaning against the mantelpiece, slightly apart from the other two. Cedric was standing with his hands behind his back, staring into the fire. Fleur Delacour looked around when Harry walked in, and threw back her sheet of long, silvery hair.

'What is it?' she said. 'Do zey want us back in ze Hall?'

She thought he had come to deliver a message. Harry didn't know how to explain what had just happened. He just stood there, looking at the three champions. It struck him how very tall all of them were.

There was a sound of scurrying feet behind him, and Ludo Bagman entered the room. He took Harry by the arm, and led him forwards.

'Extraordinary!' he muttered, squeezing Harry's arm. 'Absolutely extraordinary! Gentlemen ... lady,' he added, approaching the fireside and addressing the other three. 'May I introduce – incredible though it may seem – the *fourth* Triwizard champion?'

Viktor Krum straightened up. His surly face darkened as he surveyed Harry. Cedric looked nonplussed. He looked from Bagman to Harry and back again as though sure he must have misheard what Bagman had said. Fleur Delacour, however, tossed her hair, smiling, and said, 'Oh, vairy funny joke, Meester Bagman.'

'Joke?' Bagman repeated, bewildered. 'No, no, not at all! Harry's name just came out of the Goblet of Fire!'

Krum's thick eyebrows contracted slightly. Cedric was still looking politely bewildered.

## 第17章 四位勇士

哈利顺着教工桌子走过去。海格坐在最边上，他没有朝哈利眨眼睛、挥手，或像平常那样打招呼。他似乎怔住了，只是和别人一样呆呆地望着哈利走过。哈利穿过那扇门，出了礼堂，发现自己来到一个小房间里，两边墙上都挂着巫师的肖像。在他对面的壁炉里，炉火燃得正旺。

他进去时，肖像上的那些面孔全都转过来望着他。他看见一个皱巴巴的女巫嗖地逃出自己的相框，钻进了旁边的相框，那上面是一个留着海象胡须的男巫。皱巴巴的女巫开始悄悄对男巫咬起了耳朵。

威克多尔·克鲁姆、塞德里克·迪戈里和芙蓉·德拉库尔都围在炉火边。在火焰的映衬下，那三个身影给人的印象特别强烈。克鲁姆倚靠着壁炉台，弓着腰在那里沉思着什么，跟另外两个人微微拉开了一些距离。塞德里克背着双手站在那里，眼睛盯着炉火。哈利走进来时，芙蓉·德拉库尔转过头来，甩了甩瀑布般的银色长发。

"怎么啦？"她问，"他们要我们回礼堂去吗？"

她以为哈利是进来传话的。哈利不知道怎样解释刚才发生的一切，只是站在那里，望着三位勇士。他突然觉得他们一个个真高啊。

后面传来一阵忙乱的脚步声，卢多·巴格曼走进了房间。他一把抓住哈利的胳膊，拉着他往前走。

"太离奇了！"他使劲捏着哈利的胳膊，低声念叨，"绝对是太离奇了！二位先生……女士，"他走向炉边，对另外三个人说，"请允许我介绍一下——尽管这显得很不可思议——这是三强争霸赛的第四位勇士！"

威克多尔·克鲁姆挺直身子，上下打量着哈利，本就阴沉的脸上又暗了几分。塞德里克显得不知所措，他望望巴格曼，又望望哈利，以为自己肯定没有听清巴格曼说的话。芙蓉·德拉库尔则甩了甩长发，嫣然一笑，说道："哦，这个玩笑很有趣，巴格曼先生。"

"玩笑？"巴格曼重复了一句，有些不解，"不，不，绝对不是！哈利的名字刚才从火焰杯里喷了出来！"

克鲁姆的两道浓眉微微蹙起。塞德里克仍然很有教养地显出困惑的神情。

## CHAPTER SEVENTEEN  The Four Champions

Fleur frowned. 'But evidently zair 'as been a mistake,' she said contemptuously to Bagman. ''E cannot compete. 'E is too young.'

'Well ... it is amazing,' said Bagman, rubbing his smooth chin and smiling down at Harry. 'But, as you know, the age restriction was only imposed this year as an extra safety measure. and as his name's come out of the Goblet ... I mean, I don't think there can be any ducking out at this stage ... it's down in the rules, you're obliged ... Harry will just have to do the best he —'

The door behind them opened again, and a large group of people came in: Professor Dumbledore, followed closely by Mr Crouch, Professor Karkaroff, Madame Maxime, Professor McGonagall and Professor Snape. Harry heard the buzzing of the hundreds of students on the other side of the wall, before Professor McGonagall closed the door.

'Madame Maxime!' said Fleur at once, striding over to her Headmistress. 'Zey are saying zat zis little boy is to compete also!'

Somewhere under Harry's numb disbelief, he felt a ripple of anger. *Little boy?*

Madame Maxime had drawn herself up to her full, and considerable, height. The top of her handsome head brushed the candle-filled chandelier, and her gigantic black satin bosom swelled.

'What is ze meaning of zis, Dumbly-dorr?' she said imperiously.

'I'd rather like to know that myself, Dumbledore,' said Professor Karkaroff. He was wearing a steely smile, and his blue eyes were like chips of ice. '*Two* Hogwarts champions? I don't remember anyone telling me the host school is allowed two champions – or have I not read the rules carefully enough?'

He gave a short and nasty laugh.

'*C'est impossible*,' said Madame Maxime, whose enormous hand with its many superb opals was resting upon Fleur's shoulder. ''Ogwarts cannot 'ave two champions. It is most injust.'

'We were under the impression that your Age Line would keep out younger contestants, Dumbledore,' said Karkaroff, his steely smile still in place, though his eyes were colder than ever. 'Otherwise, we would, of course, have brought along a wider selection of candidates from our own schools.'

'It's no one's fault but Potter's, Karkaroff,' said Snape softly. His black eyes were alight with malice. 'Don't go blaming Dumbledore for Potter's determination to

## 第17章 四位勇士

芙蓉皱起了眉头。"可是这显然是弄错了，"她高傲地对巴格曼说，"他不能比赛。他年纪太小了。"

"是啊……确实令人诧异，"巴格曼揉着光滑的下巴，低头笑眯眯地望着哈利，"可是，你们也知道，年龄限制作为额外的安全措施，只是今年才实行的，既然他的名字从高脚杯里喷了出来……我的意思是，我认为既然已经到了这一步，就不允许临阵脱逃了……规定里写得很清楚，你们必须遵守……哈利要尽他最大的努力——"

他们身后的门又被推开，一大群人拥了进来：邓布利多教授，后面紧跟着克劳奇先生、卡卡洛夫教授、马克西姆女士、麦格教授和斯内普教授。在麦格教授把门关上之前，哈利听见隔壁的礼堂里传来几百名学生嗡嗡的议论声。

"马克西姆女士！"芙蓉立刻说道，一边大步朝她的校长走去，"他们说这个小男孩也要参加比赛！"

哈利尽管觉得不可思议，大脑一片麻木，却也感到心头掠过一丝怒火。小男孩？

马克西姆女士挺直她魁梧高大的身躯。她俊俏的脑袋碰到了点满蜡烛的枝形吊灯，穿着黑缎子衣服的巨大胸脯剧烈地起伏着。

"这到底是什么意思，邓布利多？"她傲慢地问。

"我也想知道这一点，邓布利多，"卡卡洛夫教授说——脸上带着冷冰冰的微笑，一双蓝眼睛像冰块一样透着寒意，"霍格沃茨有两位勇士？我不记得有人告诉过我，说主办学校可以有两位勇士——难道那些章程我看得还不够仔细？"

他短促地笑了一声，声音很难听。

"这不可能，"马克西姆女士说，她那戴着许多华丽蛋白石的大手搭在芙蓉的肩头，"霍格沃茨不能有两位勇士，这是极不公平的。"

"在我们的印象里，你的那道年龄线是能把不够年龄的竞争者排除在外的，邓布利多，"卡卡洛夫说，脸上仍然挂着那种冰冷的笑容，眼睛里的寒意更深了，"不然，我们肯定也会从学校带来更多的候选人。"

"这件事只能怪波特，卡卡洛夫，"斯内普轻声地说，一双黑眼睛里闪着敌意，"不要责怪邓布利多，都怪波特执意要违反章程。他自从

## CHAPTER SEVENTEEN   The Four Champions

break rules. He has been crossing lines ever since he arrived here –'

'Thank you, Severus,' said Dumbledore firmly, and Snape went quiet, though his eyes still glinted malevolently through his curtain of greasy black hair.

Professor Dumbledore was now looking down at Harry, who looked right back at him, trying to discern the expression of the eyes behind the half-moon spectacles.

'Did you put your name into the Goblet of Fire, Harry?' Dumbledore asked calmly.

'No,' said Harry. He was very aware of everybody watching him closely. Snape made a soft noise of impatient disbelief in the shadows.

'Did you ask an older student to put it into the Goblet of Fire for you?' said Professor Dumbledore, ignoring Snape.

'*No*,' said Harry vehemently.

'Ah, but of course 'e is lying!' cried Madame Maxime. Snape was now shaking his head, his lip curling.

'He could not have crossed the Age Line,' said Professor McGonagall sharply. 'I am sure we are all agreed on that –'

'Dumbly-dorr must 'ave made a mistake wiz ze line,' said Madame Maxime, shrugging.

'It is possible, of course,' said Dumbledore politely.

'Dumbledore, you know perfectly well you did not make a mistake!' said Professor McGonagall angrily. 'Really, what nonsense! Harry could not have crossed the line himself, and as Professor Dumbledore believes that he did not persuade an older student to do it for him, I'm sure that should be good enough for everybody else!'

She shot a very angry look at Professor Snape.

'Mr Crouch ... Mr Bagman,' said Karkaroff, his voice unctuous once more, 'you are our – er – objective judges. Surely you will agree that this is most irregular?'

Bagman wiped his round, boyish face with his handkerchief and looked at Mr Crouch, who was standing outside the circle of the fire-light, his face half hidden in shadow. He looked slightly eerie, the half darkness making him look much older, giving him an almost skull-like appearance. When he spoke, however, it was in his usual curt voice. 'We must follow the rules, and

进校以来，就一直不断违反校规——"

"谢谢你了，西弗勒斯。"邓布利多斩钉截铁地说，斯内普闭上了嘴巴，但他的眼睛仍然透过油腻腻的黑发闪出恶意的光芒。

邓布利多教授现在低头望着哈利，哈利也望着他，竭力想读懂那隐藏在半月形镜片后面的眼神。

"你有没有把你的名字投进火焰杯，哈利？"他平心静气地问。

"没有。"哈利说。他清楚地意识到每个人都在密切地注视着他。斯内普在阴影里不耐烦地发出一种表示不相信的声音。

"你有没有请年纪大一点儿的同学帮你把名字投进火焰杯？"邓布利多教授没理睬斯内普，继续问道。

"没有。"哈利激动地说。

"啊，他肯定在撒谎！"马克西姆女士大声说。斯内普摇了摇头，噘起了嘴唇。

"他不可能越过那道年龄线，"麦格教授厉声说，"这一点我相信我们大家都同意——"

"邓布利多的那道线肯定弄错了。"马克西姆女士说着，耸了耸肩膀。

"当然，这也有可能。"邓布利多很有礼貌地说。

"邓布利多，你明知道你并没有弄错！"麦格教授气愤地说，"这种说法多么荒唐！哈利自己是不可能跨越那道线的，而且正如邓布利多教授相信的那样，哈利也没有劝说过高年级学生替他这么做，我认为其他人也应该相信这一点！"

她非常生气地瞪了斯内普教授一眼。

"克劳奇先生……巴格曼先生，"卡卡洛夫说，声音又变得油滑起来，"你们两位是我们的……嗯……客观的裁判。你们肯定也认为这件事是极不合适的，是吗？"

巴格曼用手帕擦了擦自己圆乎乎的娃娃脸，转眼望着克劳奇先生。克劳奇先生站在炉火的光圈外面，脸一半隐藏在阴影中。他显得有点儿怪异，那半边黑影使他显得苍老了许多，看上去简直有点像个骷髅。不过当他说话时，声音还和往常一样生硬。"我们必须遵守章程，章程里明确规定，凡是名字从火焰杯里喷出来的人，都必须参加争霸赛的

## CHAPTER SEVENTEEN   The Four Champions

the rules state clearly that those people whose names come out of the Goblet of Fire are bound to compete in the Tournament.'

'Well, Barty knows the rulebook back to front,' said Bagman, beaming and turning back to Karkaroff and Madame Maxime, as though the matter was now closed.

'I insist upon resubmitting the names of the rest of my students,' said Karkaroff. He had dropped his unctuous tone and his smile now. His face wore a very ugly look indeed. 'You will set up the Goblet of Fire once more, and we will continue adding names until each school has two champions. It's only fair, Dumbledore.'

'But Karkaroff, it doesn't work like that,' said Bagman. 'The Goblet of Fire's just gone out – it won't reignite until the start of the next Tournament –'

'– in which Durmstrang will most certainly not be competing!' exploded Karkaroff. 'After all our meetings and negotiations and compromises, I little expected something of this nature to occur! I have half a mind to leave now!'

'Empty threat, Karkaroff,' growled a voice from near the door. 'You can't leave your champion now. He's got to compete. They've all got to compete. Binding magical contract, like Dumbledore said. Convenient, eh?'

Moody had just entered the room. He limped towards the fire, and with every right step he took, there was a loud clunk.

'Convenient?' said Karkaroff. 'I'm afraid I don't understand you, Moody.'

Harry could tell he was trying to sound disdainful, as though what Moody was saying was barely worth his notice, but his hands gave him away; they had balled themselves into fists.

'Don't you?' said Moody quietly. 'It's very simple, Karkaroff. Someone put Potter's name in that Goblet knowing he'd have to compete if it came out.'

'Evidently, someone 'oo wished to give 'Ogwarts two bites at ze apple!' said Madame Maxime.

'I quite agree, Madame Maxime,' said Karkaroff, bowing to her. 'I shall be lodging complaints with the Ministry of Magic *and* the International Confederation of Wizards –'

'If anyone's got reason to complain, it's Potter,' growled Moody, 'but ... funny thing ... I don't hear him saying a word ...'

'Why should 'e complain?' burst out Fleur Delacour, stamping her foot. "E 'as ze chance to compete, 'asn't 'e? We 'ave all been 'oping to be chosen for

## 第17章 四位勇士

竞争。"

"嘿,巴蒂把章程背得滚瓜烂熟。"巴格曼说,脸上绽开了笑容,回过头望着卡卡洛夫和马克西姆女士,似乎事情已经圆满解决了。

"我坚持要我的其他学生重新报名。"卡卡洛夫说,他的声音不再圆滑,笑容也消失了,脸上的表情难看极了,"你们必须把火焰杯重新摆出来,我们要不断地往里面加进名字,直到每个学校产生两位勇士。这样才算公平,邓布利多。"

"可是卡卡洛夫,这恐怕不成,"巴格曼说,"火焰杯刚刚熄灭——要到下一届争霸赛时才会重新燃起——"

"——下一届争霸赛,德姆斯特朗决不会参加了!"卡卡洛夫大发雷霆,"我们开了那么多会,经过那么多谈判和协商,没想到还会发生这样的事情!我简直想现在就离开!"

"虚张声势的威胁,卡卡洛夫!"门边一个声音咆哮着说,"你现在不能离开你的勇士。他必须参加比赛。他们都必须参加比赛。正像邓布利多说的,这是受到魔法契约约束的。这对你有利,不是吗?"

穆迪刚走进房间。他一瘸一拐地朝火边走去,每次右脚落地时都发出很响的撞击声,噔,噔。

"有利?"卡卡洛夫说,"我恐怕没法理解你的意思,穆迪。"

哈利看出卡卡洛夫竭力想使自己的语气显得轻蔑一些,好像对穆迪的话根本不屑一顾,然而他的双手暴露了他的内心,它们不由自主地攥成了拳头。

"是吗?"穆迪轻声说,"这很简单,卡卡洛夫。有人把波特的名字放进了那只高脚杯,知道如果名字被喷出来,波特就必须参加比赛。"

"显然,那个人希望给霍格沃茨两次机会!"马克西姆女士说。

"我同意你的话,马克西姆女士,"卡卡洛夫说着,朝她鞠了一躬,"我要向魔法部和国际巫师联合会提出控告——"

"如果说谁有理由抱怨,那就是波特,"穆迪粗声粗气地说,"可是……真有意思……我没有听见他说一个字……"

"他为什么要抱怨?"芙蓉·德拉库尔忍不住跺着脚问道,"他有机会参加比赛了,是不是?多少个星期以来,我们都满心希望自己被

## CHAPTER SEVENTEEN  The Four Champions

weeks and weeks! Ze honour for our schools! A thousand Galleons in prize money – zis is a chance many would die for!'

'Maybe someone's hoping Potter is going to die for it,' said Moody, with the merest trace of a growl.

An extremely tense silence followed these words.

Ludo Bagman, who was looking very anxious indeed, bounced nervously up and down on his feet and said, 'Moody, old man ... what a thing to say!'

'We all know Professor Moody considers the morning wasted if he hasn't discovered six plots to murder him before lunchtime,' said Karkaroff loudly. 'Apparently he is now teaching his students to fear assassination, too. An odd quality in a Defence Against the Dark Arts teacher, Dumbledore, but no doubt you had your reasons.'

'Imagining things, am I?' growled Moody. 'Seeing things, eh? It was a skilled witch or wizard who put the boy's name in that Goblet ...'

'Ah, what evidence is zere of zat?' said Madame Maxime, throwing up her huge hands.

'Because they hoodwinked a very powerful magical object!' said Moody. 'It would have needed an exceptionally strong Confundus Charm to bamboozle that Goblet into forgetting that only three schools compete in the Tournament ... I'm guessing they submitted Potter's name under a fourth school, to make sure he was the only one in his category ...'

'You seem to have given this a great deal of thought, Moody,' said Karkaroff coldly, 'and a very ingenious theory it is – though, of course, I heard you recently got it into your head that one of your birthday presents contained a cunningly disguised basilisk egg, and smashed it to pieces before realising it was a carriage clock. So you'll understand if we don't take you entirely seriously ...'

'There are those who'll turn innocent occasions to their advantage,' Moody retorted in a menacing voice. 'It's my job to think the way Dark wizards do, Karkaroff – as you ought to remember ...'

'Alastor!' said Dumbledore warningly. Harry wondered for a moment whom he was speaking to, but then realised 'Mad-Eye' could hardly be Moody's real first name. Moody fell silent, though still surveying Karkaroff with satisfaction – Karkaroff's face was burning.

'How this situation arose, we do not know,' said Dumbledore, speaking to

## 第17章 四位勇士

选中！为我们的学校争光！还有一千加隆的奖金——这个机会是许多人死都想得到的！"

"也许有人正希望波特为此而死。"穆迪说，语气里带着一丝咆哮。

他的话说完后，气氛陷入了一阵极度紧张的沉默。

卢多·巴格曼显得非常焦虑，身体不安地上下蹿动，嘴里说道："穆迪，你这老家伙……怎么说出这样的话！"

"我们都知道，穆迪教授如果午饭前没有发现六个人想谋杀他的话，就会觉得这个上午白过了。"卡卡洛夫大声说，"显然，他如今也在教他的学生疑神疑鬼，老以为有人要谋害自己。作为一个黑魔法防御术课的老师，这种素质真是少见，邓布利多。不过毫无疑问，你有你自己的考虑。"

"什么，我在无中生有？"穆迪怒吼道，"是我的幻觉，嗯？把这男孩的名字投进高脚杯的，绝对是一个手段高明的巫师……"

"哦，你对此有何证据？"马克西姆女士举起两只大手，问道。

"因为他们骗过了一个法力十分高强的魔法物件！"穆迪说，"要蒙蔽那只高脚杯，使它忘记只有三个学校参加争霸赛，这需要一个特别厉害的混淆咒……我猜想，他们一定是把波特的名字作为第四个学校的学生报了进去，并确保他是那个学校唯一的人选……"

"你似乎在这件事上动了不少脑筋，穆迪。"卡卡洛夫冷冷地说，"这真是一套十分新颖的理论——不过，当然啦，我听说你最近脑子里突发奇想，认为你收到的一份生日礼物里装着一只伪装巧妙的蛇怪蛋，就不管三七二十一把它砸得粉碎，结果发现那是一只旅行闹钟。因此，如果我们不把你的话完全当真，你也能够理解……"

"确实有人会利用貌似简单的机会达到自己的目的，"穆迪用威胁的口吻反驳道，"我的工作就是按黑巫师的思路去考虑问题，卡卡洛夫——你应该不会忘记……"

"阿拉斯托！"邓布利多警告道。哈利一时不明白他在对谁说话，接着便明白了，"疯眼汉"不可能是穆迪的真实名字。穆迪不作声了，但仍然很解恨地打量着卡卡洛夫——卡卡洛夫的脸红得像着了火一般。

"这个局面是怎么出现的，我们都不知道。"邓布利多对聚集在房

## CHAPTER SEVENTEEN  The Four Champions

everyone gathered in the room. 'It seems to me, however, that we have no choice but to accept it. Both Cedric and Harry have been chosen to compete in the Tournament. This, therefore, they will do ...'

'Ah, but Dumbly-dorr –'

'My dear Madame Maxime, if you have an alternative, I would be delighted to hear it.'

Dumbledore waited, but Madame Maxime did not speak, she merely glared. She wasn't the only one, either. Snape looked furious; Karkaroff livid. Bagman, however, looked rather excited.

'Well, shall we crack on, then?' he said, rubbing his hands together and smiling around the room. 'Got to give our champions their instructions, haven't we? Barty, want to do the honours?'

Mr Crouch seemed to come out of a deep reverie.

'Yes,' he said, 'instructions. Yes ... the first task ...'

He moved forwards into the firelight. Close to, Harry thought he looked ill. There were dark shadows beneath his eyes, and a thin, papery look about his wrinkled skin that had not been there at the Quidditch World Cup.

'The first task is designed to test your daring,' he told Harry, Cedric, Fleur and Krum, 'so we are not going to be telling you what it is. Courage in the face of the unknown is an important quality in a wizard ... very important ...

'The first task will take place on November the twenty-fourth, in front of the other students and the panel of judges.

'The champions are not permitted to ask for or accept help of any kind from their teachers to complete the tasks in the Tournament. The champions will face the first challenge armed only with their wands. They will receive information about the second task when the first is over. Owing to the demanding and time-consuming nature of the Tournament, the champions are exempted from end-of-year tests.'

Mr Crouch turned to look at Dumbledore. 'I think that's all, is it, Albus?'

'I think so,' said Dumbledore, who was looking at Mr Crouch with mild concern. 'Are you sure you wouldn't like to stay at Hogwarts tonight, Barty?'

'No, Dumbledore, I must get back to the Ministry,' said Mr Crouch. 'It is a very busy, very difficult time at the moment ... I've left young Weatherby in charge ... very enthusiastic ... a little overenthusiastic, if truth be told ...'

## 第17章 四位勇士

间里的每一个人说,"不过在我看来,我们除了接受它,别无选择。塞德里克和哈利都被选中参加比赛。因此,他们必须……"

"啊,可是邓布利多——"

"我亲爱的马克西姆女士,如果你有另外的解决办法,我愿意洗耳恭听。"

邓布利多等待着,然而马克西姆女士没有说话,只是气呼呼地瞪着眼睛。而且不止她一个人露出不满的神情。斯内普也是一副恼怒的样子;卡卡洛夫脸色铁青;不过巴格曼倒显得非常兴奋。

"好了,我们继续进行吧?"巴格曼说,一边搓了搓双手,笑眯眯地望着房间里的人,"要给我们的勇士作指导了,是不是?巴蒂,由你来讲吧?"

克劳奇先生似乎突然从沉思中醒过神来。

"好的,"他说,"指导。是的……第一个项目……"

他上前几步,走进炉火的光圈。哈利从近处望去,觉得他显得十分憔悴,眼睛下面有两道很深的阴影,布满皱纹的皮肤像纸一样白得透明,他在魁地奇世界杯赛时可不是这副模样。

"第一个项目是为了考验你们的胆量,"他对哈利、塞德里克、芙蓉和威克多尔说,"所以我们不准备告诉你们它是什么。敢于面对未知事物是巫师的一个重要素质……非常重要……

"第一个项目将于十一月二十四日进行,当着其他同学和裁判团的面完成。

"在完成比赛项目时,勇士不得请求或接受其老师的任何帮助。勇士面对第一轮挑战时,手里唯一的武器就是自己的魔杖。第一个项目结束后,他们才会了解到第二个项目的情况。由于比赛要求很高,持续时间很长,勇士们就不参加学年考试了。"

克劳奇先生转身望着邓布利多。"我想就这么多吧,阿不思?"

"是的,"邓布利多说,略带关切地望着克劳奇先生,"你今晚真的不想留在霍格沃茨吗,巴蒂?"

"是的,邓布利多,我必须回部里去,"克劳奇先生说,"目前正是非常忙碌、非常困难的时候……我让年轻的韦瑟比临时负责……他热情很高……说句实话,高得有点过了头……"

## CHAPTER SEVENTEEN   The Four Champions

'You'll come and have a drink before you go, at least?' said Dumbledore.

'Come on, Barty, I'm staying!' said Bagman brightly. 'It's all happening at Hogwarts now, you know, much more exciting here than at the office!'

'I think not, Ludo,' said Crouch, with a touch of his old impatience.

'Professor Karkaroff – Madame Maxime – a nightcap?' said Dumbledore.

But Madame Maxime had already put her arm around Fleur's shoulders, and was leading her swiftly out of the room. Harry could hear them both talking very fast in French as they went off into the Great Hall. Karkaroff beckoned to Krum, and they, too, exited, though in silence.

'Harry, Cedric, I suggest you go up to bed,' said Dumbledore, smiling at both of them. 'I am sure Gryffindor and Hufflepuff are waiting to celebrate with you, and it would be a shame to deprive them of this excellent excuse to make a great deal of mess and noise.'

Harry glanced at Cedric, who nodded, and they left together.

The Great Hall was deserted now; the candles had burnt low, giving the jagged smiles of the pumpkins an eerie, flickering quality.

'So,' said Cedric, with a slight smile. 'We're playing against each other again!'

'I s'pose,' said Harry. He really couldn't think of anything to say. The inside of his head seemed to be in complete disarray, as though his brain had been ransacked.

'So … tell me …' said Cedric, as they reached the Entrance Hall, which was now lit only by torches in the absence of the Goblet of Fire. 'How *did* you get your name in?'

'I didn't,' said Harry, staring up at him. 'I didn't put it in. I was telling the truth.'

'Ah … OK,' said Cedric. Harry could tell Cedric didn't believe him. 'Well … see you, then.'

Instead of going up the marble staircase, Cedric headed for a door to its right. Harry stood listening to him going down the stone steps beyond it, then, slowly, started to climb the marble ones.

Was anyone except Ron and Hermione going to believe him, or would they all think he'd put himself in for the Tournament? Yet how could anyone think that, when he was facing competitors who'd had three years' more magical education than he had – when he was now facing tasks which not

## 第17章 四位勇士

"那么,你至少过来喝一杯酒再走吧?"邓布利多说。

"来吧,巴蒂,我留在这里不走了!"巴格曼兴致很高地说,"这一切终于在霍格沃茨发生了,是吧,这里比办公室精彩有趣得多!"

"我不同意,卢多。"克劳奇说,语调里透着他惯有的不耐烦。

"卡卡洛夫教授——马克西姆女士——喝一杯睡前饮料吧?"邓布利多说。

然而马克西姆女士已经用手臂搂着芙蓉的肩膀,领着她迅速走出了房间。哈利可以听见她们俩朝礼堂走去时飞快地用法语说着什么。卡卡洛夫对克鲁姆打了个招呼,他们也一言不发地离去了。

"哈利、塞德里克,我建议你们回去睡觉。"邓布利多说,笑眯眯地看着他们俩,"我相信,格兰芬多和赫奇帕奇的同学都在等着和你们一起庆祝呢。他们好不容易有个借口闹腾一番,要夺走他们的这个机会就太扫兴了。"

哈利看了塞德里克一眼,塞德里克点了点头,两人一起走出了房间。

礼堂里现在空荡荡的,蜡烛的火苗已经很低,这使南瓜灯豁牙咧嘴的笑容显得闪烁不定,诡谲怪异。

"这么说,"塞德里克勉强微笑着说,"我们又成了对手!"

"我想是吧。"哈利说。他真的不知道说什么才好。脑袋里似乎一片混乱,就好像整个脑子都被洗劫一空了。

"那么……告诉我……"塞德里克说——这时他们已经来到门厅,火焰杯不在了,只有火把的光照着,"你究竟是怎么把你的名字投进去的?"

"我没有,"哈利说,抬起头来望着他,"我没有投。我说的是实话。"

"唉……好吧。"塞德里克说——哈利看出塞德里克并不相信他,"好吧……那么再见吧。"

塞德里克没有登上大理石楼梯,而是走向楼梯右边的一道门。哈利站在那里听着他走下门外的石阶,然后才开始慢慢地朝大理石楼梯上走去。

除了罗恩和赫敏,还有谁会相信他吗?大家都认为他是自己报名参加争霸赛的?可是他们怎么能那样想呢?要知道他将与之竞争的对手都比他多受了三年魔法教育啊——要知道他将面临的项目不仅听上去

## CHAPTER SEVENTEEN  The Four Champions

only sounded very dangerous, but which were to be performed in front of hundreds of people? Yes, he'd thought about it ... he'd fantasised about it ... but it had been a joke, really, an idle sort of dream ... he'd never really, *seriously* considered entering ...

But someone else had considered it ... someone else had wanted him in the Tournament, and had made sure he was entered. Why? To give him a treat? He didn't think so, somehow ...

To see him make a fool of himself? Well, they were likely to get their wish ...

But to get him *killed*? Was Moody just being his usual paranoid self? Couldn't someone have put Harry's name in the Goblet as a trick, a practical joke? Did anyone really want him dead?

Harry was able to answer that at once. Yes, someone wanted him dead, someone had wanted him dead ever since he had been a year old ... Lord Voldemort. But how could Voldemort have ensured that Harry's name got into the Goblet of Fire? Voldemort was supposed to be far away, in some distant country, in hiding, alone ... feeble and powerless ...

Yet in that dream he had had, just before he had awoken with his scar hurting, Voldemort had not been alone ... he had been talking to Wormtail ... plotting Harry's murder ...

Harry got a shock to find himself facing the Fat Lady already. He had barely noticed where his feet were carrying him. It was also a surprise to see that she was not alone in her frame. The wizened witch who had flitted into her neighbour's painting when he had joined the champions downstairs was now sitting smugly beside the Fat Lady. She must have dashed through every picture lining seven staircases to reach here before him. Both she and the Fat Lady were looking down at him with the keenest interest.

'Well, well, well,' said the Fat Lady, 'Violet's just told me everything. Who's just been chosen as school champion, then?'

'Balderdash,' said Harry dully.

'It most certainly isn't!' said the pale witch indignantly.

'No, no, Vi, it's the password,' said the Fat Lady soothingly, and she swung forwards on her hinges to let Harry into the common room.

The blast of noise that met Harry's ears when the portrait opened almost knocked him backwards. Next thing he knew, he was being wrenched inside the common room by about a dozen pairs of hands, and was facing the whole

## 第17章 四位勇士

非常危险，而且还要当着几百个人的面完成！是啊，他曾经设想过……他曾经幻想过……但那只是闹着玩儿的，是想入非非，白日做梦……他从来没有真正地、认真地考虑过要参加……

然而有人考虑了……有人想要他参加比赛，并且确保他能够入选。为什么？为了给他一个大好处？不知怎的，他并不这样认为……

那么，是为了让他出洋相？如果是这样，他们倒很可能如愿以偿……

至于是想要他的命……？难道穆迪真是又犯了偏执狂的毛病？会不会有人只是为了恶作剧，为了开玩笑，才把哈利的名字放进高脚杯的？难道真的有人希望他死？

哈利倒是能立刻回答这个问题。是的，确实有人希望他死，从他一岁起就有人希望他死……那就是伏地魔。可是伏地魔又怎么能保证把哈利的名字投进火焰杯呢？伏地魔应该在很远的地方，在某个遥远的国度，隐藏着，独自一人……虚弱无力，无权无势……

可是在哈利做过的那个梦里，就是他醒来后感到伤疤疼痛的那个梦里，伏地魔并不是独自一人……他在跟虫尾巴谈话……密谋杀害哈利……

哈利猛地惊醒，发现自己已经来到胖夫人面前。他刚才几乎没有注意两只脚把他带到了哪里。同样令人吃惊的是，胖夫人也不是独自一人待在相框里。刚才哈利在楼下和其他勇士会合时，那个飞进旁边一幅肖像画里的皱巴巴的女巫，此刻正得意地坐在胖夫人身旁。她一定是飞快地冲过排在七层楼梯边上的每一幅画，只为了赶在哈利之前到达这里。她和胖夫人都怀着极大的兴趣低头打量着他。

"好啊，好啊，好啊，"胖夫人说，"维奥莱特刚才把一切都告诉我了。谁刚被选为学校的勇士啊？"

"胡言乱语。"哈利干巴巴地说。

"绝对不是！"那个脸色苍白的女巫气愤地说。

"不，不，维奥莱特，这是口令。"胖夫人安慰道，然后她向前旋开，让哈利进入公共休息室。

肖像打开时，突然灌进耳朵的喧哗声震得哈利差点儿仰面摔倒。接着，他只知道自己被大约十几双手拽进了公共休息室，面对格兰芬

## CHAPTER SEVENTEEN  The Four Champions

of Gryffindor house, all of whom were screaming, applauding and whistling.

'You should've told us you'd entered!' bellowed Fred; he looked half annoyed, half deeply impressed.

'How did you do it without getting a beard? Brilliant!' roared George.

'I didn't,' Harry said. 'I don't know how –'

But Angelina had now swooped down upon him. 'Oh, if it couldn't be me, at least it's a Gryffindor –'

'You'll be able to pay back Diggory for that last Quidditch match, Harry!' shrieked Katie Bell, another of the Gryffindor Chasers.

'We've got food, Harry, come and have some –'

'I'm not hungry, I had enough at the feast –'

But nobody wanted to hear that he wasn't hungry; nobody wanted to hear that he hadn't put his name in the Goblet; not one single person seemed to have noticed that he wasn't at all in the mood to celebrate … Lee Jordan had unearthed a Gryffindor banner from somewhere, and he insisted on draping it around Harry like a cloak. Harry couldn't get away; whenever he tried to sidle over to the staircase up to the dormitories, the crowd around him closed ranks, forcing another Butterbeer on him, stuffing crisps and peanuts into his hands … everyone wanted to know how he had done it, how he had tricked Dumbledore's Age Line, and managed to get his name into the Goblet …

'I didn't,' he said, over and over again, 'I don't know how it happened.'

But for all the notice anyone took, he might just as well not have answered at all.

'I'm tired!' he bellowed finally, after nearly half an hour. 'No, seriously, George – I'm going to bed –'

He wanted more than anything to find Ron and Hermione, to find a bit of sanity, but neither of them seemed to be in the common room. Insisting that he needed to sleep, and almost flattening the little Creevey brothers as they attempted to waylay him at the foot of the stairs, Harry managed to shake everyone off, and climbed up to the dormitory as fast as he could.

To his great relief, he found Ron was lying on his bed in the otherwise empty dormitory, still fully dressed. He looked up when Harry slammed the door behind him.

'Where've you been?' Harry said.

'Oh, hello,' said Ron.

## 第17章 四位勇士

多学院的全体同学。他们全都在尖叫、欢呼、吹口哨。

"你应该告诉我们你报了名！"弗雷德大声吼道。他看上去半是恼怒，半是钦佩。

"你怎么能不长胡子就顺利过关的？太棒了！"乔治嚷嚷道。

"我没有，"哈利说，"我不知道怎么——"

这时安吉利娜旋风般地冲到他面前："哦，即便不可能是我，至少也是格兰芬多的一员啊——"

"你可以为上次的魁地奇比赛向迪戈里报一箭之仇了，哈利！"凯蒂·贝尔尖叫道，她也是格兰芬多球队的一名追球手。

"我们准备了吃的东西，哈利，快过来吃点儿——"

"我不饿，我在宴会上吃得够多了——"

可是没人愿意听他说他不饿，没人愿意听他说他没有把名字投进高脚杯，似乎谁也没有注意到他根本就没有情绪庆祝这件事……李·乔丹不知从什么地方翻腾出一面格兰芬多学院的旗子，坚持要把它像斗篷一样裹在哈利身上。哈利没有办法脱身，每当他想偷偷溜向通往宿舍的楼梯时，人群就向他靠拢，把他团团围住，强迫他再喝一杯黄油啤酒，或把饼干和花生硬塞进他手里……每个人都想知道他是怎么办成的，是怎么骗过邓布利多的年龄线，把他的名字投进高脚杯的……

"我不知道，"他一遍又一遍地说，"我不知道这是怎么回事。"

可是大家根本不理会，就好像他什么也没说。

"我累了！"过了大约半个小时，哈利终于忍无可忍，大声吼道，"不，说真的，乔治——我想上床睡觉了——"

他特别希望看到罗恩和赫敏，希望找到一点儿理智，可是他们俩似乎都不在公共休息室。哈利一再坚持自己需要睡觉，差点儿把试图在楼梯口拦截他的克里维小兄弟俩撞倒在地。最后他总算摆脱了众人，匆匆上楼来到宿舍。

令他大为宽慰的是，他发现罗恩和衣躺在床上，宿舍里只有他一个人。哈利把门重重关上时，罗恩抬起头来。

"你上哪儿去了？"哈利问。

"噢，你好。"罗恩说。

## CHAPTER SEVENTEEN   The Four Champions

He was grinning, but it looked a very odd, strained sort of grin. Harry suddenly became aware that he was still wearing the scarlet Gryffindor banner that Lee had tied around him. He hastened to take it off, but it was knotted very tightly. Ron lay on the bed without moving, watching Harry struggle to remove it.

'So,' he said, when Harry had finally removed the banner and thrown it into a corner. 'Congratulations.'

'What d'you mean, congratulations?' said Harry, staring at Ron. There was definitely something wrong with the way Ron was smiling; it was more like a grimace.

'Well ... no one else got across the Age Line,' said Ron. 'Not even Fred and George. What did you use – the Invisibility Cloak?'

'The Invisibility Cloak wouldn't have got me over that line,' said Harry slowly.

'Oh, right,' said Ron. 'I thought you might've told me if it was the Cloak ... because it would've covered both of us, wouldn't it? But you found another way, did you?'

'Listen,' said Harry, 'I didn't put my name in that Goblet. Someone else must've done it.'

Ron raised his eyebrows. 'What would they do that for?'

'I dunno,' said Harry. He felt it would sound very melodramatic to say 'to kill me'.

Ron's eyebrows rose so high that they were in danger of disappearing into his hair.

'It's OK, you know, you can tell *me* the truth,' he said. 'If you don't want everyone else to know, fine, but I don't know why you're bothering to lie, you didn't get into trouble for it, did you? That friend of the Fat Lady's, that Violet, she's already told us all, Dumbledore's letting you enter. A thousand Galleons prize money, eh? And you don't have to do end-of-year tests either ...'

'I didn't put my name in that Goblet!' said Harry, starting to feel angry.

'Yeah, OK,' said Ron, in exactly the same sceptical tone as Cedric. 'Only you said this morning you'd have done it last night, and no one would've seen you ... I'm not stupid, you know.'

'You're doing a really good impression of it,' Harry snapped.

'Yeah?' said Ron, and there was no trace of a grin, forced or otherwise,

## 第17章 四位勇士

罗恩脸上笑着，但那是一种非常别扭勉强的笑容。哈利突然意识到自己还披着李·乔丹刚才系在他身上的深红色的格兰芬多旗子。他想赶紧把它脱掉，可是那个结系得很紧。罗恩一动不动地躺在床上，看着哈利费力地解开旗子。

"那么，"当哈利终于把旗子脱掉，扔到墙角后，罗恩说道，"祝贺你了。"

"你这是什么意思，祝贺？"哈利望着罗恩说。罗恩的笑容显然有点不大对劲儿：简直像在做怪相。

"没什么……别人都没有跨过年龄线，"罗恩说，"就连弗雷德和乔治也没有。你用了什么——隐形衣？"

"隐形衣不可能让我越过那道线。"哈利慢慢地说。

"哦，对了，"罗恩说，"如果是隐形衣的话，我想你会告诉我的……因为隐形衣可以罩住我们两个，是不是？可是你找到了别的办法,对吗？"

"听着，"哈利说，"我没有把我的名字投进那只高脚杯。肯定是别人干的。"

罗恩扬起眉毛："他们为什么要那样做？"

"我不知道。"哈利说，他觉得要是说是为了害死他，听起来太耸人听闻了。

罗恩的眉毛扬得那么高，似乎要消失在他的头发里了。

"没关系，其实，你可以把实话告诉我的。"他说，"如果你不愿意让别人知道，可以，但是我不明白你为什么要撒谎呢，你并没有因此惹来麻烦啊，是不是？胖夫人的那个朋友，那个维奥莱特，她已经告诉我们大家，邓布利多让你入选了。一千加隆的奖金，是吗？而且你还不用参加学年考试了……"

"我没有把我的名字放进那只高脚杯！"哈利说,他开始感到恼火了。

"是啊，好吧，"罗恩说，用的是和塞德里克一模一样的怀疑口吻，"不过你今天早晨还说过，你可以在昨天夜里下手，没有人会看见……你知道，我并不是傻瓜。"

"你现在确实给我留下这样的印象。"哈利没好气地说。

"是吗？"罗恩说——他脸上的笑容，不管是勉强的还是真心的，

on his face now. 'You want to get to bed, Harry, I expect you'll need to be up early tomorrow for a photocall or something.'

He wrenched the hangings shut around his four-poster, leaving Harry standing there by the door, staring at the dark red velvet curtains, now hiding one of the few people he had been sure would believe him.

## 第17章 四位勇士

现在消失得无影无踪,"你需要上床睡觉了,哈利。我想你明天需要早点起床,接受媒体的拍照什么的。"

他猛地把帷帐拉过来遮住他的四柱床,撇下哈利一个人站在门边,望着深红色的帷帐发呆。他原以为肯定会有几个人相信自己的,其中一个就藏在那帷帐后面。

## CHAPTER EIGHTEEN

# The Weighing of the Wands

When Harry woke up on Sunday morning, it took him a moment to remember why he felt so miserable and worried. Then the memory of the previous night rolled over him. He sat up and ripped back the curtains of his own four-poster, intending to talk to Ron, to force Ron to believe him – only to find that Ron's bed was empty; he had obviously gone down to breakfast.

Harry dressed and went down the spiral staircase into the common room. The moment he appeared, the people who had already finished breakfast broke into applause again. The prospect of going down into the Great Hall and facing the rest of the Gryffindors, all treating him like some sort of hero, was not inviting; it was that, however, or stay here and allow himself to be cornered by the Creevey brothers, who were both beckoning frantically to him to join them. He walked resolutely over to the portrait hole, pushed it open, climbed out of it and found himself face to face with Hermione.

'Hello,' she said, holding up a stack of toast, which she was carrying in a napkin. 'I brought you this ... want to go for a walk?'

'Good idea,' said Harry, gratefully.

They went downstairs, crossed the Entrance Hall quickly without looking in at the Great Hall, and were soon striding across the lawn towards the lake, where the Durmstrang ship was moored, reflected blackly in the water. It was a chilly morning, and they kept moving, munching their toast, as Harry told Hermione exactly what had happened after he had left the Gryffindor table the night before. To his immense relief, Hermione accepted his story without question.

'Well, of course, I knew you hadn't entered yourself,' she said, when he'd finished telling her about the scene in the chamber off the Hall. 'The look

# 第 18 章

# 检测魔杖

星期天早晨,哈利一觉醒来,过了好一会儿才想起他为什么感到这样难过和焦虑。接着,昨天晚上的事情一下子都浮现在脑海里。他坐起来,拉开四柱床的帷帐,想跟罗恩说话,逼着罗恩相信他——却发现罗恩的床上空空的,显然他已经下楼吃早饭去了。

哈利穿好衣服,沿着螺旋形楼梯来到下面的公共休息室。他刚一露面,那些已经吃过早饭的同学又热烈地欢呼起来。他想起还要进入礼堂,面对格兰芬多的其他同学,而他们都把他当成一个英雄,想到这里他就有点儿发怵。可是如果不去礼堂,就只好待在这里,任凭自己被克里维兄弟俩纠缠。他们俩正拼命向他招手,希望他过去呢。于是,他果断地走向肖像后的洞口,把肖像推开,爬了出去,正好和赫敏打了个照面。

"你好,"赫敏说,举着手里用餐巾纸包着的一叠面包,"我带来给你的……想去散散步吗?"

"好主意。"哈利感激地说。

两人下了楼,看也没看礼堂一眼,就飞快地穿过门厅。很快,他们就大步走在了向湖边延伸的草坪上。德姆斯特朗的大船泊在湖面,在水中投下黑乎乎的倒影。这是一个寒冷的早晨,他们不停地走,一边嚼着面包。哈利把前一天晚上他离开格兰芬多桌子后发生的一切,原原本本地告诉了赫敏。令他感到非常欣慰的是,赫敏毫不怀疑地接受了他的说法。

"我当然知道你自己没有报名,"当他讲完礼堂旁边的房间里发生的一切后,赫敏说道,"瞧邓布利多报出你的名字时,你脸上的那副神

## CHAPTER EIGHTEEN   The Weighing of the Wands

on your face when Dumbledore read out your name! But the question is, who *did* put it in? Because Moody's right, Harry ... I don't think any student could have done it ... they'd never be able to fool the Goblet, or get over Dumbledore's –'

'Have you seen Ron?' Harry interrupted.

Hermione hesitated.

'Erm ... yes ... he was at breakfast,' she said.

'Does he still think I entered myself?'

'Well ... no, I don't think so ... not *really*,' said Hermione awkwardly.

'What's that supposed to mean, not *really*?'

'Oh, Harry, isn't it obvious?' Hermione said despairingly. 'He's jealous!'

'*Jealous?*' Harry said incredulously. 'Jealous of what? He wants to make a prat of himself in front of the whole school, does he?'

'Look,' said Hermione patiently, 'it's always you who gets all the attention, you know it is. I know it's not your fault,' she added quickly, seeing Harry open his mouth furiously, 'I know you don't ask for it ... but – well – you know, Ron's got all those brothers to compete against at home, and you're his best friend, and you're really famous – he's always shunted to one side whenever people see you, and he puts up with it, and he never mentions it, but I suppose this is just one time too many ...'

'Great,' said Harry bitterly. 'Really great. Tell him from me I'll swap any time he wants. Tell him from me he's welcome to it ... people gawping at my forehead everywhere I go ...'

'I'm not telling him anything,' Hermione said shortly. 'Tell him yourself, it's the only way to sort this out.'

'I'm not running around after him trying to make him grow up!' Harry said, so loudly that several owls in a nearby tree took flight in alarm. 'Maybe he'll believe I'm not enjoying myself once I've got my neck broken or –'

'That's not funny,' said Hermione quietly. 'That's not funny at all.' She looked extremely anxious. 'Harry, I've been thinking – you know what we've got to do, don't you? Straight away, the moment we get back to the castle?'

'Yeah, give Ron a good kick up the –'

## 第18章 检测魔杖

情!问题是,谁把你的名字投进去的?你要知道,穆迪说得对,哈利……我认为没有一个学生能做到这点……学生绝不可能欺骗火焰杯,也不可能越过邓布利多的那条——"

"你看见罗恩了吗?"哈利打断了她的话。

赫敏迟疑着。

"嗯……看见了……他在吃早饭。"她说。

"他还认为是我自己报名的吗?"

"嗯……不,我想不会……其实不会。"赫敏很不自然地说。

"'其实不会',这是什么意思?"

"唉,哈利,这难道还不明白吗?"赫敏无奈地说,"他是嫉妒呢!"

"嫉妒?"哈利不敢相信地问,"嫉妒什么?难道他愿意在全校同学面前出这个洋相?"

"想一想吧,"赫敏耐心地说,"你知道,引起所有人注意的永远是你。我知道这不是你的错,"她看到哈利气愤地张开嘴巴,便赶紧找补道,"我知道你并没有追求这个……可是——怎么说呢——你知道,罗恩在家里要跟那么多哥哥竞争较量,你作为他最好的朋友,又是那么大名鼎鼎——每次别人一看见你,他就被冷落到一边,对此他都默默地忍受了,从来不提一个字,我想这一次恰好使他忍无可忍了……"

"很好,"哈利怨恨地说,"真是太好了。替我转告他,只要他愿意,我随时可以跟他换。替我转告他,我欢迎他来跟我换……不管我走到哪里,人们都傻乎乎地盯着我的额头……"

"我决不会转告他什么话,"赫敏干脆地说,"你自己去跟他说吧。只有这样才能解决问题。"

"我才不想到处追着他,苦口婆心地教他成熟起来呢!"哈利说,"他什么时候才会相信我并不快乐呢,也许等我摔断了脖子,或者——"他声音很大,吓得旁边树上的几只猫头鹰扑棱棱地飞了起来。

"这并不好笑,"赫敏轻声地说,"这一点儿也不好笑。"她显得担忧极了,"哈利,我一直在想——你知道我们要做什么,是吗?一回到城堡马上就做?"

"是啊,狠狠地给罗恩一脚——"

## CHAPTER EIGHTEEN  The Weighing of the Wands

'*Write to Sirius*. You've got to tell him what's happened. He asked you to keep him posted on everything that's going on at Hogwarts ... it's almost like he expected something like this to happen. I brought some parchment and a quill out with me –'

'Come off it,' said Harry, looking around to check that they couldn't be overheard; but the grounds were quite deserted. 'He came back to the country just because my scar twinged. He'll probably come bursting right into the castle if I tell him someone's entered me for the Triwizard Tournament –'

'*He'd want you to tell him*,' said Hermione sternly. 'He's going to find out anyway –'

'How?'

'Harry, this isn't going to be kept quiet,' said Hermione, very seriously. 'This Tournament's famous, and you're famous, I'll be really surprised if there isn't anything in the *Daily Prophet* about you competing ... you're already in half the books about You-Know-Who, you know ... and Sirius would rather hear it from you, I know he would.'

'OK, OK, I'll write to him,' said Harry, throwing his last piece of toast into the lake. They both stood and watched it floating there for a moment, before a large tentacle rose out of the water and scooped it beneath the surface. Then they returned to the castle.

'Whose owl am I going to use?' Harry said, as they climbed the stairs. 'He told me not to use Hedwig again.'

'Ask Ron if you can borrow –'

'I'm not asking Ron anything,' Harry said flatly.

'Well, borrow one of the school owls, then, anyone can use them,' said Hermione.

They went up to the Owlery. Hermione gave Harry a piece of parchment, a quill and a bottle of ink, then strolled around the long lines of perches, looking at all the different owls, while Harry sat down against a wall and wrote his letter.

> Dear Sirius,
> 
> You told me to keep you posted on what's happening at Hogwarts, so here goes – I don't know if you've heard, but the Triwizard Tournament's happening this year and on Saturday

## 第18章 检测魔杖

"写信给小天狼星。你必须把发生的事情告诉他。他叫你把霍格沃茨发生的每一件事都写信告诉他……他好像早就料到会出这样的事。我带出来一些羊皮纸和一支羽毛笔——"

"别胡说了，"哈利说道，一边四下张望，看有没有人能听见他们说话；场地上空荡荡的，"就因为我的伤疤有点刺痛，他就赶紧回国了。如果我告诉他有人给我报名参加三强争霸赛，他大概会直接冲到城堡里来——"

"他希望你告诉他，"赫敏严厉地说，"反正，他迟早会知道的——"

"怎么会呢？"

"哈利，这件事不可能不被炒得沸沸扬扬，"赫敏说，口气非常严肃，"这场争霸赛是大家都关注的，而你又那么出名。如果《预言家日报》不发表文章写你参加比赛，我倒真会感到吃惊呢……你知道的，在关于神秘人的书里，有一半都提到了你的名字……小天狼星肯定情愿从你这里了解这件事，我知道他一定是这样的。"

"好吧，好吧，我给他写信。"哈利说着，把最后一片面包扔进了湖里。两人站在那里，注视着面包在湖面漂浮了一阵，随即一只巨大的触手冒出水面，把它抓到水下去了。然后他们便返回了城堡。

"我用谁的猫头鹰呢？"他们上楼的时候，哈利说，"他叫我别再用海德薇了。"

"问问罗恩，你能不能借——"

"我不会问罗恩任何事情！"哈利断然地说。

"好吧，那就借一只学校的猫头鹰，人人都可以用的。"赫敏说。

他们来到上面的猫头鹰棚屋。赫敏递给哈利一张羊皮纸、一支羽毛笔和一瓶墨水，然后她顺着长长的几排栖枝走来走去，打量着各种不同的猫头鹰。哈利靠着墙根坐下，开始写信。

亲爱的小天狼星：

　　你叫我把霍格沃茨发生的事情都写信告诉你，所以我就写信了——我不知道你有没有听说，今年要举行三强争霸赛，星期六晚上我被选为第四位勇士了。我不知道是谁把我的名字投进火焰

## CHAPTER EIGHTEEN  The Weighing of the Wands

> night I got picked as a fourth champion. I don't know who put my name in the Goblet of Fire, because I didn't. The other Hogwarts champion is Cedric Diggory, from Hufflepuff.

He paused at this point, thinking. He had an urge to say something about the large weight of anxiety that seemed to have settled inside his chest since last night, but he couldn't think how to translate this into words, so he simply dipped his quill back into the ink bottle and wrote:

> Hope you're OK, and Buckbeak -Harry.

'Finished,' he told Hermione, getting to his feet and brushing straw off his robes. At this, Hedwig came fluttering down onto his shoulder, and held out her leg.

'I can't use you,' Harry told her, looking around for the school owls. 'I've got to use one of these ...'

Hedwig gave a very loud hoot, and took off so suddenly that her talons cut into his shoulder. She kept her back to Harry all the time he was tying his letter to the leg of a large barn owl. When the barn owl had flown off, Harry reached out to stroke Hedwig, but she clicked her beak furiously and soared up into the rafters out of reach.

'First Ron, then you,' said Harry angrily. '*This isn't my fault.*'

If Harry had thought that matters would improve once everyone got used to the idea of him being champion, the following day showed him how mistaken he was. He could no longer avoid the rest of the school once he was back at lessons – and it was clear that the rest of the school, just like the Gryffindors, thought Harry had entered himself for the Tournament. Unlike the Gryffindors, however, they did not seem impressed.

The Hufflepuffs, who were usually on excellent terms with the Gryffindors, had turned remarkably cold towards the whole lot of them. One Herbology lesson was enough to demonstrate this. It was plain that the Hufflepuffs felt that Harry had stolen their champion's glory; a feeling exacerbated, perhaps, by the fact that Hufflepuff house very rarely got any glory, and that Cedric was one of the few who had ever given them any, having beaten Gryffindor once at Quidditch. Ernie Macmillan and Justin Finch-Fletchley, with whom

## 第18章 检测魔杖

杯的,我自己没有这么做。霍格沃茨的另一位勇士是塞德里克·迪戈里,他是赫奇帕奇学院的。

写到这里,哈利停下笔思索。他多么想讲一讲从昨晚开始盘踞在他心头的那份沉重的焦虑啊,可是他不知道怎样把这种情绪用文字表达出来。于是,他又把羽毛笔在墨水瓶里蘸了蘸,写道:

希望你一切都好,问候巴克比克。——哈利

"写完了。"他对赫敏说,然后站起身来,掸去袍子上的稻草。海德薇见了,赶紧扑棱棱地飞到他肩头,伸出一条腿来。

"我不能用你,"哈利对它说,一边左右张望着寻找学校的猫头鹰,"我必须在它们中间挑一只……"

海德薇响亮地叫了一声,突然飞起来,爪子深深地扎进了哈利的肩膀。哈利把信拴在一只大谷仓猫头鹰腿上,在这过程中,海德薇一直背对着他。谷仓猫头鹰飞走了,哈利伸手去抚摸海德薇,不料它愤怒地呃了呃嘴,飞到上面哈利够不着的橡子上去了。

"先是罗恩,然后是你,"哈利气愤地说,"这又不是我的错。"

如果哈利以为一旦大家习惯了他是勇士,情况就会有所好转,那么他第二天就会发现自己是大错特错了。重新开始上课以后,他就再也无法躲避学校的其他同学——而显然另外几个学院的同学也像格兰芬多们一样,以为哈利是自己报名参加争霸赛的。不过他们和格兰芬多们不同,他们似乎觉得这件事并不很光彩。

赫奇帕奇们一向和格兰芬多们相处得很好,可现在也突然对他们全都冷淡起来。一堂草药课就足以证明这点。显然,赫奇帕奇们觉得哈利盗取了他们勇士的光荣。由于赫奇帕奇学院很少获得什么光荣——塞德里克是少数几个给他们带来光荣的人之一,他曾经在魁地奇比赛中打败了格兰芬多学院——这使他们的这种怨恨情绪更强烈了。厄尼·麦克米兰和贾斯廷·芬列里本来和哈利关系很不错,现在也不跟他说话了,

## CHAPTER EIGHTEEN   The Weighing of the Wands

Harry normally got on very well, did not talk to him even though they were repotting Bouncing Bulbs at the same tray – though they did laugh rather unpleasantly when one of the Bouncing Bulbs wriggled free from Harry's grip and smacked him hard in the face. Ron wasn't talking to Harry either. Hermione sat between them, making very forced conversation, but though both answered her normally, they avoided making eye contact with each other. Harry thought even Professor Sprout seemed distant with him – but then, she was Head of Hufflepuff house.

He would have been looking forward to seeing Hagrid under normal circumstances, but Care of Magical Creatures meant seeing the Slytherins, too – the first time he would come face to face with them since becoming champion.

Predictably, Malfoy arrived at Hagrid's cabin with his familiar sneer firmly in place.

'Ah, look, boys, it's the champion,' he said to Crabbe and Goyle, the moment he got within earshot of Harry. 'Got your autograph books? Better get a signature now, because I doubt he's going to be around much longer … half the Triwizard champions have died … how long d'you reckon you're going to last, Potter? Ten minutes into the first task's my bet.'

Crabbe and Goyle guffawed sycophantically, but Malfoy had to stop there, because Hagrid emerged from the back of his cabin, holding a teetering tower of crates, each containing a very large Blast-Ended Skrewt. To the class's horror, Hagrid proceeded to explain that the reason the Skrewts had been killing each other was an excess of pent-up energy, and that the solution would be for each of the class to fix a leash on a Skrewt and take it for a short walk. The only good thing about this plan was that it distracted Malfoy completely.

'Take this thing for a walk?' he repeated in disgust, staring into one of the boxes. 'And where exactly are we supposed to fix the leash? Around the sting, the blasting end or the sucker?'

'Roun' the middle,' said Hagrid, demonstrating. 'Er – yeh might want ter put on yer dragon-hide gloves, jus' as an extra precaution, like. Harry – you come here an' help me with this big one …'

Hagrid's real intention, however, was to talk to Harry away from the rest of the class.

## 第18章 检测魔杖

尽管他们几个人在同一个托盘上移植跳跳球茎——不过,当一个跳跳球茎扭动着从哈利手里挣脱,在他脸上重重打了一下时,他们都幸灾乐祸地哈哈大笑,使人心里很不舒服。罗恩也不跟哈利说话了。赫敏坐在他们俩中间,勉强找出些话来。哈利和罗恩各自跟赫敏倒是有问有答,表现正常,可是他们俩互相躲着对方的目光。哈利觉得就连斯普劳特教授似乎也对他冷淡了——这也难怪,她是赫奇帕奇学院的院长嘛。

一般情况下,哈利肯定是渴望见到海格的,可是上海格的保护神奇动物课意味着同时会见到斯莱特林的学生——这将是他成为勇士后第一次与斯莱特林们正面相遇。

正如他预料的那样,马尔福来到海格的小屋时,脸上又牢牢地挂着他那个讥讽的笑容。

"啊,看哪,伙计们,这就是勇士,"他刚走近,估摸着哈利能听见他的话时,他就对克拉布和高尔说,"你们有他签名的书吗?最好赶紧叫他签名,我怀疑他在这儿待不长了……三强争霸赛的勇士有一半都死了……波特,你认为自己能活多久?我猜大概是第一个比赛项目开始后十分钟吧。"

克拉布和高尔讨好地傻笑起来,可是马尔福不得不就此打住,因为海格从他的小屋后面出现了,怀里抱着一大摞摇摇欲坠的箱子,每个箱子里都装着一条体积庞大的炸尾螺。海格解释说,炸尾螺之所以互相残杀,是因为它们有多余的精力没处释放。为了解决这个问题,每个同学都要用绳子拴住一条炸尾螺,带它去散一会儿步。同学们听了都非常害怕。这个计划的唯一好处,就是把马尔福的注意力完全吸引过去了。

"带这玩意儿去散步?"他盯着一个箱子,厌恶地问,"我们到底应该把绳子拴在哪儿?拴在它的刺上、炸尾上,还是吸盘上?"

"拴在中间,"海格说着,给大家做示范,"嗯——恐怕需要戴上你们的火龙皮手套,作为一种额外的预防措施。哈利——你过来,帮我对付这个大家伙……"

其实,海格的真正意图是想避开全班同学,跟哈利聊一聊。

## CHAPTER EIGHTEEN  The Weighing of the Wands

He waited until everyone else had set off with their Skrewts, then turned to Harry and said, very seriously, 'So – yer competin', Harry. In the Tournament. School champion.'

'One of the champions,' Harry corrected him.

Hagrid's beetle-black eyes looked very anxious under his wild eyebrows. 'No idea who put yeh in fer it, Harry?'

'You believe I didn't do it, then?' said Harry, concealing with difficulty the rush of gratitude he felt at Hagrid's words.

''Course I do,' Hagrid grunted. 'Yeh say it wasn' you, an' I believe yeh – an' Dumbledore believes yer, an' all.'

'Wish I knew who *did* do it,' said Harry bitterly.

The pair of them looked out over the lawn; the class was widely scattered now, and all in great difficulty. The Skrewts were now over three feet long, and extremely powerful. No longer shell-less and colourless, they had developed a kind of thick, greyish shiny armour. They looked like a cross between giant scorpions and elongated crabs – but still without recognisable heads or eyes. They had become immensely strong, and very hard to control.

'Look like they're havin' fun, don' they?' Hagrid said happily. Harry assumed he was talking about the Skrewts, because his classmates certainly weren't; every now and then, with an alarming *bang*, one of the Skrewts' ends would explode, causing it to shoot forward several yards, and more than one person was being dragged along on their stomach, trying desperately to get back on their feet.

'Ah, I don' know, Harry,' Hagrid sighed suddenly, looking back down at him with a worried expression on his face. 'School champion ... everythin' seems ter happen ter you, doesn' it?'

Harry didn't answer. Yes, everything did seem to happen to him ... that was more or less what Hermione had said as they had walked around the lake, and that was the reason, according to her, that Ron was no longer talking to him.

The next few days were some of Harry's worst at Hogwarts. The closest he had ever come to feeling like this had been during those months, in his second year, when a large part of the school had suspected him of attacking his fellow students. But Ron had been on his side then. He thought he could

## 第18章 检测魔杖

他等到大家都带着炸尾螺走开后，才转向哈利，非常严肃地说："这么说——你要去比赛了，哈利。参加争霸赛。成了学校的勇士。"

"勇士之一。"哈利纠正他。

海格浓密蓬乱的眉毛下，一双黑亮的眼睛显得非常担忧。"知道是谁把你的名字投进去的吗，哈利？"

"怎么，你相信我没有这么做？"哈利说，竭力掩饰他听到海格的话后突然涌起的感激之情。

"我当然相信，"海格嘟哝着说，"你说不是你干的，我相信你——邓布利多也相信你，大家都相信你。"

"真希望知道是谁干的。"哈利怨恨地说。

两人放眼眺望草坪，同学们现在散开了，一个个都走得很艰难。炸尾螺现在有三英尺多长了，力气大得惊人。它们不再是肉乎乎的、没有甲壳、没有颜色了，而是长出了一层灰白色、又厚又亮的硬壳。炸尾螺的模样介于巨大的蝎子和拉长的螃蟹之间——但是仍然看不出脑袋和眼睛在哪里。它们现在变得力大无比，很难控制。

"看样子它们挺开心的，是吧？"海格高兴地说，哈利断定他说的是炸尾螺，因为同学们显然并不开心。时不时地，随着一声令人惊恐的噼啪声响起，一条炸尾螺的尾巴爆炸了，推动炸尾螺向前跃进好几米，不止一个同学被拽得摔倒在地，拼命挣扎着想站起来。

"唉，我也不知道，哈利，"海格突然叹了口气，目光又回到哈利身上，脸上带着一种忧虑的神情，"学校的勇士……什么事都让你碰上了，是吗？"

哈利没有回答。是的，什么事都让他碰上了……他和赫敏在湖边散步时，赫敏说的话也差不多是这个意思。据她说，罗恩也正是因为这个才不跟他说话的。

接下来的几天是哈利在霍格沃茨最难熬的日子。记得还是在二年级的那几个月里，学校里许多同学都怀疑是哈利攻击了自己的同学，那时他的日子也差不多像现在这样难过。不过当时罗恩跟他站在一边。哈利认为，只要罗恩依然是他的好朋友，全校其他同学不管怎么样他

## CHAPTER EIGHTEEN   The Weighing of the Wands

have coped with the rest of the school's behaviour if he could just have had Ron back as a friend, but he wasn't going to try and persuade Ron to talk to him if Ron didn't want to. Nevertheless, it was lonely, with dislike pouring in on him from all sides.

He could understand the Hufflepuffs' attitudes, even if he didn't like it; they had their own champion to support. He expected nothing less than vicious insults from the Slytherins – he was highly unpopular there and always had been, as he had helped Gryffindor beat them so often, both at Quidditch and in the Inter-House Championship. But he had hoped the Ravenclaws might have found it in their hearts to support him as much as Cedric. He was wrong, however. Most Ravenclaws seemed to think that he had been desperate to earn himself a bit more fame by tricking the Goblet into accepting his name.

Then there was the fact that Cedric looked the part of a champion so much more than he did. Exceptionally handsome, with his straight nose, dark hair and grey eyes, it was hard to say who was receiving more admiration these days, Cedric or Viktor Krum. Harry actually saw the same sixth-year girls who had been so keen to get Krum's autograph, begging Cedric to sign their schoolbags one lunchtime.

Meanwhile there was no reply from Sirius, Hedwig was refusing to come anywhere near him, Professor Trelawney was predicting his death with even more certainty than usual, and he did so badly at Summoning Charms in Professor Flitwick's class that he was given extra homework – the only person to get any, apart from Neville.

'It's really not that difficult, Harry,' Hermione tried to reassure him, as they left Flitwick's class – she had been making objects zoom across the room to her all lesson, as though she was some sort of weird magnet for board dusters, wastepaper baskets and Lunascopes. 'You just weren't concentrating properly –'

'Wonder why that was?' said Harry darkly, as Cedric Diggory walked past, surrounded by a large group of simpering girls, all of whom looked at Harry as though he was a particularly large Blast-Ended Skrewt. 'Still – never mind, eh? Double Potions to look forward to this afternoon ...'

Double Potions was always a horrible experience, but these days it was nothing short of torture. Being shut in a dungeon for an hour and a half

## 第18章 检测魔杖

都能对付,但是既然罗恩无意与他和好,他也决不愿意死乞白赖地求罗恩跟他说话。可是,唉,反感和不满从四面八方朝他涌来,他是多么孤单哪。

他能够理解赫奇帕奇们的态度,尽管并不喜欢。他们要支持自己的勇士嘛。而斯莱特林们呢,他早就知道他们只会给他恶毒的侮辱——他在他们那里从来都是极不受欢迎的,因为他在魁地奇比赛和学院杯竞赛中,多次帮助格兰芬多打败了斯莱特林。但是,拉文克劳们呢,他原先希望他们会像支持塞德里克一样支持他的,没想到,他错了。拉文克劳的大多数同学似乎都以为他施展了诡计,哄骗火焰杯接收了他的名字,迫不及待地为自己赚取更多的名声。

此外还有一个事实:塞德里克看上去确实比他更像一位勇士,挺直的鼻梁、乌黑的头发、灰色的眼睛,那模样真是英俊过人。这些日子,在塞德里克和威克多尔·克鲁姆之间,很难说谁获得的赞美更多。一次吃午饭的时候,哈利竟然看见那些曾眼巴巴想获得克鲁姆签名的六年级女生,又苦苦哀求塞德里克在她们的书包上签名了。

与此同时,小天狼星那里还是毫无音讯;海德薇呢,死活都不肯接近他;特里劳妮教授又在预言他的死亡了,言之凿凿,语气比往常还要肯定;他在弗立维教授的课上学习召唤咒时,表现得一塌糊涂,结果教授给他布置了额外的家庭作业——除了纳威,他是唯一被罚作业的人。

"其实并没有那么难,哈利。"他们离开弗立维的课堂时,赫敏试着安慰他——刚才在课上,她把教室里的东西都弄得嗖嗖朝她飞去,就好像她是一块磁铁,专门吸引黑板擦、字纸篓和月宫图什么的,"你只是没有好好地集中思想——"

"真不知道为什么,"哈利闷闷不乐地说,这时塞德里克·迪戈里迎面走过,旁边围着一大群嘻嘻傻笑的女生,她们都瞪眼望着哈利,就好像他是一条特别巨大的炸尾螺,"没关系——别介意,好吗?今天下午还有两节魔药课呢……"

两节连在一起的魔药课总是令哈利不寒而栗,最近,它简直变成了一种痛苦的折磨。整整一个半小时被关在地下教室里,跟斯内普和

## CHAPTER EIGHTEEN  The Weighing of the Wands

with Snape and the Slytherins, all of whom seemed determined to punish Harry as much as possible for daring to become school champion, was about the most unpleasant thing Harry could imagine. He had already struggled through one Friday's worth, with Hermione sitting next to him, intoning 'Ignore them, ignore them, ignore them' under her breath, and he couldn't see why today should be any better.

When he and Hermione arrived outside Snape's dungeon after lunch, they found the Slytherins waiting outside, each and every one of them wearing a large badge on the front of his or her robes. For one wild moment Harry thought they were S.P.E.W. badges – then he saw that they all bore the same message, in luminous red letters that burnt brightly in the dimly lit underground passage:

> **SUPPORT CEDRIC DIGGORY**
> **-THE REAL HOGWARTS CHAMPION!**

'Like them, Potter?' said Malfoy loudly, as Harry approached. 'And this isn't all they do – look!'

He pressed his badge into his chest, and the message upon it vanished, to be replaced by another one, which glowed green:

> **POTTER STINKS**

The Slytherins howled with laughter. Each of them pressed their badges, too, until the message *POTTER STINKS* was shining brightly all around Harry. He felt the heat rise in his face and neck.

'Oh, *very* funny,' Hermione said sarcastically to Pansy Parkinson and her gang of Slytherin girls, who were laughing harder than anyone, 'really *witty*.'

Ron was standing against the wall with Dean and Seamus. He wasn't laughing, but he wasn't sticking up for Harry either.

## 第18章 检测魔杖

斯莱特林们在一起，他们似乎都打定主意要让哈利尽可能多吃苦头，因为他居然胆敢成为学校的勇士。这大概是哈利可以想象的最难熬的经历了。他已经挣扎着忍受了一次星期五的魔药课，当时赫敏坐在他旁边，不停地压低声音念叨着"别理他们，别理他们"，他看不出今天会有什么好转。

午饭后，他和赫敏来到斯内普的地下教室，发现斯莱特林的学生们都等在教室外，每个人的长袍前襟上都别着一枚大大的徽章。哈利一时没反应过来，还以为那是 S.P.E.W. 徽章呢——接着他才看清，那些徽章上都印着相同的文字，一个个鲜红的字母在地下走廊的昏暗光线中闪闪发亮，像着了火一样：

支持<br>
**塞德里克·迪戈里**<br>
——霍格沃茨的<br>
**真正勇士！**

"喜欢吗，波特？"看到哈利走近，马尔福大声说道，"它们还有别的花样呢——快看！"

他把徽章使劲往胸口上按了按，上面的字消失了，接着又出现了另外一行字，闪着绿莹莹的光：

**波特臭大粪**

斯莱特林们怪声怪气地大笑起来。他们每人都按了按自己的徽章，最后哈利周围到处都闪着那行刺眼的字——**波特臭大粪**。哈利觉得血液腾地冲上了他的脸和脖子。

"哦，非常有趣，"赫敏讥讽地对潘西·帕金森和那帮斯莱特林女生说——她们笑得比谁都厉害，"真是机智过人。"

罗恩贴墙站着，和迪安、西莫在一起。他没有笑，但也没有挺身而出支持哈利。

## CHAPTER EIGHTEEN   The Weighing of the Wands

'Want one, Granger?' said Malfoy, holding out a badge to Hermione. 'I've got loads. But don't touch my hand, now. I've just washed it, you see, don't want a Mudblood sliming it up.'

Some of the anger Harry had been feeling for days and days seemed to burst through a dam in his chest. He had reached for his wand before he'd thought what he was doing. People all around them scrambled out of the way, backing down the corridor.

'Harry!' Hermione said warningly.

'Go on, then, Potter,' Malfoy said quietly, drawing out his own wand. 'Moody's not here to look after you now – do it, if you've got the guts –'

For a split second, they looked into each other's eyes, then, at exactly the same time, both acted.

'*Furnunculus!*' Harry yelled.

'*Densaugeo!*' screamed Malfoy.

Jets of light shot from both wands, hit each other in mid-air, and ricocheted off at angles – Harry's hit Goyle in the face, and Malfoy's hit Hermione. Goyle bellowed and put his hands to his nose, where great ugly boils were springing up – Hermione, whimpering in panic, was clutching her mouth.

'Hermione!' Ron had hurried forwards to see what was wrong with her.

Harry turned and saw Ron dragging Hermione's hand away from her face. It wasn't a pretty sight. Hermione's front teeth – already larger than average – were now growing at an alarming rate; she was looking more and more like a beaver as her teeth elongated, past her bottom lip, towards her chin – panic-stricken, she felt them, and let out a terrified cry.

'And what is all this noise about?' said a soft, deadly voice. Snape had arrived.

The Slytherins clamoured to give their explanations. Snape pointed a long yellow finger at Malfoy and said, 'Explain.'

'Potter attacked me, sir –'

'We attacked each other at the same time!' Harry shouted.

'– and he hit Goyle – look –'

Snape examined Goyle, whose face now resembled something that would have been at home in a book on poisonous fungi.

## 第18章 检测魔杖

"想要一个吗，格兰杰？"马尔福说，朝赫敏举起一枚徽章，"我有一大堆呢。不过小心，可别碰到我的手。你看，我的手刚刚洗过，不想让泥巴种把它给弄脏了。"

哈利多少个日子以来积压的怒火，似乎突然冲破了他内心的一道堤坝。他想也没想自己在做什么，就伸手去掏魔杖。周围的人纷纷散开，顺着走廊避开去。

"哈利！"赫敏警告他。

"好啊，来吧，波特，"马尔福平静地说，也抽出了自己的魔杖，"现在可没有穆迪在这里关照你了——你要是有种就动手吧——"

他们都凝视着对方的眼睛，然后，说时迟那时快，就在同时，两人都采取了行动。

"火烤热辣辣！"哈利大喊。

"门牙赛大棒！"马尔福尖叫。

两根魔杖同时射出的光柱在空中相碰，转了个角度折射出去——哈利的光柱击中了高尔的脸，马尔福的击中了赫敏。高尔大声惨叫着用手捂住鼻子，一个个丑陋的大疖子正从他的鼻子上冒出来——赫敏紧张地呻吟着，紧紧捂住自己的嘴巴。

"赫敏！"罗恩赶紧上前，看赫敏出了什么事。

哈利转过身，看见罗恩把赫敏的手从她脸上拉开了。那副模样可不好看。赫敏的门牙——本来就比一般人的大——现在正以惊人的速度增长；她的牙齿嗖嗖地变长，越过下嘴唇朝下巴延伸，这使她越来越像一只海狸——赫敏紧张极了，摸了摸自己的牙齿，发出一声惊恐的尖叫。

"这里闹哄哄的在干什么？"一个软绵绵而令人厌烦的声音说。

斯内普来了。斯莱特林的学生们叽叽喳喳地争着解释，斯内普伸出一根长长的泛黄的手指，点着马尔福说："你来解释一下。"

"波特攻击我，先生——"

"我们是同时攻击对方的！"哈利大声抗议。

"他击中了高尔——你看——"

斯内普仔细打量着高尔，此刻高尔的那张脸放在一本专门讲毒蘑菇的书中倒是挺合适。

## CHAPTER EIGHTEEN   The Weighing of the Wands

'Hospital wing, Goyle,' Snape said calmly.

'Malfoy got Hermione!' Ron said. '*Look!*'

He forced Hermione to show Snape her teeth – she was doing her best to hide them with her hands, though this was difficult as they had now grown down past her collar. Pansy Parkinson and the other Slytherin girls were doubled up with silent giggles, pointing at Hermione from behind Snape's back.

Snape looked coldly at Hermione, then said, 'I see no difference.'

Hermione let out a whimper; her eyes filled with tears, she turned on her heel and ran, ran all the way up the corridor and out of sight.

It was lucky, perhaps, that both Harry and Ron started shouting at Snape at the same time; lucky their voices echoed so much in the stone corridor, for in the confused din, it was impossible for him to hear exactly what they were calling him. He got the gist, however.

'Let's see,' he said, in his silkiest voice. 'Fifty points from Gryffindor and a detention each for Potter and Weasley. Now get inside, or it'll be a week's worth of detentions.'

Harry's ears were ringing. The injustice of it made him want to curse Snape into a thousand slimy pieces. He passed Snape, walked with Ron to the back of the dungeon, and slammed his bag down onto the table. Ron was shaking with anger, too – for a moment, it felt as though everything was back to normal between them, but then Ron turned, and sat down with Dean and Seamus instead, leaving Harry alone at his table. On the other side of the dungeon, Malfoy turned his back on Snape, and pressed his badge, smirking. POTTER STINKS flashed once more across the room.

Harry sat there staring at Snape as the lesson began, picturing horrific things happening to him ... if only he knew how to do the Cruciatus Curse ... he'd have Snape flat on his back like that spider, jerking and twitching ...

'Antidotes!' said Snape, looking around at them all, his cold black eyes glittering unpleasantly. 'You should all have prepared your recipes now. I want you to brew them carefully, and then we will be selecting someone on whom to test one ...'

Snape's eyes met Harry's, and Harry knew what was coming. Snape was going to poison *him*. Harry imagined picking up his cauldron, and sprinting to the front of the class, and bringing it down on Snape's greasy head –

## 第18章 检测魔杖

"快上医院去吧,高尔。"斯内普平静地说。

"马尔福击中了赫敏!"罗恩说,"你瞧!"

他强迫赫敏把牙齿露给斯内普看——赫敏拼命用手遮住,不过很不容易,因为她的门牙已经越过了衣领。潘西·帕金森和斯莱特林的其他女生压低声音,咻咻地笑弯了腰,在斯内普背后朝赫敏指指点点。

斯内普冷冷地看了看赫敏,说:"我没看出有什么不同。"

赫敏哀叫一声,眼里顿时充满泪水。她一转身,撒腿就跑,顺着走廊跑得无影无踪。

幸亏哈利和罗恩同时冲着斯内普大喊大叫,幸亏他们俩的声音在石头走廊里造成那么大的回音,幸亏在这样乱哄哄的噪声中,斯内普不可能听清楚他们究竟骂了他什么。不过,他还是猜出了主要的意思。

"让我想想,"他说,声音特别软绵绵、滑腻腻,"格兰芬多学院扣去五十分,波特和韦斯莱各罚一次关禁闭。好了,快进去吧,不然就整整一个星期关禁闭。"

哈利的耳朵里嗡嗡作响。这简直太不公平了,他真想给斯内普念咒,把他变成无数个黏糊糊脏兮兮的碎片。他走过斯内普身边,和罗恩一起来到地下教室的后面,把书包重重地扔在桌上。罗恩也气得浑身发抖——在那一刻,似乎两人的关系又恢复到了从前那样。然而,罗恩转过身,跟迪安和西莫坐到一起去了,留下哈利独自坐在一张桌子旁。在教室的另一边,马尔福转身背对斯内普,用手按了按自己的徽章,得意地笑着。**波特臭大粪**又闪烁发亮了,在教室这边也能看见。

上课了,哈利坐在那里瞪着斯内普,脑子里幻想着各种倒霉的祸事落到斯内普头上……真希望自己知道怎样念钻心咒……那样的话,他就要让斯内普仰面躺倒,像那只蜘蛛一样,抽动,挣扎……

"解药!"斯内普说,一边环顾着全班同学,那双冷冰冰的黑眼睛闪动着令人不快的光芒,"你们现在应该准备好自己的配方了。我要求你们仔细地熬,然后,我们选一个人来试试……"

斯内普的目光与哈利的相遇了,哈利知道将会发生什么事。斯内普想要毒死他。哈利幻想着自己拎起坩埚,冲到教室前面,把它扣在斯内普油腻腻的脑袋上——

## CHAPTER EIGHTEEN   The Weighing of the Wands

And then a knock on the dungeon door burst in on Harry's thoughts.

It was Colin Creevey; he edged into the room, beaming at Harry, and walked up to Snape's desk at the front of the room.

'Yes?' said Snape curtly.

'Please, sir, I'm supposed to take Harry Potter upstairs.'

Snape stared down his hooked nose at Colin, whose smile faded from his eager face.

'Potter has another hour of Potions to complete,' said Snape coldly. 'He will come upstairs when this class is finished.'

Colin went pink.

'Sir – sir, Mr Bagman wants him,' he said nervously. 'All the champions have got to go, I think they want to take photographs ...'

Harry would have given anything he owned to have stopped Colin saying those last few words. He chanced half a glance at Ron, but Ron was staring determinedly at the ceiling.

'Very well, very well,' Snape snapped. 'Potter, leave your things here, I want you back down here later to test your antidote.'

'Please, sir – he's got to take his things with him,' squeaked Colin. 'All the champions –'

'Very *well*!' said Snape. 'Potter – take your bag and get out of my sight!'

Harry swung his bag over his shoulder, got up and headed for the door. As he walked through the Slytherin desks, *POTTER STINKS* flashed at him from every direction.

'It's amazing, isn't it, Harry?' said Colin, starting to speak the moment Harry had closed the dungeon door behind him. 'Isn't it, though? You being champion?'

'Yeah, really amazing,' said Harry heavily, as they set off towards the steps into the Entrance Hall. 'What do they want photos for, Colin?'

'The *Daily Prophet*, I think!'

'Great,' said Harry, dully. 'Exactly what I need. More publicity.'

'Good luck!' said Colin, when they had reached the right room. Harry knocked on the door, and entered.

He was in a fairly small classroom; most of the desks had been pushed away to the back of the room, leaving a large space in the middle; three of them, however, had been placed, end to end, in front of the blackboard, and

## 第18章 检测魔杖

就在这时,地下教室的门被敲响,打断了哈利的思路。

是科林·克里维。他侧着身子闪进教室,朝哈利绽开笑容,然后朝教室前面斯内普的讲台走去。

"什么事?"斯内普不耐烦地问。

"对不起,先生,我要带哈利·波特到楼上去。"

斯内普的目光从鹰钩鼻上垂下来望着科林,笑容在科林热切的脸上消失了。

"波特还要上一小时的魔药课。"斯内普冷冷地说,"下了课他再上楼。"

科林的脸红了。

"先生——先生,巴格曼先生要他去,"他局促不安地说,"所有的勇士都要去的,他们好像是要照相……"

哈利真愿意交出他所有的一切,只要能阻止科林说出最后这句话。他大着胆子用眼角瞥了瞥罗恩,罗恩正目不转睛地盯着天花板。

"很好,很好,"斯内普厉声说,"波特,把你的东西留在这里,我要你待会儿再回来,试验一下你的解药。"

"对不起,先生——他必须带着他的东西,"科林紧张地尖着嗓子说,"所有的勇士——"

"很好!"斯内普说,"波特——带着你的书包,快从我眼前消失!"

哈利把书包甩到肩膀上,站起身,朝门口走去。当他走过斯莱特林们坐的桌子时,**波特臭大粪**的字样从四面八方朝他闪耀着。

"真是了不起啊,是不是,哈利?"哈利刚走出教室,关上门,科林就迫不及待地说,"是不是?你成了勇士!"

"是啊,是很了不起,"哈利语气沉重地说——两人一起朝通向门厅的台阶走去,"他们为什么要照相,科林?"

"大概是登在《预言家日报》上吧!"

"太棒了,"哈利愁闷地说,"正是我想要的。进一步丢人现眼。"

"祝你好运!"科林说,这时他们已经来到那个房间外。哈利敲了敲门,走了进去。

这是一间较小的教室,大多数课桌都被推到了教室后面,留出中间一大块空地。不过有三张课桌并排对接着摆在黑板前面,上面盖着

## CHAPTER EIGHTEEN    The Weighing of the Wands

covered with a long length of velvet. Five chairs had been set behind the velvet-covered desks, and Ludo Bagman was sitting in one of them, talking to a witch Harry had never seen before, who was wearing magenta robes.

Viktor Krum was standing moodily in a corner as usual, and not talking to anybody. Cedric and Fleur were in conversation. Fleur looked a good deal happier than Harry had seen her so far; she kept throwing back her head so that her long silvery hair caught the light. A paunchy man, holding a large black camera which was smoking slightly, was watching Fleur out of the corner of his eye.

Bagman suddenly spotted Harry, got up quickly and bounded forwards. 'Ah, here he is! Champion number four! In you come, Harry, in you come ... nothing to worry about, it's just the Wand Weighing ceremony, the rest of the judges will be here in a moment –'

'Wand Weighing?' Harry repeated nervously.

'We have to check that your wands are fully functional, no problems, you know, as they're your most important tools in the tasks ahead,' said Bagman. 'The expert's upstairs now with Dumbledore. And then there's going to be a little photo shoot. This is Rita Skeeter,' he added, gesturing towards the witch in magenta robes, 'she's doing a small piece on the Tournament for the *Daily Prophet* ...'

'Maybe not *that* small, Ludo,' said Rita Skeeter, her eyes on Harry.

Her hair was set in elaborate and curiously rigid curls that contrasted oddly with her heavy-jawed face. She wore jewelled spectacles. The thick fingers clutching her crocodile-skin handbag ended in two-inch nails, painted crimson.

'I wonder if I could have a little word with Harry before we start?' she said to Bagman, but still gazing fixedly at Harry. 'The youngest champion, you know ... to add a bit of colour?'

'Certainly!' cried Bagman. 'That is – if Harry has no objection?'

'Er –' said Harry.

'Lovely,' said Rita Skeeter, and in a second, her scarlet-taloned fingers had Harry's upper arm in a surprisingly strong grip, and she was steering him out of the room again, and opening a nearby door.

'We don't want to be in there with all that noise,' she said. 'Let's see ... ah, yes, this is nice and cosy.'

## 第18章 检测魔杖

一块长长的天鹅绒。在天鹅绒覆盖的课桌后面,放着五把椅子,其中一把椅子上坐着卢多·巴格曼,他正在跟一个哈利从没见过的女巫交谈,那女巫穿着一身洋红色的长袍。

威克多尔·克鲁姆跟往常一样阴沉着脸,站在一个角落里,不跟任何人说话。塞德里克正在和芙蓉交谈。芙蓉很开心,哈利从没见她这么开心过。她不停地甩一甩脑袋,使一头银色的长发闪动夺目的光泽。一个大腹便便的男人手里举着一架微微冒烟的黑色大照相机,正用眼角斜睨着芙蓉。

巴格曼突然看见了哈利,迅速站起来,身子往前一跳。"啊,他来了!第四位勇士!进来吧,哈利,进来吧……没什么可担心的,就是检测魔杖的仪式,其他裁判员很快就到——"

"检测魔杖?"哈利不安地问道。

"我们必须检查一下你们的魔杖是否功能齐全,性能完好,因为在以后的比赛项目中,魔杖是你们最重要的器械。"巴格曼说,"专家在楼上,和邓布利多在一起。然后是照几张相。这位是丽塔·斯基特,"他说,指了指那位身穿洋红色长袍的女巫,"她正在为《预言家日报》写一篇关于争霸赛的小文章……"

"也许不会那么小,卢多。"丽塔·斯基特说,眼睛盯着哈利。

她的头发被弄成精致、僵硬、怪里怪气的大卷儿,和她那张大下巴的脸配在一起,看上去十分别扭。她戴着一副镶珠宝的眼镜,粗肥的手指抓着鳄鱼皮手袋,指甲有两寸来长,涂得红通通的。

"在我们开始前,我能不能跟哈利谈几句话?"她问巴格曼,但眼睛仍然牢牢地盯着哈利,"年纪最小的勇士,你知道……为了给文章增加点儿色彩。"

"没问题!"巴格曼大声说,"就是——不知哈利是否反对?"

"呃——"哈利说。

"太好了。"丽塔·斯基特说,眨眼间,她那鲜红色的爪子般的手指就抓住了哈利的手臂,力气大得惊人。她把哈利拽出房间,打开了旁边的一扇门。

"我们不能待在那里面,太吵了。"她说,"让我看看……啊,好的,这里倒是很安静很舒服。"

## CHAPTER EIGHTEEN    The Weighing of the Wands

It was a broom cupboard. Harry stared at her.

'Come along, dear – that's right – lovely,' said Rita Skeeter again, perching herself precariously upon an upturned bucket, pushing Harry down onto a cardboard box and closing the door, throwing them into darkness. 'Let's see now ...'

She unsnapped her crocodile-skin handbag and pulled out a handful of candles, which she lit with a wave of her wand and magicked into mid-air, so that they could see what they were doing.

'You won't mind, Harry, if I use a Quick-Quotes Quill? It leaves me free to talk to you normally ...'

'A what?' said Harry.

Rita Skeeter's smile widened. Harry counted three gold teeth. She reached again into her crocodile bag, and drew out a long acid-green quill and a roll of parchment, which she stretched out between them on a crate of Mrs Skower's All-Purpose Magical Mess-Remover. She put the tip of the green quill into her mouth, sucked it for a moment with apparent relish, then placed it upright on the parchment, where it stood balanced on its point, quivering slightly.

'Testing ... my name is Rita Skeeter, *Daily Prophet* reporter.'

Harry looked down quickly at the quill. The moment Rita Skeeter had spoken, the green quill had started to scribble, skidding across the parchment:

> *Attractive blonde Rita Skeeter, forty-three, whose savage quill has punctured many inflated reputations –*

'Lovely,' said Rita Skeeter, yet again, and she ripped the top piece of parchment off, crumpled it up and stuffed it into her handbag. Now she leant towards Harry and said, 'So, Harry ... what made you decide to enter the Triwizard Tournament?'

'Er –' said Harry again, but he was distracted by the quill. Even though he wasn't speaking, it was dashing across the parchment, and in its wake he could make out a fresh sentence:

> *An ugly scar, souvenir of a tragic past, disfigures the otherwise charming face of Harry Potter, whose eyes –*

## 第18章 检测魔杖

这是一个放扫帚的小储物间。哈利不解地瞪着她。

"过来吧,亲爱的——这就对了——太好了,"丽塔·斯基特说着,自己一屁股坐在一个倒扣着的水桶上,晃晃悠悠的,好像随时都会摔下去,然后她把哈利按在一只硬纸箱上,抬手关上了门,使两人陷入一片黑暗之中,"现在,让我想想……"

她打开鳄鱼皮手袋,抽出一把蜡烛,一挥魔杖,把它们都点燃了,又用魔法使它们都悬在半空,这样两人就都能看清自己在干什么。

"哈利,我用速记羽毛笔来做记录,你不会反对吧?这样我可以腾出手来,跟你正常地交谈……"

"你用什么?"哈利问。

丽塔·斯基特脸上的笑容更明显了。哈利看到她嘴里有三颗金牙。她又把手伸进鳄鱼皮手袋,掏出一支长长的、绿得耀眼的羽毛笔和一卷羊皮纸,然后把羊皮纸摊在两人中间的一只箱子上,那箱子是装斯科尔夫人牌万能神奇去污剂的。她把绿色羽毛笔的笔尖塞进嘴里,有滋有味地吮吸了一会儿,然后把笔垂直立在羊皮纸上。羽毛管竖在笔尖上,微微颤动着。

"试验一下……我叫丽塔·斯基特,《预言家日报》记者。"

哈利赶紧低头望着羽毛笔。丽塔·斯基特的话音刚落,绿色羽毛笔就开始龙飞凤舞地写了起来,笔尖灵巧地在羊皮纸上滑过。

> 迷人的金发女郎丽塔·斯基特,现年四十三岁,她的桀骜不驯的羽毛笔曾经揭穿过许多华而不实的虚名——

"太好了。"丽塔·斯基特说着,把第一张羊皮纸撕下来,揉成一团,塞进她的手袋。然后她朝哈利倾过身子,说道:"那么,哈利……是什么促使你决定报名参加三强争霸赛的?"

"嗯——"哈利张了张嘴,但他的注意力被羽毛笔吸引住了。他并没有说话,那支笔却在羊皮纸上嗖嗖地移动,笔尖滑过的地方,哈利辨认出一行新写出的文字:

> 一道丑陋的伤疤,是悲惨往事留下的纪念,破坏了哈利·波特原本应该英俊迷人的面容,他的眼睛——

## CHAPTER EIGHTEEN — The Weighing of the Wands

'Ignore the quill, Harry,' said Rita Skeeter firmly. Reluctantly, Harry looked up at her instead. 'Now – why did you decide to enter the Tournament, Harry?'

'I didn't,' said Harry. 'I don't know how my name got into the Goblet of Fire. I didn't put it in there.'

Rita Skeeter raised one heavily pencilled eyebrow. 'Come now, Harry, there's no need to be scared of getting into trouble. We all know you shouldn't really have entered at all. But don't worry about that. Our readers love a rebel.'

'But I didn't enter,' Harry repeated. 'I don't know who –'

'How do you feel about the tasks ahead?' said Rita Skeeter. 'Excited? Nervous?'

'I haven't really thought … yeah, nervous, I suppose,' said Harry. His insides squirmed uncomfortably as he spoke.

'Champions have died in the past, haven't they?' said Rita Skeeter briskly. 'Have you thought about that at all?'

'Well … they say it's going to be a lot safer this year,' said Harry.

The quill whizzed across the parchment between them, back and forwards as though it was skating.

'Of course, you've looked death in the face before, haven't you?' said Rita Skeeter, watching him closely. 'How would you say that's affected you?'

'Er,' said Harry, yet again.

'Do you think that the trauma in your past might have made you keen to prove yourself? To live up to your name? Do you think that perhaps you were tempted to enter the Triwizard Tournament because –'

'*I didn't enter*,' said Harry, starting to feel irritated.

'Can you remember your parents at all?' said Rita Skeeter, talking over him.

'No,' said Harry.

'How do you think they'd feel if they knew you were competing in the Triwizard Tournament? Proud? Worried? Angry?'

Harry was feeling really annoyed now. How on earth was he to know how his parents would feel if they were alive? He could feel Rita Skeeter watching him very intently. Frowning, he avoided her gaze and looked down at the words the quill had just written.

## 第18章 检测魔杖

"别管那支笔,哈利,"丽塔·斯基特很坚决地说——哈利满不情愿地抬起头,把目光落在她脸上,"好了——哈利,你为什么决定报名参加争霸赛?"

"我没有,"哈利说,"我不知道是谁把我的名字投进了火焰杯。那不是我干的。"

丽塔·斯基特扬起一道描画得很浓的眉毛。"不要紧的,哈利,你不用害怕自己会陷入麻烦。我们都知道你其实根本不应该报名。但你不必为此担心。我们的读者喜欢有叛逆精神的人。"

"可是我没有报名,"哈利重复着自己的说法,"我不知道是谁——"

"你对将要进行的比赛项目有何感觉?"丽塔·斯基特问,"是激动?还是紧张?"

"我没有认真想过……噢,大概有点儿紧张吧。"哈利说。他说话时感到自己的肠胃在很不舒服地蠕动。

"过去有许多勇士都丧生了,是不是?"丽塔·斯基特不依不饶地问,"你有没有想过这一点呢?"

"嗯……他们说今年要比过去安全得多。"哈利说。

羽毛笔在两人之间的羊皮纸上嗖嗖滑动,像溜冰一样来回穿梭。

"当然啦,你过去曾经面对过死亡,是不是?"丽塔·斯基特又问,一边目不转睛地盯着哈利,"你觉得那对你产生了什么影响?"

"呃。"哈利还是支支吾吾。

"你是否认为,是你过去所受的创伤使你急于证明自己的能力?你是否认为,你之所以渴望报名参加三强争霸赛,是因为——"

"我没有报名。"哈利说,他开始感到有些恼火了。

"你还记不记得你的父母?"丽塔·斯基特盛气凌人地问他。

"不记得。"哈利说。

"如果他们知道你要参加三强争霸赛,你认为他们会有什么感觉?是骄傲?担心?还是生气?"

哈利现在真的感到恼怒了。他父母活着会有什么感觉,他怎么可能知道呢?他可以感到丽塔·斯基特的目光牢牢地盯在他身上。他皱起眉头,躲开她的视线,低头看着羽毛笔刚刚写出的文字:

## CHAPTER EIGHTEEN  The Weighing of the Wands

*Tears fill those startlingly green eyes as our conversation turns to the parents he can barely remember.*

'I have NOT got tears in my eyes!' said Harry loudly.

Before Rita Skeeter could say a word, the door of the broom cupboard was pulled open. Harry looked around, blinking in the bright light. Albus Dumbledore stood there, looking down at both of them squashed into the cupboard.

'*Dumbledore!*' cried Rita Skeeter, with every appearance of delight – but Harry noticed that her quill and the parchment had suddenly vanished from the box of Magical Mess-Remover, and Rita's clawed fingers were hastily snapping shut the clasp of her crocodile-skin bag. 'How are you?' she said, standing up and holding out one of her large, mannish hands to Dumbledore. 'I hope you saw my piece over the summer about the International Confederation of Wizards' Conference?'

'Enchantingly nasty,' said Dumbledore, his eyes twinkling. 'I particularly enjoyed your description of me as an obsolete dingbat.'

Rita Skeeter didn't look remotely abashed. 'I was just making the point that some of your ideas are a little old-fashioned, Dumbledore, and that many wizards in the street –'

'I will be delighted to hear the reasoning behind the rudeness, Rita,' said Dumbledore, with a courteous bow and a smile, 'but I'm afraid we will have to discuss the matter later. The Weighing of the Wands is about to start, and it cannot take place if one of our champions is hidden in a broom cupboard.'

Very glad to get away from Rita Skeeter, Harry hurried back into the room. The other champions were now sitting in chairs near the door, and he sat down quickly next to Cedric, looking up at the velvet-covered table, where four of the five judges were now sitting – Professor Karkaroff, Madame Maxime, Mr Crouch and Ludo Bagman. Rita Skeeter settled herself down in a corner; Harry saw her slip the parchment out of her bag again, spread it on her knee, suck the end of the Quick-Quotes Quill, and place it once more on the parchment.

'May I introduce Mr Ollivander?' said Dumbledore, taking his place at the judges' table, and talking to the champions. 'He will be checking your wands to ensure that they are in good condition before the Tournament.'

Harry looked around, and with a jolt of surprise saw an old wizard

## 第18章 检测魔杖

当谈话转向他已几乎毫无印象的父母时,那双绿得惊人的眼睛里充满了泪水。

"我眼睛里**没有泪水**!"哈利大声说。

丽塔·斯基特还没来得及说话,扫帚间的门被拉开了。哈利转过头,耀眼的光线刺得他直眯眼睛。阿不思·邓布利多站在那里,低头看着他们俩,一边挤进了扫帚间。

"邓布利多!"丽塔·斯基特大声说道,一副欢天喜地的样子——但哈利注意到,她的羽毛笔和羊皮纸突然从神奇去污剂的箱子上消失了,丽塔那爪子般的手指正匆匆扣上鳄鱼皮手袋的搭扣。"你好吗?"她说着,站起身来,向邓布利多伸出一只男人般的大手,"我夏天的那篇关于国际巫师联合会大会的文章,不知你看了没有?"

"真是棒极了,"邓布利多说,两只眼睛灼灼发亮,"我特别爱读你把我描写成一个僵化的老疯子的那一段。"

丽塔·斯基特丝毫没显出害臊的样子。"我只是想说明你的某些观点有点过时了,邓布利多,外面的许多巫师——"

"我很愿意听到你无礼言论背后的道理,丽塔,"邓布利多说着,笑微微、彬彬有礼地鞠了一躬,"但是恐怕这个问题我们只好以后再谈了。魔杖检测仪式马上就要开始,如果我们的一位勇士躲在扫帚间里,仪式就不能进行了。"

哈利正巴不得离开丽塔·斯基特呢,他立刻回到了房间里。另外几位勇士都已在门边的椅子上坐定了,他赶紧过去坐在塞德里克旁边,望着前面铺着天鹅绒的桌子,那里已经坐着五位裁判中的四位——卡卡洛夫教授、马克西姆女士、克劳奇先生和卢多·巴格曼。丽塔·斯基特找了个角落坐下来,哈利看见她又偷偷地从手袋里掏出那卷羊皮纸,铺在膝盖上,吮了吮速记羽毛笔的笔尖,再次把笔竖直立在羊皮纸上。

"请允许我介绍一下奥利凡德先生。"邓布利多在裁判席上坐下后,对几位勇士说,"他将要检查你们的魔杖,确保魔杖在比赛前状态良好。"

哈利环顾四周,看见一个长着两只浅色大眼睛的老巫师静悄悄地

## CHAPTER EIGHTEEN    The Weighing of the Wands

with large, pale eyes standing quietly by the window. Harry had met Mr Ollivander before – he was the wand-maker from whom Harry had bought his own wand over three years ago in Diagon Alley.

'Mademoiselle Delacour, could we have you forward first, please?' said Mr Ollivander, stepping into the empty space in the middle of the room.

Fleur Delacour swept over to Mr Ollivander, and handed him her wand.

'Hmmm ...' he said.

He twirled the wand between his long fingers like a baton and it emitted a number of pink and gold sparks. Then he held it close to his eyes and examined it carefully.

'Yes,' he said quietly, 'nine and a half inches ... inflexible ... rosewood ... and containing ... dear me ...'

'An 'air from ze 'ead of a Veela,' said Fleur. 'One of my grandmuzzer's.'

So Fleur *was* part Veela, thought Harry, making a mental note to tell Ron ... then he remembered that Ron wasn't speaking to him.

'Yes,' said Mr Ollivander, 'yes, I've never used Veela hair myself, of course. I find it makes for rather temperamental wands ... however, to each his own, and if this suits you ...'

Mr Ollivander ran his fingers along the wand, apparently checking for scratches or bumps; then he muttered, '*Orchideous!*' and a bunch of flowers burst from the wand tip.

'Very well, very well, it's in fine working order,' said Mr Ollivander, scooping up the flowers and handing them to Fleur with her wand. 'Mr Diggory, you next.'

Fleur glided back to her seat, smiling at Cedric as he passed her.

'Ah, now, this is one of mine, isn't it?' said Mr Ollivander, with much more enthusiasm, as Cedric handed over his wand. 'Yes, I remember it well. Containing a single hair from the tail of a particularly fine male unicorn ... must have been seventeen hands; nearly gored me with his horn after I plucked his tail. Twelve and a quarter inches ... ash ... pleasantly springy. It's in fine condition ... you treat it regularly?'

'Polished it last night,' said Cedric, grinning.

Harry looked down at his own wand. He could see finger marks all over it. He gathered a fistful of robe from his knee and tried to rub it clean surreptitiously. Several gold sparks shot out of the end of it. Fleur Delacour

## 第18章 检测魔杖

站在窗边，他感到十分意外。哈利以前见过奥利凡德先生——三年前在对角巷，哈利正是从这位魔杖制作人手里购买了自己的魔杖。

"德拉库尔小姐，你先来，好吗？"奥利凡德先生说着，走到房间中央的空地上。

芙蓉·德拉库尔轻盈地走向奥利凡德先生，把自己的魔杖递给了他。

"嗯……"奥利凡德说。

他像摆弄指挥棒一样，让魔杖在修长的手指间旋转，魔杖喷出许多粉红色和金色的火花。然后他又把魔杖贴近眼前，仔细端详。

"不错，"他轻声说，"九英寸半……弹性良好……槭木制成……里面含有……噢，天哪……"

"含有一根媚娃的头发，"芙蓉说，"是我奶奶的头发。"

这么说，芙蓉果然有一部分媚娃血统，哈利想，他要把这点记在脑子里，回去告诉罗恩……接着他才想起来，罗恩已经不跟他说话了。

"没错，"奥利凡德先生说，"没错，当然啦，我本人从没用过媚娃的头发。我觉得用媚娃头发做的魔杖太敏感任性了……不过，各人都有自己的爱好，既然它对你合适……"

奥利凡德先生用手指捋过魔杖，显然在检查上面有没有擦痕和碰伤。然后，他低声念道："兰花盛开！"一束鲜花绽放在魔杖头上。

"很好，很好，状态不错。"奥利凡德先生说，一边把鲜花收拢，和魔杖一起递给芙蓉，"迪戈里先生，轮到你了。"

芙蓉脚步轻捷地返回自己的座位，与塞德里克擦肩而过时，朝他嫣然一笑。

"啊，这是我的产品，是不是？"塞德里克把魔杖递过去时，奥利凡德先生说，比刚才兴奋多了，"没错，我记得很清楚。里面有一根从一只特别漂亮的雄独角兽尾巴上拔下来的毛……准有五六英尺长呢。我拔了独角兽的尾毛，它差点儿用角把我戳出个窟窿。十二又四分之一英寸……白蜡木制成……弹性优良。状态极佳……你定期护理它吗？"

"昨晚刚擦过。"塞德里克说，咧开嘴笑了。

哈利低头看看自己的魔杖，上面布满了手指印儿。他从膝盖上揪起长袍的一角，想偷偷把魔杖擦干净。魔杖头上冒出几颗金星，芙蓉·德

## CHAPTER EIGHTEEN  The Weighing of the Wands

gave him a very patronising look, and he desisted.

Mr Ollivander sent a stream of silver smoke rings across the room from the tip of Cedric's wand, pronounced himself satisfied, and then said, 'Mr Krum, if you please.'

Viktor Krum got up and slouched, round-shouldered and duck-footed, towards Mr Ollivander. He thrust his wand out and stood scowling, with his hands in the pockets of his robes.

'Hmm,' said Mr Ollivander, 'this is a Gregorovitch creation, unless I'm much mistaken? A fine wand-maker, though the styling is never quite what I … however …'

He lifted the wand and examined it minutely, turning it over and over before his eyes.

'Yes … hornbeam and dragon heartstring?' he shot at Krum, who nodded. 'Rather thicker than one usually sees … quite rigid … ten and a quarter inches … *Avis!*'

The hornbeam wand let off a blast like a gun, and a number of small, twittering birds flew out of the end, and through the open window into the watery sunlight.

'Good,' said Mr Ollivander, handing Krum back his wand. 'Which leaves … Mr Potter.'

Harry got to his feet and walked past Krum to Mr Ollivander. He handed over his wand.

'Aaaah, yes,' said Mr Ollivander, his pale eyes suddenly gleaming. 'Yes, yes, yes. How well I remember.'

Harry could remember, too. He could remember it as though it had happened yesterday …

Four summers ago, on his eleventh birthday, he had entered Mr Ollivander's shop with Hagrid to buy a wand. Mr Ollivander had taken his measurements and then started handing him wands to try. Harry had waved what felt like every wand in the shop, until at last he had found the one that suited him – this one, which was made of holly, eleven inches long, and contained a single feather from the tail of a phoenix. Mr Ollivander had been very surprised that Harry had been so compatible with this wand. 'Curious,' he had said, '… curious', and not until Harry asked what was curious had Mr Ollivander explained that the phoenix feather in Harry's

## 第18章 检测魔杖

拉库尔非常傲慢地扫了他一眼，他只好作罢了。

奥利凡德先生让塞德里克的魔杖头上喷出一串银白色的烟圈，烟圈从房间这头飘到那头，他表示满意，说道："克鲁姆先生，该你了。"

威克多尔·克鲁姆站起身，耷拉着圆乎乎的肩膀，迈着外八字的脚，没精打采地朝奥利凡德先生走去。他把魔杖塞了过去，皱着眉头站在那里，双手插在长袍的口袋里。

"嗯，"奥利凡德先生说，"如果我没有弄错的话，这是格里戈维奇的产品。他是一位出色的魔杖制作人，尽管他的风格我并不十分……不过……"

他举起魔杖，在眼前翻过来倒过去，仔仔细细地检查着。

"没错……鹅耳枥木，含有火龙的心脏腱索，对吗？"他扫了克鲁姆一眼——克鲁姆点了点头，"比人们通常见到的粗得多……非常刚硬……十又四分之一英寸……飞鸟群群！"

鹅耳枥木魔杖发出砰的一声巨响，像手枪开火一般，一群小鸟扑扇着翅膀从魔杖头上飞出来，从敞开的窗口飞进了淡淡的阳光中。

"很好，"奥利凡德先生说，把魔杖递还给克鲁姆，"还有最后一位……波特先生。"

哈利站起来，与克鲁姆擦肩而过，向奥利凡德先生走去。他交出自己的魔杖。

"啊，是的，"奥利凡德先生说，一对浅色的眼睛突然闪烁着兴奋的光芒，"是的，是的，是的。我记得清清楚楚。"

哈利同样记忆犹新，一切就好像发生在昨天……

三年前的那个夏天，在他十一岁生日那天，他和海格一起走进奥利凡德先生的店铺，要买一根魔杖。奥利凡德先生量了他身体各部位的尺寸，就开始把一根根魔杖递给他试用。哈利觉得他把店里的魔杖都挥遍了，才终于找到一根适合自己的——这根魔杖是用冬青木制成，十一英寸长，里面含有一根凤凰尾羽。当时奥利凡德先生看到哈利摆弄这根魔杖时得心应手的样子，感到非常吃惊。"太奇妙了，"他说，"真是太奇妙了。"当哈利追问究竟有什么奇妙时，奥利凡德先生才解释说，哈利魔杖里的那根凤凰羽毛和伏地魔魔杖里的羽毛是从同一只鸟身上

## CHAPTER EIGHTEEN     The Weighing of the Wands

wand had come from the same bird which had supplied the core of Lord Voldemort's.

Harry had never shared this piece of information with anybody. He was very fond of his wand, and as far as he was concerned its relation to Voldemort's wand was something it couldn't help – rather as he couldn't help being related to Aunt Petunia. However, he really hoped that Mr Ollivander wasn't about to tell the room about it. He had a funny feeling Rita Skeeter's Quick-Quotes Quill might just explode with excitement if he did.

Mr Ollivander spent much longer examining Harry's wand than anyone else's. Eventually, however, he made a fountain of wine shoot out of it, and handed it back to Harry, announcing that it was still in perfect condition.

'Thank you all,' said Dumbledore, standing up at the judges' table. 'You may go back to your lessons now – or perhaps it would be quicker just to go down to dinner, as they are about to end –'

Feeling that at last something had gone right today, Harry got up to leave, but the man with the black camera jumped up and cleared his throat.

'Photos, Dumbledore, photos!' cried Bagman excitedly. 'All the judges and champions. What do you think, Rita?'

'Er – yes, let's do those first,' said Rita Skeeter, whose eyes were upon Harry again. 'And then perhaps some individual shots.'

The photographs took a long time. Madame Maxime cast everyone else into shadow wherever she stood, and the photographer couldn't stand far enough back to get her into the frame; eventually she had to sit while everyone else stood around her. Karkaroff kept twirling his goatee around his finger to give it an extra curl; Krum, who Harry would have thought would have been used to this sort of thing, skulked, half hidden, at the back of the group. The photographer seemed keenest to get Fleur at the front, but Rita Skeeter kept hurrying forward and dragging Harry into greater prominence. Then she insisted on separate shots of all the champions. At last, they were free to go.

Harry went down to dinner. Hermione wasn't there – he supposed she was still in the hospital wing having her teeth fixed. He ate alone at the end of the table, then returned to Gryffindor Tower, thinking of all the extra work on Summoning Charms that he had to do. Up in the dormitory, he came across Ron.

## 第18章 检测魔杖

拔下来的。

哈利从没有把这件事告诉任何人。他非常喜欢自己的魔杖,在他看来,这根魔杖与伏地魔的魔杖存在关系并不能怪它——就像他自己不能断绝与佩妮姨妈的亲戚关系一样。不过,他真希望奥利凡德先生不要把这件事告诉房间里的人。他有一种奇怪的感觉:如果奥利凡德先生泄露了这个秘密,丽塔·斯基特的那支速记羽毛笔大概会兴奋得爆炸呢。

奥利凡德先生检查哈利魔杖的时间比检查其他人的长得多。最后,他让魔杖头上喷出一股葡萄酒,然后把魔杖递还给哈利,宣布它的状态非常良好。

"谢谢大家,"邓布利多说,从裁判桌旁站了起来,"现在你们可以回去上课了——也许直接下去吃饭更便当一些,反正他们很快就要下课了——"

哈利这才觉得今天总算有了一件顺心的事。他站起来准备离开,可是那个拿黑色照相机的男人一跃而起,清了清嗓子。

"照相,邓布利多,照相!"巴格曼兴奋地喊道,"裁判和勇士来一个合影,你认为怎么样,丽塔?"

"呃——好吧,先照合影,"丽塔·斯基特说,目光再一次落到哈利身上,"也许待一会儿再照几张单人的。"

照相花了很长时间。马克西姆女士无论站在什么位置,都把别人挡住了,而且房间太小,摄影师无法站得很远,把她收进镜头;最后她只好坐下来,其他人都站在她周围。卡卡洛夫不停地用手指绕着他的山羊胡子,想使它翘成一个卷儿。克鲁姆呢,哈利还以为他对这类事情习以为常了,没想到他却躲躲闪闪地藏在大家后面。摄影师似乎特别积极地想让芙蓉站在前面,可是丽塔·斯基特总是赶上前来,把哈利拉到更突出的位置。然后,她又坚持要给勇士们一个个地拍单人照。过了好长时间他们才终于脱身出来。

哈利下楼吃饭,赫敏不在——他猜她大概还在校医院治疗牙齿。哈利独自坐在桌子一端吃饭。饭后,他返回格兰芬多塔楼,一路上想着必须完成的召唤咒作业。他上楼来到宿舍,遇见了罗恩。

## CHAPTER EIGHTEEN    The Weighing of the Wands

'You've had an owl,' said Ron brusquely, the moment he walked in. He was pointing at Harry's pillow. The school barn owl was waiting for him there.

'Oh – right,' said Harry.

'And we've got to do our detentions tomorrow night, Snape's dungeon,' said Ron.

He then walked straight out of the room, not looking at Harry.

For a moment, Harry considered going after him – he wasn't sure whether he wanted to talk to him or hit him, both seemed quite appealing – but the lure of Sirius' answer was too strong. Harry strode over to the barn owl, took the letter off its leg, and unrolled it.

> Harry –
>
> I can't say everything I would like to in a letter, it's too risky in case the owl is intercepted – we need to talk, face to face. Can you ensure that you are alone by the fire in Gryffindor Tower at one o'clock in the morning on the 22nd November?
>
> I know better than anyone that you can look after yourself, and while you're around Dumbledore and Moody I don't think anyone will be able to hurt you. However, someone seems to be having a good try. Entering you in that Tournament would have been very risky, especially right under Dumbledore's nose.
>
> Be on the watch, Harry. I still want to hear about anything unusual. Let me know about the 22nd November as quickly as you can.
>
> Sirius

## 第18章 检测魔杖

"你来了一只猫头鹰。"哈利刚走进去,罗恩就生硬地说,一边指着哈利的枕头。那只学校的谷仓猫头鹰正在那里等他。

"哦——好的。"哈利说。

"还有,我们明天晚上被罚关禁闭,在斯内普的地下教室。"罗恩说。然后,他看也不看哈利一眼,径直走出了房间。

一时间,哈利考虑是否追出去——他搞不清自己是想跟罗恩谈谈,还是想揍罗恩一顿,这两件事似乎都很吸引人——可是小天狼星回信的诱惑力太强了。哈利大步走向谷仓猫头鹰,从它脚上解下那封信,把它展开。

哈利:

我在信里不能畅所欲言,万一猫头鹰被截获就太危险了——我们需要当面谈一谈。你能保证十一月二十二日凌晨一点独自在格兰芬多塔楼的炉火边等我吗?

我比任何人都知道你能够照料好自己,而且我认为,只要你在邓布利多和穆迪身边,就不会有任何人能够伤害你。不过,似乎有人正在极力做这样的尝试。给你报名参加争霸赛是非常冒险的,特别是在邓布利多的鼻子底下这么做。

千万小心,哈利。如有不寻常的事情发生,我仍希望你写信告诉我。十一月二十二日能否赴约,请尽快告知。

小天狼星

## CHAPTER NINETEEN

# The Hungarian Horntail

The prospect of talking face to face with Sirius was all that sustained Harry over the next fortnight, the only bright spot on a horizon that had never looked darker. The shock of finding himself school champion had worn off slightly now, and the fear of what was facing him was starting to sink in. The first task was drawing steadily nearer; he felt as though it was crouching ahead of him like some horrific monster, barring his path. He had never suffered nerves like these; they were way beyond anything he had felt before a Quidditch match, not even his last one against Slytherin, which had decided who would win the Quidditch Cup. Harry was finding it hard to think about the future at all, he felt as if his whole life had been leading up to, and would finish with, the first task …

Admittedly, he didn't see how Sirius was going to make him feel any better about having to perform an unknown piece of difficult and dangerous magic in front of hundreds of people, but the mere sight of a friendly face would be something at the moment. Harry wrote back to Sirius, saying that he would be beside the common-room fire at the time Sirius had suggested, and he and Hermione spent a long time going over plans for forcing any stragglers out of the common room on the night in question. If the worst came to the worst, they were going to drop a bag of Dungbombs, but they hoped they wouldn't have to resort to that – Filch would skin them alive.

In the meantime, life became even worse for Harry within the confines of the castle, for Rita Skeeter had published her piece about the Triwizard Tournament, and it had turned out to be not so much a report on the Tournament, as a highly coloured life story of Harry. Much of the front page had been given over to a picture of Harry; the article (continuing on pages two, six and seven) had been all about Harry, the names of the Beauxbatons

第 19 章

匈牙利树蜂

在接下来的两个星期,哈利只有想到快要跟小天狼星面对面交谈了,才感到有点儿精神支柱,这是黑暗无比的地平线上的唯一亮点。随着时间的推移,发现自己成为学校勇士时的那份震惊已经稍稍淡化,而另一种恐惧开始渗透他的内心:他将要面对的会是什么呢?第一个项目一天天地逼近,他觉得那就像一个可怕的庞然大物,盘踞在他的前方,阻挡着他的道路。他的内心从没像现在这样紧张焦虑过;以前,即使是在魁地奇比赛前,即使是在最后那场为了争夺学院杯而与斯莱特林队进行的魁地奇决赛前,他也没有这样忧心忡忡。哈利觉得简直无法设想未来。他感到他的整个生命都在朝第一个项目逼近,并将在第一个项目中结束……

他也承认,小天狼星不可能使他情绪好转多少,因为他必须当着几百个人的面完成一项未知的、危险的、难度极大的魔法活动,可是在目前这种情况下,能见到一张友好的面孔也是莫大的安慰啊。哈利给小天狼星写了回信,说他将在小天狼星提议的时间守在公共休息室的炉火边。他和赫敏花了很长时间,反复研究那天夜里怎样把逗留在公共休息室里的人都赶出去,设想了好多计划。到时候如果实在没有办法,他们就准备扔一包粪弹,但愿不用使出这一招——费尔奇会活剥了他们的皮!

与此同时,哈利在城堡内的生活变得更加糟糕,因为丽塔·斯基特那篇关于三强争霸赛的文章发表了。这篇文章与其说是对争霸赛情况的报道,不如说是对哈利个人生活添油加醋的描绘。报纸第一版的大量版面都被哈利的一张照片占据,整篇文章(待续至第二、第六和

## CHAPTER NINETEEN — The Hungarian Horntail

and Durmstrang champions (misspelled) had been squashed into the last line of the article, and Cedric hadn't been mentioned at all.

The article had appeared ten days ago, and Harry still got a sick, burning feeling of shame in his stomach every time he thought about it. Rita Skeeter had reported him saying an awful lot of things that he couldn't remember ever saying in his life, let alone in that broom cupboard.

> 'I suppose I get my strength from my parents, I know they'd be very proud of me if they could see me now ... yes, sometimes at night I still cry about them, I'm not ashamed to admit it ... I know nothing will hurt me during the Tournament, because they're watching over me ...'

But Rita Skeeter had gone even further than transforming his 'er's into long, sickly sentences: she had interviewed other people about him, too.

> Harry has at last found love at Hogwarts. His close friend, Colin Creevey, says that Harry is rarely seen out of the company of one Hermione Granger, a stunningly pretty Muggle-born girl who, like Harry, is one of the top students in the school.

From the moment the article appeared, Harry had to endure people – Slytherins, mainly – quoting it at him as he passed them, and making sneering comments.

'Want a hanky, Potter, in case you start crying in Transfiguration?'

'Since when have you been one of the top students in the school, Potter? Or is this a school you and Longbottom have set up together?'

'Hey – Harry!'

'Yeah, that's right,' Harry found himself shouting, as he wheeled around in the corridor, having had just about enough. 'I've just been crying my eyes out over my dead mum, and I'm just off to do a bit more ...'

'No – it was just – you dropped your quill.'

It was Cho. Harry felt the colour rising in his face.

'Oh – right – sorry,' he muttered, taking the quill back.

第七版）讲的都是哈利，布斯巴顿和德姆斯特朗勇士的名字被挤在文章的最后一行，而且还拼错了，对塞德里克则只字未提。

文章是十天前发表的，现在哈利每次想起来，还觉得内心有一种火辣辣的、很不舒服的耻辱感。丽塔·斯基特写到他说了许多非常可怕的话，那些话他记得自己从来没有说过，更别提在那个扫帚间里了。

> 我认为是我的父母给了我力量。我知道，如果他们现在能够看见我，一定会为我感到非常骄傲……是的，夜里有的时候，我仍然会为他们哭泣，我觉得承认这一点并不丢脸……我知道比赛中没有什么能伤害到我，因为他们在冥冥中守护着我……

这还不算，丽塔·斯基特不光把哈利的支支吾吾变成了许多令人恶心的长篇大论，而且还询问了其他人对他的看法。

> 哈利终于在霍格沃茨找到了他的初恋。他的亲密好友科林·克里维说，哈利与一位名叫赫敏·格兰杰的女生形影不离，格兰杰小姐美貌惊人，出生于麻瓜家庭，她像哈利一样，也是学校的尖子生之一。

自从这篇文章一出现，哈利就不得不忍受人们——主要是斯莱特林的学生——在他经过时引用文章中的话，对他进行冷嘲热讽。

"要一条手绢吗，波特，免得在变形课上痛哭流涕？"

"你什么时候成为学校的尖子生的，波特？没准这个学校是你和隆巴顿一起办的吧？"

"喂——哈利！"

"是啊，没错！"哈利忍无可忍，大喊一声，猛地在走廊里转过身，"我刚才为我死去的妈妈哭红了眼睛，现在还要再哭一场……"

"不是——我只是说——你的羽毛笔掉了。"

原来是秋·张。哈利觉得自己的脸腾地红了。

"噢——好的——对不起。"他低声嘟哝着，接过了羽毛笔。

## CHAPTER NINETEEN — The Hungarian Horntail

'Er ... good luck for Tuesday,' she said. 'I really hope you do well.'

Which left Harry feeling extremely stupid.

Hermione had come in for her fair share of unpleasantness, too, but she hadn't yet started yelling at innocent bystanders; in fact, Harry was full of admiration for the way she was handling the situation.

'*Stunningly pretty? Her?*' Pansy Parkinson had shrieked, the first time she had come face to face with Hermione after Rita's article had appeared. 'What was she judging against – a chipmunk?'

'Ignore it,' Hermione said in a dignified voice, holding her head in the air and stalking past the sniggering Slytherin girls as though she couldn't hear them. 'Just ignore it, Harry.'

But Harry couldn't ignore it. Ron hadn't spoken to him at all since he had told him about Snape's detentions. Harry had half hoped they would make things up during the two hours they were forced to pickle rats' brains in Snape's dungeon, but that had been the day Rita's article had appeared, which seemed to have confirmed Ron's belief that Harry was really enjoying all the attention.

Hermione was furious with the pair of them; she went from one to the other, trying to force them to talk to each other, but Harry was adamant: he would talk to Ron again only if Ron admitted that Harry hadn't put his name in the Goblet of Fire, and apologised for calling him a liar.

'I didn't start this,' Harry said stubbornly. 'It's his problem.'

'You miss him!' Hermione said impatiently. 'And I *know* he misses you –'

'*Miss him?*' said Harry. 'I don't *miss him* ...'

But this was a downright lie. Harry liked Hermione very much, but she just wasn't the same as Ron. There was much less laughter, and a lot more hanging around in the library when Hermione was your best friend. Harry still hadn't mastered Summoning Charms, he seemed to have developed something of a block about them, and Hermione insisted that learning the theory would help. They consequently spent a lot of time poring over books during their lunchtimes.

Viktor Krum was in the library an awful lot, too, and Harry wondered what he was up to. Was he studying, or was he looking for things to help him through the first task? Hermione often complained about Krum being there – not that he ever bothered them, but because groups of giggling girls often turned

## 第19章 匈牙利树蜂

"嗯……祝你星期二好运,"秋·张说,"我真心希望你发挥出色。"

哈利一时觉得恍恍惚惚,感觉自己蠢到家了。

赫敏自然也分摊到了一些不愉快,但她没有朝无辜的路人大喊大叫。说实在的,哈利十分钦佩她处理这种局面的方式。

"美貌惊人?就她?"丽塔的文章发表后,潘西·帕金森第一次遇见赫敏就怪声怪气地说,"是根据什么评判的——金花鼠吗?"

"别理它,"赫敏用不失尊严的口吻说,把脑袋昂得高高的,从咯咯窃笑的斯莱特林女生身边大步走过,就好像什么也没听见,"别理它就行了,哈利。"

可是哈利没法不去理会。罗恩自从告诉他斯内普罚他们关禁闭的事之后,一直没有跟他说话。哈利曾经抱有一线希望,以为在斯内普的地下教室里腌制老鼠脑袋的那两个小时里,他们或许可以消除误会,和好如初。没想到就在那一天,丽塔·斯基特的文章发表了,这似乎使罗恩更加坚信哈利是一个喜欢出头露面、炫耀自己的人。

赫敏很生他们俩的气,她在两人之间来回奔走,试图强迫他们互相说话。可是哈利不肯让步:他坚持说,除非罗恩承认哈利没有把名字投进火焰杯,并为指责哈利撒谎而向他道歉,他才会跟罗恩说话。

"这一切又不是我造成的,"哈利固执地说,"是他的问题。"

"你很惦记他!"赫敏不耐烦地说,"我知道他也惦记你——"

"惦记他?"哈利说,"我才不惦记他呢……"

然而这是一个彻头彻尾的谎言。哈利非常喜欢赫敏,但赫敏和罗恩是不一样的。如果你选择赫敏做最好的朋友,就会少掉许多欢笑,而在图书馆逗留的时间会长得多。哈利还是没有掌握召唤咒,他似乎在自己周围形成了一道屏障,把东西都挡在了外面,赫敏坚持说多学一些理论会有所帮助。于是,他们在午饭后花了许多时间钻研书本。

威克多尔·克鲁姆也经常出现在图书馆里,哈利不明白他在那里做什么。他是在温习功课,还是在寻找能够帮他顺利完成第一个项目的办法?赫敏常常抱怨克鲁姆在那儿——克鲁姆倒从来不找他们的麻烦——但是经常有女生成群结队地咯咯笑着躲在书架后面窥探他,赫

up to spy on him from behind bookshelves, and Hermione found the noise distracting.

'He's not even good-looking!' she muttered angrily, glaring at Krum's sharp profile. 'They only like him because he's famous! They wouldn't look twice at him if he couldn't do that Wonky Faint thing –'

'Wronski Feint,' said Harry, through gritted teeth. Quite apart from liking to get Quidditch terms correct, it caused him another pang to imagine Ron's expression if he could have heard Hermione talking about Wonky Faints.

It is a strange thing, but when you are dreading something, and would give anything to slow down time, it has a disobliging habit of speeding up. The days until the first task seemed to slip by as though someone had fixed the clocks to work at double speed. Harry's feeling of barely controlled panic was with him wherever he went, as ever present as the snide comments about the *Daily Prophet* article.

On the Saturday before the first task, all students in the third year and above were permitted to visit the village of Hogsmeade. Hermione told Harry that it would do him good to get away from the castle for a bit, and Harry didn't need much persuasion.

'What about Ron, though?' he said. 'Don't you want to go with him?'

'Oh ... well ...' Hermione went slightly pink. 'I thought we might meet up with him in the Three Broomsticks ...'

'No,' said Harry flatly.

'Oh, Harry, this is so stupid –'

'I'll come, but I'm not meeting Ron, and I'm wearing my Invisibility Cloak.'

'Oh, all right, then ...' Hermione snapped, 'but I hate talking to you in that Cloak, I never know if I'm looking at you or not.'

So Harry put on his Invisibility Cloak in the dormitory, went back downstairs, and together he and Hermione set off for Hogsmeade.

Harry felt wonderfully free under the Cloak; he watched other students walking past them as they entered the village, most of them sporting *Support CEDRIC DIGGORY* badges, but no horrible remarks came his way for a change, and nobody was quoting that stupid article.

'People keep looking at *me* now,' said Hermione grumpily, as they came

## 第19章 匈牙利树蜂

敏觉得那些声音干扰了她的注意力。

"他长得一点儿也不好看!"她瞪着克鲁姆轮廓分明的侧影,气愤地嘟哝道,"她们喜欢他,只是因为他有名!如果他没有搞那一套偷鸡的假玩意儿——"

"是朗斯基假动作。"哈利咬着牙说。他一方面不愿意别人乱说魁地奇运动术语;另一方面,想象着如果罗恩听见赫敏谈论"偷鸡的假玩意儿"时,脸上会是一副什么表情,他心里又是一阵难受。

当你满心害怕一件事情,希望时间能够放慢脚步时,时间总是不会满足你的愿望,反而会加快它的前进速度。这真是一件奇怪的事。第一个项目之前的那些日子一眨眼就过去了,就好像有人把时钟拨快了一倍。哈利不管走到哪里,内心都充满了无法控制的恐慌,这种情绪就像人们因《预言家日报》那篇文章而产生的恶意评论一样,不管他到哪儿都跟着他。

在第一个项目开始前的那个星期六,学校批准三年级以上的学生到霍格莫德村游玩。赫敏对哈利说,到城堡外散散心会使他好受一些,其实哈利也巴不得出去轻松一下,根本用不着她劝说。

"可是,罗恩呢?"他问,"你不想跟他一起去吗?"

"哦……是这样……"赫敏微微涨红了脸,"我想我们可以在三把扫帚跟他碰面……"

"没门!"哈利干脆地说。

"哦,哈利,这样太愚蠢了——"

"我会去的,但我不想跟罗恩见面,我要穿上我的隐形衣。"

"噢,那么好吧……"赫敏气呼呼地说,"但如果你穿着那件衣服,我可不愿意跟你说话,因为我弄不清我的眼睛是不是在看着你。"

就这样,哈利在宿舍里穿上他的隐形衣,来到楼下,和赫敏一起出发前往霍格莫德。

哈利在隐形衣下觉得特别轻松自在。他们走进村子时,他望着其他同学从身边走过,大多数人胸前都戴着支持**塞德里克·迪戈里**的徽章,但是没有难听的议论扑面而来,也没有人引用那篇愚蠢的文章里的话。

"现在人们不停地看我,"赫敏不满地说,"他们还以为我在自言自

## CHAPTER NINETEEN    The Hungarian Horntail

out of Honeydukes Sweetshop later, eating large cream-filled chocolates. 'They think I'm talking to myself.'

'Don't move your lips so much, then.'

'Come *on*, please just take off your Cloak for a bit. No one's going to bother you here.'

'Oh, yeah?' said Harry. 'Look behind you.'

Rita Skeeter and her photographer friend had just emerged from the Three Broomsticks pub. Talking in low voices, they passed right by Hermione without looking at her. Harry backed into the wall of Honeydukes to stop Rita Skeeter hitting him with her crocodile-skin handbag.

When they were gone, Harry said, 'She's staying in the village. I bet she's coming to watch the first task.'

As he said it, his stomach flooded with a wave of molten panic. He didn't mention this; he and Hermione hadn't discussed what was coming in the first task much; he had the feeling she didn't want to think about it.

'She's gone,' said Hermione, looking right through Harry towards the end of the High Street. 'Why don't we go and have a Butterbeer in the Three Broomsticks. It's a bit cold, isn't it? You don't have to talk to Ron!' she added irritably, correctly interpreting his silence.

The Three Broomsticks was packed, mainly with Hogwarts students enjoying their free afternoon, but also with a variety of magical people Harry rarely saw anywhere else. Harry supposed that as Hogsmeade was the only all-wizard village in Britain, it was a bit of a haven for creatures like hags, who were not as adept as wizards at disguising themselves.

It was very hard to move through crowds in the Invisibility Cloak, in case you accidentally trod on someone, which tended to lead to awkward questions. Harry edged slowly towards a spare table in the corner while Hermione went to buy drinks. On his way through the pub, Harry spotted Ron, who was sitting with Fred, George and Lee Jordan. Resisting the urge to give Ron a good hard poke in the back of the head, he finally reached the table and sat down at it.

Hermione joined him a moment later and slipped him a Butterbeer under his Cloak.

'I look such an idiot, sitting here on my own,' she muttered. 'Lucky I brought something to do.'

## 第19章 匈牙利树蜂

语呢。"这时他们刚从蜂蜜公爵糖果店里出来,吃着大块奶油夹心巧克力。

"你的嘴唇不要动得太厉害。"

"好了,请你把隐形衣脱掉一会儿吧,这里没有人会找你的麻烦。"

"哦,真的吗?"哈利说,"看看你后面吧。"

丽塔·斯基特和她的摄影师朋友刚从三把扫帚里出来。他们低声谈论着什么,径直从赫敏身边走过,看也没有看她一眼。哈利生怕丽塔·斯基特的鳄鱼皮手袋碰到自己,赶紧闪身躲到蜂蜜公爵糖果店的墙根下。

那两人走后,哈利说:"她还待在村子里呢。我敢说她一定会来观看第一个比赛项目。"

话一出口,他就觉得内心掠过一阵火辣辣的恐慌感。但他没有说出来,他和赫敏很少谈论第一个比赛项目会是什么。他总觉得赫敏不太愿意考虑这件事。

"她走了。"赫敏说,目光穿透哈利,注视着街道尽头,"我们到三把扫帚去喝一杯黄油啤酒怎么样?天气有点儿冷了,是不是?你用不着跟罗恩说话!"她猜中了哈利不答腔的原因,烦躁地说。

三把扫帚小酒馆里挤满了人,主要是霍格沃茨的学生,都在尽情享受这一个下午的自由,不过也有许多哈利在别处很少见到的形形色色的魔法界人士。哈利猜想,霍格莫德是英国绝无仅有的一个纯巫师村庄,对女妖一类的家伙来说是一个安全的避风港,因为她们在伪装自己方面不如巫师那样得心应手。

穿着隐形衣在人群里穿行非常困难,说不定会无意间踩到什么人的脚,引起一些令人尴尬的麻烦。赫敏去买饮料了,哈利侧着身子,慢慢地朝角落里的一张空桌子挪动。哈利在小酒馆里穿行时看见了罗恩,他和弗雷德、乔治、李·乔丹坐在一起。他真想对准罗恩的后脑勺狠狠戳一下,但他克制住这种冲动,终于来到桌子边,坐了下来。

片刻之后,赫敏也过来了,偷偷地把一杯黄油啤酒从隐形衣下塞给了他。

"我真像个大傻瓜,独自一个人坐在这里。"赫敏低声抱怨道,"幸亏我带了点活儿来干。"

## CHAPTER NINETEEN    The Hungarian Horntail

And she pulled out a notebook in which she had been keeping a record of S.P.E.W. members. Harry saw his and Ron's names at the top of the very short list. It seemed a very long time ago that they had sat making up those predictions together, and Hermione had turned up and appointed them secretary and treasurer.

'You know, maybe I should try and get some of the villagers involved in S.P.E.W.,' Hermione said thoughtfully, looking around the pub.

'Yeah, right,' said Harry. He took a swig of Butterbeer under his Cloak. 'Hermione, when are you going to give up on this S.P.E.W. stuff?'

'When house-elves have decent wages and working conditions!' she hissed back. 'You know, I'm starting to think it's time for more direct action. I wonder how you get into the school kitchens?'

'No idea, ask Fred and George,' said Harry.

Hermione lapsed into thoughtful silence, while Harry drank his Butterbeer, watching the people in the pub. All of them looked cheerful and relaxed. Ernie Macmillan and Hannah Abbott were swapping Chocolate Frog cards at a nearby table, both of them sporting *Support CEDRIC DIGGORY* badges on their cloaks. Right over by the door he saw Cho and a large group of her Ravenclaw friends. She wasn't wearing a *CEDRIC* badge, though ... this cheered Harry up very slightly ...

What wouldn't he have given to be one of these people, sitting around laughing and talking, with nothing to worry about but homework? He imagined how it would have felt to be here if his name *hadn't* come out of the Goblet of Fire. He wouldn't be wearing the Invisibility Cloak, for one thing. Ron would be sitting with him. The three of them would probably be happily imagining what deadly dangerous task the school champions would be facing on Tuesday. He'd have been really looking forward to it, watching them do whatever it was ... cheering on Cedric with everyone else, safe in a seat at the back of the stands ...

He wondered how the other champions were feeling. Every time he had seen Cedric lately, he had been surrounded by admirers, and looking nervous but excited. Harry glimpsed Fleur Delacour from time to time in the corridors; she looked exactly as she always did, haughty and unruffled. And Krum just sat in the library, poring over books.

Harry thought of Sirius, and the tight, tense knot in his chest seemed

# 第19章 匈牙利树蜂

她掏出一个笔记本，上面记着 S.P.E.W. 的成员名单。哈利看见短得可怜的名单最上面是他和罗恩的名字。他想起那天晚上，他和罗恩坐在一起编造那些预言时，赫敏突然出现，任命他们为秘书和财务总管。唉，这一切似乎是很久以前的事了。

"对了，我也许应该吸收一些村民加入 S.P.E.W.。"赫敏若有所思地说，一边环顾着小酒馆。

"是啊，没错。"哈利说，他在隐形衣下喝了一大口黄油啤酒，"赫敏，你什么时候才能放弃这套 S.P.E.W. 的玩意儿呢？"

"等到家养小精灵获得体面的工钱和像样的工作环境那一天！"赫敏压低声音说，"我觉得应该采取一些更直接的行动了。不知道怎样才能进入学校厨房。"

"不知道，问问弗雷德和乔治吧。"哈利说。

赫敏又陷入了沉思，哈利则一边喝着黄油啤酒，一边打量着小酒馆里的人。他们都显得很轻松愉快，兴高采烈。厄尼·麦克米兰和汉娜·艾博正与邻桌的人交换巧克力蛙里的画片，两人的长袍上都戴着支持**塞德里克·迪戈里**的徽章。哈利看见秋·张和她那一大帮拉文克劳的朋友就在门边。她倒是没有戴支持塞德里克的徽章……这使哈利的心情稍微愉快了一点点……

他真愿意放弃一切，只要能够成为这些人当中的一员，坐在那里说说笑笑，除了功课以外，用不着操心任何事情。他幻想着，如果他的名字没有从火焰杯里喷出来，他在这里将是什么感觉。首先，他肯定不会穿着隐形衣，罗恩也肯定会跟他坐在一起。他们三个大概会开开心心地设想学校的勇士星期二将要面临什么样的危险项目。他会迫不及待地盼望着那一天的到来，盼望着观看勇士们完成那个项目……他会平平安安地坐在看台后排，和其他人一起为塞德里克加油喝彩……

他暗想，不知另外几位勇士是什么感觉。最近每次见到塞德里克，他身边都围满了崇拜者。塞德里克显得有些紧张，但是很兴奋。哈利偶尔也会在走廊上瞥见芙蓉·德拉库尔，她看上去跟平常没什么两样，还是那么旁若无人，镇定自若。克鲁姆呢，只是整天坐在图书馆里钻研那些书本。

哈利想到小天狼星时，内心那种紧绷绷的感觉似乎才松弛了些。再过

## CHAPTER NINETEEN   The Hungarian Horntail

to ease slightly. He would be speaking to him in just over twelve hours, for tonight was the night they were meeting at the common-room fire – assuming nothing went wrong, as everything else had done lately …

'Look, it's Hagrid!' said Hermione.

The back of Hagrid's enormous shaggy head – he had mercifully abandoned his bunches – emerged over the crowd. Harry wondered why he hadn't spotted him at once, as Hagrid was so large, but standing up carefully, he saw that Hagrid had been leaning low, talking to Professor Moody. Hagrid had his usual enormous tankard in front of him, but Moody was drinking from his hip-flask. Madam Rosmerta, the pretty landlady, didn't seem to think much of this; she was looking askance at Moody as she collected glasses from tables around them. Perhaps she thought it was an insult to her mulled mead, but Harry knew better. Moody had told them all during their last Defence Against the Dark Arts lesson that he preferred to prepare his own food and drink at all times, as it was so easy for Dark wizards to poison an unattended cup.

As Harry watched, he saw Hagrid and Moody get up to leave. He waved, then remembered that Hagrid couldn't see him. Moody, however, paused, his magical eye on the corner where Harry was standing. He tapped Hagrid in the small of the back (being unable to reach his shoulder), muttered something to him, and then the pair of them made their way back across the pub towards Harry and Hermione's table.

'All right, Hermione?' said Hagrid loudly.

'Hello,' said Hermione, smiling back.

Moody limped around the table and bent down; Harry thought he was reading the S.P.E.W. notebook, until he muttered, 'Nice Cloak, Potter.'

Harry stared at him in amazement. The large chunk missing from Moody's nose was particularly obvious at a few inches' distance. Moody grinned.

'Can your eye – I mean, can you –?'

'Yeah, it can see through Invisibility Cloaks,' Moody said quietly. 'And it's come in useful at times, I can tell you.'

Hagrid was beaming down at Harry, too. Harry knew Hagrid couldn't see him, but Moody had obviously told Hagrid he was there.

Hagrid now bent down on the pretext of reading the S.P.E.W. notebook as

## 第19章 匈牙利树蜂

十二个小时,他就可以和小天狼星说话了。就在今天夜里,他们将在公共休息室的炉火边见面——但愿别出什么岔子,最近其他事情都乱了套……

"看,海格!"赫敏说。

人群中赫然出现了海格那硕大的、头发蓬乱的后脑勺——谢天谢地,他总算不再把头发扎成马尾巴了。哈利心里纳闷,海格这么大的块头,自己刚才怎么就没有一眼看见呢。待他小心翼翼地站起身,才发现海格正压低身子,跟穆迪教授交谈呢。海格面前放着他惯常喝的大杯啤酒,穆迪则喝着他随身携带的弧形酒瓶里的东西。漂亮的老板娘罗斯默塔女士似乎对此很不满意,她一边收拾旁边桌子上的玻璃杯,一边斜眼瞟着穆迪。她大概认为这是对她的热蜂蜜酒的一种侮辱,但哈利知道不是这样。在他们最近一次的黑魔法防御术课上,穆迪告诉过大家,他不管什么时候都宁愿自己准备食物和饮料,因为黑巫师要往一只无人看管的杯子里下毒真是太容易了。

就在哈利望着他们的时候,海格和穆迪站起来准备离开了。哈利挥了挥手,接着才想起海格根本不可能看见他。可是穆迪停下脚步,那只魔眼盯着哈利所在的那个角落。他拍了拍海格的腰背部(因为够不着海格的肩膀),低声对他嘀咕了几句什么,然后两人一起回过身,朝哈利和赫敏的桌子走来。

"怎么样,赫敏?"海格大声问。

"你好。"赫敏微笑着说。

穆迪一瘸一拐地从桌子旁绕过来,俯下身子。哈利以为他在看S.P.E.W.笔记本,没想到他低声说了一句:"隐形衣真棒,波特。"

哈利顿时目瞪口呆。现在近在咫尺,穆迪鼻子上残缺的一大块看上去特别明显。穆迪咧开嘴笑了。

"难道你的眼睛——我的意思是,难道你能——"

"是的,它能看透隐形衣,"穆迪小声说,"有时候很管用呢,我可以告诉你。"

海格也低头朝哈利微笑。哈利知道海格看不见他,但显然穆迪告诉了海格他在这儿。

海格俯下身,假装在看S.P.E.W.笔记本,一边用很低很低、只有

## CHAPTER NINETEEN   The Hungarian Horntail

well, and said in a whisper so low that only Harry could hear it, 'Harry, meet me tonight at midnight at me cabin. Wear that Cloak.'

Straightening up, Hagrid said loudly, 'Nice ter see yeh, Hermione,' winked, and departed. Moody followed him.

'Why does he want me to meet him at midnight?' Harry said, very surprised.

'Does he?' said Hermione, looking startled. 'I wonder what he's up to? I don't know whether you should go, Harry ...' She looked nervously around, and hissed, 'It might make you late for Sirius.'

It was true that going down to Hagrid's at midnight would mean cutting his meeting with Sirius very fine indeed; Hermione suggested sending Hedwig down to Hagrid's to tell him he couldn't go – always assuming she would consent to take the note, of course – Harry, however, thought it better just to be quick at whatever Hagrid wanted him for. He was very curious to know what this might be; Hagrid had never asked Harry to visit him so late at night.

At half past eleven that evening, Harry, who had pretended to go up to bed early, pulled the Invisibility Cloak back over himself and crept back downstairs through the common room. Quite a few people were still in there. The Creevey brothers had managed to get hold of a stack of *Support CEDRIC DIGGORY* badges, and were trying to bewitch them to make them say *Support HARRY POTTER* instead. So far, however, all they had managed to do was get the badges stuck on *POTTER STINKS*. Harry crept past them to the portrait hole and waited for a minute or so, keeping an eye on his watch. Then Hermione opened the Fat Lady for him from outside as they had planned. He slipped past her with a whispered 'Thanks!' and set off through the castle.

The grounds were very dark. Harry walked down the lawn towards the lights shining in Hagrid's cabin. The inside of the enormous Beauxbatons carriage was also lit up; Harry could hear Madame Maxime talking inside it as he knocked on Hagrid's front door.

'You there, Harry?' Hagrid whispered, opening the door and looking around.

'Yeah,' said Harry, slipping inside the cabin and pulling the Cloak down off his head. 'What's up?'

'Got summat ter show yeh,' said Hagrid.

## 第19章 匈牙利树蜂

哈利一个人能听见的声音说道:"哈利,今天半夜十二点到我的小屋来找我。穿上隐形衣。"

海格直起身子,大声说道:"很高兴见到你,赫敏。"他眨了眨眼睛,离去了。穆迪也跟着他走了。

"海格为什么叫我半夜去找他?"哈利非常惊讶地问。

"是吗?"赫敏说,显然也很吃惊,"真搞不懂他想干什么。我不知道你是不是应该去,哈利……"她不安地环顾了一下周围,从牙缝挤出声音说道:"弄得不好,你见小天狼星就要迟到了。"

确实,半夜十二点下去找海格,就意味着必须把时间卡得很紧,才不会耽误与小天狼星的会面。赫敏建议派海德薇给海格送一封信,告诉他哈利不能去了——当然啦,还得假设海德薇同意送信才行——可是哈利觉得更好的办法是抓紧时间,不管海格找他干什么,都速战速决。他很好奇,想知道究竟是怎么回事。海格还从没这么晚叫哈利到他那里去过呢。

那天夜里十一点半,早早就假装上床睡觉的哈利披上隐形衣,悄悄穿过公共休息室来到楼下。公共休息室里还有几个人。克里维兄弟俩不知从哪儿弄来一摞支持**塞德里克·迪戈里**的徽章,正试图用魔法把上面的字变成支持**哈利·波特**。然而,他们费了好大工夫,能做到的只是使徽章上的字固定为**波特臭大粪**。哈利蹑手蹑脚地从他们身边溜过,来到肖像洞口,眼睛看着手表,等了一分钟左右。然后,赫敏按原计划从外面替他打开了胖夫人的肖像。哈利悄声说了句"谢谢!",便从她身边闪过,出发穿过城堡。

场地上一片漆黑。哈利顺着草坪朝海格小屋透出的灯光走去。布斯巴顿的那辆巨大马车里也亮着灯,哈利敲响海格的屋门时,可以听见马克西姆女士在马车里说话。

"你来了,哈利?"海格低声说,打开门,看了看四周。

"是啊,"哈利说,一边闪进小屋,把隐形衣从头上脱了下来,"什么事?"

"给你看一样东西。"海格说。

## CHAPTER NINETEEN  The Hungarian Horntail

There was an air of enormous excitement about Hagrid. He was wearing a flower that resembled an oversized artichoke in his button-hole. It looked as though he had abandoned the use of axle grease, but he had certainly attempted to comb his hair – Harry could see the comb's broken teeth tangled in it.

'What're you showing me?' Harry said warily, wondering if the Skrewts had laid eggs, or Hagrid had managed to buy another giant three-headed dog off a stranger in a pub.

'Come with me, keep quiet an' keep yerself covered with that Cloak,' said Hagrid. 'We won' take Fang, he won' like it …'

'Listen, Hagrid, I can't stay long … I've got to be back up at the castle for one o'clock –'

But Hagrid wasn't listening; he was opening the cabin door and striding off into the night. Harry hurried to follow and found, to his great surprise, that Hagrid was leading him to the Beauxbatons carriage.

'Hagrid, what –?'

'Shhh!' said Hagrid, and he knocked three times on the door bearing the crossed, golden wands.

Madame Maxime opened it. She was wearing a silk shawl wrapped around her massive shoulders. She smiled when she saw Hagrid. 'Ah, 'Agrid … it is time?'

'Bong-sewer,' said Hagrid, beaming at her, and holding out a hand to help her down the golden steps.

Madame Maxime closed the door behind her, Hagrid offered her his arm, and they set off around the edge of the paddock containing Madame Maxime's giant winged horses, with Harry, totally bewildered, running to keep up with them. Had Hagrid wanted to show him Madame Maxime? He could see her any old time he wanted … she wasn't exactly hard to miss …

But it seemed that Madame Maxime was in for the same treat as Harry, because after a while she said playfully, 'Wair is it you are taking me, 'Agrid?'

'Yeh'll enjoy this,' said Hagrid gruffly. 'Worth seein', trust me. On'y – don' go tellin' anyone I showed yeh, right? Yeh're not s'posed ter know.'

'Of course not,' said Madame Maxime, fluttering her long black eyelashes.

And still they walked, Harry getting more and more irritable as he jogged along in their wake, checking his watch every now and then. Hagrid had

## 第19章 匈牙利树蜂

海格的神情非常激动。他衣服的扣眼里插着一枝鲜花，活像一朵特别大的洋蓟。看样子他不再往头上抹机器润滑油了，但肯定花了不少工夫梳理头发——哈利可以看见他的头发上有梳子的断齿。

"你要给我看什么？"哈利警惕地问，心想是不是炸尾螺下蛋了，或者海格又想办法从小酒馆的某个陌生人手里买到了一条三个脑袋的大狗。

"跟我来，别出声，用隐形衣把你的身子罩住。"海格说，"我们不带牙牙去，它不会喜欢的……"

"海格，你听我说，我不能待很长时间……我一点钟必须赶回城堡——"

可是海格没有听，他打开小屋的门，大步走进了黑暗中。哈利匆匆跟了上去，他大为吃惊地发现，海格正领着他朝布斯巴顿的马车走去。

"海格，你怎么——"

"嘘！"海格说，然后在印着两根交叉的金魔杖的门上敲了三下。

马克西姆女士把门打开了。她宽阔无比的肩膀上围着一条丝绸披巾。她一看见海格就微微地笑了。

"啊，海格……时间到了吗？"

"晚上好。"海格说，笑眯眯地望着她，同时伸出一只手扶她走下金色的台阶。

马克西姆女士回身关上马车的门，海格把胳膊递给她，两人一起绕着临时围场的边缘走，那里面关着马克西姆女士的那几匹带翅膀的巨马。哈利一头雾水，茫然地小跑着跟上他们的步伐。难道海格要给他看的就是马克西姆女士？他随时都能看见她啊……她那么大的块头，是很难被忽略的……

不对，马克西姆女士似乎也受到了和哈利同样的待遇，因为过了片刻，她用玩笑般的口吻问道："你要把我带到哪儿去，海格？"

"你会喜欢的，"海格声音粗哑地说，"值得一看，相信我吧。不过——不要对任何人说我带你来看了，好吗？你是不应该知道的。"

"当然不会说啦。"马克西姆女士说，又黑又长的眼睫毛呼扇呼扇的。

他们还在走个不停，哈利小跑着跟在后面，不时地看看手表，心里越来越焦躁。海格脑子里有一个草率的计划，可能会使哈利错过跟

## CHAPTER NINETEEN — The Hungarian Horntail

some harebrained scheme in hand, which might make him miss Sirius. If they didn't get there soon, he was going to turn around, go straight back to the castle, and leave Hagrid to enjoy his moonlit stroll with Madame Maxime ...

But then – when they had walked so far around the perimeter of the Forest that the castle and the lake were out of sight – Harry heard something. Men were shouting up ahead ... then came a deafening, ear-splitting roar ...

Hagrid led Madame Maxime around a clump of trees, and came to a halt. Harry hurried up alongside them – for a split second, he thought he was seeing bonfires, and men darting around them – and then his mouth fell open.

*Dragons.*

Four fully grown, enormous, vicious-looking dragons were rearing on their hind legs inside an enclosure fenced with thick planks of wood, roaring and snorting – torrents of fire were shooting into the dark sky from their open, fanged mouths, fifty feet above the ground on their outstretched necks. There was a silvery blue one with long, pointed horns, snapping and snarling at the wizards on the ground; a smooth-scaled green one, which was writhing and stamping with all its might; a red one with an odd fringe of fine gold spikes around its face, which was shooting mushroom-shaped fire clouds into the air, and a gigantic black one, more lizard-like than the others, which was nearest to them.

At least thirty wizards, seven or eight to each dragon, were attempting to control them, pulling on the chains connected to heavy leather straps around their necks and legs. Mesmerised, Harry looked up, high above him, and saw the eyes of the black dragon, with vertical pupils like a cat's, bulging with either fear or rage, he couldn't tell which ... It was making a horrible noise, a yowling, screeching scream ...

'Keep back there, Hagrid!' yelled a wizard near the fence, straining on the chain he was holding. 'They can shoot fire at a range of twenty feet, you know! I've seen this Horntail do forty!'

'Isn' it beautiful?' said Hagrid softly.

'It's no good!' yelled another wizard. 'Stunning Spells, on the count of three!'

Harry saw each of the dragon-keepers pull out his wand.

'*Stupefy!*' they shouted in unison, and the Stunning Spells shot into the

## 第19章 匈牙利树蜂

小天狼星的会面。如果他们还不能很快到达目的地,他就准备转过头直接返回城堡了,让海格独自享受与马克西姆女士的月下散步吧……

可是就在这时——他们已经绕着禁林边缘走了很远,城堡和湖泊都看不见了——哈利听见了什么动静。有几个男人在前面大声喊叫……然后是一声震耳欲聋的尖厉的咆哮……

海格领着马克西姆女士绕过一片树丛,停下了脚步。哈利赶紧跟过去,和他们站在一起——在那短短的一瞬间,他还以为看见了几堆篝火,男人们围着火跳来跳去——接着,他吃惊地张大了嘴巴。

火龙。

四条模样十分凶狠的成年火龙被关在厚木板围成的围场里,用后腿支撑身子站立着,发出阵阵吼叫,呼哧呼哧地喷着鼻息——一团团火焰从它们张开的、长着獠牙的嘴里喷出,射向黑暗的夜空,它们的脖子高高昂起,嘴离地面的高度达五十英尺。一条有一对长长尖角的银蓝色火龙,正对着场地上的巫师发怒、咆哮;一条鳞片光滑的绿色火龙,正在拼命地扭动、跺脚;还有一条红色的火龙,脸的周围长着一圈怪模怪样的细金色尖刺,正在朝空中喷射一朵朵蘑菇状的火云;最后是一条黑色的巨龙,比另外几条更像蜥蜴,这条火龙离他们最近。

场地上至少有三十个巫师,每七八个负责对付一条火龙。他们拽着链条,拼命想制服四条巨龙,那些链条连接着拴住龙腿和龙颈的大粗皮带。哈利完全惊呆了。他抬起头,在上面很高的地方,看见了那条黑火龙的眼睛,瞳孔像猫眼一样是垂直的,不知是因为恐惧还是愤怒,那双眼睛暴突着……黑火龙发出一种可怕的声音,是凄厉而刺耳的哀号……

"待在那里别动,海格!"靠近栅栏的一位巫师喊道,一边紧紧拽住手里的链条,"它们喷火能喷二十英尺远,你知道的!我看见这条树蜂喷过四十英尺!"

"真漂亮啊!"海格柔声细气地说。

"没有用的!"另一位巫师大声嚷道,"念昏迷咒,数到三,一起念!"
哈利看见每位驯龙师都抽出了自己的魔杖。

"昏昏倒地!"他们异口同声喊道,昏迷咒如火箭一般射向漆黑的

## CHAPTER NINETEEN   The Hungarian Horntail

darkness like fiery rockets, bursting in showers of stars on the dragons' scaly hides –

Harry watched the dragon nearest to them teeter dangerously on its back legs; its jaws stretched wide in a suddenly silent howl; its nostrils were suddenly devoid of flame, though still smoking – then, very slowly, it fell – several tons of sinewy, scaly black dragon hit the ground with a thud that Harry could have sworn had made the trees behind him quake.

The dragon-keepers lowered their wands and walked forwards to their fallen charges, each of which was the size of a small hill. They hurried to tighten the chains and fasten them securely to iron pegs, which they forced deep into the ground with their wands.

'Wan' a closer look?' Hagrid asked Madame Maxime excitedly. The pair of them moved right up to the fence, and Harry followed. The wizard who had warned Hagrid not to come any closer turned, and Harry realised who it was – Charlie Weasley.

'All right, Hagrid?' he panted, coming over to talk. 'They should be OK now – we put them out with a Sleeping Draught on the way here, thought it might be better for them to wake up in the dark and the quiet – but, like you saw, they weren't happy, not happy at all –'

'What breeds you got here, Charlie?' said Hagrid, gazing at the closest dragon – the black one – with something close to reverence. Its eyes were still just open. Harry could see a strip of gleaming yellow beneath its wrinkled black eyelid.

'This is a Hungarian Horntail,' said Charlie. 'There's a Common Welsh Green over there, the smaller one – a Swedish Short-Snout, that blue grey – and a Chinese Fireball, that's the red.'

Charlie looked around; Madame Maxime was strolling away around the edge of the enclosure, gazing at the Stunned dragons.

'I didn't know you were bringing her, Hagrid,' Charlie said, frowning. 'The champions aren't supposed to know what's coming – she's bound to tell her student, isn't she?'

'Jus' thought she'd like ter see 'em,' shrugged Hagrid, still gazing, enraptured, at the dragons.

'Really romantic date, Hagrid,' said Charlie, shaking his head.

'Four ...' said Hagrid, 'so it's one fer each o' the champions, is it? What've

夜空，进出的火星像阵雨一样落在四条火龙长着鳞片的厚皮上——

哈利注视着离他们最近的那条火龙用后腿摇摇晃晃地站立着，嘴巴张得大大的，咆哮声却一下止住了，鼻孔里的火焰突然熄灭，但仍然冒着青烟——然后，它很慢很慢地倒下了。这条好几吨重的、鳞片乌黑的强壮巨龙轰然倒地，哈利可以发誓，这声巨响震得他身后的树木都颤动起来了。

驯龙师放下魔杖，走向倒在地上的巨龙，每条龙都像一座小山。驯龙师匆匆地拴紧链条，把它们牢牢系在铁柱上，又用魔杖把铁柱深深地钉在地里。

"想靠近点看看吗？"海格激动地问马克西姆女士。他们俩一起走向栅栏，哈利也跟了过去。刚才警告海格不要靠近的那位巫师转过身来，哈利认出来了，是查理·韦斯莱。

"怎么样，海格？"他喘着粗气，过来跟他们说话，"它们现在应该没事了——我们给它们服了安眠药剂，它们来的时候一路昏睡，本来以为让它们在宁静的黑夜醒来，它们会觉得好受一些——可是，你也看见了，它们并不开心，一点儿也不开心——"

"你们这里都有哪些种类，查理？"海格问，一边凝视着离他最近的那条黑火龙，目光里带着近乎崇敬的神情。黑火龙的眼睛仍然微微睁着，哈利可以看见它皱巴巴的黑眼皮下闪着一道细细的黄光。

"这是匈牙利树蜂，"查理介绍道，"那边那条较小的是普通威尔士绿龙——那条灰蓝色的是瑞典短鼻龙——那条红的是中国火球。"

查理看了看四周，马克西姆女士正沿着围场溜达，凝望那几条被击昏的火龙。

"我没想到你把她也带来了，海格，"查理说着，皱起了眉头，"勇士是不应该知道自己要面对什么的——她肯定会告诉她的学生的，是不是？"

"我只是觉得她很愿意过来见识见识。"海格耸了耸肩膀，目光仍然如痴如醉地盯着巨龙。

"真是一次浪漫的约会，海格。"查理说，无奈地摇了摇头。

"一共四条……"海格说，"这么说，每位勇士需要对付一条，是吗？

they gotta do – fight 'em?'

'Just get past them, I think,' said Charlie. 'We'll be on hand if it gets nasty, extinguishing spells at the ready. They wanted nesting mothers, I don't know why ... but I tell you this, I don't envy the one who gets the Horntail. Vicious thing. Its back end's as dangerous as its front, look.'

Charlie pointed towards the Horntail's tail, and Harry saw long, bronze-coloured spikes protruding along it every few inches.

Five of Charlie's fellow keepers staggered up to the Horntail at that moment, carrying a clutch of huge granite-grey eggs between them in a blanket. They placed them carefully at the Horntail's side. Hagrid let out a moan of longing.

'I've got them counted, Hagrid,' said Charlie, sternly. Then he said, 'How's Harry?'

'Fine,' said Hagrid. He was still gazing at the eggs.

'Just hope he's still fine after he's faced this lot,' said Charlie grimly, looking out over the dragons' enclosure. 'I didn't dare tell Mum what he's got to do for the first task, she's already having kittens about him ...' Charlie imitated his mother's anxious voice. '"*How could they let him enter that Tournament, he's much too young! I thought they were all safe, I thought there was going to be an age limit!*" She was in floods after that *Daily Prophet* article about him. "*He still cries about his parents! Oh, bless him, I never knew!*"'

Harry had had enough. Trusting to the fact that Hagrid wouldn't miss him, with the attractions of four dragons and Madame Maxime to occupy him, he turned silently, and began to walk away, back to the castle.

He didn't know whether he was glad he'd seen what was coming or not. Perhaps this way was better. The first shock was over now. Maybe if he'd seen the dragons for the first time on Tuesday, he would have passed out cold in front of the whole school ... but maybe he would anyway ... he was going to be armed with his wand – which just now, felt like nothing more than a narrow strip of wood – against a fifty-foot-high, scaly, spike-ridden, fire-breathing dragon. And he had to get past it. With everyone watching. *How?*

Harry sped up, skirting the edge of the Forest; he had just under fifteen minutes to get back to the fireside and talk to Sirius, and he couldn't remember, ever, wanting to talk to someone more than he did right now –

## 第19章 匈牙利树蜂

他们需要做什么——与火龙搏斗?"

"我想,大概只是从火龙身边通过吧。"查理说,"如果情况不妙,我们随时上前援救,给火龙念熄灭咒。他们要的都是抱窝孵蛋的母火龙,我不明白为什么……不过我可以告诉你,摊到匈牙利树蜂的人可没有好果子吃。它的后面和前面一样危险,你看。"

查理指了指树蜂的尾巴,哈利看见那尾巴上每隔几英寸就冒出长长的青铜色利刺。

这时,查理的五位驯龙同伴高一脚低一脚地走向树蜂,他们兜着一条毯子,里面放着一窝巨大的、花岗岩灰色的火龙蛋。他们小心翼翼地把龙蛋放在树蜂的身边。海格按捺不住内心的渴望,呻吟了一声。

"我可是数过的,海格。"查理严厉地说,接着他又说,"哈利怎么样?"

"还好。"海格说,仍然目不转睛地盯着火龙蛋。

"真希望他在面对这场危险之后仍然平平安安。"查理望着那边关巨龙的围场,心事重重地说,"我不敢告诉妈妈哈利在第一个项目里要做什么。妈妈已经为他心慌意乱了……"查理模仿母亲焦虑的声音:"'他们怎么能让他参加那场争霸赛呢,他年纪太小了!我原以为他们都不会有事,我原以为会有一个年龄界限!'《预言家日报》上那篇关于哈利的文章发表后,妈妈泪流满面,'他还在为他的父母哭泣!哦,上帝保佑,我一点儿都不知道啊!'"

哈利觉得自己不能再待下去了。他相信,海格的心已经被迷人的四条巨龙和马克西姆女士填得满满的,不会再惦念自己了,于是悄悄地转过身,开始返回城堡。

他看见了即将面对的东西,说不清自己是不是感到高兴。也许这样感觉会好一些。最初的恐惧已经过去了。如果他到了星期二才第一次看见巨龙,没准会在全校同学面前当场昏倒……即使现在可能还是会……他的武器就是魔杖——这魔杖现在看来简直跟一根细细的小木棍差不多——而要对付的是一条五十英尺高、全身覆盖鳞片和尖刺、鼻子里往外喷火的巨龙!他必须从它面前通过。大家的眼睛都望着呢。怎么通过呢?

哈利加快速度,在禁林边缘疾走。他必须在十五分钟内赶回公共休息室的炉火边,与小天狼星交谈,他不记得自己曾经有过什么时候

## CHAPTER NINETEEN    The Hungarian Horntail

when, without warning, he ran into something very solid.

Harry fell backwards, his glasses askew, clutching the Cloak around him. A voice nearby said, 'Ouch! Who's there?'

Harry hastily checked that the Cloak was covering him and lay very still, staring up at the dark outline of the wizard he had hit. He recognised the goatee ... it was Karkaroff.

'Who's there?' said Karkaroff again, very suspiciously, looking around in the darkness. Harry remained still and silent. After a minute or so, Karkaroff seemed to decide that he had hit some sort of animal; he was looking around at waist height, as though expecting to see a dog. Then he crept back under the cover of the trees, and started to edge forwards towards the place where the dragons were.

Very slowly and very carefully, Harry got to his feet and set off again, as fast as he could without making too much noise, hurrying through the darkness back towards Hogwarts.

He had no doubt whatsoever what Karkaroff was up to. He had sneaked off his ship to try and find out what the first task was going to be. He might even have spotted Hagrid and Madame Maxime heading off around the Forest together – they were hardly difficult to spot at a distance ... and now all Karkaroff had to do was follow the sound of voices, and he, like Madame Maxime, would know what was in store for the champions. By the looks of it, the only champion who would be facing the unknown on Tuesday was Cedric.

Harry reached the castle, slipped in through the front doors and began to climb the marble stairs; he was very out of breath, but he didn't dare slow down ... he had less than five minutes to get up to the fire ...

'Balderdash!' he gasped at the Fat Lady, who was snoozing in her frame in front of the portrait hole.

'If you say so,' she muttered sleepily, without opening her eyes, and the picture swung forwards to admit him. Harry climbed inside. The common room was deserted, and, judging by the fact that it smelled quite normal, Hermione had not needed to set off any Dungbombs to ensure that he and Sirius got privacy.

Harry pulled off the Invisibility Cloak and threw himself into an armchair in front of the fire. The room was in semi-darkness; the flames were the only

## 第19章 匈牙利树蜂

像此刻这样渴望与人交谈——就在这时，他猝不及防地撞上了一个硬邦邦的东西。

哈利向后摔倒了，眼镜也歪向了一边，他赶紧用隐形衣裹住身体。近旁有一个声音说道："哎哟！谁在那儿？"

哈利匆匆检查了一下，看隐形衣是不是把自己完全遮住了，然后一动不动地躺在那里，抬眼望着他刚才撞上的那个巫师的黑色轮廓。他认出了那撇山羊胡子……是卡卡洛夫。

"谁在那儿？"卡卡洛夫又问了一声，疑神疑鬼地在黑暗中东张西望。哈利还是一动不动，大气儿也不敢出。过了一分钟左右，卡卡洛夫似乎断定刚才是某种动物撞了他。他在齐腰高的地方四处张望，大概以为会看见一条狗吧。然后，他在树木的掩护下退了回去，开始侧着身子朝巨龙所在的地方移动。

哈利非常缓慢和小心地站了起来，在尽可能不发出响声的同时迅速在黑暗中穿行，返回城堡。

他非常清楚卡卡洛夫要做什么。卡卡洛夫从他的大船上溜下来，就是想弄清第一个项目是什么。甚至，他大概已经看见海格和马克西姆女士一起绕着禁林往那边走——即使在远处，他们也很容易被看见……现在，卡卡洛夫只要循着声音而去，便也会像马克西姆女士一样，知道等待勇士的将是什么了。照这样的情形看，星期二面对未知之物的只有塞德里克一个人了。

哈利赶到城堡，悄悄从前门溜了进去，沿着大理石楼梯往上爬。他已经累得喘不过气来了，但丝毫不敢放慢速度……只有不到五分钟的时间了，他必须赶到炉火边……

"胡言乱语！"他喘着粗气对胖夫人说，胖夫人正在肖像洞口的相框里打呼噜。

"既然你这么说。"胖夫人半梦半醒地嘟哝着，连眼睛也没有睁开，就把肖像打开让哈利通过了。哈利爬了进去，公共休息室里空无一人，空气中也闻不到什么异味，看来赫敏并未需要投掷粪弹来确保他和小天狼星的密谈。

哈利脱掉隐形衣，一屁股坐在炉火前的一把扶手椅上。房间里光线昏暗，唯一的光源就是壁炉里的火苗。在近旁的一张桌子上，克里

## CHAPTER NINETEEN   The Hungarian Horntail

source of light. Nearby, on a table, the *Support CEDRIC DIGGORY* badges the Creeveys had been trying to improve were glinting in the firelight. They now read *POTTER REALLY STINKS*. Harry looked back into the flames, and jumped.

Sirius' head was sitting in the fire. If Harry hadn't seen Mr Diggory do exactly this back in the Weasleys' kitchen, it would have scared him out of his wits. Instead, his face breaking into the first smile he had worn for days, he scrambled out of his chair, crouched down by the hearth and said, 'Sirius – how're you doing?'

Sirius looked different from Harry's memory of him. When they had said goodbye, Sirius' face had been gaunt and sunken, surrounded by a quantity of long, black, matted hair – but the hair was short and clean now, Sirius' face was fuller, and he looked younger, much more like the only photograph Harry had of him, which had been taken at the Potters' wedding.

'Never mind me, how are you?' said Sirius seriously.

'I'm –' for a second, Harry tried to say 'fine' – but he couldn't do it. Before he could stop himself, he was talking more than he'd talked in days – about how no one believed he hadn't entered the Tournament of his own free will, how Rita Skeeter had lied about him in the *Daily Prophet*, how he couldn't walk down a corridor without being sneered at – and about Ron, Ron not believing him, Ron's jealousy ...

'... and now Hagrid's just shown me what's coming in the first task, and it's dragons, Sirius, and I'm a goner,' he finished desperately.

Sirius looked at him, eyes full of concern, eyes which had not yet lost the look that Azkaban had given them – that deadened, haunted look. He had let Harry talk himself into silence without interruption, but now he said, 'Dragons we can deal with, Harry, but we'll get to that in a minute – I haven't got long here ... I've broken into a wizarding house to use the fire, but they could be back at any time. There are things I need to warn you about.'

'What?' said Harry, feeling his spirits slip a further few notches ... surely there could be nothing worse than dragons coming?

'Karkaroff,' said Sirius. 'Harry, he was a Death Eater. You know what Death Eaters are, don't you?'

'Yes – he – what?'

## 第19章 匈牙利树蜂

维兄弟俩试图改良的那些支持**塞德里克·迪戈里**的徽章在火光的映照下闪闪发亮。徽章上的文字现在变成了**波特臭不可闻**。哈利又将目光转向炉火，猛地惊跳起来。

小天狼星的脑袋端端正正地立在火焰中。如果哈利没有在韦斯莱家的厨房里看见迪戈里先生有过同样的举动，肯定会被吓得魂飞魄散。此刻，他不仅没有害怕，反而脸上绽开了笑容，这是许多日子以来的第一次。他爬下椅子，跪坐在壁炉边，说道："小天狼星——你怎么样啊？"

小天狼星的模样跟哈利记忆中的有所不同。他们上次告别时，小天狼星面容瘦削憔悴，周围是又黑又长的蓬乱毛发——可现在呢，小天狼星的头发短短的，又干净又整齐，脸颊也丰满起来，这使他显得年轻了，更加接近哈利收藏的那张照片上的形象，那是在波特夫妇的婚礼上照的。

"别管我了，你好吗？"小天狼星严肃地说。

"我——"哈利刚想说"很好"，但是说不出口。他还没来得及阻拦自己，就已经滔滔不绝地说开了。他已经好些日子没有这样痛快淋漓地说话了——他说到人们怎样都不相信他不是自己报名参加争霸赛的，还说到丽塔·斯基特在《预言家日报》上胡编乱造，说到他每次在走廊里经过都受到别人嘲笑——还说到罗恩，罗恩不相信他，罗恩嫉妒他……

"……还有刚才，海格带我去看了第一个项目里会出现的东西，是火龙，小天狼星，我肯定完蛋了。"他绝望地结束了自己的话。

小天狼星望着他，眼睛里满含关切，那双眼睛还没有完全摆脱阿兹卡班留给它们的神情——那种呆滞而忧郁的神情。他一直耐心地听着，没有插话，直到哈利自己把话说完，沉默下来。然后他说道："不用担心火龙，我们能够对付，哈利，不过我们待会儿再谈这个问题——我在这里不能久留……我是闯进一个巫师家庭，用了他们的火炉，他们随时都会回来。有几件事我要提醒你注意。"

"是什么？"哈利问，觉得自己的情绪更低落了……不可能还有比火龙更可怕的事情吧？

"是卡卡洛夫，"小天狼星说，"哈利，他是一个食死徒。你知道什么是食死徒吧？"

"知道——他——怎么？"

## CHAPTER NINETEEN   The Hungarian Horntail

'He was caught, he was in Azkaban with me, but he got released. I'd bet everything that's why Dumbledore wanted an Auror at Hogwarts this year – to keep an eye on him. Moody caught Karkaroff. Put him into Azkaban in the first place.'

'Karkaroff got released?' Harry said slowly – his brain seemed to be struggling to absorb yet another piece of shocking information. 'Why did they release him?'

'He did a deal with the Ministry of Magic,' said Sirius bitterly. 'He said he'd seen the error of his ways, and then he named names … he put a load of other people into Azkaban in his place … he's not very popular in there, I can tell you. And since he got out, from what I can tell, he's been teaching the Dark Arts to every student who passes through that school of his. So watch out for the Durmstrang champion as well.'

'OK,' said Harry, slowly. 'But … are you saying Karkaroff put my name in the Goblet? Because if he did, he's a really good actor. He seemed furious about it. He wanted to stop me competing.'

'We know he's a good actor,' said Sirius, 'because he convinced the Ministry of Magic to set him free, didn't he? Now, I've been keeping an eye on the *Daily Prophet*, Harry –'

'You and the rest of the world,' said Harry bitterly.

'– and, reading between the lines of that Skeeter woman's article last month, Moody was attacked the night before he started at Hogwarts. Yes, I know she says it was another false alarm,' Sirius said hastily, seeing Harry about to speak, 'but I don't think so, somehow. I think someone tried to stop him getting to Hogwarts. I think someone knew their job would be a lot more difficult with him around. And no one's going to look into it too closely, Mad-Eye's heard intruders a bit too often. But that doesn't mean he can't still spot the real thing. Moody was the best Auror the Ministry ever had.'

'So … what are you saying?' said Harry slowly. 'Karkaroff's trying to kill me? But – why?'

Sirius hesitated.

'I've been hearing some very strange things,' he said slowly. 'The Death Eaters seem to be a bit more active than usual lately. They showed themselves at the Quidditch World Cup, didn't they? Someone set off the Dark Mark … and then – did you hear about that Ministry of Magic witch who's gone missing?'

## 第19章 匈牙利树蜂

"他原先被捕过,跟我一起被关押在阿兹卡班,可是他被释放了。我敢说正是因为这个,邓布利多今年才要在霍格沃茨安插一个傲罗——就是为了提防他。当年,就是穆迪抓住卡卡洛夫,把他关进阿兹卡班的。"

"卡卡洛夫被释放了?"哈利慢慢地问——大脑艰难地吸收着又一条耸人听闻的消息,"他们为什么要释放他?"

"他和魔法部做了笔交易,"小天狼星怨恨地说,"他说他认识到了自己的错误,然后他说出了许多人的名字……他把一大批人投进了阿兹卡班,顶替他的位置……我可以告诉你,他在那里人缘坏透了。据我所知,他出去以后一直在给他那个学校的学生教授黑魔法。因此,你同时也要提防那位德姆斯特朗的勇士。"

"好吧,"哈利慢悠悠地说,"可是……难道你说是卡卡洛夫把我的名字投进火焰杯的?如果是他干的,那他真是太会演戏了。他似乎为这件事气得要命呢,还想阻止我参加竞争。"

"我们知道他擅长演戏,"小天狼星说,"当年居然说服魔法部释放了他,是不是?还有,我一直在留意《预言家日报》,哈利——"

"——不光是你,还有世界上的每个人。"哈利苦恼地说。

"——我仔细研究了那个叫斯基特的女人上个月的那篇文章,穆迪就在前往霍格沃茨就任的前一天夜里受到了攻击。是的,我知道斯基特说这是虚惊一场,"小天狼星看到哈利想插话,赶紧补充道,"但我认为不是这样。我认为是有人试图阻止穆迪到霍格沃茨来。有人知道如果穆迪在旁边,他们要下手就会困难得多。还有,没有人会非常认真地调查这件事,疯眼汉三天两头听见有人想害他。但这并不意味真有异常情况时他不能识破。穆迪是魔法部有史以来最优秀的傲罗。"

"那么……你的意思是什么?"哈利慢慢地问,"卡卡洛夫想要杀死我?可是——为什么呢?"

小天狼星迟疑着。

"我不断听到一些非常奇怪的事情,"他语速很慢地说,"最近食死徒似乎比往常更活跃了。他们在魁地奇世界杯赛上亮相了,是不是?有人变出了黑魔标记……然后——你有没有听说过魔法部失踪的那个女巫师?"

## CHAPTER NINETEEN   The Hungarian Horntail

'Bertha Jorkins?' said Harry.

'Exactly ... she disappeared in Albania, and that's definitely where Voldemort was rumoured to be last ... and she would have known the Triwizard Tournament was coming up, wouldn't she?'

'Yeah, but ... it's not very likely she'd have walked straight into Voldemort, is it?' said Harry.

'Listen, I knew Bertha Jorkins,' said Sirius grimly. 'She was at Hogwarts when I was, a few years above your dad and me. And she was an idiot. Very nosy, but no brains, none at all. It's not a good combination, Harry. I'd say she'd be very easy to lure into a trap.'

'So ... so Voldemort could have found out about the Tournament?' said Harry. 'Is that what you mean? You think Karkaroff might be here on his orders?'

'I don't know,' said Sirius slowly, 'I just don't know ... Karkaroff doesn't strike me as the type who'd go back to Voldemort unless he knew Voldemort was powerful enough to protect him. But whoever put your name in that Goblet did it for a reason, and I can't help thinking the Tournament would be a very good way to attack you, and make it look like an accident.'

'Looks like a really good plan from where I'm standing,' said Harry bleakly. 'They'll just have to stand back and let the dragons do their stuff.'

'Right – these dragons,' said Sirius, speaking very quickly now. 'There's a way, Harry. Don't be tempted to try a Stunning Spell – dragons are strong and too powerfully magical to be knocked out by a single Stunner. You need about half a dozen wizards at a time to overcome a dragon –'

'Yeah, I know, I just saw,' said Harry.

'But you can do it alone,' said Sirius. 'There is a way, and a simple spell's all you need. Just –'

But Harry held up a hand to silence him, his heart suddenly pounding as though it would burst. He could hear footsteps coming down the spiral staircase behind him.

'*Go!*' he hissed at Sirius. '*Go!* There's someone coming!'

Harry scrambled to his feet, hiding the fire – if someone saw Sirius' face within the walls of Hogwarts, they would raise an almighty uproar – the Ministry would get dragged in – he, Harry, would be questioned about Sirius'

## 第19章 匈牙利树蜂

"伯莎·乔金斯？"哈利说。

"一点儿不错……她在阿尔巴尼亚失踪了，那正是人们传说伏地魔最后出现的地方……而乔金斯知道我们即将举办三强争霸赛，是不是？"

"是啊，可是……她不大可能真的撞上伏地魔吧？"哈利说。

"你听我说，我认识伯莎·乔金斯。"小天狼星语气沉重地说，"当年我在霍格沃茨时，她也在这里，比我和你爸爸高几个年级。她是个傻乎乎的家伙，特别爱管闲事，可是没有头脑，完全没有头脑。这两样结合在一起可就糟糕透了，哈利。我认为她这个人经不起诱惑，很容易就中了别人的圈套。"

"这么说……伏地魔可能知道了争霸赛的事？"哈利问，"你是不是这个意思？你认为卡卡洛夫可能是听从伏地魔的命令才到这里来的？"

"我也说不准，"小天狼星慢慢地说，"我真的说不准……凭着我对卡卡洛夫的印象，除非他知道伏地魔已经强大到足以保护他，否则是不会贸然回去找他的。不过，不管是谁把你的名字投进了火焰杯，他这么做都是有意图的。我总觉得，如果有谁想对你下毒手，又想使一切看上去像是一场意外事故，那么这次争霸赛真是一个绝好的机会。"

"从我的角度看，这真是一个天衣无缝的计划。"哈利咧开嘴惨笑了一下，说道，"他们只要站在一旁，把事情交给火龙去干就行了。"

"对了——那些火龙，"小天狼星说，这时他说话的速度变得很快，"有一个绝招，哈利。不要经不起诱惑去念什么昏迷咒——火龙力大无穷，而且具有十分强大的魔力，不可能被一个昏迷咒打倒，需要六七个巫师同时念咒才能制服一条龙……"

"是啊，我知道，我刚才看见了。"哈利说。

"不过你一个人也能对付，"小天狼星说，"有一个绝招，你只要施一个简单的咒语。你只要——"

可是哈利举起一只手阻止了他。哈利的心突然狂跳起来，简直像要爆炸一般。他听见身后的旋转楼梯上传来了脚步声。

"快走！"他嘶哑着声音对小天狼星说，"快走！有人来了！"

哈利急忙爬起来，挡住炉火——如果有人看见小天狼星的脸出现在霍格沃茨的围墙内，肯定会掀起轩然大波——魔法部也会被卷进来——

## CHAPTER NINETEEN  The Hungarian Horntail

whereabouts –'

Harry heard a tiny *pop* in the fire behind him, and knew Sirius had gone – he watched the bottom of the spiral staircase – who had decided to go for a stroll at one o'clock in the morning, and stopped Sirius telling him how to get past a dragon?

It was Ron. Dressed in his maroon paisley pyjamas, Ron stopped dead facing Harry across the room, and looked around.

'Who were you talking to?' he said.

'What's that got to do with you?' Harry snarled. 'What are you doing down here at this time of night?'

'I just wondered where you –' Ron broke off, shrugging. 'Nothing. I'm going back to bed.'

'Just thought you'd come nosing around, did you?' Harry shouted. He knew that Ron had no idea what he'd walked in on, knew he hadn't done it on purpose, but he didn't care – at this moment he hated everything about Ron, right down to the several inches of bare ankle showing beneath his pyjama trousers.

'Sorry about that,' said Ron, his face reddening with anger. 'Should've realised you didn't want to be disturbed. I'll let you get on with practising for your next interview in peace.'

Harry seized one of the *POTTER REALLY STINKS* badges off the table and chucked it, as hard as he could, across the room. It hit Ron on the forehead and bounced off.

'There you go,' Harry said. 'Something for you to wear on Tuesday. You might even have a scar now, if you're lucky … that's what you want, isn't it?'

He strode across the room towards the stairs; he half expected Ron to stop him, he would even have liked Ron to throw a punch at him, but Ron just stood there in his too small pyjamas, and Harry, having stormed upstairs, lay awake in bed fuming for a long time afterwards, and didn't hear him come up to bed.

## 第19章 匈牙利树蜂

人们会向他追问小天狼星的下落——

哈利听见身后的炉火里发出啪的一声轻响,知道小天狼星走了。他注视着旋转楼梯的底部。究竟是谁在凌晨一点心血来潮出来散步,阻碍了小天狼星向他传授通过火龙的秘诀呢?

是罗恩。他穿着褐紫色的漩涡纹睡衣,走进了公共休息室,在哈利面前猛地停住脚步,朝四下张望。

"你刚才在跟谁说话?"他说。

"这跟你有什么关系?"哈利吼道,"深更半夜的,你跑到这儿来干什么?"

"我只是担心,不知道你——"罗恩打住话头,耸了耸肩膀,"没什么。我回去睡觉了。"

"你就想鬼鬼祟祟地到处打探,是吗?"哈利嚷道。其实他也明白,罗恩根本不知道自己无意间搅乱了什么,他明知道罗恩不是故意的,但他什么也不管了——此时此刻,他觉得罗恩的一切都那么讨厌,从头到脚,包括他睡裤下面裸露的那几寸脚脖子。

"对不起,"罗恩说,脸气得通红,"我应该明白你不愿被人打扰。好,我让开,你继续安安静静地排练你的下一次采访吧。"

哈利一把从桌上抓起一个**波特臭不可闻**的徽章,朝房间那头狠狠扔了过去。徽章打中了罗恩的额头,弹开了。

"给你,"哈利说,"给你星期二别在胸前!如果你运气好,你也可以有一个伤疤了……这就是你想要的,是不是?"

他大步穿过房间,朝楼梯走去。他隐约希望罗恩上前拦住他,甚至巴不得罗恩狠狠打他一拳,然而罗恩只是穿着那套过小的睡衣,呆呆地站在那里。哈利怒气冲冲地跑上楼,在床上睁着眼睛,气呼呼地躺了很长时间,也没有听见罗恩上来睡觉。

## CHAPTER TWENTY

# The First Task

Harry got up on Sunday morning and dressed so inattentively that it was a while before he realised he was trying to pull his hat onto his foot instead of his sock. When he'd finally got all his clothes on the right parts of his body, he hurried off to find Hermione, locating her at the Gryffindor table in the Great Hall, where she was eating breakfast with Ginny. Feeling too queasy to eat, Harry waited until Hermione had swallowed her last spoonful of porridge, then dragged her out into the grounds for another walk. There, he told her all about the dragons, and about everything Sirius had said, while they took another long walk around the lake.

Alarmed as she was by Sirius' warnings about Karkaroff, Hermione still thought that the dragons were the more pressing problem.

'Let's just try and keep you alive until Tuesday evening,' she said desperately, 'and then we can worry about Karkaroff.'

They walked three times around the lake, trying all the way to think of a simple spell that would subdue a dragon. Nothing whatsoever occurred to them, so they retired to the library instead. Here, Harry pulled down every book he could find on dragons, and both of them set to work searching through the large pile.

'*Talon-clipping by charms ... treating scale rot ...* this is no good, this is for nutters like Hagrid who want to keep them healthy ...'

'*Dragons are extremely difficult to slay, owing to the ancient magic that imbues their thick hides, which none but the most powerful spells can penetrate ...* but Sirius said a simple one would do it ...'

'Let's try some simple spellbooks, then,' said Harry, throwing aside *Men Who Love Dragons Too Much*.

He returned to the table with a pile of spellbooks, set them down and began

# 第 20 章

# 第一个项目

星期日早晨,哈利一觉醒来,心不在焉地穿着衣服,过了一会儿才意识到自己正把帽子当袜子往脚上套呢。他终于把每件衣服都穿在了合适的部位,便匆匆出来寻找赫敏,最后在礼堂里格兰芬多的桌子旁找到了她。赫敏正和金妮一起吃早饭。哈利觉得胃里不舒服,吃不下东西,就在一旁等着。赫敏刚咽下最后一勺粥,哈利就拉着她来到外面的场地上。他们沿着湖边走了很长时间,他把火龙的事和小天狼星所说的话一股脑儿都告诉了赫敏。

赫敏听说小天狼星提醒他们提防卡卡洛夫,也感到十分震惊,但她仍然认为当务之急是要想办法对付火龙。

"我们先要保证你活到星期二晚上,"她非常焦虑地说,"然后再去考虑卡卡洛夫。"

他们沿湖走了三圈,绞尽脑汁,苦苦思索一个能降服火龙的简单咒语,结果一无所获,于是他们又退回到图书馆内。在这里,哈利把他能找到的每一本跟火龙有关的书都抽了出来,两人像大海捞针一样,开始在一大摞书中搜寻。

"用魔法修剪爪子……鳞片溃烂的治疗方法……没有用,这是给那些像海格那样希望火龙身强力壮的怪人看的……"

"火龙极难宰杀,因为其厚皮中渗透着古代魔法,只有最强大的魔咒才能穿透……可是小天狼星说,一个简单的咒语就能解决问题……"

"我们再试试一些简单的咒语书吧。"哈利说,把《溺爱火龙的人》扔到一边。

他把一大摞咒语书抱到桌边放下,开始一本本地翻阅起来,赫敏

## CHAPTER TWENTY   The First Task

to flick through each in turn, Hermione whispering non-stop at his elbow. 'Well, there are Switching Spells ... but what's the point of Switching it? Unless you swapped its fangs for wine gums or something, that would make it less dangerous ... the trouble is, like that book said, not much is going to get through a dragon's hide ... I'd say Transfigure it, but something that big, you really haven't got a hope, I doubt even Professor McGonagall ... unless you're supposed to put the spell on *yourself*? Maybe to give yourself extra powers? But *they're* not simple spells, I mean, we haven't done any of those in class, I only know about them because I've been doing O.W.L. practice papers ...'

'Hermione,' Harry said, through gritted teeth, 'will you shut up for a bit, please? I'm trying to concentrate.'

But all that happened, when Hermione fell silent, was that Harry's brain filled with a sort of blank buzzing, which didn't seem to allow room for concentration. He stared hopelessly down the index of *Basic Hexes for the Busy and Vexed*: *instant scalping* ... but dragons had no hair ... *pepper breath* ... that would probably increase a dragon's firepower ... *horn tongue* ... just what he needed, to give it an extra weapon ...

'Oh, no, he's back *again*, why can't he read on his stupid ship?' said Hermione irritably, as Viktor Krum slouched in, cast a surly look over at the pair of them, and settled himself in a distant corner with a pile of books. 'Come on, Harry, we'll go back to the common room ... his fan club'll be here in a moment, twittering away ...'

And sure enough, as they left the library, a gang of girls tiptoed past them in the library, one of them wearing a Bulgaria scarf tied around her waist.

Harry barely slept that night. When he awoke on Monday morning, he seriously considered, for the first time ever, just running away from Hogwarts. But as he looked around the Great Hall at breakfast time, and thought about what leaving the castle would mean, he knew he couldn't do it. It was the only place he had ever been happy ... well, he supposed he must have been happy with his parents, too, but he couldn't remember that.

Somehow, the knowledge that he would rather be here and facing a dragon than back in Privet Drive with Dudley was good to know; it made him feel slightly calmer. He finished his bacon with difficulty (his throat wasn't working too well) and, as he and Hermione got up, he saw Cedric

在他旁边不停地嘀咕。"对了，还有转换咒……可是转换有什么用呢？除非你把它的獠牙转换成酒胶糖什么的，使它变得不那么危险……问题是，就像那本书上说的，没有多少东西能够穿透火龙皮……要么给它变形？可是给那样一个庞然大物变形，你肯定不会成功，我怀疑就连麦格教授也……除非你把咒语施在自己身上？使自己增加力量？可是它们也不是简单的咒语啊，我的意思是我们在课堂上还没有学过，我是在做 O.W.L. 考试练习题时才了解它们的……"

"赫敏，"哈利咬着牙根说，"拜托，你能不能安静一会儿？我要集中注意力呢。"

赫敏不说话了，可是哈利只觉得脑子里充斥着空洞的嗡嗡声，似乎没有空间容他集中思想。他绝望地盯着面前《对付多动和烦躁动物的基本魔咒》的索引。快剥头皮……可是火龙没有头发……闻胡椒粉……那大概只会增强火龙的火力……把舌头变硬……这是自找麻烦，给火龙再加一件武器……

"哦，糟糕，他又来了，为什么不能待在他那艘蠢头蠢脑的大船上看书呢？"赫敏烦躁地说——威克多尔·克鲁姆无精打采地走进来，阴沉沉地扫了他们俩一眼，然后抱着一摞书在远处一个角落坐了下来，"走吧，哈利，我们还是回公共休息室去吧……他的追星俱乐部成员很快就会过来，叽叽喳喳，烦死人了……"

果然，当他们离开图书馆时，一群女生踮着脚尖从他们身边走过，其中一个的腰上系着一条保加利亚围巾。

哈利那天夜里几乎没有睡着。星期一早晨醒来时，他生平第一次开始认真考虑从霍格沃茨逃跑。可是，早饭时他在礼堂里环顾四周，想到离开城堡将意味着什么，便知道自己不可能这么做。他只有在这个地方才感受过快乐……对了，他猜和父母在一起时肯定也是快乐的，但他已不记得那时的情景了。

不知怎的，想到自己宁愿待在这儿面对一条火龙，也不愿回到女贞路去和德思礼一家相处，他觉得很宽慰，心情也平静了一些。他费力地咽下那份熏咸肉（他的嗓子好像出了点儿毛病），然后和赫敏一起站起身来。就在这时，他看见塞德里克·迪戈里正准备离开赫奇帕奇的桌子。

## CHAPTER TWENTY  The First Task

Diggory leaving the Hufflepuff table.

Cedric still didn't know about the dragons ... the only champion who didn't, if Harry was right in thinking that Maxime and Karkaroff would have told Fleur and Krum ...

'Hermione, I'll see you in the greenhouses,' Harry said, coming to his decision as he watched Cedric leaving the Hall. 'Go on, I'll catch you up.'

'Harry, you'll be late, the bell's about to ring –'

'I'll catch you up, OK?'

By the time Harry reached the bottom of the marble staircase, Cedric was at the top. He was with a load of sixth-year friends. Harry didn't want to talk to Cedric in front of them; they were among those who had been quoting Rita Skeeter's article at him every time he went near them. He followed Cedric at a distance, and saw that he was heading towards the Charms corridor. This gave Harry an idea. Pausing at a distance from them, he pulled out his wand, and took careful aim.

'*Diffindo!*'

Cedric's bag split. Parchment, quills and books spilled out of it onto the floor. Several bottles of ink smashed.

'Don't bother,' said Cedric in an exasperated voice, as his friends bent down to help him, 'tell Flitwick I'm coming, go on ...'

This was exactly what Harry had been hoping for. He slipped his wand back into his robes, waited until Cedric's friends had disappeared into their classroom, and hurried up the corridor, which was now empty of everyone but himself and Cedric.

'Hi,' said Cedric, picking up a copy of *A Guide to Advanced Transfiguration* that was now splattered with ink. 'My bag just split ... brand new and all ...'

'Cedric,' said Harry, 'the first task is dragons.'

'What?' said Cedric, looking up.

'Dragons,' said Harry, speaking quickly, in case Professor Flitwick came out to see where Cedric had got to. 'They've got four, one for each of us, and we've got to get past them.'

Cedric stared at him. Harry saw some of the panic he'd been feeling since Saturday night flickering in Cedric's grey eyes.

'Are you sure?' Cedric said, in a hushed voice.

'Dead sure,' said Harry. 'I've seen them.'

## 第20章 第一个项目

塞德里克仍然对火龙一无所知……他是几位勇士中唯一不知情的。如果哈利的想法没有错,马克西姆女士和卡卡洛夫一定已经向芙蓉和克鲁姆透露了真相……

"赫敏,我们温室见。"哈利注视着塞德里克离开礼堂,在刹那间拿定了主意,说道,"走吧,我待一会儿赶上你。"

"哈利,你会迟到的,上课铃马上就要响了——"

"我会赶上你的,好吗?"

当哈利来到大理石楼梯底部时,塞德里克已经和他那一大帮六年级同学们一起到了顶上。哈利不想当着那些人的面跟塞德里克说话。每次他走近时,都会有人引用丽塔·斯基特文章里的话来嘲笑他,其中就有这些人。他远远地跟着塞德里克,看见他朝魔咒课教室的走廊走去。这使哈利有了主意。他远远地停下脚步,抽出魔杖,仔细地瞄准。

"四分五裂!"

塞德里克的书包裂开了。羊皮纸、羽毛笔和书本稀里哗啦地掉出来,撒了一地。几瓶墨水摔得粉碎。

"别捡了,"塞德里克的朋友们弯腰帮他收拾,他焦急地说,"告诉弗立维,我马上就来,你们走吧……"

这正是哈利希望的。他把魔杖插进长袍,等塞德里克的朋友们都进了教室,便匆匆走上前去,现在走廊里只有他和塞德里克两人了。

"你好,"塞德里克说,一边捡起一本被墨水溅污的《高级变形术指南》,"我的书包刚才裂开了……还是新书包呢……"

"塞德里克,"哈利说,"第一个项目是火龙。"

"什么?"塞德里克说着抬起头。

"是火龙,"哈利飞快地说,生怕弗立维教授会出来查看塞德里克在什么地方,"一共有四条,我们每人一条,必须从它们身边通过。"

塞德里克呆呆地望着他。哈利看见星期六以来他感到的恐惧,此刻正在塞德里克灰色的眼睛里闪动。

"你能肯定?"塞德里克压低声音问。

"绝对肯定,"哈利说,"我亲眼看见了。"

## CHAPTER TWENTY  The First Task

'But how did you find out? We're not supposed to know ...'

'Never mind,' said Harry quickly – he knew Hagrid would be in trouble if he told the truth. 'But I'm not the only one who knows. Fleur and Krum will know by now – Maxime and Karkaroff both saw the dragons, too.'

Cedric straightened up, his arms full of inky quills, parchment and books, his ripped bag dangling off one shoulder. He stared at Harry, and there was a puzzled, almost suspicious look in his eyes.

'Why are you telling me?' he asked.

Harry looked at him in disbelief. He was sure Cedric wouldn't have asked that if he had seen the dragons himself. Harry wouldn't have let his worst enemy face those monsters unprepared – well, perhaps Malfoy or Snape ...

'It's just ... fair, isn't it?' he said to Cedric. 'We all know now ... we're on an even footing, aren't we?'

Cedric was still looking at him in a slightly suspicious way when Harry heard a familiar clunking noise behind him. He turned around, and saw Mad-Eye Moody emerging from a nearby classroom.

'Come with me, Potter,' he growled. 'Diggory, off you go.'

Harry stared apprehensively at Moody. Had he overheard them? 'Er – Professor, I'm supposed to be in Herbology –'

'Never mind that, Potter. In my office, please ...'

Harry followed him, wondering what was going to happen to him now. What if Moody wanted to know how he'd found out about the dragons? Would Moody go to Dumbledore and tell on Hagrid, or just turn Harry into a ferret? Well, it might be easier to get past a dragon if he was a ferret, Harry thought dully, he'd be smaller, much less easy to see from a height of fifty feet ...

He followed Moody into his office. Moody closed the door behind them and turned to look at Harry, his magical eye fixed upon him as well as the normal one.

'That was a very decent thing you just did, Potter,' Moody said quietly.

Harry didn't know what to say; this wasn't the reaction he had expected at all.

'Sit down,' said Moody, and Harry sat, looking around.

## 第20章 第一个项目

"你是怎么发现的？我们不应该知道……"

"你就别管了，"哈利赶紧说道——他知道如果说出实情，海格就会遇到麻烦，"知道的不止我一个人。芙蓉和克鲁姆现在也知道了——马克西姆女士和卡卡洛夫都看见火龙了。"

塞德里克站直身子，怀里抱着一大堆沾染了墨水的羽毛笔、羊皮纸和书本，撕裂的书包从一个肩膀上耷拉下来。他盯着哈利，眼睛里有一种困惑的、几乎可以说是怀疑的神情。

"你为什么要告诉我？"他问。

哈利不敢相信地望着他。他可以肯定，如果塞德里克亲眼看到那些火龙，就不会这么问了。即使是自己的死敌，哈利也不会让他在毫无防备的情况下面对那些庞然大物——也许，换了马尔福或斯内普就……

"这样才……公平，是不是？"他对塞德里克说，"我们现在都知道了……都站在同样的起点上，是不是？"

塞德里克仍然以有些怀疑的目光望着他，就在这时，噔，噔，噔，哈利听见身后传来一个熟悉的声音。他转身一看，疯眼汉穆迪从旁边的一个教室里走了出来。

"波特，你跟我来。"他粗声粗气地说，"迪戈里，你走吧。"

哈利惊恐地望着穆迪。他听见他们刚才的对话了？"嗯……教授，我要去上草药课了……"

"别管那个，波特。请到我的办公室来……"

哈利跟着他往前走，心里忐忑不安，不知道接下来会发生什么事。如果穆迪追问他是怎么发现火龙的，他该怎么回答？穆迪会不会去找邓布利多告发海格，或是干脆把哈利变成一只白鼬？对了，如果他是一只白鼬，从火龙身边通过就容易多了。哈利杂乱无章地想着，白鼬的个头要小得多，从五十英尺的高度不太容易看见……

他跟着穆迪走进办公室。两人都进去后，穆迪把门关上，转身望着哈利，那只魔眼和正常的眼睛同时盯着哈利。

"你刚才做了一件很有风度的事，波特。"穆迪轻声地说。

哈利不知道怎样回答。他压根儿没想到穆迪会是这个反应。

"坐下吧。"穆迪说。哈利坐了下来，环顾四周。

## CHAPTER TWENTY  The First Task

He had visited this office under two of its previous occupants. In Professor Lockhart's day, the walls had been plastered with beaming, winking pictures of Professor Lockhart himself. When Lupin had lived here, you were more likely to come across a specimen of some fascinating new Dark creature he had procured for them to study in class. Now, however, the office was full of a number of exceptionally odd objects that Harry supposed Moody had used in the days when he had been an Auror.

On his desk stood what looked like a large, cracked, glass spinning top; Harry recognised it at once as a Sneakoscope, because he owned one himself, though it was much smaller than Moody's. In the corner on a small table stood an object that looked something like an extra-squiggly, golden television aerial. It was humming slightly. What appeared to be a mirror hung opposite Harry on the wall, but it was not reflecting the room. Shadowy figures were moving around inside it, none of them clearly in focus.

'Like my Dark detectors, do you?' said Moody, who was watching Harry closely.

'What's that?' Harry asked, pointing at the squiggly golden aerial.

'Secrecy Sensor. Vibrates when it detects concealment and lies ... no use here, of course, too much interference – students in every direction lying about why they haven't done their homework. Been humming ever since I got here. I had to disable my Sneakoscope because it wouldn't stop whistling. It's extra sensitive, picks up stuff about a mile around. Of course, it could be picking up more than kids' stuff,' he added in a growl.

'And what's the mirror for?'

'Oh, that's my Foe-Glass. See them out there, skulking around? I'm not really in trouble until I see the whites of their eyes. That's when I open my trunk.'

He let out a short, harsh laugh, and pointed to the large trunk under the window. It had seven keyholes in a row. Harry wondered what was in there, until Moody's next question brought him sharply back to earth.

'So ... found out about the dragons, have you?'

Harry hesitated. He'd been afraid of this – but he hadn't told Cedric, and he certainly wasn't going to tell Moody, that Hagrid had broken the rules.

'It's all right,' said Moody, sitting down and stretching out his wooden leg with a groan. 'Cheating's a traditional part of the Triwizard Tournament and always has been.'

## 第20章 第一个项目

办公室的前两位主人在的时候,哈利曾经来过这里。洛哈特教授在的那些日子,墙上贴满了洛哈特教授本人笑眯眯的眨着眼睛的照片。卢平在这里时,你经常会碰到一些十分奇妙和新鲜的黑魔法动物,那是卢平弄来让他们在课堂上学习用的。现在,办公室里放着一大堆稀奇古怪的玩意儿,哈利猜想这些都是穆迪当傲罗时用过的东西。

在穆迪的办公桌上有一个东西,像是裂了缝的玻璃大陀螺。哈利一眼就认出来了,这是一个窥镜,因为他自己也有一个,不过比穆迪的这个小得多。在一张小桌子的角上,放着一个古怪的东西,看上去有点像金色的电视天线,不过扭曲得特别厉害,不停地发出轻轻的嗡嗡声。哈利对面的墙上挂着一面类似镜子的东西,但照出的不是房间里的情景,里面有许多黑乎乎的人影晃来晃去,但都模模糊糊,看不真切。

"你喜欢我的黑魔法探测器,是吗?"穆迪问道,他一直在仔细打量着哈利。

"那是什么?"哈利指着那个扭曲的金色天线问道。

"探密器。探测到密谋和谎言时就会颤动……当然啦,在这里派不上用场,干扰太多了——到处都有学生为自己没做作业编造谎话。我搬进来以后,它就一直嗡嗡叫个不停。我不得不把我的窥镜弄坏,因为它一刻不停地鸣笛尖叫。太敏感了,方圆一英里之内的动静都能探测到。当然啦,它能探测的可不光是小孩子们的把戏。"他用粗哑的声音说道。

"那面镜子是干什么用的?"

"噢,那是我的照妖镜。看见那些鬼鬼祟祟的人影了吗?我如果看清了他们的眼白,就真的遇到麻烦了。那时我就要打开我的箱子。"

他短促而嘶哑地笑了一声,指着窗户下的那只大箱子。那上面有七个排成一排的钥匙孔。哈利正猜想箱子里会是什么,忽然,穆迪的下一个问题又把他拉回到现实中来了。

"这么说……你发现了火龙的事,是吗?"

哈利迟疑着。他一直在担心这个——他没有把海格违反章程的事告诉塞德里克,当然也不会告诉穆迪。

"没关系,"穆迪说着,坐了下来,呻吟着伸直那条木腿,"作弊向来是三强争霸赛的传统组成部分。"

## CHAPTER TWENTY  The First Task

'I didn't cheat,' said Harry sharply. 'It was – a sort of accident that I found out.'

Moody grinned. 'I wasn't accusing you, laddie. I've been telling Dumbledore from the start, he can be as high minded as he likes, but you can bet old Karkaroff and Maxime won't be. They'll have told their champions everything they can. They want to win. They want to beat Dumbledore. They'd like to prove he's only human.'

Moody gave a harsh laugh, and his magical eye swivelled around so fast it made Harry feel queasy to watch it.

'So ... got any ideas how you're going to get past your dragon yet?' said Moody.

'No,' said Harry.

'Well, I'm not going to tell you,' said Moody gruffly. 'I don't show favouritism, me. I'm just going to give you some good, general advice. And the first bit is – *play to your strengths*.'

'I haven't got any,' said Harry, before he could stop himself.

'Excuse me,' growled Moody, 'you've got strengths if I say you've got them. Think now. What are you best at?'

Harry tried to concentrate. What *was* he best at? Well, that was easy, really –

'Quidditch,' he said dully, 'and a fat lot of help –'

'That's right,' said Moody, staring at him very hard, his magical eye barely moving at all. 'You're a damn good flier, from what I've heard.'

'Yeah, but ...' Harry stared at him. 'I'm not allowed a broom, I've only got my wand –'

'My second piece of general advice,' said Moody loudly, interrupting him, 'is to use a nice, simple spell which will enable you to *get what you need*.'

Harry looked at him blankly. What did he need?

'Come on, boy ...' whispered Moody. 'Put them together ... it's not that difficult ...'

And it clicked. He was best at flying. He needed to pass the dragon in the air. For that, he needed his Firebolt. And for his Firebolt, he needed –

* * *

'Hermione,' Harry whispered, when he had sped into greenhouse three ten minutes later, uttering a hurried apology to Professor Sprout as he passed

## 第20章 第一个项目

"我没有作弊,"哈利明确地说,"我是——我是偶然发现的。"

穆迪咧开嘴笑了:"我没有责备你,孩子。我从一开始就告诉邓布利多,他尽可以发扬高尚的风格,但我敢说卡卡洛夫和马克西姆绝没有这样超脱。他们会尽可能把一切都告诉自己的勇士。他们想赢。他们想打败邓布利多。他们希望证明他只是一个凡人。"

穆迪又发出一声嘶哑的干笑,那只魔眼滴溜溜地转得飞快,哈利看着都觉得恶心了。

"那么……你有没有想好怎样通过你的那条火龙呢?"穆迪问。

"没有。"哈利说。

"噢,我是不会告诉你的,"穆迪生硬地说,"我不能偏心,是吧?我只想给你一些善意的、泛泛的忠告。第一条是——发挥自己的强项。"

"我没有强项。"哈利脱口而出,想收回也来不及了。

"对不起,我不同意。"穆迪粗声粗气地说,"我说你有强项,你就有强项。好好想想。你最擅长什么?"

哈利拼命集中思想。他最擅长什么?噢,那是显而易见的——

"魁地奇,"他干巴巴地说,"那几乎没什么用——"

"那就对了,"穆迪说,死死盯着哈利,那只魔眼几乎一动不动,"据我所知,你的飞行技术很好。"

"不错,可是……"哈利望着他说,"我不能使用扫帚,我只能带着魔杖——"

"我给你的第二条泛泛的忠告是,"穆迪打断了他,大声地说,"念一个简单而有效的咒语,使你能够得到你需要的东西。"

哈利茫然地望着他。他需要什么呢?

"好好想想,孩子……"穆迪小声说,"把它们联系起来……并没有那么难……"

突然,哈利脑子里灵光一现。他最擅长飞翔。他需要从空中越过巨龙。这样的话,就需要他的火弩箭;而要得到他的火弩箭,就需要——

"赫敏,"三分钟后,哈利飞快地冲进温室,走过斯普劳特教授身边时匆匆向她说了句道歉的话,然后压低声音对赫敏说,"赫敏——我

## CHAPTER TWENTY    The First Task

her, 'Hermione – I need you to help me.'

'What d'you think I've been trying to do, Harry?' she whispered back, her eyes round with anxiety over the top of the quivering Flutterby Bush she was pruning.

'Hermione, I need to learn how to do a Summoning Charm properly by tomorrow afternoon.'

And so they practised. They didn't have lunch, but headed for a free classroom, where Harry tried with all his might to make various objects fly across the room towards him. He was still having problems. The books and quills kept losing heart halfway across the room and dropping like stones to the floor.

'Concentrate, Harry, *concentrate* ...'

'What d'you think I'm trying to do?' said Harry angrily. 'A filthy great dragon keeps popping up in my head, for some reason ... OK, try again ...'

He wanted to skip Divination to keep practising, but Hermione refused point-blank to skive off Arithmancy, and there was no point staying without her. He therefore had to endure over an hour of Professor Trelawney, who spent half the lesson telling everyone that the position of Mars in relation to Saturn at that moment meant that people born in July were in great danger of sudden, violent deaths.

'Well, that's good,' said Harry loudly, his temper getting the better of him, 'just as long as it's not drawn-out, I don't want to suffer.'

Ron looked for a moment as though he was going to laugh; he certainly caught Harry's eye for the first time in days, but Harry was still feeling too resentful towards Ron to care. He spent the rest of the lesson trying to attract small objects towards him under the table with his wand. He managed to make a fly zoom straight into his hand, though he wasn't entirely sure that was owing to his prowess at Summoning Charms – perhaps the fly was just stupid.

He forced down some dinner after Divination, then returned to the empty classroom with Hermione, using the Invisibility Cloak to avoid the teachers. They kept practising until past midnight. They would have stayed longer, but Peeves turned up and, pretending to think that Harry wanted things thrown at him, started chucking chairs across the room. Harry and Hermione left in a hurry before the noise attracted Filch, and went back to the Gryffindor common room, which was now mercifully empty.

## 第20章 第一个项目

需要你的帮助。"

"我不是一直在帮助你吗,哈利?"赫敏悄声回答。她正在修剪振翅灌木,一双眼睛在颤动的灌木丛上睁得圆圆的,里面满是焦虑。

"赫敏,我必须在明天下午之前掌握召唤咒。"

于是他们开始苦苦练习。两人没有吃午饭,直接找了一间空教室,哈利集中全部的意念,迫使房间里各种各样的东西朝他飞过来。他仍然没有完全掌握。书本啦,羽毛笔啦,总是在飞到一半时泄了气,像石头一样落到地板上。

"专心,哈利,专心……"

"你以为我在干什么?"哈利气呼呼地说,"不知怎的,我脑子里不停地冒出一条特别大的火龙……好吧,再试一次……"

他本想逃过占卜课,继续练习,但是赫敏坚决不肯放弃算术占卜课,而如果她不在,哈利留在这里就毫无意义了。因此,他只好又花了一个多小时忍受特里劳尼教授的唠叨,特里劳尼教授用半节课的时间告诉全班同学,从当时火星与土星的相对位置来看,七月份出生的人将有突然惨死的巨大危险。

"嗯,那倒不错,"哈利大声说,已经无法按捺内心的怒火,"但愿时间不要拖得太长。我不想忍受折磨。"

有那么片刻工夫,罗恩似乎想要放声大笑。他的目光无疑是与哈利的目光相遇了,这是许多天来的第一次,但是哈利还在生罗恩的气,没有理会他。在这节课剩余的时间里,哈利一直在桌子底下用魔杖吸引小东西朝他飞来。他总算使一只苍蝇飞进了他的手心,但并不能完全肯定这是他召唤咒的威力——也许是那只苍蝇自己昏了头吧。

占卜课后,他强迫自己吃下几口晚饭,又和赫敏一起回到那间空教室。为了躲避教师的注意,他们还穿上了隐形衣。他们一直练习到午夜以后。本来还可以再待一些时候,可是皮皮鬼出现了。他假装认为哈利想把东西都朝他抛去,便开始抡起椅子在房间里乱扔。哈利和赫敏趁这声音还没有把费尔奇吸引过来,赶紧离开了那里。他们回到格兰芬多的公共休息室,谢天谢地,里面空无一人。

### CHAPTER TWENTY   The First Task

At two o'clock in the morning, Harry stood near the fireplace, surrounded by heaps of objects – books, quills, several upturned chairs, an old set of Gobstones and Neville's toad, Trevor. Only in the last hour had Harry really got the hang of the Summoning Charm.

'That's better, Harry, that's loads better,' Hermione said, looking exhausted, but very pleased.

'Well, now we know what to do next time I can't manage a spell,' Harry said, throwing a Rune Dictionary back to Hermione, so he could try again, 'threaten me with a dragon. Right ...' He raised his wand once more. '*Accio Dictionary!*'

The heavy book soared out of Hermione's hand, flew across the room, and Harry caught it.

'Harry, I really think you've got it!' said Hermione, delightedly.

'Just as long as it works tomorrow,' Harry said. 'The Firebolt's going to be much further away than the stuff in here, it's going to be in the castle, and I'm going to be out there in the grounds ...'

'That doesn't matter,' said Hermione firmly. 'Just as long as you're concentrating really, really hard on it, it'll come. Harry, we'd better get some sleep ... you're going to need it.'

Harry had been focusing so hard on learning the Summoning Charm that evening that some of his blind panic had left him. It returned in full measure, however, on the following morning. The atmosphere in the school was one of great tension and excitement. Lessons were to stop at midday, giving all the students time to get down to the dragons' enclosure – though of course, they didn't yet know what they would find there.

Harry felt oddly separate from everyone around him, whether they were wishing him good luck or hissing '*We'll have a box of tissues ready, Potter*' as he passed. It was a state of nervousness so advanced that he wondered whether he mightn't just lose his head when they tried to lead him out to his dragon, and start trying to curse everyone in sight.

Time was behaving in a more peculiar fashion than ever, rushing past in great dollops, so that one moment he seemed to be sitting down in his first lesson, History of Magic, and the next, walking into lunch ... and then (where had the morning gone? The last of the dragon-free hours?) Professor McGonagall was hurrying over to him in the Great Hall. Lots of people were watching.

## 第20章 第一个项目

凌晨两点钟时，哈利站在壁炉旁边，周围堆着许多东西：书本、羽毛笔、几把翻倒的椅子、一套旧的高布石，还有纳威的蟾蜍莱福。就在刚才，哈利才终于真正掌握了召唤咒。

"好多了，哈利，真是大有长进。"赫敏说。她显得很疲倦，但十分高兴。

"噢，现在知道下次我学不会魔咒该怎么办了，"哈利说，把一本如尼文词典扔还给赫敏，准备再试一次，"就拿一条火龙来威胁我。没错……"他又一次举起魔杖："词典飞来！"

厚重的词典从赫敏手中腾空而起，飞到房间的另一边，被哈利一把接住。

"哈利，我认为你真的掌握了！"赫敏高兴地说。

"但愿明天还能成功，"哈利说，"火弩箭比这里的东西远得多，明天它在城堡里，我在外面的场地上……"

"没关系，"赫敏肯定地说，"只要你真正集中意念，全神贯注，它就会飞来。哈利，我们最好回去睡一会儿……你需要休息。"

那天晚上，哈利一直把注意力全部集中在学习召唤咒上，内心一些茫然的恐慌暂时离开了他。然而，到了第二天早晨，它们又全都回来了。整个学校的气氛非常紧张和兴奋。中午就停课了，好让全校学生有时间到下面火龙的围场上去——当然啦，他们并不知道会在那里看到什么。

哈利莫名地感到自己像个局外人。当他走过时，旁边的人祝他走运也好，咬牙切齿地说"我们准备了一大堆纸巾为你哭泣，波特"也好，他都觉得跟自己无关。这种紧张的情绪太强烈了，他简直怀疑自己在被领去见火龙的路上就会失去控制，对着看见的每一个人念起咒来。

时间的运行方式越发古怪了，像是快马加鞭地往前跑，前一分钟他似乎还坐在教室里上第一节课——魔法史，转眼间就走进礼堂吃午饭了……然后（上午到哪里去了？没有火龙袭击的最后几小时到哪里去了？），麦格教授在礼堂里向他匆匆走来。许多人都望着他们。

## CHAPTER TWENTY  The First Task

'Potter, the champions have to come down into the grounds now ... you have to get ready for your first task.'

'OK,' said Harry, standing up, his fork falling onto his plate with a clatter.

'Good luck, Harry,' Hermione whispered. 'You'll be fine!'

'Yeah,' said Harry, in a voice that was most unlike his own.

He left the Great Hall with Professor McGonagall. She didn't seem herself, either; in fact, she looked nearly as anxious as Hermione. As she walked him down the stone steps and out into the cold November afternoon, she put her hand on his shoulder.

'Now, don't panic,' she said, 'just keep a cool head ... we've got wizards on hand to control the situation if it gets out of hand ... the main thing is just to do your best, and nobody will think any the worse of you ... are you all right?'

'Yes,' Harry heard himself say. 'Yes, I'm fine.'

She was leading him towards the place where the dragons were, around the edge of the Forest, but when they approached the clump of trees behind which the enclosure would be clearly visible, Harry saw that a tent had been erected, its entrance facing them, screening the dragons from view.

'You're to go in here with the other champions,' said Professor McGonagall, in a rather shaky sort of voice, 'and wait for your turn, Potter. Mr Bagman is in there ... he'll be telling you the – the procedure ... good luck.'

'Thanks,' said Harry, in a flat, distant voice. She left him at the entrance of the tent. Harry went inside.

Fleur Delacour was sitting in a corner on a low wooden stool. She didn't look nearly as composed as usual, but rather pale and clammy. Viktor Krum looked even surlier than usual, which Harry supposed was his way of showing nerves. Cedric was pacing up and down. When Harry entered, he gave him a small smile, which Harry returned, feeling the muscles in his face working rather hard, as though they had forgotten how to do it.

'Harry! Good-oh!' said Bagman happily, looking around at him. 'Come in, come in, make yourself at home!'

Bagman looked somehow like a slightly overblown cartoon figure, standing amid all the pale-faced champions. He was wearing his old Wasp robes again.

## 第20章 第一个项目

"波特,现在勇士们都要到下面的场地上去……你们必须做好准备,完成第一个项目。"

"好吧。"哈利说着站了起来,他的叉子掉进盘里,当啷一响。

"祝你好运,哈利,"赫敏小声说,"你会成功的!"

"是啊。"哈利说,声音听上去简直不像是他自己的了。

他和麦格教授一起离开了礼堂。麦格教授看上去也心慌意乱。实际上,她简直和赫敏一样焦虑不安。她陪伴哈利走下石阶,来到户外,这是十一月里一个寒冷的下午,她把手放在哈利的肩头。

"好了,不要紧张,"她说,"保持头脑冷静……我们安排了一些巫师在旁边,如果情况不妙,他们会上前控制局势的……最重要的是充分发挥你自己的能力,谁也不会看不起你……你没事吧?"

"没事,"哈利听见自己这么说,"没事,我很好。"

麦格教授领着他绕过禁林边缘,朝火龙所在的地方走去。当他们走近本来可以看清场地的那片树丛时,哈利发现那里竖起了一个帐篷,挡住了那些火龙,帐篷的入口正对着他们。

"你必须和另外几位勇士一起进去,"麦格教授说,声音有些颤抖,"等着轮到你的时候,波特。巴格曼先生也在里面……他会把——步骤告诉你们……祝你好运。"

"谢谢。"哈利用一种单调的、飘飘忽忽的声音说。麦格教授把他领到帐篷入口处。哈利走了进去。

芙蓉·德拉库尔坐在角落里一张低矮的木凳上。她一点儿不像平时那样镇定自若,脸色显得非常苍白,一副病恹恹的样子。威克多尔·克鲁姆看上去比往常更加阴沉,哈利猜想这大概是他显示内心紧张的方式。塞德里克不停地来回踱步。哈利进来时,塞德里克朝他淡淡地笑了一下,哈利也对他报以微笑。哈利觉得脸上的肌肉牵动得很别扭,好像它们已经忘记怎么笑了。

"哈利!太好了!"巴格曼扭过头来望着他,愉快地说,"进来,进来,放松点儿,跟在自己家里一样!"

巴格曼站在那几个脸色苍白的勇士中间,活像一个大块头的卡通形象。他又穿上了那套黄蜂队的旧队服。

## CHAPTER TWENTY    The First Task

'Well, now we're all here – time to fill you in!' said Bagman brightly. 'When the audience has assembled, I'm going to be offering each of you this bag' – he held up a small sack of purple silk, and shook it at them – 'from which you will each select a small model of the thing you are about to face! There are different – er – varieties, you see. And I have to tell you something else too ... ah, yes ... your task is to *collect the golden egg*!'

Harry glanced around. Cedric had nodded once, to show that he understood Bagman's words, and then started pacing around the tent again; he looked slightly green. Fleur Delacour and Krum hadn't reacted at all. Perhaps they thought they might be sick if they opened their mouths; that was certainly how Harry felt. But they, at least, had volunteered for this ...

And in no time at all, hundreds upon hundreds of pairs of feet could be heard passing the tent, their owners talking excitedly, laughing, joking ... Harry felt as separate from the crowd as if they were a different species. And then – it felt about a second later to Harry – Bagman was opening the neck of the purple silk sack.

'Ladies first,' he said, offering it to Fleur Delacour.

She put a shaking hand inside the bag, and drew out a tiny, perfect model of a dragon – a Welsh Green. It had the number 'two' around its neck. And Harry knew, by the fact that Fleur showed no sign of surprise, but rather a determined resignation, that he had been right: Madame Maxime had told her what was coming.

The same held true for Krum. He pulled out the scarlet Chinese Fireball. It had a number 'three' around its neck. He didn't even blink, just stared at the ground.

Cedric put his hand into the bag, and out came the blueish-grey Swedish Short-Snout, the number 'one' tied around its neck. Knowing what was left, Harry put his hand into the silk bag, and pulled out the Hungarian Horntail, and the number 'four'. It stretched its wings as he looked down at it, and bared its minuscule fangs.

'Well, there you are!' said Bagman. 'You have each pulled out the dragon you will face, and the numbers refer to the order in which you are to take on the dragons, do you see? Now, I'm going to have to leave you in a moment, because I'm commentating. Mr Diggory, you're first, just go out into the enclosure when you hear a whistle, all right? Now ... Harry ... could I have a

## 第20章 第一个项目

"好了,现在大家都到齐了——该向你们介绍一下情况了!"巴格曼兴高采烈地说,"观众聚齐以后,我要把这只布袋轮流递到你们每个人面前,"——他举起一只紫色的绸布袋,对着他们摇了摇——"你们从里面挑出各自将要面对的那个东西的小模型!它们有不同的——嗯——种类。我还有一件事要告诉你们……啊,没错……你们的任务是拾取金蛋!"

哈利看了看四周。塞德里克点了一下头,表示他明白了巴格曼的话,然后又开始在帐篷里踱来踱去;他的脸色微微有些发绿。芙蓉·德拉库尔和克鲁姆没有丝毫反应。大概他们觉得一旦开口说话,就会心慌得呕吐吧。哈利也是这种感觉。但他们几个至少是自愿来比赛的……

转眼之间,就听见成百上千双脚走过帐篷的声音,脚的主人都在兴奋地交谈、说笑……哈利觉得自己与那些人格格不入,就好像他们属于另一个物种。接着——在哈利的感觉中只是一眨眼的工夫——巴格曼已经在解紫色绸布袋了。

"女士优先。"他说,把袋子递到芙蓉·德拉库尔面前。

芙蓉把一只颤抖的手伸进布袋,掏出一个惟妙惟肖的龙的小巧模型——是威尔士绿龙,脖子上系着一个号码:二号。哈利看见芙蓉没有表现出丝毫惊讶,而是一副听天由命的神情,便知道自己的推测是正确的:马克西姆女士告诉了芙蓉即将面临的挑战是什么。

克鲁姆也证实了同样的情况。他掏出了那条深红色的中国火球,脖子上系的号码是三号。他连眼睛都没有眨一下,就一屁股坐下来,眼睛盯着地面。

塞德里克把手伸进布袋,掏出来的是那条灰蓝色的瑞典短鼻龙,脖子上系的号码是一号。哈利知道留给自己的是什么了,他把手伸进绸布口袋,掏出了那条匈牙利树蜂,是四号。他低头望着它的时候,那小龙展开翅膀,露出它小小的獠牙。

"好了,你们都拿到了!"巴格曼说,"都抽到了自己将要面对的火龙,脖子上的号码是你们去与火龙周旋的顺序,明白了吗?好了,我现在得离开你们一下,因为要去给观众作解说。迪戈里先生,你是第一个,你一听见哨声就走进那片场地,知道了吗?那么……哈利……

quick word? Outside?'

'Er ... yes,' said Harry blankly, and he got up and went out of the tent with Bagman, who walked him a short way away, into the trees, and then turned to him with a fatherly expression on his face.

'Feeling all right, Harry? Anything I can get you?'

'What?' said Harry. 'I – no, nothing.'

'Got a plan?' said Bagman, lowering his voice conspiratorially. 'Because I don't mind sharing a few pointers, if you'd like them, you know. I mean,' Bagman continued, lowering his voice still further, 'you're the underdog here, Harry ... anything I can do to help ...'

'No,' said Harry, so quickly he knew he had sounded rude, 'no – I – I've decided what I'm going to do, thanks.'

'Nobody would *know*, Harry,' said Bagman, winking at him.

'No, I'm fine,' said Harry, wondering why he kept telling people this, and wondering whether he had ever been less fine. 'I've got a plan worked out, I –'

A whistle had blown somewhere.

'Good Lord, I've got to run!' said Bagman in alarm, and he hurried off.

Harry walked back to the tent, and saw Cedric emerging from it, greener than ever. Harry tried to wish him luck as he walked past, but all that came out of his mouth was a sort of hoarse grunt.

Harry went back inside to Fleur and Krum. Seconds later, they heard the roar of the crowd, which meant Cedric had entered the enclosure, and was now face to face with the living counterpart of his model ...

It was worse than Harry could ever have imagined, sitting there and listening. The crowd screamed ... yelled ... gasped like a single many-headed entity, as Cedric did whatever he was doing to get past the Swedish Short-Snout. Krum was still staring at the ground. Fleur had now taken to retracing Cedric's steps, round and round the tent. and Bagman's commentary made everything much, much worse ... horrible pictures formed in Harry's mind, as he heard: 'Oooh, narrow miss there, very narrow' ... 'He's taking risks, this one!' ... '*Clever* move – pity it didn't work!'

And then, after about fifteen minutes, Harry heard the deafening roar that could mean only one thing: Cedric had got past his dragon, and seized the

## 第20章 第一个项目

我可以跟你说几句话吗？到外面来？"

"呃……好的。"哈利茫然地说。他站起来，和巴格曼一起来到帐篷外。巴格曼把他带到稍远一点儿的地方，进入树丛中，然后转过身望着他，脸上带着一种慈父般的表情。

"感觉怎么样，哈利？有什么需要我帮助的吗？"

"什么？"哈利说，"我——不，不需要。"

"心里有谱了吗？"巴格曼鬼鬼祟祟地放低声音，问道，"如果你愿意，我倒可以给你提供几个点子。我的意思是，"巴格曼把声音压得更低，继续说道，"你在这里处于劣势，哈利……只要我帮得上忙……"

"不，"哈利唐突地说，知道自己显得有些失礼，"不——我——我知道自己该怎么做，谢谢。"

"不会有人知道的，哈利。"巴格曼说着，朝哈利眨了眨眼睛。

"不用了，我没事。"哈利说，他不明白为什么反复告诉别人这一点，实际上他不知道自己什么时候感觉这么糟糕过，"我已经想出了一个方案，我——"

什么地方响起了哨声。

"上帝啊，我必须跑着去了！"巴格曼惊慌地说，撒腿就跑。

哈利朝帐篷走去，恰好看见塞德里克从里面出来，脸色比刚才更绿了。两人擦肩而过时，哈利本想祝他好运，但嘴里只发出了一声粗哑的嘟哝。

哈利回到帐篷里，回到芙蓉和克鲁姆身边。几秒钟后，他们听见人群里传来一片喧嚣，这意味着塞德里克已经进入场地，正面对着与他那个模型一模一样的活物……

哈利坐在那里侧耳倾听，一切比他想象的还要糟糕。当塞德里克想方设法通过瑞典短鼻龙时，人群就像一个长着许多脑袋的统一体，在尖叫……在高喊……在倒吸冷气。克鲁姆仍然盯着地面。芙蓉现在和塞德里克刚才一样，在帐篷里一圈接一圈地踱步。巴格曼的解说使一切变得更加、更加糟糕……"哎哟，好危险，太危险了。"……"他这一招可真够悬的！"……"很聪明的办法——可惜没有成功！"哈利听着这些解说，脑子里不断浮现出可怕的画面。

大约十五分钟后，哈利听见一阵震耳欲聋的欢呼声，这只能说明

## CHAPTER TWENTY   The First Task

golden egg.

'Very good indeed!' Bagman was shouting. 'And now the marks from the judges!'

But he didn't shout out the marks; Harry supposed the judges were holding them up and showing them to the crowd.

'One down, three to go!' Bagman yelled, as the whistle blew again. 'Miss Delacour, if you please!'

Fleur was trembling from head to foot; Harry felt more warmly towards her than he had done so far, as she left the tent with her head held high, and her hand clutching her wand. He and Krum were left alone, at opposite sides of the tent, avoiding each other's gaze.

The same process started again ... 'Oh, I'm not sure that was wise!' they could hear Bagman shouting gleefully. 'Oh ... nearly! Careful now ... good Lord, I thought she'd had it then!'

Ten minutes later, Harry heard the crowd erupt into applause once more ... Fleur must have been successful, too. A pause, while Fleur's marks were being shown ... more clapping ... then, for the third time, the whistle.

'And here comes Mr Krum!' cried Bagman, and Krum slouched out, leaving Harry quite alone.

He felt much more aware of his body than usual; very aware of the way his heart was pumping fast, and his fingers tingling with fear ... yet at the same time, he seemed to be outside himself, seeing the walls of the tent, and hearing the crowd, as though from far away ...

'Very daring!' Bagman was yelling, and Harry heard the Chinese Fireball emit a horrible, roaring shriek, while the crowd drew its collective breath. 'That's some nerve he's showing – and – yes, he's got the egg!'

Applause shattered the wintery air like breaking glass; Krum had finished – it would be Harry's turn at any moment.

He stood up, noticing dimly that his legs seemed to be made of marshmallow. He waited. And then he heard the whistle blow. He walked out through the entrance of the tent, the panic rising into a crescendo inside him. And now he was walking past the trees, through a gap in the enclosure fence.

He saw everything in front of him as though it was a very highly coloured

## 第20章 第一个项目

一件事：塞德里克终于通过了他那条火龙，抓到了金蛋。

"确实非常出色！"巴格曼扯着嗓子喊道，"现在请裁判打分！"

然而他没有高声报出得分，哈利猜想裁判可能把分数举起来让观众看了。

"一个下去了，还有三个！"口哨再次吹响时，巴格曼大声嚷道，"德拉库尔小姐，请上场！"

芙蓉从头到脚都在发抖。当她昂着脑袋、手里紧紧攥着魔杖离开帐篷时，哈利对她产生了前所未有的亲近感。现在只剩下他和克鲁姆面对面坐在帐篷的两边，互相躲避着对方的目光。

同样的程序又开始了……"哦，我不能肯定这样做是不是明智！"他们听见巴格曼兴高采烈地大喊，"哦……就差一点点！小心……我的天哪，我还以为她已经得手了！"

十分钟后，哈利听见观众们再一次爆发出欢呼喝彩……芙蓉一定也成功了。接着是片刻的静场，等着裁判给芙蓉打分……又是掌声雷动……然后，口哨第三次吹响了。

"现在出场的是克鲁姆先生！"巴格曼喊道。克鲁姆耷拉着肩膀走了出去，把哈利一个人留在帐篷里。

他觉得自己的身体比平常敏感多了。他强烈地意识到心脏在狂跳，他的手指因为恐惧而刺痛……然而与此同时，他又似乎游离于自己之外，好像是从某个遥远的地方望着帐篷四壁，听着人群的喧嚣……

"非常大胆！"巴格曼在高喊——哈利听见中国火球发出一声可怕的、石破天惊的尖叫，观众们不约而同地吸了口气，"他表现出了过人的胆量——啊——没错，他拿到了金蛋！"

铺天盖地的掌声像打碎玻璃一样，把冬天的空气震得粉碎。克鲁姆已经完成了他的使命——现在随时都会轮到哈利上场。

他站了起来，模模糊糊地感觉自己的双腿仿佛是棉花糖做的。他等待着。接着听见外面传来了口哨声。他穿过帐篷的入口走到外面，内心的紧张一点点增强，达到无以复加的程度。他正从树丛旁走过，穿过场地栅栏上的一道豁口。

他看见了面前的一切，就好像一个色彩鲜明的梦境。成百上千张

## CHAPTER TWENTY  The First Task

dream. There were hundreds and hundreds of faces staring down at him from stands which had been magicked there since he'd last stood on this spot. And there was the Horntail, at the other end of the enclosure, crouched low over her clutch of eggs, her wings half furled, her evil, yellow eyes upon him, a monstrous, scaly black lizard, thrashing her spiked tail, leaving yard-long gouge marks in the hard ground. The crowd was making a great deal of noise, but whether friendly or not, Harry didn't know or care. It was time to do what he had to do … to focus his mind, entirely and absolutely, upon the thing that was his only chance …

He raised his wand.

'*Accio Firebolt!*' he shouted.

He waited, every fibre of him hoping, praying … if it hadn't worked … if it wasn't coming … he seemed to be looking at everything around him through some sort of shimmering, transparent barrier, like a heat haze, which made the enclosure and the hundreds of faces around him swim strangely …

And then he heard it, speeding through the air behind him; he turned and saw his Firebolt hurtling towards him around the edge of the woods, soaring into the enclosure, and stopping dead in mid-air beside him, waiting for him to mount. The crowd was making even more noise … Bagman was shouting something … but Harry's ears were not working properly any more … listening wasn't important …

He swung his leg over the broom, and kicked off from the ground. And a second later, something miraculous happened …

As he soared upwards, as the wind rushed through his hair, as the crowd's faces became mere flesh-coloured pinpricks below, and the Horntail shrank to the size of a dog, he realised that he had left not only the ground behind, but also his fear … he was back where he belonged …

This was just another Quidditch match, that was all … just another Quidditch match, and that Horntail was just another ugly opposing team …

He looked down at the clutch of eggs, and spotted the gold one, gleaming against its cement-coloured fellows, residing safely between the dragon's front legs. 'OK,' Harry told himself, 'diversionary tactics … let's go …'

## 第20章 第一个项目

面孔从上面的看台上望着他,他那天晚上站在这里时还没有这些看台,是后来用魔法搭建的。在围场的另一端,赫然耸立着那条匈牙利树蜂。它低低地蹲伏着,守着它的那一窝蛋,翅膀收拢了一半,那双恶狠狠的黄眼睛死死盯着哈利。这是一条无比庞大、周身覆盖着鳞甲的黑色类蜥蜴爬行动物。它剧烈扭动着长满尖刺的尾巴,在坚硬的地面上留下几米长的坑坑洼洼的痕迹。观众席里发出鼎沸的喧嚣声,这些声音是友好的还是恶意的,哈利无从知晓,也不再介意。现在要做他必须做的事情了……排除杂念,完全地、绝对地集中意念,想着那件东西,那是他唯一的希望……

他举起魔杖。

"火弩箭飞来!"他喊道。

哈利等待着,他的每一个细胞都在祈祷、希冀……如果这一招没有成功……如果火弩箭没有飞来……他望着周围的一切,眼前仿佛隔着一层微光闪烁的透明屏障。它如同一层热腾腾的烟雾,围场和他周围的几百张面孔都奇怪地飘浮不定……

接着,他听见了,什么东西在他后面嗖嗖地穿过空气疾飞而来。他转过身,看见他的火弩箭绕过禁林边缘,朝他快速飞来;它飞进了围场,猛地停在他身旁的半空中,等着他跨上去。人群里发出的声音更响了……巴格曼在喊叫着什么……可是哈利的耳朵此刻已经不管用了……现在重要的不是听……

他抬腿跨上飞天扫帚,一蹬地面,腾空飞了起来。一秒钟后,一桩奇迹般的事情发生了……

当他飞速地盘旋而上,当风呼呼地吹动他的头发,当下面观众的脸都变成了肉色的小针眼,树蜂缩成一条狗那么大时,他意识到:他抛弃的不仅是地面,更有他的恐惧……他回到了他如鱼得水的地方……

这只是另外一场魁地奇比赛,仅此而已……这不过是另外一场魁地奇比赛,树蜂不过是另外一支难缠的对手球队……

他低头望着那一窝火龙蛋,辨认出了那只金蛋,它在那些安安稳稳躺在火龙前腿中间的石灰色伙伴中闪闪发亮。"好嘞,"哈利对自己说,"调虎离山计……来吧……"

## CHAPTER TWENTY    The First Task

He dived. The Horntail's head followed him; he knew what it was going to do, and pulled out of the dive just in time; a jet of fire had been released exactly where he would have been had he not swerved away ... but Harry didn't care ... that was no more than dodging a Bludger ...

'Great Scott, he can fly!' yelled Bagman, as the crowd shrieked and gasped. 'Are you watching this, Mr Krum?'

Harry soared higher in a circle; the Horntail was still following his progress; its head revolving on its long neck – if he kept this up, it would be nicely dizzy – but better not push it too long, or it would be breathing fire again –

Harry plummeted just as the Horntail opened its mouth, but this time he was less lucky – he missed the flames, but the tail came whipping up to meet him instead, and as he swerved to the left, one of the long spikes grazed his shoulder, ripping his robes –

He could feel it stinging, he could hear screaming and groans from the crowd, but the cut didn't seem to be deep ... now he zoomed around the back of the Horntail, and a possibility occurred to him ...

The Horntail didn't seem to want to take off, she was too protective of her eggs. Though she writhed and twisted, furling and unfurling her wings and keeping those fearsome yellow eyes on Harry, she was afraid to move too far from them ... but he had to persuade her to do it, or he'd never get near them ... the trick was to do it carefully, gradually ...

He began to fly, first this way, then the other, not near enough to make her breathe fire to stave him off, but still posing a sufficient threat to ensure she kept her eyes on him. Her head swayed this way and that, watching him out of those vertical pupils, her fangs bared ...

He flew higher. The Horntail's head rose with him, her neck now stretched to its fullest extent, still swaying, like a snake before its charmer ...

Harry rose a few more feet, and she let out a roar of exasperation. He was like a fly to her, a fly she was longing to swat; her tail thrashed again, but he was too high to reach now ... she shot fire into the air, which he dodged ... her jaws opened wide ...

'Come on,' Harry hissed, swerving tantalisingly above her, 'come on, come and get me ... up you get, now ...'

## 第20章 第一个项目

他俯冲下去。树蜂的脑袋跟着他移动。哈利知道它想做什么，便及时停止俯冲，腾跃而起。一团烈火喷了出来，如果他没及时避开，便会被喷个正着……可是哈利不在乎……不过是躲避一只游走球而已……

"我的天哪，他真能飞！"巴格曼喊道——观众们都在惊叫和喘气，"你看见了吗，克鲁姆先生？"

哈利盘旋着越飞越高，树蜂的目光仍然跟着他移动，脑袋在长长的脖子上转了一圈又一圈——如果他一直这样上升，树蜂肯定会被弄得晕头转向——不过最好不要把它逼得太狠，不然它又要喷火了——

哈利就在树蜂张开嘴巴的瞬间骤然下降，但这次就不太走运了——他躲过了火焰，但树蜂的尾巴向他迎头抽来。当他转向左边时，那尾巴上的一根长长的尖刺擦破了他的肩膀，撕裂了他的长袍——

他可以感到一阵剧痛，可以听见观众们失声尖叫和叹息，但看来伤口并不很深……现在他绕到树蜂的背后飞来飞去，突然，他想到一个办法……

树蜂似乎不想动窝，它太注意保护它的蛋了。它尽管不停地盘绕、扭动，把翅膀展开又收拢，收拢又展开，那双吓人的黄眼睛死死盯着哈利，但它不敢离开它的蛋太远……而哈利必须诱惑它这么做，不然他就永远无法接近那些蛋……诀窍就是要循序渐进，步步为营……

他开始不停地飞来飞去，一会儿这边，一会儿那边，小心着不要靠得太近，以免树蜂喷出火焰把他击着，但又要构成足够的威胁，确保它的眼睛一直盯着自己。树蜂的脑袋左右摆动，目光从一对垂直的瞳孔中注视着他，嘴里的獠牙全部露在外面……

哈利飞得更高了。树蜂的脑袋跟着他一起上升，脖子已经完全伸直，仍然左右摆动着，像一条蛇在耍蛇人面前起舞……

哈利又升高了几英尺，树蜂发出一声绝望的吼叫。哈利在它眼里就像一只苍蝇，一只它想拍死的苍蝇。它的尾巴又连续甩打起来，但哈利飞得太高，尾巴够不着他……树蜂朝空中喷出火焰，哈利闪身躲过……树蜂的嘴巴张得大大的……

"过来，"哈利嘶嘶地说，在树蜂上方转过来掉过去，挑逗着它，"过来，过来抓我呀……你上来吧……"

## CHAPTER TWENTY   The First Task

And then she reared, spreading her great black leathery wings at last, as wide as those of a small aeroplane – and Harry dived. Before the dragon knew what he had done, or where he had disappeared to, he was speeding towards the ground as fast as he could go, towards the eggs now unprotected by her clawed, front legs – he had taken his hands off his Firebolt – he had seized the golden egg –

And with a huge spurt of speed, he was off, he was soaring out over the stands, the heavy egg safely under his uninjured arm, and it was as though somebody had just turned the volume back up – for the first time, he became properly aware of the noise of the crowd, which was screaming and applauding as loudly as the Irish supporters at the World Cup –

'Look at that!' Bagman was yelling. 'Will you look at that! Our youngest champion is quickest to get his egg! Well, this is going to shorten the odds on Mr Potter!'

Harry saw the dragon-keepers rushing forwards to subdue the Horntail, and, over at the entrance to the enclosure, Professor McGonagall, Professor Moody and Hagrid hurrying to meet him, all of them waving him towards them, their smiles evident even from this distance. He flew back over the stands, the noise of the crowd pounding his eardrums, and came in smoothly to land, his heart lighter than it had been in weeks ... he had got through the first task, he had survived ...

'That was excellent, Potter!' cried Professor McGonagall as he got off the Firebolt – which from her was extravagant praise. He noticed that her hand shook as she pointed at his shoulder. 'You'll need to see Madam Pomfrey before the judges give out your score ... over there, she's had to mop up Diggory already ...'

'Yeh did it, Harry!' said Hagrid hoarsely. 'Yeh did it! An' agains' the Horntail an' all, an' yeh know Charlie said that was the wors' –'

'Thanks, Hagrid,' said Harry loudly, so that Hagrid wouldn't blunder on and reveal that he had shown Harry the dragons beforehand.

Professor Moody looked very pleased, too; his magical eye was dancing in its socket.

'Nice and easy does the trick, Potter,' he growled.

'Right then, Potter, the first-aid tent, please ...' said Professor McGonagall.

Harry walked out of the enclosure, still panting, and saw Madam Pomfrey

## 第20章 第一个项目

终于,树蜂竖起身子,黑乎乎的、粗糙的巨大翅膀完全展开,像一架小型飞机那么宽——哈利立刻俯冲下去。没等火龙明白他做了什么、消失到哪里去了,他就以迅雷不及掩耳之势,拼命冲向地面,冲向那一窝火龙蛋,现在不再有那对带利爪的前腿保护着它们了——他松开火弩箭,腾出双手——他抓住了金蛋——

随即他嗖地腾空而起,飞离巨龙,在看台上空盘旋,沉重的金蛋夹在那只没有受伤的胳膊底下,这时才好像有人刚把音量调了上去——哈利第一次听清了观众席里发出的声音,人们都在呐喊尖叫、鼓掌喝彩,声音震耳欲聋,就像爱尔兰队的支持者们在世界杯赛上那样——

"看哪!"巴格曼在高声大喊,"你们快看哪!我们年纪最小的勇士以最快的速度拿到了金蛋!好啊,这将会缩小波特先生与其他勇士之间的赔率差距!"

哈利看见驯龙师纷纷冲过去,平息树蜂的怒火。在场地的入口处,麦格教授、穆迪教授和海格匆匆走过来迎接他。他们朝他招手,要他过去,即使隔着这么远的距离,他们脸上的笑容也清晰可见。哈利飞回到看台上方,人群的喧哗声敲击着他的耳膜。他平稳地降落到地面,几个星期来,心情第一次这么轻松……他通过了第一个项目,他活了下来……

"真是太精彩了,波特!"他刚从火弩箭上下来,麦格教授就大声说——这话从她的嘴里说出来,已经是很高的赞扬了。哈利注意到麦格教授指着他肩膀的手在微微颤抖。"在裁判打分前,你需要去找一下庞弗雷女士……就在那儿,已经有迪戈里需要她照料……"

"你成功了,哈利!"海格声音粗哑地说,"你成功了!而且你对付的是树蜂啊,你知道查理说树蜂是最凶猛的——"

"谢谢你,海格。"哈利大声说,这样海格就不会冒冒失失地说下去,把他事先带自己去看火龙的事泄露出来了。

穆迪教授看上去也很高兴,那只魔眼在眼窝里跳个不停。

"你那一招既漂亮又干脆,波特。"他粗声粗气地说。

"好了,波特,请你赶紧到急救帐篷去吧……"麦格教授说。

哈利走出场地,仍然气喘吁吁的。他看见庞弗雷女士站在第二个

## CHAPTER TWENTY   The First Task

standing at the mouth of a second tent, looking worried.

'Dragons!' she said, in a disgusted tone, pulling Harry inside. The tent was divided into cubicles; he could make out Cedric's shadow through the canvas, but Cedric didn't seem to be badly injured; he was sitting up, at least. Madam Pomfrey examined Harry's shoulder, talking furiously all the while. 'Last year Dementors, this year dragons, what are they going to bring into this school next? You're very lucky … this is quite shallow … it'll need cleaning before I heal it up, though …'

She cleaned the cut with a dab of some purple liquid which smoked and stung, but then poked his shoulder with her wand, and he felt it heal instantly.

'Now, just sit quietly for a minute – *sit!* And then you can go and get your score.'

She bustled out of the tent and he heard her go next door and say, 'How does it feel now, Diggory?'

Harry didn't want to sit still; he was still too full of adrenaline. He got to his feet, wanting to see what was going on outside, but before he'd reached the mouth of the tent, two people had come darting inside – Hermione, followed closely by Ron.

'Harry, you were brilliant!' Hermione said squeakily. There were fingernail marks on her face where she had been clutching it in fear. 'You were amazing! You really were!'

But Harry was looking at Ron, who was very white, and staring at Harry as though he was a ghost.

'Harry,' he said, very seriously, 'whoever put your name in that Goblet – I – I reckon they're trying to do you in!'

It was as though the last few weeks had never happened – as though Harry was meeting Ron for the first time, right after he'd been made champion.

'Caught on, have you?' said Harry coldly. 'Took you long enough.'

Hermione stood nervously between them, looking from one to the other. Ron opened his mouth uncertainly. Harry knew Ron was about to apologise and, suddenly, he found he didn't need to hear it.

'It's OK,' he said, before Ron could get the words out. 'Forget it.'

'No,' said Ron, 'I shouldn't've –'

帐篷的入口处，神情显得很焦虑。

"火龙！"她用一种厌恶的口吻说，一把将哈利拉了进去。帐篷里分成了几个小隔间，哈利隔着帆布辨认出塞德里克的身影。看来塞德里克伤得并不严重，至少他已经坐了起来。庞弗雷女士仔细查看哈利的肩膀，一边气呼呼地说个不停："去年是摄魂怪，今年是火龙，接下来他们还要把什么东西带进这所学校？你还算幸运……伤口很浅……不过先要清洗一下，我再给你治疗……"

她用一种冒烟的、气味很难闻的紫色液体清洗了伤口，然后用她的魔杖捅了捅哈利的肩膀，哈利觉得伤口立刻就愈合了。

"好了，安安静静地坐一分钟——坐下！然后你就可以去看得分了。"

庞弗雷女士快步出了隔间，哈利听见她走进隔壁，说道："你感觉怎么样了，迪戈里？"

哈利不想一动不动地坐着：他太兴奋了。他站起来，想看看外面的情况，但没等他走到帐篷口，就有两个人迎面冲了进来——是赫敏，后面紧跟着罗恩。

"哈利，你真出色！"赫敏尖声尖气地说，她脸上左一道右一道的，都是指甲抓的痕迹，因为她一直在惊恐地抓挠自己的脸，"你真是太棒了！真是太棒了！"

然而哈利正望着罗恩。罗恩的脸色白得吓人，他呆呆地瞪着哈利，就好像哈利是一个幽灵。

"哈利，"他说，神情非常严肃，"不管是什么人把你的名字扔进那只火焰杯的——我——我认为他们是想要你的命！"

就好像几个星期来什么事都没有发生——就好像这是哈利被选为勇士后第一次见到罗恩。

"你终于明白了？"哈利冷冷地说，"时间够长的啊。"

赫敏紧张地站在他们俩中间，看看这个，又看看那个。罗恩迟疑地张开嘴巴。哈利知道罗恩要向他道歉，而他突然发现自己不需要听他道歉了。

"没关系，"他趁罗恩还没有把话说出来，赶紧说道，"忘了这件事吧。"

"不，"罗恩说，"我不应该——"

## CHAPTER TWENTY    The First Task

'*Forget it,*' Harry said.

Ron grinned nervously at him, and Harry grinned back.

Hermione burst into tears.

'There's nothing to cry about!' Harry told her, bewildered.

'You two are so *stupid*!' she shouted, stamping her foot on the ground, tears splashing down her front. Then, before either of them could stop her, she had given both of them a hug, and dashed away, now positively howling.

'Barking,' said Ron, shaking his head. 'Harry, c'mon, they'll be putting up your scores ...'

Picking up the golden egg and his Firebolt, feeling more elated than he would have believed possible an hour ago, Harry ducked out of the tent, Ron by his side, talking fast.

'You were the best, you know, no competition. Cedric did this weird thing where he Transfigured a rock on the ground ... turned it into a dog ... he was trying to make the dragon go for the dog instead of him. Well, it was a pretty cool bit of Transfiguration, and it sort of worked, because he did get the egg, but he got burnt as well – the dragon changed its mind halfway through and decided it would rather have him than the labrador, he only just got away. And that Fleur girl tried this sort of charm, I think she was trying to put it into a trance – well, that kind of worked, too, it went all sleepy, but then it snored, and this great jet of flame shot out, and her skirt caught fire – she put it out with a bit of water out of her wand. And Krum – you won't believe this, but he didn't even think of flying! He was probably the best after you, though. Hit it with some sort of spell right in the eye. Only thing is, it went trampling around in agony and squashed half the real eggs – they took marks off for that, he wasn't supposed to do any damage to them.'

Ron drew breath as he and Harry reached the edge of the enclosure. Now that the Horntail had been taken away, Harry could see where the five judges were sitting – right at the other end, in raised seats draped in gold.

'It's marks out of ten from each one,' Ron said, and Harry, squinting up the field, saw the first judge – Madame Maxime – raise her wand in the air. What looked like a long, silver ribbon shot out of it, which twisted itself into a large figure eight.

'Not bad!' said Ron, as the crowd applauded. 'I suppose she took marks

## 第20章 第一个项目

"忘了这件事吧。"哈利说。

罗恩局促不安地咧嘴朝哈利微笑,哈利也对他报以微笑。

赫敏突然哭了起来。

"这有什么好哭的!"哈利感到莫名其妙,对她说。

"你们两个真傻!"赫敏喊道,一边使劲儿用脚跺着地面,眼泪扑簌簌地洒到胸前。然后,没等他们俩来得及阻止,她就拥抱了他们一下,转身跑开了,这时她已是在号啕大哭了。

"真是疯了,"罗恩摇摇头,说,"哈利,走吧,他们要给你打分了……"

哈利拿起金蛋和火弩箭,觉得心情无比愉快,一小时前他简直不相信自己会有这么好的心情。他低头走出帐篷,罗恩跟在他身旁,像连珠炮一样说个不停。

"你知道吗,你是最棒的,谁也比不上了。塞德里克做了件古怪的事,给地上的一块岩石念了变形咒……把它变成了一条狗……他想转移火龙的注意力,让它去追狗。啊,那真是个很厉害的变形咒,而且真的有点管用。塞德里克拿到了金蛋,但还是被烧伤了——火龙半途改变了主意,觉得情愿先抓住他,而不是那条纽芬兰猎狗;他差点就逃不掉了。那个叫芙蓉的姑娘施了一种魔法,我想她大概是想使火龙陷入一种催眠状态——不错,也差不多成功了,火龙一下子就昏昏欲睡,可是接着它打起呼噜来,喷出好厉害的一道火焰,芙蓉的裙子着了火——她从魔杖里变出水,把火浇灭了。还有克鲁姆——你不会相信,他居然没有想到飞!不过他也很棒,大概仅次于你了。他用一种魔咒直接击中了火龙的眼睛。可惜的是,火龙痛苦地挣扎,脚踩来踩去,把那些真蛋踩碎了一半——这个他们要扣分的,他不应该破坏那些火龙蛋。"

罗恩使劲大喘了一口气,这时他和哈利来到了围场的边缘。树蜂已经被弄走了,哈利可以看见五位裁判坐的地方——就在另一边,坐在升高的铺着金布的椅子上。

"每个人的最高评分不超过十分。"罗恩说,哈利眯着眼睛朝场地眺望,看见第一位裁判——马克西姆女士——把她的魔杖举向空中。一缕长长的银丝带般的东西从魔杖里喷出来,扭曲着形成一个大大的"8"字。

"还行!"罗恩在观众的鼓掌喝彩声中说,"她大概是因为你肩膀

## CHAPTER TWENTY  The First Task

off for your shoulder ...'

Mr Crouch came next. He shot a number nine into the air.

'Looking good!' Ron yelled, thumping Harry on the back.

Next, Dumbledore. He, too, put up a nine. The crowd were cheering harder than ever.

Ludo Bagman - *ten*.

'Ten?' said Harry in disbelief. 'But ... I got hurt ... what's he playing at?'

'Harry, don't complain!' Ron yelled excitedly.

And now Karkaroff raised his wand. He paused for a moment, and then a number shot out of his wand, too – four.

'*What?*' Ron bellowed furiously. '*Four?* You lousy biased scumbag, you gave Krum ten!'

But Harry didn't care, he wouldn't have cared if Karkaroff had given him zero; Ron's indignation on his behalf was worth about a hundred points to him. He didn't tell Ron this, of course, but his heart felt lighter than air as he turned to leave the enclosure. And it wasn't just Ron ... those weren't only Gryffindors cheering in the crowd. When it had come to it, when they had seen what he was facing, most of the school had been on his side, as well as Cedric's ... he didn't care about the Slytherins, he could stand whatever they threw at him now.

'You're tied in first place, Harry! You and Krum!' said Charlie Weasley, hurrying to meet them as they set off back towards the school. 'Listen, I've got to run, I've got to go and send Mum an owl, I swore I'd tell her what happened – but that was unbelievable! Oh yeah – and they told me to tell you you've got to hang around for a few more minutes ... Bagman wants a word, back in the champions' tent.'

Ron said he would wait, so Harry re-entered the tent, which somehow looked quite different now; friendly and welcoming. He thought back to how he'd felt while dodging the Horntail, and compared it to the long wait before he'd walked out to face it ... there was no comparison, the wait had been immeasurably worse.

Fleur, Cedric and Krum all came in together. One side of Cedric's face was covered in a thick orange paste, which was

## 第20章 第一个项目

受伤才扣你分数的……"

接下来是克劳奇先生。他朝空中喷出一个"9"字。

"很有希望啊！"罗恩拍打着哈利的后背，大声嚷道。

接着是邓布利多。他给了九分。观众们的欢呼声更响亮了。

卢多·巴格曼——10。

"十分？"哈利不敢相信地说，"可是……我受伤了呀……他在开什么玩笑？"

"哈利，你就别抱怨了！"罗恩兴奋地喊道。

这时卡卡洛夫举起了魔杖。他停顿片刻，然后他的魔杖里也喷出一个数字——4。

"什么？"罗恩气愤地吼道，"四分？你这个讨厌的、偏心的家伙，你给了克鲁姆十分！"

可是哈利并不在乎，即使卡卡洛夫给他零分，他也不会在乎。罗恩为他打抱不平，这对他来说比一百分还宝贵。当然啦，他没有把这个想法告诉罗恩，但当他转身离开场地时，觉得自己的心情比空气还要轻盈。而且，为他高兴的不仅是罗恩……人群里为他欢呼的不仅是格兰芬多的学生。事到临头，当他们看到哈利所面对的挑战时，学校的大多数同学都开始支持他，就像支持塞德里克一样……哈利不在乎斯莱特林的学生，现在不管他们朝他泼什么脏水，他都能够忍受。

"你们并列第一，哈利！你和克鲁姆！"查理·韦斯莱说，他们出发返回学校时，他匆匆赶上来迎接他们，"听着，我得跑着去了，我要派一只猫头鹰给妈妈送信，我发誓要把一切都告诉她的——哦，真叫人不敢相信！噢，差点儿忘了——他们叫我跟你说一声，你还得在这里再待几分钟……巴格曼有几句话要说，就在勇士们的帐篷里。"

罗恩说愿意等他，哈利便再次走进帐篷，现在那帐篷给人的感觉完全不一样了：变得亲切而温馨了。他回想着他躲避树蜂攻击时的感觉，再拿这种感觉与他刚才出去面对树蜂前漫长的等待相比……那种等待痛苦万分，是没有什么能够比拟的。

芙蓉、塞德里克和克鲁姆一同进来了。

塞德里克的半边脸上涂着一块厚厚的橘黄色药膏，大概是为了治

## CHAPTER TWENTY   The First Task

presumably mending his burn. He grinned at Harry when he saw him. 'Good one, Harry.'

'And you,' said Harry, grinning back.

'Well done, *all* of you!' said Ludo Bagman, bouncing into the tent, and looking as pleased as though he personally had just got past a dragon. 'Now, just a quick few words. You've got a nice long break before the second task, which will take place at half past nine on the morning of February the twenty-fourth – but we're giving you something to think about in the meantime! If you look down at those golden eggs you're all holding, you will see that they open ... see the hinges there? You need to solve the clue inside the egg – because it will tell you what the second task is, and enable you to prepare for it! All clear? Sure? Well, off you go, then!'

Harry left the tent, rejoined Ron, and they started to walk back around the edge of the Forest, talking hard; Harry wanted to hear what the other champions had done in more detail. Then, as they rounded the clump of trees behind which Harry had first heard the dragons roar, a witch leapt out from behind them.

It was Rita Skeeter. She was wearing acid-green robes today; the Quick-Quotes Quill in her hand blended perfectly against them.

'Congratulations, Harry!' she said, beaming at him. 'I wonder if you could give me a quick word? How you felt facing that dragon? How you feel *now* about the fairness of the scoring?'

'Yeah, you can have a word,' said Harry savagely. '*Goodbye.*'

And he set off back to the castle with Ron.

## 第20章 第一个项目

疗他的烧伤吧。他看见哈利,咧开嘴笑了。"干得不错,哈利。"

"你也是。"哈利说,也对他报以微笑。

"你们都干得不错!"卢多·巴格曼说,他轻快地跳进帐篷,一副欢天喜地的样子,仿佛刚才是他本人成功穿越了一条火龙,"好了,我只有几句话要说。第二个项目将于明年二月二十四日上午九点半开始,在此之前,你们可以休息很长一段时间——不过我们要留一些问题给你们考虑!你们低头看看手里拿的金蛋,会发现它们可以打开……看见那里的接缝了吗?你们必须解开蛋里提供的线索——那将透露第二个项目是什么,你们可以做好准备!都清楚了吧?没问题了?好了,你们走吧!"

哈利离开了帐篷,找到罗恩,两人一起绕过禁林边缘往回走,一路上聊个不停。哈利想更详细地了解其他勇士是怎么做的。后来,他们刚绕过那片树丛——哈利就是在这片树丛后第一次听见火龙吼叫的,一个女巫突然从那后面跳了出来。

是丽塔·斯基特。她今天穿着一身艳绿色的袍子,手里的速记笔与袍子的颜色十分般配。

"祝贺你,哈利!"她说,满脸微笑地看着哈利,"不知道你能不能跟我说一句话?你面对火龙时有什么感觉?你现在觉得裁判打分是否公平?"

"好的,我可以跟你说一句话,"哈利恼火地说,"再见。"

说完,他和罗恩一起拔腿朝城堡走去。

WIZARDING
WORLD.